TOM & HUCK:

The Civil War Years

Complete Edition

Frank Fernandes

Table of Contents

CHAPTER ONE

Hooker had lost faith in Hooker. If there had ever been a general of an army that had been beaten, cuffed, and humiliated in the history of armed conflict more than General 'Fightn' Joe' Hooker, it would have to be an extreme rarity. His confidence in his own ability to lead an army had unraveled during the recent battle of Chancellorsville. His reputation was shattered as badly as the Army of the Potomac that he had so proudly led into the thick woods of Virginia. The Army of the Potomac had once again become the commissary arm of the Army of Northern Virginia fulfilling the ancient military maxim, "To the victor belongs the spoils."

Blankets, rifles, shoes, haversacks filled with spare clothing and coffee, and ammunition pouches lay scattered in mute testimony to the speed in which the northern boys had sacredly resolved to save themselves from annihilation. The Union could always be saved later.

Private Thomas Sawyer shifted unsteadily on his feet. Sweat tended to obscure his vision causing him to squint. This morning's ersatz coffee had left a bitter taste in his mouth and had given him a terrible bout of heartburn. The morning mist fought a losing battle with the creeping rays of the sun that filtered through the treetops and showered below on the uneasy lines of men clad in butternut brown and gray.

They were drawn up to witness the execution of a soldier from their division. The condemned man had been convicted of desertion under fire, attempted murder, and robbery. During the fighting at Chancellorsville, the man's regiment had been positioned near an old unfinished railroad cut in the woods. Federal forces had outflanked his regiment and had cut it to pieces. Many soldiers had run to escape certain death or capture. The unfortunate soldier had had the bad luck of being recognized by a group of staff officers who had disciplined him in the past for striking an officer and saw in his headlong flight from battle a perfect opportunity to make an example of him.

It didn't matter to these staff officers that his decision to run had been tactically correct. It didn't matter that many from his own company had run as well or that many in the regiment had been captured or killed. What mattered was that he had shamefully run from the enemy early in the fight and had been seen by nearly everyone. And of course, to make matters worse, he had been captured by Provost Guards, men specifically ordered to catch stragglers and deserters and had grievously wounded one and had escaped. He had then robbed a medical supply wagon at gunpoint and had proceeded to get gloriously drunk on the medicinal whiskey. This was his undoing. He was apprehended, tried in a court-martial and sentenced to die by firing squad.

The assembled soldiers were disgruntled and hungry this morning. Although most of the pickings on the battlefield had been gone over days earlier, most of them would have much preferred to be wandering around looking for things that may have been overlooked from burial parties or ordinance men. A gathering like this only meant that others, particularly rear echelon mule drivers and maggots would have the last chance for the thin pickings that may be left.

The gathered host was, therefore, in a foul mood. Everyone gathered in the clearing to witness the execution hoped the condemned man wouldn't botch it by carrying on and delaying the inevitable. In the same clearing, called Hazel Grove by the local people, the Federal Army had attempted to stave off the murderous attention being paid to it by Thomas 'Stonewall' Jackson. The Federal forces had assembled a battery of field artillery here when the Union center collapsed and the left flank of their army had rolled up like a scroll. They had tried to center the line and had failed. However, the artillery had bought the time needed for the entire Union Army to escape total destruction, but at a terrible cost in Northern lives.

Scattered around the clearing were shattered artillery caissons, broken wheels, ruptured cannons and dead horses and equipment of every imaginable sort. Most of anything of use had already been picked over by ordinance and quartermaster personnel. Under a few inches of dry loose baked red Virginia soil lay youngsters from Massachusetts, Connecticut, Ohio, New Jersey, and New York. In a few spots near the edges of the grove where the wounded had been brought to die beneath the shade of the trees, a fist poked up out of a too shallow grave. Dark brown spots on the green grass still attracted flies. A breeze swept the tops of the trees bringing with it the mixed smell of dogwood trees and putrefaction.

"I wished that they would get this over with," Tom said as he wiped the sweat from his brow with his sleeve. The soldier standing in ranks next to Tom burped loudly. Private Huck Finn swayed from the recoil of his violent belch.

"Excuse the pig, the hog is a' gruntin'," Huck said.

"This whole sha-bang isn't right. Making us stand in rank and wait practically all morning like this here to see a man put down like a damned sick old dog," Tom replied, ignoring his friends attempt at levity.

"What do you think they should do with him?" Huck asked. "Do you think they should give him a ten feet head start and tell him to cut back an' forth right quick?" Huck stared straight ahead trying to avoid being spotted talking in ranks. He spoke out of the corner of his mouth.

5

"Let me tell you, Tom. It don't matter if they string a rope around his neck and swing him from a sour apple tree or if they sit him down a cracker box and send him to the Almighty full of lead shot. It don't matter. They already done made up their minds. It's all a done deed. The waitin' part is for our benefit. All this here is supposed to bother you, to make you think hard about runnin' durin' a fight. That's why it don't matter an' that's why they make us wait out here like this."

Sergeant Rawlings quickly walked down the line of men and stood in front of the pair. He glared angrily at them.

"I should have knowed it was you two jackasses jabberin' away. Keep your traps shut an' your eyes to the front or so help me when this is done with I will make you eat your own livers." He stared at Huck almost eyeball to eyeball with him before he turned and strode angrily away from him.

"I sure as hell would like to know how he manages to pop up like that all the time. It ain't natural. It's as if he's some kinda' spook or haint. He comes at you right out of thin air, I swear," Huck muttered under his breadth.

The idea of eating anything, especially liver, made Huck's stomach churn. He fought back desperately against a gag reflex that was hitting him in waves. His belly was awash in bile, the result of his having eaten too many green ears of corn the previous night. He started to say something but instead tried to cover his mouth to hold back the vomit he felt welling up in his throat. He jackknifed forward and his rifle dropped from his grasp and hit the ground. He quickly stooped over to retrieve it and vomited all over his feet. Whistles, laughter and catcalls began immediately from those nearest him witnessing his plight. Rawlings once again stomped down the line of men towards Tom and Huck.

"Order in the ranks," he shouted. "You are at attention and not on a church social. No talkin' or stirrin' in the ranks. The next man that I hear laugh will wisht' he was never born. It had better be quiet damned quick so that I can hear a mouse fart in the woods if I so desire."

All was quiet again. Everyone stared blankly ahead as the sergeant walked over to Huck and whispered something in his ear. Rawlings smiled and walked back to his place at the end of the line of soldiers. He glanced at Huck with a smug look and then spotted Captain Cobb who was beginning to display interest and irritation at this most recent breach of military protocol and good taste.

Captain Theodocius Cobb was one of Virginia's proud aristocracies, a member of the Tidewater planter's class who could trace his ancestry to a particular manor house outside of London. His grandfather had been a close friend of George Washington. He came from wealth and privilege and held in low regard anyone not from his social strata. He had learned that Tom and Huck hailed from Missouri and he viewed them both as backwoods savages. He was not at all surprised that it was they who were acting badly in formation. He looked in annoyance at the pair and then at Sergeant Rawlings.

The sergeant puffed out his chest like a peacock in an attempt to appear taller when he noticed the captain's attention was focused on him. He stood ramrod straight in an effort to impress his superior officer. After his little private chat with Huck, Rawlings had looked like he was experiencing beatific visions. The sergeant felt himself clever and all powerful and glowed happily as he thought of a fitting punishment for Huck. He felt himself to be indispensable in the running of company C, a man destined for great achievements and everlasting fame. In his innermost being he felt that Cobb respected and trusted him. He imagined after the war that the good Captain would perhaps reward all the years of service with him with an important job on one of the captain's vast plantations. Captain Cobb studied Rawlings for a brief moment reflecting on how big an ass the man truly was.

Tom whispered carefully to his friend when he knew that the sergeant's attention was elsewhere.

"What did that pain in the ass have to say?" he asked.

"He said that he hopes I like my liver with onions."

Tom's eyes widened in surprise.

"That ain't good," he said.

From the rear of the assembled men, drums started crashing a loud roll. As the dead-man's march started, everyone's attention was riveted at the appearance and movement of the firing squad. They marched smartly to their assigned positions a few yards from where the coffin and pre-dug grave were. They stood at attention waiting for their next cue. Starting from the rear of the regiment and walking slowly towards the firing squad came the regimental chaplain and the condemned man. Lieutenant Custiss and Colonel Edmonds followed a few steps behind them.

The condemned man, Private Archibald Conboy, was a pathetic looking figure. His hands and legs were shackled and he hopped forward in little steps. The chaplain, taking into consideration his abnormal gait, was forced in turn to take the same rabbit like hops. Chaplain Janes was exhausted. He had stayed up all night listening patiently to the complaints, protests, and fears of the condemned man. Archibald had vehemently raged into the night. Archibald had insisted that it was all a case of mistaken identity. When this had failed to create the intended results, Archibald then had claimed that a mini-ball had creased his skull rendering him temporarily crazy and bereft of a memory. His eyes were wild looking. It was apparent to Chaplain Janes that Archibald was going to make a spectacle of himself. It was the chaplain's job to see that he did not.

Gripping the prisoner's arm tightly, Chaplain Janes could feel the man's panic rising like a fever. Archie walked towards the grave spasmodically.

"Archibald," Chaplain Janes said soothingly, "don't look at them. Look at me. Remember what we spoke of this morning. You are forgiven by the Most High. You are a new man in the eyes of the Lord. You are as innocent to him as a new born baby. You do not need the approval of man when you are in the approval of the Almighty."

"I wisht' I was a little old baby right now, parson. They don't shoot little baby boys by firing squad," Archie whimpered. The Chaplain swallowed nervously.

"A little courage now is all it will take," the Chaplain whispered. Archie continued hopping towards the grave.

"The Good Lord has placed you in his loving hands this day and will not cause you to suffer the pains of eternal damnation or the pains of man. You must believe this, my son."

Archibald's head was swiveling around like an owl as he searched the formations of men for a familiar face. He desperately looked for someone from home as he shuffled towards the waiting coffin. However, all of his company and friends were positioned on the far left of the grave and he could not make any of them out. His panic rose by the second as he neared the coffin where he was to be seated. Chaplain Janes began to read from his opened Bible.

"Parson Janes, You got to make them understand," Archie pleaded. He grabbed the Chaplains arm with his manacled hands.

"This here is all a mistake. Yassuh, it is true that I quit the fight and yassuh, it is true I shot that damned Provo fella an' robbed him, but I didn't kill him. It was self defense. Why hell, Parson, them fellas were set to kick my head round. I was drunk on top of it all. I shot him is all. The fella should know that it comes with the job. You got to tell someone that I was fixin' on comin' back after the heat died down. That's the truth. I swear. I jest' needed a few days to clear my head an' I would have come right back, yes siree-Bob. Tell someone important like an' let's make by-gones be by-gones."

Chaplain Janes looked into Archie's frantic fear filled orbs and saw that he had failed as a chaplain. Archie was going to ruin everything. Instead of a sense of peace and resignation in Archie's eyes, there stood defiantly a spark of hope blended in with quite a bit of pure terror. Chaplain Janes knew that this was a dangerous combination in a condemned prisoner and tried desperately to control his own rising fear.

"Iff'n they was, lets say, to give me another chance, why I will safely say nothin' of the likes will nary happen again, on my soul," Archie smiled. "I knows that you are good with words. Alls you gotta' do is say somethin' smart like to the Colonel here an' everything will get fixed. All this God awful whoop jamboree ain't necessary at'all. Please parson, tell the Colonel somethin' smart like as to how I was fixin' on comin' on back. I swear on my good mother's soul, may she rest in peace, that he has my word that this will never happen agin'. I was always a good soldier. Ask anybody, for heavens sake."

Archie's eyes darted to the coffin and then to the horrible yawning pit. Chaplain Janes was lost for words and instead continued to read from his Bible.

Archie remained confident that the parson would save him. Lieutenant Custiss and Colonel Edmonds joined them. Lieutenant Custiss offered him a blindfold.

"Now lets all holt' on a minute, Lootenant. I don' t believe I'll be needn' no blindfold, sir. Let's not rush things here. The parsons was jest' goin' to have a few words with the General, so you can put that danged thing away. We won't be need'n any of this so might I suggest to y'all to dismiss the whole gathrin'. Right, parson?"

Two men grabbed Archie by his elbows and led him to the coffin.

"Let's us all holt' on a danged minute, boys," he protested.

He stared dumbly at the chaplain. Somewhere in his mind, a voice screamed for him to run but he knew there was to be no escape. The Lieutenant then forced Archie to sit on the coffin as the chaplain continued to pray over him. Archie could see the firing squad that was at his front and was distracted from studying their faces when Colonel Edmonds appeared holding a large paper in his hands. Things were happening quickly, much too fast for the likes of the condemned man and he felt his life slipping away from him. He began to finally realize that the end was fast approaching. The trial, the court-martial and the last few hours sped through his mind in a blur.

"May God have mercy on your soul. May the Lord take you to His bosom this day and may you rest in perpetual light with Him and all the souls of the departed, Amen," the chaplain wearily intoned with as much care and concern that he was able.

"Parson?" Archie said weakly.

Chaplain Janes stepped to the side as Colonel Edmonds began to read from the large sheet of paper that he held in his hands. Archie's eyes were as big as saucers and his mouth hung open.

"Private Archibald. P. Conboy, the court has found you guilty of desertion under fire, robbery and the attempted murder of a Provost Guard. The penalty of death to be carried out this day, the offenses being capital crimes and the penalty to be death by firing squad in the proscribed manner of military justice. Would you have anything to say before the sentence is carried out?"

Colonel Edmond's eyes pleaded for Archie to remain quiet, but Archie felt that he must somehow make them all see reason. When he glanced over and saw the distraught face of Chaplain Janes all of his energy flowed out of his body. That look said it all. Edmonds sternly looked at Archie as their eyes met.

"Yes, I kinda figger I do. You'all know what kinda' spot we was in that day. The Yankees seemed to pop out the danged ground, there was so many of them. They kept on comin'. We fit' them hard, but it wasn't no good. I ran, but so did the whole damned company for that matter, those that was breathin' and still able. You'all know this. I want everybody to know that I ain't no dang cowart'. I only done what any normal person with common good sense would have done. I know what this here is all about and it ain't got to do with runnin'. It's because I slapped that prissy captain in the mouth and he deserved it."

Archie seemed placid now, more than Chaplain Janes had ever seen him be.

"I ain't never had a bit of luck, no how. The way I figger', better it be here and now than later. That's all I gotta' say. Good luck to all of yer' an no hard feelins'," Archie said loudly. He sat back down on the coffin.

Colonel Edmonds sighed with relief. He stiffly turned away and marched to the left of the coffin. The sun made little splotches of light dance on the brown wood of the coffin. Archie Conboy squinted in the direction of the firing squad. Birds sang cheerily in the trees.

"Ready...," the Lieutenant shouted.

"Aim."

The firing squad lifted their rifles to their shoulders. All in a matter of seconds, the Lieutenant lifted his sword skyward as thirteen men looked down their gun-sights at Archibald Conboy.

Suddenly, as if inspired with a revelation, Archie stood up to his full height and with his manacled hands stretched as wide as he was able yelled for all the world to hear. It was a plaintiff yell of wild defiance.

"I was a fixin' on a comin' back!"

"Fire."

The Lieutenant's sword flashed downward in a lightning arc as the rifles all discharged together. The shots hit Archie like an invisible fist and he somersaulted over the coffin, his feet whipping over his head as gravity deposited him in the pre-dug grave. A vapor like trail of dust curled out of the earth.

Everyone stood in silent awe over what they had witnessed. No one had ever seen anyone act in the manner that Archie had and they were stunned. Then, in ragged unison, a cheer started and ran the length of the ranks. Hats were thrown into the air as men from Archie's Division started a rebel yell that could be heard for miles. Cheer after cheer sounded from their throats like a claxon call as men began to chant his name. Colonel Edmonds looked at Chaplain Janes and offered him his hand.

"Good job, Chaplain, good job indeed, well done. I must say, however, unless his name is Lazarus instead of Conboy, I daresay that he will not be coming back any time too soon."

"Amen to that, Colonel," the chaplain said with weariness and wonder in his voice. Lieutenant Custiss returned his sword to its sheath and in a loud voice yelled to a sergeant to dismiss all present company of the firing party. Other officers in the ranks started to restore order. Sergeants roared in turn to their companies as commands were passed up and down the formation of soldiers. They all came to attention and waited to be dismissed. When it was Tom and Huck's turn to be dismissed, they turned and started back to their bivouac area.

"You gotta hand it to Archie. He died game," Huck said.

Tom looked at Huck with surprise.

"You mean he died like game. Shot down like a scared rabbit," he said with disgust.

The walk back to their bivouac area was a long one and they started trudging back. Huck remained silent, sensing the anger in his friend. The man had died well, he thought. At least he hadn't been sniveling and carrying on or crying for his dear mother like some he had witnessed. Finally, the silence grew too much for him.

"You think he died like a scairt' rabbit?" Huck asked, watching Tom's face carefully for any telltale signs of anger. Tom betrayed little emotion as he adjusted the weight of his rifle to his right shoulder.

"Of course he did," Tom said calmly. "Let me ask you a question now. Do you think he was fixin' to come back after his unofficial furlough?"

"I don't rightly know. What do they call it when a man is dyin' and he confesses to a crime? Ain't that called a deathbed confession and ain't they lawful? Ain't that jest what he did? If that's the case then, maybe he was fixin' to come back."

"Archie punched Captain Cobb in the mouth. They were looking for a reason to settle his hash. If he was smart, he should have kept on runnin' and not got caught the way he did. I don't believe he was plannin' on ever comin' back. He was just plain scared. He would have said anything if he thought it would get him off at this point. He would have claimed to be Jefferson Davis if he thought it would save him. Look, I ain't sayin' what he did was wrong. I'm sayin' they shouldn't shoot a man when his nerves give way. From what I understand, he was justified in getting out of that damned ditch he was in. That regiment was in a bind. They were outflanked. Only makes sense in what he did. Archie wasn't the only one to run that day. Like he said, the whole company ran. They made an example out of him, for punchin' the daylights out of Captain Cobb."

Huck knew what Tom was saying was true. He scratched at his crotch as he walked along. The body lice moved in accordance with a will of their own. Scratching just moved the concentrations about and temporarily eased the itching.

"He died scairt' but I ain't findin' no fault in him, mind you," Tom said thoughtfully "When the bullets start flyin', I get so scared that I feel like running too. I am not criticizing him on running. His downfall was getting drunk. If he had been a little smarter, he might have had a chance on getting away."

Huck carefully weighed what Tom was saying.

"Shootin' a fella doesn't do any of us any good. There are plenty of fellas that head for home everyday and spectacles like we were just forced to witness surely don't stop them. The whole damned thing this morning was sick." Tom stopped in mid stride and looked skyward.

"The revolution just goes on eating its own children," he said dramatically. Huck abruptly stopped.

"Who's eatin' what?"

"Never mind. It ain't important anymore," Tom said, wishing to change the subject of their conversation. Huck was totally confused by what Tom had said. This was an occurrence that happened regularly. Huck blamed this on Tom's having read too many books when he was younger. Pap had told him years ago that reading tended to drive a man crazy in time. He was accustomed to the way Tom's thought process worked but was often mystified by how he phrased things. He did not proceed with it any further. He did question how Tom could even think of eating. He must have a cast iron stomach, he thought.

They had shared a feast of green corn the other night. Huck's stomach was in open rebellion now as it gurgled and rolled. Bile once again began to erupt in his throat as the sudden image of Rawling's making him eat his own liver smothered in onions became vivid in his mind. It was just another thing he had to worry about as the residue of fried dough in bacon grease and undigested green corn welled up in his throat.

"I'm gonna be sick again," Huck said, running to the side of the road. He dropped on all fours and started heaving up. Tom turned away and stared into the thick woods that bordered the road.

"I hate to tell ya' I told ya' so, but I told you so. The way you went at them green ears last night, it ain't no surprise to me. I tried to warn you but your eyes was bigger than your stomach," Tom said.

Huck tried to stand but instead he doubled up again and fell to his knees with his hands outstretched in front of him.

"Maybe you'll feel better once it's all out of ya'. Eatin' as many green ears of corn as you did last night is one sure fired way of killing yourself damnably quick." Tom distractedly thought about how thick the woods were as Huck continued retching and moaning. Huck finally righted himself and blew a stream of something horrible out of his nose. He wiped a dirty hand over an even filthier face then reached for his canteen.

"You know, I was jest ponderin' how truly odd things are with everything in the long perspective," Tom said quietly. Huck poured water on his face and then attempted a few gulps of tepid water. He half listened to Tom between shivers.

"Remember, what you said this morning about all of that was for our benefit. How shootin' Archie was a lesson meant for us to learn by? I was jest thinkin' about our own Corp Commander. I should say, our own late Corp commander...Thomas 'Stonewall' Jackson. Old 'Bluelight' had a passel of people shot for runnin'. He shot a lot of homesick fellas', the way I figure it."

Huck's eyes rolled in his head. He slowly stood up. He nearly emptied the contents of his canteen on his upturned face.

"Do go on, if you would, Mr. Sawyer...don't mind me. I'm all ears. Green ones at that," he croaked weakly. His throat burned and he was sweating profusely. Tom ignored this last comment and strove towards the point that he was trying to make.

"It's powerful ironic that General Jackson was shot by his own people. Old Blue Light would have a man shot for runnin' at the drop of a hat and he'd usually be the one a droppin' it," Tom said convincingly, as if he had just read it out of a newspaper. Huck wiped his face with the back of his sleeve.

"You got somethin' there, Tom. He was the shootingest general we ever had, God rest him. He played hell with the Yankees and with us. I bin' a meanin' to ask you this but kept on fergettin'. Why did they call General Jackson Old Bluelight. I mean I can understand why they called him Stonewall. There stands Jackson like a stonewall. Rally around him, boys. This I can understand. On the other hand, some folks claim that General Bee was sayin' that Jackson wasn't doin' nothin' but hangin' back and was as useful in the fight as an old stone wall. But why Blue Light?"

"They say when he was riled his eyes would glow blue like. Ain't that the damnedest thing?"

Tom shifted his rifle and started to plod forward. He still stared off into the woods, admiring the beautiful early morning.

"Mighty strange how he passed on. Truly full of irony and poetic justice. Shot down and killed by the men of his own army. Many a man he had shot from his own army for runnin' away in a battle, and his own army sends him to his final reward and the Almighty. Powerful ironic. A regular wonderment," Tom said.

Huck took a few tentative steps forward to keep up with Tom. His head still spun and briefly he felt himself almost spinning into the ground. The road soon took his feet and he preceded, none the worse, as his head started to clear. He imagined his head to be filled with cobwebs and as time continued the cobwebs thinned with each step.

"I heard that it was South Carolina boys that sent him to glory. It seems like our late Corp commander was trying to figure out a way to get behind the Yankees when they all broke and ran. He was searching out a road in the dark, and that's when the Carolina boys let loose at him and his party. They thought it was Yankee cavalry coming down the road but it wasn't. It was old 'Bluelight' himself. He was killed in a case of mistaken identity." Tom stopped to let Huck catch up with him.

"It doesn't get more ironic than that. They say that if he hadn't been killed like that, that he would have found a way to get behind the Federal retreat and end the war just like that. There would have been no more Army of the Potomac," Tom said enthusiastically.

"What's this ironic you bin' sayin'. What is it?" Huck asked.

Tom looked at Huck and pointed to the side of his own face.

"Wipe over here. You're still wearing some of last nights repartee on your face," Tom said. Huck complied, wiping at his face with his sleeve.

"Irony, my friend, is what authors use a lot in their writings.

"Arthur who?" Huck asked.

"Not Arthur," Tom said, Authors. That's what they call a book writer. Perdition's sake, a book wouldn't be a proper book if it didn't have a fair dose of irony in it. They all use it," Tom said knowingly. Huck noticed the look that had started to creep across Tom's face. He knew that look only too well. It was the look that crossed his features when he was about to lecture about something that he liked to talk about. Huck had seen that look countless times before.

"That still ain't tellin' me what it is," Huck said carefully.

"You know what fate is, don't yer?" Tom asked.

"I reckon I do," Huck replied.

"Fate and irony go hand in hand. Irony is a twist on fate. Sort of like somethin' unexpected like in a persons life, outside what a body would expect in a normal given situation," Tom stated. Tom searched the immediate vicinity for a stump to sit on. Having found one, he sat down and placed his rifle against a tree. He shifted his worn slouch hat on his head as Huck sat down next to him. Huck balanced his rifle in his lap.

"I remember hearin' the Parson Janes talkin' about fate one time," Huck said. "Artillery was landin' all around us that day. Some fellas' was jumpin' from one spot to t'other. That's when the Parson Janes said that one spot was as good as another. He said to stay put. That jumpin' around was jest temptin' fate. He said that if it was your time, nothin' you kin' do can keep you from gettin' all mashed to a pulp. He said to trust in God and put your fate in him."

"Faith and fate is two different things," Tom grinned, "Your mixing up the two. He said to put your trust in God. That's faith. Fate is a different animal entirely."

"You say that's it's a twist...somethin' unexpected like?" Huck asked. He was testing new waters and simply plowed ahead.

"Yes," Tom nodded, not sure where Huck was leading with this new bit of information.

"Remember there was that time we was fightin' on the peninsular?" Huck asked.

"Yes. At Yorktown," Tom answered. Huck rested his arms across his rifle.

"That's the place, Yorktown. Remember how the Yankee sharpshooter was usin' us for target practice. There was that fella...remember, he had fair hair, what was his name?"

"You don't mean Whiggins?" Tom asked.

"Whiggins. That's the one. I forgot his name. That's the one. That fair-haired boy was pilin' rocks and branches up in front of his position, making breast-works. Goin' at it like a mad beaver. He's pilin' rocks and branches faster than anybody and the mini-balls is whistlin' in the air and sich. He's all finished quicker than anybody and he drops behind them, all safe like. He puts his head against a log and a mini-ball comes rippin' right through the cracks and blows his melon to tatters. That was

15

the damnedest thing. Is that somethin' like your fate you're speakin' of?" Huck asked. "Do I have the right mule now?"

"Yes, you got the gist of it, but it's a little more complicated than that," Tom said. "It's like this here. Suppose there's this fella," Tom continued, "and he's been getting powerful bad dreams about drowning in a river."

"That's irony. I thought it was more complicated than that," Huck quickly interjected.

"It is. There's a lot more to the story than that. Hush up a might and listen. So he figures it must be some kinda' message or some kind of sign from on high, like angels n' sich was warning him of danger comin, see?"

"Some folks would think he was a bit tetched under his headstall, maybe even hexed by devils and imps if he went a spoutin' that story around like that to the wrong people," Huck said tentatively.

"You know, I guess you know just about everything. A body can't teach you nothin'. All right, if you want to stay ignorant for the rest of your born days, it's just Jim-Dandy with me," Tom said angrily. Huck started laughing which angered Tom even more. Sensing the weariness in Tom, Huck said quickly,

"Simmer down. No need to blow your stack. Look, All I was sayin' if somebody was actin' up like that n' all, some folks would think he was peculiar." Huck grinned at Tom. "Go on now. I'm a listenin' an won't say nary a word more either."

Tom was not easily placated with Huck's promise.

"What I'm tellin' you about irony here is the way every schoolboy in the country learned it. It is a story that's textbook proper and has been taught in all the schools everywhere, word for word for a hundred years. It's the way I learned it." Tom said.

"I never heard it," Huck said stubbornly.

"You never went to school much, that's why you never heard it before. Sweet baby Jasper, you can probably count on your two hands and only have to pull off a shoe to count the number of days you ever spent in a schoolhouse."

"Pap wasn't much for me book-learning. He claimed book-learning would drive a man crazy in time."

"And you believed that?" Tom asked incredulously.

"Why, sure I did. Remember Lawyer Smith? He was the smartest man in town...smart as a whip. He could read n' writ' better than anybody in the whole town. He could quote all them famous writers from olden days and famous speeches without a scrap of paper in his hands. He went and fooled around with the wrong married woman, the buffalo hunter's woman. The buffalo hunter, why he came home one night an' found Lawyer Smith in bed with his wife. He blew Lawyer Smith all to hell with that big scattergun of his. I reckon he did not like the idea of being Coo-Cood."

"You mean cuckold. A cuckoo is a kind of bird," Tom said.

"You don't say? Anyway, at the time, it seemed to prove what Pap was sayin' and I believed it then. Now...I guess book-learnin' is harmless."

Tom shook his head and laughed.

"You're getting enlightened in your old age," he said. "There's hope for you yet." Tom pulled out a corncob pipe that was still half filled with tobacco. He struck a match on the tree he was leaning against and puffed a few times. He picked a twig off the ground and stirred the ashes in his battered pipe before puffing away again. He looked into the woods.

"These woods are thick. Ed tells me they stripped these woods and used them to smelt iron ore. That old furnace up the road has been here, he says, nigh onto a hundred years or so. They called it Catherine's Furnace, he says. They stripped the forest of all the old timber and this secondary growth sprouted. Notice how all the trees ain't all that old. It's wrapped in cat-briars and vines. You can't see more than twenty feet. No wonder they call this part of Virginia, the Wilderness. It would be a hell of a place to fight in."

"Yes, indeedy. It would be bushwhacking on a grand scale," Huck said lazily.

"Where was I?" Tom asked.

"You wuz' sayin' how that fella wuz' havin' dreams about drownden' dead in a river an' how he thought it wuz' a warnin' from on high or some sich' thing," Huck said.

"Right...so by and by, one night after waking up from one of those bad dreams he was having, he sits up in bed a spell and he hears rain coming down to beat all. He gets up and cracks the door and sees it's a real gully washer," Tom said.

"A real turd floater," Huck added for emphasis.

"Actual an' factual," Tom replied. "He can't ever remember see'n rain come down like this here before in his whole life." Tom slowly drew on his pipe. By now, Huck was hanging on to every word. The only thing that would have broken the spell he was in at this moment would have been a federal assault on their lines. Tom sensed he had his friend hooked. He let the suspense build for a little while by slowly exhaling a ring of smoke.

"Well, that ain't all of it, is it? Cause Ifn it is, that's the dumbest story I ever heard in all my days a' livin'," Huck exclaimed impatiently.

"Then, suppose he looks out and spots the river startin' to rise by the minute," Tom said carefully. Huck thought it was a question and answered quickly,

"Then he'd be a damned fool iff'n he didn't light up on out of there."

Tom ignored him and continued,

"So, he figures it would be a sight better if he was in the attic where the river could never get a hold of him. Up into the attic he clambers with a bedroll and candles."

"In case his nerves get bad, he kin smoke a pipe. Always takes the edge off me," Huck said.

"Yes...or maybe to read, I don't know," Tom said, momentarily confused by Huck's interruption.

"Wasn't you payin' attention in school when they got to that part? After all, it's your story. It's startin' to sound made up a bit iff'n you don't know." Huck said disappointedly.

"It's not important why he brought the candles for," Tom said defensively, "whether it was to read a pipe or smoke a pipe or put them on a birthday cake. It's irrelevant to the story. He just did, all right, damn it, but he's up there...you follow me?"

"Don't get riled up in lather," Huck said. "I ain't funnin' with you. I am jest' curious is all. How am I supposed to learn iff'n I don't ask questions? You got to admit yourself that you're smarter than me. Hell, your book smarter than most of us, and you use big words like there ain't no tomorrow. Like that word you jest' used. You said that it was elephant to the story. I know an elephant is big, so the way I figgers', you're tellin' me that part was big to the story."

Tom stood up and shouldered his rifle. He knocked the ashes out of his pipe against the tree and angrily stomped out the embers.

"I ain't got the time or the patience for this bullshit," Tom said. Huck jumped up.

"You got to finish the story. I'll be hanged if I would do that to you. Start a story and not finish it," Huck shouted. "That's not fair a' tall."

Tom turned towards Huck and raised a warning finger.

"I will finish the story on one condition. You got to promise that you will listen and not interrupt me again. We got a deal?" Tom asked. Tom watched as Huck's brow knotted into furrows on his forehead. Huck nodded vigorously. Tom leaned his rifle against the tree and sat down. He watched Huck to determine if he was sincere or if he was seriously confused following the plot of his story.

18

"All right then. So he's up there in the attic. He's got the candles all lit and he's feeling safe. He knows that if the river was to rise, it would not be able to drown him in the attic. Are you with me?" Tom asked.

Huck nodded his head in the affirmative.

"Now what do you think happens?" Tom waved his hand in the air to silence what may have been coming in the form of a response from Huck.

"I'll tell you what happens," he said triumphantly. "During the night, the wind blows one of those candles over and in a jump-flash minute sets the whole place a-fire and he burns to death, right then and there. That is the schoolbook example of irony, told to you proper. What do you think of that?"

Huck squinted and his jaws clenched together.

"That's irony?" Huck asked with some consternation.

"Absolutely," Tom said. "Do you get it?"

"Why sure I do. Kind of what you're sayin' is that the moral of the story is iff'n you plan on burnin' candles in an attic, don't go fallen' asleep with 'em burnin', or you might not never get up again. Not even if you wuz' to kick the window open, jump out the house and not get the flames put out on you by all the rain that wuz' a comin' down in the world. Onliest thing I can't figger out...wuz' the river that wuz risin' like hell, wuz it the Mississippi?"

Tom sighed deeply. He stood up and walked away without saying a word. Huck stood up and trotted after him. He purposely let several minutes pass and then with a flourish said,

"That damn irony is somethin' else, ain't it. I can see clearly how 'Old Bluelights' sudden departure from this vale of tears wuz' chock full of that irony. Yes sir, Chock full of it."

Tom ignored him completely, staring at his feet instead.

"If I do say so, there's some of that irony with us bein' in all of this flap-doodle don't you think?" Huck asked innocently. His comment caught Tom's attention. He glanced briefly at Huck as Huck continued shuffling down the road to their encampment.

"You ain't forgetting the trouble we had in Kansas or Henry Fowler, are you?" Tom asked.

"Never, not fer a minute," Huck said in all seriousness. "But I bin thinkin."

"And?"

"Well...bear with me now. See if this ain't some of your irony. Here we are, in a war. We are shootin' at Yankees and getting shot at by Yankees. Them fellas is all for Lincoln. Lincoln is an abolitionist. It weren't that too long ago that you and me helped a fugitive nigger escape from slavery makin' abolitionists, of a sort, out of both of us."

Tom stopped dead in his tracks. He looked at Huck with a horrified expression. Huck grinned broadly.

"They know we are from Missoura. Most of the officers, especially Cobb, think that people from our neck of the woods are half-wits and numbskulls. You go and tell that story, and they would think that you have abolitionist leanings and it would be all over. These Virginny boys are all inspired with the cause. They'd likely end up shootn' us." Tom did not want Huck to miss the importance of this point.

"I ain't stupid. I know this. This is just between us," Huck said.

"All right then, but you're forgetting that the widow Watson had freed Jim before we knew that she had."

"But we didn't know that at the time, Tom," Huck exclaimed. "Remember all we done so he could have a proper escape, like that fella in that book, the Count of County Crispo?"

"You mean the Count of Monty Cristo," Tom corrected. He did not like the direction that Huck's logic was taking. It was dangerous.

"The point is," Huck said, "that the widow Watson had freed Jim, but we didn't know this at the time. All we knowed was that Jim was runnin' and we decided to help him. We said to hell with the law an' everything to help him to escape. Now, here we are shootin' at people who believe in lettin' slaves go free. Can't you see the irony in that?"

"Stop right there. Wait one minute. For your information, not all of them Yankees are Abolitionists. I hear that some of them got their dander up, the ones we caught a few weeks ago when we drove in their picket line. When we were bringing them in, Andy called them a bunch of abolitionist scum and they didn't take to that at all, no sir." He looked at Huck inquisitively to see if any of what he had said was sinking in.

"Why most of those Yankees don't give a damn for Negroes and that's a fact," Tom said emphatically. "One of the Yankees told Andy to go to hell, that he wasn't fighting for no damned darkies. One of the Yankee sergeants said this to Andy. He said that the Colonel of his very same regiment told some Washington newspaperman that he would take his whole regiment and march them all off into a tall field of grass and stay there growing green moss on their uniforms before they would lift a finger to free them. The Yankee told Andy to go to hell."

"The devil you say," Huck said. Huck had recoiled from this new as if a rattlesnake had been placed in front of him.

"I swear," Tom said, raising his hand in the air.

"Andy Barrett said this here?" Huck asked in wonder.

"He sure in hell did," Tom said flatly.

"What did Andy say to that Yankee?" Huck asked.

"Andy told me he didn't say anything to them. He was too busy going through their pockets. He just robbed all of them." Tom could smell something cooking and picked up his pace. The encampment was very close and his appetite moved him along briskly. Huck was trying to fathom this last bit information. The confusion born out of this last bit of news was unsettling to him.

"Well, that kinda' knocks the irony out of what I was talkin' about then, don't it?" Huck mumbled. "That beats all. That puts rust all over that irony."

"Just make sure you never tell a soul what we did with Jim. And never tell anybody what happened in Kansas," Tom said quietly.

Tom could see the regiment's bivouac and hurried towards his section. Smoke clung to the humid morning air. Tom detected an unusual smell, strange but also familiar in the air. His feet hurried him along to his mess area. A small fire was smoking near the entrance of a tent that he shared with two others. A set of ramrods used for shoving a load of shot down the barrel of a rifle supported a beat up old coffeepot that was suspended above the fire.

Ed Bolls sat across from the fire reading a dog-eared newspaper. Tom and Huck shared the leaky tent, two federal shelter halves joined together by rope and meant to accommodate only two, with Ed. He looked up at the two as they approached and then went back to browsing through the crumbling yellowed newspaper. Tom lifted the lid of the coffeepot with a stick.

"Real coffee?" he asked. "Where in the world did you get real coffee?" Ed continued to browse through the newspaper.

"Last night," he answered quietly. "I bin' on picket duty since last night an didn't get a chance to get back here. I got a ride from some artillery boys. Rawlin's had give me a detail with them. I was loadin' artillery caissons and as we wuz' comin' down near that unfinished railroad cut, I tells the driver I got to piss. I wander off a bit. That's when I seed' him, a dead Yankee." Ed beamed at the memory of his good fortune. Tom placed the lid back on the coffeepot and sat down.

"Is it boilin' or do we need more fire. I almos' let it go out readin' this Yankee newspaper. It's from Philadelphia. It's a month or so old."

"Its doin' just fine," Tom said.

"Anyway," Ed continued, "I see's he's still kinda' fresh an weren't stinkin' too badly so I ambles over with a stick to see what I could find. He musta' got blown off the road an' crawled to where he was an died. He was hidden kinda' good. His haversack was blowed clear off him an' was a few paces in back of where I found him. He was one of those Dutchmen, 11th Corp. I know this when I started goin' through his sack."

Ed noticed Huck's pasty complexion as he squatted down near the fire.

"What's wrong with you...you're lookin' a tad peaked," he asked. Huck stretched out in front of the smoky fire.

"He's been up-chuckin' all morning," Tom said. "He ate some green ears of corn last night. It's a wonder he ain't got the Tennessee two-step" Ed slumped back on the ground.

"I open up his sack an' I find me aiggs wrapped in newspaper, this here newspaper in fact. I find coffee, sugar, I tell you, this fella' must of surely bin new to army life 'cause he had clean socks an' long-johns and a cookbook," Ed chortled. "Can you imagine carryin' a cookbook around with you. Damned idiot," Ed laughed.

"Where the hell did he think he was goin? Did he think he was goin' to find a fancy dining hall with lace doilies and crystal chandeliers on the ceilin' where he could show some fancy chef how to make his favorite eats." Huck began chuckling at Ed's observation.

"What did you do with the book?" Tom asked curiously. Ed poked the fire with a burning stick and looked at Tom strangely.

"I passed it out for shit-paper, it's all it was good fer." Huck pulled a plug of tobacco out of his pants pocket and cut off a section and handed it to Ed. Ed accepted Huck's generosity with a nod and a half wave.

"You found all this down near that unfinished railroad cut, ya say?" Huck asked.

"Yup," Ed replied, "down near the Brock road. Down by one of those little timber cuttin' roads that seem to pop up out of nowhere around here. Nothin' more actually than a worn out path. That Dutchman hardly looked kilt a'tall. He musta' died of fright. His pack wasn't even hardly ruint. The aiggs an' fatback was wrapped in newspaper like I says." Ed knew of Tom's predilection and love at looking at the printed word. He handed Tom the newspaper. Tom reached for the newspaper gingerly and examined it carefully looking for a date on its worn pages.

"Anything noteworthy in here?" Tom asked nonchalantly. "Yankees givin up?"

Ed spat a stream of tobacco and spittle to his side. He wiped his mouth before beginning.

"Wild injuns' are attackin' an' killin' farmers up there in Minnesota. Story there about a couple of coaches they found with ever'body scalpt an' kilt dead. They say the whole country side is a' runnin' off like the hounds of hell was after 'em." Ed wiped his mouth with the back of his sleeve again. Some of the spittle clung stubbornly to his bushy moustache.

"Injuns," he said, "is jest like rats comin' out of a hole once they start their damned foolishness. You got to get them all in the nest together like to stop their ignorance. Then it's fairly easy to wipe them out." Huck looked at Ed.

"Easy there, Daniel Boone. What the hell do you know about fightn' redskins. Hell, you're a Virginny boy from Old Williamsburg , born and bred. You wuz a cooper in regular life. You ain't no famous Injun fighter. The last injun' fightin' that was done around these parts wuz eighty years before your granpapy was born," Huck said nastily.

Tom laughed loudly. Ed looked sheepishly at Huck.

"I remember goin' to St. Lois with this farmer once on a buying trip for livestock," Huck said. "Folks used to fit up there on their way to California," he said. You should have saw the people comin' back in their wagons after they decided that they had had enough with fightn' the damned injuns' every step of the way. God, I hate injuns'. There were still arrows stickin' out of the damned wagons and bloodstains on the wheels."

Ed's face was a deep red as he stood up . His arms were enormous. He had the distinct look of a predator and did not like Huck's comment at all.

"The only good thing with those injuns' is that they are killin' Yankees. I despise the whole damned Yankee race," Ed said angrily. Tom reached to see how the coffee was doing. He could not resist the urge to smile at Huck's assessment of Ed's knowledge of being an Indian expert. He lifted the lid with a stick and breathed in the aroma of fresh coffee. Ed slapped at his hand with his stick and Tom dropped the lid quickly. Huck picked at a scab on his face and crawled into the small tent to lie down. Ed watched as Huck disappeared into the tent. Ed looked at Tom curiously.

"What he say true?" Ed asked.

"Actual and factual, Ed. I didn't go with him on that trip. I had to stay behind and tend to old man Flemming's farm. But it's true. Anyway, Huck there ain't too partial to Injuns an' neither am I. One almost killed me when I was a boy. Injun' Joe was his name. He was a real mean bastard. Don't let what he said bother you. It's just a sore spot with him anytime anybody mentions injuns'."

23

"Dirty business this mornin'," Ed said, wishing to change the subject. "I'm glad I missed out on it. That's the only time I was ever glad to be on a picket postin' that I can remember."

"Damned dirty business," Tom said flopping on his back and covering his eyes with his slouch hat.

"There's a new rumor started," Ed said, "that Lincoln is replacing Hooker as General of the Army of the Potomac."

"I wish somebody would replace me," Tom said dreamily.

"If you had been rich instead of poor as a church-mouse, you could have stayed out of this whole fracas by buying a substitute to fight in your place," Ed replied, "or if you owned twenty niggers. They let a man stay put and don't draft him, if he owns twenty niggers."

Tom grunted and turned on his side. Out of the corner of his eye, he looked up at a perfectly blue sky.

"That may be true, my friend. And if I had a little pink ass and wings, I would be an angel." Tom sighed and crossed his arms over his eyes. Ed threw a small log on the fire. Tom felt himself drifting into sleep when a few yards from where he lay, loud laughter attracted his attention. He rose up and leaned on his elbows. He watched as one of the men re-enacted the last minutes in the life of Archibald Conboy by doing a backwards cartwheel and landing flat on his back. The other men roared their approval at his performance.

"Damned fool loudmouths," Tom said bitterly. He recognized the man on the ground as Andy Barrett of his company. One of the other men he recognized as George Blakely and across from him stood John Hubert shaking with laughter.

"Andy and them is cookin' all the aiggs I found on that dead dutchy." Ed wiped his forehead leaving streaks of charcoal smudges on it. Huck emerged from the tent aroused by all of the raucous laughter that had disturbed his catnap. Ed poked Tom in the ribs with his short stick.

"Coffee's just about ready," Ed said. Tom stood up. He reached for a dented cup held in place by string to a tortured piece of leather on his belt. Ed picked up a rag and took the coffeepot off the makeshift ramrod tri-pod.

"Pass it here," Tom said.

Huck disappeared back into the tent. He materialized seconds later with a wooden bowl. Ed poured the coffee into Tom's tin-cup and then into Huck's bowl. The man who had been acting out the last few minutes of Archibald's tragic morning's drama separated from the group and sauntered over towards the tent. His hands were full.

24

"What you got there, Andy?" Huck asked.

"Aiggs and fatback, courtesy of the eyesight and luck of the right honorable Edward J. Bolls and the Lincolnite soldier, late, of course, of the Army of the Potomac." Andy grinned at his own joke. He balanced four empty pewter plates in one hand and a bowl that overflowed with eggs and strips of fatback in the crook of his arm.

"How you feelin?" he asked.

"Tolerable," Huck answered.

"You look like shit."

Andy Barrett was tall, almost six feet. His long hair stuck out from the sides of his slouch hat. He handed Huck one of the plates he was balancing. He passed another to Ed, who picked up another pewter plate and dolled out a generous portion of its contents to Tom. Huck plowed into his plate, shoveling handfuls into his mouth with his hands. Tom produced a wooden spoon and wiped it on the seat of his pants. He went right at making his food disappear as quickly as Huck did. Andy bent down next to Huck in a crouch.

"I don't want to get you all upset whils't you're enjoyin' such fine vittles, but I think you should know this. After you're little old accident at formation this mornin', I heard Rawlins' talkin' with Sergeant Alexander. I don't know what all they was a sayin' cause he chased me away. But before he chased me away, I heard him say he got somethin' special like planned fer you. It don't sound good by the way he was grinnin'. Watch your back with that sneaking, conniving bastard. Iff'n I was you, I'd make myself scarce fer a few hours." Andy cracked a huge grin at Huck.

"Thanks fer the warnin' there, Andy." Huck said nervously. Andy patted him on the shoulder and walked away. His uniform, if it could be called one, was a ragged combination of captured Federal clothing and civilian dress. The checkered pants that he had picked up somewhere were little more than rags. He resembled a scarecrow.

The cat-briars and thorny vines had left Andy's apparel in its present condition. This had been caused by their attack on the Union flank during the battle. The thick woods had seemed to be an impenetrable barrier to the Federal Corp commander. He had not believed it possible that an enemy would ever be able to launch an attack through them. He had felt safe by leaving his entire flank exposed. With the dark forest and thick briar patches seemingly offering protection for his flank, he confidently had awaited the coming day and the resumption of the fighting. No Army, no battalion or regiment could possibly move successfully through that tangled growth in line abreast and in formation without throwing the entire battle line into total disarray he had thought.

And so he had left the entire Union Flank exposed and unprotected. This was an unpardonable error. The situation was spotted by General Thomas Stonewall Jackson and after a brief meeting with General Lee, it was decided that General Jackson would take part of the Army of Northern Virginia on a flanking maneuver that would take it around the entire Union left wing. Andy's Division had started the march at eight in the morning. As the sun was slowly setting, General Jackson ordered all divisional commanders to put all lead regiments in line abreast and attack through the dense woods. The regiments had preserved their unit integrity by sometimes walking through the briars instead of around them to accomplish what their leaders had put into motion.

The briars and brambles had torn Andy's uniform to shreds and had lacerated his arms, face and legs. Scabs still covered his hands and face. At approximately five thirty in the afternoon, the first blow fell on the unsuspecting federal soldiers. General Jackson struck them in fury. The Army of Northern Virginia had boiled out of the woods in good order and formation and shattered a federal Corp.

The Union soldiers had just sat down for their evening meal when the lead elements of the Army of Northern Virginia came upon them uninvited to share their dinner. The southern onslaught had been irresistible. The only warning that the Northern men had that something was amiss was when deer and rabbits had started coming into their camp, flushed from their cover by the massive movement of Southern regiments through the woods. The federal soldiers had even taken the time to shoot at a few deer that had incredibly bounded towards them.

By then, however, it was far too late to do anything to stop or offer any kind of serious resistance to the hammer like blows that fell upon them. It had become a northern rout. The federal soldiers had run for their lives. Tom watched as Huck washed down his breakfast with the remaining coffee. Tom noticed the concerned look that had crossed his features after he had spoken with Andy. He walked over to him.

"Tom, I got to git'. Andy said he heard Rawlins cookin' up some kinda' trouble for me. That damned fella' kin' brew it up quick. I'm gonna go find me a patch of woods and lay low fer a spell. If anybody asks where I be, tell them I got deathly sick and went to the sick tent. If'n he checks on me, I'll tell him later I went and passed out on my way there."

Tom nodded. Andy had returned.

"Damned good eatin'," Huck commented. "You know, Andy, there's somethin' I bin' meanin' to ask you," He said, wiping his greasy fingers on Andy's shirt.

"Tell me somethin'. When you was bringin' in those Yankee prisoners through our lines, did any of them say anythin' that sounded odd to you?" Huck asked.

"Why hell, Huck, they all sound odd to me. They all sound like they is a' talkin through their damned noses or somethin', those that kin' speak proper American at all. The rest just kept a' jabberin' away in that Dutchy talk. Sounds like a bunch of excited barnyard animals to me," Andy said quickly.

Tom belched and spilled some coffee on his shoes.

"No, that's not what I mean. I mean did you git' into an argument with one of them?"

"Yup," Andy said quietly. "One of those Yankee scum got real mad when I called him an abolitionist nigger lovin'son-of-a-bitch an' he tolt' me to go to blazes. I had to straighten him out to the fact that I was the person holdin' a gun, not him."

Ed choked on his coffee, causing some to spill out of his nose. He started to laugh between his choking. Finally, after regaining his composure, Ed placed his hand on Huck's shoulder and said, "He stole everythin' they had and made them go through the picket line buck-naked. One of the Holy Joe's spots Andy leadin' all these shorn little lambs and gives him holy hell fer abusing the prisoners. They was all scratched an bleedin' cause Andy here was makin' them all walk through the brambles and bushes instead of walkin' on the road."

"Some of the officers ain't got no sense of humor," Andy said sullenly. Ed laughed loudly.

"One of them staff officers tolt' Rawlins what Andy had bin' up to. Rawlin's puts Andy to diggin' latrines fer the rest of the week an fillin' in the old ones. He almost dug a line to Washington, he was diggin' so long. He smelt like a thousand shit-holes fer a week." Ed laughed uncontrollably. Huck showed his sympathy for Andy by shaking his head side to side sadly and making clucking sounds. Seizing an opportunity between Ed's laughter to ask Andy a question, he asked, "Did any of them Yankees say that they wasn't fightin' fer the darkies?"

"As a matter of fact, one of them did say jest' that," Andy said with surprise. He looked at Huck suspiciously.

"But that didn't surprise me none," Andy said happily. "You know how Yankees is. They's all born liars and thieves. They git' that way early in life, I hears, from livin' in them slums they got in them filthy cities up there. Their pappy's make them go out in the streets and learn to pick pockets when they be jest younguns and crack people in the head an fish through the pockets. Ain't nobody ever tolt' you this?" Andy asked smiling.

"But yer' gotta' beg my pardon. I keep on fergettin' that you're from Missora." Andy laughed. Huck went red in the face.

"Go to hell," Huck shouted. Tom and Ed roared their approval at Huck's apparent discomfort and visible anger. He glared at his companions and then gulped the remaining coffee from his wooden bowl. He flung what little remained in it at the smoky campfire, which made a hissing sound, and angrily stomped away from them. Andy looked over at Tom.

"No offense meant, Tom," he said.

"None taken, old boy, none taken," Tom answered. He stretched out on the ground and placed his hat over his face. Ed rubbed his stomach. His face contorted and then he broke wind.

"Where the hell is he off to?" Ed asked.

"Huck heard from Andy, here, that Rawlins is plannin' on some kinda trouble for him. Huck plans on takin' a nap somewhere for a while this all blows over," Tom said, yawning widely.

"That Rawlin's is a lunk-head. He's one mean little bastard," Ed said. Huck soon returned with his rifle in his hand. He sat down next to Tom.

"Well, I'm goin'," he said. "Keep an eye open around here for me."

Ed grinned at Andy and poked him in the ribs with his finger.

"Lookit, Huck," Andy began. "I take back what I said about folks from Missora. It was wrong. No hard feelin's. I got me enough enemies, I surely don't need another. To get back on what you was askin' about, I thought it was a might peculiar when one of that bunch said, without hesitatin' mind you, that he was fightin' to save the Union and not to free the darkies. Didn't make no sense to me then an' to tell you the truth, it still don't sound right to me now," he said wearily.

"It seems to me," Andy said, "that iff'n that was true then this here war is over an we could all go home. I ain't out here in all of this to be tellin' anybody how they should run their lives or live. If we could all agree about that, then all this stinkin' business would be done with."

Andy was trying, in his own way, to simplify what politicians and statesmen had struggled with in anguish over the last decade with disastrous results. He continued, everyone's attention being focused in on what he was saying.

"But they ain't about to do that, I mean go home on their own accord. And we can't leave until they get thrown out and get so whipped that there's nothin' fer' them to do here. So the way I got it figured, there's nothin' for it till ever'body ends up killin' off everybody else. Then there won't be nothin' left but darkies, women, young-uns and wrinkled old granpaws. Ain't that a hoot?"

Andy's logic, although askew, somehow made horrible sense and they all knew this inwardly. No matter how many times they had crushed the Federal Army, there seemed to be another one gathering somewhere, ready to strike again. They all felt their chances on living to see the war's end chancy at best. Andy figured to change the subject, the gloomy mood becoming too oppressive for his buoyant nature to long endure.

"You find any money on that dead Dutchy you found?" he asked Ed.

"No money, but there was a bunch of paper with the picture of George Washington and the flag on them. Some of those were burnt to a frazzle," Ed admitted. Andy wiped his greasy fingers through his hair.

"When are you gonna git some new clothes off the quartermaster. You could git somethin wearable instead of them rags. With all the tents that was abandoned by the Yankees, there's gotta be a pair of blue federal britches around what ain't got bullet hole in them. You look like a pauper. Look at you. You're a disgrace. You look like hell. It is a wonder that Rawlin's ain't jumped on you about the way you look," Ed quipped.

The mention of Rawling's name made Huck stand up.

"Got to go. I'm off," Huck said.

"Not so fast, plowboy," Rawlings shouted. "I got plans fer' you."

Rawlings once again had seemingly appeared out of thin air. He had a penchant for doing this which annoyed his men to no end. His gaze angrily fell on the little group.

"Ain't this cozy. You boys are all sittin' around with your thumbs up your lazy behinds like you'all was in your own dear old Kentucky homes. Get on up from your lazy behinds, all of you. Boll's I heard some of what you was sayin'. You didn't happen to find any onions on that deadman, did you?"

"No," Ed stammered. Huck cringed when he heard the word onions mentioned. He knew that he was in trouble. He cursed his luck. Sergeant Rawlings walked towards Huck and poked him in the chest.

"That's too bad. Onions go good with liver. You thought I forgot, didn't you, plowboy?" Rawlings smirked evilly.

"I got a detail fer you two birds. Since you are so fond of talkin' in ranks, I will show you how you are supposed to be when you are in the ranks. Dead men do not talk in ranks so I'm gonna have you spend a little time in their company for a while. There's some buryin' to be done, up near Fairview. You will go up there and learn something from them. Find Corporal Bains and relieve a couple of his detail."

29

Huck spoke up. "But Sergeant Rawlings, buryin's gotta be all done by about now. The onliest' ones that need buryin' is the ones that crawled off into the woods to die or the ones peggin' off in the hospitals."

Rawlings interrupted Huck by standing an inch from his face.

"Finn, I done gave you a goddamned order, If you ain't out of my sight in five minutes, you will be in serious trouble. Take your friend and git'. If you can't find any dead Yankees to bury, then I'm orderin' you to find some an kill them an bury them. But you are goin' on this detail, come hell or high water."

Ed approached Sergeant Rawlings.

"Git away from me, shit-bird," Rawlings shouted. Andy avoided even looking at the sergeant.

"No one asked for your opinion, Bolls," he roared. "This here ain't none of your business, so you can take your big arms and go sit down right now. If I want your stupid opinion, I will give it to you."

Rawlings had not even looked at Ed. He had continued to glare at Huck with a smug look. He pointed down the road.

"Now, start movin' that-a-way down that there road, plowboys." He smiled at Huck and Tom and strode confidently away.

"What the hell is wrong with that fella? Why the hell do we need people like that?" Ed seethed in anger. "It's bad enough that we got to be shot at, why do we need lunkheads like that givin' us grief all the wakin' hours of every single day?"

Huck turned to Tom. "The milk of human kindness just got poured all over us again." Tom nodded his head in appreciation to the earnestness of his friend's observation and to his own memories of better days.

CHAPTER TWO

Tom and Huck trudged along the road. Tom thought about the miserable job that lay ahead The Federals had given up the field and usually that meant that their dead would be the last to be put beneath the ground.

"I hope you're right," Tom said slowly, "about all the bury'n bein' done with."

"I jest' made that up," Huck answered. "The Yankees put up a fight in Fairview Cemetery. They gave up the high ground at Hazel Grove and then went to fight in the worst of spots. In the low ground. I understand our artillery ripped them up good. If there's any buryin's still to be done, it probably will be at Fairview. Nobody in their right mind want's to pick up body parts. Bury'n bodies is no fun, it's the worse job a body kin' get'. They've been lain' out in the sun for a week. The stink clings to you, it gets in your clothes, your hair, why it even gets in your mouth. No matter how many times you change your clothes or wash yourself, it don't go away. I remember talkin' to a fella' after Sharpsburg. He was put on a burying detail fer punishment. He said it nearly drove him to desert."

They plodded along in silence. Fairview was a long way off. The late morning sunlight peeped through the dense canopy of the woods. Tom continued to look over his shoulder in the hope that an artillery team would give them a lift. Artillerymen often gave detail parties rides to wherever they may be going. Tom's hopes were rewarded a few minutes later when they spotted a lone wagon and single driver approaching them from their rear. Tom waved a friendly greeting at the driver. The teamster reigned up his mule team when he drew abreast of the pair. As Tom approached the wagon, a smell of death hit him like a hammer and he instinctively pulled away from it. He covered his nose with his hand.

"Hooo-hah, man. What have you been toting in this wagon?" he exclaimed. The driver of the offending wagon was a rail thin specimen who was even more tattered looking than Andy Barrett. On his feet were shoes that appeared to have been worn by Moses when he crossed the Red Sea. The thin man leaned forward.

"I bin' totin' rifles, britches, dead men and dyin' ones fer the last week," he said. "Kinda' rank, ain't it?"

"How do you stand it? This wagon would make a buzzard gag."

"No need to insult a man's work. You fellas' look like you could stand a ride. The thin man reached for the brake on the wagon, pulled it into place and jumped nimbly from the wagon. He then pulled out a pipe out of his breast pocket, reached into another and pulled out a tobacco pouch. Carefully filling his pipe, he eyed the two men warily. He struck a match on the wagon and it flared quickly. He drew on his pipe, still eyeing the two suspiciously.

"A good pipe keeps the smell down a tad. This hyar's fine Virginny burly. After a while, it kinda grows on you," he said.

"What grows on you, the burly or the stink?" Huck asked.

The teamster laughed.

"Both," he said. "Where you boys be headin'?"

"Burial detail supposed to be up near that Fairview Cemetery," Tom answered the teamster broke into a grin. His eyes narrowed.

"If the Provo's ever heard you say what you jest' tolt' me, you'all would be under guard as quick as a cat. You had better come up with a story a lot better than that one. Don't you boys know that all the burying is done? It ain't none of my business, but I'm warnin' you, don't use that story."

"What are you telling us, friend?" Huck asked.

"What I'm sayin' is that I ride these roads every single day and everyday I sees' boys, jest' like you, hittin' the road fer home sweet home and everyday I sees Provo's takin' them back under guard. Let me ask you a question now, friends. Who sent you on this detail and you had better have somethin', some written detail orders on you like a pass or some sich'. You got anythin' on you a' tall that says why you're out of your company area?"

The tattered soldier leaned back on his heels and rocked back and forth like an irritated schoolmaster. He crossed his arms.

"You boys gotta' know that all the buryin' being done now is jest fer' the men what die from wounds or sickness. Secondly, there ain't no hospital even close to where you boys is headin'." He exhaled a cloud of smoke. Huck leaned in towards Tom and said in a hushed voice that was full of worry,

"The man is right. We ain't got nothin' in writin', not even a company pass. Rawlin's seen fit to that. He cooked our gooses." Huck punched the side of the wagon.

"How could we have bin so stupid, Tom? That snake in the grass fixed it so that we would be a' traipsing around the woods and get picked up and put under guard. When they find out we ain't got nothin' in writin', they surely will figure that we are skedadiling' from old Marsa' Robert's army."

"We got witnesses that will say that it was Rawlings that sent us out on the detail," Tom said confidently.

"Your missin' the point. We are dealin' with Provo's, Tom. Them fellas would sooner crack your head than look at you. They treat a body worse than you or I would treat a field hand. Why do you think old Archie Conboy shot one? He had nerve, Archie did. He punched Captain Cobb in the mouth jest' over an everyday insult All Cobb did was to call Archie a lazy heathen. From what I heard, the Provo's started to whip on Archie. He couldn't fight back all that good 'cause he was drunker than a monkey, but he managed to git' one of the Provo's guns and shoot him. I surely don't want no truck with them fellas. They enjoy their jobs just a little too much fer' my taste."

Tom listened to Huck and knew that Huck was right. They had nothing to show that they were not deserting. It had happened too quickly and now, in retrospect, it appeared that Rawlings had set them up. Rawlings had clearly pulled a fast one on them, a very dangerous fast one. Tom fought against the panic that was rising and tried to resort to logic.

"Look, fella', our sergeant put us on this duty for punishment because Huck over there was talking to me in formation then dropped his rifle when he threw up on his shoes."

Tom started to sweat as he watched the stern expression of the mule driver, which had not changed. Huck's head constantly turned, half expecting any minute to see the Provost guards overtaking them.

Finally, the teamster said slowly, "This sergeant of yours kind of fixed your wagon, didn't he? And you boys went straight off without orders. Kind of hard to swallow."

Huck was becoming unnerved at the whole conversation and the irritating way that the Mule driver was treating their situation.

"You know," the thin man said pompously, "there's got to be at least a hunert' men that are absent without permission everyday. You know this, unless you're both jest' plain stupid. You know the trouble you can git' into these days without the proper pass when you travel. What's your excuse? You sound like a couple of real lamebrains to me."

Huck's fear began to turn to anger at the arrogant skinny mule driver. He quickly interrupted the man.

"You don't know Rawlings. He is a man not to be trifled with. He holds grudges against you like some people save money. He is one mean bastard who can make simply livin' a chore. When he says go I go an' I don't look back. He can raise all kinds of shades of hell for you real quick like. I jest' wanted to be away from him before he could dream up some more nonsense for me. I wasn't even thinkin'."

The teamster continued to draw on his pipe and nodded as he took in Huck's explanation. When Huck had finished, he said,

"I bin' ridin', like I sez', up and down this road fer' the last week, an' I kin' tell you I seed' enough to tell you something is in the wind. I think we's gonna' make another move right quick. They's bin' cavalry and staff officers poundin' up the roads the last couple of days to beat the band. From what I figger', this sergeant of your'n knew somethin' big was up. It does appear that he was settin' his sights on getting you two boys into some serious trouble. Suppose orders come out, let's say, right now to move. You two sorry bastards is a-wanderin' all over hell and creation. No one knows where you are and then Sha-bang," he shouted loudly. Tom jumped with the shout.

"You two are listed official like as goldbricks and deserters. Not a pleasant situation these days fer a body to be in, especially these days. They shot some poor fella', this morning, in fact fer' runnin'." He looked at both of them carefully.

"Now, mind you, if what you fellas' say is true, an' I got no reason not to believe you, then you'd be better off stickin' with me. I'm goin' up near where you boys is headin'. I gotta' pick up a load of shoes, rifles, and pants an' I got to come right back down this a' way. I got me papers all official like an' the Provo's don't hamper me a bit. They's all used to see'n me an' don't like to even come near this wagon 'cause of the stink. Tell you what. Stay with me, an' when I'm finished later today, I'll drop you off at a picket. You kin' tell an officer. Tell him that your sergeant forgot to give you a pass an' that's why you never made it up there to Fairview. Besides," he said looking around nervously, "they's still Yankee cavalry scouts aroun'."

"I thought the Federals were cleared out this side of the river?" Tom asked.

"They are, for the most part. But believe me, they is still snoopin' and poopin' around h'yar. Scouts, they be. Jist' yesterday, I was up near Salem Church. There's this fine woman lives near there I used to spark before the war...anyway, I takes me a cut to her house. Let me tell you fellas, she's somethin' else entirely. Real ladylike she is. Why she even sneezes lady-like, know what I mean? She kinda' stifles it like. The only noise you hear is a little Phhtt sound, like that there. If I tried to stifle a sneeze like that, I'd be a feared to 'cause I'd probably end up breakin' wind and embarrasin' myself in mixed company." Tom chuckled at the driver's remark.

"What about them cavalry?" Huck asked impatiently. Huck had a perfectly normal fear of men astride large horses who carried huge swords and that were armed to the teeth. The teamster leaned his back against the wagon and relaxed.

"I was jest' gettin' to that part. See, I was down this little loggin' road, you know, the ones that seem to pop up on you?"

Huck collapsed on the side of the road and buried his head in his hands. He sighed heavily. He was filled with a self-pity and self-loathing for getting caught in a dangerous predicament. The teamster had halted his story to watch Huck.

"Your friend seems a bit antsy," he said with concern.

"Something he ate, is all," Tom said soothingly. The thin soldier looked at Huck again, still not at all sure as how to read Huck's demeanor. He continued, after a while, happy to have at least Tom's attention.

"So here I be on this loggin' road after visitin' with Miss Purcell an' I hears a rumblin', the only kind of rumblin' that cavalry make. I hears' them way before I git' sight of them. Why, I tell you, they came tearin' down that road lookin' fer' a fight, like a storm. Quick like lightnin'...twenty or more of them."

"What happened? You get a look at them to make sure they were Federals?" Tom asked.

"A man don't have to see the mule that kicked him in the head to know that it was a mule what kicked him in the head," the teamster said. Huck continued to stare into the woods muttering obscenities.

"Way before they kin' spot me, I jumped off the wagon. I knew right there that I didn't want any part of that monkey show and hunkered off down a slope an' kept on runnin', I'm not ashamed to say." Tom was perplexed by this news.

"And you're sure it was Federal cavalry?" Tom asked again.

"Clean out your ears. Of course I'm sure. Put it this way. Would our cavalry be ridin' their mounts like that on our side of the river. There ain't a possible reason why they would be. The Yankee cavalry don't know how to treat their horses. They ride them to death jest like this group was figurin' on doin'. They ain't worth a tinker's damn."

What the teamster said made perfect sense.

"Did you tell anybody what you saw?"

"I tolt' my sergeant. He said to keep on the main roads and stay off the side roads, particular like Miss. Purcell's. Anyway, that was up near Salem Church, and I ain't goin' that way, today."

The mule driver indicated his wagon with his thumb and a wave.

"We might as well get goin'. Although nothin' of the likes is bound to happen like that today, there's safety in numbers. You boys always carry rifles when put on a detail?" he asked.

Tom ignored the question and nudged Huck with his foot. Huck stood up.

"We might as well go with this fella'. What he said makes sense to me," Tom said quietly to his distraught companion. The teamster climbed back to his seat and released the brake. Huck nodded dully and took a seat next to Tom. The driver clucked his mules into motion just as Huck sat down. The wagon moved with a lurch.

Tom placed his rifle across his lap. He could see that Huck was affected by the realization of how Rawlings had duped them. Huck had grown sullen and that was a bad sign. He watched as Huck ground his jaws together. Huck began to mumble incomprehensible words to himself and pull at his chin hair. Tom watched Huck's fear turned to rage. Images in the form of sadistic provost guards, Federal cavalry, and sudden death began to strongly manifest themselves in Huck's mind. He could not hold back his anger and broke like an over stressed rain-choked dam.

He gave way to loud black oaths sworn against both God and man. Indescribable blasphemies, foul imprecations, and vile obscenities gushed out in one long powerful stream. He vented all kinds of filth for the entire world to witness like a geyser.

His rage was all-inclusive. It was not this one act alone of Rawlings that had caused it. It was the end result of many compounding factors. Rawlings was simply the catalyst. Huck's anger was the end result of long endless marches, of body lice and impending feelings of doom, by strutting idiots who happily went out of their way to bring one misery, by mud and cold as well as hunger. It was the end product of the food that they were forced to eat when there was any to be eaten; His anger was against the rotten blue beef that they were expected to eat that when thrown against a wall would stick to it as if it had been glued.

Weevil infested crackers, green bacon, beans that were as hard as granite pebbles, rancid water, as well as cheese that smelled as bad as their feet and looked far worse played in his mind's eye. He vented his anger like a volcano. The wagon driver looked on in amazement.

"It's been a long day," Tom said sadly. The wagon driver smiled and nodded.

"He'll stop when he runs out of cuss words to use. You know, old Huck here never cussed like this before he joined the Army. Since then, he's learned a whole lotta' dirty words."

"I should say he has," the driver said. He was quite impressed with the litany of profanity that Huck was utilizing so effectively.

"He's got some vocabulary there."

The driver slapped at the mule with the slack reins.

"You know," he said, "when I was a boy an' said one of them there words in front of my daddy, he would say that there was jest' a limited number of dirty words a body was given to use up in their lifetime. When you used up all of yer share of cuss words, the Good Lord would take you on up to heaven because it was a sign that yer time was up." He grinned while Tom laughed at his comment.

"The Army teaches a man to cuss," the driver said. "I remember when I fust' jined up. My ears would fairly ring from all the cussin'. There was no way of getting around it a 'tall. The preacher was the worst one of them all."

Huck ran out of every cuss word that he had ever heard and stopped abruptly. He stared off into the woods, inflexible as a tent post.

"Are you quite finished, Preacher Finn?" Tom asked good-naturedly. "That was some sermon."

Huck did not hear any of what Tom had been saying. His mind had drifted away from him He was drained, his anger slowly dissolving into a clinging numbness. He slumped on the seat and leaned against Tom. He had seen too many things in the last month, experiencing events that he had tried to hide from his memory. He had been a witness to the unthinkable and a participant in orchestrated bedlam.

During the terrible fighting, with the incessant rolling thunder of rifle fire in which thousands shared in, the same numbness would begin. The smoke created by countless regimental volleys obliterated vision, encompassing all in a thick fog that blinded, choked, and confused. With the numbness came a feeling of detachment. Everything slowed down. In the vacuous embrace of the all pervading fog, he had acted as a machine, biting off the ends of paper cartridges, ramming the load down the barrel and firing at shadows and phantoms that briefly flitted in front of his gun sights. He moved and reacted by instinct alone.

Friends had died horribly right by his side. Some dropped with eyes bulging and mouths wide open in screams that were swept away by the pure power of the man made thunder. Others were decapitated in howling sheets of lead rain that filled the air. Still others were ripped from their shoes from cannon balls that bounced wickedly around their ankles to be torn limb from limb when the shell exploded.

He had moved forward keeping his eye on the regimental battle flag, spurred on by reflex more than by design. He was human flotsam swept along in a deadly eddy of a rampaging swollen river that destroyed everything in its path. His mind had vortexed in clouds of dullness. Success was measured in staying up with the flag and staying alive with the sure knowledge of knowing absolutely nothing that was happening twenty feet to one's right or left.

In the midst of thousands, he felt alone with his own mortality an open almost suffocating question. Sometimes he had found himself firing at muzzle flashes. Most of the time it was simply a matter of firing at whatever was visible for a fleeting moment when the clouds of dirty gray smoke would unexpectedly clear. Death edged him forward as he loaded and fired, all wrapped up in this blessedness of numbness. Nothing could prepare one for this. Stories about war and all it's glories mentioned nothing about the true nature of what it was like. It was mind-numbing madness with fear as a constant companion.

He was ordered to shoot at men who spoke strangely, men from cultures and places he had never known existed and in all likelihood would never have encountered if it hadn't been for the war. The different accents from the many prisoners he had seen were baffling to him. Huck drifted and floated in this numbness and as he did, he began to think back to the events that had brought him to his present condition, back to thoughts of home and Missouri and the trouble in Kansas.

The newspapers back east called the trouble Bleeding Kansas and the residents that experienced it first hand called it a nightmare. Missourians had killed Kansans and Kansans had annihilated Missourians, going at it with a passionate commitment and reverent dedication that before hand would have been hard to believe possible. A bushwhacking war had been going on for a decade before the outbreak of the war. Houses had been burned, people had been shot down in cold blood and heads had been chopped off. Livestock had been butchered out of pure meanness. This murderous discord had been born out of a legacy of hatred and sectional distrust.

In the move for compromise over the question of the spread of slavery into the new territories out West, Congress had made the mistake of putting the question of slavery in these areas to a referendum, a popular vote. This referendum was to decide the future of slavery in Kansas. Hundreds of Pro-slavery people flooded into Kansas in an attempt to sway the popular vote, while hundreds of anti-slavery forces poured into Kansas. The result was violence, murder and chaos. The opposing sides clashed in open warfare, a precursor to civil war.

Pro-slavery forces, labeled as Border Ruffians in the hostile press back east, raided Free-State people in an attempt to drive them out of Kansas. Free State militia groups attacked Missourians and on it went. People found themselves living in fear. Old grudges that had nothing to do with the issue of slavery were sometimes settled by a late night knock on the door followed by gunfire or a sudden ambush in the daylight hours. One had to be very careful whom one spoke to about certain issues and beliefs. Vendettas flourished in this atmosphere of lawlessness. Just the rumor of being pro-slavery was often all it took for a person to become a victim of the violence and mayhem that was being conducted without letup.

The sectional conflict affected Tom early one spring morning. His Aunt Polly had been found at the bottom of the well in her own backyard. Someone had caved her head open with a cavalry saber before throwing the old woman down it. Sid had been nailed to a barn door after being shot and stabbed numerous times. For some unknown reason, he had survived. His mind, however, had been destroyed by his ordeal. Old friends of the family kept Sid chained to the rafters in the attic, for his own protection as well as theirs. When it became too hot in the attic in the summer months, he was tied down in the root cellar.

Aunt Polly, it was true, had owned slaves but that had been years ago. It was still enough to get her killed. Free State militia, it was rumored, were behind her brutal death, which had shocked the small community. Someone had wanted to make an example of her. Tom had become a different person after the murder. The drunken sheriff claimed her death as a murder committed during a robbery. Her home had been ransacked of almost all her valuables, but everyone close to her suspected that she had been killed because she once had owned human beings. The killings had slackened off in the middle of the decade, but only for a short time. It soon resumed again in bloodshed and savagery.

Before John Brown had made himself infamous at his ill planned attack on the arsenal at Harper's Ferry, he had been loping heads off in Kansas. Eventually, anytime a pro-slavery person was found dead under suspicious circumstances, John Brown's name was the first on everyone's lips. It was said that wealthy abolitionists from back east in Boston financed John Brown. It was also said that many of his supporters lived in that nest of abolitionist, the Free-State stronghold of Lawrence, Kansas.

In Missouri, if you were sound on the goose, it meant that you were Pro-slavery, anti- abolitionist, anti- Lawrence, Kansas, and anti-John Brown. Anything less than this could earn one trouble. Aunt Polly's death had changed Tom. He knew in his heart that he did not believe in slavery. He had seen the misery that the peculiar institution was capable of creating in his own community. However, to even think of portraying oneself as anything but sound on the goose left one openly inviting trouble even from one's own neighbors.

Tom had read a book about the goldfields of California and when he wasn't brooding about the death of his aunt or working hard as a farm hand on Mr. Fleming's farm, it was all he talked about. He had made the place sound like paradise, Huck remembered. Fist sized nuggets of gold lay right on the surface and all it took to fulfill every life's wish was for a man to bend down and put it in his pocket. Tom lectured about California every spare minute. Talking about California and getting there were two different realities.

Huck had seen the people that had returned to St. Louis after starting out on their journey to California by land. They had decided that the trip was tantamount to putting a loaded shotgun between their eyes and pulling the trigger with their big toe. Huck remembered the wagons still fresh with the blood of their owners on them. He remembered the arrows still imbedded in the sides and the stories the survivors told.

Hostile Indians and the terror they inspired were enough for Huck. As far as he was concerned, unless there was another way to get to California without fighting Indians all the way, then he was content to let the dream lie and not pursue it. Tom continued to brood for months on end. The murder had created an outrage among the community. Tom had never gotten a straight answer from the constantly inebriated sheriff about what was being done in bringing those responsible to justice. The town sheriff, a terrible drunk, gave his version that the old woman had been killed by a pack of cutthroats and thieves, more than likely desperate criminals from a riverboat and were long gone.

He never had time to fully investigate the murder because shortly after the murder the drunken sheriff had taken an accidental permanent vacation to the Pearly Gates. The sheriff had discovered, albeit too late, that in cleaning a shotgun that is fully loaded, one should take proper precautions, especially if one has just killed a bottle of whiskey and is sitting in a dimly lit jail.

It was a close friend that let Tom know exactly who was responsible for the senseless killing and maiming and from that moment, Huck knew that their lives had been changed forever. Cecil Gordon had heard it from his father that a man had been boasting to all that would listen that it had been a free state captain of militia named Henry Fowler who had committed the horrendous crime. Cecil's father had said that a man resembling a dwarf, he was that short, and had a weasel like look with hands that resembled talons of an eagle, had stopped in at the blacksmith shop. This apparition had insisted that he knew who the killer was after overhearing various conversations about the murder.

The stranger had calmly said that the man responsible for the death was one Captain Henry Fowler, Kansas Free State militia, a man the stranger had claimed to be tracking for the last two weeks. The little man claimed to be sound on the goose after someone had asked him how he knew. There was something truly dangerous about the short strange looking man and he was gone before too many questions could be asked of him. His yellow eyes gave the man an unworldly appearance.

Huck remembered how Cecil's father and uncle had decided that the appearance of the stranger was suspicious and Cecil, one day after work, had begun to talk to Tom of what his father and uncle had suspected to be true.

"So tell me, Cecil," Tom said, "Just who the hell was the little biscuit an who the hell is Henry C. Fowler?"

"I asked my Uncle Frank if'n he ever heard tell of him 'cause he's a raider, Uncle Frank," Cecil answered proudly, "and sure as rain, he did. Uncle Frank said that they bin' a tryin' to put him down fer years as well as that short fella."

"Is that a fact," Tom replied laconically.

Cecil knew what he said would upset Tom. His Uncle and Father had warned him against telling Tom, but he felt obligated to Tom having known him all of his life. He felt duty bound to let Tom know what everyone seemed to already know.

"The man's got more lives than a damned old cat," Cecil stated, "and Uncle Frank sez' he's richer than Croesus, whoever that may be. Anyway, he got the Army protectin' him an' lives out in Leavenworth. That's why nobody kin' seem to git' to him. He rides with a bunch of abolitionists that have bin' known to raid Missora from time to time."

Tom walked into the stable that he lived in with Huck. Huck was seated on a beat up barstool playing cards with Ted Doudlass, another old friend.

"Close the damned door," Huck shouted, "do you live in a barn or what?"

It was starting to get seasonably cold out during these last days of fall. Winter was definitely on its way. Tom was glad that Huck had the stove going and smiled at his friend's joke. He could smell rabbit roasting in a pan.

"What else did your uncle Frank tell you about this Fowler?" Tom asked. The unfamiliar name perked Huck's interest.

"Who's this Fowler?"

"Fowler, Henry C. Fowler from Lawrence, Kansas. He's a captain in the Kansas Militia," Cecil said, "Pa an' Uncle Frank tolt' me that there was this fella' came into the blacksmiths not more than two days after they found Miss Polly dead. They said that this here fella' claimed Henry Fowler was the man that did it. Uncle Frank wasn't at the blacksmiths when this little fella' was there tellin' everybody that he had bin' trackin' Fowler for a week, but Pa was. Uncle Frank knew who that short fella wuz right off. That short little runt was none other than Henry Fowler's right hand man. Uncle Frank said that if he had been in the smithy's shed, that he would have spotted the fella' right off for who he was and would've sent him to hell right then an' there. You ain't never seen when my Uncle Frank gets his blood up. It's frightful. When Pa tolt him the story, why Uncle Frank was nearly frothin' at the mouth. He went plumb loco. My Uncle Frank got hisself one bad temper. He is truly frightful to witness when he get' his dander up. He acts like some kind of lunatic. Fowler and that runt fella is stone cold killers. But if my Uncle Frank had seen that runt fella, that runt fella would have been heading in only one direction out of town and that would be to the bone yard."

41

Ted placed his cards on the barrel that they used for their table.

"Anyway," Cecil continued, "Uncle Frank knows all about the both of them. He said that Fowler is friends with John Brown hisself."

"Go on out of here," Ted exclaimed.

"Actual an' factual. Yessuh," Cecil responded flatly. "Henry C. Fowler, accordin' to Uncle Frank, is one of the richest men in Kansas an' got hisself' all kinds of important friends in the highest positions in the state. He's a friend of Senator Lane an' that abolitionist bunch. He even got people in the Army on his payroll out in Leavenworth. That's why Uncle Frank an' the rest of the raiders ain't bin' able to git' him, although Uncle Frank said they tried more'n once. Every time they think they got him to rights, he slips out of it. Uncle Frank says they bin' a' try'n to put him down for years."

"Sounds to me that your Uncle Frank and his friends just ain't tried hard enough to me. Anybody can be gotten to; you just have to want it bad enough. Look at Julius Caesar, Emperor of all ancient Rome, the most powerful man in the world. Yet they still got to him. They stabbed him right in the forum."

"How did he die from bein' stabbed in the fore-arm? That ain't a serious place to get stabbed in. What happened, did he bleed to death?" Huck asked.

Tom ignored Huck entirely.

"If they could get him, then anybody can be gotten to," Tom said scornfully.

"What are you inplyin'? What Are you gittin' at you got somethin' to say, why don't you come right out with it?" Cecil asked.

"Ain't it obvious?" Tom said slowly and carefully. "They are all afraid to go to Leavenworth and kill him; otherwise they would've done it already."

Cecil's eyes widened and his face went red as he flushed with rising anger. The corners of his mouth began to twitch. Ted leaned back and laughed loudly, almost falling off the box that he was sitting on. Huck rose from his stool. Cecil stuck his finger in Tom's face.

"Take it back. Take what you said back. I am not playin'. What you said. Take it back you ain't got no cause to say what you said, I don't care about no damned Joolus Ceasar. My Uncle Frank wuz one of the first from these parts to take it to them abolitionist scum, one of the first to cross the border an' give them hell. He ain't no slacker an' no coward, so now you take it back." Cecil was infuriated.

"The hell I will," Tom said defiantly. "Your Uncle Frank is about as sure to go kill Fowler as you are, Cecil, and we all know what kind of killer you are," Tom said sarcastically.

42

"Don't make me whup your ass, Tom," Cecil shouted.

"You can kiss my ass. How does that be? Does that sound about right to you?" Tom shouted. Huck watched anger blanket Cecil like a quilt. He slowly moved towards them, expecting the worst. He did not have long to wait. Cecil's strong arms reached out in a blur of speed and grabbed Tom by his throat. With his two hands crushing Tom's throat, he lifted Tom in the air.

Tom's two feet dangled uselessly in the air and his hands clutched desperately at Cecil's constricting hands. Tom lurched forward driving his head into Cecil's nose. They both fell to the floor and began to pummel each other. Ted dove off his box as Huck began to pull them apart. Ted grabbed Cecil's ankles and pulled him off Tom. Huck had Tom in a bear hug. A trickle of blood flowed down Cecil's nose as Ted managed to hold on to Cecil.

"Will you both jest' stop," Huck shouted, "that's all we need now is for old man Flemming to come in here an' see all this here. He'd throw us all out in the cold an' I ain't partial to sleepin' in them damned dank caves this time of year. Now, never mind all this."

Cecil shrugged off Ted's hold on him with ease and angrily walked away. Tom turned his back on all of them and rubbed at his throat. Ted returned to his box and sat down while Huck reached into a bag near the barrel and pulled out bottle of whiskey.

"I was meanin' on savin' this bottle for later," Huck said, "much later when I was by myself. But I kin' see right now that what we got here is a medical emergency. Step up over here to the doctor's office, boys an' have a drink together like growed' men an' fergit' what jest' went on, ya' hear?"

Cecil chewed on his bottom lip and wiped the small trickle of blood from his nose. Tom looked at Cecil and the waiting bottle of whiskey.

"C'mon over here, now," Huck said quietly, "It ain't worth all this fussin' an' fightn', you both bin' friends way too long for all this foolishness to cause you to try an' kill each other. Remember, there's plenty of people right across the border in Kansas that would be more than happy to kill you."

Tom walked over to Cecil and looked Cecil right in his eyes.

"Cee, I take it back. I ain't got no right cause to say those things, what I said. I didn't mean a word of it. I know and respect your Uncle Frank. He's a good, stout, stand up kind of fella," Tom said.

"No hard feelin's, Tom," Cecil said. He knew how badly Tom had taken to the news of his Aunt's death and he knew that what Tom had said had been caused by Tom's anger over her unsolved murder.

Huck passed the bottle of whiskey to Cecil. While the bottle passed from hand to hand, Ted Doudlass took the opportunity to relieve the rabbit from the stove. In time, as each man gave up the bottle to the next person, he would begin a magic trick on the rabbit in making it disappear. In no time at all, the rabbit was devoured. The conversation had turned to a local girl who had eloped with a boy that they all knew.

"Mr. Harper nevah' liked Dylan Kelly 'cause he's an Irishman," Huck stated.

"Mr. Harper never liked Dylan Kelly 'cause Dylan is a half-wit," Tom said quietly. "Him running off with his daughter only proves it. That girl was no catch. She's as hairy as a poodle."

"What the hell is a poodle?" Huck asked.

"A poodle is a French dog. They are little and they got curly short hair all over their bodies. The rich French folks down in New Orleans have them," Tom replied. Huck grinned.

"How are you an' Rebecca doin? You plannin' on doin' a little seranadin' tonight," Huck asked.

"That is no concern of yours. You best mind your own business," Tom said. Huck laughed loudly at his friend's discomfort.

"Cause if you want, I kin' saddle up old man Fleming's favorite sway back mule we got here an' you an' your darlin' can go on a romantic moonlit trudge through the cow flopped fields. The onliest' thing that you got to take care of is the mule drags its foreleg a might. Landin' on yer' ass, I heard tell, can take the fun right out of a romantic evening."

Ted choked back his laughter. A broad grin spread across Tom's face.

"That is so considerate of you, Huck, as well as kindly, but I do believe I will pass on that," Tom replied grandiosely. Cecil stood up and reached for the bottle of whiskey that was quickly emptying. He gulped down what remained of it and wiped his face with the back of his hand.

"As usual, you both got it all wrong about Dylan. Mister Harper never liked Dylan 'cause Dylan is as poor as a church mouse," Cecil said. He staggered back to the crate that he had been sitting on.

"Let me tell you about Mr. Harper," Cecil began. "Mr. Harper is the kind of fella' that judges a man on how much coin is jinglin' in the pockets. If you got money, then you are square with old man Harper. He always thought Dylan was shiftless and no count, the same way he figures all of us here to be. It don't matter that Dylan is an Irishman an' talks funny. Dylan is not the brightest candle in the dark, but the fact is that the boy never had two cents in his pockets. Hell, he is poorer than us."

"That's sayin' somethin'." Ted said.

"It's the truth," Cecil answered. "You got to have money these days to be accepted by folks. It ain't like in the old days when a man might be poor but have frontier know-how that might be put to good use in the world. Them days are done with in these parts. Look at us. We are farm hands is all, yet ever' body here has got some kinda' skill. Tom here kin' put a bullet in a bumblebee's backside in flight. I seen him do it. In the old days, skills like that would feed a family. Now, those kinda' skills don't mean squat. Money is all that matters these days, and it don't grow on trees."

"You are right. Money don't grow on trees," Tom said. "It comes out of the cold hard ground."

Huck looked at Ted apprehensively. Huck sensed one of Tom's sermons approaching about California and the gold-fields as surely as he could tell of the approach of a summer lightning storm.

"Here we go," Huck said quietly.

"If we all had any sense at all," Tom said, "we would find a way of getting to California. I read a book about the gold fields out there. In California, it never snows except maybe high in the mountains. People say that a body can find gold layin' right out in the open. Fist sized chunks of gold waitin' to be plucked up like a robin's egg or panned out of the rivers with a little effort," Tom said dreamily.

"There is still free land out there for the asking where a man can still use the skills that Cee' was talking about to provide what's needed for a family. There ain't no law, no civilization an' no hostile Injun's to worry about. The Spaniards pacified them wild Injuns hundreds of years ago," Tom continued.

"You never git' tired of usin' them big words. Why don't you talk plain, for Aunt Nelly's sake. What's that pacified mean?" Huck asked.

"It means they either killed them or converted them. The Spaniards made them church goers and taught them to be like normal farmers an' the likes in these big church run farms," Tom said. "A man can be a man out there. Except for them big church run farms, it is all pretty much still wild. It ain't all fenced in like it is around here."

"You are only forgettin' one small thing," Huck said interrupting Tom. "You got to get there. California is a long way off an' I ain't partial to travelin' overland for months fightin' the damned red-skins every blessed step of the way. Them Injuns that live between here an' California ain't pacified. They are some rough old

45

devils that like to skin your melon bald with a dull stone tomahawk an' split you from your throat to yer belly. But that ain't all, I heard. They will make you run with yer gizzards spillin' aroun' yer ankles all the while beating the snot out of you if they git' their hands on you."

"Umm-mm, that is some rude behavior," Cecil said.

"Then the only way would be to go by boat," Ted said. The simply stated fact caught Tom's immediate attention.

"You are right," Tom said and smiled forlornly. "It would be the fastest and safest way to get to California, but it would cost a small fortune. None of us here knows anybody with the amount that we would need. Not even old man Flemming. I asked Flemming about loaning me what I would need. I even told him that I would pay him back two times the amount he was to give me if I was to strike it rich. He told me to try pulling my head out of my ass."

Huck pulled another bottle of whiskey from a sack.

"That ain't true, Tom," Ted sputtered.

"How would you know? You weren't there when I asked him," Tom replied.

"No. Not that, I mean we all know somebody that's got so much money that he could well afford to give us what we would need with a little persuasion," Ted said quickly.

Huck looked at Ted as if he had lost his mind.

"And pray tell, if you would be so kind, who might this person be?" Huck asked with wonder.

"Henry Fowler," Ted said reaching for the new bottle of whiskey that Huck had just opened. Ted watched his friend's expressions turn to astonishment as he pulled deeply from the bottle. Cecil was the first to react.

"You must be one full blown idjit'. I suppose Henry Fowler is gonna' hand us the money jest like that to make our trip. Huck, you had best git' the bottle away from this old boy before he seriously hurts himself with it any further."

Huck was rocking in spasms of laughter and was fighting to catch his breadth. His eyes watered from the tears. Ted became defensive momentarily as he fought back his anger.

"For heavens sake, I never meant that he would give it to us, like a loan. I meant take it from the man. Rob him. Clean him out," Ted said calmly.

The serious way Ted had said this made quite descend upon the barn. Everyone now listened to Ted carefully.

"Cecil, your Uncle Frank seems to know how this Fowler operates. We could allow your Uncle to give us what we could use against this fella' without him ever knowing that he was. Learn from your Uncle's mistakes on why they never got Fowler. Find out what went wrong with their plan and do better. Then its off to California to find those fist sized chunks of pay-dirt an' leave all this murderin' an' killin' behind forever."

And so on this one fall night the idea had started to formulate. They talked all evening and into the dawn. One off-hand statement by Ted seemed the perfect solution, a remarkable idea that would fit financial gain and revenge into one action. They would find out everything there was to know about Henry Fowler. They would travel to Leavenworth, Kansas, to rob the killer of a helpless old woman and the man who had destroyed Sid's mind. In the following day, without letting Cecil's Uncle Frank know of their intentions, they had found out many startling things about Henry Fowler.

It seemed that Henry Fowler claimed to be a direct descendant of President James Monroe and constantly let everyone know about it. He was a suspect in many killings in both Kansas and Missouri. It was rumored that he had even killed some of his own people over policy. He had apparently killed his way to the top. He was the top dog in his militia group, and he was boastful as well as arrogant. He appeared to be a rabid abolitionist who believed it was the duty of all true Christians to exterminate without mercy, all pro-slavery people they came into contact with at all times. Henry Fowler wrote articles and editorials in the newspaper that he owned describing in lurid details the many ways in which pro-slavery people would cringe and plead for mercy whenever confronting a true blue upright Christian whose holy purpose was to wipe them out.

This had hit a sore spot in Tom when Cecil had shown him one of these articles. Tom had become enraged to the point of being inarticulate. There was no doubt that Sid had pleaded for his life with his tormentors the day that they had nailed him to the barn door because in his current state that was all that he was capable of doing. His shattered psyche replayed those terrible moments of torture repeatedly. With his mind destroyed, he begged and pleaded not to be stabbed and shot by the kind people who looked after his everyday needs. He constantly screamed, shrieked, and wet his pants whenever anyone approached him. Sid had always been a delicate boy, everyone said.

Henry C. Fowler was rumored to be enormously wealthy and this fact intensified their efforts to find out more about this perplexing individual. It seemed that Henry had recently married a woman who, it was claimed, was one of the richest women in the United States. With this nest egg fallen into his lap, he had opened a bank. Money arriving from unknown sources back east was regularly deposited in his bank by couriers, each one being different from the last.

It was said that this money came from a secret society of rich abolitionists who demanded to remain anonymous. There was talk that the substantial amounts deposited in Henry's bank were slated for the most despised man in Missouri, one John Brown. After much consideration and careful discussion, a plan was devised. On a snowy winter's afternoon, they set out on a journey across Missouri to Leavenworth, Kansas, to seek retribution on a heartless killer of a defenseless old woman and those responsible in destroying Sid's mind.

What Huck remembered of the trip was the cold. At times, he had thought that he would freeze to death. They nearly had when a blizzard had swept out of the north and nearly buried them. That day, they had taken refuge in a schoolhouse even taking the horses inside for protection against the wintry blasts of Arctic air. After the sun came out, they had proceeded on their way, surviving on beans and rabbits shot along the away. As they rode, they reviewed their plans. Although Ted originally devised the idea of robbing Fowler, Cecil, and Tom were the real planners now in charge of overall strategy and logistics.

"It's all simple," Cecil said. "When we get to Leavenworth, we let it be known that we got business with Henry C. Fowler. He will probably be curious about us and think somethin' got all fouled up why he don't know nothin' about us, but that works fer' us. All's we got to do is play deaf an' dumb. We don't know why Henry didn't know nothin' about our comin'...yer follow me? We tell old Henry that our people tolt' us to go directly to the bank to deposit our little bundle. We tell him it's so much that the second batch will be comin' in the next day. The saddlebag will be filled with old papers an' sich'. We got to make sure he don't know that, so nobody looks in the bag. That's important. Then when we get to the bank, I'll put a gun aside his ear an' whisper sweet nothin's into it. We will have his ass cold. We clean his bank out an' will be gone faster than greased owl shit, take my word on that."

Ted did not look too happy with Cecil's appraisement of the ease at which Henry would be robbed.

"Are you sure we gotta' kill him," Ted asked. "It's the hangman fer sure iffn' we get caught. Why can't we jest' let him go after we rob him?"

"Because," Cecil answered slowly, "number one, that no good skunk deserves to die and number two, that man is too dangerous to let live. Supposin' he finds out jest' who we wuz', and believe you me, he jest' might. He could ride back to Missoura in a raid an' kill your ma an' pa an' mine. You want to be responsible fer' that? This way, by puttin' a bullet in his damned head, he can't 'cause he will be deader than a catfish in a bird's nest. That's why," Cecil said emphatically.

"Deadmen tell no tales," Tom said.

"Besides," Huck said, "Stealin' is a crime they hang folks fer', so it don't matter one way or t'other. If we git' caught, they will stretch our necks fer' sure. We will all be jumpin' into the air with a hemp knot wrapped around our throats."

Cecil let his horse drop back to where Ted was. Cecil was worried about Ted and it showed by the worry lines that stood out on Ted's forehead.

"Ted, the plan is gonna' work because it's simple. We done did our homework. Hell, we know more about Henry Fowler than Henry Fowler. As long as he don't stick his damned head in the bag, we will do alright. We make it plain to him straight up that the bag must only be opened in the bank. We tell him that's our orders and we took an oath. We tell him that's the way it is an' if he don't like it, that we ride away with it an' tell him that our people will contact his about the foul up in plans. Fowler is greedy an' won't let us ride away with thousands of dollars in a sack that could be goin' into his bank right then an' there. If he got his people with him, I will put my gun next to Henry's damned head. We will git' the jump on all of them that way. Believe you me, there won't be a man among them what wants to see our boy with a hole drilled through his squash. It should take less than twenty minutes an' we are on our way to Californe' by boat. Right down the Mississippi, down to New Orleans an' the gold-fields," he said convincingly."

Ted continued to struggle with his conscience.

"As fer me shootin' that louse, why, you leave that up to me," Cecil said, "I tolt' you about the time I was in St. Louis an' that Mexican fella' pulled a knife out on me. I shot him, an' that's the truth. Actual an' factual. I shot him an' never lost a night's sleep over it. The way I figger' it, I'm puttin' a mad dog down, is all. Tom's auntie was our people an' we can't jest' let them git' away with shenanigans of the likes cause they will jest' keep it up. Ole Miss Polly was sound on the goose, although she hadn't owned a slave in a long time. She needn't have been kilt' like that. An' what they did to poor Sid there is beyond belief. The poor boy will never be right in the head again. All he does is piss his pants an' wail whenever you git near him."

Cecil spit but the wind brought it back hitting him in the forehead.

"Dammit," he said viciously, "iff'n you ain't sure about how you feel about all this, then take off now. I mean it. All it will take to git' us all kilt' is one weak link in the chain."

Cecil looked at all of them harshly before continuing.

"I mean it. If any of you are unsure, then take off. I'd rather all of you know what we are about to do will make outlaws out of all of us. There ain't no goin' back whence we start. Where ever we go where there is a lawman, we will have to watch ourselves what we got planned is not fer the weak-hearted. Now tell me right now, Ted, an' be certain of yer' answer. Are you fer it?"

Huck rode up alongside of Ted.

"It was your idea in the first place," Huck jibed, "Remember?"

"Sure, I remember," Ted said angrily. He had been plagued by second thoughts about the entire venture once murder had been introduced into the plan. His idea had been a direct result of boredom, wishful thinking, and strong drink. Robbery was one thing but murder was another. In fact, he could barely remember how it was that he had even brought up the subject of robbery in the first place. It simply was not like him. Cecil was the one that had started talking about blowing Fowler's head off because when drinking, Cecil had always mentioned the Mexican fellow that he had shot in St. Louis. For Cecil, robbery and murder, it seemed, had come together as naturally as cold and snow.

"All right, then," Ted said. "I will say I'm for it and will nary say another word about it." He looked at Cecil, unsure if his voice had held any conviction at all.

"Jest' as long as I don't have to kill nobody. I am for it."

"Well," Huck said happily, "I'm sure glad that settles that. I'll meet you all at the hatters as one coon said to the other when the hounds wuz' closin' in." Relieved that the seeming breach in unity had been resolved amicably, he spurred his horse ahead with recklessness, enjoying every second of it.

Cecil motioned for Ted to draw up alongside him. He wanted to make sure that Ted had truly meant what he had just said. He was careful how he phrased what he was about to say because of the seriousness of what they were about to do. Cecil knew he would not be able to nursemaid any single one of them once Fowler was killed.

"Back home, Ted, people are startin' to take to bush-whakin' like it was normal. Like it was as normal as goin' to church on Sunday mornin' .It would jest be a matter of time before you an' me an' everybody here would be joinin' up with my Uncle Frank, jest' to protect our own damned selves. Everybody has got a side to pick. You ain't got no choice back home. There ain't a one of us that was raised fer' this sort of thing. We wuz' all raised good an' right. But now, things have all changed, everything is all different. Things changed up on us way too fast, the way we wuz' is gone fer' good an' it ain't never comin' back, no matter how much you might be a' wishin' fer' it."

Ted solemnly nodded his head.

"Becomin' a raider, well, I jest' can't see no profit in it. Don't get me wrong," Cecil said, "I am sound on the goose. But, you see, what we are doin' is doin' somethin' fer ourselves, somethin' we kin' build a future on. In California there, we kin' all start fresh like. A man don't have to fear that every stranger he meets won't put a ball in his brain. Are you followin' me? Does what I'm sayin' make sense to you at all?"

Ted was embarrassed at his own uncertainty and lack of faith in his friend.

"When you put it like that, it makes all the sense in the world."

"That's good, Ted. That's good," Cecil said wearily. They rode towards Leavenworth in silence, each wrapped in his own thoughts about the future.

CHAPTER THREE

Henry Fowler was awakened by the sounds of his wife's screeching that emanated from the downstairs living room. He pushed the covers back and shivered in the cold of the morning. He could tell just by the grating and insulting tone of her voice that she was yelling at the help again. Although he could not make out what she was raving about, he could tell by the intensity and pitch of her voice that she was thoroughly enjoying it.

Lately, that was all she actually seemed to enjoy doing. If she wasn't screaming at the maid and calling her a lazy slut, then she would be ranting at Old Josh, the groundkeeper. She despised the old man. She hated his uncultured ways and the sound his wooden leg made as he clumped about on her beautiful hardwood floors.

Henry stood, stretched, and urinated into the chamber pot. The early morning chill made him wrap his buffalo robe around himself tightly as he plodded towards the window. He threw back the thick velvet curtains and squinted from the glare of a fresh snowfall. The snow had been light during the night and the weak sun on this crisp January morning had already begun to melt some of it away. Patches of brown stood out distinctly from a carpet of powdery white snow that lay across his meadow. The brown patches reminded Henry of bread mold.

It should be an early spring, he thought, as he padded across the room towards the stairs. As he neared the alcove that joined the kitchen to the hallway at the end of the stairwell, the shrill sound of his wife's voice intensified. Her voice could raise the hackles of a hound, he thought. A picture of his wife lying dead with a broken neck and a newly bought mare crystallized in his mind and he grinned. An unfortunate accident this spring played out in his imagination. Perhaps, he thought, a bad neck-crunching fall is just what is needed for more peaceful mornings. He reached the alcove and almost walked into her. Her high pitched nasal New England twang cut him to the quick as she continued to loudly berate the old man.

"Henry, you must do something with this horrible old man."

"Now what is the rub? What is the matter?" he asked, glancing in the direction of the fireplace. The man whom he called Old Joshua leaned against the wall, warming his hands. He looked like hell. His gray hair was matted into a cone and his clothes were filthy. His jacket sleeves glistened from where he had been using it in cleaning his runny nose.

"I caught him blowing his nose on his coat-sleeve and then he reached for the coffee pot as big as Billy-be-damned. I won't stand for this, Henry. The man has deplorable habits and he smells oddly," she complained. Abigail pointed a fireplace poker at the old man and waved it threateningly at him.

"The old lout is intolerable," she screeched. Her squat head ballooned off her reed like neck. Her bird like eyes squinted in fury and her parrot like voice, when raised in anger, sounded like the whistle on a riverboat. Abigail Fowler was hideous in temperament. Joshua simply smiled at her intended threat, which infuriated her all the more.

"Don't you grin at me, you damned one-legged baboon," she screamed. Foam whipped from the corners of her mouth. She hurled the poker at him and he ducked out of its way. The poker missed his head by inches and clanged noisily on the wooden floor. Henry grabbed Abigail by her wrists. He pulled her towards him and held her tightly.

"Joshua," Henry said calmly, "If you would be so kind as to remove yourself from the premises, I daresay I would greatly appreciate it. I'm afraid my dear wife wants to kill you at this moment, and I do fear for your life if she were to slip my grasp."

"Yes sir, Mr. Fowler, but I can't understand what all this rhubarb is about. When I was lightin' the fire like she asked, I

breathed in some of the soot and sneezed. I figured it was a sight better to sneeze on my sleeve than to gunk up the coffee pot, is all."

"See the way he is," she bellowed and struggled to break free of Henry's grasp.

"The insolent swine, how dare you talk back to the lady of the house? Henry this cretin must go. This is insufferable. The nerve of the beastly cur knows no limits," Abigail screamed.

"I'll be leavin' now, sir," Joshua said. Henry watched as Joshua clumped down the hallway.

"Yes, there's a good fellow. We will discuss this matter at a later time." Joshua raised his hand in parting but did not turn around. Henry's attention turned to his enraged wife.

"If you will stop struggling and promise to behave yourself, I will release you."

Henry looked into his wife's eyes and saw madness lurking in their depths. Abigail had been an only child, spoiled and pampered beyond belief by her father. Her family was one of the richest in the country, having come from the tiny state of Rhode Island. The state and her family shared in the fact that both had started the industrial revolution in America. They owned some of the oldest and most productive textile mills in the United States and had made a fortune creating slave-cloth, a thick burlap material that was used to make cheap garments that clothed the human chattel on plantations throughout the South. However, Abigail's life was cloaked in tragedy.

Abigail had lost her mother early in life. The family had been vacationing down at the shore at a place known as Hazard Rocks. It was not named for any intended warning for the treacherousness of the slippery granite boulders but because the owner of the land was a local man whose last name was Hazard. Her mother had ventured out on one of the many smooth boulders that are numerous at the site to enjoy the crash of the breaking waves. While she was enjoying the frothy salt air, a large rouge wave seemingly came out of nowhere and without any warning swept her away to a too early and sudden watery demise. Local people for decades shunned the area because of the many drownings that had happened there regularly as far back as records had been kept and even earlier.

The ancient inhabitants of the land, the Narragansett tribe, which had still managed to exist throughout the first difficult two centuries of European contact, spoke of a demon that lived a few yards off shore in the depths of the sea. Legends told that this demon would lure and then flush an unsuspecting person to a watery grave. It is highly doubtful that Abigail's mother knew of this legend. People of her station and native people never met on any social occasions.

Abigail was raised by successions of governess' that found the child spoiled beyond redemption and with a horrible disposition. Perhaps if Abigail's mother had lived she would have been a far different person, but this is not what happened. As one of the richest young ladies in the whole of the country, and with no maternal love, Abigail grew into a vindictive, arrogant, selfish young woman who people found detestable. When her father died of accidental food poisoning, Abigail inherited his wealth estimated at the time to be in excess of several million dollars.

"Henry Fowler, release me this instant," she wailed. She struggled briefly and suddenly whipped her knee into Henry's crotch. Stars and points of light exploded in front of his wide-open eyes as he doubled over to fall heavily on the hardwood floor. His eyes slammed shut and his breathing nearly stopped. He curled into a fetal position, his face contorting into a grimace of agony.

"Ab...buhg, Ab..buhg," he moaned, and rolled over on his back, his legs bent and his knees pointed to the ceiling as waves of pain pounded into him like storm driven surf. Abigail stepped over the buckled body of her husband without care or concern.

"I told you years ago that we should get some niggers to work around here instead of that circus gimp and that Navaho whore," she said staring at the ceiling. She continued to ignore Henry's thrashing body.

"Darkies never talk back. They dare not. They are naturally lazy and dull witted, this is true. However, they never are flippant and insubordinate like the animals you have working for us now. There is always the pleasant fact that niggers work far cheaper and if you do not like their attitude, you can always get another. All of the people of my station back east have them as servants. That is what the Bible says that they are only good for. They would be better than this bunch of insolent lazy ne'er-do-wells."

Henry blinked and rolled in spasms. He was amazed at all the little specks of light that danced merrily in front of his eyes. He rose slowly to his knees and straddled the floor on all fours. Waves of nausea overcame him but in spite of it all, he managed to stagger to his feet. Come spring, he thought, come glorious spring and a wonderful day for a ride together on a newly bought mare in the country.

"I see how you act whenever that Navaho slut is around," she said, "don't think that I haven't seen you ogling her. I see you watching that harlot scrub the floor in her low cut blouse, so don't fool yourself on my account. That red nigger has to go, the bitch. I will not tolerate her or that dirty thing you call Old Joshua, scratching my floors with that damned peg leg of his. He should be shot. He is nothing but scum. He says that he is from Kansas, but I believe he is from Texas. He should not be allowed to breathe our air. If you don't make them go away, I swear by Jehovah that I will kill them both." Her voice rose to a crescendo, as did the roaring sound of Henry's pulse pounding wildly in his head.

She turned on him suddenly and screamed, "If you truly loved me, you would never let that imbecile insult me the way he does. His very existence insults me as well as that savage whore you call a maid." Her voice warbled and tears streamed down her face.

"I am telling you this for the last time." Abigail flung herself up the stairs breaking into heaving sobs. Henry grabbed the banister.

"Joshua," he croaked, "bring me a bucket of snow, and do be quick about it, if you will, my good man."

Joshua heard the weak pleas of his boss. Joshua's cracked and wrinkled face twisted into a smile. He ran his hand through his greasy cone of hair. He had been expecting this call from Henry. What a she-devil, he thought. It would be a cold day in hell before he would put up with what that man put up with. What that witch needs is a damned good whipping, Joshua thought. He hobbled into the servant's kitchen. The maid sat at the table sewing a patch on the elbow of a worn blouse that was cut low in the front. She looked up at Joshua as he plopped into a chair.

"I'll get the bucket. You will get snow," she said.

"That's a deal," Joshua replied. He had always liked Bella. In fact, her beauty struck everyone. He admired how Bella could take care of herself. Bella was a survivor. It seemed to Joshua that Abigail was more of a savage than Bella could ever be. He remembered when Henry had first hired her. Mrs. Fowler had gone mad. Henry had needed a bucket of ice that day as well.

55

Abigail constantly belittled Bella, calling her a Navaho whore, Navaho slut, and that damned Red Nigger. More recently she had started calling Bella a Lazy Slut instead of by her given name. Bella would always correct Abigail by saying that her name was Bella. Then Bella would begin to speak Navaho, causing Abigail to howl like a coyote and physically attack her. Bella always protected herself by covering up well from the rain of blows that Abigail delivered. However, Abigail would tire quickly. Then she would begin to throw objects at her. Bella would then run and Abigail would be, by this time, too exhausted to pursue her. Joshua had witnessed this on numerous occasions and on more than one time he had wanted to crash a bullet through Abigail's balloon like head.

Mr. Fowler, if he were home during one of Abigail's tantrums, would attempt to intervene. This usually ended in his having to get a bucket of snow or ice, depending on the time of the year from the outside or from the icehouse. Bella slowly rose and placed the blouse on the table. Joshua watched her pass through the door and down into the cellar where the bucket was stored. Henry was reduced to a twitching, quivering wreck after every one of Abigail's violent episodes. How a man as rich and powerful as Henry was could get use to hanging his swollen private parts time after time in a bucket of snow was beyond Joshua. It did not make sense to him. He reminded himself that for all the trouble that his wooden leg caused him, he was far luckier than some. He would not be the one sitting cross wise over a bucket of snow this morning. Bella returned with the bucket as he stood up and fastened the buttons on his coat. She handed him the bucket.

"Looks like it's gonna' be one of those days," Joshua said. "Thanks fer' getting me the bucket. Them stairs is a pain in the ass."

Bella nodded her head. She smiled warmly at him as he turned her to face him. He looked into her deep dark eyes.

"You be careful. Stay away from that witch all morning, you hear. After what jest went on, she ain't gonna' be good for a few days."

Bella simply patted Joshua on his shoulder.

"Do not worry, I can smell her stink before I see her," Bella said. Joshua laughed loudly and clumped down to stairs to get snow to fill Henry's bucket.

CHAPTER FOUR

The wagon driver clucked the pair of mules into motion. The rocking motion of the wagon had a relaxing effect on Huck as he swayed from side to side. Slowly, Huck returned to the present and stopped wallowing in self-pity and bad memories. He listened half-heartedly as the driver and Tom prattled on about the weather, generals, and other typical army gossip. The wagon driver was asking a string of questions about different units and their whereabouts which Tom did his best to answer. Huck soon became bored with the conversation and stared into space.

"The name is Childress, John Childress."

Tom introduced himself then Huck, but the teamster was more interested in gossiping than acknowledging either one of them. Huck eyed the man over and began to listen to the conversation. The questions coming from the wagon driver were unrelenting. He began to take a dislike to the man.

"You boys got any idea where Stuart is? I sure would like to know where he might be. You got any idea?" he asked.

"Last I heard, he was around Culpeper," Tom answered. The teamster seemed interested in this bit of information.

"That's reassuring' to know. This way here he'll keep The Yankee cavalry away from us down here." he said. "Yessuh...it's better that you boys stay with me. This way, if we run into any Yankee's, there is safety in numbers. Them guns loaded? I see yer' got a cap on yours so they must me. I don't cotton all too well with loaded guns in a rockin' wagon. Makes me nervous. I knowed a fella' got kilt' from a rockin' loaded loose rifle. Why don't yer' throw them in the back an' relax there instead of clutchin' them like they wuz' yer sweethearts?"

"No thanks. I'm just fine," Tom said. The driver seemed annoyed at Tom's reaction. The tone of authority in the man's voice began to grate on Huck's frail nerves.

"Suit yer selves. Yessuh...you all are better off stickin' with me. This way, if we run into any provosts, it will look like you're on some kind of official duty instead of just waltzin' around and givin' the wrong answer to the wrong people like two damned fools. Iff'n it wasn't fer me, who knows what kinda' trouble you two ding-asses might find yourselves in." He looked over at Huck.

"How's yer bowels, sonny?" he asked Huck sarcastically. "You git' everything out or are yer' still all bound up?"

"Go to hell," Huck snapped. Tom looked at the floorboards and attempted to hide a grin by covering his face with both his hands.

"Temper, temper, young sir. You will last a bit longer without getting your bowels all in an uproar," the teamster said with the same undercurrent of derision still in his voice.

"Riddle me somethin', Mr. Scarecrow," Huck asked. The muleskinner looked at him with total scorn. Tom noticed the smirk he gave Huck. Tom sensed something odd in the driver in that one fleeting instant that he couldn't comfortably label. He tried to mask his own uneasiness from both Huck and the driver. His hand clutched tightly onto his rifle.

"We playin' guessin' games now, sonny?" he replied. "Well go ahead if it will make you feel any better...ask away." The wagon driver winked at Tom. Tom forced a smile to his face.

"Why are you askin' all them questions about this unit an' that. If you wuz' always around people, you would know it already. You seem to know very little about any unit in this here army. Ain't that peculiar." Huck said.

The teamster's expression did not change as he listened to Huck's query. Tom watched him carefully, sensing something he hadn't noticed before about the man. He noticed and detected an unusual accent, as if the man was forcing himself to speak a certain way.

"I smell a rat, mister, an' I ain't gonna' be callin' it no damned rose," Huck said carefully. "I don't believe you're workin' for the Quartermaster an' this sure as hell ain't no Quartermaster wagon. I don't know where the hell you picked it up from, but no one in his right mind would order a man to ride around in this stinkin' wagon. We ain't all that desperate for wagons. No sir, somethin's wrong here an' I ain't sure I got the whole story but somethin' ain't right."

The teamster's grin looked artificial.

"How is it, you say, that you been goin' around pickin' up britches, shoes an' sich. How is it that you look like you jest' crawled out from under an out-house? Why, Andy Barrett, a friend of mine, is raggedy but you are all taters and them shoes is jest' ruins. He ain't got no choice the way he looks but not you. After every fight, you kin' always grab a new pair of britches from the Quartermaster. You say you work for them and you look the way you do. I don't think so. Why more'n half the army wears federal blue britches or Yankee shoes." Huck continued, relentless in his pursuit of a satisfactory answer from the ragged muleskinner.

"Where have you been for the last few weeks, Mr. John Childress, if in fact your name is even John Childress? You bin' a' hidin' under a haystack fer the last two weeks?" Huck was unmerciful.

58

"You bin hidin' out on the moon?" Huck asked savagely.

"How is it you ain't picked out somethin' descent to wear. You want to tell me Mr. Scarecrow?" Huck was shouting.

"You ain't on any official duty an' you sure ain't no quartermaster wagon. You bin' hidin' out from the Army fer' the last few weeks, that's why you don't know the location of any unit in this whole Corp. You are a skulker, a scoundrel who let's other people do the fightn', and no doubt, a damned deserter yourself who's runnin' away and jest' usin' this wagon as a ticket home."

The thin driver shifted in his seat and reached into an inside pocket for his corncob pipe. He still wore a grin, but by now it was see through. He tried to appear unruffled by Huck's accusations, but it was apparent it was just for show. The man lit his pipe and drew on it, thoughtfully, keeping his amused mask drawn solidly on his features. He turned and looked at Tom.

"And what do you think?" he asked Tom carefully.

"It is a good point my friend has, old boy," Tom answered, offering the wagon driver little sympathy. Huck pressed home his attack.

"If you're on official like duty, then pigs got wings an' kin' fly. I could always spot a phony, my friend, an' you fit the bill," he yelled.

The teamster slowly reigned in the mules and stopped in the middle of the road. He looked a little flush but still was in control of himself. He shook his head in a token of disbelief. His hand reached for the wagon brake as he shifted the pipe to his other free hand. He wiped sweat from his brow and chuckled.

"The only point your ding-ass friend has is on the top of his pointed head. If you follow this pin-head's story, then you are even dumber than you look. Listen up real careful like, an' if you ain't all that much of a matching set of lunk-heads, you might jest' learn somethin'." The wagon driver took a deep breath.

"If you wuz' to drive around all day in a wagon that smelt like this one here does all day, you would be dressed jest' like this. I burn these rags every few days or so when the stink starts givin' me headaches. I ain't about to be wearin' usable clothes when I'm workin'. That would be a waste. If I wuz' to do that, my sergeant would turn me inside out. So what I do, every few days or so, by and by, I pick through the discards. I wears' them until they reek, then I throws them in a pile an' burns them an' so on an' the likes."

Huck's eyes narrowed as the flawless logic bore into his mind and rang with the clarity of a gong. He saw in his mind's eye winged flying pigs.

"I bin' on active duty since the last shots were fired at Fairview an' we needed every wagon we could get our hands on, for your information, ding-ass. I've bin'

59

attached to the Quartermaster Corp since I got shot at Sharpsburg. You do remember Sharpsburg don't you? Or were you sittin' under a haystack or maybe you were on the blue moon that day an' missed the dance." The teamster tapped his pipe with his index finger.

"I can't go aroun' burnin' good things now can I?" he asked. "That would be destroyin' government property." He felt himself winning the argument and became arrogant once again.

"Now, are you understandin' what I'm sayin' or did I waste my breath on you two shit-fer'-brains?" he asked haughtily. Whatever doubts had started to erode Huck's suspicions of the teamster crystallized again with that last stinging insult.

"Show me your work orders, big mouth," Huck yelled. "Show me your travelin' orders an' shut me up. Why don't you jest' pull them out an' prove it. If you are square, then I reckon I owe you an apology. But let me tell you one thing, an' get it right the first time. If you ain't what you appear to be, I'll be damned if I'm goin' any further with you. Mind you now, I ain't gonna' turn you in. What you do is yer' own business an' none of my concern. I jest' don't want to be any where near you if an' when the Provo's catch up with you."

"Your friend can't possibly be this stupid?" The driver asked Tom.

"Try me," Huck shouted again, not fully realizing the implications of his response to the question.

"Huck's right, mister. If you are doing right," Tom replied calmly, "then we will stick with you, at least to maybe where we can explain to an officer about our not having no travel orders. But if this has all been a pile of cow flop that you've been giving us, then why, we are getting off and we are on our way. No feelings held hard. We got enough trouble to last a while. Telling anybody about you would only guarantee more."

The muleskinner sighed heavily.

"You know, you two idiots are somethin' to write home about. I kin' tell everybody back home that I met doubtin' Thomas an' his half fool brother." He started to laugh in a way that even irritated Tom at this point. The thin man wiped his hands on his pants leg.

"I surely didn't have to stop fer' you two ninnies. Why I kin' tell you that kindness curdles in a man runnin' into a pair of worthless, stupid ingrates like yourselves." He continued to nervously wipe his sweaty hands. With his left hand, he started putting his pipe back into his jersey pocket.

"Why, this will be the last time I stop for a couple of strays like you two agin'." His hand slowly started moving towards his waist.

"I suppose iff'n its work orders yer' gotta' see, then by God, all right then. I got them right here." He continued reaching into his jacket.

"Read them and be damned," the driver screamed. As he spoke, in a motion that was incredibly quick, far too fast for Huck's eyes to follow, the teamster drew a large model 1860 Army Colt out from his waistband. In a well-practiced movement, he spun towards Tom with the barrel scant inches from Tom's head and pulled the trigger.

Tom ducked and as he avoided the blast, his rifle discharged simultaneously with the bark of the teamster's pistol. The fifty-eight caliber round struck the teamster under his left eye, blowing the back of the man's head off. All that Huck saw was a red mist as he was sprayed with blood and gray brain matter. He had never even seen the pistol until it had been fired. Both men were in shock as they viewed the very dead teamster's body .Tom felt at his ear.

"I...I..I..thhink he got meat," Tom stammered, his voice trembling slightly. A visible powder burn crossed his cheek and neck. Smoke curled out of his hair.

"Let's take a look," Huck responded quickly, checking Tom over for damage. Still dazed a bit, Huck searched carefully for a wound. He looked at his friend in disbelief.

"It singed a bit, and you're gonna' have a good sized knot on yer' head, but it didn't bore a hole in it. Yer' damned lucky. He creased yer' good is all." Huck swallowed and looked at the corpse. Tom cocked his head sideways and dropped his hand from his burned ear. The dead-man's head resembled a collapsed sack.

"What in the world, do you think, caused that fella' to go wild like that. Hell's bells, we tolt' the little fella' that we wasn't gonna' turn him in. What got into him to try an' let daylight into your head?" Huck asked angrily.

"Holy hell, I kilt' that fella dead," Tom said.

"You sure did, Tom. He can't get' no deader. But I can't figger' this out. If he was a' goin' renegade, he needn't have tried to kill us," Huck said, the panic in his voice rising. He used the back of his sleeve to wipe away some of the blood and gore that streaked his own face.

"God Almighty," Tom said dully, "I killed him dead."

"I think we have established that point, Tom, an' I'm glad you did kill the little bush-whackin' runt, because iff'n you didn't, it would be me an' you layin' out in the road with the breeze whistlin' through our heads instead of him. That was some shooting!" Huck exclaimed. Tom grabbed Huck by his arm.

"That's just it, Huck. I never meant to shoot him. The rifle went off by itself. I was just ducking out of the way and it went off. I guess my hands tightened on the trigger when I tried to duck away. I never meant to kill him, I swear," Tom said.

"That's all fine an' good," Huck said condescendingly, "but first things first. Lets git'. There ain't no sense worry'n about spilled water now when the bottom is out of the tub."

"All I saw, Huck, was a flash of gun barrel when he cleared it from his coat and this crazy look he had on his face. He was going to kill us. I swear he was fixin' to blow us both to Kingdom Come. That's when I ducked and the rifle went off. I didn't even remember putting my finger to the trigger."

"That's fine. Now, lets git' on out of here. Let the fever fit the cure. We got to go before somebody comes," Huck pleaded.

"Huck, if you saw the look he gave me," Tom said.

"The hell with findin' Bains an goin' up to Fairview," Huck cried. "Lets jest' git' back to the folks we kin' trust."

"It just doesn't make sense like you say. Why was he going to murder us?" Tom asked.

Huck looked at the dead-man again. Large flies had already started to gather on the cadaver. The wind rustled pleasantly enough to rustle the leaves on the forest floor but did it not disturb the myriad flies that were gathering on the wrecked visage of the wagon driver.

"He was going to shoot us down with no more care or concern than you would a rabid dog," Tom said loudly. "Why?" he asked desperately. He started going through the corpse's pockets. Huck looked on in horror.

"Don't rob no dead-man. That's bad luck," he shouted. "You ain't thinkin' all that well, Tom. Remember, you jest' got shot in the head. Nobody would be thinkin' all that well. Now, let me help you up an' you come along real quick like with me. I'll git' you a nice cool drink."

"There's got to be more here to it than a damned argument why he was going to murder us," Tom said, busy looking for evidence. He began to strip the dead-man. Huck nervously tried to bring his friend back to reality.

"You ain't fergettin' Missora. People got kilt' fer' far less."

"I'm telling you, our late friend here has done this work before. He wasn't even mad looking; it was all business as usual. I heard of people like him before. I wonder how many poor boys he shot and put into an unknown grave without benefit of clergy or their families ever finding out what happened to them."

"Tom, think of what yer' doin'. You're in the middle of the road in broad daylight fishin' through the pockets of a man you jest' kilt' dead. For heavens sake, it looks real bad." Huck watched in amazement as Tom finished stripping the corpse.

"Huck, let me tell you something. If I'm right, then we just done something big. Real big, I tell you. If is a little word, but it's powerful in meaning," he said.

Huck scratched his head.

"Huck, you had our friend here dead to rights. This fella' ain't got no travel orders. What better way to pick up information about the movement of our army than to ride in a stinking wagon? Did you keep track of all the questions about this Corp and that Division? At the time I wasn't paying attention, but now it all makes perfect sense. This old boy is a Union man. He's a damned spy. It had all seemed like Army talk but it wasn't. He was pumping me for information."

Tom dropped the last of the dead-man's apparel in the road.

"A spy?" Huck repeated with nervousness. "You think so? Why I'll be. You know, I never believed that yarn about that dainty lady friend of his that was supposed to have sneezed so lady like. Most of the womenfolk's around these parts are poor country people. They would never try to stifle a sneeze refined-like. They would jest' let them rip. They honk like damned geese. Holy hell, Tom, I think you're on to somethin' here." Huck's curiosity was aroused. He looked about, fearfully. Tom flung another of the man's garment into the bushes.

"Let us take a look at those shoes, now," Tom said quietly.

CHAPTER FIVE

Four exhausted men rode worn out horses down the main thoroughfare of Leavenworth, Kansas, scrutinized closely by the locals. Because of the sectional conflict that was being conducted between the pro-slavery bands and the free state forces, any strange faces arriving were viewed with suspicion and hostility. The townspeople felt threatened by all strangers. The local officer of the law gave them cause for concern as he slowly began to follow them. Cecil nodded a friendly hello to the lawman. Cecil was full of confidence. Ted, however, was not.

Cecil had planned that their entry into Leavenworth would make local tongues wag and heads turn. According to information picked up by Cecil from his Uncle Frank, couriers arrived in small groups carrying enormous amounts of money. Many wealthy abolitionists from back east deposited these funds in Henry C. Fowler's bank to be used to continue to finance their cause. The more people that saw them, Cecil figured, the better. After all, it would be foolish for just one man to be carrying around that much money. By riding into town, in broad daylight, they would show everyone that they had nothing to hide.

It would only be a matter of time before one of the local people would ask them what they were doing in town. Cecil planned to play his poker hand close to his body. He would let the fly come to the web. The sheriff had not returned Cecil's nod but instead continued to follow at a distance. Although he had not confronted them directly, his presence and unfriendly demeanor caused Ted's skin to crawl. He was sweating profusely and he felt as if he needed a bowel movement.

"I take it that the fella what keeps on followin' us around and givin' us the hairy eyeball is the local Sheriff," Ted said nervously. Cecil ignored him entirely as he headed towards a livery stable. Cecil dismounted as the proprietor of the stable walked over towards the group. He stood examining the tired horses, his hands on his hips. The owner was a good eye of horseflesh and admired the animals.

"Good lookin' horses," he said, "how you boys doin' this fine afternoon? Would yer be planning' on stayin' in town a might? I would think that your horses could use the rest, they look pretty much spent." He patted the flank of Tom's horse.

"That's right. We need them curried and fed fer' the night," Cecil responded.

"Tell you what I'll do. Two bits each and I'll even check the shoes for you. Might be a little more if they be needn' shodding." The proprietor lifted up the horse's foreleg and made a careful examination.

"Looks like you've been doin' some serious traveling," he said.

Ted tensed up and looked at Cecil with a sick look. Cecil nodded.

"Where kin' a body get' a wash and a bed on the cheap?" he asked.

"The Hotel America down on the outside of that road you passed comin' by here. You probably saw it when you rode by, you can't miss it. It's kinda' beat up, but if it is cheap you want, you can't do no better."

Cecil watched Ted as he dismounted. He was beginning to shake. The sheriff watched them from across the street. The owner of the livery stood up from examining a hoof and walked towards Ted. Cecil could not help but notice that Ted was beginning to become unglued and desperately hoped that the livery owner had not noticed the high state of anxiety that Ted was starting to display.

"A harelip fella named Pete runs the place. He ain't the owner, but he's the one to see." The proprietor was curious at the exhausted state of the horses. Their shoes showed a considerable amount of wear. He failed to notice Ted entirely, too focused on his first love, horses.

"My name's Jonathan Bishop but people just call me Coolie. I do a lot of work with the Army." He pointed to the sign above the large stable door. It read Baxter's Livery and Blacksmith.

"Don't let the name confuse you. I bought it off Baxter and never got around to changing the sign. Don't make no sense, since everybody around here knows just who I am." He grinned and started to chuckle. Ted walked nervously away as both Huck and Tom stepped alongside Cecil. Cecil proceeded to loosen his saddle. He pulled the blanket and saddle from the animal and placed it on a fence.

"We have some business in town, that of a financial matter with certain parties. I would appreciate it if you would keep this between us. There may be a little somethin' more in it for you. You may be asked to do a small service for us in the near future. We will take care of you, if you do," Cecil said quietly.

"You boys are couriers, ain't you? I knew it from just looking at your horses," Coolie said quietly. Tom approached the older man.

"I'm Bill Gorman, this here is John Todd an' the other gentleman that looks a little sick is Donald Hudson," Tom said.

"Nice meeting all you gentlemen. Don't worry about a thing. Mum's the word, and if I can help you, just knock on the door. The welcome mat will be always be out for you fellas." He grinned and led Cecil's horse into the stable.

Cecil scowled in Ted's direction. He began pulling things out of his saddlebag, including a large sack filled with cut up pieces of newspaper. After a few minutes, Cecil walked into the stable and paid the owner in advance. He emerged a minute later.

"That does it for now," Cecil said stretching his arms into the air and picking up the sack.

"If you, Mr. Gorman, would prefer and stay here breathin' in the stink of horse shit, which by the way you are so full of, rather than seek out a place of higher refinement in which a man may git' a shot of pop-skull and a bath, then I suggest that you remain. As for me, I'm off to find me a harelip, a bottle of whiskey, an' a tub fulla' hot water," Cecil said.

"Maybe I'll even get somethin' to eat. We might as well spend what little we have. Throw it around, do you hear. It don't matter, cause we's all gonna' be rich," he said jubilantly. They followed him down the road. Cecil stopped and looked all three of them in the eye.

"You got to remember one thing, an' that is stick to the same story, no matter what. It will save your life. Don't be gettin' your stories mixed up an' ass backwards...that's why we rehearsed. We want to win their confidence. We want to draw their attention to us, but don't want to attract attention. That's why I asked for the cheap hotel. This way, anybody will think that we're tryin' to maintain a low profile an' stay secret like. Remember, we draw them to us. Don't go thinkin' that this is some kinda' Sunday school picnic an' sich'. What we are doin' is some damned dangerous work. so jest keep it in mind. Let caution an' good thinkin' be your guide but don't go to pieces worryin' about it." He looked in Ted's direction and punched him in the arm.

"And fer Christ sakes, Ted, you gotta' loosen up a might. You look like somebody wound your spring to the breakin' point. You're about as nervous as a damned old cat with bells on. You got to be serious but people will catch on right off and pick up the wrong signal from you if all they see is a fidget. Who the hell would hire a fidget to deliver all that money? Think about it. Keep actin' that way, an' you will surely draw the wrong type of attention to us."

Ted looked hurt for a moment, but shot back, "I am sorry about all that, sincerely, but it's that I've never planned a killin' before. I suppose it jest' gets easier every time you do, beggin' my pardon."

"Don't go sulkin' now," Cecil said. He squinted at Ted. "Iff'n you don't jest simmer down, you jest' might find yerself, beggin' yer pardon', at the end of a hemp rope danglin' in the air."

"You didn't answer my question," Ted said rubbing his arm. "That fella that started following us around, do you think he was the law?"

"Hell no, Ted," Huck said quickly, "That there fella is jest the town welcomin' committee. As soon as he finds out where we is stayin', he's sure to come over with a backed apple pie an' a big jug of sour mash whiskey."

Cecil smiled at Huck's comment.

"He was the law," Cecil said, "There ain't no doubt about it. Like I say, keep to the story. Our lives will depend on it. Make no mistake about it. We are couriers from Lawrence, Kansas, the original home of our good friend an' benefactor, Henry Fowler. Once we find out jest' who is who, then the rest will come easy. Believe me, it's all gonna be jest fine."

The America Hotel appeared to have more of it falling down than standing. Floorboards were missing on the front porch and the door hung crookedly to the side. Two figures could be made out sitting in chairs from where the boys stood in the road. As they neared the Hotel, the figures could be seen rocking in chairs. As Cecil approached, a large balding man arose from his seat. Cecil was the first to speak.

"I reckon' this is the America Hotel," Cecil shouted. His voice boomed in the late afternoon air. The large obese bald man who had stood up grinned. His hair lip was easily discernible.

"Hint sure is," he said, "you boins need a room?" The man's deformed lip caused him to sound very nasal. He wrapped a dirty shawl around his fat hairy arms. The shirt that he was wearing at one time in the distant past had been white. It was now a yellowish gray and was stained with tobacco spittle. Even though it was seasonably chilly, he was only wearing a thin shirt and a ragged threadbare shawl. His companion in the other rocking chair eyed them suspiciously. He was a short gray whiskered elfin like man whose hands resembled the talons of a hawk

"You must be Pete. Coolie down the livery says we would find you here. We need rooms an' I need a bath," Cecil said.

He warily looked at the little man. The small gnome like little man with the odd yellow eyes gave Cecil the shivers. He knew he was looking at Henry Fowler's right hand man. He looked to be the embodiment of evil to Cecil. He walked up the rickety stairs avoiding a chasm in the middle of the floor.

The heavyset clerk waddled towards the interior of the hotel. The desk counter stood like a shipwreck on a wind blasted desolate tropical island. Turning to Cecil, he said, "We don't gint' many payin' guests since all the trouble lately."

The interior of the hotel had been styled after its eastern counterparts, but that had been many years ago. Upon closer examination, all similarity to a modern hotel ended upon entering the main hall. There were holes in the floor as well as in the ceiling. The main hallway smelled strongly of cat urine and unwashed bodies. A worn ancient portrait of President Andrew Jackson hung at an odd angle above a soot-grimed fireplace.

Huck watched as the beady eyes of the dwarf turned and fastened on him. He took an instant dislike to the man. He was repulsed by his cold fish like stare and repelled by his appearance.

The evil looking dwarf gave Ted the same stare and Ted instantly started to come apart in large chunks. Ted began to show signs of imminent collapse and distress. He froze in the glare of the strange looking little man. Huck pushed Ted forward and he staggered towards the check in desk like a tightly wrapped Egyptian mummy. Huck swaggered behind him, pushing Ted in short hops. Ted had forgotten his alias and was desperately fighting to keep his nerves and emotions in check but he was, however, loosing the battle. Tom leaned on the counter of the registration desk as the hair-lipped man flopped a beaten worn book open and reached under the counter. He came up with a bottle of ink and a withered quill pen.

"Sign in the book here and it will be twenty cents"

Ted took the quill pen and twirled it in his fingers before opening the bottle. The ink had turned to paste. The fat man took the bottle and spit into it. He handed the bottle back to Cecil.

"Thanks kindly."

Tom who by now was totally astounded by the filth and decay that he was surrounded by instantly caught Cecil's raised eyebrow.

"Is it twenty cents apiece or twenty cents fer' all of us?" Cecil asked. Cecil took the quill and dipping into the bottle scratched out a name in the register that was unreadable.

"Two rooms, that's twenty cents total," Pete said.

"That's a done deal then," Cecil responded. He placed two bits on the counter, which the clerk quickly scooped up and pocketed.

"You got room eleven an' you got room ten. They is right aside each other," the clerk said. "The shithouse is innna' back. The tub is down stairs on the first floor, but you gotta gint' your own hot water from the kitchen. We ain't got no maid service, although at times a man could use one…if you get my palaver."

The man grinned a great nearly toothless smile at Ted and winked wickedly. Ted did not know how to respond to the pure degeneracy he was confronted with but merely grinned back idiotically without being able to say a word. The small man rocking in his chair suddenly emitted a fiendish cackling sound, his lips drawn back in a sneer. Huck turned in his direction. Once again, the yellow eyes of the smaller man fastened on him in a look that cut right through him. Huck straightened himself to his full height.

"Do I know you?" he bristled.

The strange little man said nothing. He continued to stare at Huck still wearing his sneer. Huck looked into his eyes and what he saw unsettled him. In that one brief second of eye contact, Huck realized that he was looking into the eyes of a killer. This was the man, he finally realized too late, that was in the livery stable that day accusing Henry Fowler of the murder of Tom's Aunt Polly. This was Henry Fowler's right hand man.

"Didn't you hear me?" he shouted brashly, "You deaf and dumb, fella?" Huck swallowed nervously. The filthy clerk pointed his beefy finger at Huck. He slammed the registration book closed.

"You had better mind your God dammed manners you God damned respect for him if you know what's good for you, you cocky son of a bitch."

Mr. Lehigh continued to leer peculiarly at Huck, his yellow eyes just slits that reflected in them an unholy yellow light. Huck turned and facing the large filthy clerk, grinned.

"Oh…well my goodness, pardon me. So this is the owner of this fleabag is it? You might try tellin' yer' boss man to try spillin' some vinegar on the floor," he said spitting on the worn boards at his feet. "It might cut down the smell of cat piss a tad."

"Don't mind my friend, here. He's had a bad day is all an' don't mean no disrespect," Cecil said quickly. "We all could use some sleep an' a drink. Where can a man git a drink around here?" he asked good-naturedly.

The heavyset man was still glaring at Huck who was practically eyeball to eyeball with him. The obese man's deformed lip curled back into a grotesque smirk. His face was beet red.

"You can try the outhouse innna' back for starters," he growled. Cecil looked at Tom, who shook his head.

"I am far too tired for all these shenanigans," Tom said quietly, wishing to defuse the situation as quickly as he could. Tom started up the stairs followed by Cecil. Ted was frozen in place. Cecil turned back to see Mr. Lehigh lock his gaze on the helpless and profusely sweating Ted Doudlass. Cecil prodded Tom with his elbow. Tom saw that Ted was in trouble.

"Come along now, Donald," Tom said loudly, "I am sure you'll feel better after you get a little shut eye. Come on, Donald."

Huck grabbed Ted by his arm and pushed him towards the stairs. He continued to stare at the clerk and as he passed him, he stopped.

"All's I got to say, slim, is that your dim wit matches yer hospitality." Huck smiled and gave Ted a final push and started to follow him up the stairs. He suddenly stopped abruptly and raising his foot, crashed it through the stairs.

"Oh my," he said, "say mister, it looks like yer' got a loose section of stairs here. Its a bit dangerous…yer' might want to tell the owner about it."

The heavyset man was extremely fast for his size. Screaming an old Anglo-Saxon obscenity, he rushed at Huck and was upon him before Huck had cleared his foot from the wreckage. He reached his beefy arms around Huck and began to crush the breadth out of him in a bear hug. Ted jumped the clerk from behind and tried to get him in a headlock, but the clerk did not have a neck. Pete swung around momentarily releasing Huck from his bone splitting grasp and bent low, throwing Ted over his broad back.

Ted flew through the air to land heavily onto the dirty floor. Pete raced back to Huck who only saw a blur approaching him before the clerk picked Huck up over his head and slammed him through the floor. Boards splintered and cracked as all the air was knocked out of him from the devastating impact. Huck groaned and almost passed out, as the clerk continued to scream insults and obscenities.

"Get the hell out of this hotel, now," Pete roared. Cecil ran down the stairs and the fat balding clerk spun in his direction as quick as a cat. Pete balled his hands into fists ready to deliver a body-numbing blow to Cecil. Cecil back pedaled away from the danger and threw both of his hands into the air.

"Whoa, big fella, I don't mean you no harm. Hold the boat there big fella," he said quickly, "sweet Jesus, lets talk an' stop all this nonsense."

He frantically reached into his shirt pocket and pulled out a fistful of loose bank notes. He waved them in front of the charging, sweating, enraged clerk. Pete's eyes followed Cecil's upraised hand that held the money. He never noticed Cecil's other hand that was behind his back. That hand held a large revolver. Cecil watched as Pete's eyes became fixated on the money.

"That's right, big fella. Look, here's some good money fer all the damages. We don't want no more trouble. Here…take it. C'mon now…you look like a reasonable fella. Take it."

Cecil watched as Pete's eyes followed the money that he waved in his outstretched hand.

"That's right, big fella…there ain't no reason in the world fer' all this broo-hah-hah…let's settle all this like proper gentlemen."

The shotgun blast reverberated in the hallway of the hotel. Cecil and Tom jumped a foot in the air at the unexpected sound. The short man with the tightly clenched eyes stood in the center of the main hall with a smoking double-barreled shotgun in one hand and a rifle in his other. He was pointing both of them at Cecil's mid-section.

"Drop the horse pistol you got behind your back, or I will drop you, wiseass." His yellow eyes glinted at Cecil in a deadly way. Cecil dropped the heavy pistol to the floor.

"Pete, back up to me a bit and kick that pistol this way. You're a bit too close to him. If I got to decorate the place with his guts, I might get some of you, too."

Pete obeyed. He flew over to the clerk's desk after booting the pistol in the direction of the shorter man. Pete reached under the counter and broke another shotgun opened and slid two heavy gauge shells into the breach. Ted looked up from the floor to see a gargoyle looking figure pointing deadly weapons at him and his friends. The gargoyle grinned at all of them evilly. Ted's final reserve of courage disappeared as quickly as a late spring snowfall. His heart skipped a beat.

"Good Lord Almighty, Mister. Don't kill me!" Ted wailed piteously. The yellow-eyed man widened his grin-revealing fang like teeth stained brown by tobacco.

"And why, if you will permit me to ask you, should I shoot your friends dead and spare you?" he asked. "Do you think you're special or something? Please...tell me. I really want to know."

Ted didn't know how to respond. He placed his hands on his head and melted into the floor. He moaned softly. His knees were bent and his head was flat to the floor. He resembled a question mark in his present posture. Huck heard Ted blubbering incantations into the filthy floorboards as Ted implored Jesus and the Apostles to save him.

"Tell your friend to stop his whining," the short man shouted, "it ain't natural."

Tom, who had stayed out of the fracas, saw his opportunity. He put both his hands in the air and cleared his throat, loudly.

"Please, sir. Excuse the deplorable actions of my associates. We have had a hard ride in from Lawrence these last few days. Harrowing, if I must say so. We have barely managed to escape with our lives. Godless Missouri border ruffians have pursued us for the last week. All of our nerves on our edge, frayed and strained to the breaking point, apparently. Believe me, sir, these are not the normal actions of anyone in this party."

The tone that Tom delivered this lie with sparked the immediate interest of the gray whiskered little man.

"You say you're from Lawrence?"

Tom nodded and slowly lowered his hands to his side.

"Yes sir, we all are. The Missouri border trash came at us about a week ago. They accosted us and we barely managed to stay ahead of them. It was touch and go for some time. Why Oscar over there, he hasn't been acting like himself and Johnny, why he's been testy all morning," Tom lied.

"Ya' don't say," the small man said with doubt and skepticism dripping in his voice. He stepped towards Ted and kicked him in the seat of the pants.

"Get up off my floor and stop your damned non-sense. You're getting snot all over it."

Ted slowly rose off the floor with his hands held high in the air.

"And put your hands down, you look stupid with them shakin' in the air like that." He still kept both weapons trained on them. Ted dropped his hands to his sides. A large wet spot covered his crotch.

Pete raised his arm and pointed at Ted.

"Look, Mr. Lehigh. That boy done wet hints' pants," he shouted. Pete threw his head back and howled uncontrollably. His deformity created a braying sound not unlike the sound a jackass would make in fear.

Mr. Lehigh walked towards the registration counter and threw the shotgun and a rifle on its flat surface.

He reached below the counter and from the shelf beneath produced a whiskey bottle and several glasses. He slammed them on the counter.

"So..." he said, "you fellas' all hail from Lawrence?"

Tom spoke up quickly, "Yes sir, we do."

"Pull up a cracker box and let's jawbone for a while," he said. Mason Lehigh poured three drinks and tossed the bottle to Ted.

"Pull on that for a while and then fling it over to Pete. You look like you could use a drink."

Mason watched Ted take the bottle gingerly, not entirely sure if the youth would be able to drink from it because of his furious shaking.

"Drink, damn it," he yelled. "What's the matter, you think you're the only man in the world to ever piss his pants? All that means is you got a strong bladder. Better men than you have pissed their pants when they thought that their time was up. Now take a healthy pull off that bottle. You look like you got the Saint Vitus Dance, the way you're shakin'. See if you can get some of that in your mouth and not on the God damned floor."

Ted meekly swallowed a gulp.

"Thank you, sir."

Ted tossed the bottle to Pete. The clerk wiped a dirty shawl on the lip of the bottle and threw his head back, taking enormous swigs. His Adam's apple bobbed as he nearly emptied its contents in a matter of seconds. Pete belched and made a whiskey face. He raised the bottle in the air to see how much was left.

"You always got to make a pig out of your self, don't you?" Mason shouted. Pete nodded his head and grinned, enjoying the effect of the alcohol.

"Get down to the root cellar and fetch me a new bottle for our guests." Lehigh looked at Pete with disgust.

"Sure thing Mister Lehigh," Pete said lazily, enjoying the warm feeling that had begun to spread to his limbs from his gargantuan whiskey bloated stomach. He handed the bottle to Ted who sheepishly looked away from the clerk in embarrassment. Pete's shoulders started to shake in silent mirth as he started to walk away. He stopped after just a few feet and pointed in Ted's direction.

"Mister Lehigh, he wet hints' pants." Once again he threw his head back and brayed loudly.

"Damn it, Pete, quit your fartin' around and do what I say. Stop your bullshit."

This time there was no mistaking the anger in his voice.

"Now, not tomorrow!" Mason shouted.

Quite unexpectedly, Lehigh stood up and grabbing the empty bottle by its neck, he reared back and hurled it with all his strength. The bottle whistled through the air dead on to its target. The fat man raised his hands in a defensive motion, but it was far too late. The bottle exploded on Pete's forehead. Pete stopped laughing and began to sprint down the hallway without even looking in the direction that the bottle had come from. Bilious rolls of fat bounced and quivered on him from the furious pounding his feet made on the floor in his frantic endeavor to instantly obey the angry command of his diminutive employer.

Huck felt the rotting floorboards shake beneath his from Pete's determined run to the basement door. He was truly amazed to see so much fat fly so quickly.

"That fella' is awfully light on his feet for a heavy man", Huck said. Mister Lehigh nodded his head in affirmation.

"That boy is as quick as a cat and strong as a bull. Don't let the fat fool you. I seen him break a bull's neck one time like you or me would snap a Goddamn stick."

Huck was impressed. Cecil was still in shock at the sudden turn of events and didn't know quite how to take the short man's mood swing. One minute, the little man was getting ready to kill them and in the next he was passing a bottle of whiskey around. One thing that Cecil did know was not to look a gift horse in the mouth. He was grateful to Tom for his quick thinking. He reached for a shot of whiskey and threw it back as the wizened little man continued speaking.

"I've known that boy all his life. I practically raised him, myself. I'm the closest thing to family the boy got. He's always had to run from a crowd of older boys when he was a youngin' cause of the way he looks. They teased him awful about it. They used to grab his lip and run him into walls with it. The bullies and gangs always set fer him. He had to learn to be fast. That's what made him so quick, you see."

Lehigh reached for a rag that was stuck in his top pocket and wiped his running nose.

"I watched them beat the hell out of him when he got caught in an alley one night. He was a tiny fat boy. They beat him all to hell. I chased them all away and wiped the dirt off him. That's when I told him that if he didn't get even with them one by one, that I would personally kick the ever lovin' shit out of him. Well, let me tell you, Pete got all those fellas one by one and kicked their heads round. He got good at it. He took to handing out beatings like a duck to water. He found out he had a true talent for it. In fact, he beat one of those bullies so badly that the boy was never again right in the head. He became a real imbecile after that beating. The boy's father came after Pete. I had to persuade the boy's father to leave town for the peace of everyone concerned. Everybody said it was simple justice for all the pain and torment that they put Pete through all them years. After that, no one in his right mind would want to tangle with Pete." Mason put the rag back in his pocket.

"On top of all that," Huck said, "he must have a head made of granite. I never seen a man take a bottle to the head like that an' then move out like a blue assed bird."

Lehigh looked at Huck.

"He pretty well almost put you through my floor. How do you feel?" he asked.

Huck straightened up from the crouch that he had been in. He slowly rubbed at the knot still in his back.

"I feel with my fingers. How do you feel?" Huck answered.

Mason laughed and threw back his shot of whiskey. He grimaced out of his pure satisfaction with the whiskey.

"Typhoid took his whole family back in 42. He was just little shit back then. He didn't have no friends, no place to go 'cause of the way he looks, so I took him in. He's been with me ever since. I'm the only family he got." Mason motioned for Ted to join them.

"All of you, find a crate or something to sit on. You too, sonny boy. Forget about Pete. He don't mean no harm. Let me tell you, if you've ever been to a hangin' then you know. Pissing in your pants is just natures way, Ain't no reason to be ashamed at all. The last thing a hanged man does is piss his pants, so let that be a lesson to you."

They all managed to find something to sit on and gathered around Mason in a semi-circle. Pete appeared a moment later with a bloody rag wrapped around his head and a bottle of whiskey. Mason took the bottle and began pouring drinks. He flipped the bottle in an underhand toss to Ted.

"You know, Pete here is very defensive towards me. Why, I remember one time down in Texas, a fella took a swing at me in a saloon. Pete stepped right in and nearly pulled that man's ballocks right off. Another shitpoke broke a bottle on his head. Pete hit that man so hard in the nose that he knocked that cowboy's eye out of his goddamned skull."

Mason squinted at Tom, his yellows eyes narrowing into slits. He thoughtfully studied Tom.

"We had to get out of there quick 'cause they were local boys, but I rode back into that Texas shit-hole about three years later and I went into that same saloon. I found out that the man that had his eye knocked out of his head never woke up. He died about two weeks after his run-in with Pete."

Mason let out a callous laugh that chilled Tom.

"So, young man, you say that some Missouri bushwhackers went for you?" Mason inquired, wiping his mouth on his sleeve.

"Yes sir, they did. They tried to bushwhack us and they started chasin' us. Their old nags couldn't keep up with us, although it was close for a time," Tom lied.

"Where did all this happen?" Mason asked brusquely.

Tom's two-step ahead mind worked like clockwork. Without hesitation, he exclaimed, " About twenty miles or so from here. I don't rightly know exactly 'cause I ain't from around these parts. I guess I was too busy trying to save myself. When we spotted them, we split up. I can tell you that I was totally lost until I got my bearings from a man and his son just two miles outside of town. Later, we all kind of met up here and that's the God's honest truth. The good Lord works in mysterious ways."

Cecil was truly astonished at the way Tom lied. He could almost believe Tom's story. He hoped that Lehigh was believing it. He took another swig off the bottle and handed it back to the fiendish looking midget. Mason took the bottle and began to pour more drinks.

"Amen," Mason shouted.

"Them dirty rotten Godless bushwhacking border trash must all die." Mason rose and screamed at the top of his voice, staring at the collapsing ceiling of his hotel as if in a trance.

"Killin' all of them can't be done sooner. It is God's will, Amen" his hawk like hands tightened on his shot glass.

"I know of a man that is pure hell on Border riff-raff. He would be very curious to know where you ran into them."

"Who may that be, sir?" Tom asked innocently. "I hope you don't mean the law. I have strict orders not to get involved with the law at any cost. They must know nothing of our intentions in this transaction."

Lehigh's was struck by what Tom had spoken.

"What are you talkin' about?" Lehigh asked slyly.

Tom looked carefully at everyone and then turned to look at the hotel's door.

"Well," he began, "I guess you know most of our story. I figure it can't hurt telling you the rest. My friends and I are couriers. We carry important, umm, documents, for a certain party who resides in this town. It is critical that we deliver these…um… documents to him. We have a sealed letter to be hand delivered to this certain party instructing him what is to be expected. We were told not to trust the law. Our orders are set and cannot be changed or we don't get paid. We received half of our pay when we left. It was deposited under our names in a bank in Lawrence. We will receive the other half after we deliver our messages to this certain gentleman. Any change in the plans and we do not receive one red cent."

Tom leaned in and whispered slowly.

"This friend of ours has no idea that we were coming in to deliver this package to him. Our employers in Lawrence wanted it to be as secret as possible. They are very important documents."

"I take it that the umm… 'Documents' is really cold hard cash," Mason smiled.

"Who you taking it to?"

"Captain Henry C. Fowler," Tom said quietly.

The face of the small man broke into a wide grin.

"Hot damn, how's that for coincidence? Me and Henry go way back. You boys are in luck. The captain is pure Dee-lightful hell on Missouri border trash. He has personally killed more of them than Cholera. He wipes them out and feels no remorse…he relishes in sending them to the infernal regions. He wipes them out quoting the Bible. It is something to behold. In fact, this is a big surprise. Henry had no idea that you boys were coming. He's going to be quite set with his documents."

Ted reached for the bottle and poured a river down his throat. His shaking visibly started increasing again.

"Truly," Tom said, "Providence has guided us here to you this day. This is truly divine guidance that has led us to you this day," Tom said with feigned surprise.

"We have signed a contract to hand deliver our package. Would you be able to arrange a meeting with the good Captain?"

"You bet your boots. First thing in the morning. Henry will be tickled pink to see you. This I promise. Lady luck has shined down brightly on you today. I will personally set up the meeting with Henry for you at first light. As for now, drink up. You are in good hands," he said loudly.

"Come now, boys, let us drink a toast to our good fortune."

CHAPTER SIX

George Blakely stepped out of the shadows of the thick Virginia forest and into the road. He rubbed his stubble on his face in wonder at what he saw. Coming down the road in a wagon were two of his messmates from his company in a swaying wagon pulled by two mules.

"Tom…Huck…Where in blue blazes did you git this wagon?"

Huck nimbly jumped from the wagon.

"George…Who is the officer of the watch?" Huck asked.

"I'm the dammed picket, can I ask the damned questions? I do believe that's how it's supposed to work," George said angrily.

"Now then…where did you git this wagon?"

Tom put the brake to the wagon, pulled it securely and stepped out. Huck ran up to George and placed his hand on George's shoulder.

"You ain't gonna' believe this. We got to talk to an officer. It's important. Tom here shot an' kilt hisself a Yankee scout."

"The devil you say," George exclaimed. He suddenly began to sniff at the air and then he pulled away from Huck. A smell staggered George as he backed away from him. George placed his hand over his nose.

"Good Lord Almighty, boy, you stink." George gagged as he stepped to the side of the road.

"You smell like an overripe latrine. You're not takin' this wagon into camp. Somebody would take a shot at you. It's bad enough around here when the wind starts blowin'. You kin still smell death in the air." George peeked into the back of the wagon from a distance and saw a bare foot. He cupped his hands to his mouth, laying his rifle across his arms.

"Post number three," he shouted.

Somewhere in the remoteness of the woods, someone yelled the identical thing. Faintly again they heard another voice pick up the call. Tom scratched the mule's head. A picket's challenge always reminded him the way dogs barked. No matter how far away from each other, dogs barked at each other in a chain reaction. George, curious as to what he had seen lying in the back of the wagon, approached it on a slant, hopping to stay downwind of it. When he cleared the rear of the wagon, he could see a half stripped body lying in the back. The corpse's head was alive with flies. George whistled shrilly.

"Yer damned near blew his head off his shoulders. Yer' a' sayin' this little skinny fella was a Yankee scout?" George asked.

"He nearly put one in my head, came pretty damned close if you ask me," Tom said calmly. A figure bounded out of the shadowy woods and came at them on a run.

"Look at his ear an' neck!" Huck exclaimed. "That's how close that skunk was to him when he let go a shot at him. He was settin' right next to him."

George placed his hand over his nose and approached Tom. He quickly glanced at Tom's ear and then retreated back to the other side of the road.

"Huck, help me let these mules, lets get them out of their harnesses," Tom said, amused at how George had approached him as if he were confronting a leper.

"Do we really smell all that bad?" he asked Huck.

"You know something…I can't rightly tell no more. Ain't that strange."

Huck unhitched the nearest mule while Tom released the other. John Hubert walked towards the wagon and then came to a dead start in mid stride as if he had hit an invisible wall. He jumped back a foot.

"Holy dog shit!" he shouted, "Boy, what a stink."

George Blakely shouted, "John, where's Arthur?"

John instantly recognized the horrendous stink. John covered his face with both of his hands.

"He's gone to git' Lootenant Custiss. What the hell are you doin' with this stinkin' wagon?"

"Tom an' Huck claim they kilt' a Yankee scout," George replied. Huck led the two mules a few yards away from the wagon and into the woods. He let them loose and they started to browse around quite contentedly. Tom then walked to the rear of the wagon. He grabbed the cadaver's ankles and pulled roughly. The body landed in the orange dust of the road, its hands flying over its head as though seeking supplication from a higher source in protest to its rough handling.

A cloud of flies exploded from the head when it hit the dust of the road after being unceremoniously dropped from the back of the wagon. Tom walked away from the body and began to push the wagon off the road. Huck and George Blakely quickly joined in helping him and soon the wagon rested in the shadows. George rubbed his hands on his shirt as he walked away from the wagon. He sniffed at the palm of his hands and made an unpleasant face.

"We aught to burn her where it stands," he said.

John Hubert was busy examining the corpse. Ed Bolls came flying down a small hill followed by Andy Barrett. Lieutenant Custiss made his way right behind them, although in a slower and more dignified manner. The lieutenant spotted the stooped figure of John Hubert in the road teetering over a very dead looking individual. George came to attention and saluted his superior officer. He offered the Lieutenant a stiff crisp salute.

"Post number three reports two of our company in the presence of a kilt' and may I add, sir, a very newly dead Yankee scout, sir."

Lieutenant Custiss removed his handkerchief from his tunic pocket and placed it over his nose. He returned George's salute as Tom and Huck acknowledged the lieutenant's appearance with a wave and a smile. The Lieutenant scowled at them, his eyes smoldering in anger.

"Is that a fact," he said.

"It sure is, Lootenant," Huck said enthusiastically.

"Tom shot an' skinned one damned sneaky Yankee scout all before noon."

Lieutenant Custiss ignored Huck's attempt at humor. The lieutenant searched the wagon and examined the naked dead-man in the road. Corporal Arthur Cook, the highest ranking non-commissioned officer at Post number three, ran down the road and went to the side of Lieutenant Custiss.

"Corporal, post sentries over this wagon. I don't want anyone even approaching it. Anyone that looks interested in what is going on here, you will detain them. Move, corporal."

"Yassuh." The corporal rolled a quick salute the lieutenant's way, came to attention, and went scampering off bellowing orders like a madman. Lieutenant Custiss turned to George Blakely.

"Private, take the rifles of the men here." He indicated Huck and Tom. George looked puzzled but he did as he was ordered. Tom reluctantly handed his rifle to George by its strap while Huck leaned his against a tree. Both of the men eyed each other in concern. What the lieutenant said next made their hearts drop into their shoes.

"You men are under arrest. Private, secure the prisoners hands." Lieutenant Custiss stepped back two paces and drew his revolver and pointed it at both of them.

"If the prisoners offer any resistance, you are to shoot. If they run, you will kill them. Are my orders clear, Private Blakely?"

George was totally confused.

"No sir, I mean Ye...Ye..ssir," George stuttered. This was not how Tom and Huck had expected to be treated. Huck's throat constricted in fear and anger.

"God-damm it. Lootenant, he said, "Tom kilt hisself a Yankee scout. We got proof. The man had a map tucked into a hidden part of his shoe an."

"Keep your mouth shut, private. For your information, Sergeant Rawlings reported you missing without permission at this evening's roll call. I see you apprehended on a picket line with a dead man. Until we get this all sorted out, you will keep your mouths shut or I will have you gagged and blindfolded, do you understand me, soldier."

Tom and Huck gaped at each other in fear. Huck's mouth dropped open at the officer's remark. George began to bind their wrists, first Tom's and then Huck's. George apologized while he went about securing them.

"Private Finn," Lieutenant Custiss said, "this matter has complicated my evening for me and if it has complicated my evening, it surely has complicated yours."

"But Lootenant, why won't yer jest listen. We got people here that will tell you straight off that Rawlings ordered us on a buryin' detail up near Fairview this very morning."

Lieutenant Custiss returned his pistol to its holster.

"Private Finn," he said, "if what you say is true, then you don't have anything to fear. If this is true, then follow orders. You have always been a good soldier, so simply continue to be one and I promise no harm will come to you. There must be procedure, private, or the whole world will erupt in chaos and confusion, both of which are not in the spirit of the Good Lord. Put your trust in him, son. However, if what you say is not true then I suppose you both will be shot for desertion and murder."

"I wisht' you hadn't said that last part, Lootenant. I was followin' yer' jest' fine till you got to that last part," Huck said wryly. Lieutenant Custiss watched as George finished his chore.

"George, I want you to go find Sergeant Rawlings," he said. "You will inform him to meet me at Captain Cobb's tent at good speed. Then I want you to assemble every man in these men's section and do likewise. Find sergeant Jenkins and tell him to relieve all of the men at this post Everyone that was a witness to what happened here tonight will be brought to the Captain's tent under Provost guard as soon as possible. Do you understand your orders, Private?"

"Yes sir, lootenant," he screamed. He was so nervous that he didn't realize he had screamed so loudly.

"Very good," Custiss said. George saluted the officer and took off running.

"As for you two, sit down under this tree."

They complied and sat down in shocked silence. Both of them were well aware of the army's ability in making mistakes and errors. They were not confident in the Army's ability to sort through a quagmire or a mystery.

"Private Hubert," Lieutenant Custiss said, "stop watching the dead man and get on over here."

"Yassuh," John roared and ran over to where the lieutenant was standing .The lieutenant watched the glum and forlorn expression of Tom and Huck. Huck, he could tell, was fuming.

"Private Hubert, you will secure the possessions of the dead man. You will fix a stretcher with some tree limbs and a blanket. You and Private Barrett will then carry the body over to the regimental surgeon. You will tell the surgeon that I said to post a guard over the body. Then you will report to Captain Cobb's tent to await me. Do you understand these orders, soldier?"

"Yassuh." John saluted and he too went off at a dead run. Satisfied that things were in order, he turned his attention to the miserable pair sitting under the tree.

"Post number three," the lieutenant shouted. Private Thornton Dean and Pete Wilson ran to him and stiffened to attention.

"One last detail for this post. You will tell your relief that no one is to approach this wagon. Arrest anyone who questions these orders or attempts to interfere."

"Yes sir," Private Wilson said loudly.

"Private Bolls, get on over here and listen well. We are going to march the prisoners to the company commander's tent. I want you to walk ahead of the privates."

"If they attempt to run, you will shoot to kill. I am giving you a direct order. Do you understand?" Ed Bolls looked horrified at what he had just heard.

"Shoot Huck an' Tom?" he blurted. "Why would I want an' go do somethin' like that fer?"

The lieutenant went red in the face. "Private Wilson get' on over here."

Private Wilson scurried over to him in a hurry.

"Private Wilson, Private Bolls is under arrest. Private Bolls, hand your weapon over to Private Wilson. Private Dean, bring that rope over and secure the prisoners' hands. Private Bolls, I will not tolerate anyone questioning a direct order. If this is the only way that you can learn, then so be it."

Ed reluctantly handed his rifle over to Pete Wilson while Private Thornton Dean secured Ed's hands with packaging twine. The lieutenant once again pulled his service revolver out and pointed the muzzle skyward. He motioned for the men to start walking.

"Listen well, all of you. You will walk to the captain's tent in an orderly way. If you decide to run, or if you do anything out of the ordinary, I will take it as a sign of your immediate guilt and I will shoot you dead. Now …proceed."

"Damn that Rawlings," Huck said bitterly.

"No talking. Move," Custiss said harshly.

They walked in silence passing both Post number two and Post number one. Both times they were challenged in the correct manner and both times the Lieutenant responded to the picket's challenge properly. When they neared the Captain's tent, Lieutenant Custiss ordered all of them to sit on the grass. The lieutenant went into the Captain's tent and emerged many minutes later with Captain Cobb who motioned Tom to step inside.

A provost guard appeared soon after. Lieutenant Custiss had a few words with him away from Huck. After their chat, the provost guard walked over and stood over Huck. He stood a few feet from him and pointed his rifle in his direction.

Lieutenant Custiss went back into the tent. He pushed the overhanging flap from his face and narrowly avoided walking into the tent post. Tom had taken a seat in front of Captain Cobb and he apparently had started telling the captain his side of the story. Lieutenant Custiss listened carefully to their conversation.

"So Huck dropped his rifle and Sergeant Rawlings came back and let into Huck. Later, after breakfast, he came and ordered both of us up to a burying detail, punishment for talking in ranks."

"I do remember the incident," Cobb said, "go on."

"He told us to find Corporal Bains. Bains, he said, was up near Fairview cemetery. He was mighty angry with us and we were glad just to get away. He never gave us travel orders, We weren't thinking We took off without any written orders, but we got witnesses that were there when Sergeant Rawlings ordered us up to the burying detail. Private Barrett and Private Bolls saw the whole thing. Anyway, sir, we took off. The last thing the sergeant said was that if we couldn't find any Yankees to bury, to find one and kill him and bury him. That fella lying stone cold dead back on the road there is a Yankee scout and I have the proof right here. He tried to shoot me in the head after we got him dead to rights for being what he was. We saw right through him."

"If what you say is true, then Sergeant Rawlings has reported you missing without permission falsely. I can't imagine that something as important as this would have simply slipped his mind," Cobb said, twirling his aristocratic mustache. It perched splendidly under his Roman like nose.

Tom continued on with his tale and omitted nothing, which seemed to annoy the Captain. However, he continued to listen in patience and when the time came for Tom to produce the map and the hidden compartment that he had found in the shoe, it caused Cobb to stand up and shout.

"I'll be damned, a Yankee spy. Let me see that shoe."

Tom pulled the shoe from his waistband and handed it over to him. Cobb greedily pawed at the shoe and when he found the secret compartment by turning the heel and twisting it to the right, he was as delighted as a child with a new toy.

"A damned Yankee spy," he again shouted. "By thunder, look at this, Lieutenant. It is ingenious. Something as fragmented as this is, you would logically think, would fall apart merely with the stress of turning it, but it doesn't. It is truly remarkable."

Captain Cobb handed the shoe to Lieutenant Custiss. The shoe was designed to look like it was falling apart. However, there was a sturdy waterproof space built into the heel, just large enough for its intended purpose.

"Inside that little place in the heel, I found this map," Tom said. "I think it's silk. It has a lot of little figures on it that I can't make out, Sir."

Tom gave Cobb the map that he had found. It was about two inches when folded, but it was almost a foot across when unfolded. The Captain took great care and time unfolding it and spreading it out on the table. Lieutenant Custiss leaned over the table for a closer inspection of it and recognized standard symbols on it that could only mean one thing. Captain Cobb instantly recognized the symbols on the map as well. Cobb was enthralled with the map.

"Lieutenant Custiss, if you would, sir," Cobb said in awed surprise. "Go and inform Colonel Edmonds that we have discovered something of grave importance that must be brought to his attention immediately. That if he would meet me at Division headquarters within the hour. General Longstreet and General Stuart must see this." He looked like he was about to burst from pure joy.

"As your trained eye can plainly see, Lieutenant," he said, "we have the symbols for cavalry and infantry units." Cobb pointed to them.

"My God, these are locations of our units identified by name and these circles marked here can only mean the position and strength of enemy divisions. This is truly a monumental find. Look at their cavalry locations."

Lieutenant Custiss studied the map and agreed with his superior officer. Tom sat in silence, not knowing what was expected of him. He knew to be silent. His spirits rose with the happiness that Captain Cobb seemed to be displaying with the map.

"I will leave directly sir," Custiss said. "You may want to know, Captain, that I have posted a guard over the wagon and the body of the Union scout. That, sir, is at the regimental surgeons. Post three is with the wagon with orders that no one is to approach it. I have also sent for all parties that were witness to the event this evening to be brought here under guard. I am sure that after finding this that someone will want to take that wagon apart later with a fine toothcomb to see if it holds any further mysteries. As for the body, I would think our people in intelligence will want to view it for identification purposes."

Cobb was impressed. "Splendid work, Lieutenant. Splendid. Where is the other soldier that was sent on this detail? You said his name was Finn, did you not?"

"He is sitting outside with the guard, Sir."

"Bring him in, Lieutenant. And get the surgeon over h'yar to look after Private Sawyer's wounds." Lieutenant Custiss saluted and quickly departed.

"Orderly," Cobb yelled loudly, "orderly, report. Where the hell are you?"

The orderly scurried in, bumping his head on the tent post.

"Captain?" he said, snapping to attention.

"Nathan, get clothes for these men, preferably something with sergeant chevrons on them. And burn those clothes they are wearing. They are affronts to the olfactory senses. Young man, nothing personal, but you reek of the smell that is produced when one pisses on a campfire."

Captain Cobb was now on fire. He bent over to continue to read the map. His eyes gleamed.

"Private Sawyer, I believe this map shows the position of the whole Federal army. Good gracious, what a find," he said.

Huck entered the tent preceded by the guard who saluted Captain Cobb. Huck slouched to attention and offered a sloppy salute in which Cobb didn't bother to return. He dismissed the orderly and the guard with a wave. Huck looked at Tom and found him to be grinning. He was relieved to see him smiling and his fears started to evaporate. Captain Cobb distractedly pulled a folding chair from behind a post and offered it to Huck.

"Sit down, Private Finn."

Huck tentatively took the chair and opened it, muttering an awkward thanks to the floor.

"I was just telling Private Sawyer that this is quite some find, possibly of monumental importance. You men just may have contributed heavily towards winning this war," Cobb said. He cleared his throat.

"We need more fellows just like yourselves in this army...clear thinking and decisive men in positions of responsibility and command instead of strutting popping-jays like that fool Rawlings. I intend to crucify him in the morning. He lied to me and endangered your lives by sending you on a wild goose chase, and I will see to his immediate demolition, you can rest assured on that. Your actions and quick thinking in ferreting out this spy are highly commendable and I also intend to promote you both, this day, to sergeants."

Just at that moment, Sergeant Jenkins entered the tent.

"Reportin' as ordered, sir."

"Are all the men who were at post three, have they all been brought here?" Cobb asked quickly.

"Yes sir, they have, they are all here and under guard."

"Excellent...we have a situation here that calls for extreme delicacy, Sergeant Jenkins. The fewer people that know what has occurred at that post, the better for all concerned. I cannot, I repeat, cannot have rumors spreading through this company or this regiment. You must all be sworn to secrecy, including the men outside this tent. There will be no talk circulating about the events that have transpired here tonight. These men have shot and killed a Federal spy and have found a telling document on his body. Keep all of the men who know what has happened tonight outside...no, even better, bring them all into this tent and then post guards. I will be leaving for Division right away and will not use my tent tonight. I suppose that I will be away all night with this business."

"Yes sir," Jenkins replied. He turned and was gone in a flash. Captain Cobb stood over the map on his field table. Thoughts pounded through his head like the hooves of a cavalry charge.

"When Nathan returns, you will inform the corporal that you are now attached to me in the role of staff. You are not to be put on any duty or detail, whatsoever. That means no picket duty, is that clear?" he asked. Tom and Huck nodded.

"I am sure that staff officers at Divisional headquarters will want to question you further on this matter. Tell the corporal to have Jenkins arrest Rawlings and detain him in this tent as well. Tell him the charges are gross misconduct of duties. That will be your first orders as sergeants."

Tom and Huck could not believe their ears.

"Now, I am off." He buckled on his sword and belt that had a holster and pistol attached to it. Cobb huffed and folded the silk map into a neat square and placed it in his inside tunic pocket. He patted it and then buttoned his gray jacket. He walked purposely out of the tent in large unnatural strides. Huck arose from his chair as the Captain left the tent.

"Time sure has a way of mollifying a situation," he said. "One minute, I'm a prime candidate fer' a firin' squad an' the next minute, I'm a military success story. If only 'Pap' could see me now."

Sergeant Jenkins and Ed Bolls appeared suddenly through the tent flaps. Ed still had his hands tied and looked to be in a state of high anxiety.

"Tom…Huck..they got the whole section under guard out there. Who the hell did you shoot, anyway? General Lee's Grandpa?" Ed asked gruffly.

They could hear the voices of many angry men approaching the tent. Ed turned to Sergeant Jenkins.

"Vernon, can't you at least tell us what we done for all of us to be in the fix we're in?" he pleaded.

Andy Barrett was pushed roughly through the flaps by a guard. He crashed into Ed who went sprawling because his hands were still tied. John Hubert, Thornton Dean, Pete Wilson and George Blakely all followed suit as they tripped and fell on one another in a chain reaction. George Blakely stepped on John Hubert's ear causing John to scream in pain. Corporal Higgins, the captain's orderly entered brandishing a lighted stick in which he used to light a small oil lamp and a pair of candles that were on the captain's field table. After they were lit, he surmised the approximate shirt and pants sizes of Tom and Huck.

"Get out of them damned clothes, you two. I'll be right back. Throw them goddamned stinkin' clothes out the tent," he said angrily. He disappeared through the flap, muttering under his breath. Vernon Jenkins helped Ed Bolls to his feet.

"Get up…you're all actin' like clowns in a circus."

Ed was grateful for Vernon's helping hand. He turned and twisted, showing Vernon his tied hands.

"How about can you loose my hands fer me. I bin on my ass three times already walkin' in the dark with them like this here," Ed whined.

Vernon pulled out his knife and cut Ed's bonds. John Hubert raised his own wrist bound hands to Vernon who cut them off as well.

"Now everybody listen up," he said, passing the knife to John who began to cut Andy's ropes for him.

"As far as I know, nobody is in any trouble. This here is for security purposes, is all. The captain didn't want y'all runnin' yer' mouths to every body you come into contact with about what went on at yer picket station this evening. It t'aint nothin' to get yer bowels all up in an uproar. Ya jest gotta' stay here a bit an' behave yer damned selves. Is that clear?"

A chorus of 'yssuh's and head nods from those assembled answered Vernon's query.

"Alright then. Sit tight and don't leave the tent," Vernon ordered. John Hubert approached Vernon holding on to his injured ear.

"Thanks for tellin' us, Vernon. The way those Provos came out of the dark and started rounding us up nearly scairt the daylights out'n me. I didn't know what to think. Them boys don't say much, but they are hell fer dedication," he said.

"I know'd it was all about that dead Yankee what's layin' next to the surgeons tent. It's all about the dead Yankee, isn't it, Vernon?" Thornton asked.

"All your questions will be answered in the morning. Again, don't leave the tent. Not even to piss. Them provost guards are all posted around this tent and you know how edgy they be. I have some business to attend to so y'all rest easy."

They all respected and trusted the word of the sergeant. He was the most dependable person that many of them had ever seen, with an instinct for combat that was uncanny. He had on more than one occasion saved many a life by his split second decisions and sense of timing. Vernon was a soldier's soldier, and no one trifled with him. He walked off into the gathering dusk. For a brief moment there was total silence, the only sound being the chirping of crickets. Huck broke the silence.

"Anybody got anything to eat," he asked.

"Arthur was makin' some sluish for tonight but I ain't seen him since all this rumpus started," Pete said softly. Everyone gathered in the cramped field tent had sought appreciable distance away from Tom and Huck because of their offensive odor. Corporal Cook pushed his way into the tent followed by the regimental surgeon.

"Speakin' of the devil," Huck said, "An' up he pops," Huck said. The Corporal sniffed at the air.

"Take them damned clothes off. Vernon said you were smellin' like a polecat an' he was right. Throw them through the flap."

They both quickly stripped and tossed the clothes through the tent's entrance. The doctor began to examine Tom's blisters. He reached into his black medical bag and ripped a small section of clean linen from a larger piece for a bandage. He then removed a bottle and a small bowl. Finally he removed a small bottle of sticky fluid and began mixing a poultice, which he applied liberally to the section of bandage.

"You've got yourself one good powder burn and the shot creased your skull, but other than that, you are the picture of health," the doctor said cheerily. "However, if the angle of that fellas pistol had been off just a single degree differently, you would be dead right now. You are lucky, my boy. Damned lucky."

Corporal Higgins, the captain's orderly, arrived with a bundle of clothes. He threw them first at Huck and then at Tom's feet. Huck quickly dressed and admired the sergeant stripes on the arms and showed them off to everyone. Andy Barrett whistled shrilly and Pete Wilson clapped his hands. The doctor wrapped the bandage around Tom's head and finished by tying the ends together.

"There you go," the doctor said happily, "now, don't remove that bandage until tomorrow night." The doctor looked Tom in the eyes.

"So, that was your handiwork that is lying outside next to my tent?" he asked. "I mean, of course, the man with the large hole in his head."

"There is?" Tom asked with surprise.

"Yes. There surely is. And to top it off, somebody is standing guard over it. I suppose that is to insure that it doesn't get up and go running off to find a cemetery because that is exactly where it belongs."

"Sorry, Doctor," Tom said.

"Not as sorry as I am, son. I may be a doctor, but I hate the sight of dead people. Always did. I guess that's why I became a doctor." The surgeon smiled, closed his bag and walked away. Tom felt his bandage. It was then that he noticed everyone staring at him. He picked up the clothes that Higgins had thrown at his feet and began to dress.

"How does it feel?" Andy Barrett asked abruptly.

"Stings a might, but otherwise than that, I'm faring good,' Tom answered.

"No. I don't mean your ear. I mean how does it feel being a sergeant. Huck said the Captain promoted you both jest like that. How does it feel?"

Corporal Cook deposited himself on the packed earth of the tent's floor.

"I got one for you, Andy," Arthur said sarcastically. "How does it feel to be as dumb as a bag of hammers?" Everyone broke into laughter. Andy nodded and laughed as well.

"What I mean to say is you being sergeants and all, why it has to make you feel strange," Andy said. "You an' Huck is the same rank as Rawlings is. Think about it.

He can't be givin' you hell now 'cause he don't outrank you. You kin' tell the man to go to hell right up front and personal. You kin tell him to stick it whar' the sun don't shine. That's gotta' be makin' you think some odd thoughts. I know I would be."

"I never thought about it like that, Andy. I guess it's all kinda' new and confusing," Tom said thoughtfully.

"Like a virgin in a whorehouse," Huck said. "The way I got it figured these stripes don't amount to a hill of beans. They's jest' fer' decorations. When Captain Cobb tells this story to God only who knows next, he wants me an' Tom to look respectable like with the new stripes. It will make him look good. He's gonna' say to whoever will listen that my two fine fellows, sergeants both, good upstanding stout hearted an' brave. who had always been shit-birds to him before, were always someone he knew to be right plucky fellows."

Corporal Cook nodded in agreement.

"You boys are gonna be pranced out in front of a lot of high rankin' officers an' shown like race horses. It only makes sense that Cobb presents you in the best light possible. Don't be too surprised when all of this is over that you don't revert right back to private shit-birds again. As fer' Rawlings, be careful when you're dealin' with him. Rawlings is a snake in the grass an' don't fergit' it," Arthur said.

"Exactly. Arthur's right. These stripes will come off us as fast as we put them on," Huck said sadly.

Corporal Higgins reappeared through the tent flap carrying a sack of hardtack.

"That's all I could find, Arthur," he said. He handed the bundle over to him. Arthur looked disappointed.

"Why, hell Nathan. I had a bunch of sluish I was makin' in a fryn' pan. You didn't see it?" Arthur asked angrily.

"I didn't have time to go to your area, Arthur. I passed a hat fer' what yer got right there. Company H is all out on double picket duty since you all are here and they weren't all that happy takin' yer places. Yer' lucky I was able to scrounge what yer got there."

A head that belligerently stuck through the flap interrupted them. All eyes were attracted to a very furious looking Sergeant Rawlings. He pushed his way into the tent.

"What kind of bullshit is this?" he shouted. He looked at Tom and Huck and exploded. "Look what we have here.

"So, you two are back already? I should have known you two were behind all this here. I told you to find Bains. I gave you an order an' you disobeyed a direct command. I got your asses cold, but I'm gonna' warm them up fer' you real good. I'll have you ridin' the rails fer' punishment till your nut sacks drop off. I'll give you so much time in the stockade you will think that you were born there."

He stared momentarily at the new sergeant stripes that Tom and Huck were wearing. Andy Barrett tried to speak but Rawlings pushed him away roughly.

"Sit down, I ain't in the mood fer' any of yer' idiocy," he said loudly. He advanced towards Huck with bad intent.

"Oh my. Do I see sergeant stripes on yer' sleeves there? That's another charge. You boys don't realize the fun we are goin' to have. Impersonatin' a non-commissioned officer. And what in the name of all that's holy are all you fools doin' sittin' in the Captain's tent when your supposed to be on picket duty."

Corporal Higgins boldly stepped in between Rawlings and Huck.

"Simmer down, sergeant. These boys are officially here as staff. That comes straight from the captain. All the rest here have been ordered to stay here tonight. You best stay here too. Vernon has somethin' he has to tell you." Nathan held off Rawlings with an outstretched arm.

Rawlings pushed Corporal Higgin's arm away, his fury and bewilderment apparent in his eyes. He glared at Huck, his eyes flaming and smoldering in an unnatural way. Rawlings screamed at Higgins.

"Don't give me that bullshit. I'm out lookin' fer' the pickets where all of you was supposed to be, an' I find company H there. Nobody knows where the hell you are. Nobody, it seems, knows nothin' about nothin' I been lookin' for an hour. I don't know if you're all layin' out there with yer' throats cut." Rawlings waved his arms over his head in confusion

"For all I know, we could have been under some kinda' sneak cavalry raid an' you all got taken prisoner. I can't find Jenkins or Lieutenant Custiss, so's I come here and I see these stupid bastards all sittin' around eatin' crackers. Where the hell is Captain Cobb? Somebody had better start makin' sense around here," he screamed.

Arthur Cook stood up.

"Huck an' Tom kilt a federal spy on that detail you sent them out on," he said. " From what I know, sergeant, and it ain't much, the Captain don't want the story spreadin' around. In fact, everybody that was there when Tom an' Huck came back with the dead-man is here."

Rawlings slowly crumbled in disbelief. He was exhausted with his raving and stress. He was dumbfounded. Andy watched Rawlings in fascination. When the sergeant sat on the folding chair and removed his slouch hat, Andy seized his opportunity.

"Tom an' Huck got put to sergeants by Captain Cobb. They's the same rank as you are," Andy said.

"That is debatable," Arthur said grinning. "I think what we got here is two temporary sergeants until this matter with the spy grows cold. Then they will revert. to their old status."

Sergeant Rawlings gaped at Huck and Tom with dumb wonder.

"I'll bet you a month's pay that you're wrong, Arthur," Tom said firmly.

"You are on, Sawyer. You got a bet." Arthur offered Tom his hand.

"One month's pay says that sergeants Sawyer an' Finn will be privates again when all this blows over," Arthur said contentedly.

Andy Barrett shouted his impersonation of an Indian war-whoop.

"Shoot him in the pants, Tom," he shouted, "The coat an' vest is mine." Encouraged by Andy's shout, Tom shook Arthur's hand firmly.

"If I ever find myself a private again, it truly will be an intolerable situation," Tom said confidently. Arthur patted Tom on the back and sat back down. He reached into the sack and pulled out a cracker.

"Anyway, Tom," Arthur said, "nothin' changes between us, except fer' the money."

Huck looked at Tom and shook his head sadly. Tom looked at Rawlings and laughed. Morning could not come fast enough for Tom.

CHAPTER SEVEN

Huck awakened from his sleep to the sound of breaking glass. He felt horrible. The effect of Lehigh's cheap whiskey played havoc with his senses. He moaned, grabbed at his head and walked unsteadily to the room's only window. He peered through the dirty smudge streaked window and saw Pete below him in the yard breaking glass out of an old door. The glare of the new day made Huck nauseous and feeble. He reached for a chair and collapsed into it. Tom, he noticed, was fully dressed and lay sprawled across the bed on the other side of the room.

Images and distorted recollections floated ethereally through his whiskey soaked brain. Lehigh had poured drink after drink until he had passed out. He could not remember coming up the stairs to his room.

Without warning, the door to his room was kicked in. It registered as an explosion in Huck's mind. Standing in the doorway with wild bloodshot eyes and a scarlet face stood Cecil holding what looked like a note of some kind. He looked like a dangerous lunatic freshly escaped from an asylum. In his other hand, Cecil clutched a revolver. He waved the crumpled piece of paper in the air.

"That no good lying stinkin' Pup," Cecil hollered.

Huck's bleary eyes widened in shock at the loudness of Cecil's yell. He swallowed dryly. His head rang with Cecil's scream of rage. The ruckus caused Tom to stir and he slowly attempted to sit up. He failed and fell back on the bed. Huck tried to speak but the words would not come. He could only make hissing noises. He tried again to speak and this time he managed to croak out something that sounded intelligible.

"What the hell's the matter?" Huck asked hoarsely.

"That dirty no good little buck-toothed weasel," Cecil raged. "That pigeon-chested poor excuse for a man."

Cecil stamped his feet loudly and booted a chair across the room. His wrath caused flecks of foam to fly from the corners of his mouth. His ire soared by the second. Cecil was livid. In his frenzy, he crumpled the paper into a ball and hurled it at Huck.

Huck picked up the scrap of paper and began to read as Cecil continued stomping around the room and bawling coarse language at the top of his lungs. Huck squinted at the paper. His lips moved as his eyes darted down the lines on the paper. Tom began to stir from Cecil's loud ravings. He watched Cecil with one eye open. Huck finished reading the letter. He crumpled the letter and flung it at Tom.

93

"Good luck and God bless all of you," Huck said weakly. "Tom, read that letter. We got trouble. Ted has decided to get religious. He's gone."

"What are you saying? Gone where? Where did he go?"

"Read the letter," Huck said with alarm.

Tom reached for the letter that had landed on the bed, smoothed it out so that it was readable and began to quickly peruse its contents. He stopped and dropped it to the floor.

"I don't understand why he.." Tom began.

Cecil interrupted Tom by picking up the chair that he had kicked earlier and smashed it into kindling by picking it up and smashing it into the wall.

"So boys," he said, mimicking the voice of a very frightened young boy, "I'm goin' home because my damned nerves are shot and I never had my heart in this to begin with." Cecil stopped suddenly and for a second almost appeared lucid. The moment faded quickly. He smashed his head into the wall splintering boards and raising a cloud of plaster dust.

"So, good luck and God bless all of you and I don't give a fat rat's ass if you all get' kilt'," Cecil howled.

"What in God's name was he thinking?" Tom asked quietly. Cecil stopped again and quickly walked over to Tom.

"He wasn't thinkin', that's the damned point," Cecil yelled.

"I tolt' him when we all started that all it takes fer' us to all get kilt' is jest one weak link in the chain. It's a hell of a time fer' him to go start gettin' second thoughts."

Huck stood up and lurched across the dingy room towards the window and threw it open. The frosty air struck him full force as he vomited violently and then sagged to his knees. Bile streaked the side of the America Hotel. Huck's hands dangled powerlessly out of the window and his head rested on the sill.

Tom struggled to his feet, his complexion an unhealthy gray. He rubbed his face and began to choke on a phlegm ball wedged at the back of his dusty parched throat. He valiantly fought the urge to empty the contents of his stomach on to the floor as Huck nearly had. Everything in the room, including Cecil, seemed to take on strange and odd angles in relation to Tom's hangover blasted vision.

"He's flown the coop. Left the nest," Cecil said, almost in a normal speaking voice. His voice slightly quavered as he fought for control. His anger slowly had begun to subside.

"I wake up an' find that letter on his bunk. This ain't good, Tom."

"Do you think anybody seen him leave?" Tom asked.

"I don't know," Cecil said, throwing his hands in the air.

"But if they did, we best find out quick. Seen' him leave alone will make them all suspicious, and we don't want that," Cecil said fearfully.

"Good riddance," Huck mumbled, "He was startin' to get on my nerves with all his damn whining an' complainin'."

Huck glimpsed Pete looking up at him. Pete continued to break the glass out of the door but then strangely stared into the bushes on the side of the hotel before glancing up at Huck again. Pete wore an ugly grin and waved at Huck. Pete's face was a mass of fat wrinkles, his eyes being just tiny slits. Huck could only wave back feebly at the fat man below him as he rocked with a gag reflex that hit him in waves. He stood back from the window and closed it half way.

"What do we tell Lehigh if they spotted Ted leavin'? Cecil asked nervously.

"Let me think on that a while," Tom said shakily. Cecil noticed Huck swaying in front of the half open window. His face and shirt were streaked with yellow bile.

"Damn boy, look at the mess you made. You stink. That's vile," Cecil said with disgust. Cecil stomped away to his room and returned an instant later with a pitcher of water.

"Here, clean yourself up. You're revoltin'."

Cecil handed Huck the pitcher of water. Huck swallowed a mouthful and spit some on the floor. He poured the rest of the contents of the pitcher on his upturned face. He shook, flung the window open, and breathed in the cool air in an attempt to clear his head. He tossed the pitcher to the floor.

Cecil dragged the room's only surviving chair over to Tom's bed. He still clutched his dated Dragoon's pistol in his hand. Cecil slammed the chair down hard on the floor, nearly breaking it and slumped into it.

"The man comes all the way across Missouri. Well over two hundred miles, faces all kinds of hardships. He has had all the time in the world while he was comin' here to back out if he wanted to and then decides to hit out at the worst possible time. He waits until we are up to our necks in it then turns as yellow as the puke runnin' down the side of this place," Cecil said flatly. He looked at his antique pistol.

"If I ever see him again, I swear I'll beat him like a drum on the Fourth of July."

Tom stood up and looking down the hall carefully and slowly closed the door.

"Hush up and listen," Tom said quietly. "Nothing changes with Ted skippin' out. We don't know for sure if anybody seen him leave or not. Here's what we say if anybody asks. We say that Ted wanted to go thank the people that gave him directions here when he got lost. We'll say that there was this little old gal that he took an interest in on that farm and was thinking of courting her with the farmer's approval."

Cecil's chin rested on his chest. He leaned back and stared at the smoke stained ceiling.

"That story," he said cautiously, "sounds like so much bullshit to me. I wouldn't believe it and I know that they won't either. You go an' tell Lehigh that story after we just got through tellin' him that we got chased by a bunch of border trash an' he will know something is wrong. Especially after he seen how Ted was actin'. He knows that Ted is a spineless yellow-belly who would never leave safety or comfort to go ridin' into possible danger all fer' the sake of some tail. These people, fer your recollections, Tom, are one hundred percent stone cold dyed in the wool killers. They ain't stayed alive fer' so long by falling fer' bullshit stories like that one." Cecil placed his pistol in his belt and stretched, raising his hands and placing them behind his neck.

"You were there, you heard the stories Lehigh was spinnin' last night," Cecil said. "How they shot this fella an' kilt that one. Hell, even if only one quarter of what he said was true, then let me tell you, we are in the company of some very dangerous sons-of-bitches. His stories are probably what caused Ted to hightail it back home."

"What do suggest we tell Lehigh then? Should we tell him that the man that put this half-assed scheme into our heads to begin with has lost his nerve and went home with his tail between his legs? Is that what we should tell him, Cee? If it is, then I guess we should tell him that it's perfectly alright for him to go about caving in little old ladies head with swords and nailing defenseless people to barn doors," Tom said angrily.

Cecil did not expect Tom's reaction. He had expected Tom's response to be more calm and deliberative.

Cecil was surprised by Tom's reaction and did not know what to say. Tom walked away but then spun on Cecil.

"I tell you what. Since my idea was, as you so strongly put it, bullshit, then suppose we hear one of yours. I'm all ears. Unless you want to go downstairs right now and put a bullet into Lehigh's head. After all, it was you that was always talking about shooting Fowler. What do you think we should do, Cee?"

Huck tried to ignore the loud angry voices that pricked his head with needles.

"I recollect another certain party that claimed that they were always trying to get to Fowler and yet they never did," Tom spat.

"What are you sayin', Sawyer?" Cecil sat up in his chair.

"I don't know," Tom shouted. "Why don't you tell me?" Tom raised his voice loudly.

"Why don't you tell us what we should do because all my ideas are bullshit," Tom shouted.

Tom was louder than Huck could ever remember him being.

"Just like your Uncle Frank, the famous bushwhacker, and just like you are. You ain't never killed a man before and don't be telling me that bed-time story about that Mexican fella you shot because I don't believe a word of it, not for a second."

Cecil looked genuinely hurt.

"I shot the damned Mexican in St. Louis in an alley when he pulled a big pig-sticker on me. I never said I kilt' him an' that's the truth, but I put a hole in him so big you could drive a wagon through, God-dammit."

Cecil stood up and faced Tom. Both men were fuming. Huck knew that they would come to blows at any second and he didn't feel all that well enough to try to pull them apart. He stood up and started lurching towards them.

"Why don't you both quit this fussin' and try to figure out what we should be doin' next. Great blazes, try usin' your heads instead of yer' mouths," Huck shouted. He walked crablike in an unsteady gait over to the window and flung the window open.

The cold air that washed over his face made his eyes pop open. Directly below the window, Huck spotted Ted Doudlass. He was surrounded by a large group of men, which included Lehigh and Pete. Ted's arms were bound and he had been beaten badly. Coolie, the owner of the livery stable, had a pistol pointed at his head. At the sound of the window being opened, Ted had looked up. In that one moment, Ted had spotted Huck.

"They hurt me real bad, Huck. I'm sorry," Ted said quickly.

Huck's heart nearly stopped beating as it fell into the pit of his stomach. The group of men looked up at the window to see who Ted had spoken to and saw Huck. They instantly started making for the backdoor of the hotel. Lehigh grabbed Ted and swung him behind a large oak tree. Coolie smashed Ted with the butt of his pistol and Ted fell on his face without making a sound.

Huck ducked away from the window. His startled and horrified expression made Cecil and Tom fly to the window. They could hear the sound of many angry voices and heavy footsteps entering the hotel. They watched as Lehigh drew his boot back and kick Ted squarely in the face. Lehigh saw them and waved.

"Good morning, cupcakes. Fine day for a killin', wouldn't you agree? Your shaky pissy friend here told us quite a little story," he said as he swung his foot and delivered another savage kick to Ted's face.

"Quite an interesting one at that. It was slightly different than the one you boys had told me. Coolie spotted Ted, here, tryin' to leave." He grinned lewdly at them.

"We had to break a few bones and fingers before he told us the truth," Lehigh shouted. Pete howled in glee and ran to the backdoor of the hotel. Lehigh pointed to the man that stood by his side.

"Boys, this is the fella' that I wanted you to meet. Boys, meet Captain Henry Fowler, of the Kansas Free State Militia. The man who is going to send all of you to hell today." Lehigh blew them a kiss perversely and then, grinning wickedly, patted his own backside.

"Kiss your ass, goodbye, boys," he shouted.

Henry Fowler smiled as he watched their terrified expressions.

"So, you Missora' scum have thought to come and try to steal from God's elect?" he boldly yelled.

"Have you come to take spoil and plunder?" Henry's face contorted in anger and turned purple.

"I shall drive hooks in your jaws, you evil doers, and thou shalt be dragged by them and taken to the bottomless pit where you will burn in hell for all eternity. Today, you shall be taken down to Hades where you will roast in the flames of hell. You will become the whores of Satan, you sodomites. Thou shall lay in the outer darkness and knash your teeth and suffer the pangs of eternal damnation," he screamed. Lehigh grinned nastily.

"Amen to that, Captain," he shouted. "And now, without further ado, let the dance begin."

The group of men that had remained with Lehigh and Fowler below the window took this as their signal to fire and all twelve rifles let loose at once. Huck, Tom, and Cecil dove to the floor as bullets poured through the framed window by the bucketful.

The room splintered and shook from the impact of the devastating fire. Huck crawled over to the bed he had been sleeping in and pulled a pistol from beneath it.

"Fats in the fire," he screamed above the roar of the gunfire to his friends. "Let's git."

Huck began to crawl to the door. He crouched low and kicked the door open. The hallway was filled with men who were as surprised as he was when he staggered, tripped and fell through the doorway, all the while firing wildly. He resembled a puppet with cut strings as he quickly fired. He fired as rapidly as he could thumb the hammer of his pistol. He twisted and crouched and slammed from wall to wall.

The men in the hallway were too bunched together for any of his shots to miss. All six shots struck six different men. Tom and Cecil dove through the doorway firing as well. In a matter of seconds, the group in the hallway had been reduced to dead and dying men. Coolie had been one of the last ones up the steps. Cecil fired and Coolie was hit in the chest. The blacksmith raised his revolver and attempted a last desperate shot at Huck and missed him by an inch. Tom aimed and sent a bullet through Coolie's brain, killing him instantly.

Huck rolled to his back and started reloading as Cecil ran to the top of the stairwell at the end of the corridor. Two steps below him stood Pete with a shotgun leveled at him. Cecil dove in a vain attempt to escape the blast of the deadly weapon. The blast tore Cecil's leg almost in half. He collapsed in a crumpled mass and Pete charged up the remaining steps. Pete stopped and fired the other barrel into the back of Cecil's head creating a fist-sized hole in Cecil's skull. Cecil's body convulsed once and then stretched and was still.

Pete momentarily stopped to witness Cecil's death throes and the physical ruin that he had caused. In that one lapsed second of judgment, Tom and Huck had time to train their weapons at him. Pete's eyes rounded in fear and surprise. The two pistols were aimed right at his head. In Pete's mind's eye, they were as big as canons.

"Only two shots to a double barrel, lard ass," Huck hissed. Pete's eyes shifted to the stairway behind him and then they darted back to Huck.

"I know you're fast, and I know what you're thinkin' fat man. But you ain't as fast as a bullet. Now, drop the shotgun," Huck said defiantly. Pete dropped the shotgun and raised his hands in the air.

"Turn and face the wall," Huck shouted. Pete did as he was ordered. Tom ran over to Cecil and turned him over on his back. Cecil's face was gone. Tom gagged and leaned against the wall. He picked Cecil's revolver from the floor and began to load it. His shaking hands made the job almost impossible. Huck shouted to Tom.

"He's dead?"

Tom could only nod his head.

"Keep Pete covered. I got me an idea."

Tom pointed the pistol at the fat clerks head and cocked Cecil's revolver. He slowly raised himself from the floor. He was shaking badly. He positioned himself away from anyone who may have been in the lower hallway. Huck staggered back to the room and crawled to the window.

"Hey Lehigh, can you hear me?" Huck shouted. "I got somethin' of yours. I got Pete," Huck yelled loudly "I got him in all his fat stinkin' glory and he's hale and hearty. You listenin? I said I got your fat darlin' baby boy. There's a bunch of your friends layin' out in the hall. Some of them are in dire need of a doctor."

Silence followed. Huck crawled back to the doorway to see how Tom was faring with Pete. Satisfied, he turned and headed back to the window.

"What do you want, dead-boy?" Lehigh shrilled in a high unnatural voice.

"How about a little tradin'. An exchange of sorts. We give you Pete without a hair harmed on his fat head and you give us Ted. Let Ted git' our horses. Bring them out front. When we're safe out of town, we will drop your baby boy off at the edge of town. Whatt'a ya say? You got a lot of people up here bleedin' to death."

Again there was silence.

"Lookit, Lehigh. Your friends need help now," Huck yelled angrily. Below him, in the yard, he figured that Fowler and Lehigh were mulling over their options. Good, Huck thought, let them stew in their own juices for a while.

In the yard, Henry Fowler was outraged at the failure of the men that he had sent up into the hotel. They had stopped firing once they had heard the furious fire coming from the second floor. They had expected to see Coolie wave and give the signal that all of the boys were dead. Now, they watched Henry pacing back and forth. Henry stopped and leaned against a tree. Ted lay sprawled at his feet. Ten other men lay in various parts of the yard waiting for Henry's orders. Lehigh spoke after a few tense moments.

"Hank, Pete' is like my own son. If we give them what they want, we can always ride these amateurs down. Hell, you got the army here on your payroll. They ain't getting away. We can doctor their horses so they will drop after a few miles or so."

Henry said nothing.

Huck waited nervously for a response. Dust reflecting the light floated weightlessly in the air. The morning beams of light that carried them streamed through the many bullet holes in the wall.

"What about it, Lehigh. We ain't got all day. Your pals ain't gonna make it if you keep on dilly-dallyin," Huck yelled brashly.

Tom strained to hear a response but only heard silence and the slight whimpering of Pete. He looked about him at the twisted bodies strewn about in the hall.

Blood was everywhere. He slowly and absent-mindedly started counting them. He counted six bodies, one of which curiously, had a wooden leg. Blood soaked the shirt the man wore. A puddle was collecting beneath the one legged man. Tom watched his chest rising and falling. Tom was shocked at the age of the man. He looked old enough to be his grandfather. Pete tried to turn and face Tom.

"Don't you move," Tom said excitedly. He placed the pistol in Pete's ear as the fat man's arms shot back into the air.

"Step back a pace from the wall and then lean your head against it," Tom ordered. Pete complied and was soon awkwardly leaning against the wall with his hands still over his head.

"You try moving again, and I will blow a big hole in that gut of yours, you murderin' son of a bitch," Tom shouted.

Tom did not want Pete to see how badly he was shaking. He moved towards the tangle of bodies and started kicking pistols, shotguns, and rifles away from the wounded men. He looked into the wide-open eyes of Coolie. Tom could not resist staring at the wooden legged man.

Abruptly, the eyes of the wooden legged man popped open and looked directly at Tom.

"I was wonderin' when you were gonna take that precaution of roundin' up the guns. I bin' watchin' you. Git me a drink of water, sonny. I'm powerful thirsty," the old man croaked. Tom jumped away from the bloody figure on the floor.

"You hold on there, old timer," Tom stammered, "my friend is working things out right now with your people. There will be a doctor here in no time."

"I heard all of it," he smiled faintly. "Captain Fowler ain't gonna' exchange nobody. And he ain't gonna work out a deal with the likes of you two. He wants you dead, plain an' simple," Joshua said weakly. "And what Henry Fowler wants, Henry Fowler gets."

Tom glanced quickly at Pete. Pete had turned his head to better listen to their conversation. When Tom turned and looked in his direction Pete hurriedly buried his nose into the wall

"For Christ sakes get me some water," Joshua shouted loudly

"I ain't gut shot, I'm just half crazy from the thirst is all." He tried to sit up and failed. His head leaned against the wall.

"Sonny, you fellas' are all new to this killin' business. I know that fer' a fact. Your friend told us all about what made you come all the way here lookin' fer trouble." He turned his face towards the body of Cecil.

"Your friend over there is dead, ain't he?" he asked.

Tom looked at the ruined body of his friend.

"Yes," Tom said sadly, "he is all of that."

Pete again started in Tom's direction. Tom caught his movement and fired a shot that hit the wall only a few inches from Pet's head. Pete cringed and froze into place.

Tom shouted wildly, "The next time you move, fat boy, will be the last time you ever move. I will put one in you, I swear."

"Pete, don't jump around so much," Joshua said sternly. "He might kill you out of nerves and how am I gonna' explain that to Mason?"

Joshua looked about at the carnage that was around him.

"Coolie caught your friend tryin' to sneak away early this morning," Joshua said uneasily. A coughing spasm choked off his words as he struggled to continue.

"Pete and Lehigh didn't believe a word of what he was sayin' so they took him to see Captain Fowler. Your friend shit his pants when he found out who he was standin' in front of. By the time they got done with him, we knew the whole story. Nothin' like this has ever happened before. I mean, somebody comin' all the distance you boys did to try to get back at what the Captain done. He said he was gonna' make an example of you boys so that it will discourage anybody else from tryin' it ever again." Joshua stopped to catch his breadth. He raised a bloody finger and pointed towards Cecil's corpse.

"You boys all wanted revenge and you found it. You found it with pure damned dumb luck. The way that fella' came through that door crawlin' and a shootin' and bouncin' off the walls, why he was so unsteady nobody even came close to hittin' him. Pure dumb luck." Joshua again pointed with his gore-streaked hand towards another corpse.

"You see that fella' layin' over there with his brains fallin' out of his head? That there is Shorty Bowens. He's the man that kilt' yer auntie. He caved her head in with a cavalry saber." He stopped to watch Tom's reaction.

"He kilt her an' threw her down a well in the backyard, verdad amigo?"

Tom nodded slowly. Joshua grimaced in a losing battle with the pain that started to attack his senses. He groaned quietly.

"Pains a good thing. It means nothin' hit my spine. Sonny, I'm all shot to hell. How about gettin' me some water, pronto. It feels like I got all the dust of old Mexico down my throat."

"Who cut up on Sidney, the fella' who was nailed to the barn door?" Tom asked.

"That piece of work was a team effort. Lehigh shot and Fowler stabbed," Joshua said through clenched teeth.

"And I suppose you were just standing around reciting poetry when all this was happening?" Tom said sarcastically.

Joshua managed a slight laugh. He looked Tom directly in the eye.

"Boy, this killin' like that ain't my style. I was in the fight with Mexico, the war. I was with Ringgold's artillery battery. They called it flying horse artillery. I seen enough killin' to last a life time. Even got my leg shot off at Vera Cruz. No, sonny boy, I wasn't there fer the killin'. I was there fer' the stealin'. When all that was happenin', I was stealin' everything that wasn't tied down. All this foolishness about slavery, that's all politics. It don't mean doodily squat to me."

"You are one fine humanitarian," Tom spat.

"Oh horse shit. You fellas came all the way across Missouri to do the same to Henry Fowler, so please, don't be givin' me no lectures on right an' wrong I am far too old to listen to that shit from a pup your age. Just git' me some water."

Huck could hear a conversation out in the hallway. He watched the antics of Lehigh and Fowler through a bullet hole in the wall. Lehigh was waving his hands in the air and Fowler was rubbing at his chin hair. Although he could not hear what they were saying, he knew that it was a heated argument. That's when he heard the gunshot in the hall. He jumped a foot.

"Tom," he yelled, "what's goin' on?"

"Pete started actin' up. I'm keeping him honest."

Relieved with Tom's answer, Huck continued observing Lehigh and Fowler argue. He also counted the men hiding in the yard. Suddenly, Fowler drew his weapon and fired one shot into the prone body of Ted. Huck leaned against the wall in total disbelief at what he had just witnessed.

"Tom," he screamed, "Fowler just kilt' Ted."

Joshua looked at Tom, sensing the fear and pain in the younger man's face.

"I tolt' you that there ain't gonna be no exchanges. You boys asses are twistin' in the wind an' Henry ain't gonna' be satisfied until you are all dead an' safely buried," Joshua intoned in a lifeless way. His voice sounded as if it were coming out of a grave. Tom's mind was swimming away from him. He was almost frozen into immobility by the dead like way Joshua had spoken his words. Tom was almost scared to the point of not being able to reason, and Joshua could sense it. He knew all too well the signs that pointed to imminent collapse and the surrender of the will to live

Joshua could see it happening to Tom in stages. Tom had never experienced so much horror in so few minutes. Joshua hoped that Tom would soon become an apathetic lump of quivering jelly. He had all the symptoms. Joshua knew he had to try something, and fast. He felt himself bleeding to death.

Huck continued to watch the movements of the men below in the yard. Lehigh continued to gesticulate frenziedly while Henry did nothing. Apparently, Huck realized, the life of the hostage meant nothing to Henry. Huck knew instantly that the man would only be satisfied with their deaths. It was a sobering and distressing fact. Huck weighed his options, which actually did not amount to much. He had counted eight men with rifles, perhaps more. There were at least two missing that he could not see anymore. They would have shifted to the front door. The men in the backyard were waiting on the word of Henry Fowler to come rushing through the backdoor and finish them off.

If that's the way it was going to be, Huck thought, then so be it. Pap had always told him that he was going to come to a bad end and now, it would appear that Pap had been right. At least with a little luck and the correct windage, he could at least kill a man who seemed to love killing. Huck vowed to take Henry Fowler' with him when the time came. To do this, he would need a rifle. There were plenty of rifles in the hallway.

Keep it up, Huck thought. Keep on arguing for just a few more minutes with Lehigh. Huck started crawling out of the room. He was so intent on this single purpose that he never heard the sound the person made who had entered the room from a side door. A rifle butt crashed into the side of his head and then there was nothing.

"For the love of Mike, git' me a little water. Your time is up, Sonny. You gambled and lost. If you help me out, I'll tell Henry to go easy on you. Chances is that he'll just hang you if I say a good word fer' you. That's if I'm around to tell him. If I ain't, then old Henry will do with you what he told everybody he was gonna' do to you. It is not a pretty story, but it is all Henry. He intends to skin you alive and make ridin' gloves outt'n yer hides. That's after he breaks every bone in your body, mind you."

All the blood was gone from Tom's face. Joshua looked carefully at Tom's vacant stare. Tom was close to breaking. He was almost entirely out of it. Joshua hoped that Pete was picking up on this. If only Pete could see Tom's current state, then he thought he might still have a chance. But Pete, he realized, was as drained as Tom. Pete had his eyes closed and was holding onto the wall expecting to be shot at any moment. The floor down the hall creaked. He turned, expecting to see the other fellow. Instead, there stood Bella with a rifle pointed at the boy Joshua had been calling Sonny. Joshua's heart leaped in his chest.

Tom turned when he had heard the floor creak. He still had his pistol aimed at Pete. Expecting the figure to be Huck, he was horrified when he turned and saw that it was an Indian woman pointing a large caliber rifle at his head. He broke out in a sweat. He knew that the woman had him.

"I mean you no harm. You must believe this," the woman said.

"Huck," Tom shouted sharply.

Bella placed her index finger over her lips as a signal for Tom to be quiet. She made her voice sound as gruffly as she was able in an attempt to disguise her voice from Pete.

"Don't move," she said.

Tom was stymied by her words. His mind worked feverishly in an attempt to sort out what was happening. Pete tried again to look at Tom but he was discouraged from doing so when Tom jammed the pistol into his ear.

"This fella' is strong as an ox and quick as lightning. The minute this fella' thinks he has a chance of going for me, he will go for my throat and I don't like that proposition at all," Tom said.

Bella nodded. Keeping the rifle trained on Tom, she slowly approached him. Pete had his eyes held firmly shut. When she was within a foot of Tom, she quickly turned and slammed the rifle butt down on Pete's head. The effect was two-fold. Pete's bulbous head smashed into the wall, breaking his nose and he collapsed like a slaughtered bull at Tom's feet. Tom slowly lowered the pistol to his side. She lowered her rifle and checked on Pete. She was confident that he was out cold.

"I had to make sure. The fat one must not now it was me or he will cause many troubles. Your friend is in the other square circle place. I put him to sleep. I cracked him good in the head. I offer both you and your not so bright friend a deal. I will show you a way out, the way I came in. No one saw me come in. You must go so that the old one here does not die. If you stay here, Fowler and his killing men will come here and all of you here will die dead."

Bella leaned her rifle against the wall and began to check on Joshua's wounds. She did not like what she saw.

"I was at Fowler's house when they brought your friend in and beat him. His name was Ted. They did many bad things to him. They broke many fingers, and he told them everything. We do not have many time or the old man here will dead soon. Fowler knows where you come from. You cannot go home. He will kill you if you try. Fowler will soon tell all his killing men to come in here shooting. He cares nothing for the lives of the men here. He will wait for night. By that time, the old one will be stiff as a boot and cold like a stone."

Tom listened. He desperately wanted to believe her.

"If you leave right now, maybe he will live."

"How do we get out of here?" Tom asked hurriedly.

"Down the stairs where Lehigh keeps the fire water there is a window. It is covered by many much broken boards and thin's there. Outside the window there is a ditch. No one can see if you crawl low. It takes you to the road. At the end, I put your horses. I know this because before I worked for the crazy woman of Fowler, I worked here."

Tom momentarily became suspicious.

"Why do you tell me this? Why should I believe you? How do I know that as soon as we get in that ditch every gun that Fowler has don't cut us down?" Tom asked warily. Bella's stare became icy.

"I could have dead you many times where you stood, stupid boy. I don't do this for you. I do it for him. The old one-legged man is a good man. He was a brave warrior a long time ago. I am a Navaho. Many years ago, Mexican soldiers made dead my family. The Mexican soldiers are bad men. The one legged man dead many Mexican soldiers in a big war. He has told me many stories about that war. The Mexican soldiers are bad people. They are like Fowler and like you. I know why you came here. When I heard, I said to myself what stupid boys. You must be much crazy. You know nothing about making people dead. You don't know that Fowler has many killing men with him. Henry pays the army many money to be safe. That is why your friends are dead and if you don't do what I say, you will dead too. And so will Joshua and he does not deserve to die by the actions and greed of stupid boys. That is why I tell you this. If you leave now, I maybe can make him not dead tonight. But as long as you stay here, he will dead. All of his blood is coming out."

What she had said convinced Tom to trust her. Hope started to flare again in his mind. He looked down at Joshua who was smiling up at him.

"Ain't some women grand," he sputtered.

"Lady you just sold a horse. Help me get Huck to his feet...no, better you get some water for the old man, but be careful. Don't let anyone see you," Tom said excitedly.

"Get your friend. Do not worry. Henry's killing men are all cowards. They are all as scared as you are. They keep their bellies low to the dirt like the snakes they really are. That is why I could come in and not be saw by them."

Tom walked rapidly to the room and found Huck sprawled out on the floor. He bent low and checked the damage that her blow had caused and found it to be minimal. There was a knot on the side of his head, however the skin was not even broken. Tom began to shake him roughly. Just as he was about to slap him, Huck's eyes opened and began to roll around in a way that frightened Tom.

"Huck," he whispered, "come out of it, ya' hear. Wake up, damn it." Tom continued to shake him and he started to make curious and strange noises. Tom placed his hand over his mouth. Finally, Huck began to come to his senses. He stopped moaning when he recognized Tom.

"Tom am I kilt'? Tell me the truth," Huck asked in a frightened voice. He felt at his head expecting to find a bullet hole. He was amazed when he looked at his hand and did not see blood or brain matter.

"No, you ain't killed. Not just yet. You just got lammed in the head by a Navaho woman," Tom said reassuringly. "How are you feeling?"

"I feel like I jest got lammed in the head by a Navaho woman. How else am I supposed to feel?"

"That's good enough for me. C'mon and get up, we're getting' out of here," Tom said with as much authority that he could muster.

"This Navaho woman is some woman. She snuck in here and lammed you in the head and then she went and got the drop on me. Are you all right? Stand still for a minute," Tom said.

Huck leaned against his friend and straightened up once he was in the hallway. His eyes rapidly adjusted to the light and he tried to avoid the carnage that he saw but couldn't. He noticed the Indian woman that Tom had spoken about sitting next to a bloody one legged man. She was administering to his wounds.

Tom whispered, "That's the woman I told you about. She says there is a way out of here through the downstairs where Lehigh keeps his whiskey. She says that there is a window that leads to a ditch. That ditch leads to the main road. She says our horses are tied up at the end of it. That ditch is hidden from view by anybody in the backyard but we got to keep low. That's how she got in here."

Tom watched as Bella lifted the old man's head so that he could drink. He gulped the water down.

"Why the hell is she willin' to help us?" Huck asked.

"She wants to save the old man," Tom replied quickly. "If we leave quick the old man might have a chance to git' some help. It looks like the only game in town."

"What are we doin' standin' around," Huck said. He bent over and drew a deep breadth.

"You all right for traveling?" Tom asked.

"Fit and dandy. If I had wings, I could fly," Huck replied. He watched as the Indian woman stood up and walked over to a man that was obviously dead. She quickly removed the man's shirt and began ripping the shirt into strips.

"Everyone here is now dead, except for Pete and Joshua. Pete will not remember who hit him, so he is no danger. I know that lout. He is even more stupid than your not so bright friend," Bella said. "Help me lift him so I can tie his wounds," she said.

Tom grabbed Joshua at the shoulders and positioned him so that he was sitting up. Bella poured a strange smelling concoction on his wounds and then began bandaging them.

"He has lost many much blood. This will stop all his leeks. Fowler is very powerful here and has many much friends in high power. He will not rest until you boys are in the earth." She ripped a shorter strip with her teeth and continued tending the older man. By now, Joshua was unconscious, his color bad. His breathing was labored, but steady.

"I tell you this. When you leave here, do not head for your home. Head south, south towards the Indian Nations, the territory. Fowler thinks you are stupid boys who will make a run for home. If you run for home, he will get the Army and his butcher boys and you will dead by tonight." She finished her work and examined Joshua. The bleeding had been contained.

"The wounds look angry. I think he will live, but he must see the white medicine man that carries a black bag and smells like whiskey all the time. Joshua is a tough old man. He really isn't that old, he just looks like it."

Satisfied, she stood up and began collecting rifles and ammunition. She checked the caliber of all the different rifles that she found and began to reload them. All the ammunition that she sorted she placed on a piece of shirt. She then re-wrapped all the different kinds in different pieces.

"South of here you will find Cherokee lake. You must remember. Follow the east shore of that lake. You will find many praying Indians there. They are my father's flock. It is where I was raised. The preacher there is a white man. He is my father. When I was little he took me into his family. From him, I learned the language of the whites and your ways. He is a good man. He was a Texas Ranger Tell him that Bella sends you to him. Tell him everything and do not leave anything from his ears. My father is not like other white men. He will help you, he will not judge you or hand you over to the bad people."

Bella tucked revolvers into both of their belts and stuffed ammunition into their shirt pockets.

"Do what I say and trust my father."

She gave Huck her rifle and a new Colt revolver.

"This pistol belongs to Joshua. See how new it is. He is many proud of it. He will not mind if I give it to you." Bella handed Tom another rifle.

"My father, his name is Reverend Harvey. He is the only man to trust. He has many much friends in Springfield. They will help you get to your California. Tell my father I will see him soon." Tom noticed that her eyes were misting up.

"I will let you have ten minutes, then I will shoot into the yard. That will keep them busy. When you hear this, ride like hell, as south and as fast as your horses can make. They look like very good animals. Don't stop for at least a whole day. If you have to, ride them until they drop dead. As long as Fowler is alive, there will never be a safe place for you in Kansas or Missouri."

"She's right," Huck said. "Henry Fowler is murderin' scum. He kilt' Ted like it was nothin'. We ain't got a choice. But I'll tell you one thing. Henry ain't gonna' get away with what he done to Ted or Sid or your auntie. If it takes me my whole entire life, I will kill Henry Fowler."

Bella interrupted quickly,

"Don't plan to live your life for revenge. Don't live for it or you will become as twisted as the thing you hate. Fowler will get what is his sooner or later. He has made many much enemies. Take what has happened to the many much dead men here and learn from it. See all this dead? They were all alive this morning, laughing and singing and living their lives. Now everything they had is gone. Go on and live your life and put death behind you. You both have many much living to do. Don't live with death for he is a bad companion. Live. You will be safe in the nations. Henry does not know anyone there, and he can be made dead like any man. He will never think you go there."

She checked the load of the rifle she held and began to walk towards a room that looked into the backyard of the hotel.

"Remember, I will start shooting in ten minutes. When you go downstairs, turn left. You cannot miss the window. Now go and have luck with you."

Huck was embarrassed at what he had said. He walked past Tom without looking at the woman.

"I'll go downstairs and check the front and the stairs," he muttered. "Don't take all day."

Tom watched as Huck cautiously moved down the stairwell and into the main hall of the America Hotel.

"I don't know what to say," Tom said meekly, "except thank you. I wish someday that I can repay you for what you've done for us today."

"Life is many much strange. Maybe someday you will," Bella said. She flipped her long black hair over her right shoulder and looked at Joshua lying peacefully on the floor. She walked into the room without looking back or saying another word. Tom rushed down the stairs. Huck was crouched near the desk. He pointed to the corridor that led to the basement and freedom. Tom went first, followed quickly by Huck.

The basement of the hotel was filled with trash and it was dark. Turning left, Tom saw the window and noticed the ditch that led out to the road. The hotel, apparently, had been built next to an old sunken road. Time had eroded it into a ditch. Bushes, broken bottles, old boards and other debris lined one side, the side that was nearest the backyard. Tom climbed through the window and started crawling as rapidly as he was able. He could hear Huck right behind him. After what seemed like an eternity of crawling, Tom stopped abruptly. True to her word, the horses were tied to a tree at the end of the ditch. All four animals were standing exactly where she had said they would be.

Huck nudged Tom with his rifle. Tom raised his index finger to his lips, trying to make Huck understand that they should wait. Huck impatiently fiddled with his rifle. Within a minute of his signal to Huck, shots rang out in the crisp afternoon air followed by a fusillade of gunfire. Tom stood up and streaked towards his horse with Huck following on his heels. He quickly freed the reins of two horses and was mounted in a blink of an eye. Looking at his friend only once to see his progress, Tom dug his heels into the side of the horse and he bolted down the road with the other animal in tow. Huck was right along side of him, heading south. Within a few minutes, they could not hear the sound of gunfire anymore.

CHAPTER EIGHT

Tom lay awake in Captain Cobb's tent staring at the seams in the canvass roof. Others in the tent slowly started to stir as the sounds of an army awakening manifested collectively in the pre dawn hours of the morning. Hacking and coughing noises from a thousand throats began to drown out the early call of wild birds. They chattered and sang to each other in the early dawn's light but could not compete with the volume of noise being produced by a half-conscious army corp. Tom stood up and stretched as he walked to the tent flap and pushed it open. Although the sun had not made its appearance, the early morning brought with it the promise of a sweltering afternoon. All of the men seemed to awaken at the same time. Years of exposure to the sounds of a camp coming to life had left its mark on all of them. No matter how exhausted they might be, once the huge anthill of a camp had been disturbed, there would be no further rest for any of them.

They were still individuals, each man distinctly different from the other; however the morning molded their differences into a sameness that bonded all of them together. Routine, the great common denominator of the infantryman, began to take over as they all stretched, yawned, and tasted the air of the new day. Soon, a thousand bladders would empty nearly in unison into latrines throughout the massive bivouac area.

The gray transitional period of night turning to day greeted Tom as he scratched his head and looked for a comfortable place to sit. Finding a suitable stump near the evening's old campfire, he had just started his downward descent when a loud voice interrupted him.

"Holt' on there. What the hell you think your doin' outside like this here? Get back inside."

Tom turned to see a Provost Marshall's guard with fixed bayonet a few steps to his left leveling his rifle at him.

"I got orders that none of you is to budge. Now git back inside if you know what's good fer you."

Tom sat down and stared down the line of tents to his front. The camp was already bustling with activity as men started to prepare fires for morning coffee.

"And I suppose that you will shoot me if I don't? Or maybe you'll just run me through on your bayonet there and pitch me into the woods so that the crows can pick my bones clean."

"Maybe," the guard said carefully and without emotion, "or maybe I'll jest point this rifle in the air and fire a shot off. My boys would be here faster than a jackrabbit, a swarmin' all over here testin' the thickness of yer' skull with a wooden baton."

Andy Barrett stepped out from the entrance of the tent and yawned in the guard's face. He had overheard their conversation.

"And jest who do you think you are talkin' to all high an'; mighty, friend?" Andy grinned widely. "This fella you jest finished threatnin' is an important man that caught hisself' a Yankee spy. He is goin' places, mister. Keep on talkin' unfriendly like to the wrong people and you might have yourself a short military career with the danged Provo's. Why hell, you might just find yourself thrown from their ranks and end up servin' with real soldiers that get' shot at, heavens forbid."

The guard shifted nervously on his feet. Corporal Cook suddenly appeared coughing heavily. He unbuttoned his trousers and lazily wandered off to attend to the needs of nature. Huck passed through the tent flap tucking his shirt into his pants. He eyed the guard with pure malice.

"Listen to old Andy there, fella. He is the wisest man I know. The man is a sage. Try some manners and loosen your bowels. You seemed to be all bound up," he said.

Ed had followed Huck out of the tent and encountering the edgy guard, pushed his bayonet aside and followed Arthur Cook. The guard looked at the enormous arms of Ed Bolls and swallowed nervously. Corporal Cook had stopped a few yards away and was laughing loudly. He unbuttoned his fly and urinated into the company road.

Smoke from hundreds of small fires added their haze to the morning mist. A quartermaster's wagon rolled slowly towards them, its driver slouched over and apparently still asleep.

"Take that old boy on this wagon," Huck said. "He's got his orders, but you don't see him all bound up and tryin' to make life complicated fer' somebody, do you? Of course not.. You could take a lesson in life from that old boy. Even write books an' sich on it, once yer' perfected it. You could call it, "How I Learned to Loosen My Bowels an' not be a Pain in the Ass For All Concerned."

"I don't give a damn. Now git back in that tent, all of you."

The guard was seething in rage.

"I swear, If'n you all don't do like I sez, by God, I'll drop one of you," he snarled.

"Will you kindly quit yer barkin' an' sit yer dog down," Arthur said, buttoning his fly.

112

"You don't want to shoot nobody and you ain't gonna' neither. I'm gonna' go see what I can scrounge up. Nathan never found that mess of sluice I had fixin' in the tent. I'm damned hungry. Tom, git' a fire started. Andy, you go fetch wood. Ed, tell Nathan where I be. I'll be back quick. I'll get the coffee pot an' the pan an' the cups. I'll even get the real coffee you got stashed."

Corporal Cook began walking down the road. He caught up with the slow rolling wagon and sat on the open backboard. He waved a hearty farewell at the Provost guard.

"I'll be right back," Arthur called. He waved again at the guard.

"And I'll be damned," the guard said softly. He lifted his rifle to his shoulder and calmly aimed at the bobbing figure of Arthur Cook. He pulled back the hammer and slowly began to squeeze the trigger. Huck pushed the barrel of the rifle down as Ed Boll's delivered a shocking blow to the very startled Provost Guard's chin. He sagged as his knees buckled. For one second the guard's mouth opened as if he were about to say something. Then his eyes closed and he fell hard on his back.

They all stood over the unconscious man. Tom bent over and retrieved the rifle. He was amazed that the rifle was primed and loaded, ready to fire.

"Where the hell do they get fellas like this clown? He was actually going to shoot Arthur. I can't believe it."

"Is he still breathin'?" Andy asked.

Huck bent down and checked the fallen man. Ed had hit the man just above the man's eyetooth. Except for an insignificant red mark, there was not a mark on the man.

"You do good work, Ed. Remind me in the future not to trifle with you. Did you all see the look on his face jest' before he keeled over? It was like his brain had taken a trip from his body. Like it jest' took off. The man is out.'" Huck stood up and patted Ed on the shoulder. John Hubert nudged the man with his foot.

"We had best git' him bucked and gag," he said. "When he comes to, he's gonna' be madder'n hell."

"If Ed had not hit the son-of a bitch, Arthur would be a dead man," Tom said, 'and I'd never be able to collect that bet that I'm going to win from him."

"I wisht' that you hadn't made that bet. It ain't like you to throw money away like that. That's usually bin my job. Must be the lump that Yankee spy fetched you that made you a little addled still."

Huck reached for his knife. He quickly removed the belt the man was wearing and cut the leather into strips which he then used to tie the man's feet and wrist. He worked quickly. Andy ripped the man's sleeve from his jacket and cut it in two with Huck's knife. He balled one of the pieces up and placed it in the man's mouth. The other strip he used to wrap around the man's mouth. He pulled on it tightly. They then dragged the man into the Captain's tent. Tom started a smoky fire and they sat and waited for the corporal's return.

The gray-blue of early morning surrendered to the coming day. Small knots of men went about preparing breakfast. George Blakely and Thornton Dean took turns watching the fire while Pete Wilson and John Hubert lost themselves in a game of poker. Huck and Tom sat as lookouts. Huck pointed to a figure heading their way.

"Look. It's Higgins. Looks like he's totin' somethin'," Huck said.

Corporal Higgins huffed his way towards them. In his arms he carried a box .He dumped it at their feet. He mopped at his sweating brow with a rag.

"I figured you boys would be hungry so I went back and picked these things up."

Huck dug into the cracker box and found fatback and hardtack crackers wrapped in brown paper. He pulled out their battered coffeepot and tossed it to Ed. The frying pan was next and he flung it at Andy Barrett.

A flurry of activity began over the rush to make breakfast. Something seemed odd to Corporal Higgins as he looked at them preparing their meal.

"Where's Arthur?" Nathan asked.

"He went back to our bivouac to git all this, but you beat him to it," Andy blurted out.

Corporal Higgins looked about for the Provost guard. Tom took Nathan by the arm and began to calmly explain to him what had just occurred. Nathan, smiling, listened carefully. When Tom had finished, Nathan's face took on the appearance of a very pained sort. He ran to the tent and emerged a second later with a very sick look etched upon his normally sedate features.

"Jesus H. Christ," Nathan said softly, looking around to see if there were any witnesses to the crime that were still around.

"You can't go cold cockin' Provo's. Didn't anybody tell you that? Do you know what trouble you can cause by doin' somethin' as stupid as thi...Holy Hell." Nathan was lost momentarily for words. His face blanched.

"You people is worst than a pack of deranged youngin's what aint got a lick of sense between them runnin' wild.' He paused and took a deep gulp of air.

"If them other Provo's come back lookin' to relieve our friend here and find him out cold and trussed up the way you got him, they will bust your ass in a dozen places. You got to git' him out of the tent. Take him a few rods into the woods there and cover him good. Don't let nobody see you do it. Cover him with a blanket and drag his ass out the back, ya hear?"

They all nodded.

"You all is like a disaster waitin' to happen. You got yourself a bomb sittin' right there in the tent. I will go find Vernon. He'll know what to do. And if you see Arthur, you tell him to stay here and not get lost again," he said frantically.

A beating drum signaled roll call. Corporal Higgins walked hurriedly away from them and soon was out of sight. John rapidly walked over to the tent to figure the best way to get the man into the woods and safely away from prying eyes. Roll call would give them the perfect opportunity because companies would be forming and less people would be about. He rushed back to the group looking frantic.

"He's gone," John cried.

"He's dead?" Andy asked, completely unnerved by John's sudden announcement.

"No, yer' fool. He's gone. He chawed right through the belt he had around his wrists like a rat," John wailed.

They all rushed in a stampede towards the tent to find it empty. Ed did not like this turn of events at all.

"That rat went back to git his brother rats," Ed said.

"Look," Pete said, "he lit out of here so fast that he didn't bother to even take his rifle."

"Them boys will be hot when they get here," George Blakely said. "I don't want to be around here when they do. Them boys shoot first and ask questions later."

"We should go back to the company area," Ed whispered, "there's safety in numbers. If we wait around here they will come an' lower the boom an..."

"What the hell are you whisperin' for?" Vernon said loudly.

They had not noticed him in the rush for the tent. He looked at the worried expressions on their apprehensive faces.

"Somebody want to tell me what's going on?" he asked. "Y' all look like somebody buggerd yer' pet goat."

"Arthur left the tent to go back to our area so he could git' some vittles. The Provo was settin' his sights on him. He was surely gonna' shoot Arthur. Ed knocked the guard out so we tied him up an' put him in the tent here. Only thing is that he chawed his ropes an' lit out of here an' is probably headin' this way at the moment with a passel of very perturbed Provo's," George said.

"Arthur went back to git sluice he was makin'," Andy said.

"Sluice ain't worth getting killed over," Vernon replied." Didn't you all see Higgins? He was supposed to bring you your things."

"Yassuh," Pete responded, "but by the time he got here, the guard was tied up already. We tolt' him about what happened an' he went to find you."

Vernon shook his head.

"Report to roll-call as usual with the exception of Finn and Sawyer. All of you, git'."

Andy Barrett let loose a shout of relief. He began to stamp out the morning's small fire with his worn out boots. He, as well as all of the others, were overjoyed that a semblance of normalcy was returning to their day. Andy was so busy stamping out the fire that he momentarily forgot just how paper-thin the soles of his boots were. He howled in pain when the embers burned through them and scorched his naked feet. He fell down and flung his boots off.

Thornton poured the remaining coffee into a cup and downed it quickly. Ed Bolls placed the cooking items in the cracker box and scurried down the road. Andy put his boots back on waved at Huck and Tom before turning and running after Ed.

"Let me handle everything when they git here," Vernon said quietly. "Don't open your mouths. All I want you to do is look important. Look arrogant if you can, but keep yer mouths shut."

Within a few minutes, trouble arrived in the form of ten very angry Provost Guards. All were heavily armed and extremely agitated. They lifted their rifles altogether like a firing squad and aimed at Tom and Huck.

"Are these the fellas what hit you, Bill?" one of the guards spoke.

"Not all of them, but they'll do fer starters." The man that Ed had struck approached Sergeant Jenkins. Vernon walked a few steps towards the angry man that the guard had called Bill.

The guard pointed his rifle at Vernon.

"Out of the way, Vernon. I'm placin' these two under arrest. They are gonna learn damned quick that you can't put yer hands on a provost guard of the Army of Northern Virginny, by God."

"I'm afraid I can't let you do that," Vernon said softly. "These men are staff, headquarters staff. They got orders that come right from Corp headquarters to report there directly. In fact, Second Virginia Cavalry is supposed to escort them. I'm expecting them to get' here any minute."

"I'll only tell you one more time, Vernon. Git' out of my way," Bill shouted.

"And I'll tell you only one more time. Do not interfere with this. Let it go. If you have trouble with this, then I suggest that you have a little chat with Captain Cobb. I suggest that you explain to him how you were going to shoot one of his men and why one of them was able to cold cock you and truss you up like a damned old turkey."

Vernon stepped up to the taller man and looked him directly in the face. His quick eyes scrutinized the man. He leaned forward and whispered in his ear.

"It would be kinda' embarrasin' to have to explain to the Captain how you let one man git' away and how the others were able to parlay you senseless. Cobb is the kinda' man that doesn't tolerate failures. He's one of those Tidewater planters. He kin' git' real nasty when he doesn't git his own way, and what he wants now is for these fellas' to report to Corp Headquarters right away."

The guard began to lick his lower lip. Vernon stepped away from him slightly.

"You are relived from this Post, anyway, as of this moment. That means you ain't got a lick of authority here no more. Captain's orders. Now, why don't you go and try doin' something useful for a change, like guardin' a latrine."

The guard was seething once again.

"One of these days, Vernon,' he said angrily.

"Don't hold your breath waiting for it. Now git', before I rip yer damned head off and kick it back to that shithole you crawled out of, ya damned rube."

The Provost Guard glared at the regimental first sergeant. Jenkins smiled back at him. He stalked away followed by all the others. Tom and Huck watched the group disappear.

"There goes a sorry bunch of bastards. They look like soldiers, but they ain't worth spit," Vernon said. "Always stayin' in the rear where there ain't no fightin' an' breakin' the heads of those that do. Many a time I seen them crack a boys head wide open when all the poor fella was doin' was lookin' fer' shot." Vernon straightened his regulation kepi on his head.

"One time, durin' the fightin' at Gaines Mill, we began to run low an' so we sent this boy back to the rear to tell somebody of our predicament. The Provo's stop him an' claimed he was skedadiling. They wouldn't even give him a chance to explain. They wopped him in the head put him in chains. We waited an' waited. Finally we ran out of shot an ended up throwin' rocks at the damned Yankees. We were forced to withdraw. If they had listened to him instead of bustin' his head open an' that boy had got back unmolested, there would be a lot of good fellas' alive today. Them Yankees poured it on when we started to withdraw. We had to run fer our lives. A hundred men got kilt' just tryin' to disengage from the action that day. I knew most of them. That's why I give the Provost guard fellas hell every chance I git."

"I do believe that fella would have shot Cook," Tom said.

Vernon nodded.

"I have no doubt about that," he said. The sergeant's attention was elsewhere, focused now on the volume of activity all around him as tents started coming down and regiments in formation moved steadily along the road. Rank after rank marched by, a sign that a large move was underway. The columns of men was unceasing. The sleepy wagon driver who had passed earlier was seen to be returning, but this time he drove his wagon on the side of the road. Corporal Higgins sat next to him and when he recognized Vernon, he bounded off the wagon and ran towards him in relief. Before he could say a word, Vernon raised his hand.

"Don't worry, Nathan. It's all taken cared' of so don't go troublin' yourself. Did you find Arthur?"

"I sure did. I passed the rest of the bunch on my way here. I left Cook with the Lieutenant," Nathan said, still unsure of the situation. He looked about nervously. The wagon driver drew up alongside them and slowly stepped down. He walked with a limp and in passing them did not acknowledge their presence and started to load the Captain's belongings in the rickety wagon.

"What happened with the Provo's, Vernon?" he asked.

"I persuaded them to see reason. Like I said, don't be concerned anymore. They realized that they had bit off more than they could chew.'

Nathan still looked bewildered.

"Sawyer and Finn are going to be paraded down to headquarters to have a nice talk with some important people. They are gonna' have a very busy day."

The road was choked with men. The amount of soldiers moving along raised clouds of dust around their trudging feet.

"If that's the case then, I had better start takin' the Captain's tent down. I hope to speak with you later and find out how you persuaded that crowd. I will see you all bye and bye."

With that said, Nathan walked away and began to help the sloop shouldered limping man.

118

"Now that we got that mess all sorted out, there's something I must tell you. The lieutenant told me it this morning," Vernon said smiling, "something that I think that you will find truly interestin'."

Vernon waited for the suspense to build.

"Sergeant Rawlings, the very man that started this whole chain of events, has been transferred out of your company and right out of the whole regiment by none other than the good Captain Cobb. He is now attached with the medical corp. in the official role as hospital gravedigger. Permanently."

"I'll be hanged," Huck said.

Vernon let it sink in before continuing,

"The Lieutenant was right there when Cobb blasted Rawlings out good. He called Rawlings a liar an' just about every foul name under the sun. He reduced the man to tears. Rawlings is no longer Sergeant Rawlings but Private Rawlings."

"More of that irony," Huck said slowly.

"The Lieutenant said that Cobb was roaring like a fresh nutted bull," Vernon said. "All Rawlings could do was make quaking sounds like a duck."

Tom could not believe his ears. The man that had constantly caused him misery and belittled him was now forced into one of the most detestable jobs in the army. The only thing that could possibly be as bad was widening latrines and filling them in, a job usually reserved for Negroes. Huck was laughing loudly and holding on to a tree for support. It took several seconds for Huck to regain his composure.

"I knew that you would enjoy that little tale," Vernon said, "but now fer business. Cavalry will be comin to escort you to headquarters. That was no bullshit story I told to those Provo's. Cobb wants you there real quick. You are ordered to stay right here for them, God only knows when. This road is chokin' up pretty damned quick with infantry. Cobb will be there waitin' for you. Oh, I almost forgot…After, Finn is to report to Company H. Sawyer is taking Rawlings place. Any questions?"

The news hit them like a thunderbolt.

"Company H," Huck wailed, "I don't know that many fellas in Company H a 'tall. Well maybe a fella here or there b-but-but…"

Tom interrupted his friend in mid stutter.

"You mean they are going to split us up just like that?"

"Why sure," Vernon replied, "Your Company would be too top heavy with sergeants. There is a need fer' a sergeant in Company H. Eli Spivey, the old sergeant of Company H, got discharged because he got shot at Chancellorsville. Eli was a damned good man. You got some big shoes to fill, Huck. The Captain feels you can do it and so do I. I talked to all of the sergeants in Company H about you. Don't worry, you'll do fine."

"Tom an' I 'jined up together. We've been together through all this since the campaignin' on the Peninsular. For heavens sake, we are from the same place in Missouri. I've known Tom most of my life. They can't jest' split us up like this."

"They can and they did. I think I know how you feel." Sergeant Jenkins took off his kepi and wiped his brow with the back of his hand.

"Most," he said sadly, "of the fellas' that I jined' up with way back in 61 are spread out pretty good. I bin' in this war since First Manassas. Those fellas' that are still above ground and in the army are all scattered throughout the Army of Northern Virginia, what with promotions and the like. The Army don't like to take a man out of his regiment, but they will if they have a need. One small consolation is that at least you're still in the same regiment. There ain't nothin' that can be done about it. I'm sorry fellas'."

Vernon placed his cap straight on his head. He looked up at the sky.

"It's gonna' be a steamer today. Take it easy fer' now. Sit under the trees. Git' some sleep while you can. Remember though, don't go wanderin' off or you may find yourselves diggin' bone pits with ole Rawlings there."

He smiled, turned and walked back to the road. He was soon swallowed up by the mass of bodies that continued to march by in a seemingly endless line. Huck sank to the ground with his back to a tree.

"The onliest' person I know good in Company H is Lawson Dunn what kin' be trusted and that boy is too card crazy fer my likens'. They are mostly people I might have peeped from time to time, but mostly they be strangers."

Huck was both disappointed and lost for words. Tom sat down next to him with his back to the tree and removed his jacket. He turned it inside out and then preceded to crack body lice he found in the seams with his thumbnails.

"Once more across the ballroom floor," Tom said to himself.

Huck did not like this unexpected turn of events. Routine made life comfortable. It was a friend that one could cling to in times of danger. Friendship meant life itself. Familiarity with routine could be worn like a suit of armor. It insulated and protected a man. Being new in a strange company did not set all that well with him and his belief in his chances of survival. Perhaps there would be people there who would resent his new found status. Perhaps he would be viewed as a foreign interloper.

Huck watched the columns of men streaming northward. There was no doubting that a huge movement was starting. The signs of a coming major campaign were irrefutable. Once again, he felt himself being drawn into and committed to organized chaos of the type he knew was going to be colossal. He felt betrayed by the bad timing of a start to a campaign. It would be starting soon.

Huck could tell just by the actions of those soldiers passing by. Row after row and in rank after rank, the sign of imminent strife was stamped on their faces and reflected in their actions. The veteran soldiers would mask their anxiety by bravado and loud bragging talk. The inexperienced men hid their uncertainty and fear with nervous laughter and foolery. After a while, it would all become contagious, infecting and spreading like a virus throughout the entire Second Corp.

Officers would try to stop it, but the wise ones let it alone. Any serious attempt to instill normal discipline would always fail no matter what was tried. Huck supposed it was simply part of human nature; all of the loud talking and wisecracking that went on at the start of a campaign strangely was consistent. He knew it would stop once they were engaged with the Army of the Potomac.

Officers that were not appreciated all that well were the chief recipients of this unruly behavior. Huck remembered the officer who had stood by the side of the road when the campaign in Maryland had begun. The officer was a martinet who was a stickler for rules and regulations.

The officer had a large moustache that took up over half his face and wore a large broad-hat so that all that could be seen of his face were his eyes and his huge bushy moustache.

Voices from the rank and file started beseeching the man to come out from under the squirrel tail that he had on his face. Hundreds of voices had picked up the chant, imploring the unfortunate officer to refrain from eating squirrel head first in the near future. Others shouted that he should pick his teeth to remove the offensive squirrel tail and still others began urging him to stop eating other things in front of the unmarried men in public. Some of their jibes had become quite rude indeed. The officer had gone scarlet in the face, that what could be seen, but had endured their abuse like a true stoic.

"I thought with all of the Captain's hurrah that he was fixin' to give us a furlough," Huck said dejectedly.

"A furlough?" Tom said incredulously, "Just where did you plan on going if he did give us one. Were you plannin' on goin' back home?"

Tom laughed bitterly and continued on his quest for more lice hidden in the seams of his jacket.

"You would have Union maniacs like Fowler chasin' you down for sport. They would stretch your neck right on Main Street. The last letter that I got from Becky says that the town is crawling with Union men. She said it's all changed. People that we knew back home are the minority now or have had to leave. The Yankees chase them out, right out of town. Home is out."

Huck knew that Tom was right. Going home was impossible. Home was solidly in Union hands and Federal authority held sway. These people in control did not take lightly to friends and families of southern soldiers. They openly persecuted all Southern sympathizers at every possible opportunity. Huck felt badly about all the people that he knew that lived in Clay County. It was a partisan war that was being conducted there by believers in The Cause.

Irregular bands of Southern cavalry used hit and run tactics against the Union forces and were usually protected by the local inhabitants of the area. The sympathetic civilian population that aided these bands of partisans paid a heavy price in burned farms and dead sons. The enemy did everything in its formidable power to eradicate these thorns in their side, including the use of fire. Whole areas were free killing zones and scorched earth policies were the norm.

Missouri was, for all intents and purposes, lost to the South. The irregular Southern cavalry bands were looked down upon by the aristocratic leadership in Richmond. The entire Kansas-Missouri imbroglio had forever soured the opinion of Virginia's proud sons towards this facet of the war. Missouri had become too ugly, dirty, and unproductive to merit any more serious attention. In the East, all eyes were focused on another western area. Vicksburg,

Mississippi was often associated with the idea of a pin that linked the two halves of the Confederacy together and a monumental struggle was underway there to hold on to the city. Holding on to the city meant that the Mississippi River was not lost. Missouri was relegated to the position of an ugly stepchild.

However, things out west were not developing along the lines that Richmond had hoped for. Federal forces were strangling Vicksburg. While the war in the Eastern Theater of operations rolled along on greased tracks, it always seemed that the West was always teetering on the brink of disaster.

General Sterling Price had been driven out of Missouri. General Johnson had bled to death at Shiloh after having his army buckled, shredded, and mauled. Tennessee was a disaster. The Cherokee Nation had sided with the South and had been throttled by the neck at the battle of Pea Ridge.

Fighting continued in Missouri, but Huck knew in his heart that home was not possible. There would be no furlough. He would have to see the war out. One way or the other, it was the only path home. He would remain and fight, but now he would be fighting with strangers. It worried him. He stretched out on the grass and closed his eyes. The heat acted as a narcotic and soon he drifted off into a troubled sleep.

He awoke to the feel of Tom's shoe in his side.

"Come on, Huck. Our rides here," Tom said. Huck stretched and looked about him. He was covered in sweat. Standing next to Tom was a very stern looking cavalryman, a corporal. His boots were so polished the daylight reflected on them like mirrors. He had the reins of three horses in his hands and his handlebar moustache gave him a fierce appearance.

"Sergeants Sawyer and Finn. I am to escort you to Corp Headquarters. Sergeants, if you will mount up, we will be off. The road is full of traffic and the sooner we start, the better."

The ride to the headquarters was uneventful except for the many delays. The road was full of men, wagons, artillery caissons, and riders were everywhere .It was time consuming as they wound their way past thousands of marching men. An army on the move was impressive in the amount of dust it was able to produce. Before long, they were all covered in a light dust. They rode along for hours and paused to let Artillery batteries pass countless times. They rode for most of the day.

As daylight started its retreat, they finally stopped at a well-kept brick house. A guard detachment on picket challenged their approach. The cavalry corporal produced his orders and they proceeded towards the front of the home. Magnolias blossomed around the porch. Staff officers were coming and going into the building like bees in a hive. Many of them wore ostrich plumes in their hats and wore high boots that ended past their knees.

They dismounted and attempted to shake off some of the dust that had accumulated during the long ride but it stubbornly clung to them. Huck removed his slouch hat and used it to bang off some of the particles that had adhered to his face. Captain Cobb had spotted their arrival from the parlor and swiftly made his way over to them.

So here you are," he said excitedly.

Tom and Huck saluted which the Captain entirely failed to return.

"Boys, I have a surprise for you…in fact it will be your honor. General Stuart himself wishes to converse with you directly. I have it on good information that General Longstreet is coming up from Fredericksburg and should be here tomorrow. Now boys, don't be nervous. Just tell the truth and shame the devil."

Cobb pulled a pocket comb from his tunic that was inlaid with Mother of Pearl and started combing Huck's stringy hair back from his forehead like a proud and

123

fussing father. Tom looked on in embarrassment. Captain Cobb spit into his hand and attempted to slick a stubborn cowlick into submission. Satisfied with his handiwork, he then turned to Tom.

"Sergeant Sawyer, please remove your hat. Corporal, give the sergeant here your regulation head-piece, if you would be so kind, sir." Cobb reached out his hand for the corporal's regulation kepi from the dismounted cavalryman. The man handed it over to the Captain with a curious look. The Captain placed Tom's worn brown slouch hat on the confused cavalry corporal.

"Don't you fret any, my good man. The sergeant is merely borrowing your hat. He will return it straight away. He must look presentable for his meeting with the General."

Captain Cobb stepped back and appraised both of his men. Tom had taken the regulation piece and had placed it on his head feeling awkward and tense. Cobb buttoned first Huck's tunic and then Tom's jacket right up to the last button. He removed a handkerchief, spit into it and began to wipe the dirt and grime off of Huck's dust begrimed face.

"Corporal, swift as you can. Give me your canteen," Cobb ordered. The corporal accommodated his wish. Cobb motioned for the corporal to spill some on his handkerchief, which he did. Cobb worked much of the filth from Huck's face. As he turned to prepare to do the same to Tom, a Major disturbed the Captain's concentration.

"I take it that these are your men?" the major asked.

"Yes sir," Cobb said readily. The major grinned warmly at all of them.

"Very well then. Men, if you would follow me," he said. The major started to walk towards the steps of the house.

"Here we go boys," Cobb said dramatically. He began to strut like a peacock towards the stairs with his head held high in the air when suddenly the major stopped dead still. He turned slowly towards the Captain and whispered ever so slightly into his ear.

"Captain, I hope you are not offended, but the General wishes to speak to the men in private. I assure you, sir, it does not reflect at all on how the General feels about your contribution to the matter that is currently at hand. He has nothing but the highest regard for you, Captain. You must understand that with what you have brought to his attention that he will be very busy. He has informed me that he will have a private meeting with you and your Colonel in the very near future. I would not be surprised, sir, that you would not be soon attached as a staff officer to this Corp's Headquarters. I believe he is of the mind to recommend you for promotion."

124

Cobb's face brightened as he snapped to attention. The Major doffed his hat gallantly to the swelling Captain and motioned for Tom and Huck to follow him. They followed the Major up the stairs past strangely dressed cavalry officers who were decked out in capes and outlandish boots that ended past their knees. Colonels, Majors, and Captains made room for them as they filed into the living room of the splendidly furbished brick house. Tom and Huck gawked at the opulence surrounding them.

Seated at a large antique mahogany and teakwood table sat none other than the scourge of the Federal Cavalry in Virginia, the man that had dashed Federal aspirations of victory asunder and had embarrassed them for many years. General Stuart epitomized to the South the notion of a perfect cavalier and looked every inch the image of one.

He rose to greet them and as he did so the buzz of conversation stopped immediately. Both Huck and Tom snapped to attention and froze like statues. The buttons on the General's tunic shone like lights.

"Are these the two men that found the map?" the General asked as he returned their salute.

"Yes sir," the Major said, amused at the statues that he had in front of him.

"Excellent. Major, if you would clear the room. This shall not take but a moment. I wish to speak in private to these soldiers."

"Certainly, General Stuart."

The major saluted and approached a young Brigadier General and whispered into his ear. The youthful General discreetly waved his hand towards himself and strode out of the room followed by every man in the room. The Major saluted General Stuart, clicked his heels, and closed the door to the room. The sound of his heels clicking sounded like a gunshot to the two frozen soldiers. They had never seen so many men of such high rank gathered together all in one place before in their lives and they were in awe. Neither had they ever been in the presence of a living legend.

General Stuart smiled at the two statues.

"For heavens sakes, boys, at ease. You boys stay like that, and you may hurt yourselves. I won't bite you, you know." He grinned and walked over to the table.

"Join me, if you will. Sit a spell with me." General Stuart motioned them towards the chairs surrounding the table. Tom moved towards the chairs and waited until the General had sat down and then he sat down. Huck did the same and watched in surprise as the General pulled out a packet of cigars wrapped in paper.

"Cigar?" he asked, offering them to the unnerved pair.

125

Tom reached for a cigar as the General placed his immaculate black boots on the top of the table and leaned back in his chair. He reached inside his tunic pocket for a match and struck it on the heel of his boot. It flared and he put it to the cigar and puffed, reading the expressions of the two. He offered the match to Tom as Huck took a cigar from him. Huck sniffed the cigar as the General handed him a match.

Huck struck the match on the seams of his trousers and puffed away contentedly. He was enjoying the cigar so much that he became oblivious to where he was. He suddenly leaned back in the chair and placed both of his filthy dust covered boots on the table's mirror like finish as well. Tom looked at Huck in horror for his breach of proper military etiquette.

General Stuart laughed a slight laugh at Huck's demonstration of his diminishing nervousness. He made up his mind right there that he liked this brash young sergeant. He also knew in his heart that these two soldiers were not Yankee agents, which he had at first suspected when he had first seen the map. The find was genuine and not a plant, of this he was now sure. All of his suspicions had literally gone up in smoke and he was thoroughly relieved.

Tom tried to get Huck's attention to warn him of his lapse in judgment in becoming too comfortable and familiar in his new surroundings but Huck puffed away like a locomotive, enjoying the fine cigar. The General noticed his attempts at this, raised his hand in a comforting gesture to Tom and winked at him.

"How's the cigar?" General Stuart asked.

"Best damned cigar I've had in years," Huck blurted. He looked up and suddenly realized that he was in the presence of one of the South's greatest legends. He noticed Tom's shocked expression. He removed his feet from the table at once and stiffened in his seat.

"Relax, sergeant. I can always trust a man who likes a quality cigar," the General said smiling. He puffed at his cigar and the smoke encircled his head. He waved his hand to disperse a cloud in front of his eyes and looked directly at both of the men seated in front of him.

"I have spoken with your captain," General Stuarts began, drawing slowly on his cigar.

"That is some tale he has told me. We have been looking for that rascal for some time…I mean, of course, the fellow that you shot and not your Captain Cobb."

"You mean you know who that fellow was?" Tom asked. He caught himself and quickly added a "sir".

"Oh indeed we do. His facial features were a bit reorganized since the last time I had spoken with him, but yes. I knew him pretty well. In fact, he was supposed to be working for us in the capacity of a spy. We had suspected, however, for some time that he was also gainfully employed as a Federal agent. He seemingly disappeared until you brought him back to the fold. He is what they call in the espionage game as a double agent. His name was George Russell Howard." General Stuart flicked an ash on the hardwood floor before continuing.

"Mr. Howard would often bring us information about the movement and plans of the Federal Army that would satisfy our people until they examined it closely based on our own cavalry reports and other agents. The information did not stand up to scrutiny. There was always something not exactly correct about it or it was old news, nothing that would hurt the Federals. That is what finally aroused our suspicions about the late George Russell Howard. In time, we would give him information that we hoped he would bring to the Federal table. Misinformation, as you will. That is eventually how we confirmed that he was a dirty agent and employed by the Federals. What you boys have found on him eliminates any doubts that we may have had. He was a major security leak for us. You men have plugged that leak quite effectively, if you will excuse the pun."

"I am sorry, general sir," Huck said. "I kin' never excuse that particular Pun. Neither will I ever forgive him. That Pun was mean- natured and a know it all type of Pun. We all would not be a sittin' here today havin' this very conversation if'n that Pun was not shot dead by my good friend, Tom. As far as I am concerned that Pun got what was comin' to him. If the Pun had been a little faster the both of us would be dead."

General Stuart laughed loudly.

"Yes, I see your point, sergeant. I suppose that particular Pun got what he deserved." General Stuart removed his feet from the table and stood up. Tom immediately started to rise as well before the General waved him back down to his seat.

"Relax, sergeant. Sit. I can't seem to sit well in chairs anymore for any length of time. It comes with the career that I have chosen," he said. General Stuart walked over to the mantle piece and lit an oil lamp. He returned with it to the table.

"I have some bad news. You know that we are short on manpower. If there had been a way to arrange a furlough so that at least you may have had the chance see your loved ones for a week, believe me, I would have done so. Unfortunately, when Captain Cobb informed me that you both hail from Missouri that option was discarded. A furlough was ruled out for the simple reason that it would be too dangerous for you. The chances of being captured by Federal forces are too prohibitive for us to venture the endeavor."

General Stuart gingerly sat down, grimacing slightly at the discomfort. It caused him. He regained his composure quickly before continuing.

"Men, I do not need to tell you that desertions are on the up rise. People leave the ranks not out of any lack of patriotism but out of an empty stomach. Our civilian population is suffering severe deprivations because the war is being conducted without let up in our own backyard."

General Stuart shifted his weight in the chair and took a long draw on his cigar. He exhaled the smoke slowly.

"Let me tell you a story. One of my very own men deserted. He was a good soldier. Soon after, he returned to us. It seems the only reason he had left in the first place was to see how his family was faring. His wife had written a letter that he showed me. I read in it that she was destitute. She pleaded for him to return to get the crops in. When he arrived home, he found the farm burned to the ground and his entire family dead. They had all been killed by errant artillery fire, Federal artillery, by the way. He was court-martialed and reduced in ranks but because of the circumstances, was pardoned. He rides and fights with us still today. In fact, he fights with a reckless abandonment, like an avenging angel. He has been taken out of his command and attached to headquarters until he gets his mind right again. He is the cavalryman that escorted you here today."

General Stuart extinguished his cigar on his boot heel and began to wrap the remnants of it in a piece of brown paper.

"Corporal Hargraves is the type of soldier that we can ill afford to lose. There was an execution in your very own division this morning. This must stop. I am going to entrust you men with information of the most sensitive kind. I must have your most solemn promise that you will never breathe a word of it to anyone. Do I have it?"

Huck jumped to his feet and placed his hand on his heart and made the sign of an x with his index finger, spit into the palm of his hand and slapped his hands together.

"You kin' trust us, General, Sir, honest Injun'. We swear we won't say nothin' to nobody."

The General leaned forward placing both of his hands on the table and slowly stood up.

"Our cause may be doomed unless some drastic measures are not taken. We are in danger of losing Vicksburg. If it does fall, the entire Mississippi River will be in Federal hands and The Confederacy we will be cut in two." General Stuart could not help but notice their concerned expressions.

"We, of course, cannot allow this to happen. Even well before this map that you have found came to our attention, General Lee had met with President Davis in Richmond. The damned politicians on the President's cabinet were pressuring General Lee to send an army under General Longstreet to Vicksburg to aid in its defense. General Lee fought strongly against this and on the narrowest of margins was able to convince the President of the inherent danger of dividing our forces in the extreme likelihood of a Federal offensive in this Theater of Operations. But it was close. Too damned close for my liking."

General Stuart slowly sat down again.

"I know what you men must be thinking. We have always destroyed every Federal Army that threatened Richmond. But you see, that is the problem in itself. The Federals are down here. General Lee's major crisis is simply feeding the Army because the Yankees are in control of the heartland of Virginia, our breadbasket if you will."

Tom was trying to let what he was hearing settle in. He had always thought that they had been winning. What the General was confiding in him hit him like a double load of canister.

"General Lee has decided to draw the Federal Army away from the Shenandoah Valley, to draw them away from our breadbasket. We will threaten Washington with a major campaign of stealth and motion in the North. We will bring the war into the backyards of the enemy, into their parlors. When we do this, the effect will be to give relief to our forces in the West. They will surely shift troops from Vicksburg to defend a threatened Washington. General McClellan, our most steady adversary, will demand more troops for any actions in the East. When this is done, we will be able to harvest crops vital to our interests. We will destroy the Federal Army in the field when they next engage us, of this, General Lee is certain. We will demand an armistice and with that will come worldwide recognition for our embattled nation. We will have won our independence from the tyranny of those people in Washington."

He watched their expressions carefully. He had thought long and hard about confiding classified information with them. It was his way of rewarding them for what they had brought to the table. He felt, instinctively, that they could be trusted.

"General Lee has seen the map that you men had found on the late George Russell Howard. It confirmed everything that he had suspected about what the Federals were up to. From what can be gleaned from the information that you have provided, there is little doubt that the Yankees are planning to cross the Rappahannock River in force and come at us, possibly very soon. They are gearing up for another go at us. We will not allow Washington to dictate where and when they choose to give battle. We are going north into Pennsylvania. We will get between Baltimore and Washington. This way, they will be forced to give battle and we can choose the place and time. We will let them bleed themselves white when they attack us, and then we will finish them. Once they are drawn out of their fortifications around Washington, I have no doubt in my mind that we will inflict a loss on them so severe that they will never be able to recover. Washington will collapse and this war will be over. That is why it is so critical that every man must be prepared to give his all. If the current trend of this war were to continue, the Federals will simply starve us into submission and then bleed us in turn to the point of our inability to wage war on the offensive. I feel, with your find, that sharing this information with you was the least that I could do since all other options in regards to a furlough are impossible. I personally wanted to tell you of the importance of your find."

Huck was impressed with the sincerity of the tone in the General's voice and the simple authority of his manner. With men like this in charge, there was no way they would ever lose. The war would be over, possibly in a few months' time. It was incredible news and Huck's mind fairly swam with the implications it brought to mind.

"If those politicians back in Richmond had won their argument, this whole army would have been deprived of the services of General Longstreet's Corp. We would have had to fight the next Yankee onslaught with one hand tied behind our back. I can tell you, frankly, that I did not like that idea one iota. The Yankee cavalry are getting better and they are starting to be more numerous than ever before. Even the quality of their mounts is improving." General Stuart rose from his seat.

"However, I digress from why you are here. Men, I can't say enough in regards to your quick actions and thinking. You have done an invaluable service for our cause. I am truly sorry about this furlough business, but I hope that after this talk we have just had that you understand. This campaign we begin may be perhaps the last action of this cruel war, I truly pray."

They were caught up in the emotions of the moment and were rendered speechless. The General walked towards them and they leaped from their chairs. He embraced them by their shoulders as he gently shepherded the pair towards the door. The same major who had helped clear the room met them.

"Major Randall, if you would see that Sergeants Finn and Sawyer have a comfortable place to lay their heads tonight after they have eaten well. Have Corporal Hargraves return them to their perspective command at first light."

The Major saluted in a crisp West Point manner and came to attention.

"Of course, sir," he said. "Sergeants, this way if you would." They all walked off the porch and into the gathering twilight of early evening leaving General Stuart alone with his thoughts. He walked back to the table and sat down. He leaned back in his chair and examined a copy of the map the two men had found. He reached for a glass of brandy as he placed a new cigar on the edge of the table. I will work a miracle with this map, he thought contentedly. I will destroy the Federal ability to wage war and support their efforts during this campaign. I will strike in their rear. I will bring the war north. I shall let the Yankees know how it feels to fight in their own towns and their own farms. I will force the war to their very doorsteps and when I begin this raid, no one will know where or **when I strike…no one.**

CHAPTER NINE

"He was visitin' his kin', I tell you. He ain't no part of this. Never was. Why don't yer' just let him go." Burton Gaines did not like the looks of his captors. The hare lipped soldier looked like a mean cuss. The cold wind blew out of a gray sky bringing with it a few premature snowflakes. The ropes that constricted his movement burned his skin when he strained against them.

The frightened youth was terrified and it shown clearly in his wide open gaze. He looked about at the bodies scattered all over the small clearing. He knew mostly all of the dead. They had been ambushed when they had least suspected it. The Yankees had been tipped off, of that there was no doubt. The fight had lasted seconds, it had seemed. The survivors had scattered to the winds. Men had been killed in mid sentence.

The amount of rifle fire that the Federals had poured into their small ranks had shredded small trees in the vicinity. The thickets that usually had hid and protected them had not been much protection in the initial few seconds and now the frightened boy and Burton were at the mercy of an enemy that was not known for practicing much of it.

"You are not in any position to be telling anyone anything," Colonel Henry Fowler said harshly.

"If you have any sense at all, then you will tell me the whereabouts of your leader. Now. I'm not going to ask you again. Where is Quantrill?"

Burton looked up at his enemy.

"I know who you are an' I know what you intend fer' me an' the boy. I know I'm done. I accept that. I am a soldier."

Henry Fowler punched the sitting man in the mouth. Burton recoiled from the blow and sat up, his lip bleeding and his teeth loosened.

"You are not a soldier. You are Missouri bushwhackers, the scum of the earth, and if you don't tell me where Quantrill is, then you won't even be that anymore. You will be carrion. You will be food for the crows. Now, tell me. Where is he?" Henry thundered.

Burton remained tight lipped and stared into the tree line. Henry drew his Colt pistol and fired a bullet into the prisoner's forehead. Burrton's head snapped back from the impact and then he collapsed sideways onto the screaming boy. Blood poured out of the dying man's forehead in a torrent.

The boy kicked the body away from him in his terror and attempt to escape the cascade of blood that flowed onto him. Henry pointed his smoking revolver at the cringing boy.

"I want you to be very careful and think well before you answer me," Henry said slowly. "You have seen what I am capable of, have you not?"

The boy nodded his head vigorously.

"How old are you?" Henry asked.

"Thirteen…al…almost fourteen."

"And what is your name, young man?"

"Lucas Gordon."

"What were you doing here, Lucas Gordon?"

"I was visitin' my brother Timothy an' my Uncle Frank," Lucas said. His voice suddenly broke and he began to cry. Henry appeared to be personally affronted by the boy's tears. He grabbed the boy by his hair and screamed into his upturned face.

"Stop your sniveling, you damned wretch and tell me where is the man they call Quantrill."

The boys stopped crying and bit his lower lip. Henry roughly released his hold on the boy's hair and stood away from him. He smiled and returned his pistol to its holster.

"I am waiting, Lucas, and I am not a patient man," Henry said calmly.

"I swear I don't know, mister," Lucas replied, fighting back his terror. Lucas knew who he was speaking to and he felt sick at heart. The man was Colonel Henry Fowler. Lucas had heard stories about this man, none of them good.

"Do you know who I am, young master Lucas?" Henry asked.

Lucas again nodded.

"You are Colonel Fowler," he said.

"You think I am a horrible man, don't you?" Henry asked. Lucas did not know how to respond. He shook and then suddenly threw up his lunch. Henry ignored him and started to pace back and forth in front of the boy.

"I am an instrument of God. Are you listening, young man."

Lucas heard the words as if they were far away, like he was in a large cave back home that he was fond of exploring.

"I shot this man to avoid senseless slaughter. No one else needs die. You rebels are but a conquered race, the same as the heathen red savages that used to hold dominion in these regions. God, in his wisdom and foresight, decreed that all this land be given to the White Man. That is why the mighty red man was laid low. He was exterminated from these parts or forced to leave. But you rebels are white men, the same as we." Henry strove to make his point, watching the boy's expression carefully to see if what he was saying was understood.

"God is a loving, a God that abhors destruction of his chosen people which is what we are. If your Uncle Frank and his kind continue in their wicked ways, it will lead to their own extermination just as surely as the heathen savage Red man was cleansed from this place."

Images of Lucas's mother flashed in front of his clenched eyes. Lucas imagined how she would cry at his burial at the cemetery.

"I can save many lives by ending all this killing and senseless bloodshed. I can save your life, young Lucas. If that man lying next to you with that big hole in his forehead had told me what I wanted to know, he would be alive. I am not a bloodthirsty man. If I can find out Quantrill's location, I will use all my power to capture and not kill them. I would kill fifty men to save a thousand. I do not want the lives of your Uncle Frank or your very own brother. I don't want any more deaths. I will find a way to take them all prisoners. This way, my people and yours will not die. After all, we are all white men. They will all be taken to a prisoner's stockade to await the end of the war. They will be safe and no harm shall come to them. You can save the lives of countless people merely by telling me where Quantrill is at this very moment. Your brother and Uncle may be seriously wounded and need the care of a doctor. You saw what happened today. It is just a matter of time before we kill them all and I do not see the purpose of it when it would be so much better to capture them. You have the power to save their lives, young Lucas Gordon or you can throw all their lives away on this foolish lost cause of theirs. It is all up to you."

Lucas looked around at the blasted bullet ridden bodies of people that he had known and respected for most of his life. In death, he was amazed at how small and insignificant they now all appeared.

"If'n I was to tell you where they be, you would take heed to see that none of them was kilt'?" Lucas asked.

"Most assuredly young man. This is the perfect opportunity to hunt them all down and put them all in the bag. They are hurt and dispersed. They will not offer much resistance and I am confident that they can all be captured in one lot. Once Quantrill is captured, I do believe that they will all surrender. That is why it is imperative that I capture Quantrill."

Lucas imagined his brother and his Uncle Frank huddled in a cold wind swept thicket bleeding to death.

"Tell me," Henry said. "I know that in your heart you can see how senseless this all is. Tell me, where is he?"

"You promise?" Lucas asked. "You promise that you won't kill them?"

Henry exploded in rage.

Henry pulled out his pistol and jammed the barrel behind Lucas's ear. His face had turned crimson.

"I have had enough of your stalling. I am losing precious daylight, and I am losing patience with you. I promise you this. If you do not tell me where he is, I will mash your fingers into a fine paste. I will break every bone in your body and grind your bones into dust. Then I will blow your head off. After, when I find your brother and your Uncle Frank, I will personally make sure they die as slowly and as painfully as I can make them. This I swear. If you tell me now where Quantrill will lay his head down tonight, I will surround them and force them to surrender without firing a shot. They will know that the jig is up. They are not stupid men. They will be taken to Leavenworth where they will be well treated and eventually return to the bosom of their families and their homes after the war is over. This I swear. If you do what I ask, I promise I will not shoot you or your family members."

"You swear to God?" Lucas asked.

"I solemnly swear this. They will not be shot. My job in these parts will be finished. Peace will return to this area and I will be freed to go where I can be of greater use to my country. This is what I live and breathe for. I will unfortunately be forced to kill you and all of them if you don't act this day with resolution and courage for the good of all. You must trust in my word, Lucas."

Lucas desperately looked about the small clearing and all of the dead bodies. He imagined himself lying among them with a large hole in his forehead. He blinked, but the image only became clearer.

"It is all up to you," Henry said serenely.

"They have a place to go to. A safe house not far from here. I heard my brother talk about it. It's down the road that the big tree is at about three miles from here. You can't miss it."

Lucas could not believe that he had spoken the words. He was filled with guilt and a self -loathing the second that he had spoken them. He looked up at Henry with hope in his eyes.

"Do you mean to say that the safe house is that farm across from Miller's Road?" Henry asked in triumph. Lucas merely nodded his head and looked down at his rope bound wrists. Henry sensed the boy was telling the truth.

Henry would never have guessed it. He knew the house and its owner. The owner was a staunch Unionist, supposedly. Henry knew that the man had one son serving with the Federal Army. A damned traitor had been in their midst all this time. The traitor would have a reckoning coming and a quick trial and immediate justice at the end of a rope, Henry vowed silently. He had been about to go charging down the road to a suspected safe house and here they were practically right under his nose at the home of a man that he would never have suspected as being disloyal to the Union. The man even flew an American flag on his house.

"You are a brave boy." Henry said returning his pistol again to its shiny black leather holster.

"You are the kind of young man that is not just thinking about his own damned self. You are thinking about others. That is highly commendable in one as young as yourself. You have done the right thing, young man. I am proud of you."

Lucas felt relieved. A diminutive officer approached the Colonel. The small man had a face as sharp as a butcher's cleaver. At his side strode a fat sergeant with a nasty smirk.

"That's it, Colonel Fowler. We went all through their pockets. We got seven of them. Eight counting this here last one you sent to hell and this little old boy makes nine. What are your plans for the little circus geek?" Mason asked.

"Hang him of course," Henry said expressionless. "You will hang all of these scum by the neck. We will leave the people of these barren thickets a clear message they will not soon forget."

"You mean you want us to hang all these dead-men and the boy?"

A grin spread across Lehigh's features.

"Exactly."

"Henry, I mean Colonel Fowler, you have one fine sense of humor," Lehigh said. He grabbed the boy roughly. Lucas shook out of fear and disbelief.

"Come on half-pint, we gotta' get busy. You're gonna' get' yer' neck elongated." Mason slapped the boy on the side of his head.

"You promised," Lucas sobbed, "you promised you wouldn't kill me."

"I said no such thing. I promised that I wouldn't shoot you, young Lucas. I never promised that I would not hang you. Unfortunately, you did not listen to me all that well. I find this a common affliction often found to be prevalent with traitors and wicked evil doers."

The sergeant walked over to a horse and unfastened a coil of hemp rope that was secured to the saddle. He played out a length and then began to make a noose, grinning in happy contentment. He worked rapidly at his task.

Tears welled up in Lucas's eyes out of anger and frustration. He was outraged at having fallen for Henry's lies.

"Damn you," the words almost choked him. He felt nauseous. All of the muscles in his throat constricted and he heard the sound of his own pulse roaring in his ears. His face burned in humiliation. Henry looked at him curiously.

"Before your neck is snapped and you descend into the pit, there is something I want you to know. You, young Lucas, are responsible for all the deaths of your friends. You see, I had you watched carefully. You were followed by one of my men last month to this very spot. This morning, you were followed again but this time you were followed by my entire command. It was just a matter of time before you would lead us to these murdering scum. I thank you." Henry smiled.

"I wonder, Lucas, that when you did awake this fine morning that you pondered on whether you would be in hell before the day was over." Henry's eyes smoldered in an expressionless face.

"I rather think not," Henry said coldly.

Pete threw the noose over the boy's neck and tightened the knot. Lucas struggled against the knot trying to slip it away from his neck but he was held firmly by the short man with the weasel like face.

"You did say to yourself, today I will make a day of it. I shall see my Uncle Frank and my brother. I will take to these spawn of Satan food and gifts of bullets to use to shoot down and smite all those that do good and are righteous in the eyes of God. Then, I will return to the safety of my abode to sleep pleasantly under a warm quilt and dream dreams of the devil and of sin." Henry's voice began to rise.

"And the next morning, with the sun rising on your comfortable farm and the cock crowing three times, you would rise early to continue to happily serve Beelzebub. But this will not happen. No indeed not, young Lucas Gordon. For tonight, your stiff lifeless dead body will twist in the wind under a cold moonlight and your damned soul will burn in the flames of hell fire. You shall be dragged to the burning lake of brimstone with hooks in your jaws and cast into hell where you will suffer the pains of the damned for all infinity."

Mason slapped Lucas in the head again.

"Stop your damned wriggling or I'll bust you upside the head with my rifle. You might as well get comfortable with the idea of having your neck broken, sonny Bob. Now stop your foolishness," Mason shouted.

Pete mounted a horse with the rope in his hand and pulled Lucas behind him. When Pete reached a suitable tree, he threw the rope over a bough and secured it taking into consideration the length that was needed to do the job correctly. Pete then hopped off his horse and both he and Lehigh hoisted the frightened boy onto the back of the animal. Lucas was paralyzed with fear. His shoulders were hunched up so high that they touched his earlobes, and his eyes were closed tightly. Fowler nodded at Pete who jerked the horse forward quickly.

"Momma," Lucas cried as he felt the horse move forward. He opened his eyes wide. Lucas went sailing into the air. His neck broke with a popping sound.

"Suffer the little children to come unto me," Henry said. He breathed in deeply a draught of frosty air and then stretched like a cat in a sunbeam. The body of Lucas Gordon eventually stopped its swinging.

"I thought for sure we had Quantrill this time, Hank," Mason said hesitatingly.

"It is simply a matter of time. I will have that brigand's head on a pole before this day is over." Henry restarted Lucas swinging by giving the corpse a hearty shove.

"Such is the fate of all miscreants and traitors," Henry said blissfully. "Now. Time invites me go."

Lehigh watched Pete begin to physically abuse a man in his section. Pete suddenly shoved the cavalryman to the ground. As the man began to rise, Pete was all over him. He pummeled the soldier to his knees and then began to kick him about the clearing. In the brief time that it had taken for Pete to win his argument, Henry had told Mason that their quarry was less than three miles from where they stood.

"As soon as you are finished here," Henry said, "follow with your section and meet me at Miller's Road. There will be a large tree there. The farm is a mile down that road. When you see us, we will already be deployed. Mason, stay mounted. I will encircle the farm with the troops I take with me now. When I begin my grand assault, and you see anyone attempt to break from my snare, you will ride them down. Kill them all. I do not want prisoners. Smite them hip and thigh."

"Don't you fret none, Hank. I will smite them as good as a body can smite" Mason answered. He watched as Pete picked the badly beaten soldier up over his head. Pete hurled the soldier through the air. The man spun several times in flight and then came crashing to earth. He hit the ground in a tangled mass. Before he came to a complete stop, Pete was on him again. He lifted the man by his throat and proceeded to shake the soldier all the while barking profanities in his face.

The soldier's head appeared to be in danger of tearing off his shoulders. Pete balled up a fist and smashed the man in the nose. The unconscious militiaman fell and did not budge.

"Captain, do not misinterpret this. We have known each other for years and I value highly all of the aid and assistance that you have rendered me in the many years of friendship. However, this is the Army and as such, you should not be too familiar with me by calling me Hank. You must learn to address me by my current rank. I do not mind at all when we are in private but in the field, the other Captains may overhear you. It may instill petty jealousies in the ranks. We must prevent discord. You do understand?"

"Why of course I do, Hank. You are absolutely correct," Mason replied.

"Good. One more thing, my good man. Tell Pete to refrain from beating a man in front of the other soldiers. Bad form, you know. Tell him to beat the man in private but to avoid breaking anything. The last man that Pete confronted is still in the hospital. We need every man fit and able."

"Duly noted. I will tell Pete to take them out to the woodshed. I will join you directly right after we decorate these trees properly with these vermin."

Henry ordered his horse brought to him and mounted. He saluted Lehigh and then spurred his horse down the road. He was followed by a contingent of Captains. Men started leaping into their saddles as a bugler sounded the charge. Henry pounded down the road in a full gallop.

"Pete, if you are finished, git' some more rope. We got a job to do and we got to be quick," Lehigh shouted.

A few frightened young soldiers huddled together after witnessing the tremendous beating that Pete had inflicted on their spokesperson.

"This one here started givin' me trouble, Mister Lehigh Sir. He said he warn't about to hang no dead man, no how. Won't be gittin' no sass from him no more," Pete said angrily. He turned towards the frightened soldiers.

"I better see dead men hangin' in the trees real soon or you'll get the same. Now move your asses, that's an order," Pete bellowed. The soldiers broke out of their huddle as Pete started to walk towards them. Lehigh had to admit Pete was a good sergeant. His men feared Pete more than they did the rebels.

Lehigh was happy. They surely had Quantrill now. The survivors of the ambush would most likely be lightly armed and horseless. They would be exhausted and on foot for the most part. The killing of Quantrill would make Henry famous. He could see Henry running for public office after the war. Perhaps senator...maybe even

President. Lehigh watched as corpses started dangling by the neck from trees. The men worked quickly and soon the grisly chore was completed.

"Should have hung them all on one tree," Lehigh said as he inspected the ghastly orchard. He shrilly screamed for Pete to mount his squadron. Pete emptied his canteen on the beaten soldier as his friends helped the beaten man towards his horse. Pete was cuffing the man and shouting loudly. Within a few minutes they were all mounted and in some kind of order. Lehigh forced his way to their front.

"Men," he shouted. His yellow eyes were almost shut in rapture. He drew a large oversize ceremonial cavalry saber, a gift from wealthy patrons in Kansas, and waved it above his head.

"Follow me." The horse took Mason's spurs but was nervous with the sword swinging about its ears and bolted down the road out of control. Mason waved his heavy sword clumsily in the air and almost lost his seating. He leaned at an odd angle and was in danger of pitching off of the animal entirely.

Pete rapidly closed in on the excited horse and helped Mason return the erratically wielded sword to its scabbard. He soon regained control and his composure. Soon Mason was in front of his charging men again. The soldier that Pete had beaten lost consciousness and fell off his mount. He was trampled to death by a horrified beardless trooper who also fell off of his horse and was so severely injured they would discover days later that the young man would never walk again. They rode their horses furiously towards Miller's road.

Frank Gordon lay huddled in a pile of leaves and watched as Henry's men dismounted and formed a circle around the safe house. From the hill that he was on, Frank had a Birdseye view of his enemies' backs. He peered at them through a small telescope and counted their numbers.

The rest of his men were behind him on a smaller hillock directly to his left. Quantrill had continued on to another safe house after Frank had suggested that the prisoners might talk about this one. Frank knew that his nephew had been captured and he feared that the boy would divulge the location of the safe house. Apparently he had.

Frank and eight other men had volunteered to stay behind and be a rear guard for the rest of the men. Quantrill, by now, was at least three miles away at another safe house procuring weapons and fresh mounts. Frank had to buy his leader badly needed time. He had to strike hard at the enemy while he had the chance. The next rally point was three miles away through thickets and bush. All of the volunteers were horse less having given their mounts to the others. In the barn were three horses that were kept there in case of an emergency. They were not finished yet.

Lucas was dead. Of this, Frank felt certain. These militia only took prisoners to get information out of them. He watched as the owner of the farm walked towards the concealed enemy soldiers. The old man had watched the activity of the Federal troopers from his window and now slowly made his way towards them clutching his ear trumpet with his right hand.

Frank was astounded when a second group of the enemy arrived and began to canter towards the old man with drawn weapons. Suddenly, an officer ran towards them bounding out of his concealment and ran frantically towards the new arrival waving his arms and gesticulating wildly. He strained to hear what the man was shouting but could not. Frank waved his hand in the air, the signal for his men to take up positions and ready for action.

The new arrivals were bunched up in a nice group. Frank figured how many that he and his men would be able to drop in the first volley. They would have their enemies' backs to them and the element of surprise on their side. Then it would be a race to the barn. Frank readied himself as he placed the telescope back into his jacket and checked his weapon.

He grimaced as he sighted in on a mounted soldier. They would rake the newly arrived mounted soldiers first with their repeating rifles and then rush the men closest to the barn. The signal for the attack would be Frank's first shot. He sighted down the barrel, took a deep breath, let half of it out and slowly began to squeeze the trigger

The rifle bucked and the mounted soldier leaped in the air and then fell forward off his horse. His men shot into the massed troopers killing several and wounding many. Those troopers not killed or wounded desperately tried to escape the deadly fire but were blasted out of the saddles before going more than a few yards. Some vainly dove off their horses and fell perforated with lead that devastated their compacted group.

Horses reared and plunged from the fast firing Henry rifles. The murderous crossfire decimated the federal cavalrymen in seconds. Frank was on his feet and running for the barn. He raced towards the concealed troopers and as one turned to hear his footsteps, Frank shot the man in the throat. Another fired and missed but was shot by one of Frank's men. They poured another killing volley into the backs of the nearest group of would be ambushers. The survivors broke and ran for their lives.

The rest of the surprised Federal cavalry held their fire as their comrades were flushed from cover and ran right into their own line of fire. They withheld their fire allowing Frank and the entire rearguard to reach the barn unscathed. Frank signaled for two men to enter the barn and quickly saddle the horses. Three horses could possibly take six men away. He knew he needed more. Frank suddenly saw his opportunity.

Several of the slain trooper's horses had not bolted away but instead were just milling about in the road.

"Deek," he shouted.

"Right here."

Deek ran over to better hear while the rest of the rearguard continued to pin the Federal troopers in place. The enemy had taken cover but their return fire was erratic and inaccurate.

"Deek, we are gonna' turn those Yankees. When we do, take a horse from the barn. Ride like hell and grab as many of those horses in the road as you can and get back here as fast as you can."

Deek nodded and went into the barn.

Frank made his way over to William Gladstone, a bear of a man, and patted him on the shoulder and leaned towards him.

"William, we have to turn them away from the road where those horses are. Deek is gonna' have a go at getting as many horses as he can. Take four men with you and get around that bunch over there." He pointed to an area directly in front of them.

"I'm going around the other way. We are gonna' roll them up like a carpet. Make yourselves sound like a hundred men. When they break, hightail it back here."

William picked four men as Frank waited for the two men that had saddled the three horses in the barn to return. When they were ready, Frank raised his hand and Williams group ran back the way they had come. Frank and his group waited a full minute and then started their movement. He began to shout, running and shooting towards the house followed by the rest of his men.

Lehigh had been struck in his heel by the initial volley. He watched in shock as his command was ripped to pieces. Mason crawled away for the cover of the nearby tree line. Pete came up behind him and scooped him up and spirited him away on a dead run. Pete was hit in his right hand but ignored the pain and ran for all he was worth. Henry had also ran back to cover with the first shots. He threw himself behind a tree and watched in horror as his men came streaming out of the far side of the woods. He watched as one of his men tumbled in a heap. It was then that he saw the group of enemy soldiers following directly on the heels of his totally demoralized men.

Henry screamed for those nearest him to fire but his men did nothing. One panicked soldier made a run for a rider less horse and bolted into the saddle. William Gladstone fired twice and the man died with his brains turned into a fine spray. Little by little, singly at first and then in groups of twos and threes, Henry's outflanked command began to melt away. There was only sporadic return fire as Deek made his way to the horses and began to collect them. He raced towards the animals grabbing as many reins as he could and made it back to the barn safely.

From the right came a high-pitched scream of defiance as Frank and his group plowed into the other side of Henry's shattered circle. One soldier turned to see where the noise was coming from and he turned towards the sound in curiosity. He was a foot away from Henry when the man's head exploded splattering Henry with gore. The blue clad trooper collapsed onto Henry. Henry ripped at his sword belt and hurled it to the ground.

Henry ran, too busy in saving his own life than commanding a retreat. Anyone that witnessed Henry's sudden departure from the fight did exactly as his leader had. Within a few minutes, all of the surviving Union soldiers were running for their lives, plowing through the woods dropping weapons and any other impediments to their flight.

The firing dropped away to nothing as Frank appraised the situation. Not one of his men had been hit and Deek had gathered four horses, more than enough to get away and make it to the next rallying point. He sighed in relief. William Gladstone approached him helping the owner of the house.

"Are you alright, Mr. Henshaw?" he asked.

"Oh I'm fine, I reckon. I lit into that ditch when the shootin' started," he said, wiping the dirt and grass from his bearded chin.

"Mr. Henshaw, you got to come with us. We got to get you out of the county. After what happened here today, the Yankees will want yer hide. Gather up some things and get ready to travel. We have friends who will protect you."

"I'm glad my wife ain't alive to see all this death an' destruction. She truly loved this place. She would lose her faith to see her beautiful garden choked with dead soldiers," he said, with a tear in his eye. Frank nodded and William helped the old man to his front door. Mr. Henshaw stopped on the porch. He knew that when the enemy returned they would burn him out.

"Gather up weapons and shot. Pick up all repeating rifles and ruin the rest. Shoot the wounded. Deek, see if you can round up any more horses. I don't believe the Yankees will be back any time soon."

Gunfire sounded as Frank's men began to kill wounded Union soldiers. Some wounded troopers screamed and some pleaded for their lives to no avail before being silenced by a single shot. Frank divorced himself from the sounds and began to think of his nephew. Tears began to fill his eyes. William returned without Mr. Henshaw.

"That old boy is strong. I didn't know that he got one grandson fightin in the Yankee Army back east. Strange, ain't it?" William asked. William had not noticed Frank's tear filled eyes as Frank turned away from him quickly.

"How many do you think we kilt'?" William asked.

"Oh," Frank said sadly, "not enough, William. Not enough."

CHAPTER TEN

Hundreds of Union prisoners streamed to the rear in all kinds of conditions, sizes, and temperaments. Tom, sitting by the side of the road, studied their faces. Some looked defiant, even angry. Others looked bemused by it all and some appeared frightened. One Federal soldier looked Tom right in the eye with unmistakable hatred. No matter how they appeared, they all shared a similar look. Stamped on all of their many different faces was the look of shame. They were ashamed and felt betrayed by their leadership. Once again, the Army of Northern Virginia had humiliated them.

They had been blasted out of their fortifications at Winchester and then had vainly tried to retreat to safety, only to be surrounded and then rounded up like stray sheep. Now they were on their way South, not as conquerors of the rebellion but as prisoners of war. They were heading South in a way that none of them had ever expected.

Tom had read the captured northern newspapers that constantly rang with banner headlines 'On To Richmond'. Well, they were on their way to Richmond, Tom thought. The more of them heading south in their present condition could only mean that the war was one day closer to ending just as General Stuart had said. Then he could go home, ask Rebecca for her hand in marriage and move to California. Tom noticed a staggering soldier who was holding a badly wounded arm. The man took one step forward, two to the side and a half pace backwards in his attempt to keep pace with the rest of the prisoners. He was in a losing battle but he stubbornly plodded along. He noticed Tom staring at him.

"Gloat while you can, Johnny. Your time will be coming soon enough," he yelled.

Tom noticed blood flowing down the soldier's arm from beneath a dirty rag that had been twisted clumsily above the gaping wound. He continued to trudge in a crablike manner down the crowded roadway as passing soldiers jostled him at every step. He swayed and rocked from all of the minor collisions.

"Hold on a bit, Billy," Tom shouted.

Tom had seen enough. The man was obviously on the point of collapse. He walked towards the soldier who grew defensive.

"If you want to fight me, you'll find me a disappointment. But if it's a fight you want, then by Jiminy, come on with it."

"I don't want to fight," Tom said, examining the man's mangled arm closely. Bone shards stuck through bare flesh. Some type of artillery shell had hit the man.

145

He had seen that type of wound before. The Federal soldier was bleeding to death with each beat of his heart.

The soldier sighed in relief.

"Good,' he said, "I'm all fought out anyway."

"You twisted this rag around your own arm now, didn't you?" Tom asked.

The wounded soldier had been expecting a caustic response from the rough looking rebel sergeant and was surprised in the friendliness of the man's voice. The few rebel soldiers he had met so far had been callous in their treatment of him.

"I had to. Everybody else was dead," he replied. He cradled his ruined arm in his good hand. So much blood had flowed onto his pants leg from his wound that it appeared as if he had been shot in the leg as well.

"You need to be riding in an ambulance and on your way to a saw bones instead of packing it down the road by foot. Come off to the side of the road with me, Johnny, and wait on me a bit."

The Federal soldier was taken by surprise by Tom's tone of voice. He shakily made it to the side of the road and Tom helped him sit down. Tom spotted a guard walking towards him and made his way over to him. Fortunately for Tom, it was not a provost guard but a convalescing infantry soldier temporarily attached as a guard until he fully healed.

Tom quickly explained the situation and the sympathetic guard nodded. Tom came back quickly to the wounded soldier's side.

"You come along with me," Tom said, helping the soldier to his feet. "Don't make no sense walking along this road and bleeding to death when there ain't a possible reason to." Tom pointed towards a group of southern soldiers lolling about under the shade of a group of trees. Tom's regiment had been ordered off of the road to let the prisoners pass and now was fully taking advantage of the situation. They sprawled about in every conceivable manner.

Tom's friends watched as he helped the wounded man towards their group. The Federal soldier walked unsteadily towards the slouching rebel infantry resting under the trees. He eyed them warily and they stared back at him in curiosity. A living Yankee was an oddity to many of them, sort of like the two-headed chicken found at the county fair. Columns of the man's countrymen filed southward to an uncertain future in an endless stream.

Tom's brigade had not participated in reducing the fort at Winchester. That had been the job of the artillery. They had battered the fort into silence. General Ewell, their very own Corp commander, had won a foot-race with the Federal forces that had tried to escape the fort. Ewell had unleashed a brigade that cut the fleeing northern soldiers off from safety and then had cut them down in large numbers when the Federals had turned to fight. Cut off and cut to shreds, the surviving Union soldiers had surrendered in mass deciding that dying in a hopeless cause was sheer idiocy. They blamed their loss on their incompetent leadership which had allowed the southern ranks to use their cannons in such a one sided way. They had surrendered in the thousands.

Ed Bolls watched as Tom aided the wounded man towards the trees. The Federal soldier gingerly lowered himself down next to a sturdy maple and rested his back against it. Tom kneeled and began to unwrap the twisted rag that wrapped the man's torn and twisted arm. The sleeve of his coat and the rag looked like the man had just cleaned fish in them. Tom could smell the unmistakable odor of the onset of gangrene.

He finished unwrapping the soldiers shattered appendage. Bone shards and maggots were practically indistinguishable from each other except for the fact that the maggots moved but the bone splinters did not. Muscle tendons and sinews hung off the arm like string. The rag had saved the man's life but had also cut off all circulation to the arm. Tom realized that the arm would have to come off and quickly.

"Where do you hail from, soldier?" Tom asked. "This may smart a might but we got to get these maggots out."

Tom took his wooden canteen and removed the stopper. He slowly poured water on the arm and picked off any clinging maggots with a twig.

"Cuba," the soldier replied through clenched teeth. The soldier's teeth ground together, his jaw working furiously and he squinted in pain. Tom tried to be as careful as he was able. He removed a clean bandage from his pack; a white piece of linen that at one time had been a sleeve of an undershirt. He re-wrapped the arm the best way he knew how and sat back. The man's complexion, Tom noticed, was a pasty yellow and perspiration stood out on his forehead.

"I am from Cuba. About thirty miles outside of the largest city on the island."

Andy Barrett overheard the soldier say this and became curious. He looked stunned.

"Cuba," he said, "ain't that down near Mexico way?"

"No, it's an island in the Caribbean Sea. It's about ninety miles off the coast of Florida," the wounded man said.

Andy became upset with this bit of information. He stood up angrily and removed his hat and threw it on the ground.

"It's like I bin' sayin' all along," he complained loudly. "We are fightin' the whole world it would appear. If it ain't them damned Dutchmen from across the sea, now we find out we're fightin' the Cubans. Next thing you know, we'll be fightin' the man in the moon."

Ed looked at the Federal soldier with suspicion.

"You say you come from Cuba. Why is it then that you don't talk that Mexican talk? You sound like a goddamned Yankee to me, and you ain't dark like a greaser," he asked.

"If it's all that important to you, my father was a whaling man from New Bedford. That's in Massachusetts. My father married a woman from Philadelphia. That would be my mother. She died when I was small but since my father would be at sea for years, my mother's sister raised me. I grew up in Philadelphia. Later on, my father bought a sugar plantation in Cuba. I've lived there since I was ten or so."

"So you are a Yankee," Ed said proudly, "I know'd it."

"I never said I wasn't. I was visiting my Aunt in Philadelphia when Fort Sumter was fired on and the rebellion began. I enlisted the next week. I have been in this war from the start."

"I think your fulla' beans," Andy shouted. "You say you're from a plantation down in Cuba. You got slaves on that there plantation, Yankee boy?"

"Hell no," the soldier sputtered. "Slavery was outlawed there years ago. We have free laborers. Free men all of them. Almost all of them are Negro who work an honest day for a fair wage. Good decent wages are the key to a successful plantation You treat people decently and you get good results. It is called progress, something you ass backward southerners don't seem able to understand." Thornton Dean leaped to his feet.

"No, you son of a bitch. It's you and your kind what don't understand, you goddamned Yankee," Thornton shouted. He puffed his chest out and swaggered over to where the wounded man was sitting.

"Go get him, Deanny boy," Pete Wilson snickered. Thornton ignored his comment as he pointed at the Federal soldier.

"You people have a lot to learn about southern folks, and we surely are givin' you Yankees a damned good lesson all about us. Look at you. You ain't a fer' real American. You're some kind of galvanized northern ferrin' scum. Hell, yer more ferrin' than American and don't you forget it. If it was up to the likes of your kind, you'd have us all mixin' in with the darkies, goin' to church socials together with them an' sippin' tea and sich with a bunch of niggers that only recently was slippin' each other into stew pots back in Africky there. They ain't all that remotely removed from cannibals. Look at what that no good goddamned nigger Nat Turner did. He kilt' little innocent white chillin' right in their cribs. My pappy tolt' me what they is capable of so don't go preachin' to me about shit. You don't know what you're talkin' about. Ass backward is we? You wouldn't know what real progress was if it came up to you an' bit you in the ass. I say to hell with you and all your kind."

"Whooo-hah," Andy whooped, "you jest' got tolt', Yankee boy. He clapped his hands and started a strange dance. Many in the company laughed at his antics. The Federal soldier ignored all their reaction to Thornton's tirade and carefully spoke so that they all could hear him clearly.

"You have just made my point. If you treated Negroes fairly to begin with, then you wouldn't have to worry about getting murdered in your sleep by them. Before the war, your whole society acted like it was an armed camp and in a state of siege. Free labor and free men, you stupid, buck toothed, inbred undereducated, subservient, servile bootlicker. Your so-called leaders are not even willing to try the concept. They refuse to give the Negro a chance at free labor, the greedy bastards. Your leaders ran this country for eighty years. The first time it appeared that they were not going to get their way, they react by trying to destroy the greatest country on the earth, like a bunch of children who are spoiled rotten. You southerners all make me want to puke."

"Good. Puke! I hope you choke to death on it," Thornton yelled. The wounded soldier appeared visibly weakened from talking.

"Slavery is wrong. Can't you see? It corrupts and degrades the soul of the slave as well as the hearts and mind of the slave owner. The slave may be under the whip but the slave owner is under the wrath of God. Your entire social structure is designed to keep the very wealthy in power. The average southerner doesn't have a chance in making a go at it. You don't seem to realize that this war will be the ruin of everything that you people hold dear. Your homes, your right to rule yourselves, all of this is about to come crashing down around your ears. You people will never defeat us. We may lose battles but we will not lose the war, of that you can be certain. For every one of us that falls in this struggle there are ten to take his place. Mark my words well this day. Someday, when this war is over, you will remember what I say. Everything you cherish will be gone. Including slavery. You're too thick headed to understand this. You go blindly fighting for the will of your slavocratic leaders. Let me ask you a question, Johnny. Do you own any slaves?"

"Never mind that," Thornton said defensively.

"That's just what I thought, shit-heel." the wounded man said, "You never in your life probably ever owned another fellow human being yet you are ready to die to protect something you never had nor probably ever will. Oh yes. That makes a lot of sense to me."

Thornton momentarily looked confused at what the Union soldier had said but could not afford to lose the argument in front of his comrades.

"Fer' your information, Slavery is in the Bible. You Yankees would twist the truth of God Hisself.' I'm fightin' fer my people's rights an' freedom from all you Godless ferrin' Northern scum. Look at the past. George Washington, the greatest American what ever lived. he had slaves. Are you tryin' to tell me he was an evil man to have slaves? Lookit' Thomas Jefferson, the man that wrote about the Fourth of July, he had slaves. You tellin' me that there was somethin' wrong with him cause if you are, then you don't know nothin' about what America is an' was, you damned fool."

The Union sergeant shook his head sadly.

"Show me," he said weakly, "in the bible in black and white where it says that Negroes have to be slaves. Show me where it specifically says blacks should be slaves and not some vague reference that you may point to about a hewer of wood and a carrier of water. Don't show me some vague character called Ham and his sons because nowhere does it say they were the color of a Negro."

This confused Thornton once again and he grew silent. He had not understood a word that his enemy had said. The Federal sergeant pressed home his attack.

"As for Washington and Jefferson, they both freed their slaves on their deathbeds and put it in their wills. I figure that they both were trying to do right and were afraid of the pains of eternal damnation. What else do you want to know, you under educated Bible spouting no mind."

Thornton had heard enough. He quickly primed and readied his weapon for firing.

"I have half a mind to put you out of your misery," he said, reaching into a pouch for a percussion cap. He placed it on the nipple of the rifle and drew back the cock. Everyone tensed at the spectacle of Thornton gone wild. The Federal sergeant ignored Thornton's threat.

"You are right in that regard. You do have half a mind. Now why don't you go away? You're starting to affect my morale. I don't have the time or the patience to teach you what you should already know."

"Son of a bitch," Thornton screamed, "you got a lot to learn yer own damned self. We will have done with you people once an' fer' all, jest' like our granpappys did with that other tyrant, old King George. We are gonna' go to that Philadelphia of yours and knock down that old Liberty Bell y'all are so proud of. We are gonna' melt it into horseshoes because you Yankees don't deserve to be called Americans any more. You Yankees is a bunch of dirty nigger lovin' sonsabitches. Keep on talkin' yer' nonsense an' see what don't happen. I'll make yer whole world come crashin' around your ears damned quick."

He pointed his rifle at the man's head.

"Go easy on the man, Deanny," Tom said, "he's hurt so bad he's ravin' out of his head, can't you tell?"

Tom began to twist a stick above the bandage to try to stop the fresh bleeding. Thornton seemed placated by Tom's assessment of the man's condition and looked about at his friends. They had all enjoyed the debate and had felt it to be a draw. To blow a hole in the man's head would be considered poor sportsmanship. Thornton lowered his rifle.

"Keep him quiet, then. I ain't in the mood to hear no more of his damned mouth," he said. He puffed out his chest and walked back to his comrades. Some gave rebel yells and many began clapping. Andy whistled loudly through the wide gap in his teeth. Pete slapped Thornton on the back and started shoving him around in play. Thornton laughed loudly and looked back at the wounded man, grinning.

The soldiers bleeding arm began to worry Tom. Something was terribly wrong. The makeshift tourniquet was not stanching the flow of blood. Tom noticed the man's eyes had started to glaze over and he wore a strange expression, almost if he were awakening from a dream. His face had started to turn waxy looking.

"In the morning, when it was cool, my father would open all the windows in the house. The windows were big. The wind would come right through the whole house. It was on the windward side of the island on a ridge facing the sea. And that breeze, why, I can tell you it was something special."

"I'm sure it was," Tom said.

"It got hot, mind you. But not hot like it gets around here. There was always that breeze coming off the sea. That view was magnificent and the color of the ocean, why, it was a color I can't even begin to describe it accurately I suppose. It was a blue and a green that would change right in front of your eyes. It was beautiful the way the sun sparkled off it in the morning. You would have to see it for any of what I'm saying to make sense."

"Maybe you ought'n not talk. Try and save your strength. I'm going to see if I can get the regimental surgeon to take a look at you so you just sit here and hold on, Billy."

Tom rose to leave when the soldier reached over and grabbed Tom's hand and held it weakly.

"I just want to say that what I said about all you southern boys wasn't true and I never meant it seriously. I just wanted to make that fellow mad. I sure did, didn't I?

I appreciate all what you have done for me. I'd like to give you something, but the guards went through all my pockets and took everything I owned. In case I don't see you again, I.."

Tom squeezed his hand.

"Don't be thinkin' like that. I understand. Now sit back an' take it easy for a spell. I'll be back directly." The soldier nodded and released Tom's hand.

Tom trotted out to the side of the road to avoid the columns of southern soldiers heading north. The road had filled as soon as the last prisoners had gone. Now, once again, the Army of Northern Virginia was on the move heading north. He had not gone very far when he heard a voice calling him from the side of the road. He spotted Vernon waving at him. He ran towards him.

"Canteens all filled?" Vernon asked. Tom nodded.

"Did you make an ammunition check?"

"Yes," Tom said quickly.

"Get your people up and ready to move. We are next in the order of march. This road is clearing up and we don't want to get tangled up with another brigade."

"I got a problem, Vernon, I got a wounded Federal over there who is bleeding to death. He's in bad shape. I'm afraid if he don't see a surgeon quickly, he's a goner. I tried to stop the bleeding, but he's leaking pretty badly. I spotted him staggering down the road."

"Show me," he said, interrupting Tom. Vernon look concerned. Tom led the way back the few yards towards the tee where the Federal soldier lay. The wounded man grinned and lifted his hand in a wave.

"Can I get some water?" he asked. His voice was just a whisper. Vernon removed his round canteen. He steadied the man as he drank.

"Tom," he said, "the regimental surgeon is through that wood there." Vernon pointed at a patch of woods to their rear.

"Cut through there about a mile, you will come to a small crick. Follow it west about another mile or so. You will find Doc preparing to move out with his people. Tell him that I said to get an ambulance here as fast as possible. Tell him it's an emergency then get back here as quick as lightning. I'll try to keep the pace down but you gotta' move quick. Tell the ambulance driver we will mark the wounded man's location with a rag tied to a tree and a stick in the road with another rag tied to it. Tom, I can't hold up the campaign for one man, so be fast. You got all that?"

"Yes, sergeant," Tom said appreciatively.

"Git',"

Tom took off at a run. Vernon watched him disappear through the sparse woods.

"Alright," Vernon shouted, "everybody up and off yer' asses. The roads startin' to thin out which means we are next in line. Arthur, form your company. C'mon let's move. Git' yer' git' goin'."

Bodies began to stir.

"Ed, find a rag to mark this man's location fer' the ambulance. Standard procedure. Let's do it quick, we ain't got all day."

Vernon stooped low and spoke quietly to the mangled soldier.

"That fella' jest' went back to get an ambulance fer' you. We're moving out. Is there anything I kin' do fer' ya'?"

The man nodded his head ever slightly.

"Could you leave me a canteen?" he asked feebly. Vernon placed his canteen next to the man's good hand. He reached up and pulled Vernon's pants leg.

'My name...is Anthony Rocha. Would one of you write that on a piece of paper or something and stick it in my pocket. I want my father to know what happened to me."

Andy came forward with a piece of crumpled newspaper that he had been saving for a bowel movement. George Blakely handed Vernon a pencil stub. Vernon smoothed out the paper and wet the tip of the pencil in his mouth. He began writing.

"Uh...how do you spell that last name you give me?"

The Federal sergeant spelled out his last name and when he was finished, Vernon folded the paper in half and placed it in the man's inside shirt pocket.

"Thank you," he said faintly.

Vernon nodded. He shouted a command and one hundred and thirty three men started walking towards the road. As Thornton passed the soldier, he stepped out of ranks and bent over him.

"I got carried away, Billy. Good luck. I hope you make it home to that Cuba. No hard feelins'?"

"No hard feelings, Johnny, and good luck to you. I'm sorry I called you all them bad names. It was just talk."

Thornton placed two crackers in a handkerchief and then removed his canteen, laying it next to the man. He ran back into the ranks.

The Federal soldier watched the column of troops until he could not see them anymore. They disappeared in a swirl of dust. He looked up at the sky towards a darkening horizon, which held the promise of a cooling shower. The wind began to pick up and as the clouds grew he began to feel a cold unlike any cold he had ever felt before. So powerful was its grip that he began to shiver. He tried to see where the sun had hidden itself but couldn't which aroused his curiosity. His chin fell on his chest and he emitted a long drawn gurgle. The wind picked at the frayed edges of the paper that had been tucked into his pocket. The wind tugged the paper out of his shirt pocket and it was swept down the road.

Huck walked slowly along the road. The farms in this part of Pennsylvania impressed him in their neatness and orderly layout. He admired their fields and the magnificent barns. The orchards, it seemed, had been laid out with the precision of a parade in mind. They stood in neat ranks that stretched into the horizon. Looking at the farms took his mind temporarily away from his current problems.

His transfer to company H had been traumatic. Just as he and suspected, he had been viewed with distrust and treated like an usurper. Its members viewed any change of routine in a company critically and this company had been no exception. To make matters worse, Huck had discovered that many of the members of company H were conscripts, drafted men and not volunteers as everyone in his old company had been.

These conscripts constantly complained about everything and were openly defiant to authority. They clung together like grapes on a vine and scorned all the other members of their company who were not from the hills of western Virginia. They did not interact with anyone out of their circle. They spoke differently than everyone in the company and had a dangerous quality about them. They were all men of the hills, heavily Scotch- Irish in origin, and extremely violent, even towards each other. Internal agreements in their group were usually settled by knock down drag out fights.

Huck had never encountered people like these men before. They were some of the most ignorant people that he could remember seeing and were the worst soldiers. However, they were marksmen to a man. He had never seen anyone shoot like these men did. One soldier had fired at a target several times and every round had gone through the same hole.

These hill people ridiculed Huck at every opportunity and openly disobeyed his orders. The lieutenant and the captain were good sorts who went out of their way to make Huck feel welcome. He shared his mess duties with the other sergeants who were all from the same small village on the banks of the James River. Huck knew a few of them fairly well. He knew some of the veteran soldiers fairly well; Lawson Dunn, Clayton Harlingen, Quintus Farley, and Obadiah Belmont, these were the old hands. The majority of the company was made up of these hostile hill people who went out of their way to make life miserable for him.

The hill men would not even acknowledge his presence at times or obey his most simplest commands, even if it were for their own good. The other sergeants would notice this and threaten the men with unpleasant details and other sundry torments. Only then would they act like soldiers leaving Huck feeling entirely impotent as a sergeant. Whenever he had an opportunity to get away from them, Huck would leave them and return to his good friends and the security of Company C. Tom would listen to Huck's plight as he poured out his frustration and anger over his current situation. Tom could feel his friend's contempt for his new comrades.

"Why don't you take the biggest mouth that is there and kick the daylights out of them. You know how bullies are. All bark. They don't like to get hit. Hell, I know how you are when it comes to fightin'. You love it, even when you know you're goin' to get licked."

"That is true, but you don't understand these fella's. Remember that story I tolt' you about them feudin' people I come across? There was that fella' Buck an' his sister Sophie an' the other boy, Harney Shepardson. Them people was killin' each other fer' thirty years. These fella's are the same kind, all cut from the same cloth. They don't play fair. They already said that they would all get' together an' stomp my guts out if I was to give them any trouble. I was a standin' right there when one of them said it. I mean I was right there. They all acted as if I wasn't. They all began laughin'. The one that said it didn't even credit me with his attention. He didn't even look at me when he was a' sayin' it. It is most perplexin'."

"You got friends here, Huck. Why, if them boys need straightening out, we could do it. The whole company would stand up for you. Them hill boys would take one look at the arms on Ed Bolls and learn to behave like church deacons Ed's arms are as thick as the Bible and twice as wide," Tom said.

"I know, but it shouldn't have to come to that. I got a million strangers tryin' to kill me dead. I do not need any new enemies at' all. These fellas' ain't like ordinary folks, Tom. These fellas' are feudin' types. I don't want a man what holds a grudge walkin' in back of me holdin' on to a loaded rifle in a battle. There are some in that group that would put a ball through your head an' then claim for all the world to hear that you went to glory a regulation hero chargin' bravely at the enemy."

"You have a point," Tom replied. "These boys are hill people?"

"Mountain and hill boys to a man," Huck said. "They claim to all be from Virginny, but I never seen Virginny boys like these birds. They say they got dragged into the army at gunpoint and are proud of the fact. Can you believe that?" Tom shook his head sadly. Huck chewed on a blade of grass

155

"I overheard one say how his family hid him out when the army come to get him oncet he knew he was corn-scripted. He said his whole family was Union people. I got Yankees right in my own company. I don't trust them, Tom. If an' when we get' in a fight, half of them birds will hit out fer' the open road, right back to the hills. I swear they hate other Virginians more than they hate the Yankees."

"You are on the horns of a dilemma," Tom said.

"Horns of a what?" Huck asked in surprise. "What the hell kind of critter is that?"

"It is not an animal. It's just a figure of speech. It is an expression the old people used to say when you had a bad problem that could not get resolved or figured out.

"Well, I don't figger' any old person ever was caught in a bind like this one here that I find myself in. What I got is fer' the books. I got them horns stuck so deep that they'll never see the lights of day agin'."

Tom bit his lower lip and suddenly pulled on his nose. His mouth flew open and he sneezed. He began to choke and laugh all at the same time.

"Easy there, don't hurt yer'self on my account. I'm glad that yer' find this all so amusing," Huck said."

"If and when them boys all break in a fight, make sure you do the same," Tom sputtered."

"Oh yes indeedy. I will be faster than a shootin' star, you may have my word on that."

"Arthur came up to me yesterday," Tom said, "with this slip of paper. He said it was for the bet we made about you and me staying sergeants. I looked at it and it had good for the next payday or kingdom come written on it," Tom said.

"Makes sense," Huck replied. "I can't remember the last time we got paid."

Tom stood up from where he had been crouching and stared off into the distance.

"Huck, I saw something the other day and it set my mind to thinking. It's been bothering me ever since."

"Spill it," Huck said.

"When we first come into Pennsylvania they began to snatch up all the niggers they could find. I asked Vernon what was goin' on. He said that orders were to grab every darkie they come across. They were going to be sent south to help pay for the war effort."

"The devil you say," Huck responded.

"Huck, these folks were free men. They weren't fugitives. I heard some of them talking. Some of them said that their fathers had been free men. It didn't do any good. The loudest of them got a beating for his efforts. It made me sick to see what they were about. These niggers were being kidnapped right in front of my eyes. They were being stolen. I saw long lines of them in chains on the road. One town we passed through, the coloreds called it Five Forks, and there were a hundred taken, stolen right from their beds. I wanted to say something, but I bit my tongue."

"That would have been a bad idea if you had," Huck said quickly.

"Huck, I thought this war was being fought about something else. I thought that this war was being fought over the rights of a free people to determine their own destiny. I thought the war was being fought because of the words of the Constitution, that we as a free people have the right and duty to rebel against any and all governments that do not serve the needs and rights of its people. I see now how wrong I was. This war is all about keeping people in chains."

Tom picked up a rock and flung it into the air. He watched its path of flight and then leaned against a tree.

"I guess it's just the Good Lord's way of chastising me for getting mixed up with the lunacy of revenge and robbery," Tom said dejectedly.

"Sounds like you are the one that's on them horns of a dilemma. You sound like you just got done reading Uncle Tom's Cabin. You are worry'n about things that you got no control over. I know why I'm fightin'. It is the same reason that you are an' you best not fergit' it. We are outlaws. We killed lawmen in Kansas. One day, when this war its over, we kin' go home. The Yankees that control home will be the outlaws then an' the shoe will be on the other foot. When we win this war, all the Yankees will be sent packin'. We will not have to worry about somebody puttin' a large hole in our heads the first time we was to walk down Main Street. It is that simple."

"I wish to God it was that simple," Tom said bitterly.

"Why hell, Tom. We bin' more fortunate than some an' more unlucky than others, but so far we come through in one piece. Look at the number of people back home that has gotten kilt since all this began. And don't fergit' we are goin' to end this war real soon, just like General Stuart tolt' us," Huck said. He hoped that Tom wasn't slipping into one of his moods. Huck had seen dark moods of despondency come over Tom that could last months.

"A couple of days ago," Tom began, "we had to get off the road to let the prisoners captured at Winchester pass before we could resume the march. All these Federal prisoners were walking and I spotted one that looked half dead. His arm was all chewed to pieces and he was bleeding bad. It appeared that a chunk of artillery

157

shell caught him good and I saw that he needed a surgeon quick. I got him off the road and tried to stop the bleeding, but it wasn't working."

Huck listened quietly, nodding from time to time and watching Tom intently.

"I find Vernon and he tells me to go fetch the saw-bones and find a wagon for him. I tell you the man had one foot in the grave. But before all this, the soldier said things that put a chill up my spine. It chilled me to the bone."

"Don't go startin' in on scarin' yer' self," Huck said.

"He said that this war would be the ruin of everything that we, as southerners, hold dear. He said that our time was coming and it was coming quick. He said that the Federals would lose battles but never the war and that everything that we know and cherish will soon come crashing down around our ears."

"That must have set well with the boys. I kin' jest' picture what some of them had to say about that," Huck said.

"What he said set Thornton Dean off. They got into a good debate. If the Yankee had not been so used up, I believe it would have come to rough and tumble with no holds barred," Tom replied.

"Eye gourgin' and nut crackin'?" Huck asked.

"Absolutely. Of course it never came to that because the man was hurt too bad, but the things that he was saying put goose bumps on me. Especially the part about how God Almighty was going to judge us and do it hard."

"Another prophet of our doom," Huck said lightly. "Tom, don't give it no mind. You know how religious the Yankees kin' get' if it suits them, like in that particular song about that damned John Brown feller' How about that other song, Battle Hymn of the Republic. God is marchin' on. Where is He marchin'? It's all a bunch of hokum. It is all a case of never mind that."

"When I got back, he was dead. Anyway, I was too late. Funny thing about that fella'," Tom said sadly. "He said that he was from Cuba. He said his pappy had bought a sugar plantation and that he was raised down there for some time. He said his mother's folks were from Philadelphia and his Pap was a whaling man. You should have heard the way he went on about that Cuba place. He said the darkies are all paid wages and the cool sea breezes and the color the lights played on the sparkling blue sea. Must be beautiful this place because of the way he went on about it. It played heavy on his mind. I kind of envied him right up to the minute he kicked the bucket."

"Where is this Cuba?" Huck asked.

"It is an island some miles off the coast of Florida," Tom replied.

"What he said don't make no sense. He said that he lived on a plantation and that the darkies got paid? Sounds like he was out of his skull if you wuz' to ask me," Huck said resolutely.

"Whoever heard of a plantation what pays its niggers?"

"You never know what might be going on in those foreign countries," Tom said, "anyway, the feller' claimed to have lived on his plantation since he was a boy. He said he was visiting friends and family in Philadelphia when the war started. The way I figure is that he got swept into it just like we did when we got stranded in Norfolk."

"If I recollect proper," Huck said, "the army appeared to be a sight better than cleaning out-houses an' paintin' an' scrapin' stinkin' fishin' boats. I wuz' eaten grass as long as it wuz' boiled. I wuz' findin' birds eggs to eat, remember?"

"Everybody thought that the war was going to be over in a few weeks. Brother, were we ever naïve," Tom said nostalgically. " I figured that the war would be over quick, and that anyone who had served would have a better foot up in life than those that stayed home. Then I could get back home and ask Rebecca to come with me to the gold- fields in California."

"That is after you asked her to marry you," Huck said quickly.

"Of course," Tom said. "It all seems like it happened a million years ago."

The crash of artillery fire immediately made their heads turn. It sounded like the faint sound of a thunderstorm to the ears of the uninitiated. The veteran soldiers knew instantly what the sound was. Tom looked at Huck with fear. Something was not right. The rolling crash of artillery fire was coming from the rear.

"It's coming from the south," Tom said haltingly.

Others sitting nearby began to rise to their feet. A low murmur began among them all. The artillery fire began to increase in its intensity at the same time. Something was definitely going on in their rear. The sound of artillery began to build in its intensity. They had expected to encounter opposition from the Federal Army to their front. The sound of an unexpected engagement commencing to their rear made many a tongue in their regiment wag. All attention suddenly turned to a rider that pounded down the road in their direction.

Men quickly made room and got out of his way. He looked like he was prepared to run people down go any person that got in his way. He tore down the road toward them at breakneck speed, his mount covered in speckled foam. When the rider spotted a group of officers in the crowd of men he reared his animal to a sudden halt and athletically jumped off his horse as only an experienced horseman could. The crowd soon swung around him. Tom and Huck hurried over to better4 see what all the commotion was about. They were both surprised to see Cobb, their old captain, desperately trying to catch his breath. He now wore the insignia of a major.

Cobb was covered in dust and was frantic looking. Several officers, including Lieutenant Custiss surrounded him as he fought to regain his poise. Vernon Jenkins trotted up to the newly promoted major pushing men out of his way. Cobb took a handkerchief from his tunic pocket and began to wipe away the sweat on his brow. He inhaled deeply.

"The damned Yankees are in back of us," he began. "They are putting on a show at a crossroads town called Gettysburg. It is surely the Army of the Potomac." Vernon offered Cobb his canteen, which the major readily accepted.

"Thank you, Vernon," he said. He swallowed a mouthful and then poured some of the contents of the canteen on his head and wiped away the excess with his handkerchief.

"General Heth was the first to come to grips with them," he continued. "So far, so good, although the fight was not planned. At first, he thought it was just militia. It turns out it was Federal cavalry and plenty of them. Right now, he is driving them off and it does appear that the Yankees will not be able to hold. That sound you hear is our artillery, not theirs."

"If it is Yankee cavalry that hit General Heth then where is General Stuart and our cavalry?" Lieutenant Custiss asked.

"That is the question on everyone's lips," Cobb replied angrily. "No one seems to know. He cannot be found. It seems that his entire command has disappeared into thin air. Anyone with information on his whereabouts, even if it is just hearsay, is to report it to Division likity-split."

"Is this a major engagement or a skirmish?" the lieutenant asked quickly.

"Orders are to turn this whole Division and take up position somewhere on the Carlisle and York road before nightfall with all speed. When you arrive there sometime tonight, staff officers will guide you into your positions. Todd, it looks like something big is up. We do not know the strength of the enemy since General Stuart's disappearance this morning. Guard these roads well. I cannot stress the importance of this. Without knowing where the enemy is, the damned Yankees might just pop up on one of these roads leading into that town and cut us in two. General Ewell is moving the entire Corp to these roads. Our division will be the first in order of march. We must make sure that the Federals don't take this opportunity and use these roads to slam us all to hell and gone. Hold these roads at all cost. If you are engaged, Third Corp will support you. Any questions?"

The lieutenant shook his head.

"Understood," he said.

"Todd, start your move now and do be quick. No one will be stopping tonight until we get to those roads. I must ride and find General Johnson. Where is he?"

"About a mile up the road," the lieutenant said rapidly..

Cobb handed the canteen back to Vernon. Cobb sprang back into the saddle as the Lieutenants saluted him. Cobb took off like a jockey out of the gate in a horse race. All of those that had been close enough to hear the exchange between Cobb and Vernon quickly began to scurry a way to prepare for the all night march and gather loose belongings.

"Sergeant Jenkins, we move as quick as we can," lieutenant Custiss shouted.

Gossip began to spread around the men like wildfire. Within minutes, as far as the eye could see, men stirred as an entire division began to move towards uncertainty

General Ewell sat alone in his tent and reread the ambiguous orders spread out in front of him for the third time. They read, "When you arrive in force at Heiddelsburg, you may move directly to Gettysburg or move towards Cashtown as circumstances may dictate." His eyes roved over the page slowly looking for something that he might have missed, especially the last few words of the closing sentence.

"As circumstances may dictate."

What in the world did they mean by that, he thought. He brooded over this line as he tried to make sense of it. Why couldn't someone on headquarters staff write a clear and concise order? This order was wrapped in mystery. It told him nothing of the on going events or the progress of the battle. This order was as vague as anyone that he could remember reading. General Ewell fondly recalled the precise orders of his late commander, Stonewall Thomas Jackson. There was no mistaking the orders of Jackson. He had grown accustomed to the neat, economical, straightforward approach of Jackson and he missed their simplicity. He remembered one of them.

Scrawled on a scrap of paper, the message contained everything a Divisional Commander need know.

"To all Divisional Commanders. We have them, attack at once, no matter how currently engaged. Attack! Attack!"

Now, part of his Second Corp was engaged hotly and the Army of Northern Virginia was strung out on many different roads with an enemy that was not supposed to be where they were. The army had yet to converge on Gettysburg. The Second Corp was north of this town with one of its trailing Divisions was attacking Federal forces without knowing the location of the main body of the Union Army.

161

Dick Ewell studied the map that lay on his field table. His head turned in jerky spasmodic movements.

Dick Ewell stood at five feet, eight inches, relatively tall for someone of his generation. His bulging eyes and sharp nose gave him the distinctive look of a woodcock. He rivaled the late Second Corp commander in his own eccentric behavior. While General Jackson was know to suck on lemons and keep one of his arms raised in the air, General Ewell, while carefully studying a situation or listening carefully to someone would cock his head very much in the manner of a bird. It was even rumored that late at night, the sound of chirping noises came from his tent when the General was alone. The General's fondness for cracked sunflower seeds only fueled the rumor of his odd behavior among the men.

No matter what personal quirks the General may have had, they did not deter from the fact that he was viewed as a dynamic field officer and had just recently been given the command of the Second Corp after the death of Stonewall Jackson. General Lee had wanted a fighter to take over Second Corp and had picked Dick over many other people. This was his first battle as a Corp commander. He had the respect and trust of nearly everyone that knew him. During the fighting in Virginia he had suffered a wound that would eventually cost him his leg. He had refused to leave the field of battle until it was certain that victory had been achieved, a victory that he had been instrumental in orchestrating. The coming fight was full of portents and signs that were unsettling to him

The primary cause for his concern was the baffling disappearance of General Stuart and the entire Cavalry Corp. Stuart had left without telling anyone of his intentions and no one, it would appear, had any idea where he may have gone. It was as if the ground had opened up and swallowed the young cavalry legend. whole.

Cavalry acted as the eyes of the army keeping headquarters informed of the precise location of the enemy's movements as well as screening the army from the unwanted prying eyes of the Federal cavalry. There had been no word of Stuart's whereabouts for the last three days. The Army of Northern Virginia was now currently blind in regards to the enemy's strength and movement. It appeared that General Heth had found Federal cavalry directly in his path. This was not a good omen.

As second Corp commander, he had ordered Jubal Early, one of his more capable Divisional commanders, to attack in support of Heth. From the confused reports that had filtered back to him, it seems that the Federal forces involved in the fighting had tried to defend two ridges. General Lee's orders had been to avoid contact with Federal forces until the army had gathered in sufficient numbers but the fight had a life of its own. The fight had come to them uninvited and this was unusual. It was not the way things were done,

Jubal Early had driven the Federals off the ridges but the attack had been met with furious Federal resistance. The Iron brigade, a Federal unit known for it's tenacity in combat, had slammed into the attacking Confederate forces and had been destroyed. The sacrifice of this brigade by the Federals was unusual in the extreme. The Iron brigade, a brigade noted for its toughness and excellence as well as for the distinctive black hats that its members wore had been sent to the slaughter without a second thought by the Federal commander. The Union counter attack had apparently given the main body of the Federal Corp responding to the Confederate drive the needed time for the Federals to take up positions on the high ground out of town. This, again, was not good news to General Ewell. If the Union forces had taken up strong positions on high ground it could only mean that they were satisfied to wait. Wait for what?

To support Early, he would now have to move his entire Corp south. It would be a footrace. He had Harrisburg in his grasp and would now have to give it up and heads towards this cross-town road hub at Gettysburg. This insignificant hamlet was going to be the scene of a desperate battle. They would be forced to fight at a place not of their choosing.

His divisions would arrive sometime tonight totally worn out with their flanks "in the air." No natural defense like a river or steep hill anchored the ends of his Corp once they went into position. The York Pike pointed like an accusing finger at one unprotected flank. If the Federal army were to enter the battle from this direction he knew his Corp could be ground to dust.

That is why he had ordered a highly expendable major recently appointed to headquarters staff to ride like hell and inform all of his divisional commanders to start their move towards Gettysburg with all haste. If this major were extremely quick he may just have time and the damned good luck not to ride directly into a federal unit and get himself killed. If this major could stay alive long enough to find the foul mouthed General Johnson somewhere near Harrisburg and convince Johnson of the urgency of coming towards Gettysburg as quick as chain lightning then perhaps he could secure his flank. Johnson would have to make sure that the Carlisle, York, and Harrisburg Pile were secure. If the Union Army appeared on any one of these roads in force before General Johnson could go into position, it was clear to him that Johnson would be cut off from support of the army and subsequently would be cut up like a Virginia ham at a Sunday picnic.

Damned that Stuart, he thought angrily. Stuart has done this army a great injustice with his disappearance. He has put the lives of thousands of his countrymen in dire jeopardy. One so young, no matter how adept at ones craft, should ever be given so much power and authority. How Stuart could act so irresponsible was as much a mystery to him as was the construction of the pyramids

It would all boil down to a footrace and a lot of luck. If Jubal could shatter all Federal counter attacks and if the roads would stay dry and open so that his artillery could deploy quickly if necessary **and if General "Bushrod" Johnson** could arrive in the nick of time to protect his unprotected flanks.. Dick Ewell scratched his baldhead. Already there were too **many "ifs" and as a trained soldier with his lines** of supply stretched as thin as they were he knew exactly the danger that he was in. The risk was great. He did not even know the topography of the land east of the town the Federals were preparing to defend.

General Lee, as outnumbered as he was, would not hesitate to attack the Army of the Potomac in the past. The problem evolving was that the Federals were content to give battle and General Lee had no idea the exact location of the enemy. All of this made him feel ill with foreboding. Of all the wrong times for Stuart to take it upon himself to go riding a raid.

"Damn that Stuart," he muttered, "damn him to hell."

The speed at which Tom and his comrades hurried towards the faint sounds of cannon fire impressed upon all of them the urgency and seriousness of the predicament that they were in. This was a battle that had not been planned, and that no one in high command had apparently expected. There was no longer loud talk or foolery in the ranks, no rowdiness or open displays of false courage. The uncertainty that they rushed towards only bred silence.

Each soldier grew reflexive and introspective. Tom plodded along, the monotony of the march pressing down on him like a weight. He began to notice odd things in the road; items discarded by soldiers who did not want these last personal items sent home if the worst were to befall them. It would be very embarrassing. Playing cards, bawdy postcards, and hastily discarded letters littered the sides of the road. Tom bent over and picked up one of the hastily scrawled letters and smiled at all the incorrect spellings and began to read it.

Deer Muther,

Ther is a. fust rait fite cuming and just want to rite you this kwik in kase sumpthing mite hapen to me. I now my bruther is yur favorite and is bekos of his club foot that you alwase doted on him. But in kase sumpthing wuz too hapen to me pleese don't let him tak ovur the farm. He is a haf-wit and bon lazi and will get you onli a krop of hartbrake and truble.

164

Tom crumpled the paper into a ball and threw it into a field. He could feel something was clearly wrong. The apprehensive glances that Vernon and Lieutenant Custiss exchanged told a story that Tom could read like a book. This engagement was not normal and Tom could sense that the coming battle would be desperate. The only soldiers that did not realize this were the recruits that the regiment had picked up at Culpeper. These young boys were full of confidence, but that was something to be expected from green troops. They alone did not realize that a fight in their rear was an abnormal situation in the extreme for the Army of Northern Virginia These young inexperienced soldiers were enthusiastic, something the older veteran soldiers were not.

Somber expressions on the faces of the older men did not daunt the spirits of the younger men hoping to prove themselves in combat against the despised Yankees. The young soldiers kept up with the hard pace that the older men set. Tom was at the rear of his company. His job was to hurry along any man falling out of column. Formations must be kept or the roads could turn into a clogged mess resulting in chaos. Once a road was choked off, the inability of commands to respond to orders would reach absurd proportions. Tom had witnessed a fist fight erupt between cavalry troopers and artillerymen during a night march on the Peninsular when the commands had become entangled.

Tom's feet ached. This pace was one of the most difficult that he could remember. The entire regiment was heading down the Harrisburg Pike in one hell of a hurry when suddenly Jacob Threats stepped out of ranks and hobbled over to the side of the road. Before Tom could say a word, Jacob tore his shoes off and flung them into a freshly plowed field. Jacob stood up, stretched, and grinned strangely at Tom.

"Damned things never fit proper. Just my luck to have taken them off a dead man with feet smaller than mine I won't be needin' them damned shoes where I'm goin' and them brogans won't be worth much after this damned road race."

Jacob ran back to his place in ranks leaving Tom with an odd feeling. The very fatalistic manner in which Jacob had spoken made Tom pause for a moment. What Jacob had said had chilled him to the bone when he had looked at the strange smile that Jacob had given him, as if he were sharing some terrible secret. He tried to dismiss the incident from his mind.

Images of a dead Federal sergeant under a tree with his chin resting on his chest with his eyes wide open played in his mind over and over again. He remembered the prophetic words of the dead man. Good Lord, Tom thought, I am spooking myself. Tom began to whistle the tune of the Bonny Blue flag. Soon, many in the marching ranks were whistling in unison.

165

The sound of canon fire began to diminish in intensity as the sun began to set. At sunset, the column began to reach the outskirts of Gettysburg. The rolling wheat fields slowly gave way to wooded ridges to their left. They could make out the buildings of the town in the distance. In the faint light, they watched as the battle flags of several Confederate regiments headed into the sleepy little town. The bayonets on hundreds of rifles reflected a blue haze from the failing light.

The lead elements of their column began a turning motion away from the town as they left the road and crossed a small stream. Hurriedly, canteens were passed to men who were known to be fleet of foot. They filled the canteens that were draped by the dozens around their necks and raced to rejoin their units. The Division moved quickly forward along a railroad track. They moved eastward and the pace began to slow considerably. In the gathering darkness they could see their cook wagons and glowing campfires shooting sparks into the air. This was a bivouac area. The Divisional baggage and cook wagons that had been in their rear had simply stopped where they were and had gone to roost when the order of march had reversed itself.

They now were preparing food, a definite indicator of a coming battle. They had already started to prepare enough rations for several days. The veterans soldiers knew that once food was prepared it meant that the battle was more than likely brewing and that high command had no intention of leaving any time soon. They knew that this was to be no skirmish but a colossal clash of arms. Most of the older men, if left to their own devices and left unsupervised over a steaming kettle of beans would easily consume the entire contents of the cauldron at one sitting, leaving the cooks to curse and rant spirited tales about the questionable genealogy of certain soldiers. Their empty threats would fall like rain on empty kettles and stuffed Confederate infantrymen.

Staff officers soon arrived and raced the length of the division directing them towards positions they were to take up. Tom's regiment halted. Within an hour, the entire division was posted in a great semi-circle across a road. A large hill loomed on the horizon, dark and full of strange sounds. It was here that the tired men were allowed to rest, but not all. Tom's sister regiment was slotted for picket duty. They could hear their protests and complaints from where they sat. As soldiers slumped to the ground, the strange sounds coming from the hill to their front became clearer. Skirmishers headed towards an ominous tree line where much of the noise seemed to be coming from. People could make out the unmistakable ring of axes on trees. The more trained ear could also make out the sounds of hundreds of men digging.

"The Yankees is definitely makin' fire pits," Arthur said. Yancey Stinson, another veteran, squinted at the hill to their front.

"They is diggin' in like the furies," Yancey said. "I surely do hope that somebody is goin' to drive them off that hill before they add the finishin' touches."

166

"Maybe it's us on top of that there hill," John said hopefully. Arthur turned and faced John with a surprised look ingrained on his face and pain in his eyes.

"You must be takin' stupid lessons with Andy. Them are Yankees on that hill an' don't you doubt it, boy. Listen up. Don't you hear it?" Arthur said tiredly. John cocked his head to the side.

"Them Yankees are makin' enough noise to wake the dead. They sound like a couple of elephants in heat, by God. Only Yankees make that much ruckus diggin' in," Arthur said.

"Think they will make us go up there tonight and root them out?" John asked.

"No," Arthur said, "I don't think so. That ain't our style. We will more'n likely let them dig in all night an' git' good and tired. They will be tuckered out good come mornin'. At first light, we will probably start the dance with artillery and commence a march aroun' their sides and then wop them good on both ends. That's more our style. Them Yankees will be forced to give up what they are spendin' so much time in buildin' "

George Blakely interrupted the conversation by practically running into the group of crouching men. He was out of breadth and was panting heavily. Arms reached out and pushed him away rudely. Someone booted him in his backside as vulgar and coarse language filled the air.

"Sorry. Tom, Vernon wants to see you," he gasped.

"Where you bin'?" Arthur asked suspiciously.

"You ain't goin' to believe what I jest' saw an' overheard from some high falutin' staff officer. I was over at the cook wagon. They found a smoke house full of bacon slabs thicker than two men put together. They got real smoked beef. They got real beef cookin' an' beans forever. I never seed so much vittles cookin' in all my life. This here Pennsylvania got some very productive farms, it do appear. You should have seen some of the fella's that was there. They weren't even waitin' fer' it to git' cooked. They were goin' right at it with their bare hands."

"What did you hear?" Arthur asked.

"We beat them damned Yankees good, today. Our boys chased them right through the town itself an' caught hunert's of them. Our boys shot them down like fish in a barrel. Some of the Yankees got so confused that they ran into blind alleys. Some tried to hide in houses. Didn't do them no good, though cause our boys went an' dragged them up from out of there." John paused to catch his breadth.

"You heard all this from that staff officer?" Yancey asked.

167

"Yes, an' that ain't the half of it. It seems that our old playmates, the Yankee Eleventh Corp is here come to get' their asses kicked good again. Kin' you believe this. The damned Dutchmen never learn. We got a Federal brigade in front of us on that hill an' the damned Dutchmen are all on another hill somewhere to the south of us. The Yankees got driven off a ridge called McPherson's or some sich' an' then flung the damned black hat fella's at us. You remember them black hat fellas. I think they wuz' Wisconsin or Michigan regiments in that Brigade. Know what? Them black hat fella's is no more. They are all gone up. That damned Yankee brigade is gone, all shot to pieces. The whole damned brigade is dead on the field."

"Vernon wants to see me? Where is he?" Tom asked.

"Down the line a might. Near the road," George said. Many eager voices began to flood the night air with questions about food and other news. Tom had learned years ago to believe only a fraction of the gossip that could be heard in a camp at any given time and stood up.

He began threading his way past hundreds of prone and standing bodies. All were lazily talking while some were listening carefully to the sound of axes biting into wood coming from the dark hill that loomed in front of them. Tom walked for perhaps a mile and spotted Vernon sitting on a cracker box in front of a small sputtering campfire. Captain Custiss stood next to Vernon with a worried expression on his face. Tom came to attention and saluted Captain Custiss returned his salute and smiled at Tom.

"Good to see you Sergeant Sawyer. Tom, we have a very important job for you and I know that you will not let us down. Vernon will give you the details. Vernon, when you are finished, I will see you somewhere near the Hanover road. Let's say in about an hour?"

Vernon nodded his head. "Yes Sir."

Couriers flew by. There was hurried activity all around as officers conferred with each other and messages were relayed back to their senders. The captain looked at Tom as if he had something to say but then instead turned and walked over to a group of staff officers bent over a field map. The busy officers acknowledged his appearance with a barrage of questions.

"Tom," Vernon began, "I'm not gonna' beat aroun' the bush. Straight out, the Captain wants you to pick six men altogether an' go up that damned hill what's in front of us an' grab us a prisoner. We need to know just what is at the top of the hill and who."

Tom's heart began to beat rapidly and his throat began to clench tightly.

"We got to know if that is the Fifth Corp on that hill. We have pickets close to the base of that hill and they are reporting that the Yankees got rifle pits already dug across the base. Them boys know we are here. So far, patrol activity on their side has been light. They tend to run only a few yards from the pits."

"Vernon, I n...never did anything like this before," Tom stammered nervously. "Why pick me?"

"I didn't pick you. The Captain did. He figures that you bin' lucky the last few days an' that your luck may jest holt' out long enough for you to git' the job done."

Tom bit his lower lip in fear.

"I know what yer' thinkin'. It is a dirty job crawlin' aroun' in the dark with out knowin' how many Yankees is out there but you kin' do it, son. It's got to be done. Nobody knows nothin' about nothin' with Stuart having jest upped and disappeared into thin air. It may be two Corp in front of us instead of jest' the one."

Vernon rose from his seat on the cracker box and lit his pipe. He drew on it slowly. Tom squirmed like a worm on a hook. He shifted his weight from foot to foot.

"You know, Tom, if old Jackson wuz, alive, we would have gone up that hill before the Yankees had a chance to put one shovel in the dirt or chopped a single tree down. But with him gone an' Stuart disappeared, it ain't developin' along the usual path. We are fightin' blind. It calls fer' different methods. This one is our only option, I'm afraid to say. All our lives may depend on what you do tonight."

Tom swallowed dryly. "When?" he croaked.

Vernon relaxed. "Right quick, as soon as you pick your volunteers. Our pickets are already waiting fer' you. See that fella over there. When you pick your men, he will show you where to go. They will take you as close to the enemy as they dare without gittin' involved heavy with them. They will show you a way aroun' the Yankee pits. After that, you got to sneak in an' go deep. You got to be quick. No more than a couple of hours at the most. Pick Arthur to lead one group an' you lead the other. Out of both of you, one should make it. Don't choose no tall fellers. Pick small wiry types. If you get' into trouble, drop what you are doin' an' get' back here. We don't want you captured. By God, Tom, be quick but play it smart. The pickets will be lookin' fer' you when you are ready to come back in. They have a password fer you to get' back into our lines. Tom, you got good instincts. Keep yer' eyes open."

"I'll do my best," Tom said stoutly. "Give me a few minute. I will be right back."

Vernon knocked his pipe against a tree and small embers fell at his feet. As he watched Tom turn to leave, he suddenly shouted, "Don't go an' get yerself kilt', you hear?"

"I will try my damndest not to," Tom said grinning. Although Tom was frightened by what he was about to try, he hid his fear well.

"How are the new boys doin?" Vernon asked. "The recruits we picked up at Culpeper?"

"They are all good boys. They will be fine," Tom replied.

"When you see Higgins, tell him to gather all the new boys together an' send them over to me. I'll be right here. Make sure you tell Higgins to feed them all. I got somethin' to say to them."

The Talk. Tom remembered the first time that he had heard Vernon give the Talk. Tom had been as green as grass to army ways at the time. That had been nearly three years ago.

"I remember when you first gave me the Talk. That's what this is all about, right?" Tom asked.

Vernon simply smiled and put his pipe back into his breast pocket. He smiled a wane smile.

"Somebody got to do it," Vernon said.

"One last question. That hill out there, it got a name?"

"Culp's hill. It's called Culp's hill. Why?"

"Just curious," Tom answered. He trotted off into the darkness to find Corporal Higgins.

All of the new recruits had been fed and all thirty-seven of them, all from various companies in the regiment, now sat in a semi circle where Sergeant Jenkins was sitting on a cracker box. Vernon could not help noticing how young they appeared. They seemed to be getting younger and younger every year, he reflected sadly. Corporal Higgins walked among them observing their behavior and waiting for Vernon to let him know when he was ready.

Higgins broke a few large pieces of rail fence across his knee and tossed the sections into the fire. Shadows played across the faces of the recruits. The fire began to flare supplying a good light as Vernon continued to study his captive audience. A few talked amongst each other nervously but most remained silent. Corporal Higgins noticed Vernon stand and he spoke loudly, "Pay attention now." He stopped abruptly and stalked towards a young man who had made the mistake of continuing to chatter away.

"You. Big mouth. Shut yer trap or I'll kick yer' danged teeth out of yer' numbskull. Listen up an' listen up good. This here is the regimental First-sergeant, the most important man we got. He's got somethin' he wants to tell you an' if yer' smart, yer just may listen to what he says an' be alive tomorrow. What he got to say will save yer' life."

The young man had frozen as Higgins stared at him angrily. Satisfied that he had their attention, Higgins stepped aside.

"They are all yours, First-Sergeant," Higgins said reverently.

Vernon began speaking in a low tone as the young men strained to hear what he was saying.

"Men, my name is Sergeant Jenkins. If you don't know already, I am the Regimental First Sergeant. I don't have to tell you that we ran across the Army of the Potomac this morning," he said. "You kin' hear with yer' own ears the sound of them diggin' in right to our front. They are buildin positions, breastworks, an' rifle pits." He carefully watched their faces.

"I am not gonna' bore you with why we are fightin' those people. This, you already know. I'm not gonna' waste my time an' talk in grand terms an' big words about this cause of ours. I reckon you've heard it all before. I will tell you this. The hopes of millions of your countrymen all ride on what you are prepared to do here in the mornin', make no mistake about that." He paused a moment. His voice became louder.

"I know you all kin' shoot. You've bin' shootin' game since you were all youngin's."

There was some nervous laughter from a few of them. Vernon again paused.

"But you never shot any game before that kin' shoot back."

Some more of the boys even grinned at this last comment. Vernon's voice grew even louder.

"This will be the first time you boys get' to see the elephant. The elephant is a nasty old beast what eats young men like yourselves fer' breakfast. He chews you up an' spits you out. He grinds your bones to dust. By tomorrow night, many of you sittin' here smilin' up pleasant like at me will be just a memory. You will be worm food. You will be cold and stiff as your daddy's boots. This is the simple cruel arithmetic of battle. I want each man to look at the other man sittin' next to him."

No one turned his head or moved a muscle.

"I tolt you to look at the man sittin' next to you. That is an order," Vernon screamed furiously. His angry manner made heads swivel about as they obeyed his command.

"You must learn to obey all orders without thought, without what you think the other fella may think of you or what the other fella' would do. When someone tells

171

you to do somethin', you had better do it or you will end up dead, dammit," Vernon shouted.

"The man sittin' right next to you, by tomorrow night, may be lying on the field dead because you failed to properly respond to a command or learn from what I'm about to tell you tonight." Vernon placed his foot on the cracker box. His voice became less tense but not relaxed. He leaned towards them.

"You kin' fergit all those fancy boyhood stories about was that was written by some idjit' that never was in a war. Git' that nonsense out of yer' head. War is not some romantic adventure like them stories say. The people that fed you them lies never seen a man die tripping over his own bowels what dropped around his ankles when a piece of shot from the artillery slashed his belly wide open. He never seen a man try to stay alive by pushing his own guts inside his own stomach with both his hands or seen a poor damned soul try to keep a friend alive by stickin' a rag in a hole in a man's chest so that the man don't bleed to death. These men who write them stories have never seen the effect of solid artillery shot goin' into a massed pack of human beings. People who wrote them there stories never seen heads and arms an' legs go spinnin' high into the air or smelt the stink of blood close up."

The young faces all looked frightened now. No smiles or nervous jabbering was heard. It had become as quiet as a congregation at a funeral.

"There is no glory in war, no adventure. I have never seen a man die gloriously; I have only seen them die bloody. There is no chivalry out here and the only honor to be found out here is in the way that you react under fire. There is nothing honorable in driving a bayonet through the throat of a man or in poundin' a man's brains out with a rock after you have shot everything you had and the Yankees still are comin' at you with bad intent. Anybody that says war is glorious is full of shit."

This was not the kind of talk that they had expected to hear from a Regimental First Sergeant. Their generation had been raised on the stories of Sir Walter Scott who had defined war as a glorious adventure, a crusade to test one's manhood in the crucible of fire and certainly not to be missed or avoided. He had imparted to them the concept of war as being almost holy; a lofty romantic belief of what is was to be a man. What they were hearing now from the man who wore the stripes of a Regimental First Sergeant was blasphemy.

"Boys, you are now in the business of butchery. We are here to kill so that we may not be killed. Not getting' kilt' is what is measured as success out here in this version of hell that you have decided to become a part of. I have bin' more fortunate than many. That is why I wear the stripes." Vernon could almost feel their apprehension and confusion.

172

"Because I wear the stripes, it is my job to see that you all fairly get' an opportunity of not bein' kilt'. This is my job. How we do this is up to each an' every one of you. Simply stated, you must learn to look an' listen. You must learn to obey every order an' command of all sergeants and non-commissioned officers without question or hesitation. You must learn to do as the veteran soldiers do. It cannot git' any more simpler than that. Failure to respond correctly will git' you kilt'."

All eyes were now locked onto every movement, motion, and nuance of this very frightening soldier whose own gray eyes were chilling.

"You may think me as crazy as a June bug divin' into a bucket of water, but if you live through this comin' fight, you will look back at what I say an' then maybe it won't sound so insane. It is my responsibility to tell you these things so that you all may be success stories an' not just a dim memory in a month's time. We are killed for lack of knowledge." One sixteen-year-old recruit standing next to Vernon appeared as if he was going to throw up.

"Rule number one," Vernon began, "is not to fire when you are out of range. Do not fire until you are ordered to fire. Do not fire until you are in effective range. You will know that you are in effective range when the man next to you is shot. If you have not been ordered to shoot, you must resist the temptation to shoot. Obey commands at all times and when you are ordered to open fire you will copy the behavior of the old hands. Watch how the veteran soldiers fire. Aim deliberately and fire coolly an' pour it into them. Keep your fire steady. Don't look to see where you shot at. Keep your fire low an' do not overshoot. A headshot will kill but the human body is a bigger target. Aim fer' that."

Vernon carefully watched their young eager faces knowing that some of the boyish faces looking at him would possibly be dead in a day's time.

"Sometimes, it is far better to wound a man than to kill him outright. The reason is that there are always men in a fight who will look for any opportunity to get' off the field, even if it means carrying a wounded man. By wounding a man, you have provided a perfect chance fer' maybe one or possibly two Yankees to get' off the field by carryin' the wounded man. Now you have taken three men out of the fight instead of the two." Vernon noticed a few of the boys nodding their heads in agreement.

"Remember, it is your responsibility to mention to any sergeant when you are running out of cartridges. If you cannot shoot, you are useless. If your rifle grows silent, you will grow silent as well. Permanently." The sixteen-year-old recruit suddenly got to his feet and began to retch. He staggered off into the night. Higgins acted as if to go after the young man, but Vernon restrained him.

"Let him go, corporal. He's got a right to be sick. He's the smartest of all of them in my book. None of you make fun of him, either fer' what jest' happened, you hear? This little incident that you jest' saw brings me to rule number two," Vernon said.

"Don't doubt yerselves' or yer' instincts," he said. "I have seen strong men crumble in a hot fight an' seen weak men turn into killin' machines. Do not be ashamed of fear. Use it. Turn it to your advantage. Let it become a tool that you kin' function with, like yer' rifle. Ever' single solitary soldier is afraid in a fight. If he ain't, there is something wrong with him. If he says he ain't afraid then you are speaking with a liar an' a damned fool."

Some of the younger ones snickered at this. Vernon waited a minute for it to sputter out.

"Fear can sharpen your survival instincts to a razors edge or it kin' turn you into a lump of jelly. Live with yer' fear an' listen to it. Never let it control you. If yer' let it control yer mind, it will surely kill you in the end." The teenage soldiers clung to his every word, totally mesmerized by what he was saying.

"Rule number three. Single out anyone who is showing signs on the enemy side of bravery. Do not let these people live. Cut them down. Do not let that man rally his people or inspire their side. Kill them quick. I will tell you a brief story to illustrate my point. In one fight, a Yankee regiment was comin' at us. The Yankees did not know that two Regiments of our division was perched on their sides because of all the smoke an' sich" He waited a moment. He looked past their faces and towards the dark hill

"The Yankee color bearer came at us, right up the center an' the Yankees followed right on his heels, over two hundred of them. When they got close, ever'body let loose, includin' our regiments on their flanks. When the smoke cleared, practically the only Yankee standin' was that color bearer still wavin' his flag. When he looked around an' saw he was alone, he stood there wavin that damned flag for all the world to see. Everybody on our side was impressed. Not one man took a shot at him. Ever'body on our side started whistlin' an' clappin'. Many tolt' him to git but he would not listen. Another Yankee regiment in back of him saw what he was doin' an' they started Hoo-rahs fer him an' started forward.." Vernon turned away from the hill and faced them all again.

"This major, a staff officer, pushes ever'body aside, pulls out a pistol an' shoots that color bearer right through his head. The rest of the Yankees seen it an' decided not to come at us. an' it was a good thing they didn't because we were low on ammunition. That staff officer turned on our captain an' gave us all a dressin' down. He was madder'n hell an let ever' body within' ear shot have it good. It seems that General Jackson had seen the whole thing what happened. General Jackson, he said,

174

had ordered him down to us jest' to kill this one color bearer. The Major had said that General Jackson had shouted that he did not want the enemy brave, he wanted the enemy dead."

The sergeant waited to see how many of them had clearly understood what he was trying to tell them. He saw that many of them were nodding their heads.

"What I want you to shoot at is any Federal soldier wearing stripes. Kill them. Officers, I want you to leave them alone. They are delightful fellows. Most of them don't know their asses from their elbows. They are a positive asset to our side. The Union Army continues to lose battle under their guidance so for heavens sake, leave them be. You kin' always spot a Yankee officer. They are fond of carrying swords and are usually to be found in the rear of their men out of danger."

Loud laughter broke out from the young recruits. The tenseness of the earlier moments began to give way. Vernon knew that they were starting to understand his words.

"Rule number four. If we are ordered to go in against artillery, do not take the time to try to shoot the gunners. If you do, your friends will be pickin' up yer' carcass with a bucket an' shovel. Gunners need to shift their elevation at targets. If we go in agin' artillery, we will rush them. We will git' under their ability to depress the barrel low enough to shoot at us. We will go in quick. This is called gittin' under the guns. If you hear the order to advance agin' artillery, move at the double quick an' don't stop fer' nothin' or nobody, Do not go to ground. If the enemy are usin' solid canon shot, the balls have a tendency to bounce along the ground an' you will not be able to git' out of the way in time. Never huddle together. I have seen one shot take the heads off a half dozen men at one time."

There was so much for these boys to learn and in such a short time. Vernon looked out at their expectant faces and he knew that some of these boyish faces now smiling would be smiling no more in the course of a few days.

"When you are ordered to fire, shoot at the fellas what hold the sponge staffs. They have to make sure that there are no burnin' embers in the barrel before the loader shoves in a bag of powder. Shoot at the buckets what hold the water. Shoot the horses. I know it goes agin' the grain to be cruel to a horse fer' all of you but do it. Federal artillery will, as a matter of course, limber up their batteries an' try to break off the fight once they see us gittin' under their ability to depress the barrels low enough to do us in. Don't let them do this because when they are a safe distance from us, they will unlimber their guns an' pound us into apple butter, Kill the horses an' the artillery-men will skeddadle. Artillerymen are not infantry. They prefer to kill at long distances an' it goes up their craw when they think of mixin' it up in close combat. They are more'n likely to run when you close with them. If infantry does not support artillery, they are almost defenseless. I have seen artillery be more noisy than dangerous when they are unsupported by infantry."

He paused to clearly think about what he was going to tell them next. He wanted this point to stick.

"Rule number five. This is most important. Remember that you are more likely to git' killed runnin' away in a fight than in advancin' towards them. Goin' backwards is far more dangerous than goin' forward fer' one simple reason. If you are goin' forward agin' the enemy you are a danger to him, a threat to his life. If you are runnin' away, all you are presentin' to him is yer' back an yer' back is a good target fer him to aim at."

Some of the tougher boys openly scoffed at the idea of running in the coming fight. Vernon carefully noted them.

"When you are ordered to charge infantry, run at them screamin' an' yellin'. Like old Slew Foot is right behind you fixin' on stickin' you in the ass with his ole' pitchfork. Scream so that all the Chinamen in far off China kin' hear you. This puts the fear of God in them and puts them at a disadvantage because you are scarin' the piss right out of them. No one in his right mind enjoys see'n a crowd of folks comin' at them with a bayonet. It is a demoralizing thing."

Vernon removed his foot from the crate and put his hands on his hips.

"If you are ordered to withdraw, watch an see how the veterans do it, Do not stampede to the rear. Retreat an' if you kin', try to keep up a fire so that you continue to pose a danger to them. Do not break an' run or you will die. Try to keep yer' front to the enemy. Follow all orders without hesitation. I have tolt' you all that chivalry is dead. It is. Honor lives. It lives in what you do tomorrow an' it will live on long after you are dead. We have always whipped those people. We are the Army of Northern Virginia."

Some of the boys began to clap loudly and a few throats roared in shots of approval and admiration for what Vernon had just said. Vernon hoped that they had absorbed at least a fraction of what he had been telling them. He raised his hand to silence them. They obediently quieted down almost instantly.

"This here is the last part. If some one you know good, a friend or relative is shot an' falls, do not stop to help them. The best thing to do fer' him is to go an' shoot the man what jest shot him. Leave the wounded. I know it is a hard thing to do, but if you don't want to end up like the man lying on the ground you must bring yerself' to leave them. There is nothin' you kin' do for him at the moment. The man that jest' shot him will shoot you if you decide to help him. Bandsmen will git' to them an' git' them help. Don't let yer' fellow soldiers down. You must carry the fight fer' the fallen friend. Load...aim...fire. Do it like clockwork. There will be times when you won't be able to even see the enemy because of the smoke. Ignore the smoke an' continue to fire until you are tolt' to cease fire. If I see any man quittin' the fight to help a wounded man off the field instead of helpin' his friends who are up to their neck in a fight, I will put my foot clean through his ass. Then that man will never be able to git' from the field with my foot through his ass, It can't be done."

Laughter broke out and rolled from the captive audience and Vernon felt relieved. Once again, as he had done many times, he had delivered the "talk." He was glad that it was finished.

"It is high time that I git' out of the pulpit an' you men git' on back to yer' companies. Tomorrow is goin' to be a long hellified day. Git' some rest. Yer' sergeants an' officers have the highest confidence in you, an' I know that you will not let us down. Listen, watch, an' learn from the veterans aroun' you. After this fight, you will all be veterans an' we will be one more step closer towards winnin' this war an' goin' home." Vernon nodded at Corporal Higgins.

The corporal took his cue and shouted loudly, "Attention in the ranks." The boys sprang to attention as Vernon walked away from the crackling fire and into the darkness. Corporal Higgins swung towards them like a large door.

"Detail, dismissed," he barked. He watched them as they dispersed and scattered into the shadows to ponder what they had just heard. He looked towards the horizon towards an ominous black hill that stood out boldly from it.

"Amen, Vernon," he said softly.

CHAPTER ELEVEN

Although it had taken the Union cavalryman all morning to become somewhat lost, by late afternoon he had accomplished the feat to perfection. He had no idea where he was at the moment and he could not have been more confused in regards to even what road he was near. The setting sun supplied him with an idea of where west was. He knew that General Greene, the man he was supposed to deliver his message to was supposedly somewhere east of the town of Gettysburg. Generals Sykes had given him the message and had told him to hand deliver it to General Greene. Under no circumstances was he to hand the message over to a staff officer.

He had followed the Baltimore Pike and had crossed Rock Creek. As he wandered along the bank of the creek, he had spotted hills in front of him, to the east and to the west. General Greene was on one of them and until he actually found him, he knew he would be forced to check all of them. All late afternoon, he had cautiously searched the hills, but they all looked the same. He had heard the crash of artillery fire to the west. All afternoon he had not seen a solitary human being. Now, with darkness approaching, all he could do was hope that he would get lucky and find someone who would know of the whereabouts of General Greene. He knew he had to be careful in the coming gloom. Pickets often shot first and asked questions later. He did not want to get shot by the same people he was entrusted to find.

He walked his exhausted horse at a snail's pace keeping a wary eye on every branch, tree, and bush that he could see in the failing light. He preferred to stay dismounted and off the trails. By keeping to the bush and walking, it made him less of a target but slowed his progress. If he were to encounter any trouble, he would have a slim chance on getting away on the pitiful tired nag that he had been given. The poor beast was probably good for one last quick burst of speed and then it would only be good for the glue factory.

He had taken a look at the orders that he had been entrusted to carry and hand deliver to the General. All they mentioned were that General Greene could expect reinforcements in the morning. They read, "Fifth Corp at Bonaughtown. Am moving with all haste towards Gettysburg. Twelfth Corp has joined with the Eleventh Corp. You will be supported. Hold with all urgency defensive ground/east." It was signed, General Sykes. During the day he listened as the battle had grown in intensity. It seemed to have increased its tempo and had grown noisier by the hour. With the sun setting, the firing had slackened and then had dropped away to nothing.

As he plodded forward, lost and alone, he began to pity himself. He wished now that he was splendidly ensconced back in Mrs. Hall's charming brothel in the Capitol. Being a general's aide and messenger had its perks. Stumbling around in

178

the dark expecting to be shot by a nervous Federal picket was a major drawback to his previously easy life.

During one of these easy periods when General Sykes had taken time out to enjoy the company of some of his cronies in Washington, the soldier had found out exactly what Mrs. Hall's fancy house had to offer. It was filled to capacity with the very rich and famous of the day. He had been amazed. He had discovered a beautiful prostitute there who was barely able to understand a word of English. After his discovery, he had called the place his home. The woman said that she was from Russia; a place that he had never known existed until then. She believed him to be an important man after the soldier had embellished his role in the conflict to a great degree. She had given in to his every whim and desire and had driven him half crazy. He did not want to lose her to a true man of means and so he had begun to hold up patrons of the establishment late at night. If they resisted him, he would give the individual a solid thrashing. It was dangerous but the payoff was enormous and he had never once been suspected since his was a face that everyone had grown to know.

He began to think of her as he peered through the underbrush. He stopped suddenly and froze still, not believing his ears. The sound of an ax hitting wood sounded clearly in the air. The sound came from his left. Finally, he thought, contact. But who was wielding that ax? He strained to better listen to its steady bite into wood and then he heard more. Many men were somewhere to his left making a lot of noise. At first, just a few sounds, and then more and more until the woods rang with the sound of people chopping.

Cautiously, he began to move in the direction of the sound. The noises grew more distinct with every few yards that he managed to cover. Now, he could also make out the sounds of shovels and pick axes at work. The soldier tied his horse to a sapling and quietly removed a cavalry carbine from the saddle. He quickly checked to see that it was primed and ready for firing. He walked forward as if he were on eggshells, desperately trying not to make a sound. He knew that he was close to his own lines now and did not want to surprise a nervous picket on sentry duty. He readied his weapon as he prudently moved forward in the twilight. Somewhere, ahead in the gloom, he heard a tree crash heavily to the ground. Fortifications were being prepared and he grew confident that it was Federal forces to his immediate front. It must be General Greene.

He had met the sixty-two year old General Greene in the Capitol. The old man was impressive. He was an engineer, graduating second in his class at West Point when most of the men involved in the war hadn't even been conceived. His family name was well known in military circles. He hailed from Warwick, Rhode Island, the same small Rhode Island town that had produced one of the American Revolutions greatest generals, General Nathaniel Greene. But it was not his connections or prestigious name that had garnered him success but the man's innate sense of fairness, intelligence, and boldness. The General had taught engineering at West Point. Many of the important generals of note in the war had at one time or another been his students there. Later, at the age when most men would have retired, he had gone on to become one of the most successful civil engineers in the United States.

General Greene was well known to be a fanatical believer in fortified positions. The way he had his men working, it sounded like he had them building a bridge. The Calvary trooper began to relax a bit. His job was almost over. The tricky part now was not to get killed by a nervous sentry. After he delivered his message, he would ask directions out of here, he thought. He did not want to dally around at the top of a hill that the entire rebel army would more than likely assault. He had no intention of waiting around for the rebel hammer to fall. He had seen firsthand the determined power of Confederate attacks and he knew that he did not want any part of it.

If a picket challenged him he knew that his best chance was to yell out loudly and identify himself as a courier. He began to think of Olga as he carefully made his way back to his horse, He pushed a branch aside and looked towards the spot that he had left the weary animal and the dispatches. Fear and panic hit him all at once. The horse was gone. His head spun around as his heart jumped into his throat. He felt red-hot needles flowing in his veins as he flushed warmly all over. It felt as if he had swallowed a rock.

He desperately tried to remember a familiar landmark and was satisfied that he was not losing his mind. He knew that the horse was supposed to be where he had left it and he had left it where it was supposed to be, next to a stunted pine. He tried to be rational. The old nag must have slipped the tether and had gone browsing towards the tree line in search of tender grass shoots. It could not have gone too far in the short time that he had left it tied to the sapling. He fought back the panic that gripped his feverish mind. His fear began to turn to anger at the horse.

"Where the hell are you," he mumbled to himself. He stooped and listened carefully. He heard something heavy crashing through the bush slightly ahead of him. He stooped low to better hear the noises. He strained to judge the sound's direction. Abruptly, a twig or branch snapped behind him, and he froze. His hand tightened on his carbine as he dropped flat to the ground. He listened to his horse whiny in agitation as pure terror began to play hell with his reason.

It must be the pickets. He quickly weighed his options. If he were to stay hidden, it would scare the pickets and that could prove fatal if they were to stumble upon him. If he shouted out who he was that could invite a hail of bullets as well. These pickets were very close and he did not want to startle them. This was not good. If the sentries had found the horse, he figured, surely they must have found the dispatches by now. If they had enough brains, they would know that a courier was nearby and not just let loose a volley in his direction once he made his presence known. He would wait and be careful and time his movement.

All of a sudden he heard a man clear his throat. The sound came from behind him. Another person whistled in a bad imitation of a birdcall. Footsteps could be heard to his front. They were all around him. He prayed that they had found the dispatches. He made out many footsteps and the person that had cleared his throat suddenly spoke in a hushed whisper that he could not make out. A few seconds went by and then he heard a voice distinctly louder cry out.

"We know you are out there. We got your horse and the dispatches. Advance and be recognized."

The cavalry trooper tried to stall. He waited a full minute before responding. He stood up carefully.

"Don't shoot, boys. I am a dispatch rider from Fifth Corp, come to deliver a message to General Greene in person. I am standing up now and I'm puttin' my carbine on the ground. My hands are in the air. I have an urgent dispatch from General Sykes to General Greene so for Gawd's sake, don't shoot. I'm comin out. Don't shoot."

He placed the carbine on the ground and raised his hands into the air. He slowly advanced towards the hidden voices He was relieved in his good fortune of running into them. The sooner he delivered the message, the sooner he could make his way back to a rear area.

"Step forward quick an' quit your jabberin'. These woods are full of rebel patrols," an angry voice whispered. The cavalryman walked in confidence towards the shapes he could now clearly make out in silhouette. He walked as quickly as he was able in the darkness trying not to make any noise. Three rifles were pointing at his chest and a sickening feeling came over him in that second of realization. Too late, he saw that he had made a serious mistake. The men were all rebels.

The trooper looked at the scarecrows that confronted him. He felt his blood superheat in his veins as the adrenaline coursed through his body. The ancient human survival mechanism, of fighting or fleeing, waged an unholy contest within his nerve-wracked mind. He felt as if he were about to jump out of his skin. Pete Wilson raised his rifle and pointed the barrel within an inch of the half maddened horrified courier's nose.

"Why don't you be a right smart fella an' put them there hands of your'n high in the air again. Fer' you, the war is over," Pete said crisply.

The corners of the trooper's mouth twitched away and his eyes blinked rapidly. His heart pounded away in his chest as he raised his hands in the air. Someone stepped forward and began to pat him down for any concealed weapons.

"Ed," a voice whispered, "tell Arthur that we got our package and we are moving on out of here."

Things swam in front of the trooper's eyes. He felt nauseous and weak. His mind screamed for action but his body seemed disconnected. He watched as his captor's heads continuously swiveled about searching the woods. Suddenly, he realized that they were as afraid as he was. These rebels were as nervous as a bunch of belled cats. In that one instant, hope soared triumphant in his heart. These rebel boys were in a high state of anxiety and the apparent fear that they were all openly exhibiting was something that might help him.

He thought about yelling for help but quickly discounted the idea. If these rebels were that afraid of what might be lurking in the darkness then he knew that he must be very close to his own lines. Confidence flooded into his soul and he felt an inner strength grow with his wild pulse rate.

"That was a damned dirty trick, you son's a bitches," he said loudly. One of the scarecrows placed his rifle on the ground and began to fiddle with a short piece of rope.

"Shut yer' yap, Yankee, an' lemme' see you put yer' hands behind your back a'fore we shut you up permanent like."

The cavalry trooper began to slowly lower his hands An inner voice screamed for him to act and act quickly. Images of a prisoner stockade flashed in his mind and with that image came thoughts of a lingering death. Dark thoughts of rivers of filth and starvation bloomed in his all too fertile and desperate mind. The southern soldier stepped behind him and he gazed into the barrel of the rifle of the soldier in front of him He watched the soldier's eyes as he began to lower his hands, and in one movement he brought his hands down and swept the rifle away from his face. To everyone's complete surprise, the Yankee trooper turned and bowled Yancey Stinson completely over.

The trooper bounded off into the night, his legs pumping furiously. He ran as if he were possessed. He ran through thick briars and bushes as branches and vines lashed his face. He stretched his hands out in front of him only when something darker than the surrounding blackness loomed in front of him. This action saved him on numerous occasions from running into trees and killing himself. He ran with his head down and put all of his energy, all of his being, into escaping. The image of his Russian prostitute flashed into his mind and it spurred him into moving even faster.

He heard footsteps behind him but never once did he look to his rear. At one time he even heard their labored breathing and their curses. With every passing second, he noticed their footsteps falling further and further behind him. He wanted to shout for joy. His pursuers could not keep up with his frenzied pace, and he knew that they dared not fire at him.

When the Union soldier had begun his dash for freedom, Pete had quickly sighted in on the fleeing man's head. He would have killed him on the spot if Yancey had not popped back up and had begun to chase the bowlegged cavalryman, ruining Pete's chances of sending a large caliber conical projectile through the madly scurrying troopers head. Pete lowered his rifle and cursed. He watched as Yancey flew after the Federal soldier, and heard Yancey cursing a blue streak as he scrambled after the escaping prisoner.

The Federal soldier was fast and Yancey Stinson was both emaciated and exhausted from the hard marching of the day but he gave it his all. Fear gave the Union man speed and since the Federal soldier had not just recently marched twelve miles at a dizzying pace like his pursuer, the Yankee quickly outdistanced Yancey who felt his stamina slipping away with every step. Knowing that he was losing the race, Yancey stopped and pulled a large knife from his boot. He sighted in on the Federal soldier's back and hurled it at him with all of his remaining strength.

He never saw the knife drive home to its target, but he did hear the man's scream of pain as well as the sound of a body crashing heavily into the underbrush. Yancey froze and scanned the darkness at the very last place that he had seen his quarry. He went into a crouch. Yancey had dropped his own rifle when the chase had started and now looked quickly about for a weapon. He found a stout branch and whacked it violently against a tree. Part of it went winging away into the night but what remained in his hand made a respectable sturdy club. He was short of breadth and he wheezed and whistled as he sucked in the night air. He began to creep forward on all fours, dragging his club along. He moved in quick spurts, watching the darkness and listening for any sound. He prayed that his wheezing would not betray his location to the enemy soldier.

Yancey was elated and quite surprised as well. This was the first time that he had ever hit anything with his knife. He knew that he had hit the soldier as he concentrated all that he had in finding his prey. He was determined to find the man and fix him good. His hands searched for signs of blood on the low grass and leaves.

"You were fast, yer damned Yankee, but not faster than a knife," Yancey said quietly to himself. "Why didn't yer' jest' give up proper, yer' nitwit."

Yancey talked to himself to ease his own fear. Although he was confident that the Federal soldier was not going to get away, he was afraid that an enemy patrol may have heard them crashing through the woods. Earlier, when they had crawled into these woods, they had been surprised at the number of Federal patrols active at the base of the hill. They were everywhere and anywhere.

"Now, with all this fuss an' feathers you caused, I ain't got no choice now but to snuff you out like a candle. Unless yer' already dead. I hope you are dead, you pain in the ass. Come out. C'mon boy, show yer damned carcass."

Yancey had been too preoccupied in his thoughts and his talking was a serious lapse in sound judgment. The cavalry trooper sprang at Yancey, driving Yancey's head into the ground. The trooper was far heavier than Yancey and he began to savagely beat Yancey. The Federal soldier straddled Yancey's chest and pinned his arms to the earth with his knees. He smashed his fist into Yancey's nose. He picked the dazed man's head up by his long hair and smashed a dozen blows into his face. The Federal soldier pulverized Yancey's features. He stood up and sank his heel into Yancey's neck and placed all his weight on it. The soldier, not satisfied that he had the proper angle to snap Yancey's neck, fell back on top of him and began to strangle the unconscious Yancey Stinson.

Between tightening his grasp on the bloody slippery neck of Yancey, he relentlessly pounded away at his victim's nose. Blood spurted and poured from his nose like a faucet. Yancey's unseeing eyes bulged then quickly began to swell into slits with the unmerciful beating. Yancey's life began to ebb away.

The trooper smiled as he saw that he was killing the rebel. The snap of a twig made him momentarily turn to see what had caused the noise. All he saw before the rifle made contact with his unprotected head was a blur. Arthur was standing over him with both hands clenched tightly on the barrel. He brought the stock of the rifle down so quickly that the Federal trooper never had an opportunity to dodge the blow. Arthur appeared determined to drive the Federals head through the forest floor. The Cavalryman took the blow full force to the top of his head and slid off of Yancey. He crumpled silently over on his side.

Satisfied that no further trouble would be coming from his adversary, Arthur turned his attention to the very still form of Yancey Stinson. He placed his ear next to Yancey's face to detect breathing. He pulled Yancey by his arms out of the bushes and more towards the scattered moonlight that broke through the canopy of the woods. What he saw shocked and sickened him. Yancey's eyes were mere slits and his nose was smashed flat.

"Good Lord Almighty,' Arthur whispered in horror. He heard the sounds of footsteps and reached for a pistol that he kept in his boot. He cocked the hammer back and lay low next to Yancey's unmoving body. He recognized Tom and Ed and put the pistol back into his boot and stood up. Tom and Ed stopped in mid stride when they saw what the Federal soldier had done to their friend.

"Is he dead?" Tom asked.

Ed stooped over the body and was sickened at what he saw. Yancey's head had begun to swell enormously.

"My God, look what that boy did to old Yancey," Ed whispered in horror. "The Yankee done banged his snout flat. I never seen anything like this here before. His whole head is blowin' up to the size of a damned pumpkin."

"He ain't dead. He's breathin', Tom. I saw the whole thing. Yancey here took off after our Yankee friend here,"

Arthur pointed to the still form of the Federal trooper. "Yancey went after him like a coon dog. He caught the Yankee but he caught one hell of a shellackin' hisself'. When I caught up to the both of them, the Yankee was sittin' astride Yancey goin' to town on him. My rifle butt an' the damned Yankee's head had a quick get together, but Tom, I got carried away a tad. I cracked the Yankee a good'n. I'm a feared I broke his head real good."

"Don't you fret none, Arthur, I know a good lawyer. Somebody get me a rag," Tom said. Ed handed Tom a rag that they had planned on using to blindfold the prisoner. Tom poured water onto it and began to clean Yancey's ruined face.

"It appears that damned Yankee bashed Yancey's face in with a mallet," Ed said in fascination. Arthur checked on the Federal soldier by kicking the man in the side. The man grunted loudly.

"Olga," he moaned.

"How do you figger' that? I thought he was dead," Arthur said in surprise. "Look what we got here." Arthur reached down and pulled a knife from the man's leg with a quick jerk. The federal soldier sat up and screamed in pain. Arthur swung quickly and punched the cavalryman in the nose. The Union trooper fell back down and went stiff. Arthur wiped the blade on the soldier's shirt

"That fella is full of surprises. He got hisself' one hard head," Arthur uttered.

"Ed," Tom spoke, "go fetch everybody. Get this fella's horse. Tell John to stay behind a few paces. Tell Johnny if he sees anything to whistle. Tell him we are moving in five minutes, as much time as it will take to tend to Yancey. Five minutes."

Ed stood up and ran into the night. Tom walked over to the Federal soldier and began to tie the prisoner's arms together. Pete Wilson gagged the trooper. As Tom worked, he noticed the prisoner's hands. They were huge. The ham like size of the man's fists had wrought havoc with the nose of Yancey Stinson.

"This boy has got huge paws," Tom said quietly. "No wonder he almost beat Yancey to death. They are twice the size of a normal man's. I ain't ever seen hands like his before."

Arthur leaned Yancey upright against a tree and wiped the unconscious man's face with the wet rag. Yancey's face was a mask of gore. Arthur then noticed something seriously amiss and dropped the rag to his side. He pried Yancey's mouth open and sighed at what he saw.

"Them big paws have deprived Yancey of all his front teeth," Arthur said sadly. Tom finished binding the Federal's hands and turned to Arthur.

"Give me your canteen," he said. Tom pulled the wooden plug out and poured water all over Yancey's head, washing away most of the caked and coagulated blood. Bloody bubbles popped from Yancey's nostrils.

"We got to get him where he can sit a horse, otherwise we got to bend him over the saddle," Tom whispered. Yancey responded to the water that was being poured on his head by emitting a load groan.

"Hush up now, Yancey," Arthur said to his badly beaten friend. "We still ain't out of the woods now, so hush up a might. You don't want to be lettin' every Yankee know we're still on this damned hill now, do you?"

Yancey moaned even louder. Suddenly, to their complete horror, Yancey struggled to his feet and emitted a scream of pure terror. Tom recoiled from Yancey's scream like an electric bolt of blue energy from the heavens had hit near him. Yancey's shocking scream thundered in the quiet night air.

"Jumping Jehosophat," Tom said in amazement.

Yancey's sudden revitalization shocked both Tom and Arthur into inaction for just a second, time enough for Yancey's reaching fingers to find Tom's rifle that was leaning against the tree. Yancey swung the rifle over his head like a club and smashed Arthur in the face. Tom dove out of the way as Arthur went crashing into the nearby vines holding onto his head. Yancey screamed like a banshee and swung the rifle again in a blind fury almost catching Tom in a vicious arc that whistled by Tom's head by an inch.

Yancey continued to scream in pain and rage. Tom leaped at Yancey and both men went crashing to the ground. Yancey struggled to his feet, still holding onto the rifle. Yancey's finger was in the trigger guard and he tightened his grasp. The rifle discharged in a roar shattering the quiet of the night. The bullet ripped through the darkness striking the worn out cavalry horse squarely in the head. The exhausted tortured animal almost appeared grateful, as its brain was blown apart. The horse sank slowly and peacefully into the tall grass. Ed leaped off the dying animal and dove into the bushes. He heard an awful scream from up ahead and stood up and ran towards the sound. As he rushed forward in the darkness, he also heard John Hubert whistling loudly, giving the prearranged warning sign of imminent danger. The enemy was heading their way.

Ed pushed away a low hanging bough of a tree. He was not prepared for the macabre scene that greeted him. Arthur stood off to the side holding onto his head while Yancey Stinson, screaming like a devil from hell, was doing his best in trying to cave in Tom's head with the end of a rifle. Yancey grew louder by the second. Time and time again, Yancey just missed in knocking Tom's brains out of his skull with his lethal swings. Arthur lunged at the swinging rifle and Tom threw himself at Yancey's feet. Ed dropped his rifle and ran into the pile of arms and legs with full force. The effect was devastating. All three men went in three different directions from the colossal collision. Tom was the first to stir and crawled over to Yancey. Tom crammed a rag into Yancey's mouth as Ed limped over and held Yancey in a bear hug.

"Son of a bitch," Arthur said weakly, "the boy has gone crazy. Every stinkin' blue belly on this hill must have heard the commotion."

Blood streamed from a gash on his forehead. He blinked away the blood that was in his eyes. They all heard the shrill whistling of John Hubert. Arthur frantically flung his jacket off and began to tear the garment into strips. He began to bind Yancey's arms behind his back while Ed held the struggling Yancey in a vice like grip. When Arthur had finished, Ed threw Yancey on the ground and sat on him.

"Tom, we got big trouble," Ed said desperately. "The horse is shot dead but I got the satchel pouch crammed down my pants. You kin' hear John out there whistlin' like a riverboat. Trouble is definitely on its way. What are we gonna' do?"

Yancey continued to struggle beneath the weight of Ed. A spattering of gunfire abruptly silenced the sound of whistling. The raucous shouts of dozens of men and shouted commands could be clearly heard by all of them.

"We are out of time," Tom said calmly. "Ed, get those papers to Vernon. Don't pass them out along the way for shit-paper. Tell Vernon everything."

Arthur interrupted Tom by grabbing Ed roughly by the collar and pulling him down to him.

"Go get' help. Tell Vernon we got more than what he sees with jest' them papers. Tell him we got a prisoner, a dispatch rider what knows exactly who an' what is on this hill," Arthur cried.

Dark shapes began to come out of nearby treeline a hundred paces to their rear. Dozens of the enemy in a long skirmish line were coming right at them, unaware of their presence but curious as to what had caused all the noise. Arthur released Ed from his grasp.

187

"You know where we will be. We are comin' out the same way we went in. The only difference is that we will be comin' out with a lot of uninvited guests," Arthur said fearfully.

Ed nodded and took off at a dead run. Tom watched as the near end of the skirmish line approached them. He bit off the paper end of a cartridge and poured the load down his rifle. He pulled the ramrod from below the barrel and drove the shot home. Reaching into a cloth pouch, he pulled out a percussion cap and expertly placed it into position and cocked the hammer back. The approaching line was just yards from them now and they had not been detected by the enemy.

Tom carefully sighted in on a shadow and slowly squeezed the trigger. The rifle bucked in his arms and the shadow screamed and fell forward while the entire skirmish line erupted in angry shouts and curses. Arthur fired and another figure tumbled into the bushes. A sheet of flame burst in their faces as the Federal line fired blindly in their direction. As the Federals began to reload, fire broke out in the Union soldiers rear.

Pete Wilson and John Hubert fired and the federals broke and ran. They could all hear John Hubert shouting encouragement to himself, something that he was well known to do in times of stress. John made himself sound like a dozen different men.

Tom and Arthur hurriedly reloaded their weapons. Tom knew that the Union soldiers would come at them from the sides and their only chance was to move out and quickly. Arthur watched as a few Federal soldiers began to crawl towards them. Arthur discharged his rifle at a highly visible enemy soldier who had more courage than common sense. The bullet killed the man and discouraged the dead soldiers comrades from coming any farther.

The surviving Union soldiers sought the safety of the darker woods. The firing dropped away to nothing to be replaced by the sounds of chirping crickets. The depth of their noise was startling in contrast to the ear splitting sounds that had been unleashed only seconds earlier. Arthur crept over to Tom.

"That was Wilson an' Hubert. I already sent Harrison and Dyson back. With Ed gone, it's jest you an' me, my friend. Not countin' our boy, Yancey here, an, the Yankee."

"When did you send Dyson an Harrison back?" Tom asked in shock.

"Who the hell tied me up?" Yancey sputtered. The cool rational way in which he said these simple words surprised both Tom and Arthur. Tom crawled over to Yancey and began to cut his bonds with the knife that had been sticking out of the Federal soldiers leg.

"Glad to have you back, Yancey. Yer' kinda' went hog wild on us fer' a spell an' we had no choice but to truss you up like this fer' yer' own safety as well as our'n. Can't say yer' kin' be faulted fer it, though you put a dent in my head swingin' that rifle the way you wuz an' yellin' like a wild Injun'." Arthur said.

Tom unloosened Yancey's last restraint. Both Tom and Arthur watched Yancey carefully and with some trepidation as he spit blood and fragmented teeth from his mouth. Yancey felt at his battered nose. His eyes were just slits set in a jack-o-lantern like swollen head.

"What happened?" his voice was slurred as if he had been drinking heavily. Tom and Arthur finished loading their rifles.

"You caught the Yankee", Tom replied, "but now we are in a fine fix. A Yankee skirmish line just came rolling at us. We got Wilson and Hubert out to our left. I just found out that Arthur sent Dyson and Harrison back. I sent Ed back to go get help. We are in big trouble. Arthur, you take Yancey back. I will go find Wilson and Hubert."

"I kin' get' back my own damned self," Yancey whispered. "You are goin' to need everybody if you plan on takin' that Yankee back. Don't you worry about me, I am jest fine."

"You look it," Arthur said sarcastically. "But if that's the way you feel, you had better get' yer' get' goin while the get' goin' is good. Find them pickets an' warn them that we are comin' in. Be careful. Them Yankees out there are plannin' on flankin' us. Don't go runnin' into them. Stay on a straight line. A beeline. Don't wander to yer' right or left or you will surely walk right into them."

Yancey stood up. He walked like a ninety year old man. He stiffly searched the sky for a familiar point of light in its vastness. Finding what he had been seeking, he slowly began to shuffle away from them. He turned towards them and said, "I will see you all bye an' bye. I wouldn't stick around in these woods too long. It appears to be an unhealthy place." He waved a farewell and slowly plodded forward. They watched him disappear.

"Arthur, I know that you have been a corporal far longer than I have been a soldier, but why didn't you tell me you sent Walleye Dyson and Harrison back without telling me?"

"You're all new to this patrol activity. I tolt them if'n we wuz' to make contact with the enemy to break off an' get' back in one piece. I thought this whole affair was bullshit, Tom. When we seed' all them Yankees when we wuz' comin' here, I thought fer' sure that we never had a chance in takin' a prisoner. Who the hell would have thought that this marble headed moron would have come walkin' right up to us fer' a howdy-doo. That is why I tolt' everybody that if we wuz' to get in a fight, to hightail it back. Nobody is left behind, if'n that's what's botherin' you, Tom. John an' Pete are already on their way back by now."

189

"Good. So what happens now?" Tom asked.

"Them Yankees are gonna' have another go at us. We got a job to do an' that's get' this hard headed Yankee back to Vernon. We will take turns totin' him out. You go ahead and scout. You carry both rifles, loaded. Help me to get' our Yankee friend here on my back, right across my shoulders."

Someone stepped on a branch in the darkness. It made a clear audible unmistakable sound. Then they heard crunching sounds. Tom heaved the prisoner onto Arthur's shoulders. Arthur shifted the load. He grabbed an arm and a leg to better balance his burden.

"That's them fer' sure. We ain't got no time. Don't wander off track. Find your star. They are definitely comin' at us from the sides."

Tom began moving. Arthur counted to five and started following Tom. Arthur glanced up in the sky but the position was too uncomfortable and instead glanced downwards at what was directly in front of him. He prayed that Tom had the correct bearing. Tom had indeed gotten his bearings and was moving along quite briskly. Tom watched for Arthur and then watched the woods. He followed the star that led him towards his original demarcation point. He had to stop when several Federal soldiers crossed his path. They did not notice him. The union soldiers were tightly packed together and were concentrating on not getting separated from each other. He watched as they approached where Tom and Arthur had been only a few minutes earlier. Fifteen minutes later, Tom squinted into the blackness ahead.

What he had thought was a tree suddenly turned towards him. Tom froze in mid-stride. The apparition slowly raised its hand in a signal for others to halt. Tom stood motionless as his heart stopped beating. Lurking shadows in the moonlight began to appear out of thin air. There were more than a dozen of them and Tom watched as the leader of the group began to follow someone very carefully. Whoever they were following were unaware of being followed. These ghosts moved differently than the others and they were very good. They moved noiselessly through the forest and quickly. They were very good at what they were doing. Tom watched the last one disappear back into the darkness. As the moonlight caught one of the ghosts, he abruptly turned and Tom got a glimpse of the enemy soldier. The man was an Indian, of this Tom was sure. Tom hurriedly retraced his steps and found Arthur Huddled on the ground with the prisoner.

"That was damned close," Arthur said.

"There were a dozen of them and they were stalking somebody. I got a good look at one of them. One was an Injun," Tom whispered.

"We are gonna' leave our friend here an go have a quick look see. If they are stalkin' somebody, it could be our half-blind friend, old Yancey boy, they figger' on snatchin'

Tom handed Arthur his rifle. They quietly hurried off to the last spot that Tom had seen the large number of enemy soldiers.

"Right over here," Tom whispered, pointing down a small clearing through the underbrush. They started to carefully walk down the small path. Arthur began a parallel walk to the path. Tom stayed off the path as much as possible. Arthur's eyes had become a little sharper than Tom's and Tom watched as Arthur went to ground and started crawling. Tom edged his way towards Arthur and watched as Arthur pointed to his own ear. Tom heard it clearly

As unbelievable as it sounded, someone was having a loud argument with someone else. Arthur and Tom began crawling at a quickened pace towards the noise. In a small clearing, bathed in moonlight, beneath a large oak tree stood a dozen of the enemy. They were in the midst of a very heated disagreement. Arthur nodded at Tom and raised his rifle.

"Shoot on three," Arthur whispered. Tom sighted on a figure and both rifles went off practically simultaneously. A scream resounded through the still night air and the enemy scattered like surprised quail.

"That will keep them honest fer' a while. Let's skedaddle," Arthur said.

He stood up and began to run with Tom closely following on his heels. They reached their prisoner and Tom stooped to have the man hoisted unto his back. Arthur had just started to lift the unconscious union trooper when the night exploded in their faces Dozens of bullets ripped through the air as the darkness was pierced by the flashes of more than a dozen rifles. Both Tom and Arthur dove for the safety of the forest floor as bullets thudded into trees and whistled over their heads.

"Christ Almighty Jesus," Arthur cried as he frantically strove to ready his rifle for firing. He pulled a pistol out of his boot and began to fire wildly in the general vicinity of the enemy. Bullets tore his hat from his head and he rolled away from the blasts that sought to end his life. Tom was readying his rifle when he heard the sound of many feet pounding towards him. He heard the sounds of many bodies crashing through the woods coming right at him Tom grabbed at his belt for his bayonet knowing that he would never have the time to fully prepare his rifle for action.

Firing from the rear of the attacking Union soldiers flooded the darkness as a volley was let loose into the backs of the charging Federals. Pandemonium erupted as a score of men were cut down from the initial fire. Some of the northern soldiers tried to turn and face the unexpected onslaught but they were mown down by yet another deadly volley that poured from the edge of the wooded glade. The rest turned and began to run in all directions.

Out of the inky blackness raced several of the panicked enemy and they headed directly at Tom and Arthur. One of the enemy soldiers made the mistake of stopping to turn and fire at his pursuers. He got off a quick shot and then turned to run. The night was blasted again by several well-placed shots and the fleeing federal soldier died in mid-stride. The bullets that struck his body made him twist and turn in flight. His body crashed heavily to the ground. The other Federal soldier ran right past Arthur without even noticing that Arthur was shooting at him with his revolver.

Arthur had emptied his revolver and had begun to reload it. Tom slowly looked to his front. Figures in slouch hats slowly began to step into the clearing and out of the line of bordering trees. They approached cautiously. There were dozens of them. Tom had no doubt that these were southern men.

"Don't shoot," he yelled.

He raised his rifle above his head with both of his hands. Arthur wisely did the same. Several of the new arrivals pointed their rifles at the pair. The rest began to chase after the broken federal soldiers.

"Come up from out of there, real slow like and keep them weapons pointed high in the air," a disembodied voice warned them. Tom and Arthur approached the group with a deliberate slowness. The soldiers began to lower their weapons when they saw that Tom and Arthur were southern soldiers.

"Am I ever glad to see you fellas'," Arthur said. He lowered his rifle. Tom slung his over his shoulders. "We got us a prisoner back in them grass shoots over yonder. We bin' a totin' him now fer' some time and.."

"So you are the birds that we are supposed to bring out," a heavyset sergeant grunted. He looked angrily at Arthur. "One of your party showed some papers to Jenkins. He showed it to the captain what showed it to the Colonel what showed it to some General. Now we got practically a company playin' peek-e-boo in these damned woods lookin' fer' you two. If you was to ask me, I think that it is a load of pure bullshit."

"How many made it back," Tom asked eagerly.

"All of them, except fer' you two jay-hoots. One of them looks like he got one mean ass crackin'. His eyes is so swelled shut, I don't know how he managed to see a 'tall an' his head is swollen big like a pumpkin. He's gittin' drunk right now on medicinal whiskey." The sergeant spit nastily into the ground. "Now where is this danged prisoner so we kin' get the hell out of these woods."

Arthur pointed and three soldiers ran forward. They spread a blanket on the ground and rolled the enemy soldier up tightly in it. They lifted their cocoon and slipped into the darkness with it.

"Let's go. These woods are crawlin' with the Yankee vermin. Don't make no sense no how to be runnin' around shootin' like this in the dark. No sense at 'tall. Which one of you shit-birds was in charge of this detail?"

"I was," Tom answered.

The heavyset sergeant grunted and narrowed his eyes at Tom.

"Well I guess you gaffed this up good and proper, didn't you, boy? You made a proper mess of things. We got a company runnin' around in the dark all fer a little old worthless piece of paper and a half dead Yankee son of a bitch."

Arthur stepped towards the big-bellied bellicose sergeant.

"You know you got a big mouth?" Arthur said angrily.

"Is that so," the sergeant said, spitting a stream of tobacco spittle at Arthur's feet.

"Yes, it is,' Arthur said. "You sound like a fust' class whiner to me." He stuck his face to within an inch of the fuming fat sergeants face. "Sergeant Sawyer here done his duty, he got us a prisoner an' he nary lost a man in doin' it. Why don't you see if'n you kin do the same, jelly belly."

"You kin' stick that bullshit whar' the sun don't never shine, corporal. You hear all that firin' goin' on. That's my men out there. Some of them is gittin kilt right now an' it's all cause of you two assholes. Don't go preachin' to me about duty. That there was a Wisconsin outfit that was settin' on jumpin' you. They got Winnebago Injun scouts workin' with them an' they are damned good trackers If'n had not bin' fer us, you two would be dead. Jest remember who pulled yer' fat out of the fire, lamebrain an' don't go a barkin' up the wrong tree. You may never know jest what might fall out of it."

Arthur began to ball up his fists; something Tom knew was not a good omen of things to come. He grabbed Arthur by his shoulder.

"Leave it go, Arthur. It ain't worth all the trouble. Let us go find Yancey and see how he's doing. Maybe he can sneak us some of that medicinal whiskey," Tom whispered.

"Uh-huh,' Arthur said, "That sounds like a right good idea. A drink would stand me good right about now."

As they neared their own lines, both of them felt relieved. Both of them dreaded having to go back in these woods in the morning. They had seen good solid defensive positions at the base. The defenses at the top were formidable, however. Tom worried as to how he would tell Vernon what he had seen. The Federals were solidly entrenched behind five-foot breastworks and were on the hill in force. Attacking the top of the hill would be disastrous. He trusted in Vernon and Captain Custiss. They would make sure that the Generals at the top would be told correctly what was in store for them if they were to assault the top of the hill in force. Just like General Stuart had said, the war was close to ending. Wherever the General was, he knew in his heart that it was for a good reason as to why no one knew his location. He recalled his meeting and dwelled on what the General had told him. The end of the war was near. Tom began to feel better.

CHAPTER TWELVE

The Federal sergeant walked rapidly towards his appointment. People in the street automatically turned their heads in his direction when he passed them. After, the buzz of their comments followed in his wake. He strolled down the street with purpose and strength and people sensed that he definitely knew his place in this world turned upside down. He sensed that he upset some people while others saw him in a totally different light. To these people, the stripes that he wore so proudly on his sleeves and his bold manner represented much welcomed change. He was a symbol of the struggle as well as a reminder to them of the average American's basic sense of fair play and decency, the very character of that nation that was now in such dire peril. His uniform fit him well and his gait was full of authority and confidence.

The Colonel of his regiment had ordered him to attend the meeting in Rochester. The sergeant knew of the man he had the appointment with and he stood in awe of him. He had always admired the man's courage and honesty. He sensed the importance of the meeting although he was not fully cognizant of its purpose. His Colonel had told him that all of his questions would be answered during the meeting.

He found the house easily enough and walked up the steps briskly in the warm July sunlight. Knocking on the door, he was greeted by a woman who cordially ushered him in to a small foyer.

"He has been expecting you, sergeant. I hope you have had a pleasant trip."

"Yes m'am, quite relaxin'. It is quite a bit cooler than what I was accustomed to in the last few months," he said.

"Yes, it is lovely this time of year, isn't it? I have heard that the regiment is in the Carolina's, is that not so?"

"Yes m'am."

"I can tell you, sergeant, that all of us are watching the movements of your regiment with keen interest," she said warmly. "We are expecting great things for it and are hoping you only the best of fortune and success. I, for one, find it truly inspiring. It is like a dream realized."

"Thank you, m'am,' the sergeant said awkwardly. She noticed that the soldier had begun to feel uncomfortable and tried to make him feel at ease again.

"Oh listen to the way I do go on. Please, Sergeant, if you would follow me. He is truly eager to meet with you and discuss the purpose of your trip to Rochester."

195

He smiled and began to follow the small woman. She led him down a small corridor, past the living room, to a large set of doors. He could hear many voices speaking loudly from behind them. Grasping both brass knobs, she opened the doors with some effort. They swung open to a good-sized study. Seated behind a desk was the man he was to meet. Several other men were seated in a semi-circle around his desk while others sat in chairs to the rear of the room next to the open windows. The man sitting behind the desk rose in welcome. He smiled broadly at the sergeant.

"Sir, I pray that you have had a pleasant and uneventful journey to our fair city. It is so good to meet you." His large lion like mane of wooly hair surrounded a finely chiseled face giving him a striking appearance. He offered his hand to the sergeant and grasped it with both of his strong hands shaking it firmly.

"It is an honor, Mr. Douglass," the sergeant said nervously. He gazed into the brown eyes of the man that had stirred a nation's conscience, a man who constantly agitated for change. This man, Frederick Douglass, demanded that the nation live up to it's own beliefs and concepts of democracy for all its citizens.

"Sergeant Watson, I have heard many remarkable things about you, all commendable if I may be so bold to say. You come to us highly recommended by Colonel Shaw. I am sure that you must have a thousand questions. Please, sir, if you would have a seat."

The sergeant sat down hoping his uneasiness with his surroundings was not too apparent. In Sergeant Watson's past, there were no elegant studies; no drawing rooms packed with well-dressed white men. Finely dressed white men of means would never sit in the presence of a field hand. It took some getting used to, the Sergeant thought. His host had waited for him to sit before he began to lower himself into the high backed simple wooden chair.

"Sergeant," Frederick began, "we have a very important task that if you find agreeable, will do our cause a great service." He waited for Sergeant Watson's response by folding his hands and placing them on his cluttered desk. Frederick's eyes bored into the sergeant's eyes.

"Suh, it would be a privilege an' a pleasure to help you in any way I can."

"Splendid," Frederick said happily, "then your trip to my humble abode has not been in vain. What we have in mind is nothing more than the raising of Negro Regiments from Philadelphia to Chicago and you, sir, will be our spokesperson, our voice and crier in the wilderness for men of color to rally to the cause of freedom." The man's oratory power had the sergeant mesmerized to his every word. Frederick stood from the desk and raised his hands in the air.

196

"Once the slave has picked up the musket and places on his breast the brass buttons and uniform of Federal service, can anyone doubt still yet that this is not a man?" His words thundered in the room.

"The sable arm will have a role in this fratricidal struggle, this terrible trial by fire. The Negro will fulfill the words of the nation's founding fathers. All men are created equal. All men have equal rights in a democracy. Hypocrisy that has lasted for almost century will be dashed asunder with the creation of these Negro regiments. We will make this country live up to its basic tenets and obligations to the family of man. Words of the Declaration of Independence that before hand have merely been hollow meaningless phrases may have new life breathed into that dry dusty parchment so that those dry bones will live again." He ignored the applause that his words had generated and continued in his deep baritone voice.

"President Lincoln has told me that he believes that the two races are so incompatible that they will not be able to live together in the same nation once freedom is attained. He believes in his heart that it is best if we were to separate entirely. He has in mind a colonization of all Negroes to Africa, an Exodus of monumental proportions. His message of forced emigration of all Negroes, no doubt, warmed the hearts of many a Confederate once his view became public," he said sarcastically.

"I can safely tell you that I, for one, have never called Africa my home. America is my home. The blood of Negroes has been shed in defending the principles of liberty and has flowed freely in this country's birth. I will never settle for anything less than being called for what I am, and that sir, is an American. We are Americans, speaking the same language, adopting the same customs and holding the same general opinions as other Americans. Our fate is intertwined. If this nation falls, then we as a people will fall and all our hopes of liberty, freedom, and equality will be sent spinning into the void for what is freedom without equality? We shall rise or fall as Americans. That is why we dare not fail in this, our most crucial endeavor."

Some of the faces in the room expressed concern after this was said. Although all were eager in seeing the end of slavery, not all believed as fervently as the speaker did in social equality. For many, this was an entirely different matter. Many of the raised eyebrows and narrowed eyes spoke volumes of meaning to the Federal soldier as he read their faces. He had never been in the company of so many men of importance and had never heard or had ever expected to hear what was being said so openly and frankly in front of so many wealthy and powerful men. This lion of a man and his bold words had caused tension in these men seated in this room. The sergeant watched the furrowed brows and the down turned mouths and realized that the words that Frederick Douglass used were intended to invoke this reaction from the gathered gentlemen. He saw that Frederick did not seem to care that he was

197

leaving many uncomfortable and he sensed that his host seemed to almost enjoy all of the negative responses from these powerful men.

"Sergeant, the one reason that you have been chosen for this assignment is that you, personally, know the dehumanizing and barbaric nature of slavery. You have had the courage in the past in ending slavery as you saw fit, as well as I did. We both chose to end slavery by escaping from it. The job ahead calls for courage, not that kind of courage that is to be found on the battlefield but courage born out of privation, cruel neglect and terror; the courage born from slavery and resistance to oppression is its name." Frederick stopped and looked about the room.

"If any in this room feel uncomfortable with the idea of equality but feel comfortable with the concept of emancipation, then he does not understand this courage. If you feel at ease with political equality but ill at ease with social equality for the Negro then you are ignorant of what this courage entails. I will agitate for equality in all of its forms if I must shake the stars, for only with equality will come the end of oppression and suffering for the Negro. But I digress, sir." He paused before continuing, assessing the stern looks that came from many of the seated men.

"I am sure that you share similar feelings about this whole matter with me and my long-windedness does you no good in determining the part you are to play in our struggle for freedom. I hope that my words did not disturb you, Sergeant Watson."

The sergeant was almost lost for words. He took a deep breath and exhaled slowly.

"No sir, they did not, although I have to say that I have never heard anyone talk how you do, so open like about freedom in front of so many people before. I am just a field hand, Mr. Douglass, what picked up what learning I could by listenin' and watchin'. What you said could earn a body a killin' if said in front of certain folks an'; I am simply not used to hearin' words of freedom spoke so wide open like before an' not see somebody reachin' in a jacket for a gun in disagreement."

For several seconds there was a clumsy silence and then Frederick Douglass threw his head back and laughed loudly breaking the spell. Several others began to chortle and chuckle and soon almost everyone was joining in on the laughter. Frederick's eyes crinkled in pure delight.

"So true. How well I do remember those times, sergeant. Those were the days that we had to have the courage of the lion but remain meek as lambs in the midst of ravenous wolves. Those days are gone forever. Now we must have the courage of the lion but act with the conviction of the righteous. No longer are we to be silenced by the whip or the gun or the rope. Bold and fearless action is required from us these days and I can see that you are well aware of this."

198

A large man in an even larger suit rose from his chair. He strode in front of Sergeant Watson and locked his gaze upon him.

"Sergeant Watson, when our host speaks of freedom and liberty, he speaks it not only for the Negro but for the white man as well. What I say here must not leave this room." The dour looking gentlemen looked at his host and then back at the sergeant.

"One more monumental loss on the field of battle may well cost us the war. Public opinion against prosecuting this war has grown and if we do not start winning soon in the East, I am afraid that the war is lost. This conflict is costing this country a king's ransom daily. If the present course of this war continues with no end in sight, there is a good chance that Lincoln will not be elected President in the next election. There are peace candidates who want a separate truce with the Confederacy and they are getting more vocal everyday. If a peace candidate is elected President, all will be lost. The Emancipation Proclamation will become a worthless piece of paper fit only to be put on the bottom of a gilded bird cage." The fat man lit a cigar and puffed slowly on it. He walked towards the window and looked out into the street.

"This would be a disaster,' he said, exhaling a small cloud. He turned around and leaned on the windowsill.

"A disaster, sergeant. If the South were ever to gain it's independence and become a separate nation, there are powers in the world that would soon sweep in like vultures to pick over America's bones. This experiment in democracy would end. Out there in the world are strong enemies to our system of beliefs. To them, our democratic government of elected officials and voting is both a frightening and dangerous thing in their eyes. They would like nothing more than to see democracy fail because freedom threatens their very power structure. This freedom that we cherish for them is a dirty word, something vile and foul. They would like nothing more than to trample what we hold dear into the muck and mire of despotism and monarchy."

A hush as silent as the grave descended upon the room. All smiles vanished from the room. The heavyset man remained quiet for a long time before continuing. He raised a warning finger in the air.

"One thing is certain. We are going to be a far weaker country when this war ends than when it began. If the South is allowed to play its hand in international politics as an independent sovereign nation, it will turn into a disaster of unimagined proportions. If the South is to win in this rebellion and gain its independence, it will be an open invitation for the invasion of the continent, both North and South, by our enemies. These buzzards will fly in and pick our bones over, rest assured." He lowered his finger and placed his beefy hands on his lapels.

"If you don't believe in what I speak of, then all I can say is let our history give you more clearly an idea of what I say. The British, our erstwhile cousins, only stay out of this war because of the political difficulty they would encounter if once having freed their own slaves in their empire would find it disastrous to support and aid a Slavocracy. Public opinion would cause the collapse of any support they may gain if they were to openly aid the Confederacy. Yet, they let the Confederate States Navy operate out of Bermuda. That island is the British Empire's Rock of Gibraltar in the Atlantic, off of our very shores. It is the official homeport of all Southern commerce raiders and their base of smuggling operations against the Union blockade. They allow the southerners to use Bermuda as a port to bring in valuable medicinal supplies as well as arms with the tacit approval of the Crown." Many important men in the room grunted and harrumphed in appreciation of the man's words.

"Twice," he said dramatically, "the British did invade our shores and twice, they were repulsed. The British are no friends of the Union. I am not so sure that if they were to invade this land if the United States would be strong enough to shatter their dreams of returning us to their fold. But if you doubt this, may I ask you this? Why do the British have strong military forces based in Halifax? Do they fear a Canadian Revolution? An Indian uprising?"

He looked around the room as if expecting to hear an answer and sensing none forth coming, he raised his fist in the air.

"I will tell you why. If we lose this war, the British intend to march an army overland and take Boston and New York by force. Then it will be on to Washington." He whipped his hand downward smashing his fist into his palm.

"They have the strongest land army on the planet and good supply bases in Canada, not to mention a navy that is incomparable, standing ready to finish us off in one bold stroke. Don't let them fool you. England claims to be a constitutional monarchy, but instead, England is a nation ruled by people who are dedicated in ensuring their own power, wealth, and privilege. They are ruled by a dangerous class system that is so rigid that it pales in comparison with the caste system that is found on the sub-continent of India. I have seen it first hand when I was the ambassador there. The English ruling class hates our system of government and despises and ridicules the populism that we so openly embrace. They sneer at men like Andrew Jackson and Lincoln. They are supreme elitists and they turn my stomach."

Some of the men rose and applauded the large man's words. He was showered with loud cheers. He acted as if he did not hear their cheers and continued to speak even louder.

"The French, under their dictator Napoleon, had plans to take back by force all of the Louisiana purchase once they had subdued the English. The Duke of Wellington knocked all of the monsters plans into a cocked hat at Waterloo. However, the French still cast longing eyes at this part of our nation. Mexico is still a hostile force to our south. They would love to have Texas and the territories gained in the Mexican War securely back in their orbit. They would love to regain the entire American Southwest. The Russians cast their greedy eyes on the Northwest part of this land in defiance of the Monroe Doctrine. Spain views Florida as a plump morsel indeed since it still controls the island of Cuba. If all the aforementioned nations were to form some sort of an alliance after Southern independence was gained and the South were to become an active partner with these despots, this unfinished experiment in democracy that we call the greatest country on the earth would be extinguished, forever." Many of the cheers faded with this dour and sobering comment. The large man walked over to where Frederick Douglass sat and leaned on the desk.

"This is why I sit in this room today. I must tell you truthfully, Mr. Douglass, what you speak of, I have a difficult time with. I do not believe in social equality. I believe that the white race is more developed and holds in it the seed of genius and civilization, while the black race has not yet reached the same degree of awareness as the white. I will not lie to you. Many in this room hold my sentiments. But I will deal with the issue of social equality at a later date. My concern, as well as the President's, is the preservation of the Union. I will do anything in my power to insure the survival of the United States. If this means placing a hundred thousand rifles in the hands of a hundred thousand Negroes then I will say that I will do it and damned be the consequences."

Some of the men began clapping

"I have never heard so much unmitigated trifling nonsense in all my life," a voice from the back of the room intoned caustically. Everyone stopped clapping to see who had the audacity to speak to the big man in such a rude manner.

"I have not traveled all the way from Kansas to listen to rambling tripe of this magnitude." A sharply dressed Colonel rose from a chair in the back of the room. All eyes fastened on him. He folded his arms and strolled leisurely in front of the assembled guests in the room.

"I believe everyone here knows me, but if you do not, allow me to introduce myself. I am Colonel Henry C. Fowler, of Kansas. I rode with John Brown when some of those gathered here were snotty nosed schoolboys. That would include your Colonel Shaw...sergeant."

The sarcastic and derisive way in which he had said the word sergeant rankled the Federal soldier. He listened and held his anger, betraying none of his feelings to the rude Colonel from Kansas. Colonel Fowler sneered at the sergeant before continuing.

"I have been fighting a war in Kansas against the Godless slavocrats since 1855. Out west, we are winning. Except for a few guerilla bands operating in the state, Missouri and Kansas are free of any serious rebel forces. You Eastern people can't seem to win out here because you have far too few fighting Generals and far too many political Generals. Once you people figure this out and act upon changing it and finally place a western General in overall command of the Army of the Potomac then you will see broad sweeping changes in the conduct of this war. Simply said, you will begin not to lose this war for the very first time."

The big man in the large suit bristled at the speaker and gave him sour glances as he slowly ambled back to his seat. The large man barely was able to contain his anger. He nearly bit his cigar in half as he fought to control his torrid temper.

"Let us get down to brass tacks," the Colonel whined. "As you may or may not know, my late wife was from Massachusetts. Her family was in textiles. Her family business that I inherited after her tragic riding accident was made partly in the production of slave- cloth. So you see, financially, I stand to lose a tidy amount in the ending of the institution of slavery." He purposely strutted in front of the large man and paused boldly in front of him.

"I know little of foreign threats to our freedoms. I care nothing about political or social equality for the Negro. I don't give a hang if Lincoln sends every Negro packing back to Africa once this rebellion is crushed. It is none of my concern. What is my concern is the total destruction of every southern institution in this land. I desire to see every form of ruin and devastation visited upon their heads. I wish to see their high places made low. They are a blight upon the earth." His voice rose by the second and he fought for self-control.

"They are all evil doers," he screamed, startling many in the room. It was a scream of rage and hatred. His face took on a purple hue and his shoulders began to shake as if were exposed to a gale wind.

"They are an abomination. They shall have hooks put in their jaws. They shall become a feast for the birds of prey and their cities will become the abode of hungry dogs and demons. They shall be dragged to the bottomless pit and shall burn in the everlasting lake of hell fire and brimstone. They shall grind their teeth together in the outer darkness," he roared.

A curious small major quickly walked over to the frothing Colonel Fowler and offered him advice by whispering in his ear. The Colonel seemed to calm himself momentarily. Everyone in the room was stunned at the evident loss of control displayed by the Colonel and mouths hung agape. His bizarre behavior had even left the big man speechless.

Henry Fowler was aware of the looks that his tirade had caused. The major gingerly took his seat but not before he had looked directly at the sergeant and smirked evilly at him. Colonel Fowler cleared his throat as he once again fought to regain his composure.

"You must excuse me if I get verbose in these matters." The veins that had stood out on his forehead and his purple coloration began to recede as he continued to wrestle with his own personal demons. He forced himself to speak in a less agitated manner but he was only a hairs-breadth away at any given moment in lapsing back to his prior state. The sergeant, his face as immobile and unreadable as a marble statue, stared at the midget major and the Colonel.

"I have contributed some monies in the formation of Negro regiments from my own personal fortune. Gentlemen, I am a patient man. I can well afford to be patient for I have no need to struggle to earn a dollar. I have more money than I will ever be able to spend in one lifetime. I can state freely that I am independently wealthy. Very wealthy."

There were many raised eyebrows from those gathered in the room. Others in the room who were as wealthy as this upstart claimed to be saw in his statement nothing more than bad taste as well as bad manners.

"What I can ill afford to be is cunctative or careless. Neither can I be slothful. I am not the type. What I find totally objectionable is that nothing is being done with these regiments. They are doing nothing in terms of winning this war. Negro regiments are either building useless fortifications or sitting on their black asses and dying from various sundry diseases. The Fourteenth Rhode Island Colored Regiment is currently sitting in a Louisiana swamp contracting malaria while some are getting venereal diseases from the local wanton women of that wretched community. This is not aiding in winning the war." The colonel waved his index finger in the air over his head and grabbed onto his lapel with his left hand. Arching his back, Henry looked each man over carefully to read his demeanor. He smiled widely.

"Gentlemen, let us all agree on one basic thing. Sambo can take a bullet just as good as a white man." He paused for dramatic purposes and turned his gaze again at the sergeant.

"When last I was in Washington waiting to have lunch with the President, I did chance to hear a delightful ditty. I was in the lobby of the hotel and some minstrels were performing. One of the lyrics that they were singing was, "Sambo can take a bullet as good as a white man." I thought to myself, what a remarkable sentiment put to song. It expressed my beliefs and I applauded the entertainers and.."

The doors of the study being flung open interrupted him. The suddenness of the interruption bolted nearly everyone upright in his chair. Standing in the doorway, the sergeant saw, was the lady that had greeted him and a sweating fat man. She looked frightened as well as annoyed.

"Pardon me, Mr. Douglass," she said, "it is Mr. Lassiter from the newspaper as you can see. I tried to tell him that you were not to be disturbed, but he barged past me saying that he had news that he must tell you."

The Colonel from Kansas recoiled in horror from her announcement.

"A damned newspaper man," he thundered. Henry pointed his finger in Frederick's face and shook it as if he was scolding a small child.

"I thought that you understood that you were to be responsible for our anonymity. This meeting was supposed to be kept at the most secretive levels. What is the meaning of this man's intrusion upon our gathering?" Henry shouted loudly. "Of all people. He is a damned newspaperman who will have all of our names in his damned newspaper before the day is out."

The small woman had braced both of her arms against the entrance to the room. The fat, balding, sweating man pushed her out of his way with ease.

"Oh my goodness!" she exclaimed.

"Mr. Douglass," the bald man shouted, "Forgive me for interrupting your meeting, but I am sure that you would want the latest news that has just this last hour come across the wire." He eyeballed those seated in the room.

"What I bring you is astounding. Someone has let the cat out of the bag," Mr. Lassiter said happily.

Frederick Douglass was more agile than anyone could have imagined. In a series of quick bounds, he collared the intruder and grabbed his arm, forcing Mr. Lassiter through the double doors in a blur.

"Excuse me, gentlemen," Frederick hastily said over his shoulder. "I must have a private moment with my colleague. I will return momentarily, you may rest assured." He kicked the doors shut. He furiously turned on the correspondent.

"Mr. Lassiter, we have been friends many years. What is the meaning of your barging into my study and belly-bumping my poor secretary out of your way in such an aggressive manner? Have you lost your mind?' Fredrick's eyes flashed lightning bolts at the shorter man. He dragged the journalist away from the doors and down the hallway away from the doors of his study.

"Mr. Lassiter, you must realize that what you have just done is no small matter. There are individuals in that room whose identities must remain secret. If their participation in this meeting were made public, it would present untold problems for many of them." Frederick stopped pushing Mr. Lassiter and released his hold on the pudgy man's arm. Mr. Lassiter rolled his hat in his hands.

"I understand perfectly, Frederick. I thought I recognized Mr. Merewether of the State Department and Mr. Hull of the War Department. Mr. Merewether, he was the portly distinguished looking gentleman in the ill fitting suit, was he not?"

"William, please," Frederick groaned. "You must keep who you have seen here today in the strictest confidence. You have always been a good friend of mine. I implore you, no, I beseech you, as a friend, never to mention whom you may have seen here to anyone. I must have your word on this."

The housekeeper opened up the doors and quickly made her way over to both of the men standing in the hallway. She stood silently behind then, not wishing to interrupt her employer. Frederick turned towards her and smiled.

"My Dear Miss. Elliot. If you would be so good as to prepare some refreshments for our guests while I am detained with Mr. Lassiter Some of your fine lemonade that I saw you preparing this morning as well as those delicious cakes I smelled baking?" he asked.

"Certainly, Mr. Douglass," she replied.

"And Miss Elliot, one more thing. Please inform our guests that I will join them straight away."

"Of course, sir." She started to turn away but stopped in mid stride.

"Mr. Douglass, I seemed to have heard someone screaming earlier while I was in the pantry. Is everything alright?"

"Emotions will sometimes rise to a feverish pitch when discussing ideas that cause such strong passions, Miss Elliot,"

"Yes. I understand."

"I assure you, Miss Elliot, that everything is under control," he said. She smiled an unsure smile at him.

"I will serve the lemonade presently as well as the sweet cakes. Excuse me, gentlemen." Both men bowed slightly as she began to leave. She stopped suddenly again.

"Perhaps I will serve the fishcakes as well. It is nearing lunch time," she said.

"Splendid idea, Miss Elliot."

She smiled and nodded ever so slightly.

"Gentlemen, if you will excuse me," she said, and walked down the small hallway. Frederick leaned against the wall.

"Now, Mr. Lassiter. I must have your vow to keep this meeting under your hat. Do I have it, William?"

"You wound me, Frederick. Of course, you have my most solemn pledge that I will never repeat to a living soul that I saw advisors of the President's cabinet in your study. Is that sufficient or should we seal it in blood?"

"What of this pressing news that brings you to invade my privacy and fairly throw all that I am attempting to gain here today into peril?"

"A coincidental choice of words, I think. What I bring you is this. Lee has invaded Pennsylvania. There is a major battle underway as of yesterday. Lee has committed at least a Corp of his army to battle at a small crossroads' town south of Harrisburg," Mr. Lassiter said excitedly.

"Are you sure?"

"Yes. It has been confirmed. You see, something incredible has happened. Someone, and I can only guess whom, has leaked it out all over the wires. I suspect that it must be someone in the War Department. The chief of security, Mr. Pinkerton, must be fit to be tied."

"Would you know the name of this cross roads town?"

"Gettysburg. But that is not where it ends. General Reynolds is slain."

"John Reynolds killed? This is a calamity."

"Listen. General Meade was given command of the Army just days ago. He has fallen back to the east of the town. He was pushed off the ridges to the west, but the Army has fallen back in good order and they seem to be fairly intact for now. It is not a rout like Bull run."

Frederick slumped against the wall, totally dispirited with the news.

"John Reynolds was one of our more capable commanders. With his loss, I fear for the outcome of this battle. God knows, we can ill afford another debacle in the field," he said dejectedly. "How is this new man, Meade?" he asked.

Lassiter shrugged. "From all reports he is a good divisional commander, but he is an unknown commodity when it comes to leading an army. He is a Pennsylvanian, though. As for his character, some say that his appearance matches his personality. I have heard him referred to as a, "damned old goggle eyed snapping turtle.""

"If Lee is south of Harrisburg, as you say, then either Baltimore or Washington is forfeit if the fight turns against us. Good Lord, if we lose this battle we may just lose the war," Frederick said.

"There is one more part of the story that I have not mentioned to you yet," Lassiter said. "This is the most unbelievable and astounding news that I must impart to you. The leak that I had previously mentioned?"

"Yes, go on with it, man," Frederick, said impatiently.

"Communiqués leaked from the War Department infer that Stuart's entire cavalry command, mind you, is not even near Gettysburg. His cavalry is reported to be raiding farther to the north. This is how I know it must be a leak. Someone in the War Department, perhaps a junior officer more than likely, wanted to make sure that this juicy bit of information did not simply sit on some duty desk along with God only knows what other useless drivel. He wanted to insure that this information would quickly be learned and passed on by everyone sitting next to a telegraph key. He put it out all over the wires and he spent a good time in doing it. Frederick, I am no military tactician, no expert, but even I know that an Army never travels in enemy territory without its scouting arm close at hand. Now, everyone knows by now that Lee is blind, including I hope, the proper military leaders. If they don't know it, they will surely know it before the day is out. Can you believe it."

"If you are correct, William, it is staggering in its implications. Astounding!" Frederick exclaimed.

"Yes, it is. Unless Lee has another cavalry corp. that no one is aware of, then Lee is traveling around in Pennsylvania blind as a proverbial bat without any way of knowing what roads are clear or the whereabouts of the Army of the Potomac. A southern blunder of monumental consequences may be occurring as we speak and I only pray that our leaders take advantage of it."

"There is Harrisburg,' Frederick said pensively. "Perhaps Stuart plans to capture Harrisburg. It would be quite a feather in his cap."

Mr. Lassiter leaned against the wall crumbling his hat in his meaty hands.

"I rather think not," William said. "I believe that Stuart has taken himself out of this fight, entirely, for some unfathomable reason."

"I hope that you are right," Frederick said quickly. Mr. Lassiter patted his friend on the shoulder.

"I must return to my office and you should return to your guests. I apologize for barging in like this and disturbing your meeting."

207

"The meeting was already beginning to be disturbing well before you made your presence known, William. Think nothing of it and I do thank you for relaying this news to me," Frederick said. William nodded and smiled.

"I have asked Mr. Holden at the telegraph office to keep me closely informed as to any breaking events. The second I hear of anything of importance, I will make sure that you will be the first to know," William replied.

"Thank you, my friend."

"I will tell no one of what I saw here today, on this you have my word. I will see my own way out. As usual." William doffed his mangled hat and began to walk rapidly down the hallway.

Frederick wasted no time in returning to his study. Opening the double doors, he was happy to see Miss Elliot placidly serving those in attendance some lemonade. She placed the pitcher on a small table and smiled at him as he made his way into the room. Henry Fowler confronted him immediately, once again thrusting his finger in Frederick's face.

"What is the meaning of that?" Henry blurted out loudly. "Of all people to have break into a private meeting of this nature. A newspaperman. Have you no sense at all?" Henry shouted. Frederick tried to ignore the violation of his space and made his way to his desk.

"Sir, Mr. Lassiter is a true friend. You can be assured that he will never mention who or what he saw here today. He has given me his most solemn pledge that he will not mention this to anyone."

"Balderdash!" Henry screamed. "He is a newspaperman. He puts his bread on his table by spreading muck and rumors. This is his job He will have our names in his filthy rag before the sun sets. If he does this, I tell you he is a dead man. I will personally send him to hell."

"Colonel Fowler, please be reasonable. There is only the remotest of chances that he has even seen you in this room. He was only in the doorway for a brief few seconds. Mr. Lassiter, although a newspaperman, is a close friend of mine. Need I remind you that Mr. Garrison in New York is also a newspaperman and one of our most staunchest supporters?" Frederick asked. There was a smattering of nervous laughter in the room. The tenseness was palpable.

"I don't give a damn," Henry shouted wildly. "I should never have trusted my anonymity to someone of your ilk. I was led to believe that you were slightly brighter than the rest of your kind, but now I can see how wrong that assessment of you was, you stupid nigger." Frederick reacted to the Colonel's words by inhaling deeply and sitting slowly down in his chair. Faces in the group looked on in shock.

Mr. Merrewether pulled on his beard and shook his head from side to side. Jim Watson kept a wary eye on the short major.

"Colonel Fowler," Frederick began, "there is no need for this."

"Listen well, nigger. I have stayed alive in this long bloody struggle by protecting my anonymity. I have seen many who did not and those people are just memories or have their lives constantly threatened. It will do me no good to have my name linked with yours. I am totally outraged by this breach in security," Henry roared.

Henry's eyes bulged and his face started to startlingly transform. Veins began to stand out on his neck and temples and he went from a reddish color to a light blue all in a matter of seconds. His skin tightened on his face.

"We from Kansas know what to do with men of his low character. The major and I will stop in on this newspaper fellow and if he gives the wrong answer to any one of my questions then there will be one less news hound in the world," Henry shouted. Frederick folded his hands on the desk. He did not look at the Colonel.

"Please, Colonel Fowler," Frederick said calmly, "There is no need to do that. He has given me his word. You may have my word that he will keep."

"Your word?" Henry yelled, losing total control of himself.

"Your word? How in the world can you expect me to trust his word or yours? The word of a man who makes his living by lies and deceit and the word of a foolish, stupid, uppity nigger that has a white woman working for him. You probably are plowing her."

Frederick fought to control his own building anger.

"Calm yourself, sir. You go too far," Frederick shouted.

"Apparently, I don't go far enough," Henry shrieked. "I will decorate the front page of his newspaper with his brains. Don't tell me to calm myself. This newspaperman does not know with whom he trifles. I suppose that I should end his miserable existence out of pure principle for his barging into a meeting that was supposed to be private. That will teach the bastard. In fact, I have just made up my mind. He must go."

"Colonel Fowler, no harm will come to Mr. Lassiter. Not by your hands, damn you. Do you understand me," Frederick shouted.

Henry was wild looking. His face changed its hue from light blue to purple.

"Who the hell are you to tell me or any other white man anything. I don't care how important you believe you are, you filthy nigger," Henry bellowed. Henry's eyes burned like coals. He walked over to Frederick's desk in a threatening way full of bad intent.

"I shall have my way with that sinner," Henry blurted out loudly. Spittle flew from his mouth.

"I shall put hooks into his jaws and drag him down to the pit of hell. He shall roast in the conflagration of the damned this very night. I will..."

Frederick rocketed out of his chair. His strong hands grabbed the front of the Colonel's tailored tunic by the lapels in a vice like grip as he pulled the startled man to within an inch of his face.

"It is my turn now and you had better listen to what I have to say," Frederick said quietly. "I have had quite enough of your infantile outbursts and threats. I warn you, do not threaten the life of Mr. Lassiter. Not in my presence and not in my home. I care nothing of what you think of me as a man. However, when you threaten the life of a friend, you have crossed over the threshold of my tolerance."

The short major leaped from his chair and went to the defense of his Colonel like a faithful dog. He was in the process of pulling a pistol from his jacket when the sergeant stood up and booted the smaller man in the face. The major's body completed a half circle in the air and came crashing down splintering the table where the lemonade pitcher had been placed. Miss Elliot screamed in terror as the pitcher hit the floor and shattered into a hundred pieces showering the major in sticky lemonade. He lay still in its puddle as the pistol spun crazily on the hardwood floor.

"Have you gone mad? Release me this instant. How dare you put your hands on a white man," Henry cried. His fear rose to the surface like a breaching whale. The suddenness of Frederick's action and his intensity had taken Henry completely by surprise. His resolve evaporated instantly in the grip of this powerful man. Fredrick tightened his grip on Henry's lapels and smiled at Henry's discomfort.

"Why Colonel Fowler, you look surprised. Don't you know that I have put my hands on quite a few white men in my time? If you had read my book, you would have known this. I have given out quite a few well-deserved beatings, including one to an overseer who had taken it upon himself to correct my un-slave like attitude with a hickory cane when I was a boy. It was a mistake that he regretted. I beat him till he bled from every hole in his body."

Henry began to shake in fear and revulsion at being manhandled by a black man. He looked at Frederick with loathing and dread.

"Do you have any idea of who I am?" Henry growled. "Take your hands off me, you damned black monkey." Spittle flew into Frederick's face, but he ignored it and tightened his grip on the quaking Colonel's neck.

"Indeed, I do know who you are," Frederick said. "I know exactly who you are and more importantly, I know exactly what you are. For those of you here that do not know who and what you are, please allow me to elaborate." Frederick's eyes blazed furiously at the Colonel while Henry squirmed helplessly in his grasp.

"You are one Henry Cadimus Fowler of the Kansas volunteer cavalry, at one time leader of the Kansas Free State Militia. You are an infamous Red leg. In the border trouble out in Missouri during the last decade, you rode with and protected John Brown. You and your Red-leg group propagated one of the worst chapters in the annals of that unholy struggle by murdering anyone and everyone that opposed your views. You killed the innocent and the guilty in a debauchery of slaughter and bloodshed that has no equal in our nation's long history. It did not matter to you. You murdered by whim and fancy and for personal profit."

Everyone in the room was stunned by what they had witnessed. They watched and listened in shocked silence at the drama that was unfolding before them. The sergeant watched the short major for any signs of motion. He picked up the Colt revolver and sat back in his seat training the gun on the diminutive major. Frederick's voice boomed like the roar of canon.

"You were financed by abolitionist groups from Boston before anyone fully realized just what kind of a lunatic you are. When it came time for John Brown to stage his ill-conceived slave rebellion at Harpers Ferry, he invited you to join him. However, you declined because by that time you were becoming very wealthy and politically connected. You didn't think that I knew that, did you, Colonel? I know this because John Brown had asked me to participate in his madness and he specifically mentioned your name at the time. I declined as well for I knew that his insane plan was doomed to failure from its inception."

Henry's eyes darted about the room. Only a handful of people on the earth knew what Frederick said was true. He was mortified.

"You claim to be an abolitionist, but you have no love for the Negro. You use our cause for personal gain alone. That makes you despicable in my eyes. You are a damned coward who prefers to stay in the shadows and play with the lives of men as if they were chess pieces. I know men like you very well, Colonel. I can read your kind like a book. Let me further illuminate for our guests what I do know about you. You were raised in some backwater hole in Virginia, am I not correct?"

Henry said nothing.

"Your father was a slave owner, too poor to have hired an overseer on the hard-scrabble farm you called home. He beat you as hard as he beat the few slaves that tilled his wretched rock garden. You proudly claim to be a direct descendent of President Monroe, but I can tell you that the weather vane above my house is closer in lineal descent from Monroe than you. You only made this claim to make yourself appear nobler in the eyes of your rich neighbors. You longed to be like your patrician neighbors and to be accepted them, but they spurned you. They rubbed your nose in your own poverty every chance that they got. You grew up with a bitter hatred of your lot in life and a jealously towards your wealthy neighbors, those tide water aristocrats whose wealth was made through the sweat and blood of Negroes." Henry struggled to understand how this man knew so much about his life.

"Yet, curiously, you coveted to have the riches and power that they so openly flaunted in front of your eyes. You vowed someday to have it all. You swore that you would bring them all low one day, to take away from them everything that they had. Your ambition in these matters knew no bounds. You courted and married one of the richest women in the country before the war. She died under mysterious conditions when she was thrown from a horse. She was an accomplished equestrian, an experienced horsewoman. You opened a bank in Kansas and the partner that you had died within a year. He was shot dead in an apparent robbery and the killer was never brought to justice. The same can be said of your partner that had helped you open your newspaper. Let's see, he died after having a big dinner at your home. How fortunate for you, it would seem. There are also suspicious deaths involved in the Free State Militia. Rivals of yours in that organization would often be found shot dead or they would simply disappear, never to be seen again. Of course, you blamed their deaths on your enemies, giving you an excuse to kill them as well, a very convenient solution to get rid of anyone who dared to stand in your way."

"I will nail your black nigger hide to a barn door for this," Henry wailed.

Frederick backhanded Henry across his mouth.

"You will listen and do exactly as I say, you damned murdering lunatic," Frederick boomed. "You will leave Rochester and never return. If you do, you may not fear what Mr. Lassiter will print in his paper about you. I will go to Boston and New York and tell interested parties there all of what I know about you. Thank God that there are not many like you among us anymore. At one time, we needed even the likes of your kind in our struggle, the lunatic fringe. Those days are over. Exposing trash like you would not hurt our cause anymore. We need to weed your type out of the movement and the sooner the better."

"Nigger, if you only knew what I have planned for you, you would be begging my forgiveness," Henry said calmly. He licked at his bleeding lower lip. Mr. Merewether made his presence known.

"Colonel Fowler, you had better shut your mouth right now. I have heard quite enough. Captain Higginson, seize the colonel. I am placing him under citizen's arrest. Mr. Douglass, release the colonel. Captain, restrain Colonel Fowler."

Frederick released his hold on Henry. The twenty-year-old captain grabbed Henry by the arms and then he placed the colonel in a chokehold. The young captains enthusiasm caused Henry's eyes to bulge from the pressure around his neck.

"Sergeant," Mr. Merewether said forcefully, "I must commend you on your quick reaction to a very dangerous situation. That man's action in pulling out a pistol threatened the lives of everyone in this room. These are the actions of the uncivilized and I intend that they suffer the repercussions of their barbaric behavior."

All of the men in the room were on their feet and were ready and willing to come to the aid of Captain Higginson if a need presented itself. There were murmurs of consent from them at the words of Mr. Merewether.

"I guess I spoke too quick about not seein' somebody reachin' fo' a firearm in an attempt to win an argument," the sergeant said. Mr. Merewether looked scornfully at Henry as Captain Higginson proceeded to half strangle Henry in his youthful ardor to do a good job.

"Captain Higginson, release the colonel, sir. I do believe you are killing him," Merewether said. Captain Higginson reluctantly obeyed but not before he relieved Henry of his side arm. Mr. Merewether looked about the room for a certain individual and when he spotted him, said loudly, "Mr. Yardtack, please leave and go find a constable at once. Tell him to come to this residence with all speed."

"This is all unheard of," Henry sputtered, rubbing his throat.

"You are correct, sir," Merewether said calmly. "Your behavior has been unheard of in the company of gentlemen, more the actions of highway men and cut throats than officers of the United States Army. You have acted most abominably. You are a disgrace to the uniform you wear and the rank that you hold."

"Fat boy, do you realize the trouble that you may be causing yourself. I would carefully think things out before taking the side of this black baboon, if I were you," Henry said haughtily. "The President of the United States is a personal friend of mine. What are you? You are nothing. You are just some comical looking clown in a bad suit. Whoever you are, I will buy your superior and will have your job and you will be out on the street peddling your fat wife's ass, you pitiful fool," Henry said shakily. He glared snidely at Mr. Merewether.

"I know many people, powerful people. I have senators and congressmen on my payroll, fatty. I will go out of my way to ruin you, if you cross me," Henry said. "I will enjoy seeing you lose everything that you hold dear."

"I warn you to be silent, Colonel Fowler," Merewether said, "or I will have you bucked and gagged, damned your eyes, sir."

213

Henry smiled a spiteful smile.

"You have no charges to bring against me," Henry shouted.

"The major is to be charged with assault," Merewether said crisply, "and you will be charged with threatening the life of Mr. Lassiter. Everyman in this room, if need be, will be subpoenaed to testify to this in a court of law. I am not clear how you think our legal system operates here in the east, but you may believe me that they are serious charges. I also intend to speak with General Halleck and bring you before a court martial. Please, Colonel Fowler, do not speak to me about friends that you have in high places that you are so familiar with because I am in high places. When I am finished with you, you will be lucky to command something bigger than a shithouse in New Orleans. I speak with the President on a daily basis and General Halleck listens well to the advice that I bring him. The Secretary of State is my brother in law and the Vice-President is an old friend, my college room mate in fact, so do be quiet, there's a good fellow."

The very mention of Halleck gave Henry serious reason for concern. "Old Brains" Halleck was a dangerous political enemy, a man that could not be bribed. Henry began to have a creeping feeling of the danger he was in. Halleck and he had almost come to physical blows once and he knew that Halleck was the one man that could easily ruin his career and future plans. Halleck despised him and would love to have an opportunity to hang Henry's scalp from his belt.

"Let us be reasonable," Henry said quietly and with as much control and charm that he could muster. "My alleged threats against the life, as you infer, of this Lassiter fellow was all bluster on my part. Certainly, you cannot believe that I was serious. I was speaking figuratively and for dramatic purposes only. Surely, you can see this." Henry furtively looked about at the men in the room to see if any in the room were willing to believe his lies. He desperately needed allies.

"All I wanted was for everyone in this room to know of my seriousness in keeping my identity in this meeting consigned to this room and this room alone. I must confess that I do have a flair for the dramatic. I see no crime in that. As for the actions of the major, here, I do agree that his actions were detestable and I say, let us prosecute him to the fullest extent of the law. I believe that he should be hanged by the neck or at least sent to prison for the rest of his natural life. Hard labor and bread and water are too good for him, I daresay. One never knows the mental state of ones' associates these days."

Merewether watched Henry squirm and it disgusted him.

"You may save all of that for the trial," Merewether said. "Captain Higginson, I feel no need to await the return of Mr. Yardtack. We will march this madman to the local jail, ourselves. He is starting to turn my stomach."

214

"For God's sakes man, consider your actions, I beg of you, and do not act in haste," Henry wailed. "It is obvious that the major has mental problems, it would appear. I know his actions are inexcusable, but reconsider, if you would, just for a moment. If there has been a misunderstanding, at least allow me to make amends and apologize to everyone, including our most gracious host. I spoke words that were unworthy of me. I have been under quite a bit of stress lately. I duly retract every thing that I have said here today, including what you all did perceive as a threat to the life of Mr. Lassiter. I intend to leave this city, never to return," Henry said desperately. Mr. Merewether looked at Henry with new interest.

"If we could come to some sort of agreement. I am a generous man. I know how to reciprocate understanding with generosity and good intentions in kind. I can fairly say that the very reason of attending this meeting was to arrange a large transfer of monies in the fitting and raising of Negro regiments for the further conduct of this war. Surely, aren't we all in agreement on this point at least?"

Frederick slowly walked towards the colonel.

"I believe that we may be able to come to a sort of agreement or understanding, as you say," Frederick said. "Would you be willing to write a promissory note in the amount that you had intended to contribute to our cause today?"

Henry leaped at the opportunity.

"Why, to be sure, of course. I am a wealthy man and money is no concern in this regard. I would be delighted. It would be my pleasure."

Frederick walked quickly over to his desk. He returned with a writing tablet, a bottle of ink, and a fine quill pen. Henry eagerly reached for them and began to write as quickly as he was able. He grinned happily while he wrote. Frederick loomed over his shoulder, carefully watching his progress.

"Colonel Fowler, please add two more zeros to the end of that figure to show all gathered here your fitting generosity and dedication to our cause so that there can be no doubt as to your sincerity," Frederick whispered into his ear. Henry swallowed nervously and shot a sick looking smile at his host. He signed his name with a flourish and handed the pen to Frederick.

"There it is. I hope that this is satisfactory," Henry said. He handed the paper over to Frederick.

"It is very generous, Colonel," Frederick said, grinning at Henry's discomfort. The amount was staggering. Mr. Merewether, always the lawyer, motioned for Frederick to let him see it. Merewether took his spectacles from his top pocket and slowly perused the note.

"This will do nicely," he said. Henry sighed in relief.

"I am glad it meets everyone's approval," Henry said. "Now, if someone would be kind enough to help me revive the major, I would like to catch the train to Albany before dinner. I have a long journey and am most eager to be on my way. I would like to leave as soon as possible," Henry said grinning at all in the room. No one smiled back at him.

"You may draw that amount from Mr. Chase's bank in New York. If you have any problems, please feel free to wire me, directly. I will make sure that the transaction will go ahead as smoothly as possible. After all, Mr. Chase is the best clerk that I have on my payroll." Henry laughed slightly at his attempt at humor.

"Now, gentlemen. I must away," he said with as much bravado and arrogance that he was able to gather from what remained of his shattered confidence. Sergeant Watson unloaded the cartridges from the major's revolver and returned it to the major's holster. Captain Higginson returned Henry's pistol to him as Sergeant Watson picked up a pitcher of water from off one of the tables and poured it on the upturned face of the major. The major awakened, sputtering and gasping. He began to curse, loudly as men picked him up off of the floor. He swayed from side to side and held on to his injured jaw.

Henry dabbed at his own bloody lip with his handkerchief and then offered it to the bewildered major.

"It has been a most productive meeting. I have learned a valuable lesson. I pray that you all do not hold any animosity or ambivalence against me. I hope that you can find the room in your hearts to forgive me. I hold no grudges against anyone in this room. I have become far too callous and unthinking because of this damned war. Now, we must be off. Major," Henry shouted in his best military manner.

"Sir?" the major said.

"Your behavior today has been atrocious. When we return to Kansas, I intend to cashier you from the ranks. You may place yourself under arrest pending a court-martial until then. You are an embarrassment and a disgrace. Now, come along and don't say another word," Henry rasped. Mason simply blinked, still confused and unsure as to what had just happened. He followed Henry obediently out of the room as the housekeeper led them to the door. No one in the room offered a farewell in their parting. They all soon broke into small groups to discuss the bizarre behavior that they all had been witness to.

Frederick Douglass peered through the window at the pair as they made their way slowly towards the train station. Mr. Merewether joined him.

"That man has eaten an inordinate amount of humble pie for today," Merewether said. "Mr. Douglass, I am a southerner by birth and tradition. My problem is that I am far too educated to believe that this nation can exist, one slave

216

and one free. It tortures me to see all of these lives lost. I wish that what we do in secret we would be able to do in the broad light of day. It is high time that we resolve this entire issue of race, something the founding fathers had clearly failed to resolve in the formation of our Republic. Now, it is the young of this generation that must pay the butcher's bill for their not standing against evil eighty years earlier."

"Mr. Merewether, I thank you for coming to my assistance. That man is a crass opportunist who cares nothing about anything but his own damned self," Frederick said sadly. Frederick turned towards Sergeant Watson.

"Thank you, sergeant. Who knows what Fowler's lapdog may have done if you had not deposited him on his backside so adeptly."

"Mr. Douglass, I had my eye on him the whole time. I know his type. That man is a killer. I could see it in his eyes when he looked at me. I know that he would have killed you. He was bold enough to kill everyone in this room to protect his boss man. I know'd how fella's like him git' oncet they start to killin'. They can't seem to be able to get' enough oncet' they gits' in the rhythms of the moment. They enjoy it too much to quit," sergeant Watson said.

"We have a lot to discuss," Frederick replied.

"Mr. Douglass. Can I ask you for a favor?"

"Since you more than likely saved all of our lives, I don't think that I can refuse you."

"Call me Jim."

"We have quite a bit to talk about, Jim."

Henry Fowler and Mason arrived at the train station as Mason's head slowly began to clear.

"Hank, what the hell happened back there? I can't hardly remember nothin'. All I know was that nigger grabbed you and that was it. I was getting' ready to blast that coon and then, boom, there was nothin'. What you said back there, about me bein' under arrest? What was that all about? What the hell did I do wrong?" Mason asked nervously.

"You did nothing wrong, my good man. The whole incident is not worth mentioning ever again, is that clear? Just remember that you need to know only one thing, Mason. Before this war is over, I am going to kill that damned uppity nigger Douglass."

CHAPTER THIRTEEN

All morning the division of Allegheny Johnson had been subjected to the deadly fire of Federal sharpshooters. Firing from a distant tree line, these Federals had kept Tom and his comrades hugging the earth and the few shallow depressions that the dips in the ground afforded. The sparse cover had resulted in numerous deaths.

The division was spread across the approaches to Rock creek and extended in a large concave arch almost three miles long. The hot steamy July air was stifling, and the sky offered no respite from the sun that was beating down on them relentlessly. This combination sapped the energy out of the huddled Confederate soldiers. The body of one of the new recruits lay sprawled a few feet from where Arthur Cook and Tom lay. Andy Barrett was on his back next to the body and continued to sedately whittle a stick's end to a fine point. As he lay there, he tried to remember the dead boy's name but only drew a blank. He could only remember that the boy had joined the company somewhere near Culpeper.

The young man had made the mistake when the firing had first commenced in trying to spot the location of the enemy sharpshooter. He had wanted to do something, to strike back at the damned vile Yankees. The long wait and inactivity of the company had caused him to become careless. As he peered over the edge of the slight mound that he laid next to, the sharpshooter had fired. The large caliber bullet struck the teenaged recruit in the throat, breaking his neck and killing him instantly. Flies buzzed around the ghastly rip in the youth's neck. His blood flowed sluggishly into the dark rich soil of Pennsylvania and his lifeless eyes stared blankly into a cloudless sky.

Andy stopped whittling to exam his work. He jabbed the sharp point of the stick into the palm of his hand to test its sharpness, He grimaced slightly at the pain it caused but was quite satisfied at his creation. He contentedly turned the stick over and began to leisurely whittle away at the other end of it. A geyser of dirt and leaves sprang upward near his elbow as a sharpshooter's bullet struck the earth, showering Andy with the debris. A second later, they heard the rifle's crack. Andy cringed and tried to make his body better fit the contours of the ground. He continued to happily whittle away.

"Hey there, Andy boy," Arthur called to him wearily, "I do believe that your Yankee playmate is startin' to git' yer range. If'n I wuz' you, and mind you, thank God that I ain't, I would definitely consider investing in some new real estate before that sharpshooter makes you a permanent part of the landscape."

"That fella' is a right persistent son of a bitch," Andy replied laconically. He continued to whittle and showed no indication that he was going to heed Arthur's warning.

"Look at that chuckle head," Arthur said sadly. "When he gits' shot, he's gonna' have this surprised look on his face. He will be wonderin' jest' how the hell did this happen' to me? You jest' wait an' see. That boy is truly an imbecile. I tell you. If'n he lives, he's got a great future waitin' for him as some towns village idjit'."

Andy grinned at them. He apparently felt himself to be in no danger although the ground around him bore the scars of many close calls. Another fountain of earth shot skyward, again closely followed by the boom of the sharpshooter's rifle. The deadly bullet missed Andy's head by a few scant inches and carved a new smoking hole in the ground as dirt and leaves were sprayed into Andy's mouth and eyes. He merely spit dirt out of his mouth and grinned stupidly at Arthur and Tom again.

"By God, Andy," Tom shouted angrily, "I have seen enough. Get out of there right now. That's an order. It is just a matter of time before he hits you and I won't sit around no more and watch this bullshit. Crawl out of that spot now, damn it."

Andy looked hurt by Tom's chastisement of him and carefully rolled to a safer spot. Tom was not in a good mood and Andy's seeming indifference to his own safety just exacerbated Tom's foul mood. After telling Vernon what Arthur and he had seen at the top of the hill, he had noticed a look in Vernon's eyes that he had never expected to see. Vernon's eyes reflected dread and fear. Tom had backed away without another word, frightened to the core by the expression that Vernon had gamely tried to hide.

Thornton Dean came crawling through the grass on his hands and knees, his butternut brown jacket streaked with sweat. Perspiration beaded his forehead like tiny diamonds. When he neared them, he rolled over onto his back and pulled his canteen from his belt. Pulling out the wooden stopper, he poured some of its contents on his head. He then tentatively swallowed a mouthful and made a face after tasting the tepid water.

"Water is as warm as horse piss," he said disgustedly. "How much longer you figger' theys' gonna' let us fry out here like this without no shade an' them dirty bastards shootin' at us the way they are? I'm about all used up an' I ain't done shit."

A bullet struck the ground a foot from where they lay. Tom instinctively drew his knees up as close as he could to his chin. The booming sounds of several large caliber Sharp's rifles reverberated in the thick summer air. Thornton buried his face in the dirt and muttered obscenities into it. He carefully lifted his head to look at Tom and Arthur.

"See what I mean? It's like this all up an' down the line. The damned sharpshooters done kilt' two fellas' in Surby's section an' the new fella', the one with the big ears who looked like a sugar bowl, he got two fingers tooken' clean off."

"You ain't come all this way jest' to tell us that the goofy lookin' boy got hisself' shot. If'n you did, I don't appreciate your comin' here an' drawin' fire to us at all," Arthur said quickly.

A bullet snapped over their heads. They all cringed as the bullet began to tumble in the air making a ripping sound, as a sheet being torn in half would.

"Vernon sent me. He wants all sergeants and corporals from all companies to meet him down near that big crooked oak we passed last night when we was goin' into position. He said to put some speed to it. I got to crawl down the line an' relay the word. Be careful crawlin' out. Any kind of motion draws their fire an' that ain't no lie. Them sharpshooters are awful eager to get' hits. It makes them riled to see a body movin'. They would much prefer to see a fella' in the condition that poor damned fella' is in." Thornton pointed towards the corpse of the dead boy and began to crawl away from them on his belly.

"This ought to be interestin'" Arthur said. He pushed his rifle in front of himself and began to slither through the sparse grass. Tom followed closely behind. Bullets slashed the air overhead seeking them out. A short scream of pain echoed in the distance followed by the angry curses of many men. Tom stopped crawling to better hear their enraged voices.

"Sons a bitches," someone shouted. "Them dirty bastards jest' kilt' Billy Bancroft."

"Dagnabbit, keep yer' heads down. Don't everybody look to see who got shot. That's jest' what they want yer' to do. Damn it, you over their, new fella', get' yer' fool head down. Git' down," a voice screamed. Tom recognized the voice of John Hubert, a veteran soldier.

"George, kin' you see Billy?" John shouted.

"Yes. He is dead. He got headshot. He's dead," George hollered.

Tom wiped at his face and continued crawling. The voices began to fade, but the bullets continued to snap and pop around his ears. Tom and Arthur picked up the pace, trying to crawl out of the deadly range and attention of the snipers.

"I will bet you," Arthur said, "that they got a whole company of sharpshooters playin' hell with us. Did you know the Yankees got a whole regiment of sharpshooters? They call themselves Berdan's sharpshooters. They wear this funny lookin' green colored pants an' jackets. I actually got to see a live sharpshooter. Last

220

night, when I went to see old Yancey in the hospital, I passed through the twenty-second boys. They had caught a sharpshooter that had made the mistake of perchin' in a tree. They had surrounded him an' forced the dirty bastard down an' he give' up. He had bin' a shootin' at fellas' whose only sin had been to try to take a piss to relieve their bladders. He finally went an' kilt' a poor fella' what had his pants down aroun' his ankles when he was takin' a squat. Poor fella' had fallen dead smack-dab into his own mess. Everybody had liked the poor fella' what got shot. He was well respected, kinda' like Vernon, so they crawled out that night to find the Yankee son of a bitch responsible. They tracked him down like a pack of hound dogs, and they treed him like an ole' coon' and took him prisoner."

"Was he one of Berdan's sharpshooters?" Tom asked.

"No. He was jest' a mean bastard what liked to kill people. No one had ordered him up that tree to take shots at anybody. He did it all on his own accord. That arrogant bastard was proud of what he done. He was arrogant right up to the minute that the boys showed him that poor fella' layin' dead in his own shit. They gave him a board and made him dig a hole. When he was finished they made him dig another one. That's when it finally dawned on the Yankee that he was in big trouble. They commenced to beat on that Yankee until he could not stand straight anymore. That Yankee pleaded fer' his life like a little old baby, but it didn't do him no good. The twenty-second boys shot him full of holes *real* slow like. They shot him in the arms, then the legs, his hands, why even his feet. They stood over him loadin' an' firin' real casual like. They must have shot that Yankee fifty times. They shot him so many times, that when they went to bury what was left, the Yankee fell apart. I never seen nothin' of the likes before. Them boys made a mess of him."

Arthur stopped crawling and slowly raised his head. He looked to see how far Tom was behind him and waited for Tom to catch up to him.

"I figger' it's safe to stand up now, but I'm still gonna' keep low. I suggest you do the same. You ready?

"Right behind you," Tom answered.

Arthur stood up and began to run hunched over as Tom followed a few steps behind. Arthur ran a zigzag pattern while Tom concentrated more on speed. After forty yards, Arthur stopped running and began to leisurely walk towards a gathering of soldiers that were standing under a centuries old oak tree. Vernon was leaning against it making small talk with Corporal Bains and Sergeant Surby. Tom spotted Huck and quickly trotted over to him.

"You look like hell. What's wrong, you got the dysentery again?" Huck asked.

"What?"

"I asked you if'n you got the runs again. You look sick."

"He ain't got the runs, Huck," Arthur said. "Me an' Tom got a chance to see what's waitin' fer' us at the top of this hill last night. There is a Union brigade sittin' on the top of that hill that looks like it growed there. They got breastworks prepared like you ain't ever seen. It looks like a castle. The breastworks got to be at least five feet tall."

"That was you makin' all that ruckus on the hill last night?" Huck asked.

"Vernon sent me an' Arthur up there with a patrol to snatch a prisoner. He said that I had been lucky, so that's why the Captain sent me up there. The Yankees were all over that hill."

"I'll say," Arthur added. "We was hidin' most of the time. We snuck way up to the top. That's when we seed what they had done to the top of that hill. It is a fort they built up there. I made up my mind right then to do the smart thing and light out. We was about to, when this old nag comes sniffin' up at us. It had dispatch pouches still on it, but the rider was nowhere to be seen. We spread out and backtracked the horse to this clearing and waited. The rider must have thought the noise he heard was the horse, but instead it was us. He walked right up to us and into our hands as neat an' clean as could be."

"We were just about to tie him up." Tom added, "and get back down when the Yankee got in his mind to try to pull a fast one. He took off running. Yancey went right after him. Yancey catches up with the Yankee and puts a knife in his leg, but the Yankee turned on Yancey and gave him a hellified beating. That Yankee had huge hands."

"That's when I caught up with both of them," Arthur said. "That Yankee was beatin' on Yancey horrible. He splittered Yancey's nose open an' fairly beat it flat. I lowered the boom on the Yankee in the nick of time, otherwise Yancey would have been kilt' fer sure. I broke his head with the stock of my rifle."

"You kilt' him?" Huck asked.

"No," Arthur replied, "that Yankee had a right hard head. I thought I cracked it like an old walnut, but I didn't kill him. Anyway, we gits' to start totin' him out of there when every damned Yankee an' his brother opens fire at us. They wuz' all around us. They shot my hat right off my head. I thought we was finished when all of a sudden our boys come wadin' right in on them. The Yankees got hit by at least two companies an' our boys finished them Yankees quick."

"So that was what all the noise was about. All of us was trying to figure out who was attackin' them last night," Huck said.

"Later, when I told Vernon what we had seen at the top of the hill, Vernon went pale, I swear. We both told him what we saw. He got this funny look and then told us to turn in," Tom said.

222

"Let me boys tell you somethin'," Arthur said. "Vernon knows that we will be goin' up that hill some time. He knows that this here comin' fight ain't gonna' be no easy win, like Chancellorsville was. This fight that's a brewin is gonna' be one rough old boy. Don't fergit', Vernon was at Malvern Hill. That fight was as bad as it kin' git', or so I have bin' tolt."

"You should have seen Vernon's face when I told him about what the Yankees had done to the top of the hill," Tom said. "He seemed to be looking into an open grave. I seen all the hope and confidence come right out of the man. You know how he is, always uplifting somebody in the worst of times. I saw his courage evaporate like rain on a hot summer day. It was all in his eyes. It scared the hell out of me."

"I seen it," Arthur quickly added. "It looked like he had saw a ghost or somethin.' The way I figger', anybody that came off Malvern Hill in one piece must have a lot of bad memories floatin' aroun' in his head."

Huck looked at Arthur and smiled.

"Don't tell me a big boy like yourself still believes in haints an' hobgoblins an' sich," Huck quipped. "To quote the late Lawyer Smith from back home, "Why sir, this is patently absurd. Do you take me fer' a country fool?"

"Believe what ever you want to. All I got to say is that Vernon is gittin' ready to tell us all how bad this one is goin' to be," Arthur replied. He pointed over towards Bains and Vernon. "Looks like Bains is spinnin' one of his yarns again. I don't want to miss this. I will see you all bye an' bye."

Arthur trotted over to the big oak tree and the group of men sitting or standing beneath it. Corporal Bains was indeed telling one of his famous stories and the laughter and hoots from those gathered indicated that it was one of his better tales. Huck wanted to join Arthur, but knew he could not. Huck did not like the way Tom looked. Huck knew that this was not the time to be distracted. People, he knew, whose minds were not clear often ended up dead from simple mistakes they would have never made if they had been thinking clearly.

"Don't be goin' and do this to yerself', Tom. You are gittin' yerself' all crazy fer nothin'. I know how you are. You got to git' yer state of mind right before the big dance. Remember what the General tolt us an' don't go fergettin' it. General Stuart tolt' us that this here fight will surely be the last one, remember? It is the end of the war. We already drove them out of that town and now we will fix them good. I will bet you any money that this is what Vernon is goin' to tell us. Them Yankees is finished. Vernon jest' wants to make sure we all know how important this fight be an' he jest' wants to make sure that we all understan' this an' don't mess it up."

"I hope you are right. I don't know anymore," Tom said wearily.

"Of course I'm right, you jest' wait an' see. Hell, if'n you can't trust the word of a General, then who kin' yer trust?" Huck asked.

"How are the mountain boys treating you?" Tom asked.

"Tolerable well now, ever since the biggest mouth of them went aroun' tellin' all the others that they should desert the first chance they got. A staff officer overheard him. The Provo's come and snatched him away faster than you kin' say, jumpin Jehosophat an' nobodies seen him since. Then the Colonel sat them all down an' had a nice chat with all of them. Colonel Edmonds tolt' them that he would personally shoot the first man of the group that even looked like he was fixin' to skin out durin' the comin' fight. The colonel said that the recent incident had caused him enough concern to actively take a strong interest in the whole company's actions in the next few days. I don't care, mind you, cause I got no place to run to."

Vernon began to get their attention by hand signals. They all gathered close together to better hear what he was about to say. He waved them all forward. Some sat on the ground so that others in the rear could see him.

"Alright, simmer down. By now," he began, "you can all figure out that we are gonna' hit them on this end. We are goin' up that hill what's in front of us. We aint' got a choice, so there it is. The Yankees got rifle pits at the base of the hill an' strong positions at the top."

There were murmurs of dissatisfaction and discontent from the gathered men. Sergeant Surby raised his hand in the air and everyone grew quiet and curious as to what he was going to say. The men of his command loved Surby because he always looked out for his people. He ran company B single-handed.

"What is it, Cole?" Vernon asked.

"Don't seem the smart thing to do, Vernon. We usually let the Yankees break their teeth on our breastworks. Why the change an' jest' what the hell are they gonna' do about all the damned sharpshooters in front of us? My poor boys bin' a' sittin' all afternoon in the broilin' sun with their heads buried in the dirt. They bin' eatin' grass all day an' they ain't got a lick of shade an' even less cover. We bin' gittin' picked off all mornin'. I already lost two men kilt' dead an we ain't doin' nothin' about it. Good men, they wuz'. If'n we gotta' cross that crick out yonder in broad daylight, them Yankees will wax our asses good."

"Lattimer's battery is going into position on Benner's hill, that's the one in back of us," Vernon responded by pointing over his shoulder. "They will hit the tree line an' the base of Culp's hill. They will hit the rifle pits. They won't be able to put much fire on the top of the hill. There are way too many trees an' sich' fer' them to do much damage, but it should solve the sharpshooter problem"

He waited to see if his answer had satisfied Surby and he quickly realized that it did not.

"I am goin' to explain why we are attackin' the way Colonel Edmonds done explained it to me. This here comin' fight is meant to keep the Yankees from pullin' troops off this hill and stop them from usin' them to reinforce their other positions where the real attack will take place. We have to make sure the Yankees stick here. Boys, we plan on pinnin' down as many of the enemy on this end so that the attack on the other end will go as smooth as glass. General Longstreet and his Corp, the Third Corp, will deliver the main blow. The Yankees ain't strong everywhere, so if'n we tie them up here, they won't be able to shift troops over to strengthen' their weak flank. They will be unable to send for help an' get' it from here because the Yankees here will be involved in a dance with us, the Second Corp." Vernon watched their faces carefully for any signs of malcontent.

"This hill is heavily fortified at the top. This fight is gonna' be tough. We must look like we are prepared and determined to crack them wide open on this hill. I repeat, we must make this attack look like the real deal, the main attack. We must convince them that we intend to roll up this flank so that they will stay put. Keep the pressure on them at all times but do not waste lives. Don't go gittin' crazy. An Army engineer who is older than Moses that knows his job put the positions the Yankees built on the top of the hill there. Fortifications could mean that the Yankees are weak here. We won't know it until we hit them. If they are, an' it looks like we kin' break them then we will drive this attack home with everything we got. If we can't take the crest, then so be it. We will have accomplished what we set out to do which is to tie them up. We must keep them tied up an' tied down. When we hear the Third Corp goin' in, we will hit them. Does everybody understand?" Vernon asked. No one moved or said a word.

"I guess no questions is good news. Good. The Twelfth Corp, Army of the Potomac, is the crowd at the top of this hill. They are a stubborn bunch. You all must know by know that our First Corp hit them, walloped them proper, and drove them through the streets of the town itself. They fell back and are perched on ridges to the west of us. Our First Corp is pretty well spent. Not all of General Longstreet's Third Corp has arrived as of yet. The Federals got pushed off McPherson's ridge and through the town, but they are far from whipped. There is plenty of fight left in them an' they are well off in artillery support. They got beat, but they are not defeated. This comin' fight is gonna' be a stand up, knockdown Injun' fight, from rock to rock an' from tree to tree. Keep your people movin' forward an' don't allow them to stall. Move forward in rushes after a volley an' cover each other's moves. Time your advances with the enemy fire. Keep a sharp eye on yer' ends an' don't allow the Yankees to git' between you. Stay in close contact by runners to who is on your flank. If the officers don't order a man as a runner, then you pick one. Support each other. Know what the section next to you is dealin' with at all times."

Vernon paused before he continued. The veteran non-commissioned men had heard this all before, but those new to command, like Tom and Huck, were learning on the job.

"If the Yankees break on this hill, orders are to push forward as far as we kin', to the next hill. If we break them here, we will have them. If they attempt to break off contact, they will leave the door wide open. We will walk right down their entire line and bag the whole lot of them, an' boys, this war is over."

Huck nudged Tom in the ribs and winked at him.

"Our own beloved Second Corp," Vernon said loudly, "is goin' in with everybody. No one is to be left in reserve. Staff headquarters believes that they are not strong enough here to come at us. Our division will cross the crick' to our front an' sweep them rifle pits. Company H of the Twenty-First Regiment has bin' hand picked by Colonel Edmonds to act as lead skirmishers. Company h sergeants, keep a sharp eye on yer' officers. They will be informed when General Longstreet begins his assault and will start our push fer the top. Once the pits are cleared, everybody is to make fer' the crest. Do not fergit' to designate somebody from each of yer' companies to fill canteens when you cross that crick'. You don't know the next time that you will see water again and the work is guaranteed to make a body thirsty." He stopped abruptly, searching his mind quickly to see if he had omitted anything. He was satisfied that he had not.

"That is all of it. Good luck to each an' everyone of you an' I will see you at the top."

The men began to break up into small groups and they ambled away trying to digest the words of the first sergeant who acted as a sergeant major. They all talked in hushed tones.

"See, Tom. It is jest' like I said," Huck commented. "Did you see the way Vernon talked about the end of this war? By God, Tom, I kin' almost feel it in my bones. This one is it. It is jest' like General Stuart tolt' us. We are gonna' end this here war right here an' right now. Then it will be safe to go home again. Then, we are off to the gold fields of California an' pull gold chunks the size of robin's eggs from out the streams. Sweet Jasper!"

Tom tried to be enthusiastic and as hopeful as Huck, but for some nameless reason he was filled with a strange sense of foreboding. He attempted to divorce it from his mind with conversation.

"It does appear that Colonel Edmonds decided to arrange your being lead skirmishers of the regiment all for the sake of the reluctant Union loving mountain

226

boys in your company. This way, if anyone of those boys decides to skin out, everyone will be able to see them do it."

"Suits me jest fine," Huck said happily.

Arthur managed to catch up with them just at that moment. He was chuckling to himself.

"What is so funny?" Huck asked.

"You should have heard the story Bains was runnin'. Every word of it was true. That boy has some funny observations about life in general. You know, I think that I would go somewhere an' pay good money jest' to listen to him go on about this an' that. He kin' tell them stories fer' hours. I laughed so hard, I thought I was gonna' piss myself." Arthur choked back his laughter.

"That sounds crazy," Huck said. "Whoever heard of a man getting' paid to make you laugh. Why, the idea in itself is enough to make you laugh."

"All's I know is that he is a comical bastard. Let me tell you what he said." Arthur said.

He broke into a fit of high-pitched laughter. He jackknifed forward and put both of his hands on his knees to steady himself. Spittle flew from his mouth and tears coursed down his cheeks. He held onto his sides and sucked in air, all the while shaking and rocking. He stopped laughing and began to giggle like a schoolgirl. Without warning, Arthur broke wind. Both Tom and Arthur stepped away from the quivering, spasmodic, flatulent Arthur Cook.

"Why don't you tell me that story later," Huck said. "I gotta' git'. With all these fellas' goin' back into position all at the same time, I do believe it will draw a lot of fire from our sharpshooter friends. I don't want to be the last movin' target fer' all of them to sight in on, git' the picture?"

"You do have a point," Arthur said, wiping his eyes. "We best get' a long," he uttered. "I will tell you the story when I see you at the top. It is a hum-dinger."

"Good enough," Huck said. "Good luck, you clay eatin' Georgia cracker."

"And good luck to you as well, you wormy Missora mule," Arthur said, grinning. Huck quickly walked away and turned back in Tom's direction.

"Don't fergit' what we talked about, now. I will see you at the top an' don't be late." Huck gave a wave and began to run towards where members of his company waited in the yellow grass. Tom watched him and saw him begin to creep backs into line. He soon disappeared from sight. Huck never once looked back.

As soldiers began to move back into position, they ran the gauntlet of the federal sharpshooter's deadly accurate fire once again. Their fire began to noticeably increase as Tom and Arthur hunched down and went to their bellies. Deadly whizzing bullets began to fill the air overhead and both men crawled carefully back to their positions under the predatory federal fire coming from their front.

Tom paused a moment to catch his breadth. He lay flat on his back. Arthur was down near his ankles with his head buried in the dirt. A bullet tore over Tom's head by a few scant inches.

"I can be truthful, Arthur," Tom said. "No matter how many times that I hear the damned sound of a bullet goin' overhead, it gives me the willies."

"It is supposed to. If it don't, then somethin' is seriously wrong with you," Arthur said.

"That last round that went over my head parted my hair. I felt the heat of it. I get so scared sometimes that I can barely think," Tom said.

"Join the club. I am scared all the time, Tom," Arthur said honestly. "It is natures way, is all. It is like the way pain works. Suppose a body didn't know what pain was. He never had the ability to feel pain. Suppose that fella' was to lean his hand on a hot stove an' leave it there 'cause he couldn't feel no pain. Why, bye an' bye, that fellas' hand would be burnt' to a stump cause he didn't know no better, see? Fear is natures way of tellin' yer' to watch yer' ass cause yer' soul may soon be partin' from it if'n yer don't."

"That makes sense," Tom said.

"Some folks, it seems, don't got this reaction to danger. Take fer' example the way Barrett was grinnin' every time he got shot at by that sharp shooter. The bullets wuz' jest' missin' him by inches, yet he wasn't showin' any concern. He knew in his heart that it was jest' a matter of time a' fore that Yankee made a mess of him, but he didn't have it in him to move out the way. You seen it. Am I right?" Arthur asked.

"Can I ask you a question?" Tom asked.

"Sure."

"You ever get any second thoughts as to what this war is all about?"

"No," Arthur said. A bullet ripped the air overhead followed by angry curses.

"I knew this was comin' when the Yankees elected Lincoln. They say this is a rich man's war and a poor man's fight, but I seed' plenty of dead rich fella's. A bullet don't respect how much money you got. This war grinds up both kinds. The Yankees picked on the wrong folks when they decided they could shove their ideas down our throats. The rich people did the only thing they could do. Slavery puts bread an' butter on their table. The Yankees started this war when they picked

Lincoln. No. I got no doubts in my mind as to what this war is all about. Now, if you are askin' as to how I feel about this war, then that is an entirely different story."

"I guess that's what I'm asking," Tom said.

Arthur looked about him to make sure that they were alone.

"I don't believe in slavery. I never did. Don't tell nobody. This is jest' between you an' me. I bin' all over, Tom. I seed' how they treat the niggers. Slavery is a cruel business, too cruel fer' my liking. I seed' niggers drop dead from the heat out in the cotton fields. I seed' how they beat an' work them to death. I seed' them treated worse than a dog. When we win this war, there will be a lot of people who feel the same way I do an' they will speak up agin' it. I truly believe this. Slavery will end some day, but it won't be the damned Yankees that end it. When the Yankees lose this war, it ain't goin' to shut up the abolitionists. They will continue to be a thorn in the side of slavery, you jest' watch. It will be good Christian southern folks that end it."

"I am flabbergasted!" Tom exclaimed.

"Don't go blabbin about what I say to nobody, you hear? This is jest betwixt' the both of us."

"You are a philosopher. You should be teaching in a college somewhere," Tom said jokingly.

"Hardly," Arthur said. "Let me tell you this an' see if it don't make sense. How much do you think the war has cost both sides money wise?"

"I can't even imagine."

"For what the North has spent alone on this war, they could have bought every nigger in the South from the planters and paid the niggers a good solid wage for twenty years to keep on pickin' cotton."

Tom howled in laughter.

"You asked me how I felt about this war. In my eyes, it is being fought because of people's stiff-necked pride. Both sides is too proud to come to an agreement or back down. Pride cometh before a fall, jest remember that. Holy hell, you got me preaching now."

"What did you think about what Vernon said?" Tom asked.

"I was more impressed by what Bains had to see than what Vernon had to say. Watch this last few yards. The land dips a might so move quick from side to side crawlin' through there. It heps' to throw their aim off."

They scrambled through the slight draw as several bullets in the process of going ballistic shrieked above their sweating brows. They made it to better cover in just a few seconds.

"I am carious to know if Andy is still among the walkers of the earth or not or one of those unfortunate ones that need a quick reckonin' beneath it. You ready fer' the last dash, Sergeant Sawyer?"

"As ready as I will ever be. Go on with it."

They crept the last few remaining yards to their old position and the fire of the federal enemy became maddening. They seemed to fire in spurts and then the fire would stop entirely. When the soldiers would become edgy and curios as to why the shooting had stopped, many would attempt to peer over their protective cover for a better look. The Federal fire would then resume in earnest and increase to a frightening intensity.

Once again, the sharpshooters were firing away at those crawling back into position with this same kind of dedication making the last few yards extremely hazardous. Tom heard several men shout out in anger and pain when they were hit and the accompanying choruses of curses when a bullet came to close to a man. The grass offered them no protection at all, just partial concealment. Any person crawling these last few yards with his weight on his elbows instead of lying straight out on his back and pushing his body forward with his feet became a prime candidate for the sniper's bullet.

Tom pushed himself forward with his legs and dug his elbows into the ground. Slowly, he pulled himself forward. He pushed and pulled himself to safety. By the time that he rolled into his old site, he was panting heavily and totally exhausted. Arthur flopped into his old position. A bullet shredded the air only a few inches overhead.

Andy lay on his back staring at the cloud speckled blue sky observing both of them. Andy appeared carefree and unruffled at the activity of the Federal sharpshooters. Fresh pock mocks on the ground indicated the many near misses from the federal fire. Smoke still curled out of some of the holes.

"Andy boy," Arthur shouted, "are you still with us?"

"Course' I'm still here. Why wouldn't I be here? Was I supposed to be somewhere else?" Andy asked in all seriousness.

"I thought by now you would have done sprouted angel's wings," Arthur said derisively, "and that you would be a' seranadin' yourself and a' polishin' yer' halo. How that Federal sharpshooter ain't bin' able to put you in the next world yet is one of God's little mysteries."

A column of dirt and leaves sprouted from the ground as another bullet slammed into the earth. The resultant shower of debris fell on the upturned face of Andy.

"It ain't fer' lack of tryin," Andy said. He squinted at the sun as he wiped the dirt from his face. The sound of thunder boomed out loudly catching everyone by surprise. Artillery fire from Benner's hill, situated to their immediate rear, began to deliver their wares in massive quantities directly in front of the positions of the crouching southern infantrymen. The forest's treeline ahead bloomed in destructive blossoms of bright orange, red, and yellow as the first shells of the Confederate artillery battery landed. The resultant gray smoke that began to pour out of the distant tree line was punctuated again and again by these deadly bursts of destruction.

Tom had jumped with the initial crashing volley that landed and gorged shallow graves out of the ground. Time after time, dirty clouds of black and gray smoke with bright yellow and orange centers erupted all through the woods that faced them. The explosions nestled at the base of the hill and then plunged into the trees on the rocky slopes of Culp's hill. The resultant barrage shredded the trees to splinters and turned scurrying Federal sharpshooters into bloody chunks. Andy rose to his knees and gazed at the hellish spectacle.

"It's about time," he screamed jubilantly. He let loose a shrill whoop of unrestrained joy and relief. In his euphoria, he abandoned what little common sense he had and rose to his feet. He screamed happily in competition with the explosions and clamor that rose to the heavens and shook the earth. Andy stretched his arms over his head and began to leap in the air in pure mindless glee. He started dancing a strange backwoods dance. He threw his tattered hat in the air and flapped his arms wildly. His behavior just a few scant seconds ago would have invited death. Now, with the bombardment at full pitch, the sharpshooter's fire had dropped away to nothing. Arthur watched the bizarre dancing of Andy with keen interest.

"He looks like some kinda' big bird a' gittin' ready to take off, don't he," Arthur shouted. "Like some kinda' half crazed pelican what got a fish hook stuck in his craw. Go right at it, Andy boy, you crazy son of a bitch."

Tom noticed the officers had started walking the line in full view of the enemy. The line extended for almost a quarter mile in a great spreading concave arch that fronted Rock creek. Tom kneeled and watched as the earth twisted and convulsed with the steady pounding from the Confederate battery of artillery. The air pulsed and the concussion from the many explosions rolling towards them made the men's breastbones vibrate. They watched the woods in front of them twist and convulse with the steady pounding of bursting artillery shells. A steady stream of these missiles roared overhead and impacted right in front of their eyes.

Artillery shells whizzed through the sky to plummet earthward in shrieking thunder. The shells shattered on the ground in hissing red-hot fragments that flew everywhere. Solid artillery balls careened along the ground with grinding fury, smashing rocks and trees, spinning, ripping, and destroying everything that they came into contact with in long smoky trails that stubbornly clung to the humid air. The smoky trails pointed to the federal line like the spread out fingers of an accusing hand. Flesh melted in the grip of this deadly power.

Torrents of these shells poured from Lattimer's position on Benner's hill as the southern gunners worked their field pieces with great speed and accuracy. Clouds of smoke rose from Culp's hill as the Confederate battery plied their ordinance at its base. All up and down the line of Johnson's Division, people began to cheer and celebrate as Andy's exuberance spread unrestrained throughout the rank and file. Some imitators of Andy's strange dance strutted and flapped imaginary wings and screamed at the top of their voices. It was a release of pure primeval energy for having been subjected to the galling enemy rifle fire and the helpless rage that they had felt at their inability to strike back at their tormentors.

It was now the turn of the Federal sharpshooters to bury their faces in the dirt and cringe in terror. The artillery raked the tree line and then started inching its way further into woods of the rocky hill. The dry underbrush crackled and blazed from the many small fires started by the shelling that the skilled southern artillerymen of Lattimer's battery were now giving their former countrymen. Many of the Federal soldiers had decided to run for their lives and the protection of the rifle pits once the artillery had suddenly shifted up the hill. But the artillery fire shifted again and caught most of them in mid stride as the gunners corrected their aim. They corrected their fire as they overshot the base of the hill and began to land shells right among the scurrying federal soldiers. These men were caught in a deluge of detonations and smoky explosions that filled the air with red-hot iron fragments and they died in the dozens.

Shell fragments tore off lower jaws, eviscerated some and flung bodies heavenward. Bodies struck the ground ripped in two while others landed sans heads or arms. The fire walked towards the rifle pits bypassing those sharpshooters who had remained with their faces pressed into the ground. These survivors watched and heard the shells screech over their heads to land now directly among the rifle pits.

The hardworking gunners of Latimer's Battery pressed the fire forward with great precision. Artillery shells began to rain down the first line of the Federal defenders. Artillery shot bounced along the ground in great arcs only to explode when their internal fusses detonated directly above a hole filled with cowering, terrified northern soldiers, blowing them into Abraham's bosom and eternity.

Some artillery shells made sounds like mighty anvils being struck when they landed on ancient boulders. Lead and metal showered the area in incinerating rain and shattered rock needles whistled in the air at odd angles just feet above the churning earth. The Battery continued to work their guns in a great destructive concert of power, flame, smoke and noise, sparing neither ammunition nor effort. Gunners sweated and strained as they shifted their Napoleons slightly in adjustment to the recoil the guns produced. They expertly sighted the guns and placed their shellfire directly on target again and again. Twelve guns continued to belch their fury at the nearby hill, rupturing the earth and leaving the federal soldiers dazed and helpless.

The infantrymen of Johnson's division, Jones Brigade, Second Corp, delighted in the pure destructive fury of the iron hurricane that was being poured out on the hill. They were awed by the expertise the gunners of Lattimer's Battery displayed in the speed and their handling of the guns. They watched open mouthed as projectiles of all sorts struck the earth, plowing furrows in the ground or bursting as they bounced and exploded at knee level. For an hour, this seemingly endless power worked the base of Culp's hill over churning men into mud and making boulders smaller ones. The ruptured earth shook and the hill spat flames at the setting sun.

Dozens of fleecy white clouds with fiery orange and yellow centers suddenly appeared over the rifle holes and breastworks of the Union infantry men who huddled in terror with their faces pressed into the brown sandy gravel. Airbursts exploded in sharp bangs that caused thousands of metal shards to shriek earthward at the huddled soldiers piercing their heads, perforating their skulls and unprotected shoulders. There was no safety to be found at the bottom of the holes that they hid in. The airborne death plastered them to the sides of their pre-dug graves.

The demoralized half-maddened soldiers began to clamber out of the pits in panic. They deserted the breastworks by squads and then by companies. The metal rich air pulverized those that did manage to get to their feet and many went tumbling headfirst back to the bottom of their holes. Union men that elected to leave the breastworks were knocked flat by the concussion of bursting shells and then were chewed up by the iron rain that fell in sheets as the distinctive airbursts dotted the base of the hill. The many detonations shimmied the sky as huge volumes of superheated air were tossed about like rowboats in a gale. The puffy clouds savagely accumulated above the base of the hill laying waste to everything that was directly below them.

"Them Yankees is catchin' holy hell now," Arthur said lazily. He reached into his shirt pocket and pulled out a plug of tobacco. He offered some to Tom who declined and then to Andy who happily pulled off a chaw.

"Air bursts. That means we will go in soon. They are getting' warmed up fer sure. Look yonder, Tom. There goes Company H into line," Arthur shouted.

Tom watched as the skirmish line dressed ranks and fixed bayonets. On either side of Company H, other regiments placed an equal number of men out front. The line stretched at the East Side of Culp's hill for more than a quarter mile. General Jones' brigade of General Johnson's Division of the Second Corp, commanded by Dick "Baldy Ewell" of the Army of Northern Virginia began to uncoil itself to ready a strike at the foe. Firing broke out from the direction somewhere to their front, sporadic and disjointed, not the sound of a general conflict. Officers with drawn pistols and bare swords stood silently listening to the ghostly sounds of the distant fight expecting it to build in its pitch. They waited patiently for the roar that would indicate that General Longstreet was smashing away at the Federal line but the sounds of battle strangely washed away to nothing.

If the officers looked puzzled, the skirmishers looked nervous. Some sensed something wrong in the apprehensive faces of their officers. It was the responsibility of the skirmishers to clear the way for the main body of the attacking Confederate brigade. They would actively engage any number of enemy skirmishers, pinning them down while the main body would attempt to outflank the enemy opposition.

"Huck's got it made, Tom," Arthur shouted. "Them lines the Yankees put at the base of the hill all got blowed to a frazzle. The artillery hushed them up. The artillery kicked the front door wide open. It sounded fer a while that somebody started poundin' hard on the back door but that done died out. Anyway, it does appear that Steuarts' Marylanders and Hays Brigade are headin, for the west side of the hill an' we stay put. Can only mean one thing. We are goin' straight up the slope of this damned hill."

"That's good, ain't it?" Andy asked.

"The damned Yankees can't be strong everywhere," Arthur said hopefully. "If'n we kin' get inside the Yankee works anywhere along the top, they won't be able to hold it. Then where do you think they will be forced to go?" Arthur asked.

"To the bottom?" Andy asked.

"Right smart answer there, Andy Boy. I will personally recommend you fer' a battlefield promotion right after this fight. You should be made, why I would say, a General at least."

"Do I git' a horse?"

"You will surely git' a horse," Arthur chuckled.

"I never had me no horse."

Arthur looked at Andy curiously.

"My pap had a horse once," Andy said sadly, "but he shot it one winter. We ate that horse fer nearly a month."

"Was it good?"

"It wasn't a bad horse as horses go. I liked him jest' fine. I felt bad when my pap shot it though."

They watched as the far left of their division began moving off to the west. An entire brigade swung into motion. This brigade was composed heavily of men from Louisiana. They were rough men who spoke with a heavy Creole accent. They were men who could march all day and sing songs all night; men who were quick to cut you with a knife if they felt insulted and quick to share a drink with you if they felt you to be a friend. Hay's Brigade soon disappeared from sight. Two other Brigades followed Hay's brigade, one made up of men from Maryland and the other, a brigade of North Carolinians.

Company H of their own regiment, the Twenty-first Virginia, began to move forward. They stepped towards the distant tree line that was engulfed in smoke from many small fires. They watched as the line disappeared in the smoke. Drummers began beating the roll for companies to come into formation.

"That settles this conversation," Arthur said happily. He stood up and began shouting loudly, "Every body up. We are movin'. It is time to git' yer git' goin, boys. Let's move, on yer feet. What do you all want? Engraved invitations to this dance ,up, boys, up."

Company C stirred itself and shook itself out. They quickly formed ranks. Within a few minutes, the entire regiment stood shoulder to shoulder in a long two-row column. Officers began to better align the battalions and posed in military postures for the benefit of the uninitiated. Hundred stood in this double row. Captain Custiss walked a section of this line, speaking briefly to some and offering encouragement to others. He stopped and began to smile and joke with first sergeant Jenkins. He patted the first sergeant on his shoulder and walked away grinning. He suddenly walked past Tom and stopped abruptly and made his way back to Tom just as quickly.

"Sergeant Sawyer, I simply wanted to say before we all go in that you should know just how important your prisoner was to us. The dispatches that you returned to us told us just who and what is on the hill to our front. Your find was integral to our planning this assault. Word has it that you will be getting a promotion after this fracas is done with. Wouldn't it be something for you to return home as an officer? Think of what the people at home would say."

"Yes sir."

"That fellow you cracked in the head would not stop talking. I do believe that the blow unhinged him. He had mental diarrhea. He told us volumes about the Federal dispositions. He knew quite a bit. He though that he was dying even though our medical people insured us that he was not. He even began speaking in a strange tongue. It was later determined that he was speaking Russian, can you believe it? Anyway, good job and well done, Sergeant Sawyer."

"Thank you sir," Tom said. Captain Custiss continued on his way. Tom looked uneasily as he glanced about at the rest of his messmates and friends. Arthur caught Tom's sick expression as Custiss walked away.

"Huck was right. You do look like you got the Tennessee two- step. You got the runs?" Arthur asked.

"No," Tom said defensively.

'You got a funny look to you. You had better stop driftin' on that cloud you are on an' git' back to earth. I kin' see it in yer' eyes, fer heavens sakes. Git yer head from out yer' backside."

"I am alright, I tell you. For my old Aunt Nellie, let it be, will you." Tom said angrily.

"I knowed' some fella's," Arthur said carefully, "they got this idea in their heads fer' one reason or t'other, that their time was up. They kept it up with these funny ideas in their heads. They went an' got careless an got themselves kilt' because of it. It was like they wisht' themselves into the grave. They done things that not even a danged recruit would be dumb enough to do." Arthur watched Tom's expression carefully.

"Don't you worry none about me," Tom replied cockily. "I intend to stay alive long enough to collect the money you owe me from our little bet you waged on me staying a sergeant. You just remember that, you old fart."

"Alright then," Arthur grinned.

"Hell, you' all heard what the Captain said. It may be me coming out of this fight a General," Tom said in jest. Some of his friends laughed at his comment.

Just as Tom finished speaking a shell whizzed overhead making many of the veteran soldiers duck. It impacted to their rear directly on Benner's hill. Several other projectiles clawed through the air to explode there as heads turned towards the direction of the hill that was being subjected to enemy counter battery fire. A southern caisson, half filled with ammunition, was hit by a shell and exploded into splinters.

"Federal fire," Andy whispered fearfully. Artillery shells thickened the air in the next few seconds. They came by the dozen and the fire was accurate. These shells whistled and hummed as the steady pounding rocked Benner's hill. Guns, horses and soldiers were enveloped in the series of blasts. Cannon wheels flew skyward, as gunners were disintegrated and horses were disemboweled. Colonel Edmonds saw the expressions on the faces of the men as they watched the Federal shells begin to rain on the Confederate Artillery position.

"Eyes forward. Keep your eyes to the front," he shouted. The men turned away but gave furtive sideway glances as the accurate Union artillery began to tell on the gunner's of Latimer's battery. Gunners raced to limber up the horses needed to draw the guns away but were cut down by bursting artillery rounds. Some of them desperately sought to escape the destruction and frantically were in the action of cutting dead horses from their harnesses when they too were struck down.

"Damned Yankee fire is accurate," Captain Custiss muttered. The Captain looked towards the setting sun. "It did appear by the sound earlier that the attack to our left is underway. Strangely, it is silent now. I do hope that our assault begins soon. We do not have much daylight left."

Colonel Edmonds turned and faced the setting rays of the sun and nodded. He watched as more shellfire sought out the lives of the Confederate gunners on Benner's hill and snuffed them out.

"That Federal fire is coming in back of this hill that is to our front. It must be coming from Cemetery hill. I am sure of it. How strange indeed that we have heard no reports of General Longstreet's attack. If the attack is underway, surely we should have heard more than just a smattering of small arms fire. We should have at least heard canon fire. Extremely perplexing, if I must say so, Captain," Colonel Edmonds said worriedly.

Another caisson of ammunition exploded from a direct hit and disappeared in a loud explosion. The ammunition stored in it also detonated from the flames. These artillery rounds ignited and went spilling around the legs of the gunners. A series of explosions caught the gunners standing near the gun that they had been servicing, and they were blown high into the air. These human missiles burned and flared brightly in the fading light. They cart wheeled and flipped through the early twilight sky and left smoky trails on their descent earthward. The sound of firing broke out on their left.

"That must be the brigade of General Steuart," Colonel Edmonds noted. "It sounds as if he is engaged. What is the meaning of our delay? If the Yankees put artillery at the top of Culp's hill, I fear we will not be able to come to grips with them. They will fire right down our throats. I pray that we hear soon of General Longstreet's attack."

Captain Custiss nodded and continued to observe the beating that Lattimer's battery was receiving. He watched the mayhem through his long single piece telescope.

"Sir, if you would. It appears that Lattimer's battery is attempting to disengage from Benner's hill." Captain Custiss handed the Colonel his spyglass. He peered through it carefully.

"Not all, Captain. Some remain. It is good that the battery leaves. The position was untenable. They have done all that is humanly possible to aid us. We must go in soon."

Colonel Edmonds watched as a Confederate field piece soared high in the air, its round that was stuck in the muzzle exploded, peeling the end of the gun like a banana. The gunners disappeared in the bright flash. He turned away sickened at what he had just seen. One Confederate gun answered the Yankee fire. The gunners were stripped to the waist and worked like men possessed. Colonel Edmonds handed the telescope back to the Captain.

He had time to sight in on the one gun crew when another federal shell landed among the Confederate gunners. The resultant explosion ripped one gunner's head from his shoulders and tore another in two. Captain Custiss turned away from the carnage occurring on Benner's hill.

In the next several seconds, Lattimer's battery was incapable of returning the Federal fire. The young commander of the battery was lying mortally wounded next to a shattered gun. Without any return fire from the southern artillery unit, the Federal fire intensified. Using a new invention, a French range finder, the Union artillerymen now tore the Confederate position on the hills to shreds. They drenched Benner's hill in fire.

"We must go in, If need be with cold steel alone," Colonel Edmonds said loudly. Captain Custiss inwardly cringed with the Colonel's bold statement. He could not believe his ears. Even with the technological advancement that had occurred with the development of the rifled musket in the last fifty years, men like Colonel Edmonds still took heart with the archaic principle of a bayonet charge.

The new rifled bored muskets killed at a far greater range than did the smooth bore muskets of the last century. Captain Custiss knew that a bayonet assault was as old fashioned and outdated as a knight in amour challenging a fully loaded canon. If one were close enough to stick a man with a bayonet, Captain Custiss reasoned, then it would be more than probable that your enemy would have ample time to send a bullet through ones head well before one could jab the enemy with a knife attached to the end of a rifle.

"We shall sweep them off this hill at the point of the bayonet," Colonel Edmonds repeated, "or we shall all die in the attempt." Again, Captain Custiss winced at the words of his superior officer. Colonel Edmonds attention became riveted on a group of horsemen galloping towards him.

"Aha," he said happily. "I see General Johnson riding this way with staff officers from General Jones' headquarters. Let us see what presents itself."

General Johnson rode towards Colonel Edmonds. He reined his horse in tightly and quickly dismounted. His face was crimson and flecks of white spittle lined the corners of his mouth.

"Captain, if you would hand me your glass, sir," he asked. The captain handed his telescope over to the General and stood out of his way. General Johnson focused the glass at the destruction occurring to the Confederate battery positioned on Benner's hill.

"Fuggin' Yankees. Damn them to hell. They have fairly immolated Lattimer's battery," he cursed.

General Johnson, considered by many to be the most profane officer in the Army of Northern Virginia, let loose a string of obscenities. His blue streak caused some of General Jones' staff officers to hide their smiles and look away. The numerous and inventive way the General used the vulgarity that described the act of human sexuality punctuated his sentences from beginning to end. He would use the phrase so many times that it would become impossible not to hide ones wonderment from the world, especially if it happened to be a young lieutenant unfamiliar with the General's informal manner of speech.

Woe to that young man that smiled when the General was seething in rage and liberally sprinkling his expressions with the word. The staff officers dismounted and stood by the roadside. The General handed the Captain the small telescope.

"Colonel, everything is fuggin' goin' awry. It appears now that General Longstreet and the Third Corp have already started their attack earlier. The fuggin' sun is about to fuggin' set an' here we stand an' sit, late for the fuggin' ball."

The staff officers continued to look away from the General. General Johnson hiked his trousers up and stretched.

"For some unknown fuggin' reason, General Ewell has just now been fuggin' notified of Longstreet's attack. He has ordered us in. No one heard a fuggin' thing an' no one from Longstreet's staff informed Dick Ewell. Fuggin' cooperation is fuggin non existent between the fuggin' corp commanders these days. We did nothing all fuggin' morning except take casualties. The fuggin Yankee sons' of bitches pulled units off this fuggin' hill an' used them to reinforce their other side of the fuggin' line. Longstreet went in unsupported. The Yankees brought their fuggin' artillery forward an' fuggin' deployed them on fuggin Cemetery hill while we sat around with our fuggin' thumbs firmly implanted in our fuggin' backsides all morning an' fuggin' afternoon. This has got to be the most fuggin' unplanned, fuggin' uncoordinated, fuggin ill conceived attack I have ever had the sad fuggin' misfortune to witness. This is a fuggin' debacle of the first fuggin' magnitude. Dick is back in his tent howling fuggin' mad an' he has a right to be, dammit."

While Captain Custiss was amused at the litany of profanity that gushed from the mouth of the General, it was obvious that the General's language was burning the ears of the genteel Colonel's.

"This fight was fuggin' unplanned. Lee got it in his head that he can fuggin' whip them here. Lee figures he can whip them with frontal assaults all the time. This fuggin' fight keeps on fuggin' consuming brigades an' fuggin battalions like a fuggin' wildfire. There is word now that old John B. Hood got fuggin' shot. The first corp is fuggin' been all used up. That's all I know. I just got finished talking with Dick and he holds my exact fuggin' sentiments. He has ordered the whole division forward at once. The firing you hear is General Steuart's Brigade goin' in. Daniel is on his right. To Daniel's right is Williams. General Jones, your brigade commander, holds this end of the fuggin' line. To your right, Colonel, is no one."

Colonel Edmonds nodded in understanding.

"We are going ahead with this attack in the fuggin' dark," General Johnson said with disgust. "Caleb, I am sending you in. I have 'Extra Billy' Smith's Brigade holding a position on the York road. There have been fuggin' reports of Union activity around there. Personally, I think that all the reports are fuggin' Federal stragglers, but fuggin' better safe than fuggin' sorry. I am sending him to you directly. I want you to understand this, Caleb. If you break those fuggin' Yankees, that I will support you. Stay in close contact with Walker's and Nicholl's Brigades, and I will inform General Jones to be ready to turn towards General Steuart's Brigade to support him if Steuart can outflank any part of the Yankee works. Caleb, yours is the best fuggin' regiment in the fuggin' Brigade, and you are the best fuggin' regimental commander I have. You must take the crest of that fuggin' hill. I am sending you straight up that old bastard."

"Understood, sir. I will plant the colors on its summit by this evening."

"That's the fuggin' spirit, Caleb. I know you will. Caleb, you got to move fuggin' quick. If we can break them son's a fuggin' bitches, then we can push forward to fuggin' Cemetery Hill. If this does occur then we will have the Baltimore Pike. If we secure this fuggin' road and we turn the entire fuggin' Yankee flank, them shit eatin' Yankee sons a' fuggin' bitches are all done."

The sound of distant and scattered gunshots came from their front. It was not steady but highly erratic. To the trained ear it meant that the skirmishers of Steuart's Brigade were coming under heavy fire from Federal advanced positions.

"That is Steuart. If he turns any part of that flank, then you stop your advance up the hill and turn in towards him. If you see that the Yankee's are abandoning the crest, then by all means, take it and then turn towards Steuart's Brigade. Use your discretion, Caleb. Turn right along the entire line. If you see that General Steuart is heading for the Baltimore Pike, then support his action by covering his flank. The Yankees might just counter-attack so be ready. If we hit them hard enough, it might knock that idea right out of their fuggin' heads."

General Johnson shouted to one of his staff officers.

"Donny, grab that old fuggin' cracker box and bring it here." The General reached into his pocket and pulled out a crudely drawn map. He pointed to a straight line on it as he spread it open on the box.

"This fuggin' map is not exact so bear this in mind. This here is the Baltimore road. It leads right to the base of Cemetery fuggin' hill, the very same hill that the Yankees ran to when we whipped their fuggin' asses. See this other fuggin' line here? This one is the fuggin' Emmetsburg road. Longstreet was supposed to secure this fuggin road but this fuggin' fight is so disjointed that I don't know if he has attained his objective or not. See this fuggin' ridge that runs alongside it? If Longstreet has secured this road and has succeeded in breaking their line anywhere along here, then we will fuggin' annihilate them. He will secure the Taneytown road that runs kinda' fuggin' parallel to it. They will be hit from two fuggin' sides and we will have them fuggin' cold."

Another Federal shell exploded on the hill setting off a load of ammunition that had been stored in a caisson.

"I don't give a fuggin' care how many Yankees are in the forts outside of Washington City. We will find a fuggin' way to come through the fuggin' backdoor. If we just continue to fuggin' sit around doing nothing, an opportunity to destroy them fuggin' Yankees may disappear like a fuggin' fart in the wind. That is why Dick has ordered everybody forward. I am telling this to as many people as I can. I can't fuggin' emphasize enough just how important it is for all of us to do the utmost in this endeavor. Where is General Jones?"

"He is to the left of Benner's hill," Colonel Edmonds replied.

"Good. I got to go. You be fuggin' careful, Caleb."

"Yes, indeed I will be sir, and may I say good luck to you as well." Colonel Edmonds saluted as General Johnson returned his salute and mounted his horse. The General and his staff rode away in a cloud of dust.

"General Johnson delights in turning a phrase on its ear," Captain Custiss said softly. "I don't fully understand it, Colonel. How is it possible that General Longstreet has started his assault along the Emmitsburg and Taneytown roads and yet we have heard nothing of it? Surely, it is not that far distant from our present location. We should have heard the firing," the Captain said thoughtfully.

"That is a mystery, Captain, one that I cannot answer. I do hear our skirmishers, however. We must go in soon. What in the world are they waiting for?" Colonel Edmonds said desperately.

Tom and the soldiers of C Company watched as the last remnant of Lattimer's Battery limbered up a gun and departed as quickly as they were able amid the bursting Federal shellfire. Three canons remained, stubbornly dealing out death in a long-range contest of wills.

It was an unequal contest as the Federal fire dropped one southern artilleryman after another. The destruction of Lattimer's Battery left many a soldier with a sinking feeling in the pit his stomach. The earlier cheers had given way to silence. Many of the men gripped their rifles with a fatalistic resolve. Hundreds of grim faces peered towards the gloomy hill. Tom was awash in melancholy.

Pete Wilson spat on the ground and wiped his runny nose on his stiffening sleeve. He watched as a shell slammed into one of the remaining canons. The projectile landed directly on top of the brass Napoleon and it disappeared in a ball of fire. The gunners who had been working the gun merely seconds before were evaporated in the blinding flash. Nothing remained of them. Another shell landed on another caisson. Bodies tumbled through the air and for a slight moment were visible. Then all were consumed by the secondary explosions caused by the ammunition in the caissons being set off in a chain reaction. The surviving horses went hurtling away from the destruction in every direction, galloping away in stark terror. The last gun of Lattimer's battery was now silent. Every gunner lay wounded or dead as Union artillery fire continued to work the hill over.

The sound of ripping gunfire from his immediate front made Tom turn away from the scene of calamity that had overtaken the last gun on Benner's hill. The sound of his regiments skirmish line encountering heavy resistance and the steady gunshots that hung on the humid air was a sure sign that something was about to happen and soon. Pete glanced upwards as the sun began its decline into the western horizon.

A mounted group of Staff officers made their presence known as they cantered towards the vicinity of Colonel Edmonds. The Colonel could be seen listening carefully to what they said. Edmonds pulled out a gold watch from his pocket and glanced at it as the staff officers saluted the Colonel and trotted their horses down the line of soldiers. Pete and the rest watched as the Colonel said something to

242

Captain Custiss. The Captain saluted and walked towards Company C. The Captain faced them and then did an about face, as if he were on a parade ground. Custiss drew his sword from his scabbard. Pete's eyebrows arched on his forehead.

"We are for it now, boys," Pete said loudly

"What the hell are we waiting for now?" Arthur asked with total undisguised frustration and anger in his voice. Andy looked down the ranks of soldiers to better see who had spoken the words they all felt. He realized that it had been Arthur who had said it and then he whistled shrilly through his teeth. Before the whistle had died away in the air, Colonel Edmonds walked to the front of the regiment. He held a sword in one hand and a pistol in the other. He raised his sword high in the air and came to attention. The drummer boys began to crash a beat that was instantly picked up by the other regiments of General Jones' Brigade, a steady sound that was as familiar to many of the soldiers as their own names. It was the signal to prepare to advance.

"Gentlemen," Colonel Edmonds shouted over the steady pounding of the drums. "Today, once again, we show the world that we are the finest infantry in the world. Thus always to tyrants. Men, forward the regiment. To the top."

The Colonel turned towards the shrouded hill. He pointed his sword at the distant haze as the entire line stepped forward. The regiments on both ends of the Twenty-first regiment stepped lively towards the distant enemy, a triple row of men that stretched continuously for a half a mile. Elbow to elbow, the brigade swept forward towards the Federal brigade anchored at the top of the hill.

General Jones was mounted on a gray speckled mare and stood off to the side as the brigade swept towards the prominence on the horizon. He saluted the color guard as they walked past. Colonel Edmonds who brought his sword up to his face and then swept it downward in a quick motion returned the salute.

Tom felt goose bumps rise on his arms, and a chill ran the length of his spine. He had told no one of his chat with the General. The conversation played out in his mind over and over again. The end of war was in sight. Tom peered at the haze that clung to the horizon and at the menacing hill before him. A sound like a bumblebee zipped over his head, first one and then several more. The Federals were overshooting the skirmishers ahead of him. The thick July air made the regimental flag droop. The smoke of many small fires and hundreds of expended cartridges wafted about the battle flag.

The constant sound of rifle fire became sharp as they rapidly approached the creek before them. Tom gingerly stepped into the water and was surprised at its depth. He lifted his rifle over his head and grabbed at his cap pouch. First Sergeant Jenkins was already across waving the men forward.

"Move," he shouted, "You are not takin' a bath. Git' yer git' goin'. Sergeant Sawyer, move your people forward. Let's go."

Tom pulled himself out of the water and began to align the men of the company into rows. Regiments on either side did the same so that there still remained unit integrity throughout the Brigade. Tom glanced back at the creek and noticed a gray clad body floating face down. One of the reluctant Union loving mountain boys of company H, one of the skirmishers he thought to himself.

In the fading light, he glimpsed at the enemy rifle pits and breastworks that was at the base of the hill. The wind blew the clinging and concealing smoke away in patches. The skirmishers of company H were involved in a deadly shootout ahead of him. The federal defenders were in a desperate situation. The edges and rim of the federal rifle pits were studded with dead and wounded men, all wearing Union blue. The Northern soldiers had been caught in the bombardment and had suffered greatly. Now, with a ferocity born of their suffering and terror, they grimly held onto the pits and blazed away stubbornly at the men of company H and the approaching main confederate battle line. They had seen their comrades blown down and crippled by the artillery fire and had witnessed their comrades ripped to shreds when some had decided to abandon the pits and join the main line at the top of the hill. They knew that running away now was impossible and so they cursed and lashed out in fury at the rebels that they saw coming at them.

The skirmishers fired from behind whatever cover was available and they fired by squads and in volleys, pinning many of the Union men to the bottom of their holes. The heady rebel yell echoed in the air as the main body of the brigade crashed into the federal defenses. Smoke curled up and over the brown slash in the earth that the Federal soldiers were so resolutely defending. Smeared red in places with human gore, the trench was packed with blue clad soldiers who fired rifles and then reached for loaded rifles passed to them by wounded men at the pit's bottom. The federal soldiers kept up a murderous fire at the advancing southern infantry of Jones' Brigade, but they were slowly being ground down.

Several marksmen from the first line of skirmishers had positioned themselves in trees and began picking off the most accurate of the Federal soldiers. These marksmen dropped the defenders to the bottom of the hole causing a disturbance in the rate that the wounded soldier could load and hand the readied weapons to the soldiers who were still able to fire. The assembly line began to wear down as the main assault line came at the rifle pit like an avalanche.

The men of company H and company C conducted the assault like a well-oiled machine. They fired and maneuvered in tandem, as they grew closer to the defensive positions of the Union soldiers. Finally the rebel line was muzzle to muzzle with the defenders. What once had offered protection to the northern soldiers now quickly became a death trap as southern soldiers fired down into the pit from the sides, front, and rear.

The resultant slaughter of the Union men was extreme. The fight flickered and went out of most of the Federal soldiers. Some chose to turn and run but these men did not live very long or run very far as volley after volley from the men of company C cut them down. The futility of running and resisting became readily apparent seconds after the last fleeing man lay broken in death and bleeding on the ground. All of the Union defenders left alive threw up their hands in surrender.

The men of Company C flowed right past the Federal rifle pits in jubilation, ignoring the dejected enemy soldiers. They loaded weapons and began the ascent up the face of Culp's hill. The base of Culp's hill was devoid of the enemy. The advance skirmishers of the regiment now joined the main assault line. Tom looked among their numbers for Huck but not spotting him began to climb with the rest of his comrades. The different companies began to merge quickly together. Soon regiments began to mix with other regiments as the uneven land forced many of the men to all move towards areas where climbing was easier. The brigade surged up the hill as all eyes sought to glimpse the prize through the rocky woods, the summit of the hill. They sweated and cursed and pushed each other forward up the course of the steep slope.

As they neared the top, a slashing curtain of rifle fire greeted them. Aimed deliberately low, bullets smashed into shins and thudded into stomachs. Men screamed and dropped with the first volley. For some of the men who had been shot, it was the first and only indicator of just how close they were near peak. The woods were thick and in the growing darkness, visibility was limited. Men dodged for the nearest cover, a rock, a boulder or a fallen tree. Wounded men rolled down the hill bowling over others who scrambled forward frantically seeking cover or someone to shoot at. Bullets clipped benches off trees and careened into the air when they struck a boulder. These boulders covered the slope resembling a sleepy herd of browsing elephants in the darkness. Men began to accumulate behind them as the Federal fire increased in volume. No longer sure that they were doing the most damage by firing in volleys, the Federal officers had ordered independent fire. They fired from behind a log breastwork that was three feet high and from a trench that covered them from enemy fire. They leaned over these logs and fired a shadow at its base. They fired independently and in constant rotation. As one group fired, they stepped away to let others fire. Their action wore the attackers out as bullets tore into their unprotected ranks. The air hummed with the amount of bullets that flew towards the crouching southern infantrymen of Jones' Brigade.

The noise sounded as if thousands of bees were angrily buzzing around in defense of a disturbed hive. The firing was non-stop and deafening. Arthur screamed to be heard although he was standing right beside Tom.

"They keepin' they'a fire low on purpose," he said as he crouched behind one of the boulders. "Iff'n you wuz' to try lyin' down, you'd git' head shot fer' sure."

Men sought shelter and protection from the deadly fire. One recruit tried to hide behind a sapling that could not have been more than a foot in diameter. The intense fire was riddling his coat sleeve and jacket. His canteen took a direct hit and flew apart. He twisted and turned and miraculously was not hit but the small tree was being chopped to slivers. All around the terrified boy lay southern soldiers who had fallen in the initial blast of the Federal guns. Some of the wounded soldiers lying on the ground began to be repeatedly struck by the endless gunshots being leveled at them. The noise drowned out their screams of agony.

Arthur could clearly see that the boy was in trouble. He screamed and waved at the boy to get his attention. Finally the boy spotted Arthur. The Corporal waved for him to run to him but the horrified boy refused to budge. He shook his head vigorously as tears coursed down his face. He continued to contort his body to the shape of a tree. A bullet struck the stock of his rifle ripping it out of his hands and sending it flying down the hill. Another bullet struck his pewter cup.

"For God's sakes, jump aside boy, run to us," Tom screamed. The boy stared blankly at them twisting and turning his small body. The wounded that lay at his feet continued to be struck repeatedly and they died. Their bodies were still subjected to bullets even after death had freed them from their torture. They started to come apart. The boy watched as a man's head became detached form his shoulders and began to roll down the slope. The head came to a stop, but another bullet struck it and it continued its descent down the hill. A bullet scooped out another dying man's brains and splattered the young man with gore. Still the boy refused to move. He was frozen in place.

Arthur raised his rifle deliberately at the boy and aimed two inches above the young soldiers head. He fired and the bullet slammed into the tree. The boy turned to see Arthur standing behind the cover of the boulder with a smoking rifle in his hands. Arthur pointed the rifle directly at the youth and waved for him to run towards the boulder once more. The recruit shook his head more adamantly than ever.

"Is that so? We shall soon see about that," Arthur said, angrily grabbing Tom's rifle. He snatched it to his shoulder and fired. This time the bullet ripped a chunk of the boy's lower ear off. The frightened boy at his ear and dashed toward the boulder. When he was within reach, Arthur grabbed him by his hair and threw him to the ground. He leaned into him without letting go of the boy's hair and yelled so loudly that everyone heard exactly what he shouted into the frightened boys face.

"The next time I order you to do somethin', by all that's holy you had better do it or I will drop you myself. Do we have an understandin', soldier?" he bellowed He released his hold on the boy. The young man landed hard on his posterior, dazed but none the worse for his experience. He quickly began to rummage around on all fours for a serviceable rifle. They watched him carefully. He loaded a rifle and aimed and fired at the top of the hill. Arthur smiled and handed Tom his rifle.

"That young man is a fight'n hellcat," Arthur said. Ed Bolls fired from behind the cover of the boulder and ducked for cover. Bullets struck the boulder causing sparks to fly in the gathering darkness.

"A lot of danged bark and no bite," Ed screamed, as he rapidly loaded his weapon. Tom loaded and popped up over the top of the rock and fired towards the top of the hill. He twisted and dropped back down as quickly as he was able. The entire top of the hill resembled a volcano with the amount of gun smoke that hung above it; Hundreds of rifles discharging all at the same time heightened the illusion. A cascade of fire boiled from the peak as the Federal soldiers fired by company. Any motion towards gaining the top by direct assault was clearly impossible. All along the rebel line, individual Confederate soldiers braved this fire to take a shot at the flashes that they were briefly able to see in the man-made ground fog.

Tom fired at the Union breastwork and ducked back to cover. Others did the same, again and again. They all knew that they were not doing any appreciable damage to their blue clad enemies. However, the fire of the Union men was causing casualties among the southern ranks every second. Lawson Dunn of Company H darted into position to fire when a bullet struck him in the chest, knocking him down. He rolled a few feet and came to a stop, completely out in the open. Lawson sat up and tore at his shirt, trying to determine how badly he had been hit. A small half a moon rip in his flesh was an inch below his collarbone. He looked completely surprised as he felt at it. Another bullet struck him in the temple and he fell heavily on his side. The blood spurted from the wound and he shook violently. He drew his knees up towards his chin. Bullets slammed into his body and he began to slide down the incline.

Tom watched as John Hubert bent low to reload his rifle. The top of his skull peeled back as cleanly as soft-boiled eggshell is cracked with a spoon at breakfast. John stood stark still and his lips drew back revealing a horrible grin. His eyes rolled up in his head and he tottered backwards a few steps. Another bullet smashed into his forehead and he went flying down the hill in a spray of blood and gray matter, his arms flailing over his head. They huddled behind the rock as though taking shelter against a storm's icy bite. The gritty reverberations of the bullets striking stone whined and groaned all around them.

"This is no good," Arthur shouted. "Theys killin' us."

Rock chips rained down at them from the steady pounding the boulder was receiving from the Federal line. The Union position was less than twenty yards from where they hid. The Confederate attack had stalled. The southerners returned fire but their volume diminished as ammunition began to dwindle. They were not inflicting damage to their foes and the veterans began to hold back their fire. They huddled all along the line and discussed what was to be done. Vernon Jenkins tore past crouching soldiers as he made his was way to the top.

"Sawyer, Cook…Where are you?" he hollered.

"Over here." Tom shouted. Vernon made his way over to them with bent shoulders.

"We can't afford to stall." Vernon shouted into Tom's ear. "If we stall, we are gone up. They will kick the shit out'n us. Some of the boys on the left are actually in the main works up there. The Yankees pulled off some units. Some of the trenches at the top were empty. We got to try to support them up there an' the only way is to keep the pressure in them. From what Custiss has told me, some of those crazy Louisiana boys, Hays Tigers, pushed right in through to Cemetery hill but got stuck in some of the Yankees abandoned fightin' holes. They can't go forward and they can't go back so they appear to be stayin' put. Colonel Edmonds is goin' to try and link up with whoever is at the top. See that large boulder over there that looks like the prow of a boat?"

"I seed' it," Arthur said. Tom took a couple of seconds to see it in the diminishing daylight.

"The Yankees line in front if it is shaped like the letter 'C' with the empty part facin' our way. Colonel Edmonds is right over there. Get as many people over to him as quickly as you can. Start spreadin' the news…use everybody that is still with us in your section. When you have a fair amount, come back here. There is another regiment from "Extra Billy" Smith's Brigade that is supposed to be comin' to us. When you see them, feed them into the line over there with Edmonds. Captain Custiss and me are goin' to hit them on this side. There are more of us here than you think, Tom. No more than and hour, you got it?"

"Yes, Tom said.

"Good. Make as much noise as you can when you go in. If they think they're bein' hit by a fresh brigade, they might jest break an' run. I'm countin' on you, son."

Vernon bounded away into the darkness, his shouted commands ringing loudly in the night. The Federal fire had stopped being deadly accurate due to the darkness. The shooting that had been very low was now wildly high, clipping leaves from overhead branches. The clipped leaves and branches began to accumulate on the men's heads giving them the appearance of being ancient Roman statues. They would occasionally wipe the wreathes off their heads.

Tom's spirit was buoyed up from Vernon's orders. At least Vernon knew what needed to be done. He had a plan instead of uselessly trading shots in the dark. It made perfect sense now. They would use the cover of darkness to take the top of the hill. The Yankees could not hit what they could not see. They would rush them in the darkness and overwhelm the enemy. Tom began to inform all the surviving members of his section what they had to do. Huck had been right all along. This was truly to be the end of the war. The way home began at the top of a hill.

CHAPTER FOURTEEN

Rebecca sat on her porch patiently awaiting the return of Bella. She watched as Doctor Waters and his sons decorated the front of his home across the street in red, white, and blue bunting in preparation for the Fourth of July celebration later in the week. With her brothers and father away fighting in the Confederate States Army, the holiday did not hold the same meaning for her as it did in the past. In her small town, the celebration of the birth of the United States no longer brought neighbors together but instead divided them.

Only pro-Union people celebrated the holiday these days. The picnics and fireworks were events that she was no longer able to attend even if she had desired to, which she did not. If she were to show up at any of the scheduled holiday activities, she would be shunned by some and castigated by others. Her pro-southern friends and family would label her as a black Republican and traitor to the Cause and her Unionist neighbors would snub her.

People she had known all her life would no longer speak to her or greet her in passing on the street because her father and brothers were away fighting for Southern independence. The local business community detested all known southern sympathizers. It was only due to the kindness of Mr. Kantz, the local grocer, that she was able to buy the necessities of life. Mr. Kantz was a German fellow who had known her all her life. He was one of the few people in town that had not turned against any of the people whose relatives were now involved in open rebellion against the Federal authority in Washington.

While she sat waiting, she fanned herself with one of Tom's infrequent letters and watched a group of happy Union soldiers involved in horseplay. The town always seemed to be filled with soldiers these days. It was not even noon and already the heat was stifling Bella had left the house earlier in the morning in anticipation of the steamboats arrival from St. Louis. Today was the day that it would be arriving with mail and Rebecca hoped that it would arrive with a letter or letters from Tom.

She had not received a letter from him in some time. The interval between the times he posted a letter and the time she received one would often be months. It was not an inordinate amount of time, considering the route the letter traveled which was quite considerable. Tom sent all of his correspondence to Bella's stepbrother in Richmond. He, in turn, had a friend whose sister was able to post the letter in Baltimore. Even though the country was divided on major issues, it appeared that the Post Office was not. Rebecca's town was in Union hands so if she mailed a letter addressed to Tom, more often than not, it would find him. She would mail the letter to Baltimore and the circle would work backwards and Tom would eventually receive her mail. It was time consuming, but it worked.

Rebecca truly enjoyed Bella's company. It had not taken any time at all for her to like her. She had appeared at her door one day with the first letter from Tom. Bella had traveled all the way from the Indian Nations to deliver it in person. In the letter, which was dated a month after the fall of Fort Sumter, Tom had recounted to her the terrible series of events that had transpired to them in Kansas. He told of the deaths of Cecil Gordon and Ted Doudlass, something he obviously felt very guilty about. He made no excuses for himself. In the letter, he made it clear that he was writing to insure that Ted and Cecil's families should know of their deaths. Bella also spoke in length of the tragic circumstances of that day. She spoke in great detail and omitted nothing, even referring to Tom and Huck as those two stupid boys as well as telling of the unwanted advances of her former employer, Henry Cadimus Fowler towards her.

She had wanted nothing in return from Rebecca and was preparing to leave when Rebecca insisted that she spend the night. That had been three years ago. Since that time, Bella had often written to Bella's stepbrother in Richmond as well as Bella's stepfather, Reverend Harvey. Bella had gotten a job working for Doctor Waters while she taught school every day, excluding of course, the summer months and harvest time. They shared expenses and had become very close.

Rebecca had found the added income that Bella provided very helpful and her supportive company relieved her loneliness. She had not received a letter from her father and brothers in nearly two years, although a local boy, the brother of Cecil Gordon, had told her that they were all right. He rode with the rebel guerilla leader, William Clarke Quantrill, and he had it on good authority that they were at Vicksburg, Mississippi. Since this area of her home state was now fully in Federal control, she had not seen him in months, either. All she knew that Vicksburg was surrounded by Federal forces and the local newspaper related stories everyday about its imminent collapse.

Bella had been gone a long time. The soldiers in town had single-handedly taken it upon themselves to escort Bella to the post office down near the wharf. The blue uniformed boys would wait for her across the street, seemingly engaged in a lively banter with Doctor Waters. When they spotted her leaving, they would take up an escort and by the time she arrived home, she would have been walked and talked to for many a mile by the love stricken soldier boys. Bella was a beautiful woman although she didn't seem to understand this. She never spoke a word to the soldiers and it was rumored among them that she was a mute. Their attention angered her, yet she remained tight-lipped in their company. The faces of the young soldiers were forever changing as they were shifted or transferred from one place to another so that none of them ever found out that she could speak.

Rebecca wiped the sweat from her brow. She stood and pushed the door open. Her father had made an ice shed in the basement and earlier she had made a trip down there and had broken off a large chunk of ice in which to make a pitcher of fresh lemonade. She walked into the kitchen with the intention of getting a cooling drink when she heard the door slam shut. She stopped and reached for a glass in the cupboard. Bella was back.

"I was just going to get a drink, Bella. I will fix you one; I will bet you that you could use one. Any mail?"

There was no response. Rebecca became curious and placed the glass on the table.

"Bella?" she said cheerily.

She turned around and walked towards the parlor and when she cleared the corner, she froze. A dirty man with an eye patch holding a pistol was in her front room peering from behind the curtain out at the street. He was covered in dust and his large mustache and beard completely covered his face.

"What in God's name do you think you're doing in my home." Her fear rose as he simply stood silently and looked at her with his one good eye. Panic began to grip her.

"Rebecca, its me. I don't rightly fault you with not recognizin' me. I have changed quite a bit," the strange man said grinning. Her mind swam away from her and she felt faint. There was something familiar about the man.

"Rebecca, I ain't any ghostie or haint It's me, Ted Doudlass."

"But you're supposed to be dead." Her hand flew to her mouth. Her fingers tingled and she became dizzy.

"Well I ain't, not by a damned sight."

Rebecca reached for chair and flopped into it. She placed her hand over her wildly beating heart as Ted sat down on the couch next to you.

"Rebecca, are you all right? You look a little flushed. Let me git you a drink."

"There's lemonade with ice. In the kitchen Fix yourself one as well. I was going to get Bella one and.. Ted, everyone thinks that that wicked man out in Leavenworth killed you. Your family...everyone thinks that you're dead."

Ted walked into the kitchen as Rebecca tried to regain her composure. She heard him filling the glasses and he returned a moment later. She took the glass and pulled a chunk of ice from it and began to rub her temples with it. Ted examined the ice in his glass and then began to gulp down his drink. He wiped his mouth with the back of his sleeve.

252

"Don't tell anyone you seen me. It's better off for my family that everybody thinks I'm dead. The Yankees will leave them alone. I fight with Quantrill. The Yankees treat our kin bad. They let a buildin' fall on top of some women that were kin of some of the fellas I ride with. They were crushed to death in it. I don't want anything of the likes to happen to maw or paw. Promise me."

"Of course," she said.

"How are they?" he asked.

"They are just fine. Tell me what happened, Ted." He removed his filthy jacket and walked over to the window and looked out of it nervously.

"I guess the place to begin with is Kansas. I don't remember everything; it's all kinda' hazy. I understand that Cecil Gordon was kilt, but Tom and Huck got away. Alex Gordon tolt me that he writes to you?"

"After they thought that fellow Fowler had killed you, they managed to escape. They rode out to the Indian nations where the father of the woman that had helped them to get out of the hotel, a Reverend Harvey, befriended them. From there, he managed to secure them passage on a boat that was leaving New Orleans headed to San Francisco. You remember, that's all Tom used to talk about. Anyway, the captain' received a wire telling him that his wife had taken ill just as they were leaving, and the captain took the ship and left for Norfolk. When the boys got there, they were stranded. Shortly after, the war broke out and they joined up. Tom wrote that that it was the only thing that had kept them from starving."

Ted returned and sat down.

"I remember that they caught me and took me back to that fella Fowler's house. They beat the daylights out'n me, even broke my fingers. I tolt them everything." He breathed deeply. I'm responsible fer getting Cecil kilt. It's somethin' that I'll take to my grave." He paused a moment.

"Rebecca, they beat me like some kinda animal. This big harelipped fella named Pete, I remember, was good with his hands and knew where to hit you where it hurt the most. He nearly punched the life out of me. That's all I remember. I woke up a day later half froze an' in the back of a wagon with a hole in me so big that when the wind blew it whistled right through me, I swear. I was more dead than alive. What happened was this farmer seen them shoot me an' durin' all the shootin', slipped me out of there an' hid me under some hay in a wagon. That farmer was no friend of Henry Fowler. He later tolt me the reason why I didn't bleed to death was that the blood had frozen around the bullet hole. Fowler had shot me an' left me fer dead an' some old farmer what was sound on the goose took me into his home and brought me back to health. I was in an' out fer a month. If that farmer hadn't picked me up, threw me onto his shoulder and hid me in the wagon and done what he did, I would not be here sittin' with you havin' this here conversation."

"Why are you home. You must realize that the Yankees know that you fight for the South. This town is full of Union soldiers. They will surely hang you if you are found here," Rebecca said.

"The less you know, the better it will be for you, just in case somethin' was to go wrong. The reason that I ducked into here was that I seen an Injun woman that was at Fowlers house the day he shot me. I didn't want to get spotted by her and I ducked in here. I didn't even know if you still lived here or not, but I couldn't afford to get seen by her."

"You must have seen Bella. She is the woman that I spoke about. It was she that helped Huck and Tom escape. She ran away from that evil man shortly after."

"You mean she ain't with Fowler?"

"No. In fact, she lives with me. Bella stays here with me. She can be trusted. Her step father is the one who had helped them."

"It is a small world," Ted said. "That is a relief."

"Here, give me your glass. I will refreshen it." She walked into the kitchen and prepared the drinks. As she carefully poured each one, she suddenly heard the front door open. She immediately recognized Bella's voice.

"I know who you are," Bella said. "You are the boy that Henry made dead many years ago. I never forget faces even if you are a dead boy spirit. Have you come to make me bad medicine because I could not save you from Fowler, evil dead boy spirit? I could not save you, evil dead boy spirit, but I did save the stupid boys."

"Lady, please put that gun down. It jest may go off. You don't want to send me to the Almighty. We are all friends here."

"Quiet, evil dead boy spirit. You want revenge because I could not save you. What evil have you done to Rebecca who is good? Tell me, or I will shoot you."

Rebecca nearly dropped the pitcher. She ran into the parlor. Ted's hands were both high in the air. Bella had a Colt revolver pointed at his nose.

"Bella, " Rebecca said slowly and calmly, "Please, put the gun down. This is Ted Doudlass, a friend of mine. We have known each other since we were children. He is no spirit at all. He is flesh and blood."

"I sure as hell am. Look." Ted pulled his shirt back over his head and turned around to show Bella his back. There was an indent in his back that one could place a stack of silver dollars in. He turned around and exposed an exit wound that was slighter larger.

"See. It went clean through," he said. "It took a couple of ribs with it and a hunk of my lung, but other than that it didn't hit much of anythin' valuable though I might add that I don't ever want another one of the likes. This here is plenty enough. I ain't no spook, lady. I ain't no evil dead boy spirit."

"You lie many much to me, trickster. You forget that I know Fowler dead you." She pulled back the hammer of the pistol and her finger tightened on the trigger. Her eyes were coal black and they sent a shiver up Ted's spine.

"Rebecca, do somethin'. I do believe she is gonna test her theory about whether I am flesh an' blood by sendin' a bullet through my melon."

Rebecca was frantic. She knew Ted was in serious danger.

"Wait! Don't shoot. I can prove to you that he is no dead boy spirit. Remember after Tom and Huck escaped..Got away? Remember that you told me that Henry was angry that the boy that he had shot had gotten away as well. That's because he wasn't dead. He was just hurt. Badly. He is no trickster. He is a friend of mine," Rebecca pleaded, "Please put the gun down."

Bella looked at Rebecca with doubt. Ted stared at the pistol as Bella's hand tightened on the trigger.

"Remember, you said yourself that Henry was angry after the shoot out that everyone had gotten away. Remember how you told me that when you shot into the yard that they all charged the house together? Remember that you said that you crawled out the basement window and then walked through the front door after Henry found the Hotel empty?"

"I walked through the front door like nothing happened. Henry told me that I was in much danger. Later, he was much mad because he couldn't find the dead boy. But I know that Henry had dead you, trickster, because when Henry deads a man, they stay dead."

"Bella is everything an always?" Rebecca asked.

"No.You say then, that Henry thought he made this boy dead but he did not dead him?"

"Exactly. He was simply shot very badly..Almost dead, but not quite. A farmer rescued him and nursed him back to health. Do you understand?"

"Then you only had a half foot in the spirit world. You are a half dead boy spirit. I have seen many much full dead spirits before and they can be powerful. A real pain in the ass if you are not careful. You can only make half bad medicine. You are not much." She grinned at Ted. "Henry would be very much angry to know this, that you are not dead. It would frost his ass." Bella placed the hammer of the

255

pistol in a safe position and stuck it into her waistband. She pulled her shirt over it and walked to the table.

"No letters from the boat man today. Do you have a frosty drink?" Bella asked. Ted was relieved that the gun had been put away. He still held his shirt up near his chin.

"I will get us all a cool drink. I think we all could use one. Excuse me, Ted," Rebecca said. Bella stared at the healed wound.

"I had a friend, he was shot the same day that you were. In the hotel he was shot many much times. He lived but he was in bed for almost a year. I tended to him. He was a good man. When he was well he got the wagon and went to Lehigh's hotel. The same one that he got many much shot to hell in. He said he needed to get out and mix with people. I told him not to go. He went anyway. They say he got drunk and fell out of the wagon, they say that it ran over his neck. He died. But I believe that Lehigh made him dead by having Pete break his neck. I ran away right after I heard. He must have gotten drunk and talked too much."

"Sorry to hear that," Ted said sympathetically.

"Not as sorry as old Joshua was. He was not that old, he just looked it."

Rebecca returned with a pitcher of lemonade. She pulled three glasses out of her apron pockets. She handed out the glasses, first to Ted and then Bella. She picked up the pitcher and carefully began pouring the drinks.

"You were stupid boys. You came to take money from Henry Fowler to go to California and take gold from the ground. You did not know that Henry Fowler is a man who takes money from people and then takes their lives and puts them in the ground. Henry's wife was many much rich. She died. She fell off her horse and broke her head. This is what Henry said. I do not believe it. I believe Henry broke her head. She died. I will not miss her because she was a bad person." Bella sipped on her glass of lemonade.

"Henry is a bad man. He finds it much easy to dead people and takes their money than take gold from the ground. People are gold to Henry. If you have many much money, Henry will dead you and take it. He has made dead nearly everyone that had money. He gets away with it because he knows how. He gives other people like him some of the money, other people in power. That is why no one can get him. He has the Army and the law in his back pocket. I knew you stupid boys did not know this when you came into town. When they beat you and made you talk, I thought they would hang you as fast as they could. You are many much lucky they didn't. If you had dead Henry, all of his friends would have tracked you down. They would have much angry against you for making dead a man that made them many much money. Henry has taken much but Henry has given much."

Ted drank in Bella's amazing good looks and decided that she was possibly the most beautiful woman that he had ever seen. She had a funny way of turning a phrase and sounded like a muleskinner but besides these flaws she was stunning. Her brown skin was perfectly smooth. There was not a fault or blemish that he could detect. He studied her features. Her eyes were sparkling pools of magic and her raven black hair fell spilling off of her shoulders to land below her knees.

"Henry looked all over for your friends but I had them in a safe place. I had them go to my father's home in the Nations. Henry knows no one there and could be made dead like any man there. Why do you come here? There are many much blue soldiers here. You must know that if they find you, they will dead you on Main street."

"You know, that's somethin best not be talked about. Let me tell you, when I saw you, I thought Henry had to be here. I figured the jig was up, that's why I ducked in here. Anyway, I'm not all that concerned. The eye-patch is convincing enough. I tell anybody what asks that I got my eye shot out fightin' the rebels at Pea Ridge. I'm an invalid out of Federal service is my story. The eye patch is real. I lost my eye about a year ago fight'n the Yankees."

"If you stay around here, you will lose many much more than an eye," Bella said. There had been no intended acerbity in her remark. She was being honest. The white men's war was an enigma to her, so convoluted to her that merely thinking about it made her feel addled.

"You white people kill each other. You have known each other. You all went to the same schoolhouse and the white church. You all were born by the same white medicine man, Doctor Waters, but you make each other dead with no more care than shooting the fox that comes to take the fat red hen. The blue soldiers say they fight for freedom. You gray soldiers say the same thing. Is this something you cannot share? Why don't you find out what this freedom is and cut it in two and share. Even little children share."

"It is not as simple as that," Ted replied. "I have no choice, never did." He rubbed his hand over his hairy face.

"I did not plan on living the life that I lead. It was forced on me. It has been rammed down my throat and no one ever asked me if I liked the flavor. This life I got, It's the only one I got. I learned this layin' in a bed fer almost six months. Until someone kin show me some way better, I guess I'll keep on doin' what I gotta do to stay above the ground. It ain't easy."

Rebecca nodded her head in agreement.

"There has been so much killing. It seems like it will never end," she said.

"I would like nothin better than to sit down in the town I was born'd in, right here in the company of friends and family and rest like some little old boy. The way it stands though, I can't because somebody will slip up on me an' put a ball through my head an' that's a sad fact."

"When will all the dead making stop?" Bella asked.

"When the war is over. When all the old scores are settled. Wars don't last forever. They got to end sometime. Somebody will win and somebody will lose. When that happens, the killin' will stop."

"You think wars stop but this is not so. My people have been in a war with the Mexican soldiers for so many years, the number is too big to say. The Mexican soldiers killed my mother, father, uncles, aunts, brothers and sisters and all of my people. They still do. I tell you a little story. The man in the Indian Nations where I hid your friends was not my real father. He was a Texas Ranger. He told me that all of my people had been lined up and made dead. My people are Navaho. They lived on the land for as long as there is memory of things. These Mexican soldiers made dead everyone, the old and the young. He was sent to punish the Mexican soldiers. He said they followed their sign, the sign of the Mexican horse soldiers and made them all dead. They showed them no mercy. He said they decorated the lances of the Mexican soldiers with their heads and left them as a warning. When he returned to the Navaho village, my people's village, he said he found me under a pile of dead people. He brought me home and raised me as his child. He was a good man that had been made sick by making dead all those Mexican soldiers so he gave up making people dead. He put away his guns, forever. He gave up war as a young man puts away his toys and says that he is no longer a boy but a man. He became a minister man and preaches the word of the risen Christ. The only way to make no war is for you to stop making dead people. If you believe all wars end because they end, then you are not so bright, half-dead boy. I am hungry. I will pick many much green beans. Are you eating with us?"

"Of course he will,' Rebecca said quickly.

"I will wring a fat hen's neck. We shall eat well. You look like you could use a good something nice to eat. You are a bony looking man. You look like you could play your ribcage like a washboard in a jug band." Bella left without saying anymore leaving Ted smiling.

"Is she always so direct?"

"Her honesty and simplicity has endeared her to me. I have never met anyone so open and frank before in all of my life. She phrases things a bit oddly, did you notice?"

"Yes, particularly when she had her gun to the tip of my nose and was callin' me an evil dead boy spirit. I caught that right away."

They both broke out in laughter.

"Her father, a most delightful man, wanted her to live in both worlds. I will always stay in touch with him. Bella never learned to read and she really loves for me to read his letters to her. He is a gentle man of God. He wrote to me saying that Bella can speak Navaho, Cherokee, and Spanish. In the summer months, Bella would travel to a Cherokee family and they spoke very limited English. Mr. Harvey wanted to imbue her with a sense of her Indianess. They taught her to respect the old ways. She is very serious when she told you about seeing ghosts. She believes everything has a spirit. Even a rock or a tree or a stream of water."

"Do you think she would have shot me?"

"Most assuredly. If I had not come running, I am sure she would have. Perhaps not to kill you, but possibly to disable you."

"That's comforting to know,' Ted replied. Ted rose and walked over to the window. He snuck a look out into the street.

"I hate to run, Rebecca, but I've stayed too long as it is. I got somethin' to do an' the lives of people depend on me getting' it done."

"Please, Ted. Stay for dinner at least."

"I would love to, but I ain't got a choice. There ain't no way out. But you tell Tom an' Huck when you write to them that you seen me." He walked towards the door and put his coat back on. He opened the door and doffed his hat.

"Thanks fer everything, Rebecca. That cool drink was a breadth of fresh air." He looked about the house recalling memories of happier times.

"Like a breadth of fresh air, indeedy. I will see you again. Take care, Becky." She watched him as he passed through the door and down the steps. He turned towards the river and soon was out of sight.

Bella looked at Rebecca with doubt. Ted stared at the pistol as Bella's hand tightened on the trigger.

"Remember, you said yourself that Henry was angry after the shoot out that everyone had gotten away. Remember how you told me that when you shot into the yard that they all charged the house together? Remember that you said that you crawled out the basement window and then walked through the front door after Henry found the Hotel empty?"

"I walked through the front door like nothing happened. Henry told me that I was in much danger. Later, he was much mad because he couldn't find the dead boy. But I know that Henry had dead you, trickster, because when Henry deads a man, they stay dead."

"Bella is everything an always?" Rebecca asked.

"No. You say then, that Henry thought he made this boy dead but he did not dead him?"

"Exactly. He was simply shot very badly..Almost dead, but not quite. A farmer rescued him and nursed him back to health. Do you understand?"

"Then you only had a half foot in the spirit world. You are a half dead boy spirit. I have seen many much full dead spirits before and they can be powerful. A real pain in the ass if you are not careful. You can only make half bad medicine. You are not much." She grinned at Ted. "Henry would be very much angry to know this, that you are not dead. It would frost his ass." Bella placed the hammer of the pistol in a safe position and stuck it into her waistband. She pulled her shirt over it and walked to the table.

"No letters from the boat man today. Do you have a frosty drink?" Bella asked. Ted was relieved that the gun had been put away. He still held his shirt up near his chin.

"I will get us all a cool drink. I think we all could use one. Excuse me, Ted," Rebecca said. Bella stared at the healed wound.

"I had a friend, he was shot the same day that you were. In the hotel he was shot many much times. He lived but he was in bed for almost a year. I tended to him. He was a good man. When he was well he got the wagon and went to Lehigh's hotel. The same one that he got many much shot to hell in. He said he needed to get out and mix with people. I told him not to go. He went anyway. They say he got drunk and fell out of the wagon, they say that it ran over his neck. He died. But I believe that Lehigh made him dead by having Pete break his neck. I ran away right after I heard. He must have gotten drunk and talked too much."

"Sorry to hear that," Ted said sympathetically.

"Not as sorry as old Joshua was. He was not that old, he just looked it."

Rebecca returned with a pitcher of lemonade. She pulled three glasses out of her apron pockets. She handed out the glasses, first to Ted and then Bella. She picked up the pitcher and carefully began pouring the drinks.

"You were stupid boys. You came to take money from Henry Fowler to go to California and take gold from the ground. You did not know that Henry Fowler is a man who takes money from people and then takes their lives and puts them in the ground. Henry's wife was many much rich. She died. She fell off her horse and broke her head. This is what Henry said. I do not believe it. I believe Henry broke her head. She died. I will not miss her because she was a bad person." Bella sipped on her glass of lemonade.

"Henry is a bad man. He finds it much easy to dead people and takes their money than take gold from the ground. People are gold to Henry. If you have many much money, Henry will dead you and take it. He has made dead nearly everyone that had money. He gets away with it because he knows how. He gives other people like him some of the money, other people in power. That is why no one can get him. He has the Army and the law in his back pocket. I knew you stupid boys did not know this when you came into town. When they beat you and made you talk, I thought they would hang you as fast as they could. You are many much lucky they didn't. If you had dead Henry, all of his friends would have tracked you down. They would have much angry against you for making dead a man that made them many much money. Henry has taken much but Henry has given much."

Ted drank in Bella's amazing good looks and decided that she was possibly the most beautiful woman that he had ever seen. She had a funny way of turning a phrase and sounded like a muleskinner but besides these flaws she was stunning. Her brown skin was perfectly smooth. There was not a fault or blemish that he could detect. He studied her features. Her eyes were sparkling pools of magic and her raven black hair fell spilling off of her shoulders to land below her knees.

"Henry looked all over for your friends but I had them in a safe place. I had them go to my father's home in the Nations. Henry knows no one there and could be made dead like any man there. Why do you come here? There are many much blue soldiers here. You must know that if they find you, they will dead you on Main street."

"You know, that's somethin best not be talked about. Let me tell you, when I saw you, I thought Henry had to be here. I figured the jig was up, that's why I ducked in here. Anyway, I'm not all that concerned. The eye-patch is convincing enough. I tell anybody what asks that I got my eye shot out fightin' the rebels at Pea Ridge. I'm an invalid out of Federal service is my story. The eye patch is real. I lost my eye about a year ago fight'n the Yankees."

"If you stay around here, you will lose many much more than an eye," Bella said. There had been no intended acerbity in her remark. She was being honest. The white men's war was an enigma to her, so convoluted to her that merely thinking about it made her feel addled.

"You white people kill each other. You have known each other. You all went to the same schoolhouse and the white church. You all were born by the same white medicine man, Doctor Waters, but you make each other dead with no more care than shooting the fox that comes to take the fat red hen. The blue soldiers say they fight for freedom. You gray soldiers say the same thing. Is this something you cannot share? Why don't you find out what this freedom is and cut it in two and share. Even little children share."

"It is not as simple as that," Ted replied. "I have no choice, never did." He rubbed his hand over his hairy face.

"I did not plan on living the life that I lead. It was forced on me. It has been rammed down my throat and no one ever asked me if I liked the flavor. This life I got, it's the only one I got. I learned this layin' in a bed fer almost six months. Until someone kin show me some way better, I guess I'll keep on doin' what I gotta do to stay above the ground. It ain't easy."

Rebecca nodded her head in agreement.

"There has been so much killing. It seems like it will never end," she said.

"I would like nothin better than to sit down in the town I was born'd in, right here in the company of friends and family and rest like some little old boy. The way it stands though, I can't because somebody will slip up on me an' put a ball through my head an' that's a sad fact."

"When will all the dead making stop?" Bella asked.

"When the war is over. When all the old scores are settled. Wars don't last forever. They got to end sometime. Somebody will win and somebody will lose. When that happens, the killin' will stop."

"You think wars stop but this is not so. My people have been in a war with the Mexican soldiers for so many years, the number is too big to say. The Mexican soldiers killed my mother, father, uncles, aunts, brothers and sisters and all of my people. They still do. I tell you a little story. The man in the Indian Nations where I hid your friends was not my real father. He was a Texas Ranger. He told me that all of my people had been lined up and made dead. My people are Navaho. They lived on the land for as long as there is memory of things. These Mexican soldiers made dead everyone, the old and the young. He was sent to punish the Mexican soldiers. He said they followed their sign, the sign of the Mexican horse soldiers and made them all dead. They showed them no mercy. He said they decorated the lances of the Mexican soldiers with their heads and left them as a warning. When he returned to the Navaho village, my people's village, he said he found me under a pile of dead people. He brought me home and raised me as his child. He was a good man that had been made sick by making dead all those Mexican soldiers so he gave up making people dead. He put away his guns, forever. He gave up war as a young man puts away his toys and says that he is no longer a boy but a man. He became a minister man and preaches the word of the risen Christ. The only way to make no war is for you to stop making dead people. If you believe all wars end because they end, then you are not so bright, half-dead boy. I am hungry. I will pick many much green beans. Are you eating with us?"

"Of course he will,' Rebecca said quickly.

"I will wring a fat hen's neck. We shall eat well. You look like you could use a good something nice to eat. You are a bony looking man. You look like you could play your ribcage like a washboard in a jug band." Bella left without saying anymore leaving Ted smiling.

"Is she always so direct?"

"Her honesty and simplicity has endeared her to me. I have never met anyone so open and frank before in all of my life. She phrases things a bit oddly, did you notice?"

"Yes, particularly when she had her gun to the tip of my nose and was callin' me an evil dead boy spirit. I caught that right away."

They both broke out in laughter.

"Her father, a most delightful man, wanted her to live in both worlds. I will always stay in touch with him. Bella never learned to read and she really loves for me to read his letters to her. He is a gentle man of God. He wrote to me saying that Bella can speak Navaho, Cherokee, and Spanish. In the summer months, Bella would travel to a Cherokee family and they spoke very limited English. Mr Harvey wanted to imbue her with a sense of her Indianess. They taught her to respect the old ways. She is very serious when she told you about seeing ghosts. She believes everything has a spirit. Even a rock or a tree or a stream of water."

"Do you think she would have shot me?"

"Most assuredly. If I had not come running, I am sure she would have. Perhaps not to kill you, but possibly to disable you."

"That's comforting to know,' Ted replied. Ted rose and walked over to the window. He snuck a look out into the street.

"I hate to run, Rebecca, but I've stayed too long as it is. I got somethin' to do an' the lives of people depend on me getting' it done."

"Please, Ted. Stay for dinner at least."

"I would love to, but I ain't got a choice. There ain't no way out. But you tell Tom an' Huck when you write to them that you seen me." He walked towards the door and put his coat back on. He opened the door and doffed his hat.

"Thanks fer everything, Rebecca. That cool drink was a breadth of fresh air." He looked about the house recalling memories of happier times.

"Like a breadth of fresh air, indeedy. I will see you again. Take care, Becky." She watched him as he passed through the door and down the steps. He turned towards the river and soon was out of sight.

The steam engine chugged along through the Pennsylvania woods spewing clouds of dirty smoke into the humid July air. The windows of the baggage car were open to allow what little breeze there was to cool the occupants of the cramped compartment. Jim Watson sat next to a well-dressed individual whom he had been introduced to in Frederick Douglass' home. Jim was not in uniform. It had been decided that both men would pose as important members of a church back east. He wore a top hat and a fine suit, as did his companion. It was hoped that two well-dressed black men traveling in tandem would not be accosted or harassed by local people. The curiosity they would spark would cause tongues to wag instead of fists to fly. Hopefully.

Jim kept a large knife in the small of his back for emergency purposes. Benjamin Robinson, his traveling companion, favored a 32-caliber derringer pistol concealed in his boot. They rocked back in forth to the rhythm of the train on the uncomfortable stools that they sat on. Sergeant Watson gave a sideways glance at Mr. Robinson who was enthralled at the moment with the scenery. Jim thought of the monumental task ahead, to create Negro Regiments. They were to organize local churches in the community and sponsor recruiting rallies in cities starting in Philadelphia and ending in Chicago. He was proud to be a part of it.

Frederick Douglass had confided to them of the day's events at Gettysburg, They had talked into the early morning of the people they were to meet, many of them old hands in the Underground Railroad. The next thing that he knew was that he was on a train with Mr. Robinson traveling to Philadelphia and a meeting with members of the major Negro churches in that city. Jim watched as the conductor walked through the baggage coach. The beefy conductor avoided looking at them and closed the door. An engineer stood on the other side of the door and peeked in on them through the glass.

"So that's them," the engineer said. The conductor laughed. He pushed the peeping engineer away from the coach and into the next car.

"A couple of fancy niggers. See what they're wearing. Hell, I ain't even got a coat like the one that big nigger is wearin," the conductor said angrily. "What the hell is the world comin' to? First, that ape in the White House frees them. I suppose the next step is amalgamation."

"I had to see this," the engineer said. "Bill told me you knocked them down a peg. How did you get them niggers out of your coach?"

"I told them that no niggers is gonna' ride with descent white people on my train. I told them I don't care if they got fancy watch fobs and top hats and put on more airs than some belted Earl over in London, England. I told them to get cracking. You know, they both didn't say a damned thing although I wished they had. If any one of them had given me any lip, I would have thrown their black asses right off the train. I got a nigger knocker right under my desk, I would have bust that big gray haired nigger in his head."

The engineer snorted and began to laugh.

"I got to get back. We are getting' some strange flags. Somethin' is up and I'll be damned if I know what the hell is goin' on. Don't be surprised if we make a stop somewhere up the line. I'll let you get back to your friends there in baggage."

The conductor turned and went back into the baggage compartment and sat down at his desk still avoiding the two men who sat uncomfortably on their rocking stools. The engine lurched ahead and the sound of the train made clicking noises as it passed over the tracks. The conductor leaned back in his comfortable chair and placed his feet on his desk and pretended to be reading the newspaper. Ben Robinson continued to stare out of the window but Jim watched the conductor carefully. The conductor made a fuss of clearing his throat.

"It says here that Vicksburg is about ready to fall," he said nonchalantly, still avoiding looking at them. He waited to see what their response would be. If they said a word, he intended to inform them that he wasn't speaking to them and for them to mind their own goddamned business or out they would go. They remained quiet, however, and their lack of concern annoyed him. He folded his newspaper and placed it on his desk. For the first time since he had spoken to them earlier, he looked directly at them.

"What kind of work are you boys into? I must be frank. We usually don't get too many well-dressed niggers on this train. Are you barbers? I heard of coon barbers in New York City that made plenty of money cuttin' naps off niggers heads." He smiled and placed his hands behind his head. His query went unanswered.

"You niggers deaf?" he said. "I asked you niggers a question. Don't you hear good?"

"It is, "Don't you hear well", not 'good', you simpering ignoramus and our business is our business and no concern of yours, " Ben said. "I would appreciate that in the future you would stop trying to make idle conversation with us. You are not fooling anyone in this baggage car, except possibly your self. You can't stand our presence, so why keep up this idiotic pretence of civility. I find this charade irritating at best. You see, I don't communicate all that well with stupid people, a fault that I have always been guilty of, I must confess."

Ben Robinson had not even looked at the conductor but had continued to stare out of the window. The conductor's face twisted in hatred. Ben looked directly at the conductor.

"What in the world is the matter? Don't look like what I tell you is some sort of surprise. When you forced us out of the coach, which I may add, that we paid for like anyone else on this train, I could see in your eyes that you wanted an excuse to throw us off your train. There were plenty of witnesses and you would have been seen as simply exercising your authority over two troublesome Negroes. You would have been applauded. That is why I said nothing. However, in this tiny baggage car, there are no witnesses. If you wish to speak with someone then speak to yourself and leave us in peace. Does that register in your little pitiful pea brain or should I write it out for you?"

The conductor was flabbergasted that a Negro had the audacity to speak to him in this manner. No one in his life had ever put him down so elegantly as this finely dressed Negro had and he was in shock. His hands began searching for a wooden baton that he kept under his desk when the whistle blew loudly, startling him further. There were not supposed to be any whistle calls until they neared the next stop. He flew from his seat and out the door in a blur to see what was the emergency.

Jim looked at his companion as if he had two heads.

"You tryin' to git' us kilt', Slim?" he asked crossly. "You should see that yo' Alligator mouth don't get yo' hummingbird ass hung from a tree an' mine along with it."

"Relax, Mr. Watson. I knew that tub of lard was fairly expecting us to react the way I did. I guarantee it. I have been around whites of his ilk for the last decade and have learned much about human nature, especially the northern peckerwood variety. I know the species all too well. He would have been suspicious of us if all we did were to mutter a "Yassuh" into the floor like a couple of field hands. He would have made life miserable for us, all the way to Philadelphia. The way to shut down a bully is to confront him. I confound and confuse them. He was a bully. Now, he will go around telling everyone so proudly how he bested a couple of uppity niggers on his train and he will believe it in his own little mind. He will embellish it and add to it until someday he will tell the story to his grandchild perched on his knee."

Jim smiled. "You somethin' else, Mr. Robinson. Good gracious." Ben walked over to the conductor's desk and picked up the newspaper. It was dated July 3, 1863. It was a day old. Today was the Fourth of July. A lot had happened in the last 48 hours. The meeting in Rochester at the home of Frederick Douglass had occurred on July 1st,. A mysterious man in an ill-fitting suit had given him a list of names and a bankroll that could have choked a horse. This "Mr. Burke" had told that it was to be a whirlwind trip and they were on the train within the hour and heading towards Philadelphia.

The shrill whistle of the train blew again and the train noticeably began to slow. The whistle sounded again in a series of sharp blasts and then one long one. Ben and Jim looked out of the windows and spotted a church spire in the distance. They noticed a parallel set of tracks that ran next to their own and a water tower on the horizon. The train began to shudder and jerk as the cars began to bump into each other.

"We ain't supposed to be stoppin' here. What do you suppose is wrong?" Jim asked. The train finally stopped and Ben walked towards the door.

"Let's go see," he said. They stepped out of the car. People bustled everywhere. The sound of the worn locomotive's hissing competed with the sound of many church bells ringing wildly.

"Mr. Watson," Ben said, "This is still Saturday, isn't it?"

"I was about to ask you the same thing. It sounds more like a Sunday than a Saturday afternoon."

They began to walk towards the many buildings near the small station and as they walked past people, they began to notice a festive air, like it was a holiday. People talked and buzzed about each other and they were all smiling. Faces began to look deliriously happy. Ben stopped in mid stride and grabbed Jim's arm.

"Jim, that lady up ahead. I was able to read her lips. Do you see her, the one with the big carpetbag? If I am correct, I believe she just told the man that she is with that Vicksburg has surrendered."

"You read her lips?" Jim asked. "What do you mean you read her lips? What are you sayin' son? You ain't into that voodoo, is you? I ain't followin' you all that well."

"I will explain later. I must verify this. Good Lord Almighty, I think she just said that Lee has been beaten and driven from Pennsylvania. Wait one second." Jim continued walking, completely baffled by his companion's statement but hopeful that it was true. Ben walked towards an older man and stopped. The older man had a bag in his hand that he clutched to his chest as Ben approached him.

"Pardon me, sir," Ben said. The man looked warily at him and turned his back and walked away without acknowledging Ben's presence. Ben continued studying the different faces in the crowd and noticed a man looking at him. He walked towards this man.

"Excuse me, sir, if I may bother you for just a moment," Ben said boldly. The man did not turn or look away but looked at Ben just as boldly.

"How may I be of assistance to you, young man?" he asked.

"I believe that I have just heard someone say that Vicksburg has fallen? Can this be true?"

"Indeed, I have and it is true. That is why the bells are ringing. Here is even more staggering news. Lee has this day been broken at Gettysburg and threatens us no more. He has been beaten. It is on the telegraph. Can you imagine, all on the Fourth of July. Truly wonderful and marvelous news worthy of a day of Thanksgiving. General Pemberton has surrendered Vicksburg and General Grant has taken control of the city and at Gettysburg, General Meade has won the day. It seems as if the hand of God has touched this day. This day has surely seen evidence of answered prayers, but you must excuse me, young sir. I see my dear wife struggling with the conductor. It seems that she took an instant dislike to the man for some reason and is giving the poor man fits and I must bid you leave, good day, young man." He doffed his hat and hurried away towards his wife. Ben hurriedly returned to Jim's side.

"Jim, we may be witnessing the beginning of the end of this dreadful war. It is true. Vicksburg and Gettysburg are both victories." Ben watched as the man he had just spoken with walked towards a woman who was trying to pull a large carpetbag from the grasp of the same conductor who had forced them from their passenger coach. The conductor held onto the bag when suddenly the woman drove her fist into the man's face. He staggered and fell heavily to the ground.

"Hot damn, did you see that? The little lady kin' hit like a mule," Jim shouted. Her husband placed his hand on her shoulder and quickly led her away. People flowed around the semi conscious conductor as an engineer ran towards his fallen associate.

"We should see if we can inquire about sending a wire to Philadelphia informing our friends of our delay. I still don't have any idea why we stopped out here," Ben said. He began to move with the crowd again. They passed the conductor who was sitting upright but was too dazed to stand.

"Listen to those church bells. They are music to my ears," Ben said.

"Ben, I have to say this. I never heard a colored man talk the way you do except'n for Mr. Douglass. Lord, that man kin talk pure jewels. But you, Mr. Robinson, you give him a run for his money, yassuh you do."

"Excuse me, Jim. I didn't hear you."

"It's not important. Lets us go find that telegraph office," Jim replied.

They looked down the track and saw the smoke of an approaching locomotive. They walked as quickly as they could to the embankment away from the tracks.

"I understand now. We have been shunted to the side so that this train may pass us," Ben said. Both men stood and watched as the train drew closer towards them. As it grew nearer, they could clearly see that the train was loaded to bursting with wounded Union soldiers. Over the sound of the ringing bells and the racket of the steam engine could be heard a moan like the sound of a winter wind. It was the sound from hundreds of the dying soldiers on board. The train rolled past them and disappeared around a bend but the stench that trailed behind it clung to the humid air.

Neither of them said anything once the train had passed them and they continued towards the station. In the distance, they could make out the telegraph office.

"There is a question I bin meanin' to ask you."

"Yes, what is it?"

"Where did you learn to talk the way you do? I mean you talk better than any white man I evah' seen. Only colored man that talks the same way is Mr. Douglass"

"He is a superb orator, isn't he," Ben said smiling.

"I don't know what that means, but if it means he talks good then the answer is yes," Jim said.

"Yes, it means he speaks well," Ben replied.

"The way you done tolt that conductor yo' mind, I never heard anythin' of the likes in all my born days. That old boys mouth flapped open as though he was a fixin' to catch flies like a bull frog."

"Fair question. I ran away from slavery when I was fourteen. That was in Delaware. Mosses helped me, Miss Tubman. The "General". I got all the way to Toronto with her help. Through various connections that would take forever to explain, I found myself sailing to England and I was attending Oxford College within the year. I was fifteen, almost sixteen when I started studying. I have always had a knack for mathematics. I cannot explain it. I studied physics, particularly physics and engineering. I graduated in two years. I stayed on and was working on my doctorate when Miss Tubman contacted me and here I am."

"You a doctor, Ben?"

"Not a doctor that takes care of people. I don't fix broken bones or make poultices when you are sick. I was studying to be a doctor of science."

"You don't say. That England. That's a far place, ain't it?"

"It is across the ocean. There is no slavery over there. Do you know, Jim, that this is the last civilized country to have slaves? Something is wrong when the greatest democracy in the world is a slave nation."

They could see that the telegraph office was crowded and it would be a long wait. Jim leaned against a tree.

"Jest' how old is you. It don't matter none, I'm jest curious."

"I am almost nineteen. I will be nineteen in a month," Ben said.

"What kinda' place was that Oxnard College?"

"Oxford was like being on another world. It was a place older than the United States. It was amazing. They are doing things there today that our grandparents would swear was sorcery if they were alive to see it. They are creating things like raw power that flows down a wire. They study electrical energy. They are studying the building blocks of all matter, the smallest particles known to man. I wrote a paper, a dissertation on the atom that some hailed as a break through piece of research, although I did not have the time to continue working towards what I saw as a distinct possibility. I believe that it will someday be possible to split the atom to release the very essence of all power, the very same power that the sun releases. We will harness it to make this world a paradise."

This strange young man again baffled Jim.

"That adom you speak of. It ain't got nothin' to do with your Adam's apple in yo' throat?"

"No. The ancient Greeks gave us the concept of atoms. I will leave my mark in the world of science. It is my passion. I have these dreams, Jim."

"It's good fer a man to have them. My dreams made me free. I'm sorry that I'm sich' an ig'orant man, I barely understood anythin' you jest' said."

"No matter, my friend. I have put all that behind me for the moment. What is most important is the job that we have been given. I want you to know that I am committed to our goal, one hundred percent. I believe that Mr. Douglass has picked me to be the mouthpiece and he has picked you to keep our mission strictly bordered within the framework of common sense."

"All I know, Ben, is that if Mr. Douglass said it would free all our kin iff'n I was to jump off a high bridge with my behind painted purple, I wouldn't even give it a never mind. I'd hit that rail runnin', high assin' it off that bridge without a care."

270

"Listen to those bells, Jim. There must be churches for miles around ringing in celebration the past few days' events. I do not believe that I will ever forget this moment. The irony of this being the Fourth of July and the news of the great victories achieved will never be wasted on me."

"Sorry, Ben. There you go again leaving me scratchin' my head as to what your sayin'. What is Iron-ee?"

"I will be happy to explain it to you, Jim. Suppose, let us say, that there was this fellow that was experiencing a repetitious dream. Let us say it was a nightmare that came again and again to him. Let us further say that in this nightmare, he saw himself being drowned in a powerful rising river."

CHAPTER FIFTEEN

Hundreds of dead and dying men lay together under the stars. The occasional whine of a tumbling bullet blended with the cries of the delirious and the moans of the wounded. The night crept sluggishly forward towards the dawn stubbornly refusing to give in to the coming morning. Death still ruled the night so powerfully that the normal sounds of insects on this warm summers night were noticeably missing. They too had been hushed by the touch of battle like the hundreds of twisted bodies that lay broken and shattered on the ground.

The exhausted survivors on each side had called a halt to the slaughter so that the maimed and blasted bodies of the wounded could be gathered in a gruesome harvest. An occasional shot rang out in the night as a nervous and bone tired soldier fired at a lurking figment of his overworked imagination.

The Confederate wounded that fell a few paces from the abatements of the Union defenses at the top of the hill were left exactly as they had fallen. No help would be forthcoming to them from either side and they were left to choke out their last remaining breadths alone. No truce had been arranged.

There had been one white flag seen, the shameful mark of surrender. Confederate soldiers, advancing to the crest had received a volley at point blank range when a returning Federal Regiment had returned in strength to the thinly held line. The Confederate soldiers had been nearly annihilated in the initial fire and a few shocked survivors fashioned a flag of capitulation. The Union men had waved the rebel soldiers forward into their lines when suddenly an enraged rebel officer had dashed the flag from the hands of its bearer to the earth and entreated his men to continue the fight. The Federal soldiers saw this as dirty work and not playing by the rules. The Confederate officer was quickly dispatched to a better world by a thunderous volley of well-placed shots. After this incident, there were no more white flags accepted by either side.

Bleeding bodies carried in blankets or shelter halves flittered among the shadows of the boulders and trees dragged and pulled by comrades who moved in dull shock. The attack in the dark had failed although it had been close. Returning Federal regiments had returned to the top and had tipped the weight of the fight in the Unions favor. They had delivered death to the attackers over and over again as the Confederates pushed closer to the peak only to be stopped short by the murderous intentions of the Federal defenders. The Federals fired coolly and did not loose their heads. The Confederates came at the Union men like waves on the ocean only to be broken at the top as surf is on a beach.

Tom lay exhausted in a hollow next to a boulder. The body of Arthur Cook lay wrapped in a blanket at his feet. Pete Wilson lay a few feet away from him. Pete had taken a long time to die but he had eventually succumbed to his wound. Tom watched as a group of soldiers struggled past him carrying a bloody burden. They staggered by him but he did not recognize any of the men. Similar processions were being repeated in front of him as solders dragged and pulled men off this hill of death.

Tom had dragged Pete by the wounded man's arms until he could not take another step. Pete had never regained consciousness. His brains oozed out of a ragged hole behind his ear. Pete's ragged breathing finally had stopped after what had seemed like an eternity to Tom. Tom stood up shakily and held onto a rock for support.

"Where the hell do you think you are a'goin? Y'all better sit down 'for you fall down," Thornton said weakly.

"I got to get back up there," Tom said.

"You don't even know how bad yer' hit. Why don't you find out a'fore you go and bleed to death."

"It ain't that bad. How's Andy doing?"

"I do believe he died. He ain't a'makin' them strange guhglin' sounds no more. Holt on a might, let me see. No, he's still suckin' wind but I don't know fer' how much longer. He is all shot to hell an' gone. Draggin' him down this hill would jest' make him die quick. He don't seem to be suffering."

"What about you. How bad are you off?" Tom asked.

"I'm pretty well spent. This here is where it all ends fer' me. I seed' plenty of fellas what were shot jest' like me an' every one of them curled their toes. I ain't fixin' to travel all the way down this here hill to lie around with a bunch of strangers and up an' die anyway. I'm in good company here and here is wha'r I intend to stay."

He started to laugh, but the weak laughter turned into a coughing fit. Blood began to leak from the corners of his mouth. He wiped it away with his sleeve.

"Damn," he sputtered. Thornton wheezed and hacked up more clotted blood. "My goodness."

Tom leaned against the rock.

"There'll be stretchers up here, as soon as it starts to get light. You are going down with them and that's an order. You're still soldier enough to listen up and do what you're told."

273

Thornton placed his head against the rock and stared up into the northern sky.

"We almost had them, Tom. We were close. I seed' Threats jump right amongst the Yankees. A lot of our boys did. A whole section made it into their works. Then the Colonel yells, "Up boys an' give them the cold steel. Follow me," he yells, and ever body gits' up to follow him and then everybody got kilt', jest' like that. The way the Colonel went up them last few feet, I thought he got shot out of a cannon. He got everybody kilt' yellin' an' wavin' his damned old sword. I nevah' seed' anythin' like that fire before. A whole company was gone in a flash, jest' like that."

Hundreds of dead and dying men lay together under the stars. The occasional whine of a tumbling bullet blended with the cries of the delirious and the moans of the wounded. The night crept sluggishly forward towards the dawn stubbornly refusing to give in to the coming morning. Death still ruled the night so powerfully that the normal sounds of insects on this warm summer's night were noticeably missing. They too had been hushed by the touch of battle like the hundreds of twisted bodies that lay broken and shattered on the ground.

The exhausted survivors on each side had called a halt to the slaughter so that the maimed and blasted bodies of the wounded could be gathered in a gruesome harvest. An occasional shot rang out in the night as a nervous and bone tired soldier fired at a lurking figment of his overworked imagination.

The Confederate wounded that fell a few paces from the abatements of the Union defenses at the top of the hill were left exactly as they had fallen. No help would be forthcoming to them from either side and they were left to choke out their last remaining breadths alone. No truce had been arranged.

There had been one white flag seen, the shameful mark of surrender. Confederate soldiers, advancing to the crest had received a volley at point blank range when a returning Federal Regiment had returned in strength to the thinly held line. The Confederate soldiers had been nearly annihilated in the initial fire and a few shocked survivors fashioned a flag of capitulation. The Union men had waved the rebel soldiers forward into their lines when suddenly an enraged rebel officer had dashed the flag from the hands of its bearer to the earth and entreated his men to continue the fight. The Federal soldiers saw this as dirty work and not playing by the rules. The Confederate officer was quickly dispatched to a better world by a thunderous volley of well-placed shots. After this incident, there were no more white flags accepted by either side.

Bleeding bodies carried in blankets or shelter halves flittered among the shadows of the boulders and trees dragged and pulled by comrades who moved in dull shock. The attack in the dark had failed although it had been close. Returning Federal regiments had returned to the top and had tipped the weight of the fight in the Unions favor. They had delivered death to the attackers over and over again as the Confederates pushed closer to the peak only to be stopped short by the murderous intentions of the Federal defenders. The Federals fired coolly and did not loose their heads. The Confederates came at the Union men like waves on the ocean only to be broken at the top as surf is on a beach.

Tom lay exhausted in a hollow next to a boulder. The body of Arthur Cook lay wrapped in a blanket at his feet. Pete Wilson lay a few feet away from him. Pete had taken a long time to die but he had eventually succumbed to his wound. Tom watched as a group of soldiers struggled past him carrying a bloody burden. They staggered by him but he did not recognize any of the men. Similar processions were being repeated in front of him as solders dragged and pulled men off this hill of death.

Tom had dragged Pete by the wounded man's arms until he could not take another step. Pete had never regained consciousness. His brains oozed out of a ragged hole behind his ear. Pete's ragged breathing finally had stopped after what had seemed like an eternity to Tom. Tom stood up shakily and held onto a rock for support.

"Where the hell do you think you are a'goin? Y'all better sit down 'for you fall down," Thornton said weakly.

"I got to get back up there," Tom said.

"You don't even know how bad yer' hit. Why don't you find out a'fore you go and bleed to death."

"It ain't that bad. How's Andy doing?"

"I do believe he died. He ain't a'makin' them strange guhglin' sounds no more. Holt on a might, let me see. No, he's still suckin' wind but I don't know fer' how much longer. He is all shot to hell an' gone. Draggin' him down this hill would jest' make him die quick. He don't seem to be suffering."

"What about you. How bad are you off?" Tom asked.

"I'm pretty well spent. This here is where it all ends fer' me. I seed' plenty of fellas what were shot jest' like me an' every one of them curled their toes. I ain't fixin' to travel all the way down this here hill to lie around with a bunch of strangers and up an' die anyway. I'm in good company here and here is wha'r I intend to stay."

He started to laugh, but the weak laughter turned into a coughing fit. Blood began to leak from the corners of his mouth. He wiped it away with his sleeve.

"Damn," he sputtered. Thornton wheezed and hacked up more clotted blood. "My goodness."

Tom leaned against the rock.

"There'll be stretchers up here, as soon as it starts to get light. You are going down with them and that's an order. You're still soldier enough to listen up and do what you're told."

Thornton placed his head against the rock and stared up into the northern sky.

"We almost had them, Tom. We were close. I seed' Threats jump right amongst the Yankees. A lot of our boys did. A whole section made it into their works. Then the Colonel yells, "Up boys an' give them the cold steel. Follow me," he yells, and ever body gits' up to follow him and then everybody got kilt', jest' like that. The way the Colonel went up them last few feet, I thought he got shot out of a cannon. He got everybody kilt' yellin' an' wavin' his damned old sword. I nevah' seed' anythin' like that fire before. A whole company was gone in a flash, jest' like that."

Hundreds of dead and dying men lay together under the stars. The occasional whine of a tumbling bullet blended with the cries of the delirious and the moans of the wounded. The night crept sluggishly forward towards the dawn stubbornly refusing to give in to the coming morning. Death still ruled the night so powerfully that the normal sounds of insects on this warm summer's night were noticeably missing. They too had been hushed by the touch of battle like the hundreds of twisted bodies that lay broken and shattered on the ground.

The exhausted survivors on each side had called a halt to the slaughter so that the maimed and blasted bodies of the wounded could be gathered in a gruesome harvest. An occasional shot rang out in the night as a nervous and bone tired soldier fired at a lurking figment of his overworked imagination.

The Confederate wounded that fell a few paces from the abatements of the Union defenses at the top of the hill were left exactly as they had fallen. No help would be forthcoming to them from either side and they were left to choke out their last remaining breadths alone. No truce had been arranged.

There had been one white flag seen, the shameful mark of surrender. Confederate soldiers, advancing to the crest had received a volley at point blank range when a returning Federal Regiment had returned in strength to the thinly held line. The Confederate soldiers had been nearly annihilated in the initial fire and a few shocked survivors fashioned a flag of capitulation. The Union men had waved the rebel soldiers forward into their lines when suddenly an enraged rebel officer had dashed the flag from the hands of its bearer to the earth and entreated his men to continue the fight. The Federal soldiers saw this as dirty work and not playing by the rules. The Confederate officer was quickly dispatched to a better world by a thunderous volley of well-placed shots. After this incident, there were no more white flags accepted by either side.

Bleeding bodies carried in blankets or shelter halves flittered among the shadows of the boulders and trees dragged and pulled by comrades who moved in dull shock. The attack in the dark had failed although it had been close. Returning Federal regiments had returned to the top and had tipped the weight of the fight in the Unions favor. They had delivered death to the attackers over and over again as the Confederates pushed closer to the peak only to be stopped short by the murderous intentions of the Federal defenders. The Federals fired coolly and did not loose their heads. The Confederates came at the Union men like waves on the ocean only to be broken at the top as surf is on a beach.

Tom lay exhausted in a hollow next to a boulder. The body of Arthur Cook lay wrapped in a blanket at his feet. Pete Wilson lay a few feet away from him. Pete had taken a long time to die but he had eventually succumbed to his wound. Tom watched as a group of soldiers struggled past him carrying a bloody burden. They staggered by him but he did not recognize any of the men. Similar processions were being repeated in front of him as solders dragged and pulled men off this hill of death.

Tom had dragged Pete by the wounded man's arms until he could not take another step. Pete had never regained consciousness. His brains oozed out of a ragged hole behind his ear. Pete's ragged breathing finally had stopped after what had seemed like an eternity to Tom. Tom stood up shakily and held onto a rock for support.

"Where the hell do you think you are a'goin? Y'all better sit down 'for you fall down," Thornton said weakly.

"I got to get back up there," Tom said.

"You don't even know how bad yer' hit. Why don't you find out a'fore you go and bleed to death."

"It ain't that bad. How's Andy doing?"

"I do believe he died. He ain't a'makin' them strange guhglin' sounds no more. Holt on a might, let me see. No, he's still suckin' wind but I don't know fer' how much longer. He is all shot to hell an' gone. Draggin' him down this hill would jest' make him die quick. He don't seem to be suffering."

"What about you. How bad are you off?" Tom asked.

"I'm pretty well spent. This here is where it all ends fer' me. I seed' plenty of fellas what were shot jest' like me an' every one of them curled their toes. I ain't fixin' to travel all the way down this here hill to lie around with a bunch of strangers and up an' die anyway. I'm in good company here and here is wha'r I intend to stay."

He started to laugh, but the weak laughter turned into a coughing fit. Blood began to leak from the corners of his mouth. He wiped it away with his sleeve.

"Damn," he sputtered. Thornton wheezed and hacked up more clotted blood. "My goodness."

Tom leaned against the rock.

"There'll be stretchers up here, as soon as it starts to get light. You are going down with them and that's an order. You're still soldier enough to listen up and do what you're told."

Thornton placed his head against the rock and stared up into the northern sky.

"We almost had them, Tom. We were close. I seed' Threats jump right amongst the Yankees. A lot of our boys did. A whole section made it into their works. Then the Colonel yells, "Up boys an' give them the cold steel. Follow me," he yells, and ever body gits' up to follow him and then everybody got kilt', jest' like that. The way the Colonel went up them last few feet, I thought he got shot out of a cannon. He got everybody kilt' yellin' an' wavin' his damned old sword. I nevah' seed' anythin' like that fire before. A whole company was gone in a flash, jest' like that."

"I thought they had some sort of plan," Tom said quietly. "I thought they had an idea on how they were going to take the top of that hill. I figured we could rush them in the dark like Vernon said. God sakes, the fire coming off that hill had us all lit up and in plain view right out in the open. It was a slaughter. We never had a chance."

Thornton moaned and grabbed at his chest.

"Good gracious," he said faintly, "That's a right curious feelin'. Tom, sit with me a spell. I'll make a deal with you. If'n I'm still kickin' when them stretcher fellas get here, I'll go down with them to that aid place. All right? Jest' sit with me is all I'm askin'. I got some strange sensations takin' holt' of me."

Tom staggered over to Thornton in the darkness. His eyes had become accustomed to the shadows and faint shapes that were around him. He lowered himself down next to Thornton.

"You got a deal, Deanny boy," Tom said.

"I am fairly busted up proper, Tom. I feels things movin' around inside me playin' hell. Must be all the lead rattlin' around inside me there."

Tom recognized a voice in the distance and he strained to hear what was being said. It was the loud voice of Vernon Jenkins.

"Put that damned fire out, you idjit' What the hell is wrong with y'all anyway?"

278

"We got a wounded man here," a voice sounded in anger.

"I don't give a hang if you had Jeff Davy's granmaw over there with you. Stomp that damned fire out you moron or I will stomp a hole in yer damned backside," Vernon shouted.

""Who the hell is over here? Ain't there nobody with you ain't got no common good sense. Where the hell is your sergeant."

"They ain't any sergeants or an officer either. Everybody is kilt' or wounded," a voice said wearily in the dark.

"You're lightin' up the whole area an' ruinin' people's night vision. Now stomp that fire out good." Tom could hear Vernon stomping out the fire and slowly stood up. A faint dot of light in the darkness blinked out of existence.

"You new fellas' got a lot to learn in a short time. Stomp it out good. You, big fella', come this way. You see that tree down there, the tall one? Walk that way. When you get to that tree, walk about a hunert paces to the left. Find the stretcher-bearers an' bring them back fer your wounded man. Can you remember how to git back here?"

"Yes sergeant."

"Go. The rest of you, come with me."

"Vernon," Tom shouted, "Over here."

"Who's that?" Vernon yelled in response.

"It's me. Tom."

"Tom, you holt' on. All right, follow me, single file. Watch the man in front of you. Hold on to his belt if you got to until you get your night sights back. Let's go. Move, damn it."

Tom steadied himself against the rock and watched for the approach of the sergeant. He heard them before he saw them. Soldiers followed in Vernon's wake all in a long single column. It reminded Tom of ducklings following their mother.

"I'm sure glad to see you," Tom said.

"You men file down there a few rods an' wait on me. Try not to step on the wounded." Vernon looked Tom over quickly.

"You hit?"

" I got shot, but it went clean through," Tom replied.

"Where?" he asked with concern.

279

"Right high in the shoulder muscle. I think the shot was pretty near spent when it hit me. Nothings broke, I know that. It just bled like the dickens. It went through the fleshy part, knocked me down and spun me around like a top."

Vernon watched as the night-blind soldiers walked groping on to each other and stumbling in the dark. He shook his head sadly.

"Fer Chrisakes all of you. Stop an' sit right where you are until you git yer vision back. That's right, sit, God-dammit. Right where you are. Lord sakes, yer makin enough noise fer a battalion. Hell. You might draw some of our own fire down on us, Sit, Now." Vernon screamed. The soldiers complied and sat down. Vernon looked at the bodies lying at his feet.

"Who's with you?" he asked.

"Arthur's dead. So is Wilson. Thornton's here. Andy's here, but he's not doing so good. I ain't seen nobody else since we were ordered down the last time. Vernon, what happened?"

"Some of our boys got in their line. I would say nearly all of company H. We almost had them. Then they started feedin' men back into the line an' we couldn't hold. That's when the good Colonel decided to charge with the bayonet without layin' down a good solid base of fire to keep their heads down. Custiss hit them on the left an' fer' one minute, they went to ground. It looked like it was goin' to work. But they popped right back up jest' when the Colonel was goin' forward. When they finished with the Colonel, they shifted back over to us. We couldn't stay. Don't you fret none. We will fix them tomorrow, that's fer' sure. They ain't all that strong anymore…not after tonight. We seen the best they got to offer an' we nearly busted them wide open. Right now, we got to restore some kind of order. Regiments are all mixed in together an' it has to get all unraveled before the sun comes up. They tell me that we are settin' up a few yards back, out of their range. We got to get the wounded out an' down to a sanitary station."

Vernon walked past Tom and examined the still form of Andy Barrett. He slowly stood up.

"Andy is gone. Barrett wasn't all that much in the brains department but the man never flinched. Never." He looked at Thornton who was slowly trying to stand up.

"Easy there. How you doin', Deanny boy?" Vernon asked.

"I do believe I am gone up, Vernon."

"You are way too mean to die, Deanny. The devil is too afraid of you for him to welcome you into his kingdom. He's afraid you might give the place a bad name."

Thornton attempted to laugh but was wracked with a coughing spasm for his efforts. Vernon helped him down to the ground.

"You ain't out of this war, yet, Deanny boy. Not by a damned sight so stop feelin' sorry fer yer' damned self. I'm gonna' get a couple of these new fellas and you will be totted out of here. There is a station set up right down the hill, about a half mile from here so you jest 'hang on."

Thornton nodded and leaned back, obviously in quite a bit of pain. Vernon helped Tom to lower himself to the ground as well. He returned a minute later with an improvised stretcher. A jacket had been lashed to a couple of stout tree branches. Soldiers carefully rolled Thornton into it and began to slowly carry him down the hill.

"Company H got into their works?" Tom asked.

"That's what they tell me," Vernon said, "But nobody is all that sure because nobody came back down to tell the story. A few wounded fellas, but that is it. I ain't heard no serious shootin'. Fer all we know, they might all be still up there huddled down waitin' fer first light."

"Think so?" he asked hopefully.

"Won't rightly know until the mornin'. Now, as fer' you. You got to get taken cared' of. I can't afford to lose you right now. Follow them fellas down the hill and get that wound looked at."

"I'm alright, Vernon. Honest. It ain't nothing but a scratch. I'd feel the fool goin' down with this little old thing."

"Let's take a look at it." Vernon helped Tom to remove his shirt. He carefully looked at the rip in his upper chest.

"Looks clean. It went through muscle. It would appear a ricochet an' damned fortunate it hit you where it hit. If it had had a little more power it would have bounced off a rib and plowed a furrow into your chest an' then you would be in serious trouble. Turn around."

Tom did as he was told.

"It came out in yer' armpit. It's all banged up pretty good. You better have the doc look at it anyway."

"He's going to be busy. Others need him more that I do. I got to go find Huck."

"You can't. The Yankees are way too trigger-happy tonight an' you ain't all that steady. You lost a lot of blood. Come on down the hill with me. He might be down there already. Trust me, I'll find out. I need every old hand I got, Tom. We lost some damned good fellas tonight, Arthur included. Them boys over there was startin' a fire. Can you believe it? That's because there was nobody around to tell them any different. I need you to help sort them out. I need you down that hill. Tom, they didn't give you stripes for no good reason. Whether you know it or not, or even like it, you are a leader and have responsibilities. That's just the way it is. You got to do it now."

Vernon shouted loudly, "One of you, get over here. We got a wounded man here that needs a hand getting' off this slope."

A young soldier appeared and offered Tom his arm. His head was spinning and he was nauseous. There was something familiar about the young man. Tom looked closely at the boy. The bottom of his lower ear lobe was missing. It was the young soldier who had been forced to come to cover by Arthur Cook's well-placed shot. The boy helped Tom down the hill and he looked at the blanket wrapped body of Arthur Cook.

"Alright, men," Vernon said, "Follow that sergeant down the hill an watch where yer' goin'."

Ted Doudlass walked rapidly towards Mr. Flemming's store. Walking stride for stride with him was a shorter man. The man's hair was a dark brown and he sported a short mustache. His drooping eyes gave him a sleepy look. William Clarke Quantrill was non-descript in appearance. There was nothing about him that would indicate to the world at large that he was the leader of a band of irregular Confederate guerillas that at the moment were tying down hundreds of badly needed Union cavalry and infantry in the pursuit and intended destruction of his small group. William Clarke Quantrill had successfully thwarted every attempt the Union forces in Missouri had made in destroying his force of guerillas and he carried the war to Federal outposts all over the state.

He looked more like an owlish schoolteacher than a feared leader of desperate Southern guerillas, something that he actually was before the outbreak of hostilities. Even fewer people knew that before the war he had been an abolitionist, raised in Ohio. When he had first mentioned his intent on visiting Ted's town, many of his people had tried to dissuade him. After all, he was a highly wanted individual with a price on his head. His purpose on coming to the town was to procure much needed powder and ammunition. He had insisted that the sleepy little town was the perfect place to achieve his ends and could not be convinced otherwise.

On this hot July afternoon, they were steps away from accomplishing what he had in mind. They bounded up the steps of the store as Ted held the door open. Ted looked around the place. Nothing had changed. The place looked exactly like it had when Ted was a boy. The very same candy jar filled with hard candy still stood in the same place as it had ten years ago.

Mr. Flemming, the owner, stood behind the counter involved in a one sided conversation with a Federal soldier. Ted and his captain started to browse about the store keeping one ear open to the conversation that Mr. Flemming was having with the soldier.

"This here is a Smith and Wesson caliber pistol number two Army revolver. You can't beat this weapon, soldier. I got a new shipment of Colts in not more than a week ago if you want to look at one. They was all still packed like the day they left the factory way back east. I don't sell no shoddy weapons, soldier. But they ain't cheap. You got cold hard cash then I'm the person you need to talk to. I don't take no credit. Now, what is it going to be?"

The soldier seemed flustered and he looked around, catching both the attention of the two browsing men in the far aisle. He sheepishly looked at them and then leaned into Mr. Flemming and whispered as not to be overheard by them. Mr. Flemmings eyes smoldered and he scowled. He slammed the pistol back into its container.

"I had you figured fer a gold-durned deadbeat. If you expect me to wait fer my money, sonny, then you don't know business. This is my life. You expect me to give you a revolver worth forty-five dollars and wait fer you to come back after you git paid and pay me. You must be crazy from the heat. You soldier boys are all alike. One day yer here an' the next day yer off chasin' that Quantrill bastard or Injuns or bandits. I can't keep track of the number of you fellas that pass through this town no more." He placed the wooden box under the counter next to the display glass on the bottom shelf. The soldier looked embarrassed and glanced again at the two other men who were fingering the bristles on a broom in the next aisle.

"You gotta yell my business all over the store?" he said angrily.

"Let me tell you something, sonny. Maybe you didn't hear so good before. Look at my lips," Mr. Flemming said slowly.

"Cold hard cash, on the barrelhead. I'm not a greedy man. If you had, let's say, thirty-five dollars, we could have done business, but since yer jest tolt me that you ain't got but sixteen whole dollars you must learn to shit or git off the pot. If you can come up with the added money, I will give the revolver to you fer thirty five dollars today. I'll even throw in enough bullets so's you kin' shoot every Reb or Redskin fer' a month of Sundays. I aim to please. That's what makes a good businessman. Why don't yer' go ask some friends to lend yer' the money. If they say no, why not take a chance with the sixteen yer' got on yer'. There's always a poker game to be found. Hell, yer' might git lucky, sonny boy. If yer' do, you know where you kin' find me."

The soldier smiled.

"It's a good deal I'm givin' yer'," Mr. Flemming said.

"You're a hard man," the soldier said. "Don't be too surprised if you don't see me in just a while."

"That's the style, sonny. I'll be waitin' right here."

The soldier glanced briefly again at the two men in the shadows, turned and left the store. Captain Quantrill eased his way towards the counter.

"These damned soldier boys," Flemming said. "Just 'cause they's in the Army, they expect credit. I'll probably never see a hair on his head again. They come an' go around this town like flies on a turd. He'll be gone tomorrow, you kin' bet on it. Now, gentlemen, what kin' I do fer' you?"

"I am interested in buying ammunition and powder. A substantial amount," Quantrill said. Ted remained in the aisle and nonchalantly hefted a shovel. He kept his eyes trained on the door and one hand near his pistol.

"I got enough powder and shot to start a war. How much we talkin' about," Flemming said, quite interested in his new customer.

"I got every caliber made," he said proudly.

"I will be needing five thousand rounds in the categories described forth wit on this inventory ledger. As you can see from this document, I am a buyer for the Second Colorado Cavalry. When we were in St. Louis, I received this telegraph informing me of my commanders need for this purchase, seeing that we will be meeting our escort in less than a week."

Flemming reached for the invoice and his spectacles at the same time. He perused the paper and the items on it, making odd satisfied noises as if savoring every morsel of a fine meal. Ted watched Flemming carefully for any outside signs of recognition but he was so absorbed with the items on the list that he never gave Ted a single glance.

Ted thought to himself what a greedy old fornicator Flemming was. He had always appeared to favor Southern independence; at least he had always talked a good talk about it. Now, here he was, happily selling weapons to a man that was poised as one of their enemy. It seemed to Ted that Mr. Flemming's allegiance to homespun southern beliefs had eroded with the south's recent reversal of fortune in this county over the last two years.

"This here is some list you got. I see here that you are instructed to secure two hundred pounds of powder as well as fifty pounds of shot. This is gonna' be quite a load. I suppose you have a way of getting it to Colorado 'cause I don't make deliveries."

284

"We have a man that will come by directly. What I need to know is when can you fill my order?"

"This here is a tall order but it will be ready when your man comes. I'm here all by myself here today. My son's wife took ill and he's tendin' to her. Nothing serious, jests' some kinda' summer flux. Lets see. All told, about an hour. I'll stack it in back where your man kin' load it on his wagon. You do have a wagon?"

Quantrill nodded and turned to see what Ted was doing. Ted was doing his part to perfection, ready to drop the first wrong person that walked through the door.

"Let me do a quick bit of cipherin' here," Flemming said quickly. "I'll give yer' a quick figure."

"No need. My man will have all the funds necessary for the transaction. His name is Mr. Burns. If there are no further questions, then we will be going."

"No sir, everything will be ready fer Mr. Burns when he arrives. It's bin' a pleasure doin' business with you, young man," Flemming said cheerily. Ted began to inch his way towards the door, keeping his face away from Mr. Flemming. Captain Quantrill doffed his hat gallantly.

"Good day to you, sir," He said courteously.

Flemming waved a farewell as Quantrill walked for the door.

"I hope yer kill a passel of redskins, sir. Maybe a rebel or two while yer' at it," Flemming shouted. He walked towards the rear of his store to prepare the order as his two customers walked out the door and down the steps.

"He seems more'n happy to be servin' the damned Yankees, the old bastard," Ted said angrily. "That old son-of- a-bitch use to say that Yankees was a money grubbing crowd of foreign born trash. Hell, he was pro-southern all his life. He was a good friend of Frank Gordon. I can't believe the changes in the old coot," Ted said with disgust.

"It is a good thing that we did not have to use your familiarity with the old man in this mission. With his current state of mind since his revision, he may well have tried to turn you in to the authorities. Do you think he recognized you, sergeant?"

"No sir."

"Good. This is why I insisted in doing this my way. I knew that this town would be easy enough. It is totally isolated from all the rest of the war. It is a little undisturbed backwater town. It may as well be on the moon. Did you notice all the militia? The riverboats drop them off and they get shuffled off rapidly, it would appear. You heard the old man. They don't stick around here for too long. This is perfect," Quantrill said happily.

"What next, Captain?" Ted asked.

"We ride to the caves. That should take an hour. Then we get sergeant Burns to pick up the goods. We wait for him and then we go. It could not be any simpler."

"It seems to me, sir, that after we meet Burns that we have some time to kill. It will be probably better for the wagon if we travel in the daylight instead of at night. We wouldn't want to run into a rut and throw a wheel or break an axle."

"What are you suggesting, sergeant," Quantrill asked.

"How does a home cooked chicken dinner with all the fixin's sound to you, Captain. Even ice cool lemonade to wash it all down with?"

"Real ice?"

"Yessir. It is a long story, but when I was scoutin' through town this mornin', I ducked into a lady friends house when I thought I had spotted some trouble. I tell you, sir, she thought she had seen a ghost on account of my premature reported demise."

They walked leisurely towards their horses. The captain was amused with the story and was beginning to feel the tenseness peel away in layers.

"Anyway, as I was leaving, she invited me to stay fer dinner. I couldn't then because I had to get back to the command. But now, with what we know, and. with all this free time on our hands, why I thought I might broach the subject with you, sir. Her father and brothers are away fightin' on our side at Vicksburg. She can be trusted, sir."

Captain Quantrill placed his elbow in the palm of his left hand and stroked his moustache. He stretched his neck and tried to appear to be dissatisfied with the activity of his sergeant.

"I am disappointed with your judgment, sergeant. Is this how you conduct a scouting mission deep in enemy territory? By visiting lady friends? Did you not realize the seriousness of what we do here?" Quantrill said sharply. "Must I remind you that dalliances with the opposite sex often is a delicate proposition at best? This was never on the agenda."

"No suh,"

"This will take careful consideration. We must present a good image to all of our southern brothers and sisters and as such, find your idea very sound. Splendid idea. Now, let us get to those caves and sergeant Burns. Do you think the young lady would mind if we brought him along."

"I am sure she would not, Captain."

"So much the better. I do believe I could get used to your hometown. Now, let's get going. We have pressing needs for this ammunition. I haven't told anyone of this yet. I intend to capture Lawrence, Kansas. I will put that town to the torch. We will destroy that nest of abolitionist scum and I must have this ammunition. We shall make Kansas bleed like it never bled before.

The Confederate regiments of Jones, Steuart, and Williams had established their lines a few hundred feet from the summit of Culp's hill. Tom had asked many people if they had seen Huck but no one could say with any certainty that they had. Everyone had seen at least part of company H breach the Union defenses and set up housekeeping in the empty Federal line. After that, no one could say what had happened. The fight had been too confusing, too uncoordinated in the darkness.

Some of the wounded from company H sullenly sat waiting for medical attention. These men claimed to know nothing of what happened to their comrades. They said that they were wounded on their way to the top and had dropped out of the fight early. Even Vernon could not find out anything of substance about what had happened to the members of company H, all that Vernon could say that the last anyone saw of them was when the company had poured into the Yankee defenses. Ed Bolls and George Blakely sat with Tom. Yancey Stinson, who had not taken part in the attack, had sneaked away from the hospital and had rejoined the company. His face was still swollen, however, the jack-o-lantern look that had been hammered into his features had diminished to a great degree.

Many of the members of company C were missing. At least a dozen men were known to have been killed and at least three times that number wounded. Many of the wounded had refused to be sent to the rear. The survivors sat around and helped each other dress their wounds. Tom had eventually fallen into a fitful sleep. As the sun slowly crept into the sky, the Army of Northern Virginia began to prepare for the coming day. They knew what to expect. They were going straight up the hill and even though they had failed that night, there was renewed confidence that they would drive the enemy from their positions.

In the early morning while the sun was still just a promise in the sky, many of them were already checking the amount of ammunition they had and their supply of percussion caps. Canteens were collected and men were designated to fill them. They all speculated on what the day would bring. Tom sniffed at the morning air and saw Ed Bolls and George Blakely checking their weapons. Ed began to check Tom's wound for him. He removed the rag that someone had given Tom earlier and used a slightly less filthy rag to rewrap it. Tom's chest and shoulder were an ugly purple and black. His armpit was equally discolored.

"You got to get this looked at. Have someone pour some whiskey in it. That there's a damned ugly rip you got fer' yourself. It would appear that it bounced around yer' armpit before it was finished goin' through yer' chest," Ed said. "It's all black and blue, like you got hit with a big mallet."

"There ain't no time for that, "Tom replied.

George finished cleaning his rifle and then checked the sights. He began to pick his nose.

"There's plenty of time, Tom. Hell, you got more time than money. Why don't yer' do what Ed said. Find the doc. Let him take a gander at it. You don't want to lose yer' arm."

Flies buzzed around Tom's wound and he brushed the air with his hand to dissuade them from landing on his flesh. During the night, flies had already laid eggs in the gash in his chest. Tom simply shook his head. They knew how stubborn Tom was and decided to try again later.

"Suit yerself," George said. "I was talkin with Ogden an' he heard from somebody that we plan to hit them mid-day. He heard that Third Corp is goin' to go at them again."

"Can you tell me how he managed to hear that?" Ed said sarcastically. "Somebody write it down on paper fer him? That boy is deaf as a post. Remember at Sharpsburg in front of that old Dunker Church. A caisson went up while he was practically on top of it. It blew his ears out. He is as dingy as they come."

"I don't know how he come by it, but that's what he tolt me. He can still speak, you know," George said defensively.

Tom ignored their conversation while Ed and George continued to argue over mundane things, partly to keep their minds off the deaths that had cut their number down to just a handful of souls. Tom shut their voices off and fell into a deep hole of self inflicted guilt over Huck's disappearance. Yancey was soon involved in the pointless bickering. The sun inched higher in the sky.

"And I suppose Ogden tolt you about the Yankees recruitin' nigger soldiers as well," Ed spat.

"If the Yankees are low enough to use nigger soldiers, then you know they must be hard up. It's a sure sign that they are whipped," Yancey said thoughtfully.

"Niggers won't fight an' if they do, they will surely make a mess of it. Even worse than the Yankees have already," Ed stated knowingly.

George chuckled at Ed's observation and then he stopped still, his laugh frozen in his throat as he heard a sound coming at them through the air. The first volley of Federal Artillery thundered in the distance. A whistling sound preceded the rumbling of the artillery. It was as though time itself had locked into place for one instant as their eyes met in disbelief. The Federal fire from a battery of artillery landed in one devastating second.

Yancey was thrown yards skyward by the blast of an exploding artillery shell. He landed on his back and sat up with his left arm missing. Another shell struck a boulder, splitting the artillery shot in half. One half of the projectile struck Yancey directly in his swollen pumpkin like head and took it off his shoulders. His body sagged forward still in a sitting position. The hot blast from the explosion washed over Tom as he flung himself flat on the ground. Corporal Bains dove to the earth next to him. George Blakely tried to crawl away from the fury of the Federal barrage and as he rose to run to the shelter of a boulder, a shell landed on his head. His body sprayed into the air in bits. The resultant explosion tore Ed Bolls in two.

The shrapnel riddled Corporal Bains, and Tom was flung into the air and landed in a hole beneath a tree. He did not move. The Union bombardment decimated Tom's regiment tearing gaps in the southern ranks. They could not move out of the path of the well-placed destruction. They could only endure the horrific carnage. It was just ten o' clock in the morning.

Books and papers lay scattered around the small room. There were books on the floor, under the desk and on the windowsill. Bundles of newspapers were stacked like logs and piled to the ceiling. An old sailor's trunk was stuffed to overflowing with telegraph messages. It was if a tornado had been spawned in this small room and had driven papers and things into every crevice and corner. This was the only room in the modest house that was in this condition. Miss Elliot, Frederick Douglass's housekeeper, kept the rest of the home clean and in order. She had been barred from ever entering his study after she had decided to take it upon herself to tidy up his study.

She had first sorted all the papers that she saw into piles according to their sizes. She had then gathered and compiled stacks based on the thickness of the documents. She had discarded year old newspapers by the wheelbarrow full. Ancient telegraph messages were incinerated in the fireplace making a cozy warm fire as she went about her business of making order out of chaos. All the scraps of paper with names and dates were collated alphabetically and tied up securely with twine.

She cleaned off his desk and placed books back on the shelves. She dusted the entire bookcase and polished his desk until it the hard oak wood gleamed. Miss Elliot then went right at cleaning and picking up miscellaneous scraps of papers on the floor that she put in a binder. When she could see the hardwood floor, she scrubbed it on her hands and knees and then polished it as well. The floor twinkled in appreciation.

After her Herculean labor, she stood back and admired the fruits of her hard labor. There was neatness and a semblance of order where there had been none before. She was satisfied. A great man like Mr. Douglass, she felt, deserved a clean study and this room was now clearly worthy of him. When Frederick returned home from his trip to Boston and New Bedford, the shock of what she had done to the room caused him to rage to the point of apoplexy. He could not find a thing. After his anger had subsided, he made Miss Elliot solemnly swear never to enter his study again.

Frederick sat at his desk reading the most recent casualty list from the fighting at Gettysburg. The battle had ended on July third with the repulse of General Pickett's Division at the center of the Union line. This had occurred almost two weeks ago. There had been much criticism towards the inaction of the commanding officer of the Union forces in not following up his victory by smashing the retreating forces of the rebels. Some argued that General Meade had purposely allowed the Army of Northern Virginia to retreat back down into Virginia unmolested. These men spoke of how the Union army had failed, once again, to destroy Lee's retreating columns by Meade's inability of hurling the Army of the Potomac at the defeated foe and ending the rebellion in one fell swoop.

The Army had indeed defeated Lee's latest assault upon the Union but it had been nearly wrecked in the process. From the amount of dead, wounded, and missing men it was clear to Frederick that the Army of the Potomac was not in any hurling condition anymore. He knew that the sentiments of many of Meade's critics were men with a political agenda, men who wanted to cause scandal in Lincoln's administration so that Lincoln would not be nominated for President in the coming election.

His eyes scanned down the list of the known dead in the newspaper column and he was appalled. The names seemed to go on forever. As he read the names, a scriptural passage from the Bible came to mind. "Saul has killed his thousands and David his tens of thousands." How singularly odd for that one passage to come to mind with all that he had experienced in the last few days.

He had received a telegram informing him that his son had suffered a wound but was expected to recover. His sons regiment, the fifty-fourth Massachusetts, had tried to wrest control away from the rebel defenders of a fort that controlled the approaches to the city of Charleston, South Carolina. Although the attack had failed with a high cost in human lives for the attackers, it had demonstrated to the world that Negro troops could and would fight as bravely as their white countrymen. They had very nearly taken the enemy position and by all reports his son and his comrades had conducted the operation with determination and valor.

Frederick viewed the results of the battle as a moral victory. This fight, he realized, would possibly silence forever those in the north who had repeatedly prophesized that the Negro was incapable of military service. He remembers when he had been accosted in the streets of Boston by a man who had said those very words to him at a rally not more than a month ago. Frederick's response to the man's statement was a history lesson. He had told the fellow that Rhode Island had fielded a regiment of Negro soldiers during the American Revolution and that Lafayette had been quoted as saying that the regiment was probably the best led, equipped, and dressed unit in the Continental Army both highly motivated and disciplined.

The regiment, the First Rhode Island, had demonstrated coolness under fire and an ability to gain its objectives at many battlefields during the war. Frederick had also told the pompous ass that at the Battle of Saratoga, perhaps as many as a third of the Colonial soldiers engaged in the battle had been Negroes. The man had quieted very quickly when a few learned gentlemen in the crowd had readily concurred with Frederick's statement.

He was saddened to learn of the death of the Colonel of the regiment. He had met young Shaw this last spring in Boston. He lamented the loss of this fine young man and thought what a tragedy for his family. A knocking at the door to his study distracted him.

"Yes, Miss Elliot?"

She opened the door but did not cross over the threshold of the room.

"Mr. Douglass, Mr. Lassiter from the newspaper is in the parlor. He has said that he has some news for you, something in the way of a telegram." She had been just washing the evening meals dishes away and her hands were still wet. She wiped them nervously on her apron.

"Thank you Miss Elliot. If you would be so kind to inform Mr. Lassiter that I will be with him momentarily."

"Of course," she answered. She started to leave but stopped short.

"Mr. Douglass, if there is nothing else then, I will be leaving for home as soon as I finish this evenings dishes. There is a fresh apple pie in the pantry and."

"And I am sure it is succulently sweet," Frederick said quickly, beaming a huge flashing smile in her direction. She blushed and began to back out of the doorway. His way of emphasizing and phrasing his words lately always seemed to bring a rosy hue to her cheeks and a smile to her face. Frederick playfully waved to her as he watched her depart and then began to rapidly scoop up telegrams and stuff them in his pockets as he hurried to meet Mr. Lassiter. Frederick opened the door to the parlor as the very rotund Mr. Lassiter struggled to his feet, rising from the sofa like a huge observation balloon.

"Mr. Lassiter, what a pleasant surprise. Are you out walking on this beautiful summer night in the dim hope of burning off some fat?" he teased, "or do you bring me some good news?"

Mr. Lassiter laughed heartily.

"No, my friend. I bring you news. Whether it is good news or bad, only you can determine this. Here, I have received several telegrams from Mr. Robinson and Mr. Watson. See for yourself."

He handed Frederick several telegrams as Frederick took them and sat on the sofa. He pulled out his reading glasses and began to go through all of them very quickly.

"I hope they bear good news," Mr. Lassiter said. Frederick was so absorbed in reading them that he paid Mr. Lassiter little attention. Mr. Lassiter decided that it was time to go. He was to meet some friends in a local pub and was eager to be on his way.

"I can see that whatever it may be it has your undivided attention. I'm off."

"Hurrying home to enjoy your good wife's delicious cooking, no doubt," Frederick said half-jokingly.

"Her cooking has made me the two men that I am," Mr. Lassiter said, patting his enormous stomach. "Good evening, sir. I will, as usual, see my way out. Have a good night, my friend."

"And you as well."

Frederick read and then re-read the messages. Mr. Watson and Robinson would be returning to Rochester soon. They mentioned in the telegrams that they would be arriving with two unexpected guests. How very strange as not to mention their identities, Frederick thought. From all that he had understood from their last correspondence, their mission to Philadelphia had been highly successful. The large Negro community had rallied to their cause and had already funneled hundreds of new men into Federal service. They must feel secure in the infrastructure that they had created if they felt confident enough to return to Rochester so soon and leave the organizing in other hands.

Very good. If this were the case, they would soon be heading to Chicago to begin the process there. Frederick wondered who the guests could possibly be. They must be important to the cause for them to be coming to Rochester with no mention of their identities. Splendid. Frederick rose off the sofa and headed towards the pantry and the aroma of freshly baked apple pie.

Jim Watson listened carefully to the words of the clergyman as Benjamin busily scratched notes into a small notebook. On this hot steamy day, July 6, 1863, in the

City of Brotherly Love, Jim glanced at the frenzied writing activity of his young companion. Benjamin wrote at a speed that Jim found incomprehensible.

"Gentlemen, I don't know what more to say. Our people need help and they need it now. When the invaders found any colored people, they would put them in bonds and herd them south like cattle against their will. Their homes were burned and their livestock joined the coffle lines as well. Many people went into hiding. They are starving and desperate, not knowing that Lee's forces have been driven from our soil," The reverend was trembling slightly in frustration and anger.

"They are wandering around the wilderness like the Israelites of old. Certainly with the connections you gentlemen have in regard to finances, something can be done. We in the community have raised and contributed as much as we can. I am begging you for your help in this matter."

"We need men who know where these folks would hide out at an' kin find them quick," Jim replied, "And fast horses. Maybe a wagon or two for the old folks what are ailing'"

"Would you know as to the number of people that have been uprooted? I'd rather think the number small at best," Ben said.

"Hundreds, sir," Reverend Ellis said sadly. "Mothers with babes in their arms wander in the woods, the very young and the very old, they all wander in the wilds like Moses in the desert."

They were interrupted by a young man who rushed into the rectory of the church out of breath.

"Pardon me, Reverend Ellis. You wanted me to tell you the minute Bunky arrived. Well, sir, he is here in all of his glory. He is right outside."

"Send him in at once. Gentleman, Mr. Carter, Bunky as we call him, is one of the oldest free men of color who lived near Gettysburg. Let him tell you what has occurred," Reverend Ellis said.

The young man soon returned with an elderly man. The old man looked as if he had undergone an ordeal of some sort. The younger man helped Bunky to sit in a chair. His eyes darted from the Reverend Carter to the two neatly dressed men who stood at his side.

"Bunky, this is Mr. Robinson and Mr. Watson. They are our friends. I hope that you are faring well," he asked loudly.

"Putty well fo' a man my age, jest crawled out of a hole in de ground that I be hidin' in fo' the last free days. Yassuh."

Reverend Ellis smiled. "Bunky, these men are here to help us. The world must know what has happened. Please tell them like you told me what happened when the rebels came." Reverend Ellis had again said this quite loudly.

"What in de wold are you hollerin'? I kin' hears you jest' fine. It's muh' wind dats' gone, not muh' ears, lan' sakes." He looked at the stranger's expressions trying to read them by their demeanor.

"When de sessech come, I was weedin' in a patch ob' greens. My gran'son come runnin' through de' fields an let out a whoop, otherwise dey' would'a had all of us. Yassuh. Them sessech boys went round throwin' ropes on all de' colored people. Me an' mine, we went away as fas' as we could an' hid out under a fallen tree. My gran'son's wife, his fo' 'chillin' and me. We stayed put. Nearly starved when muh' gran'son crept along back to the house to fetch vittles."

"You witnessed the rebels kidnapping people? You saw this with your own eyes?" Ben asked.

Bunky shrugged his shoulders.

"No," he said calmly. "Not with muh' own eyes. Can't say I did, suh. By dat' time alls I saw wuz' Five-Folks' buhnin'. Dey' buhnt' all'a Five-Folks' out of spite. All I saw wuz' de' smoke."

This Five-folks, I mean Five-Forks, I take it as being the Negro community near Gettysburg?" Ben asked, writing rapidly.

"Yes. It was a thriving community founded long ago by some of the first freed men of this state," Reverend Ellis said quietly.

"Dey' cotched' muh' gran'son. Dey' roped him together in a long coffle an' started makin' dem' all head souf'. But muh' gran'son was too smart. He got away, come back with sumpin' ta' eat fo' us. We went back an' de' farm was ruint'. Dey' took everthin' an buhnt' de' res'."

"What happened to those that had been warned of the rebels?" Ben asked.

"Dey' is scattuh'd all over hell n' creation. Mus' be a hunert' or two folks wanderin' aroun', too scary to come out cause dey' still think the sessech is out lookin' fo' dem'."

"Mr. Robinson, there are hundreds of people in the same condition as Bunky and his family, war fugitives, wandering in the woods. We will get you as many wagons, guides, and horses that we are able. Bunky here is ninety years old. He has lived at Five-Forks since its inception. It was a solid community of hard working self sufficient people of at least a hundred souls, founded shortly after the American Revolution by free-men. Now they are scattered all throughout the area living like vagabonds or slaves."

294

Ben looked at Jim who simply nodded his head.

"Dey' is Sessech boys wanderin' through de' woods. Dey' is all done in, all shot to pieces. Dey' is tryin' not ta' git cotched' jes' like us. I seen dem' but dey' din't see me, Nossuh," Bunky said.

Bunky was fascinated by the speed in which Ben used his pencil.

"How many did you see?" Ben asked.

"Mo' den' I wanted too. Too many. Dey' is all hurt an' scairt'…an' dey' is thin as scarecrows. No fat on dere' bones a't'll. Evu'hbody is jest' tryin' ta' stay out ob' each ober's way, now. Yassuh. Let muh' gran'son talk. What he got to say will bring a man to de bohl'n point. Yessuh."

"Reverend Ellis," Ben said carefully, "Our forces have been mauled severely. But it would appear that the Rebels have been hurt as badly or they would not have retreated back into Virginia. Lincoln has a victory at Vicksburg practically on the same day that Lee has been driven out of Pennsylvania. Nearly about the same time, we hear that a Negro regiment assaulted a near impregnable fortress in the harbor of Charleston, South Carolina. These cannot be mere coincidences. They are a sign from the Almighty that we are living in the year of Jubilee. Think of this. The birthplace of Southern rebellion to Federal authority is now under siege. The birthplace of this war that has caused so much misery and death will fall. I, for one, do not believe that the Northern press in Ohio or Indiana will strongly object to tens of thousands of Negroes volunteering to join in regiments or battalions to smash that city down. The people of this country are sick of this war and desperately want to see its end. This war is a death struggle. Both sides were not aware of just how much suffering this war would bring when it began, but no one is delusional about the price this country has paid in lives over the question of one human owning another. This is a struggle the likes of which the world has never seen before." Ben took a moment to catch his breadth.

"Our mission here can wait. I am sure, after the last few days that we will have more recruits than we know what to do with. I believe we should organize later and act for the moment. I pledge you our support, Reverend Ellis."

Bunky spoke clearly and for all to hear, "Revun, this man speaks the truthf' bettah' den' I eber' heard. De' year ob' Jubil-lee has truly come."

"Amen to that," Reverend Ellis intoned.

"Hallelooliah," Bunky shouted.

CHAPTER SIXTEEN

Tom regained consciousness slowly. His mind floated out of the deep recess it had been driven into by the concussion of the blast that had nearly killed him. He had been hurled yards through the air and had landed in a shallow depression underneath of a tree. Fallen boughs and branches from the splintered tree covered him. Someone had begun to dig a grave but had not completed it before the artillery fire had descended upon him. The hole had saved Tom's life.

He cracked opened his eyes slightly. A light rain fell on his burned upturned face. It felt refreshing and he licked the corners of his mouth where droplets of water had accumulated. A nagging unrelenting thought drifted in his mind. He could not remember where he was. An even more bizarre problem presented itself when he tried to remember his own name.

Water droplets continued to condense on his charred beard and slowly trickled into the corners of his mouth. His tongue was swollen and his throat was brick dry. Thirst prompted his first attempt at movement and when he did he felt a sharp pain in his chest. He stopped his moving and stared into the early morning sky attempting to shut out the pain. He focused on the stars that he could see between the breaking rain clouds.

He felt quite comfortable in this activity until a pain blasted through his head like a hatchet blow. He moaned quietly as if not to wake anyone sleeping near him. He moved his hands to his head and his shoulder. His body protested the movement by becoming quite vocal. Pain shouted its message all through his body. Most of the hair that remained on his head was burned. Remains of clumps of charred crust circled his ears. The hat that he had always worn was just a remnant; it too was burned into his skull.

Despite the agony it caused, he felt at his face. He quickly pulled his hands away as he touched the burns that covered it. He fought to sit up and began to remove what was left of his jacket. The back of the jacket had been ripped out. His trousers were burned to his skin and were more rags than a garment. He felt at his chest and pulled away his hand in revulsion. The wound on his chest was covered with maggots. He felt something moving under his arm and found maggots there as well. He brushed them off the best he could and attempted to stand up. His view of the world quickly narrowed as he passed out and flopped back into the hole.

The early sunlight painted his morning a bright orange as the light played on his closed eyelids. He felt movement on his burned face as if someone were stroking his face with a tiny paintbrush. The flies buzzing about his face and crawling up his blood clotted nose made him sweep his hand across his face and when he did he yelped in pain. The rain had stopped falling and he saw that the morning sunlight colored the sky in pale blue. The gray clouds were retreating in column away from him.

He took notice of his surroundings. He could see with the growing light that he was in the company of dead men. Bloated bodies were everywhere, swollen and distended in the later stages of decomposition. Oddly, they all looked alike and he did not recognize anyone of them. Some of the bodies were so swollen that they had split their trousers. Many had simply burst open. Flies clouded the pungent air above them. Tom saw a headless body sitting stark upright a few yards from him.

Tongues stuck out of bloated faces and their eyes were just tiny slits giving all of them a fish like quality. Lips were swollen across their grotesquely swollen features and their arms were bent like they were about to fight someone. Curiously, some of them were frozen into the positions of horseless riders. All of them had been dead for quite some time.

Tom wondered just how long he had lain among them. He attempted to stand but fell over again. However, this time he did not pass out, but gamely struggled to his knees. He stood and started to walk but again came crashing down. He crawled as his body demanded relief from the oppressive thirst that he felt. His tongue clung to the roof of his mouth and he became exhausted after only a few feet and had to stop. The pain pounded at his senses and as he rested, many images came to mind. He began to slowly piece things together all disjointed and unfocused, but memories nonetheless.

He remembered Huck's disappearance and the Federal artillery barrage. He remembered getting shot and seeing Arthur Cook die. In his mind, he saw Pete Wilson drive a bayonet into the chest of a Federal officer who, although mortally wounded, still **managed to aim and fire his pistol into Pete Wilson's head.**

He stood up and began to stagger down the hill. He fell a few times but he managed to stay on his feet most of the way down the gentle incline. As he walked past the Federal positions at the base of the hill, he noticed many graves marked by boards from ration boxes. All of those interred were Federal dead.

He stopped when he spotted a canteen and he shook it and found that it was empty. He kept it and continued on his shaky way until he could make out Owl Creek. He wobbled towards the creek and finally arriving on the banks, he stuck his head into the cool water and drank his fill. When he looked around, he noticed a body a few paces upstream that had washed onto the bank. The body was clad in butternut brown and its pants were Federal blue. Its skin was bloodless, almost transparent to the eye.

Tom sank his canteen in the water up to his elbows and filled it. He poured some of it on his head and then corked the wooden canteen. He had no idea of where he was going or what he was going to do and so he started to follow the bank of the creek. He staggered forward like a drunken man.

When he reached a bend in the flow of the creek, he suddenly saw a man in civilian clothes calmly washing what appeared to be a pane of glass in the water. The man was so preoccupied in his task that he never heard Tom approaching him. Tom became aware of a large wagon under the nearby trees with writing on its side. It read, 'Matthew Brady Photography Company" He walked stiffly towards the busy fellow and stopped a few feet short of him. The man finished rinsing his plate of glass, satisfied that all of the chemicals on it had been washed free of its surface. He carefully laid the glass plate on a wooden crate to dry. It was at that moment that he looked up and saw Tom.

What he saw was an apparition from the grave. The explosion from the bursting artillery shell had burned Tom's face, hair and beard. His jacket was ripped and his pants were shredded. Her was covered in the blood and body fluids of George Blakely when George had evaporated from the direct hit he had taken. Tom's eyes were sunk into his skull and his half burned beard could not disguise his hollow cheeks. He stood there rocking back and forth watching the terrified expression of the strange man in civilian garb. The man stared at Tom for several seconds before speaking.

"I have no money," he said in a strange accent.

"Neither do I," Tom said in wonder.

"I have been warned by the authorities that there are many southern stragglers of low quality that would take the gold fillings from a man's mouth if the opportunity presented itself to them. They are reputed to be men of low character. They are said to be desperate scoundrels, drunkards and despicable cutthroats all. These men avoided the fighting by deserting the battle only so that they would be able to rob the dead. I pray that you are not part of their company."

"They sound like quite a cast of characters," Tom muttered. "No sir, I am surely not one of those goldbricks. I don't want no trouble and I mean you no harm. I have had enough trouble in the last few days to last me a lifetime. It would appear that I must have been blown up somehow."

"Blown up?" Mr. Gardner asked.

"Yes. Blown up. There appears to have been quite a bit of it going around the last few days, but I fortunately do not seem to be able to remember my own incident with any clarity. In fact, I don't even know what day today is."

"It is July 8."

"I have been out for sometime. I got shot. Then I got blown up, best as I can figure."

"I take it that you are a Rebel?"

"Twenty Second Virginia volunteers, Jones Brigade, Johnson's Division, Second Corp, General Ewell commanding, Army of Northern Virginia, Robert Lee commanding. I prefer to be called a Southern soldier but what is in a name? Mister. I am powerful hungry. My stomach is touching my backbone. If you could spare a bite, I would be forever indebted to you and I would be on my way. Like I said, I don't want any trouble," Tom said exhaustedly. Mr. Gardner realized that the man was on the point of collapse.

"I think that there is some breakfast left. My assistant could not keep anything down and lost his appetite. It is the terrible smell of this place, you understand. He has been throwing up all morning. Come now; let me help you over to the wagon. My assistant has been absolutely useless to me all morning. He would appear to be a delicate youth."

Mr. Gardner helped Tom over to the wagon and a small-unattended campfire. A large black frying pan with a sturdy lid had been placed on the dying embers. He steered Tom towards a portable canvass studio chair. Tom lowered himself into it. It was the first of its kind that he had ever seen and it was quite comfortable.

"Billy," Mr. Gardner shouted, "We have a guest. Bring another cup from the trunk."

A curly headed youth stepped out of the wagon and on seeing Tom, froze in his tracks. The man was obviously a rebel soldier, a dirty blood smeared vision from hell.

"Don't stare now, boy. Go and fetch the cup, there's a good lad," Mr. Gardener said. "I have some coffee as well."

Billy entered the wagon and returned seconds later with a cup that he handed to Mr. Gardner. Mr. Gardner poured coffee into the cup and handed it to Tom.

"Thanks kindly," Tom said. He blew on the cup and then drank slowly. Billy stared at Mr. Gardner waiting for an explanation for why they were being hospitable to an enemy soldier. Mr. Gardner lifted the lid of the frying pan and inspected the contents. He picked up a fork and began to turn the sausages, which sizzled and smoked. He put down the fork and picking the frying pan up with a rag, scooped out the remaining scrambled eggs onto a pewter plate. He stabbed a fat sausage and laid it next to the eggs. Mr. Gardner handed a plate carefully to his guest.

"Can I ask you who won?" Tom asked weakly. Mr. Gardner had been so wrapped up in thinking of the photograph that he intended to take of Tom that he did not hear his question. He started to hand the fork to Tom.

"Beg pardon, I didn't quite catch what you said," Mr. Gardner said.

"Perhaps I should phrase my inquiry a little more clearer. I asked you who won. You must excuse me, sir, I am still a bit dingy. Did I mention to you that I got blown up?" Tom reached for the fork and dropped it. Mr. Gardner watched as Tom fought to control his emotions. His shoulders shook and he doubled up on himself. Mr. Gardner placed the plate on the ground. Tom whimpered quietly onto his hands. He remained this way for several minutes Mr. Gardner rose and stood next to him. After a while, Tom regained his composure.

"I'm sorry" Tom mumbled.

"That is perfectly alright young man. Take your time. The eggs can wait." Mr. Gardner said sympathetically. Take your time, you are among friends and you are safe."

"I don't want to be a burden to you," Tom said quietly. Tom was embarrassed by his momentary outbreak of emotions. He looked up at Mr. Gardener.

"Nonsense," Mr. Gardner said. You are no burden. In fact, you are an asset at this point. I am burdened with an assistant that has already told me that he is leaving. He is much too delicate for all of this. All of this destruction is too much for the boy. He is free to go. That leaves me in the quandary. In this business, it is imperative that I have help. If you are agreeable to the proposition of being my assistant, I would be very grateful. I will teach you to be a photographer. I think that is better than being a prisoner of war. How does that sound to you?"

"I guess that means we lost," Tom said.

"Lee has been driven out of Pennsylvania and has retreated into Virginia. It is more than apparent that you have done all that could possibly be expected of a soldier. Perhaps it is time for you to think about yourself for a change. This war is far from over, but it could be for you if you choose."

Tom thought this over. Possibly everyone he knew had been killed, including Huck. He knew that it was a miracle that he was still alive and he had his fill of the war. Tom reached for the plate of food.

"I reckon that you have found a new assistant," Tom said.

The column of rebel prisoners, guarded by their federal guards, trudged down the road. The Union soldiers were under orders to shoot any rebel soldier who tried to escape, although all of the southern soldiers heading to the railhead were in no condition to try to escape. Most of them bore one wound or more. One of the wounded southern soldiers had decided that he had had enough of his captors. He had decided to rid himself of their company the first time an opportunity presented itself. These Yankees were bullies and he hated bullies. They pushed and prodded men forward with their rifles and beat any man who protested the rough treatment.

The man wore a makeshift bandage around his head made from and undershirt. The blood had caked around the edges and his face with streaked with his own blood. It covered a rip on his cranium. Ahead of him, a fellow prisoner walked slowly ahead on the point of collapse. The man grabbed the fellow by his arm and bore some of his weight. The surprised prisoner saw that the man who had come to his aid was a sergeant.

"Thanks, kindly. It's a Christian act what you do an' I'm beholdin' to yer. I'm about all done in, but every time I ask's these sons-a-bitches iff'n I kin sit, they start pushin' me forward. I'd like to know why we are in such a hurry fer."

"You would do the same fer me," The sergeant said. He saw that the fellow that he was helping had been shot in the arm. It hung down uselessly to his side.

"I sure would. These damned Yankees ain't got a pint of kindness for us. They jest keeps on yellin' and hollerin' the dirty bastards. They ain't fed us once. I suppose they will onc't they git' us to the railhead. That's what I heard one say to the other."

"Where did they git you," the sergeant asked.

"I wuz with Archer's Brigade. We got pinned down takin' this cut through one of the ridges. There was an old railroad cut there. We got pinned down. We couldn't go forward nor backwards. They was all around us in a blink. They got most ever-body. They even got Archer hisself.' How 'bout you?"

"I was with the Second Corp, we got ordered to take the top of the hill durin' the night. We had laid out all day in the sun, then they tell us to take the hill when the sun was settin'. We went up thet' there hill and most of my company got into the Yankees works. Only thing we didn't figure was that they got help an' while we was getting low on shot, why thet's when they hit us. I fired my last cartridge an' this old boy jumps at me. I lammed him in the head and then another one comes at me fixin' to run me through with the bayonet. I took holt' of his rifle an' made like I was tryin' to take it away from him. When he pult' it back, I let him have it good, and ga-goonk, I pushes it into his stomach with everything I had an' he keels over. I think I got him low with the stock in the nut sack 'cause he warn't movin no more after that."

"You're a right funny fella," the man laughed weakly.

"Oldest trick in the book, I ain't makin' this up. I turns and this fella cracks me good, but I didn't go down. I had thet other fellas' rifle so I returns the favor an'

301

swung it like a club. Down he tumbles into the hole. By that time I was jest tryin' to git the hell out of there. Then the curtain come down on me and out go the lights. That's all I remember until I felt somebody pullin' on my legs, draggin' me out from under all them bodies. Best I kin figger, they thought I was dead until I started into cussin' them. Next thing I know, I'm walkin' here with you'all."

"They's more n' more fellas comin' in all the time," the wounded man said. "A few days ago there were jest a few dozen. Now they's gotta' be a few hundred with us. I can tell you that I don't like the idea of goin' to no prison camp. From what I heard it's a death sentence."

"Don't take no heed to them stories, what you hear from people is mostly made up," the sergeant said with sadness in his voice. "Seems like these days you can't take nobody fer their word. Even a General's."

"I hope yer' right, sergeant. I heard stories about a prison camp up there in New York somewhere. They say a hunert' men die there a week."

One of the guards had been noticing the conversation. All talking between prisoners was strictly forbidden and he made his way over to the two of them. He shoved the wounded man from behind who fell heavily to the ground. The other soldier grabbed out to steady the man, but he was to late. The wounded man fell face forward onto the ground and screamed in agony. He held his wounded arm and looked at the guard with hatred. The sergeant stripped off his shirt and ripped the arm from it. He quickly fashioned a sling and helped the man to his feet. The guard looked at both of them warily.

"No talking is allowed. Now get going." The guard threatened them with his rifle. The bayonet glinted in the late sun of the afternoon.

"What is the matter with you, can't you see this fella' is in a bad way? What yer want an' go do somethin' like that fer'," the sergeant shouted loudly. The young Federal soldier began to feel intimidated by the bellicose southern sergeant. He nervously looked about him at the many faces of the prisoners that had witnessed the ugly incident. Many of them were muttering under their breaths and looked at him with utter contempt. The boy did not like the many rebel soldiers who had begun to crowd around him.

"Sergeant Kile," he shouted loudly, "Sergeant Kile, we got a smart mouthed Johnny here causing trouble."

The Confederate sergeant put both of his hands in the air.

"Whoa, young fella'. Holt' on there boy. I don't want no trouble, Yank. All's I want is fer' you to have some kinda' consideration fer' a fella' what's hurt an' can't cause you no harm."

He turned to see a Federal sergeant rapidly approaching him in the company of some very angry looking blue clad soldiers. Before he could say another word, the Federal sergeant smashed his fist into his face. He staggered a few feet and tears immediately filled his vision, a natural reaction from the impact, but he did not go down. He recovered quickly.

"All of you had better mind your own business and get heading down that road if you know what's good for you," the Federal sergeant announced loudly. The crowd of men began to break up as the rest of the column of soldiers swung around them. Another man helped the wounded soldier, and he started to head away. As the southern sergeant turned, the Federal moved and stepped in his way.

"Not so fast Reb. We know how to treat troublemakers. I can look right at you and see nothin' but trouble right in your eyes."

"I guess you ain't as stupid as you look, then, Yank, 'cause trouble an' me go hand in hand. But not this time. That boy knocked that fella' to the ground. Anybody kin' see that the man was hurt. He did it out of his havin' a mean streak, plain an' simple."

The Yankee sergeant delivered a blow to the sergeant's mouth and this time the rebel was knocked to his knees. He wiped his bloody mouth and slowly struggled to his feet, his hands balled up in fists.

The Federal soldier pulled out a revolver and pointed it directly at him.

"Don't sass me. That will teach you to talk back, you damned traitor," he said.

The Confederate sergeant looked at the Federal soldier with a gleam of murder in his eyes. It was so stark in it's intent that the Union soldier stepped a few feet away from him. He cocked the pistol.

"C'mon Johnny, let's do it."

The Confederate soldier continued to stare at him. The Federal sergeant was aware that more of the prisoners were starting to stop and take note of what was occurring. This one unruly rebel soldier was once again creating an ugly scene.

"Keep that crowd movin', dammit,' The Federal sergeant shouted. Several Union soldiers began shoving and threatening the prisoners. They moved away reluctantly.

"Head down that- a-way," the federal motioned with his pistol towards the woods.

"The hell I will. You ain't trapsin' me out in the woods so you kin' shoot me like a sick dog. You gonna' shoot, then do it here in front of all these fellas'. Maybe if they see you shoot an' innocent man, maybe it will start some real trouble."

"You got one minute to start heading that-a way or I will give you a new set of nostrils high on your forehead, bumpkin."

The Confederate yelled loudly to the passing prisoners.

"Go to hell, you chicken shit bastard," he roared. "Put that pistol away so you an' me kin' tangle. Then we'll see who the better man is when you ain't holdin' all the cards. Put it down if you got the nerve. A fair fight, jest' you an' me"

"Some of the prisoners looked anxiously at the spectacle but they were prodded and shoved forward like cattle. Some continued to watch as they trudged along before the guards who pushed them along noticed them. Several more Federal soldiers appeared, frightened at the disturbance.

The Federal sergeant smiled.

"We got us an attempted escape here boys. One rotten apple can spoil the whole barrel."

He blew a whistle that hung from his neck. All the Confederate soldier heard was the sound of many footsteps coming in all directions at him. He swung wildly and connected, but then he was overwhelmed. They held him and beat him savagely. A whole platoon of northern men continued to keep the prisoners moving forward. Two-dozen men began to kick and stomp him towards the woods. They picked him up and pummeled him again until they were exhausted. They made a circle around him and took turns beating him. His beaten was hidden from the eyes of his fellow prisoners. The soldiers beat him until their fists ached. In their frenzy, they beat him out of his clothing. His shirt and pants were so saturated in his blood that they simply came apart as they pulled and tugged to stand him up just to knock him down again.

They grabbed his arms and his legs and flung the naked body into the woods to hide what they had done, quite satisfied that they had killed him. The Federal sergeant looked at the bloody body and decided not to waste a bullet on a dead man. They grinned and slapped each other on the back and walked quickly towards the disappearing column of prisoners congratulating themselves on a job well done. It was July ninth, 1863.

The relief wagon that Reverend Ellis had secured for Jim and Benjamin was intercepted by a Union cavalry patrol five miles from the battlefield site. Two volunteers rode in the wagon while Ben and Jim rode fast horses. The Federal soldiers searched the wagon containing clothing, blankets and medical supplies and the troopers questioned all of the relief party. The Union cavalrymen were astounded at the group's request and their intended mission, which Ben had stated so succinctly and eloquently. The captain of the cavalry troop was quite impressed by the young man's directness. He was not impressed with the youth's long-windedness, however.

"Jah, I huff' heard enoughf. You will come mitt unser gruppen und huff' a nice chat mitt Colonel Horche. He will tell you vhat' you are to do. These roads are still verboten to civilians.Forbidden. Der rebel stragglers disguise themselves as der civilians und try to get away."

"And just how long will this take," Ben said impatiently.

"I think you talk sehr schmart, but I do not think you verstandt der danger you are in. Der roads und der woods still hold der rebels stragglers. Gott ein himmel, it is a wonder that they haven't killed all of you chust for your horses. You are not their favorite color. You are fair game to them. We patrol to stop them. If we see them, und they don't surrender ve finish them. They are Kaput. If they see you, you are Kaput. Niche var?"

This was new and frightening news for both Ben and Jim.

"Ve see your people, ve send them into camp. I tell you this. Der colonel, he vants to help you, if he permits you then so it is. It ist all in his goodt hande, Jah? Now, I am a busy man. Please follow me."

They watched the captain gallop to the head of his troop. Jim signaled the wagon driver to try to stay up with the troopers. The captain slowed his mount to a canter as he drew abreast of his lead riders. Ben put spurs to horseflesh and the horse bolted forward overtaking both the captain and his lieutenant. The captain ignored the rambunctious Ben as he raised his arm at the approach of one of his flanking scouts. He signaled a complete halt to his men. His hand signal called a walk to the troop ,and as they slowed a rider approached them in a slow trot. He saluted the captain.

"Captain Mueller, we got contact," the rider said.

"Jah. Und how many?"

"Can't know for sure, captain. They tried to bushwhack an ambulance team. We heard the shooting and come in quick. They scattered into the woods. Sergeant Goff said to ride ahead and let you know."

"Any casualties?" the captain asked.

"Yes sir. One of the wounded men being transported died when the ambulance crashed into a tree. The ambulance driver ran with the first shot and the wagon went down the road out of control and smashed into a tree. It's all in pieces." The cavalry trooper looked suspiciously at Ben and Jim.

"What's with the contraband, Captain?" he asked. Captain Mueller ignored his scout's question entirely.

"Find Sergeant Goff. Tell Goff to keep this road open. Tell him that B troop vill be here in less than vun hour. The contraband, I think, ist none of your problem."

The cavalry corporal smiled a toothy grin.

"Yessir, Captain. Understood. I thought for a minute these contraband were our reinforcements, Captain."

"Always der funnyman, eh Turner? Shtop being a verdamnt funnyman, corporal. I huff seen a lot of dead funnyman in this war. Go," the Captain shouted angrily. The corporal saluted and raced away. The captain turned to Ben.

"You see. It ist sehr dangerous. They try to shteel der viskey from der ambulance und der horses. They are desperate, these rebels. Dey vould chew you up und schpit you out. You shtay mitt mir und C troop."

"For how long?" Ben asked.

"You huff anoder place to go? You are strange to me. I huff never heard a Negro speak der Inglish like you. I am vrom Hanover. Mien Inglish ist not so goot. Not even as goot as yours."

He looked at Ben for an explanation.

"I come to America to fight mitt Segal. Herr General Segal, now there ist ein mann. I fought mitt Segal for freedom in mien landt, against der tyranny. It vas not so goot in mien country und ve lost der war. Dot vas a long time ago, Jah? But today, I shtill fight for der freedom. Now I fights mitt General Custer. He ist chust a young poy, but he fights mitt der big palls, as you Americans say. Ve are der First Michigan Cavalry."

"It is my pleasure to meet you, Captain Mueller," Ben said.

"Jah, I am almost sure. Now, if you will keep up mitt der little vagon und try not to get all your schmart brains blown out all over your goot suit, you must not get in mien vay again. I vill be very busy so don't follow me closely, ever again, niche vart? It vill definitely not be goot for you."

The captain bellowed a command so loudly and so elemental in its Uhlan savagery that it startled Ben.

"Sehr goot! C troop. Jah, Mitts mir! C troop, with me. At der gallop." The cavalry troop followed Captain Mueller as he wheeled part of his command directly at a thin patch of forest. Ahead Ben could se an ambulance wagon. Several bodies were strewn in the road. He watched as the captain and his men disappeared over a hill and then they were gone. The rest of the federal cavalry rode along with Ben and Jim staring intently ahead into the distance. It was 8 p.m., July ninth, 1863.

In the brief time that Tom had been with Mr. Gardner, his condition had steadily improved. Mr., Gardner had even shaved Tom's head and put a smelly ointment on his burns that apparently worked. He had been given new clothing that belonged to the photographer and he looked exactly what he was now, a photographer's assistant. Billy had recently departed, and Mr. Gardner diligently taught Tom what was expected of him in his new role. During the night, Tom would explain the causes and reasons of his being in the Army of Northern Virginia, and Mr. Gardner would teach Tom the great mystery of capturing images on glass plates. Tom told Mr. Gardner his story and Mr. Gardner shared in kind about his trade.

"After the captain of the steamship arrived in Norfolk, Huck and I were on are own. We got odd jobs like cleaning stables and sweeping floors but the looks people would give you because you were not in uniform and fighting for the cause got to us. We couldn't make ends meet and we were destitute. Finally, we enlisted. Everybody figured the war would be over in a couple of months. That was almost three years ago," Tom said as he finished washing a photographic plate.

Mr. Gardner examined a series of photos that he had allowed Tom to take and develop. He scanned the photo with a critical eye.

"No one expected this war to last this long," Mr. Gardner said. He continued to study the photograph. He looked at the image with a magnifying glass. He sighed and sat down.

"Tom, I must tell you this, son, and I hope it doesn't go to your head. The photographs that you took yesterday. I was looking at them. Somewhere in me was a little voice screaming for there to be a flaw, a mistake, something that was obviously wrong or something that I could teach you about the craft. I guess it was my vanity. These photographs are flawless. They are absolutely perfect, the lighting, the composition. Everything is perfect. Tom, in all my years in this business, I have never seen anyone learn the basic techniques as quickly as you have. You seem like you have been doing this all your life, not someone who first was introduced to the art less than a week ago."

'That's because I got a good teacher," Tom said.

"No. I tried to teach Billy and I took more time with him than you but he was inept at best. My boy, you have an inherent God given gift. Heed well what I tell you. The speed that you mix the needed chemicals with total accuracy and speed, why, I have never in all my days seen anything even remotely coming close to this. You surpass me. You mystify me."

Tom looked at the photographs that he had taken. It was a series that he had taken of the Federal dead of the Iron Brigade. They lay where they had fallen near McPherson's woods. This Union regiment had slammed into the vanguard of the Confederate Assault on the first day of the battle and had blunted the southern attack. They had paid dearly in their endeavor. The Iron brigade, possibly one of the best in the Army of the Potomac, had been shattered. The dead had been a shot that Tom had asked to take, and Mr. Gardner had allowed him to take them.

"You like them?" he asked.

"They are masterpieces. They are magnificent. This quality of work is not usually found in a novice. I think you have found your calling. If someone had told me that you had never taken a photograph before these, I would call them a bald faced liar."

"Maybe it's just beginners luck," Tom said.

"And maybe you should acknowledge a God given gift," Mr. Gardner said flatly. "Anyway, we must be off this morning. We are to meet Matthew. Gather everything up quickly now. I want Matthew to show you a technique called stereoscopic photography. It's putting two images together for a panoramic sweep of the subject. Truly innovative," Mr. Gardner said enthusiastically.

"I'm going for a bowel movement. Start packing," Mr. Gardner said as he looked about for paper.

Tom began to gather the plates of glass in their wooden crates into the wagon. As he hefted one through the door, he turned to see a group of blue uniforms around him. He had been replaying Mr. Gardner's words in his head so intently that he had never even seen their approach. He glanced around nervously for Mr. Gardner, resisting strongly his urge to run from the group of curious soldiers.

"Good morning," one of the soldiers said. Tom did not know what to say or do. Mr. Gardner was no where in sight. He ignored them and continued to load the wooden crates.

"Hey, bald man. Are you deef? And what is with your face, it's all burned up. Hey, fella. I'm talking to you," the Union sergeant said angrily. Tom put down his crate and faced the Union soldier. He shrugged his shoulders and grinned.

"Par le tout ser ville plait," Tom said. The Union soldier pointed his revolver at Tom. Tom noticed the whistle that hung around his neck.

"What the hell did you just say?" the sergeant asked angrily.

"Je roi le quois le semena? Tom sputtered.

308

"He's talkin' Frenchy talk, sergeant Kile. I heard them talk like that when I was down in New Orleans. This fella is a frog, ain'' I right, Frenchy?"

"Boos se swant sur le pont," Tom said quickly. Sergeant Kile returned his revolver and looked at Tom as though he were insane.

"Damned foreigner, are you. You speekee dee english, froggy boy?" he said loudly.

Tom shook his head. Mr. Gardner appeared walking out of the woods. He was tightening his belt and buttoning his fly.

"Good morning gentlemen. How are all of you this fine morning." Mr. Gardner said.

"Just fine," the sergeant said, "Now that there's somebody around here I can talk to. Your boy here can't talk American."

"Coot de witt bolanger de-haul assi," Tom said. Mr. Gardner nodded his head in agreement.

"Vraiment. Oui, Mon ami." Mr. Gardner said.

"What he say. That foreign talk sounds like a bunch of gibberish to me?"

"He reminds me that we must be on our way, and quickly. We have an appointment we must keep and the sun waits for no man. Now, how may I help you."

"We was just curious. I never seen a photograph wagon before. Just wanted a peek, is all. We just got through taken a bunch of rebel scum to the rail head down the road and we was just goin back when we spotted you here."

"I see," Mr. Gardner said. He turned to Tom.

"Toute le monde sera la. Vit..vit," he said brusquely to Tom and waved his hands at him. Tom took his cue and hurriedly went back to loading the wagon.

"How the hell did he get all burned up like that?" the sergeant asked.

"He is new to this country and my own French is pretty bad. We carry a lot of volatile chemicals needed to take the photographs and when he was mixing a batch, I mistakenly gave him the wrong orders and the resultant explosion was most dreadful. It blew him right out of his shoes, I'm afraid to say. In fact, we carry enough chemicals that if the wrong amount was mixed incorrectly, the explosion would be similar to a thousand pounds of gunpowder going off all at once."

Tom came out of the wagon holding two large bottles of chemicals.

"Le oui .oui c'est la plume?" Tom asked, "Cou le d'jour dehaul assi?" The soldiers faced blanched with Tom's sudden appearance. They began to back away from Tom and Mr. Gardner.

"Non, Non. Quelle idiot. C'est la boom de la boom boom. Idiot," Mr Gardner said angrily. Tom began to walk towards the soldiers who backed further and further away from them.

"Boys, it is time to go. Good luck there fella'," Sergeant Kile said, quickly turning away. They practically scurried away from Tom and his employee.

"Does anyone want their photograph taken? I can give you a good deal," Mr. Gardner shouted to his rapidly disappearing guests.

"Thanks but no thanks," one of the soldiers shouted. They soon were over the hill in the road and out of sight.

"They were some mean looking cusses," Tom said. Mr. Gardner patted Tom on his shoulder.

"How is the arm? Let's take a look at it."

Tom removed his shirt and Mr. Garner helped Tom unwrap the bandage.

"When I first saw this, it was full of maggots. But I believe if it hadn't been for all of those maggots you would have died of gangrene. The maggots had eaten all the dead and torn flesh. When you lay out there in that field of dead all those days and nights, they ate all the poison out and left you with a clean wound. The exit wound is just as clean. When we stop, I will put more of the sulfur powder on it. Don't overwork it just because you are feeling better. Take it slow now and get the horses. I will take care of the rest. I can't wait to see Mr. Brady's expression when I introduce you to him. Now, off with you. We have a busy day ahead of us and many miles to travel."

The next few days flew by. The meeting with Mr. Gardner's superior, Matthew Brady, had not taken place so Mr. Gardner continued to instruct Tom in taking photographs. Tom's skills with processing the photographic plates grew daily. His newly acquired expertise at all facets of photography continued to baffle Mr. Gardner. They commented on the weather and small talk as they headed away from Gettysburg. Mr. Gardner saw something ahead that struck his interest.

A group of Federal cavalry had three southern soldiers in custody. They sat next to a rail fence and looked up at Mr. Gardner in defiance.

"Tom, stop the wagon. Prepare me several plates. I must have this," he said.

Tom stopped the wagon and did as he was instructed. Mr. Gardner hopped from the wagon and walked towards a mounted Federal officer. The officer showed interested in the photography wagon and the man who approached him.

"Good afternoon, Captain. What do we have here," he asked.

"Goodt afternoon. Jah, what I got ist some stragglers. Ve are giving der horses rest. Ve hoff been riding hard all day. You are der famous photograph mann, Jah?"

"Yes, I am. Captain, I must have a photograph of these three soldiers, preferably standing next to the rail fence. Would you mind if I shot them?"

"No, take your photograph. You call this a' Shot'?"

"Yes," Mr. Gardner said happily. Captain Mueller laughed and scratched his head.

"This I think ist funny, Jah. Better you take your 'shot' of them than me. If I am to take my "shot' of them, you vill hoff no photograph. Men, listen. Dis ist a Photograph man. He asks me if he can take a shot of der prisoners. I say better for them to be shot by him than shot by us, niche var?"

"Thank you, Captain?"

"Kapitan Mueller, First Michigan Cavalry. I hoff always been interested in this business. May I vatch how you take the "Shot?"

"By all means," Mr. Gardner said.

Captain Mueller dismounted and keeping one hand on his revolver walked a few paces towards the prisoners.

"Der mann ist a Photograph mann. He vants to take der photograph. Kooperate mitt der mann, Jah. Do vhat he says. Be goot poys or I vill give you der teufel. I will make life hell for you."

The prisoners both stood up. Mr. Gardner could see that Tom had parked the wagon and was busily and skillfully preparing the equipment needed for the picture. He noticed that two of the prisoners had scavenged a lot of gear from the surrounding fields. The men had realized that they were going to go to a prisoner stockade so they had collected as many items as they could. They wore this extra gear like insulation against the dangers and deprivations they knew they would face. Mr. Gardner saw that the third prisoner was not. The man obviously had been beaten because his cheeks were still puffy and bruised.

"Assistant, bring me a bowl filled with flour and one of my brushes. I will show you a trick of the trade," he shouted to Tom.

"Soldier, I would like to take a photograph but I need to disguise the, um, damage that someone has inflicted on your face. I hope that you don't mind. I promise that I will not harm you."

"Do what you got to do," the man said.

Tom brought the requested items and handed them to his mentor.

"Take careful attention. I will touch the subject up so that the bruises will not be noticed," Mr. Gardner said. He dipped the small brush into the flour as Tom held onto the bowl. The prisoner looked up at the sky and suddenly looked at Tom. For the first time, Tom looked at the man's battered face and then each man froze as each had seen a ghost.

"Tom, if you paid for that haircut, then you should try get your money back. You got robbed," the soldier whispered.

"Huck," Tom blurted out. Mr. Gardner saw that the Captain had caught the exchange of greetings. Mueller approached the group with a curious look on his face.

"You, soldat. How do you know this mann, hier?" he said quickly. Huck was lost for words. Captain Mueller watched Tom carefully.

"Soldat, I huff' given you der question, jah. Maybe you do not hear me so goot. So I ask you again. This time you give mir der answer, jah? How do you know this mann hier?"

Huck looked into the distant tree line and remained silent. Tom suddenly grabbed Huck by both his shoulders.

"I can answer this question, Captain. This man is my cousin from Maryland. I can't believe it. Mr. Gardner, even you didn't recognize Huck. This is unbelievable," Tom cried. "I didn't recognize him either at first, Mr. Gardner, because his face is swollen so."

"You men are der family?" Mueller questioned.

"We sure as hell are. His daddy is my daddy's brother," Tom said convincingly. Tom embraced Huck in a bear hug and began to pound him on the back in affection.

"Easy there, cousin. I'm all banged up," Huck said.

At the mention of the identity of the rebel soldier, Mr. Gardner realized that this was the person that Tom had mentioned countless times in their conversations together. Mr. Gardner jumped fully into the story.

"My Huck, how you have changed. It has been three years since I have last seen him, Captain. He used to work in the studio with his cousin. I have known both of them since they were ten years old. What a strange turn of events," he said grinning.

Captain Mueller shook his head.

"Ist dot so?" he said suspiciously.

Mr. Gardner sensed the suspicion of the Captain and acted quickly.

"Captain, may I have a word with you in private. Please?" he asked.

The captain walked a few feet away from them with Mr. Gardner.

"Captain, what I am about to ask is very irregular. I would not do this for merely anyone. The lad's parents died in a terrible coach accident when he was fourteen. The only family he had left was Tom, my current assistant, who I already had recognized when he was very young as having extraordinary talents in this profession. I practically raised the both of them."

The Captain nodded his head thoughtfully.

"Certainly you can see that fate has delivered this young man into our hands. So many young lives have been lost in this cruel war. You can see for yourself that the young man is undone. He has been cruelly beaten. He probably would not survive the rigors of life in a stockade."

"How is it that der mann ist ein Rebel soldat und der odder boy ist not?"

"Captain, my studio is in Washington. You surely have seen how the city is, I am sure. There are rebel sympathizers that live in the capitol of our very own nation. He probably got carried away with all of the adventure and joined the army when he was in Maryland, probably to visit the graves of his dear parents. I know that he now regrets ever having lifted a hand against our great country. If you could see in your heart to release him to me, I will guarantee that he will never again lift a finger in disservice to his true nation."

"You vant I should turn him over to you?" Captain Mueller asked in astonishment.

"What is one more rebel prisoner, Captain. It will cost us more to confine him, feed him and clothe him in confinement anyway. That is if he survives. He is a good boy. Captain, I will be bluntly honest with you. I do this not out of just humanitarian reasons. I confess that I could use his help. Like I said, he knows quite about the business and I desperately need his help."

The captain smiled and then began to laugh.

"I thought so. In America there is always der chase for der geld, der money. I should huff known."

"I will make the deal even sweeter. The next time that you are in Washington, I will take your portrait for free. No money," Mr. Gardner said. He reached into his inside pocket and pulled out a card and handed it to the captain.

"So, you vill take a free 'shot' of me." Captain Mueller turned his back on Gardner and strode threateningly over to Huck.

"Soldat, lift der hande, der right vun."

Huck did as he was told.

"Repeat after me," the captain said, as he watched Huck raise his hand in the air.

"Icht shvear nehvar again to make der fight against mien country. So help me, Gott."

Huck repeated the words. Captain Mueller turned and faced Tom and Mr. Gardner.

"Goot. I now pronounce you paroled on der feldt. He ist all yours. You may now kisst der bride."

The smoky fire snapped and popped as Mr. Gardner listened to Tom tell of the harrowing series of events that had transpired the very last time that he had spoken to Huck. He had learned a small part of Tom' story over the last few days but in Huck's company Tom had told the full story in more horrifying detail and deep emotion. The full realization of what Tom had been through made Mr. Gardner shudder as Tom told of his role in the fratricidal conflict. Tom recounted in detail all of the names of the men that he had seen die or had been wounded. Mr. Gardner learned that this young man had seen practically every person that he had known in the last three years die violently.

He reflected inwardly on his own role in the great and horrible events that he was now a witness to. He was, as a man, preserving a record of the ghastly war. The record was one done in light that would exist for the coming unborn generations to reflect upon and wonder. Perhaps these yet born would be the ones who would be able to put down for countless others the causes and reasons for so much sacrifice, death, and destruction. Maybe they would be able to see his work, one day and give light to the darkness of the war. Perhaps this was enough. He stood up feeling small and insignificant. He walked towards the wagon still wondering at the reasons behind why his country had self-destructed.

"That's about it," Tom said finishing his story. "As far as I can figure, there ain't nobody left. That shelling was the worst I ever experienced. The only reason why I'm even here is that I got blown into a hole under a tree. Somebody had not finished digging a grave and that's what saved my life. Nothing above ground could live through that bombardment."

Huck moaned softly as he changed his position on front of the fire. He watched Mr. Gardner walk towards the wagon and enter it.

"What about Vernon?" Asked Huck.

"I'm not sure. He wasn't with our group when the artillery started hitting us. I don't know. That artillery hit us like a chain lightning. Some if the shells hit the tops of the trees. The metal came out of the sky like rain. It caught us all standing around. I hope he is alive, but I wouldn't want to bet on it.

Tom saw that Mr. Gardner had lit a candle and was rummaging around in the wagon for something.

"What is it with that fella?" Huck asked.

"You mean Mr. Gardner?"

"Yes, Huck answered. "I don't get it. He went out on a limb for me. He could have just buried me in a deep hole, yet he didn't. What fer?"

"We got whupped. We will lose this war. I ain't never seen nothing more clearer in my life. Nearly getting killed has opened my eyes. What the General said about the war being almost over? Remember? This battle was supposed to end the war. I guess the Yankees did not read the script because they won this fight," Tom said angrily. "That was bullshit, all the General told us. If I had wanted to get killed fighting, I could have stayed some and got killed fighting. It seems that this war will never be over but it is for me. Vicksburg has fallen. The south is all done and so am I. This battle was our high water mark. It is all down hill from here."

Tom tossed a small log into the fire.

"Think of this. Every soul, every living human being that we know has been killed. They are all gone. I was never all in fire with the "Cause" to begin with and I sure as hell don't want to die in a losing cause. I got caught up in it all by circumstances and not by any loyalty that I felt for the Confederacy. My loyalty was with the good fellas that I served with all them long years and they all gone up. I will miss them all dearly but there ain't a damned thing that 'I can do for all those poor fellas. Certainly getting killed won't bring them all back. Both of us have come within a hairsbreadth of getting killed. I have done all I can do and so have you. It's high time that we start thinking about ourselves for a change. High time," Tom said.

Mr. Gardner returned with a bottle. He handed it to Huck who threw back a wealthy amount of its contents. Huck passed the bottle to Tom and Tom drank moderately from it. He passed it to Mr. Gardner. Mr, Gardner had obviously taken a few belts off of it while he was alone in the wagon because his words were already slurred and his eyes were starting to look watery.

"Great photographs, my boy," he said. "Mr. Brady will be surprised when I tell him that it was not I who took them. He will surely put them in the exhibit that he plans in Washington and you will be a part of it. You too, Huck.

"I don't know nothin' about them photographs," Huck said.

"Thass' alright. We will need someone in other capacities. I mean in the way of lifting and carrying. That is if you are up to it. How do you feel?"

Huck laughed causing Tom to smile.

"Put it this way," Huck began. "I received a fair amount of beatings from my Pap when I was a youngin'. Old Pap there gave me plenty of practice in takin' a whuppin'. If an ass whuppin' could be marked down like in school, then I passed with high grades. I am a scholar in the way of takin' an ass whuppin'. That is the only reason why I'm alive. This beatin' was the worst I ever got in all my born days. Them boys was so intent in stompin' my brains out that they were kickin' and punchin' each other in their enthusiasm to beat me to death. I played possum every time I came to, but that didn't last too long. I figured I could outlast the bastards but I'd b e a liar if I tolt you that I did. Plain truth is that they figured they had kilt' me. I was sure that they wuz going to."

He reached for the bottle that Mr. Gardner handed him and threw another healthy amount of the whiskey into his stomach. He made a face as the alcohol burned the inside of his mouth.

"I came to cause there's this big nigger pourin' water on my face. I'm laying there buck naked and they takes what they got and wraps me up. His whole family was there watchin' out, all scared like. I had blood comin' out of my ears and my teeth was all loose. They had hidin' in the woods an' had seen the whole thing, from the start to finish. They took care of me. They shared what little they had with me. I owe them my life. We kept movin' about steady fer the next day or so an' then 'I realized who they be hidin' from. They wuz' hidin' from us. I knew that they would be better off without me, so I thanks them an' start down the road. Not even five minutes later, that big Dutch man puts a gun next to my head. I knew the jig was up. Those other two fellas gave me some clothes what they had so I could at least look like a soldier an' not a rag muffin. Shortly after, you show up."

He poked at the fire with a stick to turn the log on its side.

"Tom," he said. "What you said is true. The war is over fer me as well. They got us listed as kilt or missing an' all I kin say about it is good. Let sleeping dogs lay. I have done fit my last battle of this whole stinkin' murderous business," Huck said firmly. "Mr. Gardner, if I keep in knittin' up like the way I am, I will help you in any way I kin'. That medicine you got works wonders. Smells like rotten eggs but it works. I'm not nearly pissin' as much blood as I was a day ago."

"Mr. Gardner." Tom said. "I need to write a letter. I have to let someone know that I am still alive. Do you think that I could post a letter by and by?"

"To be sure. A sweetheart back home perhaps?"

Tom said nothing. He smiled and reached for the bottle of scotch.

CHAPTER SEVENTEEN

Henry Fowler listened attentively to the man sitting in front of his desk. Major Lehigh had insisted that he listen to what he had to say.

"I can't say fer sure that the man he was with was Quantrill, but I sure as hell knew who the other fella was," Mr. Flemming said.

"There's a good fellow. Please, take your time and leave out nothing," Henry said.

"I never fergit a face, Colonel. It is part of my business to know people. He had an eye patch over his eye and he had a scruffy lookin' beard, but like I sez, I never fergit a face, Especially his. He was always a pain in the ass when he was a boy. He used to whine and carry on whenever he was in the store an' he didn't have no money to buy no candy with. Sometimes I would slip him a piece of rock candy just to shut the little bastard up an' get him out the store."

Henry grew impatient but hid it well. He pretended to enjoy the man's company.

"I see," he said. "And what was the name of the fellow with the eye patch?" Henry asked.

"Ted Doudlass," Mr. Flemming said. Henry's eyebrows arched in surprise. The boy that he had supposedly killed all those many years ago outside of Lehigh's hotel was alive.

"Continue, "Henry said, writing the name quickly on his ledger.

"He comes' into my store with this short fella' with brown hair and a brown moustache. A mousy looking fella' with droopy lookin' eyes. He don't think I spot him, see. I heard tell that Doudlass got shot to death by the law in Kansas right before the war began along with his friend, Cecil Gordon. Everybody knows that Frank Gordon, the uncle of the boy what got kilt', rides with Quantrill. That Frank, he is a wild one. The man has got a temper that can melt hell when he's riled. There ain't a more furious bastard alive when he gets his dander up. I seen him demolish a bar full of these ig'orant shitkickers from Kansas once. He…"

Henry fought to keep his emotions in check. He refrained from jumping across the table and seizing the man by his throat. Henry hated long homespun tales. He despised the unsophisticated common man. He smiled pleasantly at Mr. Flemming.

"Quite. Please continue Mr. Flemming. I am a busy man. What exactly are you implying?"

"Well, like I said, I was kinda' surprised to see that he was still alive. He don't let out who he is and stays in the shadows. The other fella', he pulls out this paper what got bloodstains on it. It's a voucher to buy one hell of a lot of shot and powder. This mousy fella' claims to be a buyer for the Colorado cavalry, but I sees right through it. I never fergit' a face an' I kin' spot a pile of cowflop before I step into it, believe you me," Mr. Flemming said proudly.

Henry imagined the old man with a rope around his neck hanging from a large maple right outside of his office.

"Yes. Part of the business savvy that you have accumulated over the many years of being a merchant," Henry said condescendingly.

"Exactly. You're a smart man, Colonel, a good judge of horseflesh I'll bet," he said enthusiastically. "Anyway, they bought a hell of a lot of shot an' powder. I'm thinkin' to myself, just who the hell this short fellow was an' then it comes to me. We got southern sympathizers in town that hang together thicker then fleas on a mangy dog's back. I seen pitchers' drawn in the paper what this fella' Quantrill is supposed to look like an' he fit the damned bill. It all began to make sense. Doudlass was friends with the Gordon boy what got kilt' and that boys uncle rides with Quantrill. That fella' was Quantrill what was in my store. I swear on it."

With the mention of the name, Henry grew ecstatic. If he could kill or capture Quantrill, it would make his name a household word in this part of the country. Henry thirsted for fame and power.

"Quantrill," Henry screamed. "That brigand must be eradicated from the face of the earth. This Doudlass fellow, if I remember correctly, was supposedly killed in Kansas along with Cecil Gordon, although his body mysteriously disappeared in the confusion of the gunfight. It was assumed that his friends somehow were able to retrieve the body and escape. I remember reading about it in the newspaper. Five deputies were killed that day and those responsible were never brought to justice. Would you happen to know what happened to them?"

"Is there some kind of reward out fer them?" Flemming asked.

"Yes. There is a reward of five hundred dollars on each of their heads," Henry said.

"Good. One of them was named Thomas Sawyer an' the other, he went by this odd name his pap gave him, Huckleberry Finn. His friends called him Huck. That boy was a son-of-a- bitch, real squirrelly. His father was a mean drunkard', used the beat the boy like a dog. They lived in this rat hole shack down by the river. Sawyer was a conniving, scheming little bastard but that Huck was a pip."

Henry had known the names well. Doudlass had told all under the brutal questioning. Pete had beaten the names out of the Doudlass youth. What Flemming was saying was true. Henry rose and extended his hand to Mr. Flemming. He offered a most charming smile to his guest.

319

"Mr. Flemming, the information that you have provided us may just prove to be invaluable. I want to thank you for coming forward with it. You have done a patriotic dead in contacting Major Lehigh and I will forever be in your debt if it aids us in catching this mad dog killer."

Flemming released Henry's hand that he had been pumping and his expression changed quickly.

"Let's get somethin' straight, Colonel. I ain't come all this way to do a patriotic deed like you say. Five hundred dollars each is a whole lot of money. I know that there is a reward fer' that devil Quantrill an' more n'likely fer that Doudlass boy. I come here to make a deal. I did not go runnin' to the law when I saw them the first time. The law would have collected the reward money an' I'd just end up as the man who owned the store where Quantrill and his man was shot dead. There ain't no money in that." Flemming sized up the Colonel and boldly proceeded.

"What I want is to go fifty-fifty. I ain't that good with a fire arm no more, but if I could get you to loan me a good man with steady hands, we will put that bastard an' his friend in a pine box. Fifty-fifty."

Henry smiled. He wanted to rip the older man's throat out with his teeth.

"Colonel, I am a realist an' the most real thing to me is cash on the barrelhead. Patriotism won't feed yer', but green backs will. When this war ends, I intend to end up with more money in my pockets than when it started."

"I understand you perfectly," Henry said. "My sergeant will be at your business establishment as soon as it is humanly possible. I assure you that you will get your just rewards in this whole affair. Now, sir, if you would. The Major and I have much to do and the sooner we begin the better. We will contact you as soon as we are able. You will not be forgotten. The sergeant will escort you to the train."

Pete entered and Mr. Flemming followed him out of Henry's office. Mason entered and closed the door. They watched as Pete led Mr. Flemming down the street and towards his hotel.

"So, what do you think, Henry?" Lehigh asked.

"It was Quantrill. There is no doubt. The Doudlass boy and the other two that escaped me must certainly ride with that scum. I failed to make an example of Doudlass, Sawyer and the other cretin, Huck. If Quantrill is bold enough to ride into town with just one man, then he will feel comfortable enough to do it again. I want you to go to this town, Mason. Select your men carefully, only those you consider trust worthy. Keep the number small. Find out the names of all southern sympathizers in this town and watch their comings and goings. See where all these rats live. Start with the Gordon household, then the Doudlass's and the rest of them. Do not trust the telegraph and do not use it. Send all information to me by courier only. This town sounds like a nest of rebels. If Quantrill rears his head again in that stink hole, we will have him. Start today."

"The job's as good as done, Henry," Lehigh said. He turned and started to walk away.

"Mason, one last thing,'' Henry said.

"What is it, Henry?"

"Make sure Mr. Flemming never reaches the town alive. Make sure he disappears and is never found. I want that sinner dead before tonight is over.'"

"Henry, that son-of-a-bitch is already drawin' flies but he just don't know it yet. He will disappear like spit on a hot griddle."

Henry sat down as Mason walked out of his office. Henry's latest attempt at gaining a general's star had failed. The trip to Washington had been a disaster and the secret meeting in Rochester had almost landed him on the hot plate of his most deadly enemy, General Halleck. 'Old Brains" would have taken Henry to the wood shed. All that he had managed to do was to secure the position of Deputy Regional Adjutant. At least it kept his rank a Colonel.

With the capture of the outlaw Quantrill, all that would change. He knew that in the future, higher office demanded that he hold the rank of general. First it would be Senator Fowler and then who knows. The stars were the limit. Henry was wealthy and had all of the correct political connections. He had all the time in the world. The office of the Presidency beckoned him forward and once that was achieved all of his enemies, 'Old Brains' Halleck included, would feel his wrath. But he knew of one person especially who would be the immediate recipient of his revenge and that would be that dammed uppity nigger Douglass.

Matthew Brady was beside himself with anger when Mr. Gardner told him who his assistants were. Rebels soldiers. Mr. Brady could not believe how foolish Mr. Gardner had been to take under his wing the two men. If the press were ever to learn that these two men were rebel soldiers who traveled with the army in sensitive areas, anything might happen to them. They could be accused of spying for the south and summarily executed.

"Have you entirely lost your mind or are you so profoundly ignorant as to jeopardize my business and good name in this way and not even realize the implications or what could be the consequences of your actions?"

Mr. Gardner was stunned.

"Why don't you simply pull out a pistol and shoot me in the head. It would be far faster than what you do to me with this bit of information. You are ripping my guts out with this stupidity and I don't need this," he shouted.

"Calm down, Matthew. They will surely hear you," Mr. Gardner said quietly.

"I don't give a tinkers damn. How stupid can you be? There are some in the army that consider us a nuisance at best. If word were ever to get out that we travel in the company of two rebel soldiers dressed as civilian Photography assistance, my name would be ruined. My name would be dragged through the muck and the mire. The trust that I have built up with the army, my reputation, my credibility, and my life's work would be gone in a flash. These two could be shot as spies. Did your small pea brain ever think of that you blithering idiot."

"But Mr., Brady," Mr. Gardner began.

"But my ass. They have got to go, no if's, and's, or but's possible. They are a liability to me and I won't tolerate anyone or anything that would put my business at risk. No one ever gave me a handout when I first began. I created my business with just the sweat of my brow and my own two hands. If you wish to take in every stray you find, do it on your own time, not mine, damn it."

"Please, just listen to me Matthew. One of these fellows is a diamond in the rough. He takes photograph like he has been doing it all his life. You have seen the series that he has taken. They are perfect. Matthew, he would be an asset for us. He.."

"If their identities were ever discovered, the authorities would never trust us again. They would never let us near a battle site. You would end up your days taking photographs of naked whores assets in Mrs. Hall's fancy brothel in Washington, and you would deserve it, you twit." Matthew punched the wall of the wagon with his fist. Outside of the wagon, Tom and Huck listened to the loud discussion between Matthew Brady and Mr. Gardner.

"That is some kind of Donnybrook they have going," Tom said nervously.

"Donny who?" Huck asked. Tom listened closely but he could not make out what was being said.

"It does appear that Mr. Gardner's boss is not too happy with our being here. This argument only will have one loser and I am sure it will be us," Tom said with concern.

"Lets git'," Huck said. "This new fella' here might up an' turn us in to the next bunch of Yankees he sees."

"You have an uncanny reflex action simply to run when the squeeze is on. Now, I'm not saying that it is entirely wrong. I know that it often works. Discretion is the better part of valor. But think of what you have said and think of the fix that we are in," Tom said patiently.

"You got a plan?" Huck asked hopefully.

"No. I do not. But I do know that running is out. Where the hell are we going to run to?" Tom asked in despair. "Where are you going to take off to? The roads are crawling with Federal cavalry. Look around, there ain't even a fair patch of woods to hide in, just farm fields. Even if there was, how long do you think that you could go unseen eating roots and tree bark before some old fat farm dog would give you away? Use your head. You know they grabbed you the first five minutes you were alone and walking down road. Great furry blazes."

Mr. Brady came out of the wagon followed by a very worried looking Mr. Gardner. His forlorn expression said it all. Mr. Brady paced about nervously waiting for Mr. Gardner to break the bad news to them. Mr. Gardner looked balefully at his feet. He could not look Tom in the eyes. Mr. Brady saw that his assistant could not bring himself to do what needed to be done. He stopped wringing his hands and walked towards them.

"Boys, I don't know why Mr. Gardner has allowed this to happen. He should have known better. I take it for a serious lapse in judgment on his part," he began calmly. He tried to be friendly and smiled at them.

"The truth of the matter is that from here on in, you fellows are on your own. Please. Hear me out. It is not personal but strictly for business reasons why I make this decision. We, as photographers, travel everywhere the army goes. We travel in areas that are restricted to the public, areas that are very sensitive to the conduct of the war. We are allowed to do this because of the trust that I have built up with certain Army officers and politicians over the years. At first, they were hostile to me, but they have grown to accept my intrusion into their very secretive world. I remember when I was photographing a supply depot at Whitehouse, Virginia. I was detained and questioned by the guards who accused me of being a spy." Huck looked at him with distrust while Matthew continued to smile.

"We have been in staging areas and a host of other places that I dare not mention for obvious reasons. If in your travels with us, your true identities were discovered, that you were, in fact, two rebel soldiers traveling in some of these places in civilian dress you could be charged with espionage and shot as spies." Mr. Gardner sadly shook his head in agreement.

"I am sorry, Tom. What Matthew said is true. I did not even think of the consequences for you if someone were to question who you were," he said.

'The ramifications for my business would be calamitous. All the trust that I have been able to build over the past few years with the Army would come crashing down around my ears. I would be ruined," Matthew said. He grew serious and the smile vanished.

"So what you're sayin' is that you are givin' us the boot," Huck said.

"Yes, I'm afraid so. You are on your own for your own good as well as mine. Look at it this way. The only reasonable thing for you to do is to turn yourselves in to the proper authorities," Mr. Brady said.

Huck turned his back on Mr. Brady and walked away laughing. He soon returned grinning happily.

"Why, I would have to say that it is truly a good idea, one that I will take right to heart. It is a pure gem. Let me see if I got this right," Huck said dramatically. Mr. Brady grew nervous by Huck's dramatics.

"I'll go sit on that rail fence and patiently wait fer' the boys that nearly put me in the next world to come by. When they get here, I will introduce my self to those sons-a-bitches and let them finish what they started." Huck was yelling and Mr. Brady backed away from him.

"This time," he yelled, "They will beat my brains out. Sounds like a plan to me, how about you, Tom?"

"Mr. Gardner get the wagon ready for travel," Mr. Brady said. Mr. Gardner was pained and troubled by the whole situation.

"Perhaps if we could find the local officers of the law instead of the army. We could explain the situation.." Mr. Gardner began. Matthew turned on his assistant and exploded.

"What the hell is wrong with you? The matter is settled, you idiot. Hasn't anything we discussed sunk in to your numb skull? Do you not grasp any of it?" Mr. Brady was enraged and turned towards what he considered to be the problem at hand and pointed at them.

"It was not I that put you in the situation you both now find yourselves in. I had no part in that. I have no sympathy for any person that would raise their hand against the finest democratic government on earth. You followed the whims of your greedy leaders, those traitors who thought only of preserving the institution of slavery and nothing of preserving the Union. They would destroy freedom to preserve their privilege, their wealth, and their power that brought them such fabulous riches. You have made your bed, now you can lay in it, damn you." Mr. Brady reached in his belt for a large Colt army revolver and pointed it at Huck.

"I wish you only the best of luck. I wish you no harm. My business must come first, however, and in this matter I will not yield. I have worked too hard to lose it over something that can be easily avoided. That is the way it has to be. Now, for Christ's sakes Mr. Gardner, if you would prepare to move the wagon out, please. If not, then you can stay here with your new friends and try to explain to Federal soldiers that you are not a rebel soldier as they most certainly are."

324

"Yes sir," Mr. Gardner said. He walked away, looking over his shoulder at the sad scene that he felt responsible in creating.

"Tom, if this can be any sort of consolation," Matthew began, "the photographs that you have taken are excellent in the extreme. The series of dead from the 'Iron Brigade" and the one you took of Huck sitting on the fence and the other rebel soldiers standing by it are works of art. I can't even tell that Huck's face was swollen by the way you worked the lighting. Never before in my life have I seen a relative novice with such an innate sense of this craft in all my years experience as a photographer. You have a gift from the Almighty, son. It is almost supernatural in its implications. It is as if fate has decreed you to be here at this point in time in history so that Mr. Gardner and myself would recognize this remarkable talent. When this war is over you must come and see me at my studio in Washington. I will have a job waiting there for you. Mr. Gardner, are you about ready?"

Mr. Brady offered Tom his hand and they shook.

"Good luck son, and remember what I said."

Tom simply nodded. Mr. Brady offered Huck his hand, but Huck walked away instead. Matthew hurried to his stallion and hurriedly mounted, keeping a wary eye on Huck. Mr. Gardner set out in the wagon and they soon disappeared down the Hanover Road. It was a speck against the brown and green of the road as Tom sat down by the roadside. The grass that bordered the road waved with the afternoon breeze.

"I hope he posts the letter I gave him," Tom said. Huck dropped down to his side and started to chew on a piece of long stemmed grass. They sat in silence for some time when Huck suddenly stood up and began to remove all of his clothing.

"What for?" Tom asked tiredly.

"You think I am teched', don't you?" Huck asked. "Good, 'cause that is exactly what I want the next group of Yankees to think. I want them to think that I have gone around the bend," he said, throwing his pants into the ditch by the road.

"I want to make them think that I am stark ravin' looney, naked as a jaybird and crazy as a bedbug. They don't shoot crazy people, Tom, but they sure as hell shoot spies. Them clothes that I had on before the two soldiers give' me was taken off dead men, but at least they was soldier clothes. Mr. Gardner made me throw them away an' put on his spare duds. Them duds kin' git' me shot and so kin' your'n."

Tom saw the logic of his friend statement of fact clearly. He stood up and began to strip as well. Huck flung his shoes into the field.

"The way I figgers', when the Yankees come, the most that they will do is laugh. Tom, I am way too busted up to catch another thrashin'. I am still pissin' blood. Another bangin' like the last one, and I'm off to the Pearly Gates, beggin' yer' pardon."

Tom looked at Hucks body. It was a mass of blue, red, and purple bruises and he knew this to be true. As he removed all of his clothing as well, he felt as if he was having a burden lifted from his shoulders. He felt free, His cares and concerns melted away with each piece of clothing he flung away. When he finally stood naked, he stretched. The sun felt good on his injured chest.

"I should have done this days ago," he said.

It was almost intoxicating, this absence of dread. He had been in a state of depression for so long that the exhilarating sense of well being made him feel like a young boy. Once again, Huck and he were about to turn the world upside down and he felt the power of those earlier days grip his soul.

"Now what?" he asked.

"Any direction is as good as t'other," Huck said. He grinned happily like fool. Huck began to sing the words to "The Bonney Blue Flag'. As they began to walk towards the distant horizon on this beautiful July afternoon, Huck's voice boomed into the air. Tom laughed as Huck began to murder the lyrics to the song. Before long, they were both howling made up verses at the top of their lungs, shattering the stillness of the Pennsylvanian farm fields. They felt like they were Titans, as if they were about to storm and take by force Mount Olympus and lay waste to the ancient gods. They felt in control of their destinies, totally alive and indestructible.

The late owner and founder of Petersburg, Missouri's only brothel floated along with the current of the river. Small fish nibbled on her finely manicured toes and her hair floated about her head like a halo. She drifted along until she hit a sandbar and a passing riverboat's wake lifted and deposited her fully onto it. Several hours later, passing crows had begun to strip the body of its flesh. Another riverboat passing closely by the ever-shifting sandbar caused the wake of the boat to wash her free of it. She continued on her unscheduled trip down the river.

Pete had placed the Madam into the river on the direct orders of Major Mason Lehigh. Mason had kept the enraged Madam busy as she argued her salient points of non-cooperation with Mason's business proposition while Pete had stolen around her and sneakily placed the barrel of a derringer next to the back of her skull. She was abruptly removed from the business community by its small pop, the noise of the fired derringer being barely loud enough to disturb the sleep of her lazy Persian cat lying on her bed. She was wrapped in a rug and deposited in the river, not a fitting end for someone who had such finely tuned entrepreneurial skills as she had.

When Mason and Pete had first arrived in Petersburg on Henry's orders, they had learned of a house of ill repute that just bordered the small town. The owner, a middle aged woman, had followed the course of the army and saw a potential goldmine in a dilapidated house not a mile from the busy wharves that constantly flowed with soldier boys. Seeing its vast potential, the Madam had invested a little money into the building's renovation. Soon, the Madam was seeing a tidy profit flow into her project. Soldiers and sporting men were there every night in droves.

She was able to hire talent from all up and down the river and she became wealthy practically overnight. Profits stacked up and she expanded into a casino. Profits from the casino enabled her to expand and so on it went. Before too long, her establishment was competing with the better bordellos of St. Louis. Rumors circulated all the way to New Orleans about the fine fancy house up near St. Louis drawing more play for her tables and clients for her prostitutes.

Meanwhile, some local residents of Petersburg began to object to the house being in their town. The Mayor was on the payroll of the Madam as were all of the New Chamber of Commerce members. Anyone who protested too strongly about the whorehouse was admonished to be quiet. If that failed, they were bribed. If this did not bring the required results, then the person was labeled as a southern sympathizer and was hounded from town, ostracized, and cut off from the basic needs of everyday life. Most gave up in time and moved away.

There had been a sheriff in town a few years earlier, a terrible alcoholic, but he had accidentally shot himself to death cleaning a loaded shotgun in the dim light of the town's one room jailhouse. His sudden demise had been as much a shock to the towns' people as it had been to the sheriff. His unexpected departure had been due to his love of drink and misadventure with a loaded firearm and everyone had felt badly about his messy end. His position was never filled again because no crime that was noteworthy had occurred in the town in over a decade and people soon forgot that there had ever been a need for a sheriff in the first place. That is until the fancy house had reared its ugly head in their small town.

Certain religious families stubbornly bonded together and refused to move. For a brief time, there was cooperation between the pro-union faction and the pro-southern faction. These people, in a meeting, had decided to hold elections for a new sheriff, figuring that their man would be elected and enforce the town's ordinances about prostitution in the towns limits. An election was duly held and duly tampered with. Certain monies from the burgeoning account of the madam of the house insured that her own candidate was elected as the new law in Petersburg. The coalition fell apart.

The new sheriff had been the Madam's favorite barkeeper and muscle in the brothel that she had run in St. Louis. He was a burly mean type who loved to throw his weight around the town. He intimidated everyone including the Mayor. His favorite pastime during the weekends was to slip behind a boisterous soldier and deliver a bone-crushing blow to the back of the drunken soldier's head.

He would then drag the intoxicated soldier out of the establishment by his heels and throw him into the street as a warning to others. You were allowed to spend your money on the ladies, to gamble, and to drink. But the message was clear. If you could not control your liquor you would end up with a concussion at best with your pockets turned inside out in the middle of the street.

One time some drunken soldiers had stood their ground against the sheriff. The sheriff had seemingly backed down and had offered to buy them all a drink on the house. The soldiers had accepted his generous peace offering. He had ordered several more shots for his new friends and when they had been sufficiently plied with enough expensive bourbon and their guard was down, he proceeded to easily shoot them all to death at the bar. Many well paid witnesses had stepped forward to say the sheriff had killed them all in self-defense and the matter was officially closed.

Once the townspeople realized just who and what they were all dealing with, all opposition from the good people of the town ended abruptly. The pro-southern families moved away to the fringes of the town to support each other the best way they could. The sheriff reigned supreme in town and his word was the law.

Everything was looking positively lucrative for the Madam until the arrival of Major Mason Lehigh. Mason, upon arriving in Petersburg to conduct his spying operation, had learned of the Madam and the huge profits that she was accumulating every week. It peaked the Major's interest. Since his mission was to gather information, no one in town knew that Mason was even connected to the military. Mason made three other soldiers live outside of town in drafty tents while Pete and he lived in relative luxury at the Madam's hotel.

They posed as sporting men of wealth since Henry had provided them with a large weekly stipend to conduct the operation. The three soldiers began to conduct a survey of all known southern sympathizers in town and outside of the town limits. The hotel became their headquarters. Mason and Pete dressed extremely well and spent a lot of money gambling Henry's money away and the pair lived lavishly. The soldiers dressed shabbily and did all the work. They reported daylily to the diminutive major. One of the soldiers would then take all pertinent information relevant to the activities of all known southern sympathizers in the area back to Henry Fowler. Henry would in turn, hand the courier a large sum of money for the continued conduct of the undercover operation underway.

Henry would then have a myopic Army clerk transfer the information to a card system. The cards, all the same size, were filed in several large containers. The cards soon mounted up and Henry knew quite a bit about everyone and everything that went on in the town of Petersburg. He knew everything except for the knowledge of the fancy house. Mason had kept Henry ignorant about the Madam for his own very personal reasons.

Mason had almost immediately on arrival at the house cast his greedy eyes on the Madam's business venture. One day, after a week of seeing the profits generated there, Mason had approached the Madam with a proposition. He broached the subject of creating a partnership with her. She laughed in his face. He patiently tried to explain to the haughty woman that it was not intended to be a laughing matter and that she should seriously consider his offer. He would insure her total protection. She said that she already owned the town and for him to drop the matter if he knew what was good for him.

She had thought the little man harmless but for safeties sake, she had wanted the sheriff to run the dwarf out of town. When she went to find the sheriff, she discovered that he had disappeared into thin air one rainy summer's evening. People all throughout the town looked upon the sheriff's disappearance with favor but the Madam viewed the incident with alarm. Pete had intercepted the sheriff that rainy night and had killed the man with a shotgun blast to the throat. He threw the head into the river and then had taken the body to a patch of evergreen woods outside of town. The incredibly agile Pete had climbed a tree like a monkey carrying the body of his victim and had lashed the body securely to the very top. He tied it so securely in a heavy rope cocoon that there was no way possible that the body would ever see the earth again.

Once again, Mason entreated the woman to reconsider. The second meeting had occurred in the woman's office. Lehigh was cordial and polite but the Madam remained adamant. He pleaded with her that she would have overall control of all daily operations and that in return, he would make sure that she would remain untouchable in the town. All that he wanted was fifty percent of the weekly take. He mentioned that with his protection, no one like himself would ever be able to place her in an uncompromising position ever again. He mentioned that as it stood, that she was defenseless with the sheriff gone.

She had almost relented, but her pride had gotten the better of her. She stood up and began to cuss him out and then attempted to physically beat him. This was the greatest mistake of her life. Pete, who had been peeking through the keyhole snuck in through another door and had placed the derringer next to her curly head and removed her forever from the roles of the Petersburg Chamber of Commerce.

Pete had bundled her body into a carpet and had rowed out to the middle of the river past the town and had thrown the Madam into the chocolate waters of the Mississippi. Mason and Pete became sole proprietors of the only fancy house for miles around and hired one of the older women to head the daily operation. Since

Lehigh was always seen throwing money around and he was living in the hotel, his concocted story about buying the Madam out was accepted by many but not all. When one of the girls, a friend of the late Madam, began to question the legitimacy of Lehigh's story about the so-called 'sale', she was fired and sent packing by the new management.

Pete escorted her out of town and she too disappeared up a tree, thanks to the coordination and brute strength of Pete. After that, no one questioned the new business arrangements and Mason grew wealthy beyond his wildest imagination. The soldiers were drawn to the establishment like flies to a sugar cube and the money rolled in without letup.

Lehigh and Pete sat in the hotel's large dining room feasting on roast duckling, mashed potatoes, and peas. They were alone. Pete picked up a gravy boat and drowned his portions until the gravy overflowed his plate and flowed onto the table. It slowly dripped onto his leg. Lehigh stopped eating to watch Pete as he began to shovel mashed potatoes and peas into his mouth. The napkin that Pete wore around his neck to protect his expensive new suit was speckled with the drippings that poured out of his half open mouth. Pete was not aware that Mason had stopped eating to watch him. He was oblivious to the fact that his boss was not appreciating his dining habits and he continued to shovel food into his mouth in a blur.

Pete did not chew the food but rather swallowed it whole. Ripping a drumstick off the half a duckling on his plate and grabbing a biscuit, Pete plunged the biscuit into the pile of food and jammed the drumstick, bone and all, into his mouth. His jaws stripped the meat from the bone like a threshing machine and then he spat the bone onto the floor. He crammed the biscuit into his mouth before the leg bone had time to hit the floor. Lehigh had seen enough.

"By God, boy," he shouted angrily, "You have all the manners of a rutting pig."

Pete looked sheepishly at Mason, completely unclear on how he had offended him. His fork was in suspension between his mouth and the plate.

"Look at you. Half the damned food you shoved in your mouth is on the damned table. Look at the mess you are making. You shovel food in your pit like there ain't no tomorrow. Why don't you just dive headfirst into the plate and be done with it."

Pete could not look Mason in the eye. Instead, he stared at the floor. His cheeks were stuffed with food and some of it continued to fall out of his open mouth. Mason stood up and backed away from the table.

"Disgustin' is what it is. So help me, if we wuz' to go into some fancy eatery in St. Louis, the management would throw you out on your fat ass for making such a disgustin' spectacle of yourself the way you do."

Pete continued to stare at his shoes. The fork had not moved an inch from its last position although some of the food had slid from it landing on the floor.

"Put that fork down and close yer' yap, you slack jawed moron. You're droolin' all over the place. Look at me when I'm talkin' to you, boy. When I got somethin' to say to you, you are like a fart in a bottle," Mason shouted, "But when a skirt walks by you suddenly turn into a spry ' Wide Awaker."

Pete closed his mouth and sat straight up in his chair making eye contact with his benefactor. He placed the fork on the table.

"I'm gonna' learn you how to be respectable if I got to kill you to do it. You are gonna' learn to eat proper like a descent person, like a man of wealth and breeding, or you can eat out in the barn with all the rest of the barnyard animals. I will get a special trough built for you and pour the slop in it fer you every night."

"Yes sir, Mr. Lehigh," Pete mumbled. The door swung open to the dining room and banged loudly into the wall. Sergeant Neely entered the room panting and out of breath, his forehead etched with worry lines. He came to attention and saluted the Major. Lehigh threw his napkin in anger on the table.

"How many times do I got to tell you not to salute me, you damned fool. Am I wearin' a goddamned uniform? Are you?" Mason shouted.

"Sorry, Major Lehi…" Neely stopped in mid-syllable, aware of the mistake that he had made. Mason continued to glare at him.

"Just what the hell is it, anyway," Mason asked anxiously, "You spot our man or what?"

"No sir, but I seen somethin' else interestin' enough. I seen that injun' squaw that used to be Henry…I mean Colonel Fowler's maid, the one that he was crazy about? She lives in town with the local school mom, a Rebecca somethin' or other. I spotted her down by the wharf headin' for the Post Office. She's the kinda' woman you don't soon forget."

"The hell you say," Mason said happily. "Boys, it looks like we hit paydirt. All the chickens are comin' home to roost. Perfect," he said. Mason sat down as Neely leaned forward and placed his hands on a chair. His eyes darted towards the full meal that lay in front of him. The delicious aroma coming from the table caused his stomach to begin to roar as he licked his lower lip in helplessness.

"I'm sure the Colonel will want to know this recent turn of events. Sergeant, report back to the Colonel with this. Tell him what you seen an' tell him we got work. Leave today. Tell him to send more money an' three more men."

"Yes, Mr. Brown," The sergeant said. Mason grinned at Neely's use of his alias.

"Good job, Neely. Now, get going," he said. Neely tore his gaze from the table and nodded his head. He left to begin the six-hour trip back to St. Louis. Pete looked curiously at Mason.

"I don't get it, Mr. Lehigh. Why do you figure Bella is in town?" he asked.

"I ain't too sure, but somehow they are all connected to Quantrill." Mason poured himself a shot of whiskey and sat back in the plush leather seat. He placed his shoes on the table and leaned back.

"Bella saved old Josh the day of the shoot out in the hotel. He would have bleed to death. She got them boys out, but I'll be damned if I know how she did it. Josh never said how she did that. I don't think he even knew how she did it. How that Doudlass boy disappeared is a mystery."

Mason sipped at his drink. He took a cheap cigar from his vest pocket and bit the end of it off. He lit it and puffed contentedly on it.

"That Doudlass boy rides with Quantrill. This we know. Bella helped them boys to escape the shoot out at the America Hotel that day. This we also know. They must be all pretty comfortable comin' here. Good. We will bag the whole lot of them right here in this rat's nest."

Pete did not know whether it was safe to resume eating again. Mr. Lehigh had been terribly angry. He gazed at his food and then at Mr. Lehigh. Mason picked up a napkin and blew his nose into it. He tossed the shot of whiskey back and wiped his mouth on the sleeve of his expensive suit.

"Old Joshua made a bad mistake. He forgot who he was talkin' to," Lehigh said.

"That's why you tolt' me to break his goddamned neck," Pete said quickly, happy that Mr. Lehigh was no longer angry with him.

"You know, I felt bad about havin' to kill Josh. We rode together a long time. He was a hell of a good man. I wish he had not gotten so drunk that night and started flappin' his gums about what happened in the hotel that day. When he tolt' me that it had been Bella that got those boys out and saved his life, I knowed' right there and then that he was a dead man. Henry had to know and you know the rest," Mason said. "You kept him drinkin' an' I slipped out and tolt' Henry. Henry said to kill him and that was that. Henry don't play no games."

"I did a good job, didn't I? I broke his neck good," Pete said proudly.

"Yes, you did. He never knew what hit him," Lehigh drew heavily on the cheap cigar and released a cloud of smoke.

"I don't know how she knew that Joshua was killed. Must have been some kinda' woman's intuition. The next day, she was gone. Henry wanted that woman bad," Mason said.

"Who didn't," Pete chortled. He threw his head back and brayed loudly. Lehigh rose up from the table and viciously delivered a backhand blow across Pete's large rubbery lips. Pete recoiled away from the blow and nearly flipped the chair that he was sitting in over before he caught his balance. He held unto his bleeding mouth with both of his hands, his eyes registering a dumb surprise at what Mason had done. Lehigh sat down and pointed a bony finger at Pete.

"You got to learn to be more careful like what you say. If you said that in front of the wrong people, and it got back to Henry he would kill you. I did not mean it that way, you dirty minded lummox. I meant that Henry wanted her taken cared of. I know it nearly broke his heart when he found out. He figured that Bella had planned the whole botched robbery attempt with them boys. He probably was right, now that we know what we just found out."

Pete continued to hold onto his bleeding mouth. His eyes stared unblinking at Mason as blood trickled onto the table and mixed with the puddles of gravy.

"Henry come all to pieces. He started blubbering like some little old baby. Henry was sweet on that squaw an' probably still is. She was a beauty. He grabs me by my collar an' looks me dead in the eyes. She is a sinner that will burn in hell, he goes. She will have hooks driven into her jaws, he goes, an' will be dragged to the lake of burnin' fire, he goes or some sich'. I asks him if I was to do all that, put hooks in her jaws and the likes and he looks at me funny and says no. He tells me just to shoot her in the head."

Pete continued to stare at Mason and he listened carefully, afraid to say another word. Lehigh looked at Pete.

"Go rinse yer' mouth out with salt water. Then go find Timmins. I want him to find out all about this school mom, this Rebecca. Now get and do what I tell you."

Pete sprinted out of the dining room and flew out the door. Mason sat back still enjoying his cheap cigar. Bella's appearance in town was an unexpected twist. His little yellow piggish eyes squinted as his normally suspicious mind tried to fit all the pieces together. One way or another, this bit of information would please Henry. He knew that Henry had been jealous of Old Josh's relationship with the squaw. He also knew that Henry still carried a flame for the injun' woman. This ought to be interesting. He leaned back, poured another whiskey and puffed on his stinking cigar as the sun began to set.

CHAPTER EIGHTEEN

Frederick shook hands with Mr. Robinson and welcomed his guests into his home. Besides Mr. Robinson and Sergeant Watson, Frederick shook hands with the two strangers that had arrived with them. These men were the ones mentioned in the telegram. He smiled at his guests while he showed them the way to the parlor.

"I received your message just last week informing me of your unexpected trip back to Rochester. I pray that everything is all right. You did not mention in the telegram the purpose of your return trip and it concerned me," he said. Frederick remained standing while the men seated themselves.

"Let me set your mind at ease, sir," Ben replied." The community of Philadelphia welcomed us with open arms. We were so successful in organizing there that we felt it was safe to leave the city and return home for a brief interlude. The organization that we created is in highly capable hands."

"Splendid. I knew that it could not be otherwise," Frederick said, still grinning. "As for the purpose of our meeting here today," Ben continued, "we find ourselves in a peculiar position. I could not very well mention the circumstances in the message because of a very delicate situation we find ourselves in."

Frederick could see that Ben was choosing his words carefully.

"I see," Frederick said. "And just what is this delicate situation that you mention?"

"Mr. Douglass, I would like to introduce to you Sergeant Thomas Sawyer and Sergeant Finn, recently members in good standing, but now detached from service not of their own choosing, from the Army of Northern Virginia, Confederate Sates Army."

Frederick's smile vanished. He was flabbergasted but retained his composure. He sat back in his chair patiently waiting for an explanation as to the reasons and causes of why the enemy was sitting comfortably in his parlor.

"I suppose it best at this point to let Jim take over," Ben said with hesitation. He was not able to read all that well the reaction of Mr. Douglass. Frederick turned to Mr. Watson who stood up from his seat.

"Mr. Douglass, I knew these men here since they was boys. They are the boys that helped me escape from slavery many years ago," Jim said.

Mr. Douglass pulled at his beard and looked at both of the strangers.

"Is this correct?" Frederick asked.

Both of the men nodded their heads, unwilling to speak.

"Hmm, *interesting*. One of you helped Jim escape down the river. Mr. Watson has told me the story. It is quite amazing in retrospect. Even more so is the odd name. Huck, I believe it is. You are named Huck?" Frederick asked.

"Yes," Huck said. "Huck is short fer Huckleberry."

"You must pardon me. The name is strange. I mean you no disrespect, young man, but your parents could never in all good common sense have named you Huckleberry."

Tom began to smile as he watched Huck begin to squirm in his chair.

"When I asked Jim what your real name was, he could not answer me because even he did not know," Frederick said.

"I reckon that is true. There ain't but a handful of people in the world what knows what my Christian name be, an' half of them has passed on," Huck replied. Tom patted his friend on the shoulder and spoke loudly.

"Tell the gentleman your given name. It is a civil thing to do, you know."

"Yes, by all means. Please, you are among friends," Frederick said pleasantly. Huck looked angrily at Tom and nervously at Frederick.

"My friend here gets a kick out of this. He rides me about it, that's why there ain't many what knows what my first name truly be. I reckon your right, after all what Jim and Ben has done fer us, it's the gentlemanly thing to do. Ben here more'n likely saved our lives so the least I can do is be respectful an'..."

"Quit stalling and tell the man," Tom said. Huck looked annoyed. He took a deep breath.

"My Pap named me Hezekiah after my great grand Pa who was supposed to have bin' some important big wig in the Revolution, some kinda' general or some sich'. He came from Virginny. Pap said he liked to fight and drink even way up till he dropped dead in his tracks. He was fightin' with a neighbor about the neighbors cows gettin' in his hemp fields when he keeled over, but Pap remembered him when he was little and the name stuck. That's what my Pap tolt' me. When I was a young'n, that name was too big a name for me to chew on. No matter how hard I tried to say Hezekiah, all that come out was heck. I was heckin' all over the place cause I could nary say the name to save my life. All's I could say was that my name was Heck. Pap, they say, got a laugh out of the way I said it an' he starts to call me Huckleberry soon afterwards."

Tom began to choke on the laughter he had been attempting to hold back. He could not hold it in and began to hoot loudly.

"See that," Huck said, "Every time I mention the story he breaks up like this here. He never gives me no rest with it."

Tom tried to control his laughter but the harder he tried the more he hooted. Tears began to fill his eyes.

"It ain't the name, honest. It's just the way you tell it..I swear," he choked. Everyone in the room began to laugh. The tension in the room was instantly dissipated by Huck's unintentional humor.

"According to Mr. Watson, you men are from Missouri. How is it then that you were members of the Army of Northern Virginia? You both are a long way from home," Frederick said.

"It's a long story," Tom replied.

"Please, indulge me," Frederick said. "I am fascinated that this reunion has ever happened. It instills in me the belief in the word we call fate. Do continue."

"Before the war, things got bad in Missouri," Tom began, "people took to killing folks all about this time like it was nothing. One day, some Kansas people come to town. They were probably just passing through. Anyway, they killed my Aunt Polly and hurt Sid something horrible."

Jim had told both of them to fully tell their part as to what had caused them to leave home. Ben especially had mentioned to leave nothing out. When it came time for Tom to tell of the murder of his Aunt, Tom began to choke up. Huck saw that Tom was having some trouble relating the story to Mr. Douglass because of the emotions involved so Huck jumped into the story.

"You see, Mr. Douglass, Tom's Auntie had owned slaves an' that's the reason why these Kansans kilt' her. This fella' we found out kilt' Miss Polly an' threw her down a well. Sid got hisself nailed to a barn door an' shot an' stabbed so many times that the poor fella' lost his mind. He is so addled to the point now that he will never be good fer nothin' no more. All he does is moan an' shake an' piss his britches."

Frederick nodded gravely.

"We found out who done it one night. He was a well-known son-of a bitch an' we all swore an oath to get even. We traveled all the way across Missoura to kill him, an' we nearly froze an' starved to death but we got to where this fella' called home," Huck said.

"What is the name of this individual?" Frederick asked.

Tom spoke slowly and clearly.

"His name is Henry Fowler."

Frederick turned quickly towards Jim and Ben in disbelief.

"I demanded some kind of retribution for what he did against my kin'. I needed to see some kinda' justice, even if it were my own. The law didn't give a hang. The damned drunk of a sheriff told me that it was a pack of river ruffians, thieves and cutthroats that killed my Aunt. He did not care as long as it was one of our people, he didn't care. It wasn't anything of the sort. It was that dammed murdering Fowler that did it," Tom said passionately.

"I see," Frederick said calmly.

"I will be honest with you. Not only did we plan on killing him, we also planned on robbing him. We needed a stake that could take us out of Missouri and Kansas permanent. I read a book. It was called, 'Two Years Before the Mast'.

"I have also read it," Frederick said.

"In the book the Gold fields of California were mentioned. I figured that if we could get money from Fowler, we could get away from all the killing," Tom said slowly. "It was all a dumb dream. Things fell apart so fast it seemed that everything we planned went up in smoke."

"We got caught with our pants down," Huck interjected. "They read us like a book an' set us up. One of our friends was caught and he talked. They knew why we come and what we planned to do. Fowler owned the law so he came at us with all he had. Two of our friends died in a shootout with the law in this fleabag hotel. We barely made it out of there alive."

"If it hadn't been for this Indian woman, we would have been killed for sure," Tom said. "She showed us a way out of the hotel and a way for us to get away," Tom continued. "She gave us the name of her adopted father who lived in the Indian Nations. We got there and we told him our story and he set us right. He even set us on a boat to California but even that went wrong. The captain received a telegraph as we left New Orleans informing him that his wife had taken ill in Norfolk. The next thing you know, we are in Norfolk. Shortly after, Fort Sumter got fired on and the war was on. We got caught up in it."

"We jined' up right after Manasas," Huck said. "Been with the army nigh unto two years."

"Two long years. It was the biggest mistake in my life, trying to get revenge the way I went about it. I feel like the Almighty has chastised me for my sins over the last few years, his way, so to speak, of teaching me a well deserved lesson."

Frederick nodded his head solemnly.

"I never was all on fire with the 'Cause" to begin with, neither has Huck. I seen a lot of downright dirty things most recent that I don't agree with nor will I ever.

337

People were thrown into chains just because of the color of their skin. I never believed it right. If this war is truly being fought like Mr. Robinson says, for the freedom of all men, so that freedom can be enjoyed by all, then I will be the first to tell you that the last two years of my life have been spent on the wrong side. It is crystal clear to me. I am done with it all. My soldier days are over. All I want is to get back home and get on with my life and live in peace."

"Amen," Huck replied wearily. "Just fer the record, Mr. Douglass, Tom an' me ain't no deserters. And we ain't no skulkers neither. This last fight at Gettysburg there, why let me tell you it was a mean one. Everybody we knowed more than likely got their selves kilt in it. The damned artillery almost blew Tom here into the next world yonder, an' I got cotched and nearly thrashed to death by these northern Yankee scum. Beggin' your pardon," Huck added quickly.

"No offense taken, young man," Frederick said.

"Them devils whupped me to within an inch of life. I have caught my share of thumpings. Why hell, Mr. Douglass, I caught whuppins' and was raised with them like some folks are raised at goin' to church every Sunday. My Pap would wake up on a Sunday after his crazy drinkin' and thump me nearly hollow every Sunday mornin'. These Yankees, I don't know how many, beat me an' left me fer dead."

"Mr. Douglass," Jim began. "When we was recruitin', shortly we started we got news that the rebel army had started to grab colored people an' force them into slavery. Reverend Ellis begged for help. All our people were hidin' out not even knowin' that Lee had gotten whipped. There was old men an' women with babies starvin', not knowin' anythin' wanderin around the woods."

Frederick listened and his facial expression did not change. He was paying careful attention to every word being spoken.

"Yes," Ben said. "I decided from many witnesses that the Confederate Army was involved with countless illegal kidnappings throughout the area of Gettysburg. We learned that an entire community of Five-Forks had been burned out and many of the inhabitants thereof enslaved. As such, I determined that we must act. People who had been uprooted from the surrounding countryside were roaming the woods as vagabonds and fugitives in their efforts to escape from the clutches of these detestable slave catchers. The situation was intolerable. We secured fast mounts and left the city on a mission of rescue. We found the old and infirm, starving frightened children and desperate escapees from the long coffles heading south." Ben stopped and watched Frederick's demeanor but his face still remained mask like.

"We fed them, clothed them, gave them aid in every way possible. We organized a grassroots-building project. We scoured the woods and found a hundred people and set them on their feet again," Ben said happily.

"And what eventually happened with these people?" Frederick asked.

"I can report to you with all confidence that they are all doing fine. In fact, Jim had a new born baby named after him in appreciation of his efforts. Isn't that so, Jim?" Jim laughed.

"Yessuh, Mr. Douglass. Everything worked out just fine," Jim said.

"Tell me, how did you manage to find our two guests?" Frederick inquired. His question was directed at Jim. He eagerly answered the question.

"We was comin' down the Baltimo' Pike, makin' one last round of the woods to see if we had missed any folks. I spots two fellas', nakid' as they was on the day they was born walkin' north an' singin' like they had no care in the world. Well, Mr. Douglass, I reigned the horses up nex' to them. I was thinkin' they was crazy men let loose from some loft or cellar where they stores crazy people. I heard tell that is what white folks do with members of their family what turn lunatic. I figured in all the fightin' and commotion that they might have slipped they' tethers an' was roamin' free."

Frederick smiled.

"Let me try to explain," Tom said. "I was knocked senseless by the explosion of a federal artillery shell that practically landed on top of the men that I had been talking with. The explosion killed all of them and nearly blew me out of the clothes that I was wearin' .It picked me up and threw me yards threw the air. I landed in a half- dug grave. Everyone above the ground died. I didn't come too for days. I laid right there among the dead. When I did come too, I found this fella' taking photographs."

"Interesting," Frederick said, "What was he photographing?"

"Everything and anything. He was taking pictures of the entire battlefield. He even took pictures of the dead."

"How macabre," Frederick said softly.

"This fella', a Mr. Gardner, why, he fed me an' clothed me. He even made this concoction of sulfur powder or some sich' an' put it on my wounds. He took to cleanin and changin' the dressin' of my burns daily. I became his student. He would teach me how to mix the chemicals an' prepare the photographic plates. He said that I had a natural talent for it. He even let me take a few photographs. I never had done nothin' of the sort before, and Mr. Gardner was a good teacher. I love taking photographs. The whole concept of taking photographs was a mystery to me but not after he showed me how."

Tom stopped speaking to catch his breath. He hesitated and when he did he noticed Jim encouraging him in his recounting of the tale. Jim was smiling and nodding his head. Tom realized that he was getting off his topic and returned to it.

"One afternoon, when we were traveling down on the Emmitsburg road, Mr. Gardner seen a group of rebel prisoners sitting on a rail fence being guarded by a group of Yankee cavalrymen. Mr. Garner insisted that he wanted a photograph of them. When I was setting up the equipment he told me to fetch a bowl of flour and some brushes to touch up one of the prisoners that had a battered face. That is when I recognized the beat up fella' was Huck. We both thought each other had been killed in the fighting."

"Remarkable. Prisoners you say. How did you manage to secure your friend's liberty from the guards?"

"Mr. Gardner did some fast talking to an officer in charge. He somehow convinced the man to release Huck into our custody. This officer fella' was a big likable Dutchman that was interested in photography. He let Huck go with us as incredible as it may sound."

"Truly fascinating. How did you chance to meet Ben and Jim Watson?"

"I was jest' coming to that," Tom said. "When Mr. Gardner's Boss arrived the next day and learned who we were, he was not happy. Mr. Brady…he is Mr. Gardner's boss, said that if found in civilian clothes and in his company, that we could be shot for spies. He said that his business would be ruined. He chased us away at gunpoint. I can honestly say at this point that I did not want any trouble. It was the last thing on my mind."

Huck nodded his head in rapt attention to all of the details that Tom was hurriedly infusing into the story. He was prepared to jump in if he felt that Tom had omitted anything of importance.

"We were alone. Traveling around in civilian clothes did not seem to be too wise. We had survived too much simply to be shot as spies" Tom said.

"It was my idea to strip off the duds that we wuz' wearin'," Huck said proudly. "Strippin' them off that way we did, I figured that when the Yankees cotched' us again, that they would be too busy laughin' at us to shoot us as spies. I was a hoppin' that they would think we wuz' crazy an' not shoot us on sight. I wuz' way too busted up to take another ass crackin' from them Yankees. We started singin' real loud too. Only somebody crazy would be out struttin' aroun' nekid' an' singin' made up looney songs."

"They wuz' a comical sight," Jim said. "When I fust' caught sight of them an we commenced to talkin', I didn't even recognize either of them. Huck's face wuz' all swollen an' beat up an' Tom here looked like an' old man since his eyebrows wuz' all burnt' off an' he wuz' bald. I asked them what they thought they wuz' doin bein' nekid' an' singin' like wild men. That's when they tolt' us what they had jest' bin' through an' they promised to behave they' selves. We took pity on them an' offered them a ride to Philadelphia. So we begin talkin' an' so, bye an' bye, I asks where they wuz' from. One of them, I think it was Tom, sez' that they were from Missoura'. I ask him where in Missoura an' he ups an' says Petersburg. I nearly fell out the wagon when he said that. That's when I knowed who they wuz'. Even though I hadn't seen them in years, I knowed who they be."

"Quite a tale," Frederick said. Ben tried to discern if Mr. Douglass intended his remark to be sarcastic or not.

"Sir, I did not know what to do, frankly," Ben said. "They could not stay with us in Philadelphia. People would begin to talk or ask too many questions. If word were to get out to our enemies that we were harboring rebel stragglers, it would be our undoing. Something drastic had to be done."

"Mr. Douglass," Jim said, "I couldn't let them be taken to no prisoner stockade. They were both in bad shape. I knew they would never live through that. I could not let that happen. After all, they wuz' responsible in heppin' me git' to freedom."

"That is when I decided to come to Rochester with all good speed. I could not think of any other option," Ben said nervously.

Frederick kept his face a solid granite block. He stood up and looked out to the street from his parlor window. Finally, after what seemed like an eternity to Ben, Frederick turned to face Ben.

Ben…Jim…What you have done is nothing more than what I would have expected from you. What you have done is both a selfless display of Christian charity and love. from aiding the destitute who were roaming helplessly in the fields to helping your friends in their time of need. I can only admire your courageous spirit and your wisdom. If you had acted in any other way, I would have been disappointed. I am very proud of both of you."

Jim sighed in relief.

"Thank you, Mr. Douglass," Ben added.

"The only problem now is that what we can do for these men. Gentlemen, I am sure that you have had time to mull things over on your journey here. What direction do you thing we should take? I am open to suggestions. But let me tell you one thing I know. I know all about this fellow, Henry Fowler. He was in this room not less that a month ago. He is a dangerous individual, highly unstable and prone to revenge. Did you tell them that you had met the man, Jim?"

341

"Yessuh, when Tom told me the name of the man guilty of killin' his auntie, chills went up my spine."

"This you should know. Henry Fowler," Frederick began, "murdered his way to power. If you think he was powerful then, he is even more so because of the war. He has been promoted to Colonel and holds the title of Deputy Military Adjutant of Missouri. His job is to clean up Missouri of all Confederate irregular forces there. If you men were to return home, you would be sticking your heads into the lion's den. After the incident that happened at my home, I know that I will have to watch my back. He is ambitious and ruthless, not the type who easily forgives slights and insults and definitely not someone who will ever cease hunting for the men who tried to kill him once and escaped."

"That is a risk that I have to take," Tom said.

"Tom here is sweet on a little ol' gal back home," Huck said. "He's bin writin' her for almost two years. He wants to go back home an' see her. Sort of pop the question to her. Nothin' kin' change his mind, he's dead set on it."

"You see, sir," Tom said, "Rebecca, that's her name. Her father and brothers were away fighting as Vicksburg. I haven't gotten a letter from her in quite some time now. With Vicksburg fallen, there is no way of knowing if any of then are alive. She could be all alone in the world. I got to get back. If I can get home, I am sure that she will come with me. I don't figure on staying around home too long knowing that Fowler is looking to hang us."

"I see," Fredrick said. "Far be it from me to stand in the way of love. I suppose the first thing we should do is to procure new identity papers for you. I know someone in the War Department that my help us in that regard. We can get papers stating that you are two discharged Union veterans whose time of enlistment has run out. That should not be too difficult. The hard part is getting you two home."

"Sir," Ben said. "I have taken the liberty of wiring some of our friends in Canada, some of the old Underground Railroad network in anticipation of your approval of getting them home safely. I have even contacted the "General" herself. I told her the entire story and she has promised to help us in every way possible."

"I don't know how to thank you," Tom said.

"Young man, what you have told me today has repaid me in a way you may never know. You are our prodigal son returned to the fold of humanity and I see that as a payment higher than any gold that you may have ever found in the goldfields of your California."

"Hot damn, Tom," Huck shouted. "We are going home."

342

Sergeant Timmins had obeyed the major's orders to the letter. Mason had instructed Corbett to find out everything that he could about the woman that Rebecca lived with and to do it as discreetly as possible. Within a short time he learned that the woman was an unmarried schoolteacher. Her brothers and father had enlisted in the Confederate army and were away fighting at Vicksburg. Since Vicksburg had capitulated to Federal forces and because of the Union's staunch policy of not exchanging prisoners at this juncture of the war, there was every likelihood that none of them would ever see home again for a long time.

She apparently did not have a beau, although Timmins could not see why. She was an attractive young woman. He often described her as pert in his dispatches, which annoyed Mason. All of her friends were hard-core southern sympathizers. Many of the rebel sympathizers had been driven from the town and people from all over Kansas now occupied their residencies. The homes had been abandoned and soon filled by people whose loyalty was strictly with the Union.

She, on the other hand, had not been driven from town and Timmins figured it must be out of desperation that she hung onto the home in the dim hope that one day her family would return to her. He had found out the interesting fact that Bella had taken up boarding at her home shortly after the death of Joshua Mulvaney. Timmins watched the house this early August morning and was not surprised when he saw Bella leave the house and start working in the garden.

Under Bella's care the corn was the highest he had ever seen in a little stick and stone garden and the string beans grew like weeds. She fed the chickens every morning and slopped the hogs as well. After, she would leave to work at Dr. Water's home as a housekeeper, returning around four in the evening. Timmins watched her move about at her chores, Even at this distance across from the home in the backyard of a loyal union man, there was no mistaking that Bella had every asset and charm that any woman could possibly be given in his world.

It was no wonder that Henry had gone practically crazy over her and mooned for her like a love struck pimply faced adolescent. She was knockdown good looking. He hoped that Henry ordered her killed soon. He would definitely relish the work. His mind played with the idea of what he would do to her before he slit her pretty throat. He also hoped that Henry ordered Rebecca killed as well. The backdoor opened and Corbett backed into the bushes next to the barn he was leaning against.

He was surprised to see Rebecca walk into the garden and stretch. She straightened her bonnet before helping Bella remove weeds from the strawberry patch. Bella bent low and popped a strawberry into her mouth. Corbett could tell they were laughing but was too far away to hear what they were laughing about. He was more interested in letting his eyes linger on the blouse of the voluptuous Indian woman that showed her figure quite nicely when she had bent over.

343

She stayed in that position for several minutes and Corbett's eyes locked into place. Bella kept smiling in her revealing position. She knew that Corbett was looking right at her and would not take his eyes off of her opened blouse. Rebecca did as she had been told and sat on the ground and pulled weeds.

"He is at the corner of the barn hidden by weeds. Did you see him when you come from the house? He has been there since early before the sun comes out," Bella said. Rebecca continued to laugh. She found a ripe strawberry for herself and examined it carefully. She put the strawberry up into the air and shifted it slowly towards her neighbor's barn.

"You are right. It is the same man that was there yesterday and the day before. What does it mean, Bella? Who is he?"

"Finish quickly then follow me into the house. Weed carefully and take your time. I will tell you. Do not look at him when I leave you. I will meet you in the big chair room," Bella said, trying not to frighten her friend.

Bella knew exactly what it meant and it meant big trouble. This was no admirer; this was not some lovesick teenage soldier boy. She had recognized the man as Corbett Timmins. She knew that he was one of Henry's most faithful and dependable killers. Bella had overheard a conversation that Henry had with the man about a killing committed in Missouri that Corbett was responsible for. This pig of a man enjoyed killing and looked forward to killing like some people enjoyed a fine cigar or a good dinner. This animal had boasted to Henry that he had personally dispatched thirty-seven people to the infernal regions and looked forward to more business in the future with Henry. Bella placed her hoe next to the shed and slowly walked into the house.

She went directly to her room and pulled a pistol out from under her bed. She checked her loads to make sure that the humidity had not spoiled any of the cartridges and stuck the pistol into the small of her back. She wrapped a shawl around her waist to insure that the pistol would be hidden and secondly to hold it securely in place. She heard the downstairs kitchen door squeak on its hinges and listened carefully for the sound of Rebecca's footsteps entering the parlor. She skipped down the steps, feeling guilty about bringing this trouble into her friend's life. Rebecca was kind and good. She was determined to make things right at all costs.

"Bella," Rebecca cried, "I'm so frightened. Who is that man? What does he want?"

Bella grabbed Rebecca by her arms.

"He is just a man. He is no devil spirit. He is a man and nothing more."

"Maybe we should tell Mr. Gates. He will know what to do. Maybe he can perhaps talk to the man and..."

"Mr. Gates is a nice old man but he is too old and wrinkled like a prune. Believe me, I know what has to be done. I want you to stay inside and lock the doors. After today, I promise you that we will no more have him watching us and following us around like brother four legs. Trust me. Now, when I leave, bolt the doors. I will be back as quickly as my feet can make me."

"What are you going to do?" Rebecca asked.

"This man will talk to my good friend I have. Do not ask questions. There is no time."

"Do be careful," Rebecca pleaded.

"You must learn to trust me and calm down. Now, lock the doors."

Bella walked down the steps and began walking down the street. Rebecca slid the bolt back and leaned against the door with all of her weight. She remained this way for only a minute and then hurried to bolt and lock the back door in the kitchen. She wondered as to whom Rebecca's friend was that was going to set things right.

Timmins watched as Bella left the home and began to follow her. He saw her head towards the docks and then she did something out of the ordinary. Instead of heading towards the Post Office, she picked up speed and began to nearly run towards a group of abandoned homes that were precariously perched close to the river.

The bank of the river had at one time been further away from the current shoreline. A few years ago, the channel had changed slightly and the homes that had been many yards from the river's edge had now had their foundations soaked and water lapped at their front doors. They had all been abandoned and now stood silent, falling into disrepair as the river soaked into their timbers.

Timmins wondered what she was up to. She looked to be in one hell of a hurry. At this early hour in the morning, few people were up and on the street. Everyone was still in bed. What was she going to shantytown for and why in such a blasted hurry? Maybe she was going to meet somebody. Could it be that she was going to meet Doudlass? He walked carefully trying to keep his feet from getting wet. He looked down and tried to avoid a big puddle. He nimbly jumped across it. When he looked up again, she was gone.

"Damned sneaky little squaw bitch," he muttered. He drew his revolver as warning bells began to go off in his head.

"Where did you go? Come out now. I got a present for you," he whispered quietly. He looked into a window to see if he could spot her on the other side. The house was slowly rotting into the river. Some drunks had apparently used the house because empty bottle littered the floor. Some one in the past had lit a fire on the floor. The house was so saturated with moisture from the river that the house had not caught fire. He was not paying proper attention in locating Bella as he should have been because when he rounded the corner of the collapsing house, he heard a noise behind him. He spun towards the noise. His surprise was total.

Bella stood behind him with a dirty wet blanket wrapped around her hand. He heard the muffled explosion and then his world erupted into excruciating pain. His pistol took flight from his hand and he went sprawling headfirst into a mud puddle. The bullet had slammed into the back of his leg and had exited his kneecap. The pain coiled like a serpent around his senses and then sprang to every nerve cell in his surprised brain.

He grabbed at his blasted knee as his eyes slammed shut. His face was covered in mud. Bella kicked him in his face as he tried to turn over and he stretched out in the puddle as if it were a king sized bed. Muddy bubbles popped to the surface of the stagnant water from the corner of his mouth. His eyes slowly opened and he rolled over onto his back holding on to his wrecked knee. He desperately looked for his weapon.

"Good morning to you, Corbett Timmins. Nice way to start a day. I know who you are so don't lie to me. If you lie to me, I will dead you."

"Goddamned you, bitch," Timmins screamed.

Bella calmly wrapped the dirty blanket around her hand that held the pistol and fired. The bullet struck him in his other knee shattering his kneecap and blowing out a large section of muscle and gristle from the back of his leg. He grabbed at his leg and howled in agony. The shot had not been loud, the blanket having muffled its sound and the river and the closeness of the houses drank in the sound. In town, no one had heard the report of her revolver.

Bella stood over Corbett with the revolver pointing at his midsection. His eyes watched in horror as she rotated the next load into position to be fired and pulled back the hammer.

"Henry has sent you. Why?" Bella asked.

"I'm gonna kill you, redskin...you are a dead wom..."

Bella fired the revolver again. The bullet pounded into his thigh, a few inches from his groin. The round ripped a part of his buttocks off on exiting his body. Corbett screamed in helpless rage. He fell on his back into the mud. He shivered in pain and shock. He rose slowly to lean his weight on his elbows.

346

"Don't shoot me any more, for Christ sakes. Don't shoot me no more," he whimpered. "What do you want to know...I'll tell you, jest' don't shoot me no more, goddammit."

"Henry sent you," Bella said, "Don't speak, just nod your head yes or no. He knows I am here?"

Corbett nodded in the affirmative.

"Are there many with you?"

Timmins shook his head in a negative response to the question.

"He sends you here to dead me?"

Corbett did not appear to have heard the question. He closed his eyes and bit into his tongue. Bella cocked the pistol and prepared to get his attention again. Corbett heard the telltale sign of the revolver being readied and opened his eyes quickly.

"Henry is in love with you. He did not send me to kill you. He wants you back. He told me to keep an eye on you an' make sure that you are alright an' sich'. He wants to have a sit down talk with you...dinner an' wine. The fella is in lo..."

Bella fired a bullet shattering Corbett's elbow. He shrieked loudly and flopped back into the puddle. He slowly rose up in the puddle.

"I asked you nicely to stop doin' that," Corbett shouted angrily.

"Tell me another lie and I send you to the whiteman spirit world without your important parts." She aimed the revolver at his groin

"Alright," Corbett sobbed, "Hell...it won't hurt to tell you. Henry found out that the Doudlass fella an' Quantrill was in town. He knows somehow that you an' that pert school mom might know when Quanrtrill plans on comin' back here to buy more ammunition. There, dammit all to hell, are you happy now?"

"No," Bella said coldly.

"Look, I told you everything I know. Henry will skin me alive when he finds out I told you what I did. What more do you want?" Timmins pleaded.

"I don't want many more. You have told me plenty."

Corbett gave a sideways glance at his left boot to see if the large Bowie knife that he kept there was still in place. The ebony handle peeked over his cuff.

"Good. Now that I told yer' everything yer' wanted to know, how about leavin' me in peace. I figgers I kin' still sit a horse. I will have a right bad time getting to my feet though. The way I have it is that we are fair and square. Yup. Fair an' square. Iff'n you was to help me to my feet, I figures I can hobble out of here. What

347

do you say? Help me up to my feet? I kin' get to my horse an' I am out of yer life for good. I got to get away from here after what I tolt' you. Henry now is my number one worry, not you. C'mon an' help a poor fella out now."

Bella started to walk towards him. Corbett reached out with his left hand and slowly started another movement with his right hand towards his boot. He smiled. Bella raised the pistol and fired sending a red-hot bullet through Corbett's head. He flopped on the ground in the manner of a fish out of water a few times and then went rigid, the smile still etched on his surprised face.

She quickly stripped the body naked and pushed it into the dark waters of the river. Corbett's body bobbed on the surface and then an undercurrent pulled it under the surface. It soon was swept southward along with the other flotsam and debris the muddy river carried with it. She threw the smoking blanket into the river and quickly walked towards Rebecca's home.

William Clarke Quantrill had made Kansas bleed like it had never bled before. On August 25, 1863, he had attacked and burned the city of Lawrence, Kansas in a rampage the likes of which was unheard of in the annals of the sectional conflict up to this time. He had killed two hundred and fifty men, young boys and old men in cold blood. The slaughter had been ruthless and nearly total, few men between the ages of sixteen and sixty having escaped the wrath of the former school teacher, abolitionist, slave catcher, rustler now turned war chieftain.

He had made the streets of Lawrence run red with blood and in doing so had created a clamor so loud that it reached the highest office in the land. The conscious of a nation demanded justice for all the victims. Overnight, the name of William Clarke Quantrill had become a household word. The attack stirred the ire of a people fast becoming sick of the war and the endless casualty roles it produced.

In one bold stroke, this former son of Ohio had burned his name into the hollowed halls of the infamous insuring his own demise in the process. There would be no safe refuge for him now anywhere inside the continental borders of the United States. No efforts would now be spared to track him down and lay him low. No expenses were too great to spend in hunting down the mad beast as a war weary people hungered for revenge. For Henry C. Fowler the attack at Lawrence had been a Godsend.

A month before the raid, Henry had circulated to his political supporters in Washington several anonymous letters stating that the current military commander of the area had proven ineffective in the capture or death of elusive Confederate irregular forces in Missouri. These men were politicians who all had received generous donations to their campaigns from Henry.

The second thing he did was to send various newspapers signed affidavits saying that Quantrill had been seen in various towns buying bullets in quantity. Henry then sent three handwritten copies to a friend in the state department detailing the surveillance mission that he was conducting in one of the towns that Quantrill had been spotted in. This information was then sent to all of the politicians that Henry had supported in the past.

When Lawrence was burned, these politicians demanded that the current military commander be removed from his position for incompetence. He was promptly sacked. The officer was sent packing after being made a scapegoat in the matter and sent to a dead end military posting in California. Since Colonel Henry C Fowler was the only one who seemed to have a plan, his name was touted by all of those politicians that Henry had in his deep pockets. They demanded action and Henry Fowler was thought by many to be the man that would bring Quantrill to quick justice and his promotion to brigadier general was approved in less time than any other person in the history of the war.

Henry had what he had long coveted. He became a general and his base of operations began to grow overnight. Men and supplies were shuttled into Henry's determined effort to hang Quantrill's head on a pole. He stood in his ornate office of his new headquarters and admired himself in front of the full-length mirror that was hung on his door. He struck fierce posses in front of it keeping his eyes on the bright golden stars that perched on his narrow shoulders. He liked what he saw.

General Henry Cadimus Fowler, master of the fate of all sinners and God's own instrument of justice and righteousness in this God forsaken nest bed of traitors. He was the master of all he surveyed and dispenser of immediate death to any who stood in his way. Henry needed others to revel in his newfound omnipotence. That is why he had sent for Major Lehigh. He was disturbed from his self-admiration by a slight knock on the door.

"Entre", Henry said. A tired looking Captain with severe bags under his eyes entered the room.

"General, Major Lehigh has just arrived with C troop."

"Thank you Captain Barlow. Please send him in. By the way, young captain, you look dreadful. We cannot have this; we must keep up our image. Get some rest if you would."

Captain Barlow was a veteran cavalry soldier just recently attached to Henry's command from the fighting back east in Virginia. He had been ordered to this new command and sent west to aid in the efforts of the newly promoted General Fowler.

"Beggin' the General's pardon, sir, but I will not have an opportunity for that. You have ordered me to patrol the Boston Mountains. We will be leaving tonight, sir."

Henry hated to be corrected by a subordinate. He fought to control his anger.

"Captain, you will obey my orders. I don't care what you may have thought I had ordered you to do before. I am giving you a direct order now. It necessitates that I countermand my previous decree. We cannot have you hanging around here looking like some damned raccoon or some blasted panda bear from far off Khitai. I order you to sleep, so sleep. Crawl into a bed and sleep," Henry said shaking in rage.

"Does this mean that my patrol is not to take place tonight, sir?"

"You will patrol when I tell you to patrol, you insignificant insubordinate cockroach. I care not if you are a graduate of the Military Academy. Remember this, young captain, we must look as good as we patrol. If your tiny mind can fathom this then one-day you too may find yourself in a position of command like myself instead of being merely one of my ground worms. I most seriously doubt it though. Who has ever heard of a general that resembled a damned raccoon? The very thought is preposterous and runs counter to all military logic. I suppose that you have read Clausterwitz?"

Captain Barlow stared blankly at the ceiling.

"I haven't had too much time to read lately, General Fowler. I've been way too busy killing rebels and burying my own good men to read, sir."

"Indeed. No matter. Now, send in Major Lehigh and away with you. Crawl into your bed and sleep, young captain. The next time I speak with you, you had better look like a captain in my command instead of a damned Panda bear."

Henry waved his hand in an effeminate gesture that was not lost on the Captain who saluted crisply.

"Yes sir," he said. He closed the door and shook his head in disgust.

West Point had not prepared him in the proper way to react to amateur soldiers. He held this General in contempt as he did all politically appointed General officers. Captain Barlow motioned to Major Lehigh to enter the office   and passed him in the foyer. Another political military hack, he thought bitterly, except this one was an elf. He closed the door and exhaustedly walked away wishing that he was back with the good men of the Second Rhode Island cavalry.

Mason walked into Henry's new office quarters like a strutting gamecock.

"Hank," he said, slamming the door shut and almost breaking the mirror.

"Nice place ya' got here. The place kinda' suits you," he said, offering Henry a halfhearted salute.

Henry ignored his comments and sat down behind his massive mahogany desk. Mason awkwardly sat down, not too sure if Henry had found out somehow that Pete and he had become the towns only whoremasters. He hoped that Henry was just acting high and mighty and did not know the truth about what was going on in Petersburg. He had paid all of his men good money to keep their mouths shut. When he was ready to tell Henry the truth, all of his ducks by then would be in order. He knew only too well how Henry felt about sinners. Pete had been left in charge with instructions to keep the men out of his business. Mason ordered Pete to make any soldiers that were too nosey to disappear.

"Let us forego the banal trivialities, Mason. I received your message last Monday about the sudden and curious demise of the late sergeant Corbett Timmins. What do you know of this?" Henry asked brusquely.

Mason felt relieved at once with Henry's inquiry. Henry did not know of the brothel, of this he was certain.

"Damndest thing, Hank. I told you that Bella was in town, right? I ain't kilt' her just yet. All's you got to do is say the word and I'll send her damned soul spiralin' down to hell so fast, she won't even know what hit her."

"No, we don't want to frighten our quarry away from our snare. Keep her alive but watch her all the time. No harm will come to her until we have learned everything that we may from the coquettish temptress." Henry folded his hands in front of his face and went dark in his eyes.

"What about Corbett? He was a loyal and faithful man, one of my best workers, excluding our good friend, Klaus, of course. Who killed him?"

Mason despised Günter Klaus. He was a murderer who killed on his whims, a moody dangerous individual who had even killed members of Henry's own entourage for no apparent reason. Henry forgave him for his ways because he seemed to be able to smell danger and had saved Henry's life on more than one occasion.

"Corbett uped an' vanished one day. About a week later some little boys raftin' an' fishin' come across him rottin' dead on a sandbar in the middle of the river. Timmons was pretty much all bones. Somebody dispatched him to the next world with a gunshot 'cause there was a hole bored straight through his noggin', He didn't git' drunk an' fall in the river, that was certain."

"Perhaps it was one of Quantrills minions that killed our unfortunate and erstwhile associate?" Henry asked glibly.

"You have been keeping careful records of everyone that comes through the town, have you not? All strangers in town are documented and filed; I have received new cards every week. Is there any chance that you may have slipped up?" he asked carefully.

"Not that I know of," Mason said.

Henry jumped up from his seat and pointed his finger in Mason's face. His face went purple and flecks of foam appeared as if by magic in the corners of his mouth. This outburst caught Mason completely by surprise.

"I have nearly spent a fortune on this enterprise and one of my best men becomes fish food and all you can say is I don't know? Obviously someone killed Corbett. He did not shoot himself in the head," Henry screamed.

"No, Henry. Of course not." Mason was accustomed to Henry's wild mood swings but he somehow sensed this one to be different. Henry had always treated Mason as nearly an equal. However, Henry had somehow changed. For the first time in their relationship, Henry appeared to be threatening Mason, a feeling that Mason was not all that comfortable with. Henry stretched on his toes to appear taller than what he was and his eyes bulged wildly.

"I want you to find out who killed Corbett. Here me out. Whoever has killed Corbett is the key in apprehending and killing Quantrill. Understand one thing, my small major. I will skin you alive if you fail me. I swear this and don't think that your big fat ape like friend will be able to save you. I will cook him slowly over a pit of flaming railroad ties and feed him to you bit by bit as you are flayed alive in front of his eyes. If you fail me, Mason, heaven nor hell will keep my fury from you. Do you understand me? Do you?" Henry roared.

If any other man had threatened Mason in this manner they would be dead before they hit the floor. Mason blinked in disbelief at the way Henry was treating him. In this one second of realization between blinks, Lehigh knew that things between them were irrevocably changed.

"I understand perfect, General," Mason said without emotion. With that said, Henry deflated like a balloon. He slowly sank back into his chair satisfied that he had made his point.

"Good. It is so important that all of my subordinates comprehend my edicts to the letter, even you, Mason. I know that you will not fail in your assigned mission, and that is precisely why I have allowed you to serve me."

Henry reached for a box that sat on his desk. He opened it and offered Mason a cigar. He lit it and sat down again and fumbled at a drawer in his desk. Opening it, he placed a jeweler's box in front of Lehigh.

"I am glad that what I had to say is a thing of the past. It is so difficult to balance the pain with the pleasure, Mason. It is not like it was in the old days. I have much more responsibility as you can see. Sometimes it becomes unbearable. I hate to treat old friends in such a manner but it is for your own good, don't you see. It is my sacred duty, proscribed by forces way beyond our mere mortal means that drive me. I do what needs be done. It is the will of Jehovah. Now, no more sad faces, please. I know how to reward good work and loyalty."

He tossed the box to Mason who caught it in his right claw.

"Open it," Henry said smiling.

Mason opened the box and saw that it contained two small golden eagles, the symbols of rank for a Colonel. They had been Henry's eagles.

"Congratulations, Colonel Lehigh," Henry said. "And you can inform Pete that he is promoted to Captain, both he and Neely. Mason, I am sending you back, posthaste. Pick another two good men. Keep the home that Bella is living in under surveillance twenty-four hours a day as well as the Gordon home. Keep the cards coming. I am setting up a new system of identification for everyone in town. I need you to contact the mayor of town for me and inform him that he is to have a meeting with me. My men will come for him in a few days; He is to be our new business partner and chief informer so have him ready to travel."

"It is done," Mason said flatly.

"When Quantrill next comes to town, he will find that it is under my total control. I will continue the pretense of looking for him so that he does not grow suspicious but I know in my bones that he will come to us and then we will have the fiend."

"I am leavin' as soon as I get my two new men. Anything else, General?"

"Yes. How did Bella look?"

"Fit as a fiddle." Mason grinned lewdly.

"Not for long she won't Colonel Lehigh. Not for long."

Ben placed two bundles wrapped in brown paper and tied with string in front of Tom and Huck. They curiously looked at the bundles as Ben seated himself at the kitchen table.

"Gentlemen, if you would open the packages that I have placed in front of you," Ben said. Tom reached for his and undid the package. Huck tore at the brown paper biting the string in two. He was surprised at what he found. Tom pulled a blue Union tunic from the paper and light blue federal trousers.

"It has been decided that you travel as two recently discharged Union soldiers. We believe it safer for you to wear the uniform as not. No one notices soldiers these days but they would notice two military age men in transit. You would get a lot of curious stares and comments these days as to why you were not serving the nation in this its darkest hours. Everyone your age is in the army and you would stand out in a crowd attracting the possible attention and interest in those men whose job it is to ferret out deserters from Federal service. Hence the subterfuge of posing as Union veterans returning home to the arms of their loved ones."

"These here duds is beat up," Huck commented looking over the threadbare uniform. "Any reason why it is we got to look like refugees from an outhouse?"

He tried on his faded blue tunic.

"Indeed there is. I was just getting to that," Ben said. He handed both of them envelopes.

"These are your identity and discharge papers. Mr. Douglass is responsible for these papers and they were not easy to procure. The identity papers are authentic however the dates of discharge are not. They are perfect forgeries. Memorize everything on them because your lives may very well depend on them."

They removed the papers and began to read them. As they read, Ben continued.

"We have a friend of considerable influence in the War Department who was told the entire circumstance as to how you became our guests. This man of means went to work and in less than a week he was able to produce what you are now holding in your hands."

Ben watched as Tom's eyes devoured every word on the pages. He noticed Huck struggling with the material. Hucks eyes squinted and his forehead was a mass of wrinkles. Huck's lips moved like a ventriloquist's dummy.

"You can see that one paper has been made to appear as old as the date in the right hand corner. These are the forgeries. These are your new identities. The other paper does not look so old because it is not. These are your discharge papers," Ben said.

Tom nodded his head while Huck shuffled his papers from one hand to another.

"These are the true identities of two Union soldiers who were reported missing in almost two years ago. The paper was aged with tannic acid and tea, believe it or not. Familiarize yourselves with the names and dates on these and commit it all to memory. You must know all pertinent information and must pay careful attention to detail. Need I remind you of the penalty for an enemy soldier apprehended in the uniform of a Union soldier?"

"No, that you do not. I am well aware," Tom said. "You say that these two Yankees...I mean Federals were reported missing?"

"Yes, Privates Patrick Daniel Shay and Jonathan Prout were reported missing at the battle of Shiloh. They were members of the Second Indiana. The unit, by the way was mustered out of service this last May when the term of the enlistment's expired. See the date in the corner?"

"These ain't their clothes, are they? I don't cotton to wearin' no dead boy clothes no how," Huck said resolutely.

"Huck, if they were reported missing in action, tell me how the hell would these be their clothes?" Tom asked.

"You askin' me or tellin' me. They could be from the dead boy's kit. He never said they lost the kit," Huck said quickly trying to defend himself from Tom's telling logic.

"Good Lord," Tom said, finding it hard that Huck had just said what he did.

"No," Ben said trying to restore some peace and to end the coming debate quickly. "The clothes are old but you can believe me Jonathan and Patrick Shay never had worn the uniforms."

"That's all you had to say and it's right settlin' to know this," Huck said contentedly.

"I guess that I am Jonathan ," Tom commented dryly. "So you say these two poor fella's were reported missing at Shiloh. What if they had just plain run. I mean deserted. Suppose these fella's are alive and well and are walking around somewhere and we bump into them?"

"Good point," Ben said. "Our friend in the War Department forwarded us the after battle report. The Second Indiana had indeed broken during the afternoon of the first day and were taking refuge on the banks of the Tennessee River when they came under severe artillery fire for a while. When the smoke cleared, their entire section had been decimated. This was the last tine anyone ever saw them alive again. There is more than probable reason to believe that they were killed at this time and their bodies thrown into the river from the galling artillery attack. There is even less reason to believe that they are alive because they had no place to run to even if they had wanted to. The Confederate Army was to their front and the river to their backs. No, it is not possible that they survived. They are gone," Ben said.

"There is no need to think that they are alive or that you could possibly meet them. You are not going anywhere near their hometown, so the chances of an encounter with anyone that may have known them is nil."

"Artillery fire you say," Tom said. "Poor bastards, I know what that's like."

"Look Tom, we got demoted to privates. Ain't that a kick in the seat of your britches," Huck laughed, fingering the single stripe on the sleeve of the Federal tunic.

"Later, when you try on the uniforms, you may want to tell us if they fit. We took into consideration your height and your weight. Since you are going to pass as two discharged Union soldiers going home, we did not want to have you wearing tailored uniforms. The more disheveled the better," Ben said.

Tom had put his entire uniform on and it fit him very well. Huck was dissatisfied that the pants were a little too short.

"Now, for more important things on tonight's agenda. We have sat down and through many hours of diligent thought and correspondence with friends scattered in almost every imaginable location we have devised a plan, a route for your passage home," Ben said. He reached into his bag.

"It is intricate and very complex but we believe it will work. We are sure of it. Everything will hinge whether or not you can convince your lady friend to leave with you. If you can, we will get you to California," Ben said confidently.

"Don't worry about her leaving with lover boy here. She will follow old Romeo to the ends of the earth, ain't that right, Tom...you silver tongued devil." Tom acted as if he had not heard him.

"Tom showed me a letter she wrote him a while back. She is in love with our boy here, crazy middle of the road howlin' mad fer him."

"I never showed you any damned letter, you story teller. Anyway, even if I had, you wouldn't have known what was in it because you can hardly read all that well. That is because you have neglected your education so dreadful like when you were a young boy," Tom said.

"You are illiterate?" Ben asked worriedly.

"No, I am a Baptist. Does that make a difference?"

"Ben asked you if you could not read," Tom said.

"I kin' read a bit an' write my name. I ain't totally ignorant. But to answer your question let me tell you somethin. Tom has always had a soft spot for Rebecca, even when we were young'ins. I remember when she was nothin' but skinny knees, freckles, buck teeth and pig-tails. She liked our boy here way back when. Later, just before all the trouble, Tom here would be seen skulkin' around her front porch practically every night where she lived like an old tomcat. Believe me, she will come with our Lothario. Bet you didn't think I knew that word now, did you Tom." He laughed loudly.

356

"As long as you are able to read and comprehend the information that we have provided you and can sign that name, I suppose it will be alright. Back to the issue at hand, gentlemen."

He cleared the table and then placed a map upon it. He carefully spread it open. Tom and Huck edged warily towards the map as Ben doted over every wrinkle attempting to make it smooth and easily readable.

"This is a map of Canada, the central United States and Missouri." He pointed to a specific area on the map.

"This is the Rochester and Buffalo area right here. This is where you are now. Please follow me carefully. Buffalo over here is the first goal on your journey home. You will arrive in Buffalo in two days, no more, no less. From here as you can see, you are going to take a boat ride, a boat ride to Canada." Ben watched their expressions carefully. He pointed at a dotted line on the map.

"From your landing here at Nanticoke, you will go overland to the city of Hamilton and then on to the shore of Lake Huron. From here you travel to Goderich where you will stay with our friends for a day. Then once again, you will be met by our people and they will take you to a ship and you will travel by boat to Makinaw, Michigan. From here, it is simply a two day trip home. Down lake Michigan to Chicago, Illinois."

Both of them looked duly impressed with the map and its many dates and names as well as the many different colored lines, some dotted and some not.

"At Chicago you will be met by our people who have arranged the final leg of your journey home. You will travel by stage overland to Joliet, Illinois and then to Peoria. There you will embark on a barge that will take you to a landing near this town of Pitsfield where you will get on a flatboat and be home, a days travel at best. You will have twenty-four hours to convince your lady friend to leave. You will travel to St. Louis in style, on a riverboat. As you can see, there are names and dates and specific times on the map. You must keep to the schedule. If for any reason you are unable to do so, you must be sure to contact them by telegraph. Arrangements can then be made to rectify any problems, but gentlemen, there are no guarantees. This you must understand. It is all up to you."

"Seems easy enough," Tom said.

"In St. Louis you will go to the bank named on the map. You will secure all the rest of the finances needed to pay for a first class stateroom on a steamer that will be waiting for you in New Orleans. Then you are on your way to California, San Francisco, to be exact."

Ben straightened up from the table and put his hands in his pockets.

"Boys, I must let you know something that you will find interesting. The entire cost of your trip has been paid due to the generous donation given to Mr. Douglass by none other than one Henry Fowler. Mr. Douglass persuaded Fowler to donate this huge sum of money when Henry found himself in a delicate position on his most recent trip to our host's home. So, there it is. I hope the irony is not missed by either of you."

"I know all about that there iron-ee. It is a powerful thing that seems to follow a body around, ain't it?" Huck said.

"And to insure your safety, Jim will be traveling with you. He knows many of the people along the way in the way of safe houses where you can receive help if you need it. He will visit his family in Illinois before moving on to organize in that area. We know that the Mid-West is not so tolerant as in the east about Negro soldiers but we know that he will be successful. By the way, the money that you draw in St. Louis from the aforementioned bank is more than enough for your trip to California. Frederick did not want you destitute once you arrive in San Francisco."

"I am overwhelmed by all of this effort," Tom replied.

"As for me, it has come to my attention that there is a regiment forming in Connecticut of Negro soldiers and I have decided to enlist in it. It is to be called the 29th Connecticut Colored infantry regiment."

"Ben, you are one of the smartest people that I have ever met but you don't know what war is truly like," Tom said in shock.

"I intend to find out. I have to do this. I can't ask others to do what I am incapable of doing. I have to test my own resolve, my own endurance of the unspeakable or I won't be able to live with myself. Years from now, if we are all alive and hale, I want to be able to say that I did all that I was capable of in this terrible war. I want to be able to say that I had a hand in ending it. That is why I am enlisting as a private. I leave tonight. Mr. Douglass thinks I return to Philadelphia, but they don't need me there anymore. They will continue the work and they will do it well. Once I have time, I will wire Mr. Douglass and explain the reasons of what I do. So you can see, we are all starting on a great journey, fraught with many unknown perils and prone in uncertainty. But we must all do what we must do and I pray that one day, when this war is over, we may all gather together to remember this moment as a sort of turning point in our lives. A turning point that was something truly upstanding and right in our lives. Until that day, I will think of you always," Ben said.

"Ben, you be careful," Huck said, offering Ben his hand. As Ben reached for Huck's outstretched hand, Huck suddenly hugged Ben and then backed away as quickly. Ben patted Tom on his shoulder.

"Good luck to all of us and goodbye," Ben said. He walked away and they heard the front door shut behind him. Tom looked at the floor.

"There goes one damned good fella'," he said. Tom noticed something strange as Huck turned around. There were tears in Huck's eyes.

"What is the matter with your eyes. Did you get something in them, Hezikiah?" Tom asked.

"Go to hell and be damned," Huck said. He wiped his hand over his face and walked out the backdoor of the kitchen and into the night.

CHAPTER NINETEEN

Frank Gordon stood up from the small crackling fire and threw his remaining coffee in his cup on the ground.

"When Bob makes his move, I am backing his play. A lot of fella's are gonna' do the same. I' m not telling' you what to do, but you got to come to some kind of decision 'cause it is surely comin' soon."

"How soon you figure?" Ted asked.

"Don't rightly know. Maybe tonight," Frank said quietly. "I already talked to Bob. He knows how I feel. I told him that I would stand with him. He knows that whatever happens that I am all done with it. I'm through. I am goin' home to get my wife an' the boys an' then I'm headin' west."

"Any idea where?"

"No, I don't have a clue as to where. All's I know is that I ain't stayin' in Missoura no more. This war is lost with Vicksburg gone an' the Yankees makin' holy hell in Virginia. Old 'Marse' Robert got beat an' beat solid. Best thing is to end the war by some kinda' cease-fire. But neither side is willin' to end it that way. One sides got to be layin' at the feet of t'other down an' out for the war to end."

"You truly believe that we will lose this war?"

"There is no doubt in my mind. Those lunk-heads in Richmond lost Missouri. They will go on to lose the war. That is a fact. Anyway, our gallant leader has done made the biggest mistake in his dumb life by burnin' that Lawrence Kansas the way he did. I am glad we stayed out of that one. Bob did not have the opportunity to stay out of it. It made him sick an' that's why he is the way he is."

"You think it will come to gunplay when Bob makes his move?"

"Possibly. Quantrill deserves everything he got comin' to him. Lawrence is a black mark agin' his name an' agin' everyone what rides with him. It is one thing to ride under the banner of the black flag, but it is a total different matter as to what he did. They ain't gonna rest until they plant that little murderin' sawed off runt under the soil. The roads will be full of Yankees wantin' to get their names in the paper by killin' the little bastard."

"And just how many here feel the same way Bob does?"

"All of the old hands. The younger boys what joined us later still look up to the nutless sack of dog shit. I am glad that Bloody Bill is not in camp. I particularly don't trust him an' that boy that worships the ground he walks on."

"You mean Dingus?"

"That's the one. Frank James' little brother. What is that boys real name, I fergit'?"

"Jessie," Ted replied.

"Jessie, that's it. That boy is a wild one. He got a crazy look about him. Frank seems to be normal but that Dingus is trouble. If'n he pulls down, I will put one in his brain box, the sick puppy. Frank will have to go too, an' that is unfortunate because he is a likable fella'."

"Home is crawlin' with Yankees, Frank. I know 'cause I seen it when I was there with the Captain not too long ago. Everything is all changed up. What I mean to say is that there are a few families what are still sound on the goose, but it ain't the same place you remember."

"I don't plan on stickin' around town anyway. Like I said, I'm goin' home, grab Natalie an' the boys and then I am gone. Natalie's Granmaw was full-blooded Cherokee injun. Maybe we will head that way towards the nations to find some of her people fer a spell. Who knows?"

Ted mulled his options over. Frank was right. Staying with Captain Quantrill and continuing to fight in a losing cause did not make sense. Many of the younger boys were fighting for revenge alone, something that Ted was not.

"When you head home, I will go with you. I will say I am for it. You kin' depend on me. There is a certain lady that I will get to see there.'"

"Who is that?" Frank asked.

"Rebecca. Do you remember her; the family lived right on Main Street. When I was home last, I ran into her."

"I sure do. She comes from good stock. You sweet on her?"

"I reckon," Ted replied slowly. Frank could only smile at Ted's uneasiness with his question. He looked about to make sure that their conversation was not overheard by unwelcome ears.

"Bob knows that the command has gotten too big. What Quantrill has done is a death sentence fer' all of us. He knows the only chance we got is to break up into small groups like it was before. Bob will make sure that men with families an' sich' will be free to leave. The rest will be stickin' together fer defensive purposes only until the war ends. Bob figures there might be a pardon fer all of the fella's what leave. Safety lies in small numbers. Bob don't want to fight no more. His main purpose now is to live to see the end of all this bullshit an' I can't blame him. What

Quantrill done in Lawrence has stuck all our heads in a hemp noose. I was hopin' that you'd join us."

"Seems like the only sane thing to do," Ted said.

"Frank," a voice called out in the distance. "Best you get on over here. I think you will be interested in hearin' this."

"Great balls of fire. It's startin'," Frank said in surprise.

"What is?"

"What we were just talkin' about. That was the signal. Bob is goin' to call it a showdown right now. I had a feelin' that he might. Watch yourself Ted. If any gunplay breaks out, don't get involved. Take off an' get to the horses. Grab as many as you kin an' git'. Meet me by the crick where that big oak overhangs it. You got it?" Frank checked the condition of his pistol and placed it back in his belt. He straightened his broad brimmed hat.

"Got it," Ted said.

"Shows about to start. My God, I never thought that it would come to this. I bin' fightin' nigh' unto ten years. I lost Cecil in this war an' my nephew Lucas. I am spent. I know the fire has gone out of the chimney when you got to worry that your own people might cut you down."

Frank walked quickly towards the center of the encampment followed by a surprisingly calm Ted Doudlass. Ted could se that Bob and his band of supporters were grouped about the tent of Captain Quantrill. The tent was not a real field tent but rather two shelter halves looped together and supported by two large saplings. Captain Quantrill sat on a cracker box reading a newspaper. Bob waited until everyone was standing around him. Bob began by clearing his throat. The Captain took no interest in him.

"Captain, may I have a word with you?"

"Can it wait, sergeant? I'm a little preoccupied at the moment," Quantrill said without looking up from the paper.

"I'm afraid it won't, Captain."

The way that Bob said this peeked the Captains interest and he placed the paper on the ground. He looked up and saw that at least a dozen men stood around Bob. People in camp began to wander over, curious as to what was happening. Quantrill saw that the men surrounding Bob were practically all of the older men, men in their late twenties. He removed his wire-framed spectacles and placed them on top of the newspaper.

"Alright then sergeant. What is this all about?" he asked.

"Captain, what I got to say ain't easy. I thought long an' hard on it. Me n' some of the fellas here have been talkin' things over an' we have decided to ride out. We are through with all of this. This command has gotten way too big. We feel that if we stay together like this, it will be jest a matter of time before the Yankees catch us all flat footed. Smaller groups will be safer fer all concerned."

"Is that so," Quantrill said. He did not like what he was hearing. This was a direct threat to his authority and he knew it. The younger teenaged boys could not believe their ears.

"Yes sir, that is exactly so. Nothin' you say is gonna' change this. After what happened in Kansas this past August, it is a sure bet that the Yankees will do everything possible to nail all our hides to the barn wall. Stayin' large like this only makes it easy fer' them. We started out as small bands. That is what guerilla fightin' is all about. We were never meant to try to go up against a battalion of infantry or several troops of Federal cavalry. The Yankees got ten times the manpower than us. It's jest' a matter of time before they simply swamp us. Stayin' small will allow us to live, to stay alive. Stayin' big like this is jest' waitin' fer' the headman's ax to fall. We tried your way an' its not goin' to work."

"Sergeant," Quantrill said slowly, "you of all people should know that I can not allow for this to happen. We have struck a blow for southern independence. All of the newspapers in the country are writing about what we did. We let the world know that the war is far from over here in the west. We must and will strike another blow for freedom."

The Captain was nervous over what was occurring but dared not show it in front of the younger soldiers. He looked at the faces that supported the sergeant and saw that they were his most reliable non commissioned officers that he had. These men were the veterans. If they were to depart, he was lost. He tried to be diplomatic and attempted to garner a patriotic response from their ranks.

"Surely you can see that. Leave now, why man, don't be ridiculous. Right now, the whole state of Kansas is quaking in terror and Missouri too. What we did in Kansas gave hope to every true loyal southern man and woman in this part of the country. We inspire people to believe that all is not lost, that somehow we will emerge triumphant and..."

He was interrupted by a loud hoot of derisive laughter. Everyone turned to see who had the audacity to interrupt the Captain in such a manner. Sergeant William Gladstone pushed his way to the front still chuckling. He was a large rough looking man and he stepped right in front of Quantrill.

"Please, don't give us any of that old horseshit. Save it fer the pimply faced boys what don't shave none or the whores at Natchez. None of us is buyin' any of it. Not now."

The captain's jaw dropped open.

"Bob here," William said, "Is too much of a good man to give you both barrels, you sack of monkey puss, but I ain't a'scared of the likes of you, you crazy murderin' lyin' stinkin' pup. What you done in Lawrence was an abomination. I was there an' seen it with my own eyes an' it made me want to puke to think that some of our boys was capable of that. All these young'ins that ride with you don't realize this 'cause they don't know their asses from their elbows. They live fer revenge an' killin'. You young boys look at this maniac as some kinda hero. Some hero...killin' little boys an' old men. Innocent people got butchered. I got no qualms about killin' Yankees. I have killed a passel of Yankees an' I don't feel a bit of remorse. They deserve killin' if they wear a uniform an' shoot back but this wasn't any of the likes. This was murder. You killed because you had some kinda' personal grudge agin' them. That is why we are leavin'. You deserve to git' your neck stretched for what you done and the sooner the better, you slick talkin' dung pile."

"William, you are perilously close to earning yourself a court martial," Quantrill said. He felt his control over the men slipping away.

"Blow it out your ass, Captain. We ain't takin' no more orders from you, you cross eyed, buck toothed little weasel."

"Lieutenant Richards, arrest Sergeant Gladstone," Quantrill shrilled. "This is clearly mutiny and insubordination."

Frank placed his revolver behind the lieutenant's ear and his hands shot into the air. Bob, at the same moment, had calmly pulled his large Colt from his waistband and placed the barrel against the forehead of the Captain. Suddenly the whole camp was pointing a loaded weapon at someone else. It was a complete standoff. Quantrill responded quickly.

"Everyone put the weapons down. That is an order," he said.

No one moved a muscle and not an eye flinched or blinked. Fingers slowly began to tighten on triggers. Dingus aimed directly at Ted Doudlass nose.

"Put the weapons down, goddammit," Quantrill shouted boldly, in total control of his emotions. He did not show a bit of fear. Guns began to lower but they were not put away. Everyone was so accustomed at being ordered by the captain that the lowering of guns had been a simple reflex action. Both side glared angrily at each other. Bob looked Quantrill in the eye.

"I know it is over when we start pointin' guns in each other's faces. I am leavin' with these men, Captain. If you want to shoot me in the back, here is your chance," Bob said, walking away.

All of Bob's supporters carefully watched the faces of the younger men. They began to back out of the encampment. They did not show their backs, however, to their former comrades. Slowly they disengaged apart and withdrew into the shadows. Within minutes the sound of many horses leaving in a hurry could be heard from those in the camp. The silence that followed was as dreadful as that found in a wake. The young boys were left to wonder as to what had just taken place.

"Men," Quantrill finally said loudly, "Remember what you have witnessed here today. It is something that you will be able to tell your grandchildren one day. Today, you saw the Lord sorting out the flax from the wheat. Remember it well."

With this said he withdrew into his tent and closed the flap. He sat down and stared at the candle that flickered on a cracker box. He knew what Bob had said was true. He knew that his end was just a matter of time. He was doomed. At this moment, he wished that he were back in an Ohio schoolhouse teaching spelling to snotty nosed eight year olds.

The fishing vessel rolled in a light swell. It was a day out of Mackinaw, Michigan and a chill wind swept across its deck from the north. Tom and Huck stood at the railing looking out from the bow of the boat. The bright moon splayed silver fingers of light across the dark surface of Lake Michigan. A sailor passed them coiling a length of rope.

"Pretty damned cold night for September, eh boys?" the sailor asked. They both nodded their heads as the sailor passed them.

"I thought the Yankees liked the cold," Huck said.

"It would appear that not all of them do. Not that one, anyway," Tom answered. He shivered as he fought his hands and the wind trying to light his pipe. He cupped his shaking hands to protect the feeble flare of his match from the frigid wind and sucked strongly on his pipe.

"Mind givin' me a light, I left mine back in the cabin. I don't wanta' go back in there the way Jim is snorin'. I believe it would not be safe for me. The way he is suckin' all the air out of the room there I'm feared I might jist up an' suffocate from lack of breath."

Tom laughed and handed Huck a wooden match He struck the match on the railing and then flung the match into the water.

"Funny thing, I don't remember him ever snorin'. Ain't that strange?" Huck asked.

"People change," Tom said objectively.

"That is gospel," Huck said. He drew on his pipe and blew a cloud out into the frosty night air. Tom noticed Huck's brow knot up into a furrow, a sure sign that Huck was reflecting seriously on an idea.

"I know I have changed with all we seen this last few weeks. Them waterfalls at Niagara we seen, if somebody had tolt me about something like them I would have said that they was spinnin' some kind of yarn. You know what I'm thinking?"

"How should I know what you are thinking. What do I look like, a gypsy with a crystal ball?"

"I am startin' to think that niggers is jist' like people like us. I'm startin' to think that there ain't a hell of a lot of difference between us at'all."

Tom leaned against the railing and looked at Huck. He smiled and shook his head.

"I beg your pardon?" he said.

"I am serious. I think that niggers do a better job at being people than a lot of white people I knowed in my life," Huck said adamantly. Tom laughed and stared into the horizon.

"You laugh. You think I'm daft? Alright. I will prove it to you. Remember old man Flemming what owned the store?"

"Yes, I do, the old skinflint," Tom said.

"He had this big house and he lived there all by hisself," Huck began. "All his youngin's had growed' up an' moved away. We worked our tailbones off for that old fart on his farm. I hope I don't have to remind you about that fact."

"I still have the blisters," Tom said.

"While him and his tight assed boy ran the store, we ran his farm an' made money fer' him with all them horses an' growin' the corn an' the wheat. We made plenty of money fer him. He had the store on Main street with plenty of room in the back an' enough room in the attic for a dozen fellas an' sich'. What does the old geezer make us end up livin' in? His house with all them empty rooms in it? His store with enough room in it to house a heavenly choir? No. That old bastard made us live in his damned old barn. When it snowed, the snow would come right through all the damned spaces in the walls. The roof leaked like a strainer. You could put enough wood in that old pot-bellied stove of his until it glowed red and yet still every mornin' there was ice in the piss bucket. Your trousers were frozen solid so that you could lean them against the wall before you put them on."

"Whatever is your point?" Tom asked, entirely amused with the story that Huck was telling.

"I am gettin' to it. Hold yer horses, will you. What was I sayin'?"

"You were relating an interesting analogy, similar to a parable in form and context, as to how you have ascertained with a determined amount of observation from our shared past that there are no discernable differences between the Caucasian race and the Negroid," Tom said. "A hypothesis that not only a few scant months ago would you have dared to broach the subject with many of our late constituents and fellow cannon fodder would have been greeted with the most vulgar responses imaginable."

"I was?"

"As far as I was following you, yes, you were," Tom replied.

"I'll be damned. I did all that there? How was I doin'?"

"Pretty damned good. It was keeping my attention until you ran out of steam. Do you know where you were going with it?"

"No, But that don't make a never mind. My point is that all the colored people we seen lately who had us in their homes treated us like we wuz' members of their own family. I kin' honestly tell you that I don't understand why they don't hate white people. What is truly an amazing wonderment is that they don't. They truly don't. Hell, let's say Iff'n I wuz' to kidnap some fella', let's say a fella' from Scotland across the sea, and bring him here in chains an' work him like a mule. Bye n' bye, let us say, supposing that fella's children should somehow git' to become free. I know how people are. I would have to keep one eye over my shoulder at all times because them people would be comin' to find me an' usher me into a pine box."

"You do have a point. Well put," Tom said. "I applaud your analogy."

"You applaud my what?" Huck asked.

"That means I understand the point that you made, is all." Tom drew on his pipe as the smoke curled over his shoulder.

"I don't mean to say that there ain't no differences an' the likes. Of course there are. But the differences don't outweigh the plain fact that I have seen many niggers..I mean colored folks that jest' happen to be the color they are to ever feel the way that I used to feel towards them. I look at Jim an' I don't even see his color.

367

All I see is the man. A man that snores like there ain't no tomorrow but a man regardless."

Tom tapped the ashes out of his pipe.

"I am turning in. Tomorrow is going to be a long day, we got plenty of traveling to do, according to the map that Ben gave us. You should think about doing the same," he said.

"You think I'm wrong fer' thinkin' like this?" Huck asked.

"You go ahead and think anyway you want to," Tom said. "It is a free country. But if it makes you feel any better, I think what you said is right. I could not have said it any better." Tom headed towards his berth. Huck glanced up briefly at the star speckled sky and followed Tom below deck.

"The blankets smell like fish," Huck said.

"What do you expect," Tom replied, "This is a fishing boat. Hell, you lived in a barn and woke up with the smell of warm horse apples in your nose for years and you never complained about it once."

"That is because I am kinda' partial to the aroma," Huck said. "Fish stink."

"So does your feet" Tom said.

Bella watched Rebecca tear at the envelope of the letter, the first one that she had ever seen Rebecca receive. Bella had faithfully gone to the riverboat landing where the post office and telegraph office was located everyday excluding Sundays for the last three months. She had arrived there bright and early on her way to work and the people there had become accustomed to her routine. To her complete surprise, the man at the post office handed Bella a letter addressed to Rebecca. After her housekeeping chores were finished at Doctor Waters home, she had hurried home and presented the letter to her friend who now sat at the kitchen table frantically tearing at the weather beaten envelope.

"It is from Tom. I recognize his handwriting," Rebecca said nervously. She was practically in tears.

"I will let you hear your talking papers alone," Bella said turning to leave.

"Don't be silly. Please ...sit down."

Bella reluctantly sat down, not wishing to offend Rebecca.

"Are you sure? I know many people who listen to Talking Papers and wish to be alone. My father tried to make me learn the pictures in the way of the signs that make the Talk, but I was never many good at it. Much people believe that all women would be wasting time in doing this when they should be learning how to cook and sew and grow many corn."

"That is terrible," Rebecca said as she pulled the pages out of the envelope.

"Reading and writing should be taught to everyone. It makes us all better people." Rebecca pressed the folded pages out flat on the table and began to read. Bella watched as Rebecca's eyes began to move across the top of the page.

"It is dated July 18, 1863," she said. She began to read the first page. Bella continued to watch Rebecca's expression and intensity. Rebecca's eyes raced across Tom's letter.

July 18, 1863

Pennsylvania, near Gettysburg

Dearest Rebecca,

I hope this letter reaches you and yours and finds you all in good health and happily together. I am writing to tell you that I am coming home. I do not know exactly how but there is nothing in this world or the next that will keep me from you.

What a fool I have been the last few years. My dearest one, please forgive me. I thought that wealth would win your heart for me. That is why I left the way I did, without telling you anything. I planned to make a fortune in California and return in a year or so with enough money that you would be impressed enough with me to answer yes when I asked you to be my wife. I now know how wrong I was.

I realize now that the greatest thing a man can have is life and the love of a good woman. As long as I can breathe I have everything that I will ever need in my life because I have you. What is measured as wealth for me these days is your love. Wait for me, my sweet Rebecca.

I am not certain when or even if this letter will ever reach you, but I pray to the merciful Father that it does. I am no longer a soldier. As you must know by now, we were badly beaten in a town called Gettysburg. Huck is alive and we are together but we were both nearly killed. Suffice it to say that neither of us are a prisoner of war. In a sequence of events that would simply be too lengthy to write about, we are both ordinary citizens now. The war is over for both of us and he is returning home with me. I think he believes he needs to protect me. You know how he is.

But do not doubt for a minute that I will soon be at your door. Without you, I am a half a being, like one half of a pair of scissors. Never doubt my love for you. When I come home and take you in my arms there is a question that needs to be asked and I hope you will answer yes. Think long on it, sweetheart. Think not in haste. My life will be full of trouble. I am a wanted man. I offer you nothing but my heart and soul. But with you with me, I can conquer any adversity that may befall me. I must close this letter as I have just run out of paper. I love you

Always,

Thomas Sawyer

Rebecca's eyes were misting over and Bella felt awkward.

"Does your Talking Paper speak well the words that you wanted to hear?" she asked.

"Yes, it does. Thomas promises that he is returning home. And soon. This letter is almost four months old. He could be here any day now," she said happily. Rebecca looked at Bella and noticed a strange expression pass over her friends face.

"Bella, why do you look all concerned when I say this? Is something the matter?"

Bella shifted nervously and began to rise from her chair. Rebecca reached out and took her by the hand and held it tightly.

"Don't look away from me. I saw that look just then. You are trying to conceal something from me. What is it, Bella? You know that you can tell me anything."

Bella sank back into the chair.

"I beg of you. Tell me this instant. It has something to do with Thomas, doesn't it?"

"I will tell you. First, you must tell me if your heart is brave. What I speak you must listen well and have a brave heart. Is your heart brave?"

"Yes. Now tell me."

"I know your heart is brave. I watched you when you were listening to the Talking Paper with your eyes. It is this. Remember when I told about that bad man, Henry Fowler."

"Yes."

"Henry Fowler has many men here and they watch this house and many houses of people that you know well, people whose heart favor the gray soldiers who fight the blue white men."

370

Rebecca looked confused.

"What do they want from us? They must know that some of us will never leave. They cannot force us away from our homes that we have lived in all of our lives. Why are they doing this? We have not done anything wrong for them to treat us like this," she said angrily.

"They do not want your homes. They want your lives. They know that Quantrill came to this town. They know he was in your house. The half-dead boy spirit that walks with the eye-patch did not tell you that his friend was Quantrill when he brought him home on that fat hen Sunday eating day. The man that watched this house told me what they do here before I made him many dead and threw him into the great muddy water that goes past where the river is trying to drown the houses."

"You killed someone? Oh my goodness Bella, what have you done?" Rebecca asked horrified.

"His name was Timmins. He was a bad man that made dead many people for many money. Before I made him dead, he told to me how Henry Fowler sets a trap for Quantrill and the half a dead boy spirit that was with him on the fat hen eating Sunday."

Rebecca's mind raced with the shocking news.

"Remember when I tell you how I helped your Thomas and his not too bright friend escape the trap that Henry set for them in the hotel many years ago? Henry knows that I am in town. He wants to dead me the same way he made old Joshua dead. Henry sends his evil little Totem man and his fat friend with the split face here. I have not seen them but I feel it they are here. If your Thomas comes to this town he will get trapped.. This is how Henry makes dead many people. He has Timmins or the short man or that no good Neely dead people for him."

Rebecca fought to remain calm.

"Thomas is in terrible danger then. Bella, we must warn him somehow before he arrives."

"This is sure that I know. When Henry has killed Quantrill and the half dead boy , he will come for me. He will try to send my spirit to the house of my southwest grandfather's and I do not think I am ready to go there. Not just yet. We must try to save your Thomas. Do you love him? Do you love him to do anything to save his life?"

Rebecca nodded. "Yes. I do."

"Henry is used to getting what he wants. If they are watching us, we must watch them. I must find the short little totem man and his fat boy. I must make them dead as I can. If you cut off a rattlesnake's head, it becomes a harmless thing whose rattle is given to crying babies to play with. This is what must be done to save Thomas. Listen well, my friend. I have a plan."

Lieutenant Neely bounded up the stairs of the hotel two at a time as he made his way to Colonel Lehigh's room on the second floor. He carried in his bulging pockets the weeks reports compiled on all the southern suspects in town and any unfamiliar face that had appeared in town. After the death of Sergeant Timmins, the eight men of the detail always traveled in pairs. Timmins had become slack and careless and had paid the ultimate penalty. The danger of what they were doing in this town had become readily apparent to them all when they had found the rotting corpse of Timmins. When they had first started their duty in town, many had taken the job lightly, considering the job as a lark. All that had changed with the discovery of the body.

The wounds that Timmins had suffered before he had received a fatal gunshot had seemed cruel indeed, as if someone had wanted to torture the man before they had ended his life. Timmins had not died in a drunken brawl or a stupid gunfight. This was apparent to Neely. Someone had probably tortured Timmins for information and it was more than likely someone who had wanted to know why he was in town. It was true that Timmins had enemies all over the state of Missouri and Kansas. It was apparent to Neely that Timmins had grown overconfident in his assignment and had allowed an enemy to surprise him. Timmins, Neely figured, had been set up.

Neely did not know who had set Timmins up, but it only made sense that Timmins had met his end by a person or persons that knew who he was. The only person that knew who Timmins was in this town was the Indian squaw, the one that had worked at Fowler's home. The squaw had seen Timmins and Fowler talking together countless times. Neely also knew that the Indian had seen Fowler speaking on many different occasions with himself as well. Timmins had mentioned on the day before he had disappeared that he was planning on watching the house that Bella was staying at. Neely told this to Lehigh and he had simply said to watch the house but stay a good distance from her. He had told him that when it came time to have a day of reckoning, the squaw bitch was the first to go.

Neely had felt good knowing this. He made the landing at the top of the stairs and made his way to Mason's room. He knocked briskly at the door and waited. Mason who was dressed in a suit that was almost two sizes too big for him opened the door.

"Make it quick, Neely. I got to sample some of the new talent comin' in from New Orleans today. Put the papers on the desk over there," he said, "anything new at all to report?

Neely began to unload the papers from his pocket onto the desk.

"No, Colonel Lehigh," he said. "Colonel, it's startin' to get a little cold in those tents. The men were asking what happens when the weather starts to change for the worse?"

"Make big fires, Neely."

Neely was disappointed in the answer. He received in one week what it would normally take him half a year to earn as a lieutenant of cavalry. Although Lehigh made sure they were paid extremely well, the idea of sleeping in a freezing tent did not appeal to any of the eight men on the detail.

"Lookit Colonel. This ain't gonna sit all to well with the others. We was wonderin' if we could all come into the hotel whence it turns cold. We will pay for the rooms. Its just that them tents don't keep a chill off a man at all and none of us is getting any younger." Mason relented.

"If you pay, I don't see why you can't. Hell. I was thinkin' it might be better for all of you to get out of them uniforms and be legitimate. I even talked with Henry about it and he agreed. The last time I talked to him, he said that he was arranging everything with the mayor." Mason walked over to his desk and pulled out a mahogany box.

"Open her up," Mason said.

Neely walked over and opened the box. Inside a velvet backdrop were one sheriff's badges and eight deputies badges. Neely didn't know what to say.

"Henry paid a good amount for them badges. The boy's stars are silver, solid silver, but your star is gold, solid gold. You men are now the official law in this town startin' today. We can't have the law livin' like a bunch of owl hoots now, can we?" Mason laughed."

"Fowler paid the mayor a handsome fee, but he can well afford it. The mayor takes orders from us from this point on and he don't ask no damned foolish questions either if he knows what's good for him. Neely, old boy, we own a town."

Neely was dumbfounded. "You mean I'm the sheriff?"

"Jobs pay twenty five dollars a week. Plus what Fowler is payin' you, you should be all right, don't you say! Beats rustlin' cattle like in the old days, don't it. Pin that star on, sheriff," Mason said.

Neely pinned his badge on.

"I got a plan for this place, Neely. What Henry don't know, won't hurt him. I got a box of hundreds of dollars under the bed. Neely, I'm bustin' this old house out. I'm gonna' start come spring in makin' this place the biggest, largest cat house north of St. Louis. I got new girls already lined up and comin' in and if they meet my approval they will start immediately. **Neely, I tell you, we are all gonna' be rich. But you gotta' understand on thing. Henry might not approve of all of this 'cause he's a Bible pounder.** The man hates sin and sinners, so we got to keep this all quiet. I need **men that are gonna' be loyal to me if this here is all gonna work out for our benefit. Do you follow me, Neely"**

Neely nodded. "Yes sir, Colonel Lehigh."

"Stop that Army talk, Neely. Call me Mason. What I'm tellin' you is after this war is over, Fowler's star is gonna' continue to rise. Maybe someday he'll be president of the whole United States…who knows. But that don't mean that we will necessarily go with him. This here can be our thing and our's alone. If that is to happen, Neely, I will need men who are loyal to me and me alone. People who will be able to back me up if anyone tries going against us. That includes Henry. The way I figure it, we all could be as rich as Henry is in jest a few years. Can I have the support of you and the rest of the detail?"

"I would shoot old Henry hissself if he tried to interfere, Mason. That is a fact," Neely said.

"Good. That's what I expect to hear from you. Make sure the rest of the men are square with this. The first man that offers any opposition, I want you to shoot that man between the eyes as an example, no questions asked. Do you understand me, Neely?"

Neely smiled. "I sure do Mason. I sure do. No problem." Mason offered Neely his hand and they shook.

"It's good to have a partner I can depend on," Mason said, grinning.

Twelve year old Fenton Gordon watched as his eight year old brother Clayton ate a frog. He knew in his heart that it was wrong of him to let Clayton eat the frog, but the gusto his older brother displayed in eating the frog had dispelled all of his objections. Clayton simply enjoyed and relished the attention his older brother showed in his eating of the amphibian. Watching Clayton eat the frog was more fun than spying at the soldier that constantly was near their farm.

When the stranger had first appeared, Fenton and his brother had looked upon it as an enjoyable interlude that broke up the boring monotony that transpired day after day on their insolated farm. After a while, it too had become boring. The stranger in the blue uniform no longer made the game interesting. He no longer hid himself like he had at first. The game had been to sneak up on the stranger and watch him without being seen.

The soldier now made it too obvious that he was watching the house and no longer hid. This took the fun out of the game. In fact, the strange soldier no longer wore a blue army soldier's jacket, but now dressed in regular everyday clothes. He even waved at them when they waved at him. Fenton watched as the last vestiges of the frog disappeared down Clayton's throat. Clayton giggled and wiped his freckled face.

"One of these days your gonna get sick so bad your gonna' poop purple and roll up into a ball."

"Mr. Gates sez that the Frenchies down New Orleans eat frogs all the time and you never hear tell of any of 'em getting sick," Clayton replied.

"I bet you they don't go ahead and eat them raw the way your doin'. Keep on eating raw frogs and when you get sick, I'll tell maw what you have been up to."

They walked towards the farm house. The weather had been unreasonably warm for October. Clayton had probably eaten his last frog of the year. Soon the frog pond would be asleep under inches of ice, and the winter would grip this part of the world in its icy embrace.

The boys stomped up the back steps of the house making sure that any mud would drop off long before they entered the kitchen. They intently watched their feet as little clots of mud flowed from their feet from their intensive stomping. They looked surprised to see their Sunday school teacher sitting at the kitchen table with their mother.

At once Fenton became nervous with her presence in the kitchen. Last Sunday, he and some friends had climbed up on the roof after class and had spit on some of the students and had thrown dirt clods at others. Retribution sat at the table with his mother and Fenton swallowed hard as he realized that Rebecca's sudden appearance could only mean trouble.

Rebecca smiled at both of the boys. Clayton gave his best frog-eating grin and waved a pleasant hello at Rebecca. Fenton smiled uneasily. He immediately detected that something was wrong from her expression, but Rebecca was valiantly trying to conceal her feelings. She was as nervous as his mother, he realized. Something was wrong and it had little to do with the spitting dirt throwing incident. Fenton was both relieved and frightened.

"Boys, say hello to your teacher," Natalie Gordon said.

"Hello, Miss Rebecca," the boys chimed in unison. Natalie Gordon then said something that made Fenton even more suspicious.

"Miss Rebecca and me got something to talk about. You boys go out and play a bit."

"Yes'm," Fenton said, relieved to know that what ever Miss Rebecca was going to say to his mother had little to do with him. Clayton waved a parting gesture at

Miss Rebecca and followed his brother out the door. They clomped down the stairs. Clayton recognized the worried expression on his brother's face.

"Maw will skin you if she finds out you wuz' on the roof of the church throwing dirt balls and spitting tobacco juice," Clayton said.

Fenton said nothing, hoping that if it weren't talked about too much, it would go away. He walked towards the barn intending to check on the two cows the family owned when he noticed something odd. The soldier was missing. He usually stayed at the tree spying on the house until sundown and then he would leave to return early the next morning. He was nowhere to be seen and it wasn't ever near sundown.

"Look Clayton, over yonder. The soldier is gone."

Clayton spun his head around to see if what Fenton had said was true. He was just as surprised as his brother to see that the soldier had indeed left. Clayton shrugged shoulders as Fenton began to walk over to the spot the soldier usually was. As they neared the tree, Fenton spotted a puddle of blood on the ground, not much, but a puddle nonetheless.

"Maybe he got a nosebleed like I use to," Clayton said, "and decided to ride back into town."

Fenton spotted the soldier's horse tied to a tree a few feet away in the underbrush. When Clayton spotted the horse, he grabbed his brother by the arm. Fenton froze still and Clayton looked at the reason. The soldier's head was a bloody mess. He was trussed up securely with rope and lay a few feet away from the horse.

"Holy Mosses," Fenton said loudly. Both of the boys looked at each other as fear gripped them. They both began to run back to the house as fast as they could.

CHAPTER TWENTY

Lehigh, Pete, and Sheriff Neely waited at the pier for the arrival of the riverboat that carried General Fowler. Henry had telegraphed Mason informing him that he would be arriving on the afternoon of October 22, and as most of the riverboats arrived at Petersburg either early on the morning or by late afternoon, they were expecting him well before sundown.

"Neely, remember now. No talk about any business arrangements. Nothing about the cathouse. If Henry does know about the hotel then we could have an awkward moment. You sure that you tolt' everybody to keep their damnable mouths shut now, didn't you?" Mason asked nervously.

"Everybody knows the stakes, boss. If Henry knows anything about it, he found out by someone else and not us. That you can rest easy on now."

Mason was startled as he heard a riverboat whistle. The Captain of the riverboat gave the chord to the whistle another tug. His boat was full and he had made good time. He looked forward to spending an hour or two at the hotel outside of town. The talk was that it was the biggest, fanciest house of ill repute on this part of the river. In fact, more than one of his passengers were fancy ladies, of this he was sure. There were also quite a few sporting men as well as the usual assortment of soldiers all heading into town.

In fact, one of the oddest passengers on board was a general. The captain had never seen a general dressed as this one was. When he had boarded as St. Louis, the second officer had made a comment that he should see the strange apparel that the General was wearing. The Captain had at first been shocked into silence when he first viewed his most important passenger.

Henry wore a sky blue uniform with a bright red sash. Gold epaulets, larger than he had ever seen, adorned his shoulders. A large gold encrusted sword with a mother of pearl handle set the sword off. But the most imposing thing that this strange General wore was the large naval style hat. It was purple and blue speckled with silver. A large ostrich feather stuck out from the crest. The hat hearkened back to the era of Napoleon.

The Captain fought back an urge to laugh as he passed the strangely attired Federal general. There was no doubt of the man's rank, for there on his shoulder sat the largest two stars he had ever seen. They were the size if an average man's fist. The Captain laughed silently into the palm of his hand. He had decided that he had seen everything. Being a captain, he thought it undignified to acknowledge this finely dressed buffoon a greeting. Ordinarily, he would have asked if the general needed anything and would have made the man of importance very comfortable.

377

The captain passed the absurdly dressed officer without even making eye contact. When he and his first officer were safely back in the privacy of the pilothouse, they had laughed until tears streamed out of their eyes. The captain leaned over and tugged at the ship's whistle again and gave a series of staccato blasts that warned an approaching flatboat heading towards the riverboat of the captain's intended desire to land at the pier before the flatboat. The captain glided towards the pier and the crew began to heave lines to people at the dock. They quickly secured the riverboat to the moorings.

The flatboat began its approach to the dock a few seconds later. Mason began to pace nervously on the dock as he awaited Henry's appearance down the gangplank. Henry had telegraphed him the day before telling him that he was arriving for an inspection and that was all. Mason wondered what kind if inspection it was supposed to be. He hoped that Henry had not found out about his business activities in town. If he had, he knew it would mean trouble. He hoped that he could at least explain himself to Henry. He intended to say that the hotel fancy house was a front, an undercover ruse to keep suspicious minds at bay while the operation was being conducted in earnest.

If Henry failed to buy it, Mason was prepared not to back down from Henry. The last meeting that Mason had with Henry had been an eye-opener for Mason. Henry had never before threatened him and Mason was not the kind of person to back down from anyone. Mason had realized that Henry had gotten to the point where he felt he could threaten his life. If that was the case, Mason thought, then it was time to remind Henry that there were some men who could be threatened and some that could not be. Many a man had looked upon the small stature of Mason Lehigh and had not taken him seriously enough. These men's bodies were buried all over Kansas and Missouri.

Mason had talked it over with his men and had planned well in advance for any and all situations that may arise. Two of his men were on the roof of the telegraph station with Lehigh in plain open sight for their high-powered sharpshooters rifles. If Henry planned to arrest Mason on the dock, they were ordered to open fire. If Henry did not, they would go back to the hotel and have an early dinner. If any trouble were to arise, Mason had ordered Pete to take careful attention and at the proper signal, all of his loyal men would burst into the hotel's dining area and kill Henry and whoever was there with him. Lehigh's men would take care of any of Henry's men that were away from the dining hall.

Mason hoped that it would not come to this. Henry had always been an eccentric, one to put in airs and be high faultin', but Henry had changed. Mason reminded himself that whatever may happen, it was not personnel but purely business. Mason still respected Henry but he would not be treated with disrespect by anyone. If Henry had to go, then Henry had to go.

378

Many people began to walk down the gangplank, soldiers by the score followed by civilians of every conceivable type. A few dozen sporting ladies caught Mason's eye. He was not prepared for what he saw next. Gunter Klaus came down the gangplank followed by fourteen of the most dangerous men that worked for Henry. They were dressed in tailored uniforms and were all above the rank of Captain. Colonels and Majors all of them and some of the most feared men who had ridden with Henry during the border fighting.

Gunter Klaus wore the insignia of a full colonel and led Henry's men down the plank and onto the pier. Henry was last. Mason spotted Henry's strange apparel and fought a desire to laugh. Henry walked down the plank as if he were part of a royal procession. Gunter recognized Mason on the dock and headed the group towards where he stood. Mason feared and loathed the demonic Gunter Klaus, a foul tempered lout of a man, that he had seen murder a man in St. Louis for no apparent reason.

The victim had walked past Klaus from the other side of the street. Klaus had turned and fired one bullet into the bald pate of the unknown person who collapsed dead into the road. When Mason and the rest of their group were safely away from St. Louis and the law, Mason had asked Klaus why he had killed the stranger.

Gunter had chilled Mason's blood with the explanation he had given and Mason had never forgotten what Gunter had told him. From that point on, Mason knew that Gunter was a maniac and not to be trusted. Gunter had grinned and said that he had just gotten an urge to kill the man for no earthly known reason. He said that he had just felt like killing someone at that moment. Mason quickly looked Henry's entourage over and shuddered. If Henry knew anything and wanted to make a move against him, he definitely had the talent and backup to do it.

Some of these men had the uncanny ability to sense danger and more importantly, to correctly react to it. All were fanatically loyal to Henry and would have had no qualms in shooing their own grandmothers dead if called upon to do so by Henry. If trouble were in the brewing and if Mason were to survive, he knew that it would take careful timing and a whole lot of luck. He was well aware of what kind of trouble that these men were capable of wreaking in a very short time.

The group drew abreast of Mason, Neely, and Pete. Gunter looked Mason in the eye for a split second and Mason froze in panic. Mason desperately tried to keep his mind a blank in an attempt to disguise the terror he felt. Gunter passed him and then for some unfathomable reason, Gunter looked directly at the roof of the telegraph office. He stared at the roof intently and then turned and walked towards the building. Mason inwardly squirmed like a worm on a fishhook and fought back his desire to open fire on Klaus. The group with Henry got out of the way as Henry approached Mason.

Mason properly saluted. Henry did not respond but stared at Mason strangely. Mason said nothing as his stomach dropped into his shoes. Finally, after what seemed like an eternity to Mason, Henry saluted and snapped to attention like a Prussian Junker.

"What have you got to say?" Henry asked haughtily.

Mason felt his hand inching towards his pistol. He was not sure whether to give his men the signal to open fire but was within a hairs distance of pulling his pistol out and blasting Henry in the forehead with it. He tried to grasp what Henry had asked him for a clue as to what Henry was thinking. Henry simply glared at Mason as if Mason had two heads.

"Damned your eyes, Colonel. What have you got to say? What is the matter? Does the cat have your tongue?" Henry scowled at the smaller man. Mason's hand continued to make a careful descent to his weapon. The signal for Mason's men to open fire was that he would yell loudly, "This calls for a celebration." He would fire one shot into the air. After that signal shot, Mason was to dive away while everyone would open up on the general. The men on the roof would shoot him while the men in the telegraph office would pour forth from the office and cut down every living soul that had come with Henry. Suddenly, Henry beamed a huge silly grin at Lehigh.

"About the uniform, man…about the uniform. Isn't it splendid?" Henry asked, as he pirouetted in front of Mason.

"I had it specially made for me in New Orleans by some Frenchies right off the boat from Paris. Extradinary workmanship, I dare say. Feel the quality of the materials. The fabric, why it fairly breathes like a living creature. They have told me that the style is all the rage in Europe. It is copied by all the finer minds of men of good taste, like myself. What have you got to say about it?"

Mason swallowed dryly

"I asked you what do you have to say about it, old man. You are astounded, aren't you? That is the effect that it has on people, I am fairly sure. If you want, we can go to New Orleans and I can have them make one for you as well. I offered to do the same for Klaus and the others, but they all declined. They all said that they were unworthy to wear such fine raiment's. I, of course, could see that such an exquisite uniform would be wasted on them. They are all crude and oafish men who would only bring disgrace to such a fine uniform. After all, Mason, you can't make a silk purse from a sow's ear."

Mason sighed in relief. Henry began to laugh at his own joke and pulled out a dainty lace handkerchief and dabbed at his nose. He then made a show of placing it back into the sleeve of his jacket. He strutted around the dock as he did as people began to gawk at Henry's garish uniform. Many began to make snide comments.

Henry apparently did not hear them. He was too busy enjoying their stares. However, Mason did. He scowled dangerously at everyone and the people making these rude remarks drew away instinctively away from his evil predatory stare and Mason's intimidating manner.

People who at first only had wanted a glimpse of the strangely garbed general now were being pushed and shoved away from him. Once having walked the perimeter of the dock, Henry's entourage now made a protective cordon around their boss. All comments and curiosity faded abruptly as Henry's men bullied and threatened everyone standing near Henry. People scurried away from them in abject fear. Soldiers, in passing, would nervously avoid all the officers they saw. They would go out of their way, staring at their feet and walking into the backs of the men in front of them who were also trying to avoid the fierce looking majors and colonels that were with Henry. Henry ignored all of this and watched a barrel-laden flatboat that had just pulled onto the dock being unloaded.

"I am thankful that this flatboat's cargo consists of whiskey instead of pigs," he said. "As for pigs, Mason, the sheriff of this town looks like a street rag picker from the slums of New York. If the man is going to wear a star of such fine quality, the least he should do is dress appropriately for his position. That goes true for the rest of the shabbily dressed deputies. Those stars and badges cost me a pretty penny, not to mention having to buy off what posses for a city council and the mayor, the spineless greedy maggots. This is my town, Henry. Make sure that they dress well," Henry said loudly.

"As the French so aptly put it, my good man, D'Estat est moi. They represent me, the law and order here. They must not look like riff-raff. They must look like gentlemen."

"I don't know all about that, General Fowler. With our being undercover so to speak in this town, it may draw attention to us. Hell, Henry, half of them don't even wear the badges. Neely here is the only one and maybe Covington and Amos Dinwiddie. That's plenty to show these local piss pots who the damned boss is out here. The rest of our people is all hidden in the shadows."

"Good idea. That seems logical enough. Good work, Mason. I commend you on it. The less people that know of our operation, the less chances that that Quantrill may find out about us being here. Good work. We shall have that fiends head on a silver platter before too long. Need I remind you of the consequences of failure?" Henry stood on his toes and towered over Lehigh.

"No sir," Mason said convincingly sheepishly.

"You, my most trusted loyal servant, shall be instrumental in bringing this effort to completion, this I have no doubt. I have spent a fair amount in this effort. I will see results. Anyway, Neely's star is big and shiny but not nearly as big and shiny as mine. You remember that. Now, we must away."

"What was that, Henry?" Mason asked. Henry stared angrily at Lehigh. Mason blinked a few times trying to understand what Henry had said.

"Oh...I get' it...why sure, Henry...I mean General Fowler. We will away together to the most comfortable and luxurious place in this whole half-assed town, Wait till you see it. I got us a carriage waitin' yonder. Wait till you see this place. The people in charge of it are true blue Union people an' they cooperate with me one hunert' percent."

"I expected nothing less from my most important operative. After all, Mason, it is my town, isn't it?"

"General, this here town is all yours, lock, stock and barrel."

Mason grinned widely. He walked ahead and when they came to the carriage, he opened the door for his boss. Henry majestically strode towards the carriage and entered it followed closely behind by the midget Colonel. Henry was duly impressed with the opulent velvet interior of the stately coach.

"General, there is a small thing about my headquarters. It is a whorehouse," Mason said boldly.

"My man, I could not care if it was the whale that swallowed Jonah, as long as the pursuit of our mission gains us the required results." Mason grinned and slammed the carriage door firmly. Henry leaned back in the seat and admired his rich surroundings.

"After we have our man," Henry said, "we shall drive all these whore-mongers and sinners from my town. We shall burn this nest of iniquity down its foundation and the smoke will rise in triumph to the heavens. On this you can be sure, my good Colonel."

Mason disguised his dread at Henry's words. He looked out of the window at the passing soldiers and sporting men who were headed to his establishment to spend their money on ferro, blackjack, and fancy ladies. We shall see about that, Mason thought.

Tom and Huck walked into the dock after climbing out of the flatboat. Tom would have twenty four hours to find Rebecca and convince her to leave with him. The flatboat would be heading down the river to St. Louis and eventually to New Orleans. The trip was already arranged and paid for well in advance.

The boys gave curios glances about them, astonished at the changes the town had been through in the last four years. In their federal uniforms, they blended in with the crowd that bustled around the dock area. They begin the walk to Rebecca's house on Main Street. It was October 22, 1863.

From the open doorway of the Gordon barn William Gladstone and Ted Doudlass watched the sons of Frank Gordon as they ran panic stricken towards their home. In their haste to tell their mother about the soldiers who lay bound, gagged, and bleeding in the woods, they had become obvious to everything. Their legs pumped furiously as they ran and their eyes bulged in terror.

"Looks like Frank's boys found our little friend." William said quietly.

Frank had wanted to first check out his farm from a distance before riding in. What he saw had infuriated him. A man siting directly across form his home was nonchalantly looking in the kitchen window with spyglass. A buckboard and an old horse were tied to the apple tree in front of the house. Frank watched as the strange man watched his home obviously taking his time and seemingly not interested in leaving anytime soon.

Frank had come back in an agitated state. He was, in fact, almost incapable of speech. He raged, bellowed, and roared. The blood of his Viking ancestors banged and pulsed in his head eradicating all reasoning and logic from his mind. The blood lust he felt manifested itself in an immediate need to destroy what he perceived as a direct threat to his family. The berserker spirit that gripped Frank was truly frightening to watch. His face contorted and his eyes were almost out of their sockets as he screamed obscenities to the blue sky.

Ted and William had never seen Frank act this way and for a while they feared for their own safety. He was temporarily insane, his rage being all inclusive against this strange interloper with a spyglass that had the gall to watch his wife, children, and home. The only people who had ever seen Frank react in this manner had been his enemies, and they could never talk about what they had witnessed because they were all dead as a result of Frank's fierce anger. William and Ted watched as he slowly returned to normalcy. He soon began giving orders to them.

Deputy Edgar Covington lazily watched the goings on at the Gordon Homestead interested in the owner of the buckboard and the owner of the old mare tied up in the front yard. He knew that it was owned by the local school-mom. She was on his enemies list. He kept his eyeglass trained on the kitchen window and focused all his attention paying little notice to his immediate surrounding.

Edgar turned to investigate a sound in the nearby brush, a rock thrown by William Gladstone. As he turned to see what had caused the noise, Frank Gordon placed the barrel of his revolver in this ear.

"Put your goddamned hands up in the air and don't make a noise you son of a bitch, or it will be your last sound you ever make. What the hell do you think your doin' staring through that there thing at my house? I hope you ain't love struck with the lady of the house 'cause she just so happens to be the woman I married," Frank said.

"It ain't so, I swear," Deputy Covington pleaded.

He put his hands in the air as Frank stood at arms length and pressed the barrel of his pistol against the forehead of the deputy. Frank noticed that the man wore an impressive deputy sheriff's star on his overcoat. Frank pulled the man's pistol out of man's waistband and tossed it away into the underbrush. William grabbed the man's arms and twisted them behind his back as Ted quickly secured them with a length of rope.

With this hands bounded securely, William pushed him into the woods and away from the road and the house. They went a few rods onto a grove of small trees. Edgar looked at one of the men and nearly emptied his bladder. The man had an eye-patch, a blonde beard and moustache and his hair was long. He knew he was looking at Ted Doudlass, one of the men that he was supposed to watch for. There was no mistaking the man's identity. He felt nauseous with the realization that he was a prisoner of men who were known to ride with the devil, Quantrill.

Edgar looked frantically about him, his heart beating nearly out of his chest in horror. They were leading him to his death and realization of it's almost made him faint with fear. He knew he did not want to die. For the first time in his life, he had enough of the creature comforts to actually enjoy living. The money from the whorehouse and the company of the fancy ladies made life sweet.

Now, he thought that was about to all end. His throat constricted with the idea of his own oblivion. Life had been had for Edgar. He did not grow up with a silver spoon in his mouth. He had grown up hardscrabble…first as a minor cow rustler and then had moved on to horse thievery. The image of himself lying dead in the woods with a bullet in his head made his legs grow weak and his skin go clammy cold.

"Who the hell are you with this damned star pinned to your goddamned coat?" Frank asked angrily.

"I'm Deputy Sheriff…Deputy Sheriff Covington."

William stepped in front of the anxious deputy and balling up his fist delivered a staggering blow to the man's mouth. Edgar landed on his back. Tears from the pain flooded his eyes. His lower lip had been split in two and blood flowed freely from his abrasions and cuts that his teeth had caused to his mouth. He rolled his tongue rolled across his teeth to see if any had knocked out.

Edgar was tough. He was determined to die like a man and not a whimpering coward. Many times in the past when he had killed a man he had always been embarrassed for them and made to feel uncomfortable by their carrying on and in some cases, their tears. Although he was terrified, he was determined not to show fear. Ted and Frank quickly brought him to his feet.

"Wrong answer, Tulip," William said gruffly. "You better start givin' the right answers around here. I know who the law is around here and it ain't you, sweetheart. Don't bullshit me, I was born and raised in this town."

The deputy continued to try to blink away his tears that filled his eyes.

"Things have changed around here, is all I'm sayin. I'm the deputy I tell you...the law," Edgar said with conviction. He hoped that the tears that filled his eyes would not be construed by his captors as weakness. It had been a natural reaction for his eyes to water after being hit the way he had.

"Start talking, deputy, or things are gonna start changing on you for the worst. What the hell are you doing looking through my window with that goddamned thing?" Frank asked.

He brandished the spyglass at Edgar like a medieval mace. Frank watched the deputy as he blinked away the tears that has been caused by the blow he had received to his face. Edgar fearfully looked about for help from any quarter. He prayed that one of the boys would come by. Perhaps Frank would not kill him in front of the boy. Maybe he would have enough time to plead his case for mercy if the boys came by.

"Let me kill him, Frank. Hell, I'll even dig the hole," William Gladstone said. He grabbed the deputy by his throat and lifted him off the ground.

"I'm gonna' make you die miserably slow, you little piss ant useless you answer the man. What are you doin' here?" He flung the deputy to the ground. Frank grabbed Gladstone by the arm and led him a few feet away from the sprawled Deputy.

"William, I need answers right now, not corpses. Let me try it my way. You can catch more flies with sugar than you can with vinegar," he whispered.

Frank walked over to the Deputy and began to lift him to his feet as Ted helped him. When they had him standing, Frank backed off.

"William, git' me the bottle of whiskey," he said. "What was your name again son?" I didn't catch it."

"Edgar...Edgar Covington."

"Edgar, I got a problem and I'm gonna' need you cooperation. I am trying to stay in control and not put a bullet in your head. Do you understand the predicament I'm in?"

Edgar nodded hopefully. At least this murdering bushwhacking scum was willing to talk. Perhaps there was a chance that he would not die this day. Edgar attempted a feeble smile.

"I come home and see a man looking through the window of my house. Now, normally I'd kill you just for that, but I will try not to as long as you help me. Do we have an understanding, Edgar?"

"I hope you don't kill me. If you did, you would be killing me for the wrong reason. I ain't interested in your wife or ever causin' harm to your boys. I swear on my soul."

"I don't necessarily want to, like I say, kill you. I'm trying not to, but if you don't help me to help you, then I guess I will let William try it his way, and believe you, me you don't want to know the things he has in mind for you."

Gladstone pulled a large Bowie knife from his boot and waved it in front of the frightened Deputies nose. William handed the bottle of whiskey to Frank.

"Ted, untie Edgar's hands. Don't go tryin' nothin' stupid, Edgar. You will be dead long before you hit the ground."

Frank pulled the cork out of the whiskey bottle and handed the bottle to Edgar. When Ted untied him the deputy reached for the bottle.

"Swish some of it in your mouth...then have a good pull," Frank said. Frank watched as the Deputy complied. He grimaced as the alcohol burned the split in his lip and the cuts his teeth had caused in the inside of his upper lip. He then took a long pull off the bottle.

"My teeth is all loose," Edgar said faintly.

"Whiskey will tighten up what's loose and loosen what's tight," Frank responded. "Go on, have another drink." Frank watched as the Deputy drank. He handed the bottle to Frank.

"Good. Now let's us all sit around and have a sensible talk like reasonable men. Edgar, I am going to be honest with you. I rode with Quantrill. That is all over with now. I've come home to get my wife and children and them I'm gone. I presently don't want no trouble with you or anyone else. I am done with the war. All I want now is to be left in peace. Let me tell you something, Edgar, my boy. The war is lost. I know this and you know this. The only ones who don't know this is the young ones and the damned lunkheads that are too inspired with the cause that lead them. When this war is finally done with, Missoura' is gonna' have a lot of young men who don't know nothin' else but to raid, plunder, and kill, 'cause that's all they growed' up with. I ain't gonna' have my boys raised in a place like that. You take my word, Edgar. Missoura' is gonna be full of bandits, raiders, and outlaws, As for me, I'm leavin'. Am I makin' sense to you?"

"Yes, you are," Edgar said.

"Good. I ain't fightin' with nobody or no one, Edgar. I bin' fightin' for nigh onto ten years. I'm sick of it. But let us be clear on one thing. I will fight to the death to protect what's mine and I will kill for the same, Edgar. I'm beggin' you to answer truthfully. If I think for a minute that you are lying to me, don't think that I will not hurt you real bad before I kill you." Frank drank from the bottle and handed it to Ted.

"So tell me now, how are you a deputy on this town? I never seen you here before until today and all of our Sheriffs in the past were local men. Most were good men although every now and then we got some that were no good fer nothin'. I remember a fella...he was and affable drunkard who blew his face off one rainy night while cleaning his shotgun. He made a right horrible mess out of the Sheriff's office. His brains was all over the damned jail. After that, we kinda had no Sheriff 'cause everybody felt bad with what happened to the last one. That there was a tragedy...Ted, do you remember the last time we had a sheriff in town?"

"Can't say that I do, Frank."

"How is it that you are a deputy, Edgar? Think careful before answering 'cause I might go off like a shotgun myself and that would surely be a disaster for your longevity."

"Colonel Mason told Neely that the General bought the town so that's how I'm deputy. Half the fella's don't wear the star but Neely does to please the Colonel. I suppose that's why I do."

"Who are these people...this Colonel and General?"

"That would be Colonel Lehigh and General Fowler. General Fowler...why he's some General. He's been fightin' just as long as you have. He was a Kansas Jayhawker from way back. Good friends with Senator Lane and those boys from the trouble back in the 50's. He goes way back. Colonel Lehigh is in charge of the operation out here, we know all about you rebels in town. We know all your names. That fella over there, we been waitin' for him to show up for quite some time now. He rode into town with Quantrill last summer. My job was to watch your house, and if he showed up there or you showed up, I was to report directly back to the Colonel so we could spring the trap and catch the whole lot of you. I never was spying on your wife. I swear."

"I believe you Edgar. How many of you are out here?" Frank asked.

"Usually seven or eight, depending. Today, General Fowler is comin' to town for some kinda inspection. That means trouble for the Colonel 'cause he runs the whore house in town and is makin' money like there ain't no tomorrow an' the General don't take to sinners and the likes. We are all sidin' with the Colonel if there is any trouble. The colonel pays us well. I was supposed to watch just half a day today and take up position on the telegraph office's roof for the General's boat to arrive. Any attempt that Henry made on the Colonel, and it would be the end of Henry. The Colonel don't give a damn about any of you. Hell, I'm even kinda partial to your two boys. Ask them if you don't believe me...but I never was disrespectful to your wife. You gotta believe me."

William Gladstone handed the bottle to Edgar. He walked behind him.

"I believe you Edgar. Now say good night," Frank said.

"What?" Edgar asked. William Gladstone smashed Edgar in the top of his head with a rock. He pitched unconscious over on his side.

"I hope you didn't kill him, Frank said, "I was just startin' to like him."

"Frank, we gotta get out of here. Me and Ted will tie him up your new asshole buddy over here...Buck and gag him. Go get your family...we ain't got no time to waste. Accordin' to old Edgar here, if he was tellin' the truth, the cat fur is about to fly...we'll take up watch in the barn. Did you notice that buckboard and old mare in the front yard. Any idea who might be visitin'?"

Ted spoke up. "Frank, you remember Rebecca...that's her Father's rig. I'm sure of it."

"Boys, I will be with you directly." Frank walked towards the house and used the cover to the barn to mask his approach to the front door. He opened the front door carefully and strained to hear the voice of his wife and another woman. They were speaking in hushed tones as he pushed the door open and entered the parlor, He drew his weapon. Frank Gordon was home after being gone for three years. It was October 22, 1863. It was nearly noon. Frank inched his way towards the kitchen and the sound of his wife's voice.

Bella sat in front of Rebecca's dressing table and thoughtfully stared at her image reflected in the mirror. She had been relieved when Rebecca had told her that she would be visiting the Gordon farm sometime this morning. For what she had in mind, it would be crucial that Rebecca not be home for her plan to work. On the table she had arranged a pile of empty thread spools from Rebecca's sewing box, a bowl of sugar water, a bowl of crushed dogberries, and a bowl of flour. She cared for Rebecca but sometimes Rebecca's nervousness was a major distraction. Better that Rebecca did not know all of her plan.

388

Rebecca was to inform all the families that had been spied on of their general situation. Rebecca would do this one family at a time. Bella was already to put her plan into effect. She eyed her long black hair and sighed. This is where she decided to begin. She reached for a large empty spool of thread and began winding her hair around it. She wound her hair as tightly as she could, and when she finished she applied sugar water to the spool. She tied it with a short piece of string. She worked quickly and in silence. Soon her whole head was full of spools.

Satisfied at her work, she then began to take a small dry cloth and rub the flour into her brown skin. She began to take on a ghostly appearance. She applied another cloth to the crushed dogberries and worked the color into her lips and cheeks. Her lips took on a purple hue and her cheeks began to take a rosy color as she worked the berries lightly into her face. She stood back and looked at her work. She took out the spools and her hair fell to her shoulders in ringlets held into place by the sticky sugar water. She fingered the curls into spirals that ringed her oval face.

Her next project had taken her several days to complete. She had taken one of Rebecca's slips and with patience and a great deal of creativity had made it into something that she had seen the fancy ladies of the hotel wear. She completed the look with a parasol and an embroidered shawl of lace. She quickly dressed and when she was finished, she stared at the transformation. She looked exactly like what her Father had called fancy ladies. She remembered him calling them painted circus ponies. She rubbed excess flour from her face. She was proud of her whorish look that reflected from the mirror. It renewed her confidence in her own abilities.

She placed her fully loaded single action Colt pistol behind her back and secured it with a leather thong. She bounced up and down to see if it would fall out if she had to run. The pistol stayed on her back and did not budge. She shifted her shoulders and turned to the mirror to see if it could be detected by a casual glance. It could not. She looked long and hard at her reflection in the mirror. This was the day to put into motion what she knew must be done. She had felt responsible for the trouble she thought she had caused Rebecca and she was determined to rectify the problem.

She had taken great care to find out if Lehigh and Pete were in town and she had been rewarded by her diligence. She had spotted Pete and Lehigh in town. Either man had not seen her. Lehigh seemed to have shrunken in size and Pete had appeared to have become wider, but there was no mistaking the pair. Bella walked down the stairs and as she did she continued to test the position of her pistol by slightly bouncing. As she did, her bosom became more noticeable in the dress that she wore. She did not notice this. Instead, she stopped at the bottom of the stairs and looked about her.

She had spent some fond memories in this house with Rebecca. She felt Rebecca to be her sister; she had become so close to her. If this was the day her spirit would join her ancestors, Bella was prepared. She resolved to place all worry in a special place that only she knew about. She was as calm as she was when going to one of her Father's sermons. She opened the door and walked down the stairs in the direction of the hotel. She kept her mind focused and walked towards the riverfront and dock on Main Street.

Carriages passed her as well as men in pairs and in larger parties. She felt their eyes on her. As she neared the dock, she noticed a large number of people watching the goings on of one particular carriage. She could not help looking into the carriage as it drew next to her on its way to the hotel. The carriage was extremely expensive looking and would have attracted attention simply by the way it looked. It was obvious by the way that people stared and watched the carriage that someone of importance was riding in it. She curiously looked inside the carriage and there in full view, enthralled in conversation were Pete, Lehigh and Henry Fowler.

They were so involved in what Henry was saying, that her presence in the road went completely unnoticed by them. She covered with her face parasol and looked away quickly from the carriage. She continued on her way to the hotel, devoid of concern for her own safety. She was so focused on what she was going to so, that she never even realized a man in a carriage had pulled up next to her and was speaking to her. She stopped and began to listen to what he was saying. She watched his lips like a person who had a hearing problem.

"I see that you are going my way. You must beg my pardon in assuming this, you see. I am new to this town, but I have heard quite a few stories about the entertainment that can be had here. Quite a few stories indeed."

His eyes were focused on the ample cleavage that her bouncing on the stairs had exposed. The man's eyes were fixated on her bodice. He was practically leaning out of his buckboard for a better view of what had his complete and undivided attention.

"May I offer you a ride?"

He lifted up his hand to silence any objections that Bella may have voiced.

"No, I do not offer a ride, I demand that you accept. I will have no other answer. It would be criminal to let a beautiful woman as yourself walk while there are lesser women who ride in comfort."

He offered her his arm. She looked about and then climbed aboard the buckboard with a little aid from the stranger. He clucked the old nag into motion. The Buckboard was a rental. Mr. Gates and his son were making a fortune from the never-ending amount of people that wanted to ride the mile and a half to the hotel in comfort.

The carriage business was booming for them and they shuttled passengers from the dock to the hotel every time a boat landed. For an exorbitant fee, they rented carriages to those that didn't mind paying the cost. They had even gone so far as to purchase the fanciest carriage ever seen in three counties, a magnificent antique from the last century, and rented its use for the exclusive rights of the big wheels at the fastest growing cat house in the state.

"I do this as an act of Civic responsibility, mind you now, and not merely because of a predisposed nature or predilection. I do it because it is merely the way I was raised and nothing more, of course. After all, we are not savages."

His eyes played over her so much that he didn't really guide the old nag. The horse knew the way by now from the daily routine and plodded along like a machine.

"You are quite exotic looking. I have been in New York on many business ventures. Me, myself, I am originally from Hartford, Connecticut...well outside Hartford. I came out here just before the war as a salesman of sorts."

He could not keep his eyes off her nearly exposed breasts. Bella caught the direction of his gaze and quickly fixed the front of her dress. He disappointedly stared ahead.

"I take you as a foreigner. Wait...let me guess. You are Portuguese are you not?"

He smiled waiting for her to speak. Bella had never heard of the term before in he life. She had no idea of what he was talking about. To her the words sounded like "porch geese." She looked at him oddly and said nothing. She kept her attention on the whereabouts of Henry Fowlers coach and paid her new acquaintance little attention.

"I take your silence as my being correct. I assume it of course. It is an amazing gift, I do believe I have, of being able to look at a person for the first time and determine his or her, I may add, national origin. Don't get me wrong, young lady. I am not now, nor have I ever cared for the trend that was so prevalent just before the war. I mean of course, the detestable and narrow view of those damnable "Wide Awakers"

The man took a minute from his ramblings to pick his nose.

"I believe that there is plenty of room in America for the world to come to our dinner table. Anyone who would find fault in anyone's origin just because they were unfortunate enough not to have been born in the United States in a half-wit. Those Wide Awakers and their provinciality in this regard was truly on aberration. I can tell you that I have always been against the rampant nativism they preached, yes indeed. Anyone can climb above their origins to become an American. It is the

391

inherent nature of all of you foreigners to overcome your inferioty and become Americans. This is what I deem to be you people's saving grace."

Bella had not grasped practically anything that he said. He continued to prattle on.

"You say many words." Bella finally replied.

"I beg your pardon?" he asked.

"You have big eyes," Bella said disgustedly. She watched the fancy antique carriage ahead as the strained chassis swung on its unconditioned springs as the wheels shimmied. It traveled at a good speed and Bella watched it disappear in the traffic.

"Excuse me, did you just say I have bigot's? Of course we have bigots. Do you understand?"

Bella nodded.

"That is precisely what I have been speaking about. I do not contaminate myself with their prejudicial and mean spirit of belief. They are heavily bigoted those Wide Awakers. If there ever was a political movement of more inane irresponsible attitudes, it was the Wide Awakers."

"You say I am porch geese?" Bella asked, pointing at herself.

"Yes", He smiled. "Of course you are Portuguese." He pointed to his own chest.

"I am not Portuguese. I am an American. I am as Yankee as a person has the pleasure of being. My family came across on the Mayflower. I knew of a man in Lisbon, Connecticut, he was Portuguese. He had many lovely daughters, none as lovelier than you. May I ask you, without deterring one iota from the respect that I have for you, whether you are a sporting lady or not…a lady of leisure?"

"I am porch geese painted pony," Bella said.

"That, my dear, is the best news I have heard all day."

The hotel loomed before them. People thronged on the huge veranda and red, blue, and yellow Japanese lanterns were hung everywhere. Men in expensive suits sat in wicker chairs speaking to scantily clad woman of east virtue. Soldiers in groups of almost a dozen gawked at the sights displayed on the expensive porch. In the foyer of the structure, men stood elbow-to-elbow and nearly belly-to-belly, smoking expensive cigars and exchanging ribald tales. The action at this hotel continued twenty-four hours a day, seven days a week. The flow of people was non-ending. A hundred people entered while a hundred seemed to be leaving.

Prostitutes and sporting men congregated in the gaming room gambling huge sums of money while other women served the players watered down drinks. Bella looked around to see if she could spot Henry's distinct carriage but she could not. Her escort had continued to blather words at her, which she found difficult to comprehend. She continued to nod complacently to all of his questions.

"I hope you will let me buy you a drink," he said confidentially, "money is no consideration. I have accumulated so much money, in fact, that I will never be able to spend it in one lifetime. The war, you know. I have made a fortune supplying certain people in Hartford lucrative contracts with the government, which I have handsomely profited from. I suggest that we play some easy game of chance and then retire to the restaurant for a good meal."

Bella hopped out of the carriage and stole away from her enamored host who called after her in frantic and incorrect Portuguese. His pleas entreating her to stop were left behind as she danced up the steps and into the great hall of the hotel. People were everywhere and quite a few were intoxicated. Drunken soldiers and pie eyed politicians bounced along the walls, holding on to the red velvet tapestries that covered the entire length of the spacious main room.

Portraits of nudes were situated above the bar and the roof was covered by mirrored chandeliers reflecting the glow of the many lamps, giving the entire room a certain excitement and character. The grand stairway wound up to the second floor making the entire room seem huge and palatial in appearance. A thick red carpet with diamond patterns covered the floor. Several women immediately began to notice her, as she passed a group that was standing together, one of them tapped her shoulder.

"Some place, ain't it homey. If your waiting for the audition stay with us. There looks like there is plenty business to be had here for all of us."

Several of the women began to snicker at what she had said.

"See the tiny peckerwood standing over there with that funny dressed soldier. He said to wait right here for him. People say he owns this place. I ain't never seen a place like this in all my born days."

Bella hid her face when she saw that the woman had been speaking about Lehigh and Fowler who stood only a few scant yards away. She turned and walked quickly towards the bar.

"What got into her?" she heard the woman ask angrily. "Stuck up bitch."

Bella walked away as quickly as she could without drawing attention to herself. She peeked in the direction where she had seen Henry lecturing to Lehigh and his associates. Henry was gesturing widely with his hands and pointing to various patrons of the hotel. She could see that he was losing control of himself Lehigh was trying to lead him into the main dining room, but Henry was too angry and worked up to even listen to Mason. Henry's voice rose in intensity and Bella, along with quite a few other people, were more interested in what the strangely garbed man with the purple face was saying.

"These perverts will all burn in hell," Henry screamed.

"Please, Henry. Not now," Mason pleaded. "Let us away, as you say, to the dining room. These no good damned sinners ain't worth a breath of your effort to try to save them from getting' a pitchfork in the ass from old Beelzebub."

Henry stopped his angry raving.

"Yes…I think you are right. They are not worth saving. When it times time to burn the rat nest down, Mason, I want you to make sure that as many of these perverts are in here as you can possibly get. Order the bartender to serve free drinks that night. Then, when they are all in here doing their perversions, I want your men to board up the doors. Nail them shut, do you hear me? Only then will you set this devil's playground to the torch. Their fat will roast in the conflagration as surely as their rotten souls will burn in hell for all eternity."

"We will make their fat sizzle, Henry. Don't worry none. You have my word."

Henry smiled at the people who stared at him.

"You sinners will have a reconciliation with the Almighty God Jehovah sooner than you think. Revel in your wickedness, you Sodomites, while you still may" Henry touched Mason on the shoulder and whispered into his ear.

"If they only knew what we have in store for them, eh old man." Henry threw back his head and laughed.

"We got us a good meal planned tonight, Henry. Follow me so's we can talk away from these wicked evildoers and sich. Right through the doors and into the dining room."

A huge table was set up and the aroma of roast pig filled the room. Mason stopped and grabbed Pete and pushed him through the door away from Henry.

"I want you sittin' at the table. Neely as well. Henry is going along with everything so forgit' the part about comin' in shootin'. Get the rest of the men in here and off the roof of the telegraph office. I want everybody in the dining room. Don't mess this up, Pete, I'm countin' on you. Get back here likity-split."

Pete nodded. Mason walked to the table admiring the platters of food that were neatly laid out. His men followed him in and waited for Henry to sit down before they seated themselves. Henry made himself comfortable as Mason sat down at his left.

A waiter with a steaming pot of coffee began to fill cups, starting with Henry's. Henry waited for the boy to finish pouring his coffee. Henry studied the young man.

"It's too bad that the innocent will burn along with the guilty but such are the ways of nature. Take that young boy serving us coffee, for example. For him, this is merely a job. He probably has not tasted any of the perversions going on around here. Yet, when it comes time to burn this hellhole down, it is more than likely that he will perish in the flames as well. Better that he dies uncorrupted in his youth, you see."

Henry waved his left hand in the air.

"However…who knows really…he maybe already contaminated by the wiles of all the wonton women of this Gemmorah. That is why he must roast along with all the rest. We will take no chances. This will be a righteous town if I have to kill every man, woman, or child in it. Where are the owners of this entrenchment of evil? Will we meet them?" Henry asked.

"No sir. Not likely. They are out of town," Mason said warily.

Henry leaned closely to Mason and whispered in his ear, "Regardless of the fact that they are Union people. When it comes time to raze this cesspool of corruption, I want then to burn as well." Mason nodded his consent.

"I'll burn all their asses up for you, Henry. You can count on it."

"Good. Splendid. What are the owners like? They must be rich. Do they have important friends in high places?" Henry asked.

"Why, in fact, they are rich. But for them having important friends and the like, I would say not. They like to keep in the shadows. They are out of town most of the time and let one of the women watch the books. She's and old whore that is just glad to have a chance to earn a dollar," Mason lied. He blew on his coffee. Mason caught Henry looking as him oddly.

"They's just two old coots…no family…no friends," Mason added quickly.

"My good man. Me thinks that you have overlooked a prime opportunity here," Henry said. "I am surprised that you, with your good business sense, did not see it. It surprisingly jumps up and bites one on the nose, in fact."

"I'm not following you so good, Henry. You lost me," Mason replied.

"Follow this carefully then. How much money do you think this place generates in a weeks time?" Henry asked.

"To tell you the truth, I don't know how much," Mason lied.

"I tell you that just by what I have seen here in this short time it must be a handsome amount. Where do the old men put their money? Do they deposit the money in the bank in town?"

"No, I don't think that they do, now that you ask."

"Perfect. On the night that you choose to fire this den of iniquity, arrange a meeting with them and the old whore that runs the place. When they are all together, I want you to shoot the old whore in the head. Make sure that you get all her brains on the old geezers. That will show them that you mean business. Threaten them that the same will happen to them if they don't get all the returns from the past month. Tell them if they don't, they are deadmen. Tell them that they will live if they do this and die if they don't. They will surely comply. When you have the money, have Pete break their necks. You will keep forty percent and I will take sixty. Then nail all the doors shut and burn all the damned wrenches." Henry sipped his coffee.

"Forty percent. Sounds good to me," Mason said slowly.

"It is much better to steal from the wicked. It satisfies my soul. Now...on to other matters. I was with Jim Lane a few weeks ago. The story he told me of his narrow escape at Lawrence sent chills up my back. The day Quantrill attacked, Jim Lane was barely able to escape with his life. He jumped out a window still in his night shirt and ran into the woods."

"You don't say."

"That is why it is imperative that we catch this brigand. I want him dead. I need you to chop his head and hands off. Put them in pickling spice and alcohol and send them to me. I know of a taxidermist that has offered to mount his head on a board for me. I intend to hang it in my study. His hand, I will have the same artist turn them into ashtrays. When I was in Washington this summer, I did chance to see in the lobby of the hotel an ashtray fashioned out of an elephant leg. You know that I met with the President. He is exactly as reported by General McClellan. The man is unnatural height. He is an ape, quite simian in appearance. Lincoln is an ape."

Henry sipped on his coffee.

"Mason, the game is politics. This next election, Lincoln is out. This last "sha-bang" they fought, they lost nearly twenty thousand apiece. Everybody that I speak with is sick of this damned war. This is why General McClellan will beat "old honest Abe" in next election. This last fight at Gettysburg, that's the second time Lee was on his way to Washington. We will not let the Capitol fall. We will go rolling merrily along. Lincoln will be seen for what he is, a complete baboon. Little "Mac" will be elected President and he will end the war in a "a negotiated peace.""

"We made a lot of money out of this war," Mason said hopefully, "what happens when it ends?"

"We will make even more money, my dear fellow. The climate is right," Henry shouted, "and it is such a big country."

Henry's attention was distracted by the appearance of a prostitute with raven ringlets of hair and dark purple lips that slinked her way towards him.

"Need I embarrass you further by your lack of knowledge regarding the works of great ancient writers, particularly those of Rome's classic periods. I would, I am sure, just confound your ignorance. Let me simply say that there has never been a successful slave rebellion against any true power. This war has been turned into a war to free the niggers making it in effect a slave rebellion by that baboon, Lincoln. May I remind you now of Sparticus."

Mason squinted his eyes trying to remember where he had heard that name before.

"Sparticus... hmmm...wasn't he the huge nigger that his owner used to have wrestle all the time?" Big nigger with good speed and hands?" Mason asked.

"I daresay you know nothing of what I speak. Hear me, this rebellion will fail. All of the uppity niggers will go to hell, including that damned nigger Douglass and that ape in the White House. Lincoln will fail. There will be a peaceful resolution to this war when Little Mac is elected President. The niggers will be put back in chains."

Henry made a display out of tasting his wine. First he sniffed it and then sipped at it with his little finger pointed at the ceiling. He pulled his monogrammed handkerchief from his sleeve and daintily dabbed his lips with it. He waved it at Mason in small circles.

"I have thought ahead and will be at the right place at the right time when this entire travesty finally is resolved. The rich southern planters will need niggers and they will be desperate for them. They will have to deal with me. With my connections, I will have men knocking every damned free nigger in the head and will put them on ships and send them south. I will corner the market in niggers. After all this bloodshed and destruction from this war, no one in the north will give a damn about the legal rights of the blacks You and I shall take a trip to Rochester with a few dependable men. I shall personally cut the tongue from Mr. Douglass' head. Then I shall burn it clean with a hot poker and stick him in a barrel and take that damned coon south with us. I intend to sell that black bastard very cheaply to some poor buck toothed shit farmer in Arkansas. All those rich southern perverts will give me any amount that I ask. They will come begging to me for niggers to pick their cotton. I will have all those southern gentlemen eating from the palm of my hand. This you can count on, Mason. That black monkey Douglass cost me a fortune the last time that I saw him and I vowed to all that is holy that I would see to the ruin of…"

Henry watched the seductive approach of the painted prostitute as she wiggled her way towards the dining table. He was struck speechless by her whorish beauty.

Gunter Klaus sprang from his chair a few seats down from Henry. He desperately grabbed at his holster for his pistol. A bullet smashed into his forehead. He stiffened, and a very surprised look encompassed his features. For several seconds he shook violently and then he fell forward, his face landing in a bowl of steaming mashed potatoes.

Majors and Colonels dove out of their chairs in all directions as chaos ensued. Henry could not react. He tried to stand but his legs wouldn't obey. He watched in fascination as the prostitute leveled her pistol between his eyes. She calmly fired at his head just when Lehigh shoved Henry to the floor. The bullet ripped off Henry's lower ear and he screamed in pain. Mason covered Henry's body with his own small one.

A Major took deliberate aim at her and fired and missed killing a waiter. As he drew back the hammer of the pistol to fire again, Bella sent a lead bullet into his eye. He danced a strange sort of jig. In his death throes his finger tightened on the trigger and the pistol bucked in his hand. The bullet bore into a very surprised looking Colonel's temple blowing the entire side of his head into a spray of flying pieces of brain tissue and fragments of skull. The Colonel uttered a groan and sat back in his chair. He hung there momentarily suspended by a split second between life and death, and then he collapsed onto the floor. The Major continued his macabre dance of death and then his body doubled over and he went twirling into the table.

By now, other startled officers had begun firing at the crazy woman who had just attempted to kill their meal ticket. They began to fire furiously at the bizarre apparition, this hellish angel who calmly fired and seemed to hit everything that she aimed at.

Bella did not have the chance of killing either Mason or Henry now as the room erupted in gunfire. A bullet tugged at the sleeve of her dress as she backed towards the door. A Colonel fired at her head and missed. The badly aimed shot found a home in the chest of a heavily perfumed Major with mutton chops who fell backwards with a piece of roast beef still dangling from his lips.

Bella continued to fire. A Colonel began to run towards her firing wildly, with his left arm in front of his head holding it in front of himself as if it were a shield. Bella fired and he went rolling onto the floor, moaning in agony. She fired again and hammer clicked onto an empty cylinder. She slammed the heavy door shut. The door splintered and shook from the intense firing of the men still in the dining hall.

People ran and some screamed. Drunks were pushed to the floor as panic broke out in the main hall. A crowd of people ran to the entrance trampling any one who was too drunk to run, Bella put the pistol in the small of her back and ran for her life. The doorway of the dining hall burst open and several angry cursing men poured out, all firing at Bella's back.

Patrons were hit from this wild fire and fell dead or dying. Bella pushed forward in the careening mob and almost fell when she reached the veranda. Men were leaping on horses and a half naked woman ran towards the road in terror.

Henry's men lost sight momentarily of Bella as she tripped and fell. They quickly spotted her as she rose and flung herself down the stairs. The crowd flowed like a stream around her affording the gunmen little opportunity of a clear shot of her. Infuriated that she would escape their vengeance because of the cover the crowd provided her, Henry's men began firing into the backs of the crowd cutting scores of people down.

Bella dodged and jinked her way towards a young patron who was so scared witless that he was trying to mount his horse from the wrong side. Bullets continued to thud into flesh all around her. Bell reached out and ripped the bridle out of the startled young mans hands. He began to protest the action when Bella reared up and punched the dapper young stalwart in the groin. He fell on his back releasing the bridle.

Bella leaped into the saddle and the horse jolted as if it were in the Kentucky derby. Bullets whizzed over her head as Henry's men emptied their revolvers at the desperate woman on horseback. Bella hung low to the side of the horse allowing herself the greatest amount of cover the horse's body could provide. She felt the horse shudder as it was repeatedly struck by bullets. The horse thundered down the road with flecks of blood and foam whipping from its flaring nostrils.

Henry appeared on the veranda holding his shredded ear. Blood had cascaded down from his wound straining his sky-blue uniform a dark crimson. He had managed to staunch the flow of blood with his monogrammed handkerchief. Lehigh stood at his side. Henry's men had begun to reload and some were racing for whatever means of transportation that was at hand to continue their pursuit. Some jumped astride horses while others knocked people from their buckboards and carriages.

"After the harlot, men. I offer a thousand dollars to the man who kills that damned Jezebel. After her now brave boys."

Henry drew his ceremonial sword and waved it in a circle above his head nearly striking a staff officer in the face with it.

"Mason, that was too close, much too close. The Ides of March came stealing towards me in the form of a hellish painted strumpet. I will have her painted head on a pike before this day is over. This assassination attempt can only mean one thing. Quantrill is in town. He sent the whore to kill me, there is no doubt. Gather everyone, Mason, we are after the fox."

"Henry, you ain't gonna believe who that Jezebel was. You ain't gonna believe it," Mason said in wonder.

Dead and dying people of both sexes lay on the veranda, in the bar, in the doorway, and on the steps. Blood was everywhere.

"Mason, I am in no mood for a guessing game. If you know the identity of that damned witch, then out with it." Henry said. He cradled his wounded ear and looked about at all the dead sprawled around him.

"That was Bella, Henry. There ain't no mistakin' it. She was gussied up so that when she came sashaying over to the table, I couldn't make hide nor hair of her. But when she started flingin' lead around the pace, that's when I recognized her and pushed you down on the floor. That girl can shoot. If I hadn't pushed you down she woulda' blown your head clean off."

"Why didn't you notify me that she turned into a fallen lady? My God, man. If I had known that she had turned to a life of debauchery and sin, I would have had her shot immediately. That would have been the first thing on my agenda on my trip here. I would have shot her as you would a horse with a broken leg. It would be the only way to save her soul, if those people really in fact so have souls."

"She ain't a whore, Henry Why she was after your hide is anybody's guess. Henry, I live here. If I had seed' her here, believe me, I woulda' remembered her. I can't figger' why she would want to do a damned fool thing like this," Mason said.

Neely, Pete, and the rest of the Deputies came riding into view at a full gallop. Neely leaped from his horse and nearly landed on a corpse. He caught his balance and hopped over the body of a well-dressed fat man. A cigar was still clinched firmly in the cadaver's teeth. Peter stooped over the corpse and removed the gold ring from the corpse's stiffening hand.

"Holy hell, Colonel Lehigh. This place is like a slaughter house," Neely said quietly.

"Mason, arrange for a doctor to see me in your quarters immediately before my system is poisoned. Arrange to have D troop leave my headquarters. Telegraph them now and inform Captain Barlow to board his troop in a transport, horses and all. Don't worry about the cost. Have them leave immediately. Take charge, Colonel. I'm not feeling all that well." Henry looked on the point of collapse.

400

A Major made his way over to Henry.

"General Sir, Colonel's Klaus , Grofton, and Thomas are dead. Major Rafferty is wounded...mortally I'm afraid. Major Langhorn has been killed as well."

Mason shook his head."

"I tolt' you that was some shootin'. Six shots and she got meat every damned time."

Henry grabbed the Major for support. "Mason, gather the men that I have left. Round them up...tell them I don't want Bella shot...not right away. Also send some men to Flemming's store to see if Flemming's son has seen Quantrill. Report to me in one hour. I am going to lie down...my head is pounding and send me a doctor. Major, help me to the Colonel's room."

"Pete, show the Major to my room."

"Yes, Mr. Lehigh."

Pete helped the Major to half carry Henry over some of the bodies that littered the doorway.

"After the fox...Mason," Henry mumbled.

"What happened?" Neely asked.

"Bella came in shootin'...kilt a fair passel of Henry's men. She tore on out of here with all of Henry's men shootin' at her to beat the band. What you see is the result. Neely, Quantrill just may be in town, If he is, we are gonna' make sure that Henry dies a hero. Now. This is what you got to do."

CHAPTER TWENTY ONE

William Gladstone watched the antics of the two Federal soldiers as they peered into the home of Rebecca. Frank had asked William to reconnoiter the house in the chance that the house was more than likely being watched as well. After Rebecca had told Frank what was goin' on, he had made up his mind to leave that day.

Rebecca had insisted in returning home. She planned on packing a few things and retrieving the few dollars that she had been saving. She also wanted to leave a note on the door of Reverend Grimes telling where she could be found.

Natalie had found some paper and Rebecca scrawled a quick message and Frank had told her that he would leave it on the Reverend's door. William was to check out the house and only if it were clear would they allow Rebecca to return to her home. Frank would return to where his family, Ted, and Rebecca waited for them outside of town near the caves. William was to return in an hour. If he failed to return, then Frank would know that he was in trouble and plans could be made accordingly.

William carefully watched the two as they stuck their noses against the pane glass like schoolboys. William pulled both of his pistols out and cocked them. The two Federal soldiers never heard him as he stepped out from behind the shed and made his way towards the pair. When he was within earshot, he pointed the pistols at their midsections and cleared his throat. The two Federal soldiers turned towards the noise. Their hands went straight into the air.

"I'm glad you Yankees know the drill. Damned peepin' Toms. You sons' of bitches got a lot of nerve pesterin' good folks the way you do. I ought to drop you sacks of shit where you stand. If you damned Yankees are heeled, I would suggest strongly that you drop them on the ground. Be slow. Pull them out butt first and throw them yonder." William nodded towards the gate of the garden a few feet where they stood. Both of the men were grinning at him.

"You Yankees hear me, or are you both jest scairt' stupid? If you think you're faster than greased monkey shit, then by all means, pull down on me. I ain't kilt' me a damned Yankee in a while. I'm gonna' tell you jest' one more time. Drop them pistols you got or I'm a gonna start droppin' both of you silly lookin' bastards."

"If you shot us, you'd feel mighty poorly afterwards," one of them said. The one that had spoken continued to grin at him. William was getting edgy and his fingers began to tighten on the trigger. He had not seen anyone else around and he began to wonder why they continued to smile at him.

"Is that right? And why would that be? There ain't nobody around to help you grinnin' ya-hoots. Even if they are tipped off by the gunshots, it wouldn't help you two none. You'd still be deader'n hell. You tulips are tryin' to bluff the wrong poker player."

"You'd regret it, Mr. Gladstone, because you'd be killin' your own neighbors, that's why." Tom said.

Something was familiar with the voice and the smile. It drifted in his memory like a vivid dream that quickly dissipates on awakening. He could not place the face in his mind and it troubled him.

"I ain't never heard tell of no Mr. Gladstone, tulip," William growled.

"Mr. Gladstone…it's me, Tom Sawyer, and this here is Huck Finn."

William did not lower his pistols. He glared angrily at the two men.

"What made you two boys turn agin' your own kith' an' kin'. You think I'm gonna' be tickled pink seen' you boys in Yankee bluecoats…well, your sadly mistaken'. I ought to stop talkin' and start shootn'."

"We ain't no damned Yankees. This here was the only way we could git home. It's a long story Mr. Gladstone," Huck said quickly.

"If'n' I remember correctly, you two boys were always good fer makin' up stories and sich'. If that is you, Huck, I remember when everybody thought you got drowned in the river. I spent nearly a day rowin' out on that river lookin' fer your stinkin' carcass. The mosquitoes nearly ate me alive and you weren't even in the river. You was hidin', is all, if my memory severs me correct."

"You can't fault me fer somethin' I did when I was jest' a young'n, can you?" Huck asked.

"Reckon I can't, but I kin' fault you fer gittin' Cecil Gordon kilt over in Kansas.."

"We didn't have anything to do with it, Mr. Gladstone We were in a shootout and he got killed," Tom replied. "Look, I come home to find Rebecca. If she's around, she can tell ya', I'm sound on the goose. I was with General Lee and Stonewall by God Jackson. Find her, she'll tell you; we aren't any Yankees, Mr. Gladstone. Do you know where she is?"

"Maybe yes… maybe no. Now drop those pistols. I know ya' got them cause I spotted them in your britches. Drop them an' I mean now," William said angrily.

Huck tore his hat off his head and threw it on the ground. He began to kick the ground in a cold fury.

"If this don't beat all. We get help from our deadliest enemies and now we're gonna' get shot by our friends what known us our whole damned lives. I don't get it. The whole world is crazy or maybe it's jest' me," Huck shouted.

"Huck go slow. Now ain't the time for a temper tantrum," Tom said.

"I don't rightly give a damn anymore. Shoot me, Mr. Gladstone, and have done with it if you've a mind to. Shoot me down cause I am through with all of this shit. You'd be doin' me a favor cause I can't figger nothin' out no more. I'm about as confused as a body kin' git'. I'm howlin' crazy."

Huck threw back his head and howled like a wolf. William put his pistol in his belt.

"Quit yer' damned pissin' and moanin' boy. You always wuz' a pain in the ass. We ain't got time fer' your shenanigans. We got work to do and we ain't got much time to do it in."

"Do you know where Rebecca is, Mr. Gladstone?" Tom asked.

"Rebecca is down near the caves waitin' fer' me to get back. So is Frank by now. Don't worry, son, she's safe. You don't know this, but the Yankees have been layin' a trap in town. Seems like Quantrill came to town sometime this summer. He got spotted. They've been a waitin' for him since then. They's bin' spyin' on everybody what's sound on the goose ever since. Rebecca came to Frank's wife Natalie tellin' her what's bin' goin' on. Natalie didn't know nothin'. All's she thought was that there was law watchin' the house because Frank rode with Quantrill. I spotted you two lookin' in Rebecca's house here. I thought it was more Yankees a playin' games. We caught another son of a bitch at Frank's home not more than an hour ago when Frank came back here to get his family. I cracked his head and tied him up good. We ride into this hornets nest not knowin' any of this at all. You ain't seen anybody else snoopin' around hyar?"

"No sir," Tom said.

Huck reached down and picked up his hat. The sound of gunfire rippled in the air. At first it was distant, but with each second it grew closer. William ran to the shed where he had tied his horse and came back with a shotgun. All of them ran to see what all the gunfire was about.

A woman on horseback was riding pursued by two men on horseback and three men in a buckboard. They were blazing away at the woman who rode madly down Main Street heading directly towards Rebecca's home. Suddenly, the woman sailed through the air and landed on the ground as lightly as a snowflake. She accomplished a front shoulder roll and was off and running. The second her feet hit the ground she began sprinting towards the house.

404

The rider closest to the fleeing woman ran out of ammunition and threw his pistol to the street. Cursing, he drew his cavalry saber and spurred his animal towards the woman with the intention of skewing her on the end of his blade. William made the rider out to be a Federal colonel. That was enough for William.

He stepped into the road with his shotgun aimed at the quickly approaching colonel on horseback. The colonel was so intent on delivering his fatal blow that he never saw William coming towards him.

"This way little bit," William bellowed. "Run tidally winks, run."

William fired his shotgun from his hip. Eight marble-sized balls spread in a cone like pattern from the barrel and hit the colonel full in the throat at point blank range. His throat disintegrated and his head flew off his shoulders. The headless body of the colonel stood up in the stirrups and dropped the sword. The horse streaked past William. The headless body bobbed crazily in the saddle as the excited horse raced down Main Street out of control.

Bella tore past William and past Tom and Huck without even glancing at them. She raced up the steps and threw herself through the door. The second Federal soldier tried to stop his horse as quickly as he could before he came within the lethal range of William's double-barreled shotgun. He attempted to fling himself off the horse at the last second but it was too late. The shotgun blast hit him in the chest. His feet never cleared his stirrups as his chest was ripped to pieces from the impact of the load.

His chin fell on his chest and he toppled off his terrified horse. Tom and Huck ran towards the swerving buckboard firing and cocking their pistols as fast as possible. They both unloaded their pistols into the compacted mass in the buckboard.

One of the three Federal officers in the buckboard aimed and fired. The shot hit William and knocked him off his feet. All twelve shots fired by Tom and Huck found human flesh. The men fell in every direction out of the buckboard and the buckboard overturned. The horses dragged it down the street. One of the men tried to rise again, but he fell forward into the street firing his last shot into the ground. Tom ran forwards the fallen William Gladstone. He could see that he was still alive.

"Git' back to Frank. Tell him what happened. Tell him to git.' The damned town is crawlin' with Yankees," William choked.

Huck ran over and both men lifted William and dragged him into the house. The woman came down stairs with a box of ammunition. She sat on the floor and quickly began loading her pistol. They laid William on the floor.

"Do like I say, dammit," William gasped. The bullet had hit him in the chest.

"Rebecca's father has many guns in the chest. Get them. How badly hurt is the man who looks like a bear?" Bella yelled.

"Lady, what the hell is going on?" Tom asked.

"Get the many guns, Tom." Bella stood up and scurried over to the door and slammed it shut. Neighbors looked out of windows, there was no escaping the horror of a disembodied head lying in the street. Rebecca's neighbors looking out on the street began to worry. The war was coming home.

"I know you. You're that injin' woman that was in the hotel in Kansas…the one that got us out of there."

"Pay attention," Bella shouted. "There are many soldiers in the street and they do no look happy. They are going to rush the house. I have not many bullets. Get the many guns or you will never know what this is all about because you will be dead. Do It now. You and the speckled faced not too bright boy I cracked in the head many years ago. Do it now."

A bullet noisily ripped through the window. Tom dragged himself toward the wooden loveseat in Rebecca's parlor. He flung back the seat and found two shotguns and an ancient musket that probably had last been fired in anger during the war of 1812. Tom shook the loveseat. He heard shotgun shells rolling around in it. He began to greedily collect shotgun shells and he threw a shotgun to Huck.

The front door was kicked open. One of Henry's men who had been in the buckboard staggered through the door. He was covered in blood and was holding his throat. Blood pulsed and flowed between his finger's. The door hit the wall with a terrific force as the dying man aimed and fired at Bella. She had raised her pistol to fire but the man's appearance in the doorway had been too sudden. His shot tore the weapon from her hand and ripped her middle finger from her hand. Blood spurted from hand and she screamed in agony. She rolled backwards and away from the enraged gunman.

The bloody soldier pulled the hammer back to fire. Tom fired. The man's shin exploded severing his leg in two. He hopped on one leg and fired at Bella hitting her again. Again, Bella screamed in pain. Huck frantically chambered a shell onto his shotgun. The gore streaked Major drew the hammer back on the colt again to fire. William Gladstone hurled his knife at the man striking him in the chest. The blade sank into his heart. He fired into the ceiling and collapsed onto Bella.

She kicked the dead man off of her and quickly tore a piece of her dress to fashion a bandage for her hand. Huck ran to the door and slammed it shut. Tom peered through the window. Soldiers were everywhere with the men jumping off horses while others shouted commands. Bella felt at her leg. The bullet had hit her in the thigh and had gone through without hitting bone.

"It burns like fire," Bella said grimacing. "and he took my finger. I will not need it on the other side anyway."

"The next time you fella's kill a body make sure they stay kilt," William groaned. "Reach over there and git my knife. I feel naked without it. How many are we talkin' about out there?"

Tom pulled the knife out of the dead man. William crawled and placed his back against the wall. He pulled out a pistol and handed it to Tom as Tom returned the bloody knife to him. He pulled out a second pistol and threw it to Huck. Bella finished wrapping her wounds and threw a box of cartridges to Huck.

"There's got to be twenty or thirty of them out there and the crowd just seems to be gettin' bigger by the minute," Huck hollered.

"One of you go upstairs and see if they surrounded us yet. My horse is in the shed. I got a Sharps rifle and a Henry repeater on my saddle and enough of ammunition to last us till Sunday. If there's a chance to get them, git 'em. If they rush us, we don't stand a chance with jest' a shotgun and pistols."

Huck bounded up the stairs. Angry voices and whoops came from the street.

"Lady… I hope you don't mind me askin' but what the hell is goin' on here?" Tom asked quietly.

"Good question," William said weakly.

"Henry Fowler and all of his evil men have made a trap. Henry is in town. I tried to kill him in the big house where painted circus ponies lay on their backs and make money with what they have between their legs. I missed. They chased me. I think we will never get out alive now. If I had dead them, the rest of them would be lost. They are all cowards…they would have all run away."

"You must be Bella. Rebecca tolt us about you. Tom…help me over to the window," William said.

"They saw Quantrill in town last summer. They bin' layin' traps for that damned fool ever since. We all tolt Quantrill thet' comin' into this town wuz' a bad idea, but he wouldn't listen. They must think they hit the mother load…that's why they are so all fired up in stretching us all horizontal. They are sure as shit goin' to come at us and they are gonna' come with everything they got." William tried to struggle to his feet. Tom helped William to stand.

"Are you bad. Let me see," Bella said.

"Don't worry none. I've been worse. I'm not gonna peg out jest yet."

Bella ignored his protests as she opened his shirt and looked at the wound. She quickly removed his shirt and probed at the rip in his flesh.

"It hit your rib. It did not come out. Your rib is broken. The bullet must come out. I do not believe it is deep, though. I think it is in the rib bone. It hit a bullet from what you wear around your neck. See. If it had not hit this bullet it would have bounced off your rib and gone into your heart."

Bella handed William a twisted bullet that he had worn in a bandoleer that has crisscrossed his chest. The bullet had hit the shell casing and had flattened it. William took the twisted bullet and looked at it closely.

"I'll be damned," William said.

"The bullet must come out or it will turn green like the grass and smell like bad cheese. Then you will dead." Bella began to remove all of his clothes from the waist up.

"Quit fussin', there ain't no time." William tried to push her away, but she pushed right back. He slapped her hands and she slapped back at his hand as she continued to strip him.

"You're a right feisty little minx, now ain't yer,"

"Stop it," Bella said angrily.

William grinned. Huck returned down the stairs in leaps.

"They's getting' ready for fun and games, but they don't appear to be in the back. I'm goin' for it," Huck said.

He took large strides towards the back door. Bella picked up her pistol and slammed William in the side of the head with the butt end. He rocked over on his side. Bella took the knife and began to cut at the wound. Within a few seconds, she had the bullet. She ran into the kitchen and returned with a pitcher of water and a clean washcloth. Tom handed her a strip of cloth he had torn off a shirt in the closet. She cleaned his wound as Tom kept a careful watch out the parlor window.

"I must start a fire in the stove. I will burn his wound closed."

Huck put one pistol in his belt. He used his thumb to cock the hammer of the pistol in his right hand. He took a deep breath as if he were diving under water and ran to the shed. He found the horse just as William had said. He located the bandoleers of ammunition. He quickly pulled out the Sharps rifle and then the Henry repeating rifle. He tied the rifles together with a piece of rope from the saddle horn and slung them over his shoulder. He then began to rapidly wrap the bandoleers of ammunition around his waist and over his shoulder.

He looked up and heard voices. He grabbed his pistol and laying on his stomach began to low crawl towards the sounds. Three Federal soldiers were being pushed at sword point by a red faced Colonel towards the unguarded back door of Rebecca's home.

"Quantrill's inside that house, soldier. I don't give a fat rat's ass if your on furlough or not...your still a United States soldier, Private, and I am a friggin' Colonel. That means you got to do what I tell you or I will have you put up against a wall and shot for cowardice. Now get in there. Rush that house, Goddamned you."

They looked at the house with hesitation. The Colonel put his pistol next to the most frightened looking soldier's head and fired. The boy jerked and fell forward. Blood and smoke poured from his blasted skull.

The two young Federal soldiers stared at the terrible Colonel and then began to move cautiously towards the house. One opened the door with his rifled musket and stepped inside slowly. There was shotgun blast and he was flung backward through the air and landed on a rosebush, He convulsed and died as his body bounced off the thorny bush.

The other boy leaned in the door and fired. As he began to duck away, his head popped like a balloon as a shotgun blast took him full in the face. He spun off the back porch and onto the ground. Someone from inside slammed the door shut. The Colonel fired several times at the door and began to back away. Huck whistled loudly through his teeth. The startled Colonel turned in his direction.

"Soldier", he said. "I am Colonel Hogg. Quantrill is in that house. I need you to go root that swine out of there. You will be hailed a hero all across this great nation, son."

Huck smiled and did not say a word.

"Soldier I order you to attack that house."

"The onliest thing I figger I will be attackin' in any due time is you, Colonel. Allow me to introduce myself, suh. My name is Sergeant Hezikiah Finn, Second Corp, General Jones' brigade of Johnson's Division, Army of Northern Virginia General Robert E. Lee commandin' How do you do?"

Huck raised his pistol and emptied it into the body of the Colonel. The man staggered backwards as the first three shots hit him in the chest. As he fell backwards, Huck watched his bullets punch the life out of the man. He watched as the light in the man's eye went out as surely as if one had blown them out like candles. The rest of the shots hit the man in various parts of his body as he crumpled to his knees and fell over sideways lifelessly. Huck ran towards the back door and kicked it open.

"It's me. I'm comin' in. Don't shoot," Huck screamed. He lurched through the kitchen door and threw the rifles on the table. He saw William lying in a puddle of blood.

"He got hit again? Is he dead?" he asked.

"No, I had to get the bullet out. I made him sleep like that time many years ago when I made you go to sleep. Do you remember?"

"I surely do."

"Take the rifle and get back to the stairs that are up and look out the window. I must start a fire and burn his bullet hole with a big metal spoon. I want to say, before anything happens that I am sorry I hit you. I want to say that I am, as you whites say, scarred shitless. But if this is the day that I go to the house of my southeast Grandfather's, I want you to know that I will fight till they dead me... If Henry gets his hands on me he will dead me anyway. I have nothing to lose. I am just sorry that I did not dead all of them..Henry...Lehigh...Neely...I thought I was doing many good. I have gotten all of us dead. I am sorry."

"As long as you can wiggle your ears or other body parts, you ain't dead," Huck said. "Don't worry about a thing, young lady. You got me and Tom over there to protect you, rest assured."

"Help me barricade the backdoor. I don't want no more surprises poppin' in here unannounced," Tom said.

They pushed a huge cabinet in front of the door and then walked to the kitchen. Bella was bent over and had just started lighting the stove. Huck found his eyes roving over Bella's form. Tom slapped him in the ribs.

"For Christ sakes, stop gawking' and help me turn the table over and lean it against the door, will you." Bella went to the parlor to check on her patient.

"She got the nice bumps, don't she?" Huck asked playfully.

"I'll give you some nice bumps in a minute. What do you want...Sharps rifle or the Henry?" Tom asked.

"You take the Sharps...you're the sure-shot. I'll take the Henry. This way, when they rush us. I can get from the front to the back upstairs real quick through the halls. You ought to start see'n what you kin' hit from that parlor window. This ought to be interestin'...some homecomin' ain't it?"

"You said a mouthful," Tom replied.

Mason and two of his Deputies arrived at the house directly across from Rebecca's. Men were milling about aimlessly but many had rifles. A fat Major was arguing with a thin older gentleman. The older man was visibly upset while the Major looked like he was getting ready to strike the older man.

"This intrusion into my home is intolerable. We are true blue Union people. Why don't you invade the home of all these damned southern traitors that we have in town? You come in and scare my poor wife witless then your people start breaking my windows. This is my home, damn you man and I..."

The major drove his head into the face of the elderly man's face knocking him to the ground. Blood flowed from his shattered nose. He held onto his nose and whimpered and groaned. Mason smiled.

"Son of a bitch wouldn't shut up, Mason," the fat Major said.

"I don't care if you blown his brains out," Mason laughed.

"What's the situation here?" he asked.

Colonel Dodge...we lost him. Somebody took his head off with a shotgun. Colonel Bleir is starched like a shirt in a Chinaman's laundry. We got Major's Rainy and Cornett missing in action and Colonel Hogg took some men to the back of the house and ain't come back. We heard a few shots but ain't seen nothing of him since and Major Dowling is dead."

Mason looked at the old man as he struggled to his feet.

"I am a doctor, a well-respected member of the community and a good friend of the Mayor I'll have you know. How dare you treat me in this manner. I will see you in court. You will rue the day you landed a hand on my person," the Doctor whined.

"So you're a doctor, eh?" Mason asked cynically. He grabbed a soldier's rifle and smashed it across the elderly man's mouth. He reeled backwards and fell against the side of the house.

"Now you need to see a dentist. Maybe that will teach you to keep yer damned mouth shut, Deputy Towers, arrest this traitor. Throw him in the damned jail. If he resists arrest, you are ordered to shoot him."

Mason walked into the doctor's home. The parlor had been turned into a fortress. Men with rifles aimed out of the windows watching the home across the street.

"They ain't fired a shot at us, Colonel. Like I said, we heard some shootin' from the back, but nothin' since then."

"It's gotta be Quantrill," Lehigh said. "Major Garnett, I want you to find every able bodied soldier in town. We need men. I sent for Captain Barlow and D troop, but they won't arrive until tomorrow at best. Any man that resists, shoot them down on the spot. Make examples of them. Send a man to Flemming's store and tell Neely to have Flemming break out every weapon in his store and all the ammunition. If young Flemming says a word in protest, hang him. Then send Neely to get Henry…I mean General Fowler and tell him to tell the General that we have Quantrill trapped here on Main Street. Tell Neely to tell the General that he will be missing out on a great moment of he doesn't get here quick. You got all that, Garnett?" Mason asked.

"Yes sir."

"Good…get' going…one more thing. Send somebody out on the street there and pick up old Dodge's head before the General gits here. It may upset the General to see that head laying out in the dusty road like that."

"What should I do with it?" Garnett asked.

"I don't know an' I don't care what you do with it. Throw it up on a roof. Just get it out of the damned road, yer idjit. Tell Pete and Neely to ride back with the General. They know what to do after that. Garnett, you got one hour…git." Garnett left. Mason looked at the house. There was plenty of daylight left. He smiled.

CHAPTER TWENTY TWO

Mayor Jared Clifton wheezed as he walked up the grand-staircase of the hotel as he made his way to see Henry Fowler. He was bothered by asthma whenever he was stressed, and today he was highly stressed. News had come to him of the many deaths that had occurred at the hotel. The gouts of coagulated blood that had pooled on the ground and the floor and not been cleaned away, although the bodies had been taken away.

They were stretched out in the ball room. Twenty-seven men and woman in the first stages of rigor mortis lay cooling on the hardwood floor. The Mayor had seen several prominent citizens of his political flock stretched out in a most undignified manner on the floor. It was then that the wheezing had begun.

As he made his way to Henry like a dutiful vassal, the wheezing increased to the point where he sounded like he was playing the harmonica. A Major stood with his hands on his hips at the top of the stairs.

"Stop right there. What do you want and who are you?"

The Mayor stopped and tried to catch his breath.

"I'm the Mayor. I must see General Fowler immediately." He gasped.

The Major patted the wheezing man down quickly for weapons. Satisfied, he motioned for the man to proceed. Two disheveled Federal soldiers stood at attention at the door to Lehigh's room. They were battered and bruised and stood ramrod straight at port arms. They had been caught hiding below the bar after the shooting had ended. They had been impressed into Henry's service at gunpoint.

When they had objected, they had been pummeled, throttled, and beaten by Pete who almost had broken their necks in his enthusiasm. After Pete had gotten through with them, they obeyed every single command to the letter.

"I'm here to see the General," he wheezed.

"Let him in," the Major shouted.

One of the soldiers banged twice on the door and opened it allowing the Mayor to walk in. The room was dark. It took a minute for the Mayor's eyes to adjust to the dim light. The curtains were drawn, and a dim light from the candle flickered in the darkness. Henry sat at the desk. His head was wrapped in linen like a mummy. Two officers stood next to him. When the Mayor had entered the room, the two Federal soldiers had drawn their weapons and pointed them at Jared's face.

"Put down the weapons men. It's simply the Mayor and not another assassin," Henry said.

"Henry, there are bodies stacked like cordwood in the ball room. What in God's name happened here?" the Mayor asked.

"There was an assassination attempt on my life this afternoon by one of Quantrill's minions. A fallen lady obviously was sent by that murderous devil when he found out I was in town. All of the deaths that have occurred here can be blamed directly on his attempt to kill me. We are scouring the town as we speak here and I am sure his apprehension and death will occur before the day is out. You will be famous. Jared, the toast of the country. You will be an instant celebrity for being the man whose town it was in that the wily Quantrill was finally bought to justice."

"What am I going to tell the families of the slain? This will be very embarrassing I can't very well tell the widow Hopkins that her husband was shot dead in a whorehouse very well now, can I?" Jared sputtered.

He began to wring his hands which annoyed Henry.

"Stop being such a ninny, Jared. We can say or do anything we like after the day is over. If it makes you feel better and places a balm on your feeble conscience, we will say that he died gloriously in the service of his country while apprehending the mad dog Quantrill. After we have Quantrill's dead body, we can place anyone you choose in the vicinity of the corpse and claim they died heroically. What I am going to ask you is that you control the telegraph office. I will send one of Mason's Deputies with you to make sure that this news is not leaked out all across the country before we are ready. Do this, Jared, and you will be rewarded handsomely. Are we clear on this?" he asked.

"Yes, General Fowler."

"Good. You may go now. Away with you then and remember well what we spoke of." Henry watched the Mayor depart.

"Greedy maggoty fornicator. I have paid him his last dollar. After Quantrill has been killed, Major, I want you to shoot that man. Then we will pile all the bodies in the bar room, soak their heathen carcasses with all the alcohol in this abominable place and light it up."

Henry began to unwrap his head from the makeshift bandages. He grimaced in pain.

"My head feels like some infernal red savage is pounding away using my skull for a tom-tom. Why hasn't the doctor arrived to stem the poison that is surely spreading throughout my system by now? They must have some blasted quack that passes for a doctor in this one horse shit-hole of a town. Why hasn't Mason sent him to me?" Henry lamented.

Two knocks sounded on the door, followed by the door opening and two officers drawing their weapons again.

"Ah good, surely this must be him presently," Henry anxiously said. He was disappointed when Neely entered the room and snapped to attention. Henry angrily waved his hand in a mock salute.

"Where the hell is the doctor, Neely? Why hasn't Mason sent him to see me as I had requested?"

"Beggin' the General's pardon, sir, but the doctor is busy tendin' to some of our wounded that we got when Quantrill and his men were chased into a house on Main Street, sir. Colonel Lehigh has him trapped, sir. He asks the General to come to his headquarters, so that the General may share in the victory. He said you oughtn' not miss out on this great event, beggin' you pardon, sir."

"He has Quantrill trapped in a house, you say?" Henry asked incredulously.

"We got him trapped in that house tighter than a barrel of monkeys, General," Neely replied.

Henry became ecstatic. A huge grin appeared across his face as all previous feelings of pain were pushed away in his euphoria.

"I knew it. This is my crowning glory," Henry screamed jubilantly.

"I knew that Quantrill could not resist coming back here to purchase more weapons and powder. I knew it," Henry shouted.

"Colonel Mason also suggests that the two officers that you have would best put to better purpose rounding up all the stray soldiers in the town .The Colonel cannot spare nary a man, sir. We have the house surrounded but we need more men if we are to capture Quantrill before sundown," Neely lied.

"I was a genius to put my trust in Mason. That is a very good suggestion, one that will be put into effect immediately."

Neely was amazed at how easily it was becoming. Everything that Mason had told him to say to Henry had worked like a charm. Henry's reactions were precisely what Mason had told him that would be. Neely continued in his treachery.

"Colonel Lehigh had taken over the Flemming store and is using it to channel men to the encircled house, but he says he need dependable men there. He said it's important that this be done as quickly as possible, sir. He wanted me to stress the urgency of that last request, General."

"Colonel Teal...take Major's Burns and Smith with you. Take charge of the situation at he store. Funnel as many men with weapons to Colonel Lehigh with as much haste as possible"

Henry raised his hands skyward.

"Gentlemen," Henry said dramatically, "a moment like this comes once in a man's lifetime. May God have mercy in any man that does not fulfill his duty because I surely won't. You have your orders."

Both of the men saluted and left as quickly as they could move.

"General...you won't be needin' the soldiers you got by the door. Wouldn't they be put to better use with the officers down at Flemming's?" Neely suggested.

Henry pushed Neely aside and ran to the door.

"You soldiers catch up with Colonel Teal. Tell him that General Fowler ordered you to help him. Now leave."

The two frightened soldiers ran down the stairs after the officers. Henry slowly closed the door.

"You know Neely, there will be many good things coming out of all this. You should thank your lucky stars that you have bet the right horse in all of this. I am impressed with the entire operation, yes indeed."

"Colonel Lehigh ordered Pete and me to escort you to the Colonel." Neely said.

"Good. I can't think of a better bodyguard. Come, good Neely. Time invites me go," Henry said with a flair.

As Henry walked out the door and into the hall, he saw Pete. Henry walked past him, too preoccupied in thought to notice the queer glances that Pete was giving Neely. Neely smiled and winked. Pete's face broke into a wide grin. Pete threw back his head and brayed like a donkey.

Deputy Eb Wyngard, Deputy Glen Wright, and Major Garnett were in Fleming's store. Major Garnett was not interesting in returning to the command of Colonel Lehigh. He knew that there was going to be a fight and he wanted no part of it. The staff officers that had accompanied Henry on the detail had been nearly wiped out. Major Raymond Garnett, although fiercely loyal to Henry Fowler, did not want to press his luck and get involved in the coming fight if he did not have to. He thought about the deaths of all of his compatriots.

Gunter Klaus had been shot in the head by that ring-tailed floozy that had popped out of no where and had shot into the group of seated officers, Major Rafferty, Colonel Thomas, Colonel Grofton, and Major Langhorn had all died on the dining room floor. Colonel Dodge had had his head blown off and Major Blier's chest had been opened up like a can of beans by a shotgun blast. Major Dowling had been riddled by gunfire and had bled to death in the middle of Main Street. Major's Rainey and Cornett, along with Colonel Hogg, were missing, presumed dead.

Out of the original group that had landed at noon time, there were just four staff officers left. Eleven men were dead. Garnett was going to make sure that he wasn't number twelve. This was safe duty compared to trying to rush a house full of desperate rebels. It was so much safer to simply wait for the whistle of a riverboat to sound than trying to pick up just a few stray soldiers off the street. Boatloads of soldiers would arrive eager to sample the pleasure of the fancy house. Garnett would commandeer them at gunpoint and Mason's men would lead them to the slaughter.

The disgruntled soldiers would often protest, but if they protested too strongly, Garnett was always ready to kill the biggest protestor. Garnett had killed one man who had become too vocal in his objections in taking part in the proceedings. He had fired one well placed shot through the man's open mouth. The man had toppled into the river. One minute the man had been arguing that he had done his part in quelling the rebellion and was heading home to his loving family. He said there was no way in hell that he was going to fight anymore. The next, minute, he was a nameless corpse floating with the sluggish current of the mighty river as it wound its way past the trouble town.

Garnett waited to hear the whistle for the next boat and wiled away his time in small talk with Wyngard and Wright. He idly flipped the wooden matches at a body hanging from a rope in the store. Aubrey Flemming hung from the rafters. His face was discolored and his tongue stuck out. He had not died of a broken neck, but in fact had slowly strangled to death.

Young Aubrey Fleming had taken over the store after the mysterious disappearance of his father. He had strongly objected to Mason's appropriations of weapons and ammunition from the store and had paid with his life.

"Duty here must have been a bed of roses with Lehigh, eh fella?" Garnett said. He flicked another unlit wooden match at the corpse.

"Real soft duty…livin' in a whorehouse an all."

"It warn't all like that there. We lived in tents for a long time outside of town…it got cold. That's when Neely asked Lehigh if we could stay in the hotel. We wuz' freezin' our asses off. It warn't all that easy duty a'tall," Wyngard said angrily.

"We had to catch the comings and goings of every asshole that came through town. It got to be a chore writin' all their names down and followin' them around. Shit, we had a list of names and turned them into Mason every week. Do you know how many fools got off that boast in a goddamned week?"

"No idea," Garnett said, "but I kin' imagine." Garnett walked over to the corpse and gave the body a push. It started to sway and then began to twist around in a tight circle.

417

"I guess it all paid out though," Garnett said. "We got that bastard Quantrill and that's all Henry ever wanted. Boys, let me tell you somethin'…Henry has lived for this moment. I bin' with him since "59". I ain't never seen him caught up in anything like this since he got the bug up his keester for the injun' that used to work for him. What the hell was the squaws name?" he asked.

"Bella," Wright answered.

"Yup…Bella…he was crazy about that woman. She was a good lookin' squaw. Anyway, with Quantrill dead it will mean Henry will have us stop bein' out in the field now. We were chasin' every lead and rumor for the last three months about the whereabouts of that skunk. Things will begin to return to normal with that bastard dead. Me, for one, I'm glad it's the end of the trail. I'm getting too old fer' sleepin' out under the stars no more."

Major Garnett bored with swinging the corpse and turned to see both men standing with weapons drawn and pointed at hi midsection. He quickly turned to look behind him, thinking that someone or something was the cause for the men to be pointing guns in his vicinity, but there was no one behind him. His head spun back towards them.

"What's going on, boys? Quit yer johnny ass'n and put those pieces away," Garnett said sternly.

"Sorry Raymond. You come here at the wrong time, is all. Nothin' personal about this, mind you…but this is the way its got to be."

"What the hell are you talkin' about, Eb." Garnett demanded.

"You wuz' always a decent fella' to us, Ray."

"Just wait a durn' minute. What the hell is this all about. You can't be plannin' on jist' gunnin' me down like this here. What the hell have I done?"

They cocked the hammers back and Garnett watched their fingers tighten on the triggers.

"Stop fartin' around. Put them guns away. It ain't funny no more."

Both men looked at Raymond Garnett with cold steel in their eyes. The major knew that from the dead look in both of their eyes that he was in serious danger.

"You can't be plannin' on killin' me. Not here…not now…not like this. We got Quantrill trapped in town. We are gonna' all get famous an' rich from this. I knowed' you fellas fer' years. Christ Almighty…we bin' through some tough times together. Why hell, Eb, I brought you to meet Henry for the first time cause I admired your work. Put the guns away and let us talk. Look…I'll even put mine down first. See. The least you kin' do is let me hear why yer' plannin' on taking me

418

down. I got a right to know…don't you think? See…I'm puttin' my piece down. You kin' do this for me. I always treated you boys fair and square now didn't I?"

As Garnett removed his pistol from his hostler, he suddenly flipped it smartly into his hand. He managed to fire only one shot that ripped the air over Eb Wyngard's head missing him by an inch. Wyngard and Wright had been ready for such a move. They unloaded their weapons into the fat Major's stomach. He fell heavily to the floor, holding onto his belly.

"What fer?" he croaked.

Deputy Wright stepped across his body and fired a shot into Garnett's head.

"That's what's fer', Raymond," Eb replied coldly

Blue smoke curled out of the deadman's ears. Wyngard and Wright dragged the dead Major to the back of the store and waited patiently for the last of Henry's men to arrive. They did not have to wait long. Coming towards the store were Colonel Teal, Major Burns, and Major Smith followed by two soldiers they had never seen before.

Wyngard and Wright waited behind the counter with their hands down by their sides. Each man held two fully loaded Colt revolvers. They watched as their old friends, Lester Teals, Basil Smith, and Alphonso Burns walked towards the door. Teal stopped and ordered the soldiers to stand guard.

"Go fer' Lester fust'," Eb whispered. "Don't listen to anything he says. I swear the son of a bitch kin' read minds. The man is the luckiest person I knowed'. He must have a horseshoe up his ass. As soon as he gets in the door, start shootin' and don't miss."

Wright nodded.

Teals entered the store. Alphonso Burns and Basil Smith followed a few steps behind him. As soon as Lester opened his mouth in greeting, he was hit by a hail of gunshots. Bullets struck Teals in the arms and chest as Wright emptied first one pistol then the next into the twisting Teals.

Lester fired once, striking Wright in the forehead. Wright plunged to the floor. Burns and Smith were killed instantly in the first second of the deadly barrage of gunfire. Lester aimed and fired again, hitting Wyngard right between the eyes. Eb slammed into the counter then careened against the wall. He stood still for a second and Lester shot him again through the heart. Eb smashed face first into the floor.

Lester Teals drew back his lips and laughed weakly. His eyes rolled up into his head and he fell backwards. The two frightened soldiers crept to the door and looked in at the carnage. The green recruits threw away their rifles and ran towards the woods, grateful to be alive and intending to stay that way for as long as humanly possible. They deserted the Army, leaving Federal Service behind them forever.

Mason sat at the doctor's dinner table sipping a glass of wine. He wanted to speak to all of his gathered deputies in private before the arrival of Henry Fowler. He looked at his men and did a quick headcount. Five men stood in the kitchen.

"Where's Edgar Covington?" he asked

"Nobody's seen Edgar all afternoon," Deputy Felix Bloom answered quickly.

"He was at the Gordon house this morning, but he never made it to the roof of the telegraph office like he was suppose to." Mason rubbed the stubble on his chin and put his feet on the table.

"Gordon rides with Quantrill, that's a known fact. We can assume they killed him then. Bloom, take a horse and get over to Flemming's store and see what's taking Eb and Glen so long. Get back as quick as you can…we're starting to lose daylight. Alright then, Martin…you got somebody watching the back of that house like I tolt' you?"

"Sure do, Mason. I got fourteen men in the back there under the command of a veteran sergeant what's clear on the situation. He's dependable…one of the few. Mason…most of these boys is green as grass but that Sergeant has got them so that nobody can come out that backdoor and live. By the way,…we found Colonel Hogg dead along with three other soldier boys."

Deputy Warren Bretchel interrupted Bloom.

"We found Tory Cornett under the carriage that overturned and got dragged down the road. He got stuck somehow under it. Anyway….he's deader that hell."

Mason nodded.

"Good. So the only guard dogs that Henry may possibly have left are Lester Teals, Alphonso Burns, and that half wit Smith. Looks like Henry's shit out of luck. Everybody knows the situation. Henry plans to take away our bread and butter, meaning my house of ill repute. We can't let this happen. Henry lost his goddamned mind. That uniform he was wearin' was the frosting on the cake."

There was laughter from many of those gathered in the kitchen.

"Henry was a good man in his day, but he's too queer lately. I put up with a lot, but when he threatened my life, then I made up my mind that Henry has served his purpose and has got to go. I want you to know that at least Henry will die a hero. When the shooting starts, Neely will put a bullet through Henry's head. When we get Quantrill, we will tell the world that Henry died sending Quantrill to hell where he belongs. It's the last we can do for old Henry."

Many of the men nodded solemnly, and there were many low murmured comments of consent.

"Things are going so well for us at this time that I couldn't have planned it any better. When Klaus got his brains blown out and fell into those mashed potatoes, I almost shit myself in pure delight. He was the most dangerous man that Henry had, but I don't have to mention that…you all knew him. The next person that we have to watch out for is that damned Lester Teals. We will wait till Bloom comes back. If everything's still goin' to plan then we don't have to worry about old Lester anymore. If Lester if alive, then drop him on the spot but be careful. He is one dangerous luck ridden son of a bitch. If you see a hair on his ass, don't try takin' him yourself. Get help. Is that understood?"

"There was a chorus of agreement by the assembled men.

"Good. Then let's get on to the plan. Deputy Smallwood," Mason said slowly, "just how many people do we have?"

Melvin Bay Smallwood took out a crumpled piece of paper and smoothed it out and began to tally the numbers on it.

"As it stands right now…we got thirty seven people in the front and fifteen in the back. Martin is right, Mason. Most of these boys is green as grass…they never been near a fight. We got no officers in the group. We got seven veteran soldiers, two of which are sergeants and understand that if Quantrill is kilt', they will get a thousand dollars apiece. I told them just what you said, Mason. By the way…I know it ain't none of my business but did you mean that last part…about the thousand dollars apiece?"

"Hell no. We will take care of them alright, that's fer' sure, but not exactly how they figger'," Mason said.

Everyone in the room began to laugh.

"Alright, we got the coal oil and the torches?" Mason asked.

"We got torches, ammunition, and rifles…hell, we even got enough powder to blow that house to the moon," Smallwood said happily.

"Let us remember what butters our bread. The town butters our bread. I don't want to see this town go to the moon," Mason said.

"We will burn them out only when we run out of men. Burnin' is the last thing we want. We will send every soldier boy in this town at that damned house, whether they are blind, crippled or crazy before we set fire to the house. The wind is pickin' up an' it could get hairy lightin' fires right now. Alright then, this is it. When you hear two quick shots fired, everybody goes in. Remember, this is our bread an' butter. No one walks on our bread an' butter."

William Gladstone regained consciousness. He smelled chicken cooking, and for one second before the pain hit him he felt hungry. He noticed that the sun was setting and he felt at his broken rib. As his hand touched the bandages, he realized that the smell of chicken was the smell of his own burned flesh.

Bella sat on the floor near him loading an old musket. She had two pistols ready in front of her. She spoke without looking at him and continued to load the old smooth bore musket.

"I had to burn the wound. You bled many. Your rib is cracked, but you will heal," she said.

"If I live that long," William muttered.

He sat up on the couch. He felt a little nauseous and he was lightheaded. He looked in the fading light and saw Tom sitting by the parlor window adjusting the sight on his Sharp's rifle. William stood up shakily and wobbled over to the window and looked out. Across the street, men were gathered in the street and they were coming straight at them.

"Looks like I woke up just in time fer' the dance," he said.

"Huck...they are coming," Tom shouted.

"We got movement in the backyard. Sweet Jesus," Huck yelled from upstairs.

William watched as at least ten men begun to run for the house. Bella threw William two pistols. He caught them and placed one at his feet. Men with lit torches followed in the wake of the men rushing the house.

"They's gonna' try to burn us out. Tom...take the men with the torches out. Bella...you and I will start droppin' all the brave boys in front."

A volley of fire came from across the street followed by a shattering volley from the backyard. The house was ripped by gunfire. In the kitchen, plates and cups in the cupboard were shattered, and in the parlor portraits hanging on the wall went flying. A bullet struck the rifle Tom was holding. It jumped out of his hands like a living thing. William ducked as rounds buzzed and snapped all around him. The front door was struck repeatedly. Large caliber bullets impacted on the door, sending rippling tears all throughout its frame.

The volume of bullets that tore onto the house made it seem as if some angry giant had decided to tear it down. Bullets plowed into walls making objects in the house dance as they were hit and went spinning about. Tom grabbed the Sharp's rifle as he lay with his back on the floor and checked the weapon for damage. The bullet had hit the front sight. Holes began to smash about the window frame showering him with plaster and wood chips.

422

The first group of attackers made it to be base of the small hill that the house stood on and began to fire at the windows and the door. By now, the door was a splintered remnant of what it once had been. A sergeant and two soldiers made a rush for the porch. One soldier kicked at the door. Bullets continued to thump into it. A federal sergeant and two other soldiers made a rush for the porch and made it there unscathed. One soldier began to kick at the fragmented door even as bullets continued to thump into it. As he drew back his foot to kick it in, he was struck by several bullets from the fire directed at it by the men at the base of the hill. His momentum sent him crashing through it and he plowed head first and landed on the hallway floor.

Bella fired at the twitching figure. The Federal sergeant leaned over to the window and fired blindly into the house. The pistol flash burned the shoulder of William Gladstone. He grabbed the soldier's pistol with one hand and fired into the sergeant's chest with the pistol in his right hand. The sergeant pitched through the window. William used the wounded soldier for cover and killed the third soldier who had just entered through the smashed front door. Two forty-five caliber bullets punctured his cranium and he fell forward onto the other twitching dying soldier.

Bella continued to fire into both of them and began to scurry quickly away from the open doorway. Tom looked up and saw another group of soldiers begin to rush the house. The ones at the base of the hill waited for these reinforcements before attacking. They continued to blaze away. Tom aimed and fired in a blink of an eye. The bullet caved in a young man's chest. He had been running at full speed until the bullet had smashed into him sending a broken shard of his breastbone into his aorta. He rolled onto the ground and lay still.

William headed for the door passing Bella who was frantically loading her revolver. William laid out on the floor and quickly emptied both of his pistols into the running mass of blue clad figures. Three of the soldiers also rolled on the ground as twelve shots tore into flesh and bone. William pushed away from the door. Tom raised his rifle and fired at a soldier who was trying to get a clear shot at William. The soldier had raised his head just for a moment. Tom fired and the soldier died with his brains spraying all over the man lying next to him. Tom could hear the steady fire from Huck and the Henry rifle.

The volume of fire began to slacken as Tom looked out the window and saw a third group start their dash across the road, Huck ducked down as the window sill exploded.

"Tom," Huck screamed, "they're on the back porch. I can't get a clean shot at them."

Tom began to crawl towards the kitchen. The door was being kicked open. He picked up William's shotgun and fired at the door. A scream pierced the air. Tom fired another barrel off and hid next to the stove. Bella picked up the shotgun and began loading it. Tom drew his revolver from his belt and stood up. In two short hops he made it to the small back window. He took a chance to see if he could spot anyone on the porch through it. He peeked out and came eyeball to eyeball with a buck toothed freckled face sixteen year old frightened Federal soldier. The boy looked at Tom in horror. Dropping his rifle, the boy ran form the window and off the porch.

A bearded Federal soldier peered into the darkened kitchen window in curiosity. Tom fired his revolver in the man's face, setting his beard alight from the muzzle flash and killing him instantly. Bella walked into the small bedroom off the kitchen and fired booth barrels into the floor again. She loaded the shotgun and picked up the old smooth musket. She began kicking at the hole she had made in the floor. Tom watched as she squirmed through the hole, pulling the shotgun and musket along with her.

It was dark in the crawlspace and cobwebs were everywhere. She pushed them aside and dragged herself to the front of the house. She spotted the soldiers huddled at the base of the hill. She pushed herself along and finally arrived at a spot in which she was looking down their ranks from the side. She worked quickly to remove some of the intricate latticework that decorated the small space from the foundation. She sighted in on the group of soldiers who were unaware of her presence. She balanced the shotgun and pulled the shotgun's trigger with her right hand finger.

The blast ripped into the soldiers. She fired the second barrel and the group at the hill began fleeing for safety of the house across the street. Two bodies remained at the foot of the house. Bella watched as the soldiers ran and was grateful for the brief respite. She looked across as men began to push the fleeing soldiers back attempting to restore order. It was then that she spotted Henry Fowler standing on the front stoop waving his huge sword and screaming in helpless frustration.

She picked up the musket and slowly and carefully aimed at Henry. She held her breath and slowly squeezed the trigger. The musket boomed and the mini ball sped across the street missing Henry by a foot but striking Neely directly in the nose. Neely had just raised his pistol to put a bullet through Henry's head when chaos had erupted in the form of several wounded men striking to the rear of the house. Mason had just signaled to Neely to shoot Henry.

Mason had stepped into the road to halt the rout of the soldiers as Neely quietly placed his revolver to Henry's head. The bullet battered Neely with such force that Neely jumped straight up into the air. He landed on his feet with a hole in the back of his head one could put a baseball through. Neely's ruined head spun downward and he crashed to the ground. Bella had put too much powder in the barrel and the

424

resultant shot had been very powerful. Neely was dead before his body hit the ground.

She screamed in pain as the ancient musket's muzzle ruptured showering her in lead fragments. The pain from her hand almost caused her to pass out. She watched as Henry dropped his oversized sword and began to steak down the road in the direction of the hotel. All the soldiers that were in the road turned and Bella saw them lose all interest in the battle as a headless rider on a heavily foaming horse barreled its way towards them. They scattered in a directions. The headless rider was held in place by rope and as the horse thundered towards the men, its arms rose and fell like some kind of huge bird.

Ted Doudlass and Frank Gordon were right behind the headless horseman. The demoralized soldiers attention had been glued to the bizarre sight of the headless Colonel Dodge's last trip through town. By the time they saw Frank and Ted, they were being killed. Frank fired two shotguns into their ranks and Ted emptied two loaded pistols. Frank threw his shotgun into the road and pulled out two loaded LeMatt Revolvers and began dropping soldiers. Frank spurred his animal right into their ranks and he decimated them.

Ted dropped his empty pistols and pulled out two double barreled shotguns and fired again and again. Men dropped singly and in pairs. Deputy Towers fired from the doorway and struck Ted in the chest. Ted fired and hit Deputy Tower's blowing off his arm. Towers hit the ground and began to bleed to death. Deputy after deputy died from Frank's devastating attack. When all twelve chambers of the LeMatt were emptied in both revolvers, Frank fired off the shotgun shell housed below the barrel into the remaining people in the road. He drew his sword and decapitated Deputy Smallwood with one steady strike. Smallwood fell as his head sailed through the air.

Mason watched his men drop like rain and decided that he had had enough. He ran towards the door of the Doctor's house, trampling the dying Towers in his headlong flight. Pete was right behind him. All of the men in front of the house were dead, dying, or fleeing for their lives. Twenty bodies were left lying in the street. Frank listened to the sounds of the gunfire still coming from the rear of Rebecca's home. He pulled out a Henry repeating rife and raced his horse down the road followed by Ted Doudlass. Bella had witnessed the mayhem and started crawling back towards the hole in the floor.

William Gladstone had also witnessed the debacle in the front of the house and started to walk towards the kitchen. The backdoor fell apart as a big Federal soldier crashed his body through the door. Tom shot the man as another then another man piled into the kitchen firing crazily. One Federal sent a bullet into the elbow of the man in front of him. The man yelped in pain and fired striking Tom in the knee. Tom fell. Bella fired a shotgun into the men and they all went down.

One man fell against the stove and fired at William. William fell. Huck hobbled down the steps and blasted the soldier out of existence. Deputy Martin pushed his way in followed by Deputy Granger. Granger and Martin fired at Huck who tumbled down the remaining steps. Granger fired again at Bella and Bella went crashing to the floor. Frank Gordon and Ted entered the backdoor shooting both Granger and Martin to pieces. A bullet plowed through Martin's head knocking his eye out. William fired and killed Deputy Granger, the last enemy alive in the kitchen. In just a few seconds it was over. Smoke filled the house.

Tom rose on his one good leg and leaned against the wall. Frank helped him to an overturned chair and righted it for him to sit. He was amazed to see his old friend and neighbor.

"Mr. Gordon. I'm sorry about Cecil," Tom said.

"Don't worry about that now. William, you still kickin'?" Frank asked.

William rose off the floor. A bullet had creased his skull. Blood flowed freely from his scalp.

"I'm fit as a fiddle," William moaned. William reached down and helped Bella to her feet.

"Come on up here with the living, Tiddlywinks. Hell's-bells what a circus, eh Frank? That was good timin'. I thought we had all gone up. This little bit here is a fightin' she-devil."

Bella had been hit by a bullet that had passed right through her shoulder. Huck pushed William away from Bella.

"She's got a name," Huck said angrily, "so stop callin' her little bit and Tiddlywinks fer heavens sake. Them names sound like names fer some kinda' racin' horse. This lady is somethin' special so start treatin' her as sich'."

Huck had been shot several times. Blood soaked his shirt. Bella began to administer to him. He fell against her and slowly slid to the floor. Bella's keen eye ascertained the damage to Huck.

"He is shot many times. We must find the Doctor or he will dead. I can't do the many things that a Doctor will do. Please...find Doctor Waters."

"Ted, they got the doctor locked up in the hoose-gow. I saw that dwarf smash him in the face and then they bundled him off. Go spring him." Frank said.

Tom looked for the first time at the man called Ted. His mouth fell open.

"Ted? Ted Doudlass? How the hell are you?" Tom blurted.

"I have bin' better," Ted said. Blood flowed down his leg and puddled on the floor.

"Howdy Tom. We got a lot to talk about. I'll explain everything later. It's good to see you."

"Likewise…I am sure." Tom could not believe his eyes.

"Ted, after you git' the doc, get over to the telegraph office and burn the place down. Grab one of those torches out in the front." Frank noticed for the first time that Ted had been shot.

"Are you shot bad?" he asked.

"No, Frank. It's just a flesh wound. I'm fine. I'll meet you all back here in a few minutes."

"Listen everybody, we got to travel," Frank said.

Tom watched as Ted turned and left the kitchen.

"You look like you have seen a ghost. He is the half dead boy spirit that walks with a patch on his eye," Bella remarked casually. "I don't think many much of the half dead boy spirit in the past, but now I am glad the half dead boy spirit walks with an eye-patch is on our side. He pulled our fat out of the fire. The half dead boy spirit cannot be killed because he is a half a ghost and had already half died. It is a funny trick. Don't worry. Tom, you will get used to the half dead boy spirit all over again. I did. We sill have many trouble. Henry is still alive." Bella said.

"Not for long," Tom sputtered, "I intend to fix that situation here and today. He's the reason all of this got started and I don't care if I got to crawl to put him in hell."

Bella began to work on Tom's knee. She made a tourniquet and then braced his knee with a board and tied it tightly.

"The bullet did not shatter the knee. It was an inch above, but the bone, I think, is broken." Bella said weakly.

"Can you ride?" Frank asked.

"Yes I can," Tom said in great pain.

"Good. Now let us go find this Kansas Jayhawker and finish it once an fer all," Frank said. There was something truly frightening with the look that Frank gave Tom.

Chapter 23

Deputy Felix Bloom teetered on the point of collapse as he made his way to the telegraph office. He had been shot several times and was bleeding heavily. It took all of his concentration and effort to plod the half-mile to the telegraph office. Things had not worked out like they had been supposed to. The sight of the headless colonel had enervated everyone to the point of absurdity. They had stood around and had been slaughtered like sheep by the two mounted whirlwinds that had roared among them. He knew he was lucky only to have been shot three times. In close combat, those LaMatts that one of those devils used was a horrendous weapons.

He had witnessed his close friend, Warren Bretchel, take three shots in the chest from the revolver. Warren had staggered from the impact of the bullets that shredded his internal organs to small chunks. He had never seen the people that killed him. He had been to busy trying to rally the green soldiers that had deserted their posts when the headless Colonel had ridden amongst them flapping its arms and terrifying the already panicked men. All attention had been riveted in the dead Colonel Dodge and that had been their undoing.

All the Deputies were killed in the first few seconds of the surprise attack. Whoever these men were, Felix thought, they had known exactly who to kill. The sad fact was that for all of his talking and planning, Mason had run like a frightened schoolboy. Felix had also seen the great Henry Fowler reduced to a quivering jelly kneed dirty yellow coward. Felix had made his mind that it wasn't going to end just yet. He would go to the telegraph office and let everyone know just what had happened, even if he had to write the message in blood. Henry Fowler was a sniveling cur and Mason was just as bad. Bloom staggered past the deserted docks and opened the telegraph office. The Mayor was seated behind one of the desks.

"Where's the regular fellas' that work here?" Felix asked.

"I sent them home as General Fowler has instructed me, to make sure the news of the great victory here today is not leaked prematurely to the world. I know how to operate the keys. It is my hobby you know," Jared said. Jared was frightened by the appearance of Bloom. The man's face was ashy and he was covered in blood and gore. Felix laughed.

"Great victory...what a joke. Mr. Mayor, for your information, this town is now in rebel hands. Quantrill and his men have killed all the true blue Union men in this town. I suspect that they will commence the slaughter soon like they did over in Lawrence last August. So if you don't mind, I suggest that you wire to the nearest office and let the world know what has happened."

"Where is General Fowler? I must see him to confirm this. Where is the Colonel Lehigh. For God's sakes man, where are all of General Fowler's brave staff officers?"

428

"They are dead, Mr. Mayor. As for Henry and Lehigh, the last thing I saw of them was their backsides hightailin' for cover. Now, if you will," Felix pulled out his revolver and pointed at the Mayor.

"Start workin'. Telegraph St. Louis and tell them what went on here. Tell them about the cowardice of Fowler and Mason. Tell them this town is in Rebel hands."

"I can't do that. General Fowler is very powerful. I would be ruined," Jared whined.

"I'm a fixin' to ruin you permanent if you don't start clicking them keys. Get me a pencil, Mayor. I will make sure you put down what I tell you."

Jared handed Felix a paper and pencil.

"Please…think of what you are doing. Think of the trouble that Henry can cause us all." Jared whined.

Felix began to scrawl his message. When he was finished, he handed it to the Mayor.

"I can't send this," he complained. Felix placed his revolver next to the wide eyed Mayor's head.

"So help me God, if you don't send this I will aerate your skull. Now send the damned message."

The Mayor started clicking away at the keys. Within a few seconds, it was finished. Jared was in tears.

"This will finish me," he cried.

"Tell them to confirm the message. Tell them to send it back word for word," Felix ordered.

The Mayor tapped out the message. Within several minutes, the message came back and Felix picked it up.

"Read that back to me, and you had better pray that you did it right," Felix said. The Mayor cleared his throat.

"You have ruined me." He began to read.

"Quantrill attacked Petersburg. Stop. All loyal Union men killed. Stop. Henry Fowler showed cowardice in the face of the enemy. Stop. Send troops. Stop. Request Captain Barlow. Stop. That's it," Jared said sadly. He suddenly sprang to the window and looked out on the wharf.

"Oh my," Jared said loudly.

Felix looked out of the window to see what had caused the Mayor's odd reaction. Walking towards the office with a torch was one of Quantrill's raiders. Jared dived to the floor.

"I'll be damned," Felix said through clenched teeth.

Felix opened the door and aimed at the raider's chest.

"You damned muderin' Missoura' scum," Felix screamed.

Ted was just clearing his pistol when the first bullet struck him. Ted grabbed his chest and dropped the pistol. He fell backwards as he was struck a second time. The lit torch flew out of his hands and landed on the roof. Ted fell sideways into the river. He rolled over onto his back. The current twisted him into the deep water and he was pulled under the surface of the mighty river.

Felix crumpled the ground. He looked up at a beautiful October sky as stars just began to show. He breathed in deeply, exhaled, and then his heart stopped. His head fell to the side. Jared ran out of the telegraph office. He saw that the roof was starting to burn due to all the tar that had been used to repair the hole in it. The roof snapped and popped cheerily in the night. Jared ran away.

Mason and Pete reached the hotel. Mason's shorter legs and stride had compelled Pete to pick Lehigh up and tuck him under his arms. Pete ran effortlessly with the shorter man. Mason had his revolver trained to the rear expecting at any moment to be overtaken by Quantrill's men. Pete bounded up the steps and released his hold on Mason.

Mason slammed and slammed the door shut. Pete raced over the bar and vaulted it. He reached for the shotgun and shells that he kept from habit behind the bar and when he found it, he bolted over to Mason's side.

"What happened to Mr. Fowler?" he asked.

"He ran. He simply ran. I see Neely gettin' ready to shoot him. Hell, I gave him the signal to go ahead. The next thing I know, Neely jumps up in the air and lands back down with a goddamned hole in the middle of his face. Then that headless horror comes flying down the road flapping his wings followed by a million of Quantrill's men. My people were trying to get those bastards back in the fight and then all of my people started getting shot and all those green soldier boys saw the headless wonder come flying right at them and it broke their will to live it seems. Shit...they started runnin' into each other like a bunch of silly sons of bitches. I turned and saw Henry lighten' right the hell out of there. Holy hell Pete, they kilt' everybody. Every single deputy was kilt' in jest' a few seconds. I never seen anything like it."

Mason caught movement out of the corner of his eye and spun with his revolver drawn. Henry Fowler descended the grand staircase dressed in an even more garish uniform topped off with a Zouave turban with an ostrich plume. The uniform was a brilliant yellow. The short Zouave styled jacket was royal purple.

"Mason. What is the meaning of being here? Why aren't you out there with your troops leading them to victory? What have you got to say for yourself, Colonel Lehigh?" Henry screamed.

"I guess I can ask you the same thing, Henry."

Mason lowered his pistol.

"I had to return of course to properly attire myself for battle. One cannot lead men if one is not properly attired for battle. Must I have to remind you of this? Must I do everything? Now, I demand that you return to your troops unless you are here to tell me that the day is won and you have Quantrill's head in a bucket."

Mason and Henry turned in the direction of Pete and began to laugh his strange braying laugher. Pete could not stop laughing. He waved his hands in the air and walked down the length of the bar. He pulled a bottle of scotch off the shelf, broke the bottle on the counter and began to drink huge quantities of alcohol, still laughing his odd laugh.

"Henry, I don't know how to tell you this. Hell, I'm not sure you will even understand what I'm about to say. Everybody is dead, Henry, and those that ain't are runnin' like hell to get away from here. This town is in rebel control now, Henry. I suggest that we get out of here directly before they find us and do us proper," Mason said wearily.

Henry pursed his lips.

"You say our military forces have been defeated?" Henry asked.

"Now you're gettin' it Henry."

"And that Quantrill is in control of my town?"

"That's about the gist of it, Henry."

"We must retreat in order. This must not be a rout. We shall retreat in good order. I shall not run into the woods in my nightshirt like Senator Lane. I will retreat so that years from now people will speak of this moment with awe. Our retreat will not be like Napoleons retreat from Moscow. Our retreat will be one that will be written into the history books for the future generations to ponder and pause in awe and contemplate."

"Good idea, Henry. Now…If you don't mind there is something I have to get from my room. Pete, stop your fartin' around and get by that front window. If you

431

see anything or anybody, start shootin'. Henry, I suggest that you find some kind of firearm around here. Check in the ballroom. I think some of your fancy colonel's and major's are still armed. At least I know Klaus is still armed. He never got a chance to even pull his piece out. You might have to wipe some mashed potatoes off it though."

Mason laughed loudly and shook his head. He ran up the stairway to his room. Henry walked over to a chair and sat down.

"This is just a temporary setback, Sergeant. We will emerge victorious. You see, I have a plan. We will let the enemy think that he has won a victory. He will think that everything is going his way. You will see. I had the foresight to order Captain Barlow and D troop to come here yesterday morning. They will probably land sometime tomorrow. We will retreat out of town and signal the boat before it gets to town. Then we will surround the town and attack. Captain Barlow is a good soldier even though he resembles a raccoon at times with those black circles constantly under his eyes. I have warned him countless times about it. Of course, he doesn't listen. Regardless, he is a good man even though he is a graduate of West Point and thinks his family has money. What does that pup have on me? So you can see that this setback does not hamper our plans at all. Quantrill will feel comfortable and he will use the time to slaughter the good citizens. Again, all part of my plan. This will be their eventual downfall. This I guarantee, my obese Sergeant. The greater the struggle...the greater the glory." Henry folded his arms confidentially.

Mason returned with a huge carpet bag.

"I was just saying to the Sergeant, Colonel, that we will wrest victory from the jaws of defeat. I had ordered Captain Barlow to this battle ground. He will arrive tomorrow. We shall signal the boat from the shore by lighting a signal fire from the shore. Once this is done, we shall surround the town and slaughter all of the wicked murdering scum."

Mason was astounded with Henry's revelation.

"Henry, that is all well and good, but I think that you overlook one thing. The problem is getting out of here in one piece to light that signal fire. Pete, keep your eyes peeled, I'm gonna' scrounge up some weapons and bullets."

Mason hurriedly scurried to the ballroom. He started to gather a pistol and ammunition when he heard Henry scream in terror and the door break asunder in a loud crash. Pete's shotgun went off and then he heard a furious exchange of gunfire.

Mason peeked out from the ballroom. A wild looking rebel soldier had ridden his horse up the porch and had smashed right through a locked and bolted door. The raider held the horse's bridle in his teeth and was blasting away at Pete with two

432

LaMatt pistols. Another raider rode his horse into the ballroom. Pete dove out the window.

Henry once again screamed in horror and went running up the grand staircase. The first rider dug his heels into the side of the animal and rider and horse went up the stairwell in a flash. The other rider was obviously in agony. He dismounted from his horse and collapsed on the floor. Mason quietly backed away from the door and walked as quietly as he could towards the window. Mason heard Henry scream again.

There was a series of shots and Mason heard an upstairs door being kicked open. There was another series of shots and the sound of breaking glass. Mason began to slowly open the window trying not to make a sound. Suddenly, a yellow and purple flash passed in front off his eyes as Henry's body hurled out the second story window in a spray of broken glass. Mason had the window almost open.

"I hope you're not leaving on my account, Lehigh," Tom stood with a pistol pointing at his head. Lehigh dropped his weapon to the floor. Lehigh squinted at Tom.

"I know you. You're that fella' in the America Hotel we caught that day. Holy Christ, if this don't beat all."

Mason threw the carpet bag at Tom and leaped headfirst through the window. The carpetbag knocked Tom down. Mason sailed through the window. By the time Tom painfully arose and looked out the window, Mason was gone. Frank came back down the stairs and jumped off his horse. He helped pick Tom off the floor.

"Did you get Henry?" Tom asked.

"I believe so. I must have hit him a few times. He went through the window." Frank looked out the window but did not see any bodies.

"Lehigh got away clean. So did that harelip. They must have got Henry and took off." Tom said. He opened the carpet bag. It was filled with money...thousands....and thousands of dollars. Frank's eyes bulged.

"Mother of mercy," Frank uttered. They both grabbed a fistful of money.

"If what Henry said if true about more soldiers comin' in a boat, we ain't got much time, Frank," Tom said. Frank put the money back in the bag and closed it.

"You should have let me shoot Henry through the window when I had the chance, Frank," Tom said.

"All's well that ends well," Frank grinned. "The hell with Fowler. I shot him so many times he ain't gonna' live. He'll go crawl away in a hole somewhere and die, believe me. We got to get back to the caves and get out of here. But I'm gonna' burn this place to the ground before I go. Give me your arm, I'll help you up on your horse."

Tom stumbled over to his horse and with Frank's help hoisted himself into the saddle. Tom rode out into the porch and down the steps. Frank followed him a few seconds later. Before leaving, Frank had drenched the bar and the floor with several bottles of liquor and then had thrown a match at the floor. The flames spread rapidly. They backed off a distance and admired Frank's handiwork. Soon the hotel was a roaring conflagration. Frank turned and started to ride away. Tom hugged the carpetbag and spurred his horse after Frank.

William Gladstone watched as the telegraph office slowly slid into the river. The sparks flew into the air and started small fires in the dried grass and leaves nearby. The dock had just started to burn as William dismounted. A dead body smoldered on the dock. William noticed a Deputy star on the corpse. He looked around for Ted but was satisfied in his mind that the sad scenario was more than likely true. The Deputy had been shot by somebody and that person was more than likely to have been Ted. Where he was now was anyone's guess.

William assumed Ted to have been killed by the Deputy and more than probably had fallen into the river. William looked and watched the roof of a tool shed begin to burn. The whole town was in danger of burning. Flames spread everywhere spurred on by a strong wind. He rode back to tell Frank the news.

Doctor Harrington Waters made his patients comfortable. Tom, Bella, and Huck lay in a wagon. Doctor Waters had stopped Huck's bleeding and was fairly certain he would recover. Bella would as well. Tom's knee was pretty well ruined and would be touch and go if he were ever to walk normally again. He was sure that he was crippled for life. The bullet had not hit the kneecap but instead had sent many fractures throughout it. He would watch it carefully in the next few days. If it looked like an amputation was needed, he would take the leg off above the knee.

Doctor Waters youngest boy, Harriman Waters, arrived with another wagon. Seated on the wagon was the Doctor's wife, a woman several years younger than himself. Their home was just beginning to burn.

"Pa...the soldiers left kegs of powder in the bedroom...when those flames hit it, it will blow it to smithers. We got out everything we could."

There were crowds of people streaming out of Petersburg. The rumor of slaughter and the fires caused by Lehigh's Deputies and unwilling troops had caused a flood of fugitives. Mayor Jared Clifton had also fueled the rumor of impending death and destruction and had started a major stamped of terrorized citizens. His harrowing tale of the death of a raider magnified his own sincerity in the belief that they were all about to be slaughtered. Doctor Waters walked around the wagon and patted his wife on the knee.

"Stop worrying, Mother. Quantrill has not come to kill us all in our beds. These stories that you hear are all unsubstantiated. It has all been a terrible mistake caused by the actions of a few despicable men in power. Frank has told me everything. I brought him into this world. I have known him all his life. Although I cannot abide with his secessionist viewpoint, he has no reason to lie to me and the actions of the Union soldiers that were here so recently leaves no doubt in my mind. I know he is telling me the truth. Now, son, take your mother away before we are all blown to kingdom come."

The son slapped the reins on the horse and they drew away from the front of Rebecca's home, joining a crowd of refugees. Doctor Waters watched William Gladstone and Frank Gorgon approaching him on horseback.

"Time to go, Doc. How you standin' up?" Frank asked.

"Fine young man. I will heal as well as your friends. My wife and son are leaving just now. My home is full of gunpowder kegs just waiting to go off like Chinese firecrackers. There is nothing for me here. Where will you go?" he asked.

"All of us is headin' for the nation. Natalie's grandmother was full-blooded Cherokee. It seems as if Bella knows all of them, what's left there. She used to spend time with them in the summer. Small world ain't it? We intend to put as much distance and this war between us as we can. Tom talks about going to California and Rebecca's goin' with him. We got time to decide, but we ain't got no time here. That wind is pickin' up. This whole town is goin' up."

"To think…all of this is ruin caused by errors, confusion, and stupidity," the doctor sighed.

He stepped into the wagon and followed Frank and William down Main Street. The flames burned wildly whipped by the winds. The flames finally reached the kegs of powder stored in the first floor bedroom of Doctor Water's home. The detonation was fearful. The resultant shower of flaming lumber spread the fire everywhere. The town burned brightly in the night. The inferno roared out of control.

In the morning there would not be a single building standing. The town of Petersburg had blinked out of existence on the October night never to be inhabited again. In time, no one would even know that it had ever existed at all.

Henry Fowler slapped at an insect that had plagued him all night. On this unseasonably warm night, the insect had taken upon itself the singular duty of trying to fly up Henry's nose and commit suicide before the cold change in the weather made it an after-thought in the bug world. Henry moaned as he slapped his face. The metal armor that he had worn under his bright purple tunic had saved his life, but the incredible wallop that the LaMatt revolver's bullet had packed had covered him in welts and bruises. He groaned and looked up at the rising sun.

"Men...wake up. Now is the time for us to render justice to the infidels. Light the signal fire. I expect Captain Barlow to arrive forthwit. Then I will have that Quantrill's head mounted on an oak board. Arise, everyone," Henry shouted.

Pete stood and shook Lehigh awake. Pete was not feeling all that well. The bullet that had struck him in the buttocks had stripped a pound of flesh from him. He could barely stagger to his feet.

Lehigh awoke and helped Pete lean against a tree. Lehigh had slept fitfully all night. After they had revived Henry, they had followed the bank of the river and had rested in the reeds. Henry had been unconscious from the plunge from the second story room. Pete had lifted him up and they had run into the night. Lehigh was bruised but none the less for wear.

"Henry. I don't think it's too wise to be yellin' this early. We don't know who may be out there listenin'," Lehigh said.

Lehigh was interrupted by the whistle of a boat. As they came across the turn in the narrow part of the river, they could make out a riverboat towing several barges. The barges were crammed with soldiers and horses.

"See," Henry screamed happily. "It is Barlow come to the rescue just as I planned. Come...let us get to town. They will not stop for us here. The town is smoking...its ruin streaks heavenward. Quantrill is hopefully busy slaughtering all the good citizens. I tell you, their deaths will not be in vain. Let us away to the docks. We will see my plans come to fruition as surely as the sun sets in the west. Follow me."

Henry pushed the bushes away from his face and began to walk towards the town. Lehigh and Pete limped after Henry who had his head held firmly in the air like a king. Smoke from the fires wafted across the street as they began to pass row after row of destroyed homes.

"Mr. Lehigh...I don't think I kin' keep up with Mr. Fowler. My ass cheeks is painin' me smartly. You want I should break his neck for you now or later?" Peter moaned.

Lehigh let Henry get a few feet further away before he turned on Pete.

"Look you moron," Mason hissed. "You had better forget everything we ever talked about in regards to Henry. Think, for God's sake, you blithering idiot. Do we have the hotel anymore?...No. We ain't got a pot to piss in or a window to throw it out of. I had over twenty thousand dollars or more in a carpet bag that I had to throw at some skinny bastard just to escape with my hide. Do you think I want Henry dead now?"

Pete shrugged. Mason leaped up at Pete and punched him in the eye. Pete covered his eye with both of his hands and took a few steps backwards.

"Now you listen up and listen up good. I don't know fer' sure if Quantrill was in town or not. If that's Barlow comin' into town and Quantrill was in town then Henry has a chance to go at Quantrill again. Do you understand anything?"

Pete nodded.

"What do you understand?" Mason yelled.

"I understand I don't wanna' get hint' no more, Mr. Lehigh." Pete was in tears. "I'm feelin' powerful bad, Mr. Lehigh."

"Good fer' you, boy. Let me say this again…Henry is all we got. Henry is our bread and butter. If I ever hear you talk about breaking his neck again, I swear I will knock the ever lovin' shit out of you. You got that?"

Pete nodded.

Henry turned towards them.

"No dawdling in the ranks, Colonel Lehigh. We are almost there. Look…riders are coming this way. Quickly, if you will. We must maintain some kind of military formation and decorum now, shan't we. Hurry…they are almost here."

Mason quickly ran and drew abreast of Henry as Pete limped over and made it to Mason's side just as two riders came upon them. Both of the men wore the insignia of captain.

"Captain Gendron, I cannot belief mien eyes. There must have been a verdamnt circus in town. Ve huff' a midget, und der fat mann und a circus clown heir."

Captain Gendron covered all of the men with his revolver.

"I see some dead men in der road, but I zee' no circus animals…no circus tent. Chust' a fat man, a midget, und a clown. Vas ist loss?…Did der elephant knock over der candle unt set der tent on fire? Ist dot what happened to burn der whole town down, jah?"

"Captain, I'll have you know you are addressing a superior officer. Where is Captain Barlow? I am General Fowler."

"So, my name ist Captain Mueller. I vass sent here to find you, Herr General Fowler."

"Where are Colonel's Johnson and Major Hemmings? Why aren't they here to greet me?" Henry asked nervously.

"Because, Herr General, they are all unter' arrest pending an investigation," Mueller said. "Now, Please Colonel dwarf, if you would please, place your weapon on the ground or Captain Gerdon vill shoot you in za head, nicht var? Do you understand, jah?"

"What? What is the meaning of this?" Henry screamed loudly.

"Der meaning is dot you, Herr General, are unter' arrest unt facing der court-martial for conduct unt' becoming of unt' offiseer, misappropriation of military funds, extortion, bribery, gross misconduct of duties, cowardice unt' murder. Der last vun ist a capital offense, nicht var? The list ist rather long, Herr General fancy dressed Circus clown. You want me to continue? I don't think so. Now…drop all your weapons. I will not ask nice again."

"You fool. As we stand here, Quantrill is getting away," Henry shouted.

"For your information Herr General, Quantrill attacked a town in southern Missouri two days ago. Unless der man can fly like a great winged Teufel, there ist no possible way that he was here like you say. We received a telegraph yesterday stating that this town was unter attack by Quantrill. All reports of the whereabouts of Quantrill end up on General Halleck's desk in Washington. You are familiar with Herr General Halleck?"

Henry swallowed heavily.

"You see, it seems that someone telegraphed your headquarters informing of your cowardice. I chust happened to be there unter' orders from General Halleck. He wanted to know why ist der reason for all der Majors und Colonels on your staff. You are a bit too top heavy mit feldt grade offiseers. I vas at your headquarters investigating for almost three days before this message comes. It seems that a Mister Flemming's body was found outside of town. He was last seen speaking' mit you. You huff ' been a naughty boy, Herr fancy dressed circus clown. You huff a goot offiseer in Kapitan Barlow but he ist der only vun. In fact, he is going back east to rejoin his command as we speak. Nothing will happen to him. Der mann needs der rest is all. You huff' been running the poor man into the ground after Quantrill. All der rest of your staff offiseers are der murderes, cuthroats und theives..like yourself. I huff' seen many other things that are highly questionable in your command. When I informed Herr General Halleck of what we find, he ordered your immediate arrest. After all, he ist the chief of der Army, nicht var?"

Henry was speechless. Mason looked at Henry and saw him shrink inwardly. Captain Gendron dismounted as several soldiers came at the party standing in the road. They secured Henry, Pete. And Mason's hands behind their backs. Henry was stunned and looked at the mounted officer with terror in his eyes.

"Vass ist der matter. You are dresset like der circus clown but you can't machen like der funnyman now, can you General Fowler. I think not so. I want to tell you one thing, Herr General not-so-funnyman now. I huff' been a soldat for twenty years unt in all mien time, I huff' never seen un offiseer of your type before. You are der total disgrace even to that ridiculous uniform you wear und to all men of arms. If you were in mien country, I would split you open like der chicken und kick your guts in der sewer for der pigs to feed on," Mueller said bitterly. He turned to his men.

"Everyone, back to der barges. We huff no need to stay in this desolation. Kapitain Gendron and Sergeant Valdez, you will find any survivors of this town und escort them to headquarters for der disposition. Troop und prisoners, mitt mir," Captain Mueller shouted.

Henry and Mason trudged towards the barges. Pete hobbled as best as he was able and soon they were boarding the barges for the trip back to St. Louis. Henry desperately sought a way out of the situation that he was in but his mind kept on drawing blanks. He was in serious trouble and not even his money could buy him out of his trouble. He knew that any charge of cowardice leveled against an officer in these times spelled an end for that person's military career.

As the barge cleared the docks after loading the horses, a solitary figure stood on the shore watching its departure. Deputy Edgar Covington could not believe the destruction he saw of the town. Every building was gone. He walked towards the ruined dock and bent over the charred remains of a body lying in the road. He reached down and pulled a blackened sheriff's badge from the still smoldering shrunken corpse. It read Sheriff Neely. The cheap gold paint had burned off the metal badge. Edgar took a last look at the ruins all around him. He threw the badge as far as he could into the river. He then pulled his own badge out of his pocket and flung it. It skipped across the small waves the barge had caused. He then began a long walk to somewhere.

Epilogue

Frederick Douglass would eventually marry his housekeeper. He would become the ambassador to Haiti and stay involved with civil rights the rest of his life. When asked by a young man of color what one could do to improve the plight of African-Americans in the country, Frederick was known to have said, "Agitate...Agitate...Agitate."

Benjamin Robinson enlisted in the 29th Connecticut. In the last days of the war, Benjamin fell at the Battle of the Crater at Petersburg, Virginia. His regiment would be one of the first to enter the city of Richmond when its defenses finally collapsed in 1865. Two soldiers of this regiment would guard the wife of Robert E. Lee at her home in Richmond after the city fell into Union hands. She asked the commanding officer to remove the black soldiers. Their presence was too offensive, she had said. The soldiers stayed at their posts. It was too late to accommodate the wishes of certain people's sectional beliefs by this time. There were too many young men resting in the earth...too much blood had been shed in the ending of slavery.

Edgar Covington would become a lawyer and later a judge. He would be credited with the creating a ranch in Wyoming for orphans. He had two fine children and when he died, no one would have ever guessed that at one time in his youth the distinguished Judge Covington had been a rustler, a killer, and an owl-hoot. He died in 1914, a highly respected member of his community.

William Clarke Quantrill, the ex-Ohio school teacher and Confederate raider, was usurped from power by two of his own lieutenants and lost popular support within his band of followers. Even young Jessie James and his brother left his band to follow one of the disloyal lieutenants, Bloody Bill Anderson. William Quantrill, fearing that he would face death if he surrendered at the end of the war to the Union forces in Kansas or Missouri, decided to travel to Kentucky to surrender to Union forces there. He was shot and killed in Kentucky by Union supporters of a local militia group.

Jessie James and his brother would survive the war. Frank Gordon's prophecy about Missouri turning into a place of bandits became true with both James brothers becoming the most famous bandits in American history. Jessie would die before the end of the century, shot by a member of his own band. Frank would live to be an old man. Bloody Bill Anderson was killed by Federal Forces and his head ended up on a pole. Someone made a death mask of William Quantrill's entire head. It resides in a refrigerator to insure that the wax does not melt on sultry Kansas nights.

William Gladstone, with his split of Lehigh's money, left Oklahoma and traveled to Texas. He opened a bar and married a local woman. In 1865, he was shot dead by a black soldier over an argument involving a redheaded prostitute. His death sparked a race riot in which fourteen whites and nine black soldiers died. It was one of the first race riots in United States history involving civilians and soldiers.

Frank settled in Oklahoma with his wife and two sons and in 1903, oil was discovered on their land. They became millionaires. Fenton Gordon would become a doctor and serve with the United States Medical Services in the construction of the Panama Canal. Clayton would become and oil man. The Gordon family, to this day, is involved in the oil business. Frank passed away in 1915 and Natalie would pass away in 1940. She would live to see her great grandchildren born into wealth.

Henry Fowler's meteoric rise to rank in the Army crashed to earth just as quickly as it had risen. Dr. Waters, Mayor Clifton, and a score of soldiers that had survived by fleeing the destruction and deaths that day at Petersburg testified against Henry at his court-martial. The black mark that he would make if all the truth were known forced the Army to cashier him from its ranks to avoid embarrassment. He was slipped under the rug. All of Henry's powerful friends disavowed even of having ever known a certain Henry Fowler. Henry's great wealth protected him to some extent. Hundreds of bribes were paid out, and by the time he left the army, Henry was practically penniless.

Henry left Kansas in disgrace. Pete and Mason followed him to Colorado where in 1869, Henry bought a played out silver mine from a local drunk. Henry believed that the mine was his way out of obscurity. He made Pete and Mason work the mine like slaves. In 1871, Pete discovered one of the greatest loads of silver on the North American continent. Henry sold shares and all three men became multi-millionaires overnight.

Mason was instrumental in ordering elevators into the shaft. However, being frugal and somewhat money hungry even with his millions, Mason had decided to cut corners in the construction of the elevators. He pocketed the extra money out of pure greed and habit. On the morning of October 22, 1872, Mason had invited Henry to see the marvel that he had made.

On that day Henry, Pete, and Mason boarded the elevator for the decent in comfort to the bottom of the shaft, eighty seven feet below the surface. Mason would have been better off spending the extra money and not pocketing the funds because halfway down, the main cable gave way. The broken cable ripped through Henry's jaw. Henry screamed in pain as it pierced his neck, tore under his tongue and ripped through his upper jaw.

As the weight changed, the cable shifted and plunged down the shaft with the counter weight. It pulled Henry out of the elevator car and he went plunging down to the bottom of the shaft. Mason had also neglected proper ventilation procedures. The overworked mechanism at the bottom of the shaft broke into flames from the friction, igniting deposits of natural gas at the bottom of the shaft. Henry was dragged by a cable to a fiery death. The elevator containing Mason and Pete struck the earth, crushing Henry to paste and shortening Pete to Mason's size in a millisecond. The resultant cave in buried them in tons of rubble. They died leaving no heirs.

Captain Mueller stayed in the Army. When General Custer requested his services with the seventh cavalry for a campaign in the Dakotas, Captain Mueller was glad to join him. In 1876, Custer, along with his entire command, was killed at the battle of the "greasy grass", otherwise known as Custer's last stand. Captain Mueller died during this action. Because Captain Mueller's orders were mishandled, no records exists that he ever served with Custer during this campaign and no record exists that he was ever killed in the engagement. He was listed as absent without leave by a myopic clerical worker, the same person that had mishandled his transfer orders in the first place.

Tom married Rebecca in 1865. Huck was his best man and Bella was the Maid of Honor. A year later Rebecca and Tom reciprocated the honor for Bella and Huck. It took nearly another year for Huck to recover sufficiently enough so that he could travel. With the money that they had, there was no pressing need to go to the gold fields to get rich. They settled down and bought a ranch out in the hills of a sleepy town called Los Angeles

Tom never walked right again and soon became depressed with the fact that he was no longer capable of doing ranch work. He and Rebecca left California and traveled east. Tom, enthralled with the art of photography, became an expert with film and opened a studio.

Thomas Edison heard of this photographic wizard and soon hired him to work on his film needed for the infant motion picture industry. Eventually, Tom's innovative talent reaped Mr. Edison success. Thomas Edison went on to monopolize the movie industry at the turn of the century. Other people became dissatisfied with Edison's tyrannical domination of the industry and rebelled. They looked for a place in which movies could be made all year instead of in an indoor sound stage and they looked for someone who had been with the industry since its inception to lead them.

Tom was a well known and respected person in the industry and when he suggested a ranch in California whose owner was having a difficult go at making a success of it and wanted to sell it, these people were very interested. Huck's sons had all grown and moved away and Huck's increasing age made it feasible to sell the ranch to this group of movie makers.

Nestled in the hills of a sleepy town, the ranch had everything that these rebel filmmakers wanted. There was ample daylight, the weather was great and the price was perfect. Tom became the group's anchor person and within a few years the ranch began turning out movies. They called the ranch and studio, Hollywood.

Tom grew wealthy and Huck made a tidy profit in the sale of his ranch. Huck moved into the city and bought a house not far from Tom's residence. Tom eventually retired to spend his days in his laboratory. Huck in his late sixties, converted a beat up saloon into a theater and learned everything about running a projector. He thoroughly enjoyed his new second career and the theater was a huge success. He often showed select audiences first showings of feature movies at his theater inviting some of the biggest stars of the day and other important leaders of the community.

Everyone knew Mr. Finn and everyone looked forward to these special events. One evening, Rebecca appeared at Huck's home, something that occurred regularly. Huck greeted her with a peck on the cheek and looked out the doorway disappointed that Tom was not with her.

"Good evening, Rebecca. Where's the old boy?" he asked. His curiosity was aroused in the anxious state of Rebecca.

"Come in…what's the matter, he didn't fall down again did he? I tell him he's gotta' walk or his leg will stiffen up like a broom handle. I know, I get stiff every now and then and it ain't from just the alcohol either."

"He's fine. I left him in his laboratory. He asked me to tell you that he's had a breakthrough in making his color film. I asked him what color the film was going to be and he laughed and said you would understand. Huck, I have to show you somethin'. I…here, look at this." She handed Huck a letter. He reached into his jacket and put his reading glasses on.

"Tom knows that I'm showin' that new movie tonight, supposed to be a lot of big wigs there. Tom knows the fella' that made the movie…a Griffin something or other. Why even President Wilson hisself' talked about this here movie…called it history done in light. It's called The Birth of a Nation. Supposed to be about the war 'tween the states. I know he wanted to see it 'cause I was talkin' to him about it yesterday. Must be somethin' here for him to lose all interest in it."

Huck began to read the letter as Bella entered the room. She had just finished the evening dishes.

"Good…I was just going to call you. Sandra brought over the draperies that you wanted."

"Oh wonderful. How is she?"

"That daughter of her's is giving her fits. I said good, now she knows what she put me through. Sandra took after her father and now my granddaughter has taken up right after both of them." Bella watched as Hucks lips moved while he read the letter.

"Stop moving your lips when you read. You look like a frog trying to catch a fly," Bella said sharply. Huck raised his hand in the air. Bella laughed.

"Yesterday, Sandra had her at the beach. Sandra said she turned around and that little rascal was gone."

"Jumpin' Jehosophat," Huck shouted.

"That was very similar to Tom's reaction," Rebecca said.

"Will someone please tell me what's going on?" Bella asked.

"Can you believe it," Rebecca said. "It's a letter from George. I remember telling him about the war when he was little. He had always been interested in it. I had no idea he would do something like this," Rebecca said.

"You mean your son, George?" Bella asked.

Huck sat down.

"So many years ago," Huck said, "sit down for a minute Bella," Huck said.

"Young George was apparently writin' a book in his spare time about what happened to me and his father during the war. He was doin' research and found a certain bank in St. Louis with an account under our names. It was the money that Frederick Douglass deposited in it for our stake to California. We never got to St. Louis. That money has been sittin' there collectin' interest for fifty years. According to George there is seventy-nine thousand dollars that the bank says is ours. All we gotta do is go there and claim it."

"My goodness," Bella said.

"Tom said that he would see you tomorrow morning about planning the trip. Isn't this incredible? Rebecca said. Huck looked at his watch quickly.

"I got to git', I forgot the time. Tell Tom I will have Gordon pick him up in the automobile. Rebecca, take care. Bella, start figurin' out a way to spend our money. I will see you later this evening."

Huck walked briskly towards the theater a few blocks from his home. His mind drifted in the past and he hardly noticed the crowd congregating at the door. He nodded at a few people and made his way to the projection booth. His assistant had already prepared the rolls of the film and everything was ready to go.

Huck peered at his audience. At his signal, the house lights dimmed and he flicked on the projector. Huck began to watch the movie. After thirty minutes, Godfrey Hall, Huck's assistant, began to notice the older man visibly getting upset.

Huck began muttering things under his breath. Suddenly Huck stood up and flicked the projector off. Cats calls and loud whistles erupted from the audience. Huck clumped angrily down the stairs and walked to the stage as Godfrey turned the house lights on. When the people saw the old man appear on stage they grew silent.

"What's the matter, Mr. Finn," someone called out, "did you. forget to pay the electric company?"

"Shut yer mouth. If you can sit here and think what you are seeing is the way things were then you are the dumbest people ever to have breathed air on God's green earth," Huck said loudly.

"This here movie is an abomination and a disgrace. This ain't the way it was at all. The Negro ain't like these here white men in painted black face rapin' and killin'. This here is all a lie and a pretty damned dangerous one at that…let me tell you all somethin'. The black man has fought for freedom in every war we ever fought and he always came out on the short end of the stick. I knew a man, a colored man, when I was a boy who taught me about people. People, goddammit. I knew another colored man during the war who was the smartest man I ever met. He got kilt' fightin' for his peoples freedom in the War Between the States and there ain't a man in this here room that could hold a candle to him for brightness. This movies is a disgrace to what's good and right. There is good and bad in all people but I learned a long time ago that there are some colored folks that do a better job at bein' people than any white people I knowed' and that's the God's honest truth. My life was saved by a big black man who shared what little he had with me when I was beaten an' left for dead, beaten by a bunch of white men. For God's sake, the coloreds never went on a warpath and kilt' white people the way the wild injuns' did. I remember when I was younger an saw the wagon trains comin' back to St. Louis filled with arrows. They kilt' white folks by the hundreds. I remember when Custer got hisself' and his whole command wiped out. Thirty years age they was all cryin' for the injuns' head on a silver platter. Now, they call them the Noble Redman. What bullshit. The blackman never went on no massive killin' spree, although I can't figger out why…Lord knows he has had enough reasons to. And somethin' like this movie is simply a way for some idiot what never was in the war because he was too young to have been in it to shape peoples minds about the black folks. This is a twisted sick thing he's doin' here I won't abide by it."

Huck stopped to catch his breath. He was shaking in anger. Catcalls and booing began, someone yelled out loudly, "Nigger lover."

Huck pulled out a large Army revolver, model 1860. He fired a bullet through the ceiling and everyone jumped up.

"You will all shut up, now," Huck shouted. There was not a sound to be heard.

"If I see anybody headin' towards the exits, I will put a bullet in their collective asses."

No one stirred.

"Good"' Huck said calmly, "I'm so glad I have your attention. I'm gonna' tell you a story so listen up good and you may learn somethin'. Huck began carefully and slowly.

"My good friend Tom and I were thick in the woods at a place called Chancellorsville. There was no town there just the big old tavern what got burnt to a frazzle durin' the fightin' that took place there a few days earlier," he stopped and shook his head.

"That was 1863…fifty six years ago." He drifted in his thoughts and then said quietly, "How the hell did I get so old?"

People began to fidget in their seats and he caught himself. He glared at them with the pistol still pointing in their direction.

"If I recall proper, the General of the Yankee's, a General Hooker I heard, got his bell rung good. He was leanin' against one of those columns of that old tavern when a cannon ball struck it. Some say the shock of it caused him to become screwy. They say he lost faith in hisself'. At the time I was with Jones brigade, Johnson's division, Second Corp, Army of Northern Virginia. We was drawn up in a clearin' to witness the execution of a soldier from our division. He had run durin' the fight'n and had shot an' robbed a member of the provost guard. I can still remember it like it was yesterday."